x^2

GREEN LIGHT
BRIDGE

ISBN: 978-0-9965924-9-9 - *print*
978-0-9965924-8-2 - *e-book*

COVER IMAGE
Jonathan Rice

BOOK DESIGN
timmyroland.com

For my wife, partner, and best friend, Victoria.

*You are the reason for everything
that's good in my life.*

$$x^2$$

x² BOOKS
WORLDWIDE

GREEN LIGHT
BRIDGE

LARRY BLACK

x² BOOKS
WORLDWIDE

$$x^2$$

1 Travis

Travis was floating eight inches above his bed when he woke. In the split second before he hit the mattress his eyes flew open wide, his heart hammering against his chest, damp with sweat. His room was bathed in light. Could it already be morning, he wondered? The clattering whir of the water cooler echoed in the stillness of the room's illumination, the bent blade tapping steadily against some metal support.

He could see his entire room in perfect detail. No shadows or dark corners persisted, just stunning light that practically vibrated in whiteness along his walls making his black light posters flat and colorless in the brilliance. The light danced along the clutter on the large folding table against the wall, sparkling against the debris of a Hunchback of Notre Dame model near completion, illuminating the whip marks carefully painted red as they crisscrossed Quasimodo's hump. The lamp on the table flickered impossibly fast like a strobe light then exploded with sharp pop, scattering shards of white glass across the surface of the table. The well-loved Thingmaker glowed impossibly bright orange, waves of heat rippling upwards along with the strong smell of Plastigoop residue that ran in rivulets across the table, fastening Matchbox cars to the Formica surface.

Lifting his head, the fourteen-year old boy looked across the bed and saw his little brother sitting up, eyes wide in amazement. Travis looked past his brother to the window and stared at the backyard of his home, shining bright in the same strange light. He could see past the edge of his yard, over the chain-link fence into neighbors' yard more than half a block away. The late summer heat had turned to steamy stillness in this daybreak that seemed utterly wrong in every way. Travis realized there were no cicadas, no crickets, only the rhythmic clicking of the water fan still blowing the moist cool air across an otherwise motionless room. Travis felt his brother's hand slide into his and grip tightly.

The door to the bedroom opened quickly and Travis watched his dad creep into the room along with his mom. A moment later, his older sister ran into the room, hair tangled across her face, her smiley face t-shirt hiked up over her rear end showing pink bikini panties that glowed in the eerie brightness. Travis and Andy followed the teenager out the side door of their room that was off the screened-in back porch. The concrete steps were cool to Travis's bare feet as he scrambled down and walked out into the middle of the back yard with this family looking around at the living daylights lighting up the neighborhood. Travis stopped in between his Dad and older brother, Trey, who was already out in the yard, having made his way from the porch where he had moved to escape the crowded boys' bedroom.

Out of the corner of his eye, Travis saw more movement and watched Mr. and Mrs. Clemmons standing together across the fence looking up into the night. Looking further down the fence line, he saw the Roland sisters in their old maid nightgowns and sponge curlers staring up into the daytime brightness as well. Three more houses down he saw Emily Moon with her mother and across from her, his best friend, George with his parents all looking toward the sky.

As his eyes rose, he noticed the brightness was radiating down from a silent source above the

1

neighborhood. The light was as bright as the sun, yet somehow didn't burn or cause his eyes to close. Instead, Travis felt his eyes grow wider and more and more of the white light flooded in. He felt his arms rising up toward the light, finally releasing his hold on Andy's hand. Within his body, Travis felt a whirring, a noiseless tremble, like a tuning fork sliding into a glass of water. His feet rose up on tiptoes that gripped the flat cool blades of the St. Augustine lawn, as if he would simply float away if he relaxed his muscles.

Travis felt like the top of his head had been effortlessly and painlessly removed and the shimmering rays spotlighting Maple Street were pouring in a rich stew of memories, places, feelings, and wisdom into his mind that couldn't be explained or contained. In that moment, he simply felt like he was watching a hundred, maybe a thousand different television screens of the most vivid realistic events he had ever seen. The images were beyond description, no context or framework with which to understand them. It was a deluge of energy that caused him to be everywhere all at the same time. Although without understanding, he knew the light was permeating his mind and had been doing so for his entire life. He saw images from his early boyhood days, terrible and wonderful memories swirling and colliding. He held his breath as wave after wave of light raced within him, wondering how long he had now been standing underneath it. The hours had turned into days or even months. He gave himself completely to the light, feeling every hair, every pore, every molecule dissolve into its sunlike infinity. He sucked in his breath as the wave moved through his chest and belly, vibrating and exploding into silver.

The darkness was almost deafening when it came. A slight breeze lifted the sycamore and maple leaves and the buzz of cicadas increased as if an invisible hand were turning the radio volume slowly up. Murmurs of voices filled the softness of the night. The light had vanished making the night seem oppressively dark, palpable. Travis suddenly realized he was laying on the cool ground while everyone else was standing looking around for the brightness that had moments ago vanished. He felt the grass tickle his bare back and legs, his ears filling with the sounds of insects and the voices of neighbors. He looked up and saw Trey's tanned hairy legs and knees with tell-tale scar, Andy in his arms firmly hugging the older boy's frame, while turning his head back and forth searching the sky. The clusters of families and neighbors with faces upturned and searching were lit up once again as the light, now miles away, pulsed brightly; hovering and blazing like a supernova. Once again it winked out, causing the summer air to shimmer and hum once again with insects.

"Now what the hell was that?" Travis heard his dad say walking toward the fence line, gesturing with Mr. Clemmons toward the place the light had just disappeared. The dim light was filled with the shadows of neighbors in nightgowns and underwear who had not yet quite figured out they were out in public wearing much less than they normally would. Trey stepped over Travis. The husky teenager gently dumped the little boy on the ground.

"Hey Numb Nuts, why are you down there?" Trey croaked in his deep voice.

"Dunno. What just happened?"

"That light woke everybody up." Andy added.

Travis stood up and looked toward the back fence and caught sight of Emily once again. The young girl hugged the thin nightgown around her skinny frame and waved slightly. Travis waved back, becoming aware he was only wearing his Fruit of the Looms, stupidly putting his hands down in front of his crotch in a vain attempt to cover up. The neighborhood appeared ready to get back to bed and he watched from the shadows as one by one the families disappeared inside.

"Let's get back to bed," Travis's mother said as she turned and climbed back up the stairs to the porch. Travis looked up and saw the vast star field of the Milky Way stretched out against the velvety sky. The boy stood looking up until his dad called again from the porch to come inside. He turned to go but suddenly realized his nose was bleeding. He wiped his nose on the back of his hand and then on his underwear. He started up the steps and noticed Trey was standing in front of one of the big Sycamore trees in the back yard. Travis watched the sparkle of his big brother's pee rocket against the dry grey bark as he emptied his bladder in a seemingly endless stream. Travis heard his dad yell through the open screened window of his parent's bedroom.

"For God's sake, it sounds like a racehorse out there. Get back to bed."

Travis started laughing and then turned ran back inside, allowing the screen door to bang hard against the frame. It ripped open again and a rolled pair of socks sailed past his head as Trey came inside. Travis dove inside his bed, but sleep didn't come.

2 Jack

Both men sat up in the tent, breathless and totally awake, hairs on their head and arms prickling and standing on end. Jack could have sworn he was floating out in the lake just a few moments before, having some vague memory of a weightless tranquility before the light woke him. A soft hum vibrated through the stuffy, moist air inside the canvas walls of the tent. Jack looked around and his young son was also wide awake, standing upright, gazing up at the illuminated roof, his small arms raised upwards as if waiting for the light to stoop down and pick him up for a ride on its shoulders. Without speaking, Jack grabbed the boy and crawled out of the tent, feeling Tim, Jack's life-long friend, push out of the flap right beside him. The men stood gazing at the unfathomable brightness of the light, their eyes widening; whiteness blinding their vision. Jack felt his son grow lighter in his arms and he gripped the toddler tighter as a rush of images and energy opened the top of his head in a dizzying torrent, knocking the man and boy backward to the damp earth.

Jack opened his eyes and felt Tim's arms around him, helping him sit up. Instinctively he reached for his boy and felt small arms tighten around his neck. He looked into the face of his friend who was pale and shaking in the dim light.

"Holy shit, Jack. What the fuck was that?" Tim croaked in a low whisper.

"No idea," Jack whispered back. "Is it gone?"

"I think so. Are you ok?"

"I think I am." Jack pulled his boy into his lap. "What about you kiddo?"

"It morning, Daddy."

"Sure seemed like it for a minute, didn't it."

The air filled again with the soft chirp of crickets and croak of frogs around the lake. The casual lap of waves moved the small boat around in the brown water, anchored nearby the campsite. Jack heard the splatter of Tim emptying his bladder against a nearby tree and suddenly felt an intense pressure himself. He leaned over to put Joey on the ground, but the little boy clung tighter. Shaking his head, he put the boy up on his shoulders and relieved himself into the bushes.

"Daddy pee a lot. I pee my diaper."

"Well thank goodness for that," Jack whispered with a chuckle. "Let's go back to bed." The man crawled back inside the tent, settling back on top of his sleeping bag, his boy still clinging to his neck. Tim crawled inside and slid his bag over and right against Jack, lying close and still.

"What the hell was that?" Tim croaked.

"Hell if I know. Military plane or something, I guess."

The men continued to lay still, wide awake, unable to relax or find sleep again. "There weren't no motor or jet sound, no rotors, nothing," Tim said.

"Yeah, I know. It's weird for sure."

"Why'd you fall down?"

"I don't know. Just couldn't stand up or something. Buddy, let's try and sleep. This kid is gonna be nuts if we stay up."

"I told you not to bring him."

"Yeah, well I wouldn't be here without him. I told you Lori was flipped out again. We had to get out of the house."

"Well, it wasn't the fishing trip I had in mind with a baby along. Christ."

"Yeah well, my life isn't what I had in mind either," Jack muttered. Looking back over his shoulder he added, "Murphy, are you gonna move back over to your side of the tent?"

"Nope, I'm good right here," Tim said, sliding over even closer to the other two in the tent. Jack sighed and turned on his side away from his friend who reached over and wrapped his arm around his shoulders, spooning close.

"Oh, for God's sake," Jack whispered trying hopelessly to find sleep again.

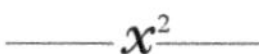

Carl Washington held his daughter's hand as they stared up at the sky. They had gone out for a late evening walk which had taken them out of the Norton community, across the tracks, and up Sycamore Street to Park Street. They walked all the way to the park, past the city pool, stopping at Freeman's long enough to get a large Grape slush. Carl noted the surly face of the high school boy who had served them, that knowing look of someone who was wondering what the hell you are doing in this part of town. But Carl had been walking or driving from Norton up to Maple Street since he and Mike played football together. He just smiled at the pimple-faced boy and invited him to have a nice evening.

Carl and Mary sat on a picnic table and drank their slushes. He had never really played in this park as a child. Back then, he would have been chased down the street by boys throwing rocks more than likely. The night was still, hardly any wind and after their walk, Carl's shirt stuck to his back which was beginning to get a bit tight in the middle. He had always had a flat belly, lots of muscles. But now, after college and Viet Nam were years behind him, he had grown wider and flabbier, like most of the other men his age in town.

He and Mary finished their slushes and laid back on the table and stared at the stars. Carl pointed out constellations and told stories of his college days or the few parts of his military service he talked about. He shared his current struggles to make the washateria successful. He talked of his ongoing work to try and get the Norton community water supply cleaned up and the status of the legal case against Hi-Gro and the owners. He felt there might finally be some real movement in the case and held out hope that the hundreds of families harmed by the toxic site would get reparations of some kind.

He stretched his arm out and Mary lay in the crook of his arm. It was strange that his son, Yancy, rarely showed any interest in taking a walk or hanging out with his father. The boy seemed as different as he could be from Carl. He seemed distant and lost, preferring to play with friends or stay near home. Maybe it was just his age. Did twelve year old boys really enjoy hanging out with their fathers? He had never been given the chance.

But Mary had been his constant companion on his walks or long Saturdays at the laundry for a long time. He felt closer to her than to his wife, wondering these days if they were actually going to make it. Delois had no stomach for the politics and constant struggles Carl found himself in the middle of, trying to make a difference for his family and the others in Norton. It was his legacy. He'd felt this way all his life and he had to believe it would make the world a better place for Mary, Yancy, and all the other children.

Mary wrapped her father's strong brown arm around her shoulders. Her soft long curls tickled his face. Now that she was wearing her hair in a picked-out afro, she looked older than ever. He wondered what time it was. They had stayed out far later than they should have. He just had so much on his mind. These days, it seemed the only way to clear his head was to walk. But he was so tired now. Maybe he could just shut his eyes for a few minutes before they walked back home.

Carl's eyes flew open sometime later. For a moment he was alarmed that Mary was gone, then even more so as he looked to his side and saw his daughter floating six inches above his arm and the picnic table, where she had been lying. The sky directly above them was awash with light, silvery and intolerably bright. Mary dropped down on the table as if someone had released a stone from their grasp. She sat up and stared at the light. It flowed over them both in a tight circle of twenty feet in diameter. Within that small space it was complete daylight. Outside that, inky darkness hovered at the perimeter. Seconds later, the light vanished with no sound. It moved some miles away to the southwest and flashed again. Then it appeared to zoom back to the west and vanish.

Mary reached over and grabbed Carl's arm. "Daddy, what is it?"

The two sat still for a good two minutes before looking at one another with frightened gazes. Carl glanced at his watch.

"Oh shit, we gots to go," he swore grabbing Mary by the hand again and taking off at a jog. He didn't want to run fast. It was bad enough he was out this late in the white part of town. If he was seen running, there was no end of trouble that could find its way into his life.

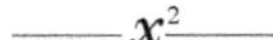

$$x^2$$

JL Martin stood on the large wrap-around porch of his large two-story colonial house pissing into his wife's zinnias when the lights hovering over Cowhill caught his eye. He stood still holding his dick long after he was finished urinating, trying to puzzle out what in the hell could be shining a light down over some neighborhood in the little town. Best he could tell it was over by the City Park. The air was so still and the sweat ran off his bald head down his back and into the crack of his ample ass. Funny, he thought, the ever-present cicadas had stopped their thrumming as well. The only thing he could hear was the air conditioner compressors and some faint giggling from the bedroom behind him.

The sultry night was like a moist blanket to his naked skin. He lit a Tiparillo and took a deep draw and sent the smoke high into the air above his head. The light had stayed on only a minute or so. When it extinguished, he assumed it was gone. Then it almost seemed like smaller points of light began to rain down, like a slow moving firework. He watched as a streak appeared in the sky that headed southwest over toward the lake. It hovered for a moment and then dissipated. He looked out beyond the edge of the roof to see the palate of stars glittering in the velvety night. Just as he turned to go back inside, behind him a wide flash of bright white illuminated the entire porch, like a floodlight pointed at the house. As he whirled around, JL saw a green glow and a simultaneous whump, as something struck the earth over the hill to the east of the house, rattling the windows of the house like a sonic boom.

"What was that?"

The dark college student stood beside JL now, her large round breasts outlined by the silvery moonlight creeping into the edge of the porch. Her full lips hung open as she looked around trying to find the source of the light and sounds. The dark triangle between her legs was thick and curly, just the way he liked it. Her hair was flattened down in the back but still a puffy, wiry mound in front. He tried to think of her name. Dimonte or LaFonda or some ridiculous Afro-stupid name. What is it with these young colored girls, he thought? What happened to completely respectable names like Ruby or Mabel?

"Just dry lightning or something, darlin'," JL said sliding in behind the girl. As he brushed against her large round ass, he stirred. He reached around and gripped her breasts, tweaking the eraser-shaped nipples in his fingers as she moaned and leaned her head back against his. JL gripped her arms and bent her forward until she was leaning over the porch railing.

JL began to move inside the girl as a tall figure stood close behind him, large strong arms reaching around to help him drive deeper inside the coed. Joe Wilson was a defensive end for the East Texas State Lions. Joe was a completely reasonable name for a colored boy, he was pleased to think. Whenever he had a college girl over, which was as often as he could get the house to himself, he tended to invite a football player over as well. He liked three-way sex, two guys and one girl. JL felt the young man move behind him and grip his ample waist. He gasped as Joe positioned himself and slid deep inside. Throbs of pain coupled with tingles of ecstasy filled him as he rocked back in forth; sandwiched between the students, cries of release echoing in the still air, sweat gluing the trio together.

"Yee haw, ride 'em cowboy!" JL shouted to the sky.

3 The Starchild

The being knew his vessel was beyond repair and would last only a short time. His curiosity had pushed him farther and farther this time, far beyond where his father had insisted he go. But it was a big galaxy and there was so much to learn, so much to experience. It had always been sustainable before. Even now, he was not clear which miscalculation had doomed him, but he was finished nonetheless.

The emotions and energy were better at night. He could sort through them, enjoy them, experience so much. He had attempted it during the light hours and was overwhelmed with the mental onslaught. So much confusion, so many conflicting emotions. His world had none of this to offer, at least none so primal or primitive. But they also resonated with incredible vibration within him. He assessed he had experienced a vast number of new emotions and mental images in just the brief partial orbit. His father would want to share his experiences. Surely he had explored these on his own. Wasn't it he who had mentioned this blue world and pointed it out not that long ago?

The journey had proved longer than he calculated and he had rushed the planning. He was too eager to explore and experience. So many dead planets, so many gas giants, so much empty space. This world was so rich in those unimagined emotions and experiences. The others in his instruction group had long wondered if there was more. Now he knew, there was so much more. But he also wondered if his curiosity had cost him more than he was prepared to give.

There was only so much time left. He had already sent out the distress beacon. He cringed imagining the wrath of his father, the worry of his mother. But it had been worth it. His mind processed the situation and calculated the only possible solution: in his language, it was called hmurthagah 'ia; the spreading of one's consciousness into other organic, sentient organisms to hibernate, to incubate, until the a'asa'hmurthgah; "the gathering" could begin. It would keep him safe and hidden. And those he hid within would not know, or at least, he hoped so. But even this filled him with excitement and anticipation. Living as a dissociated organism, what would he know? Would the experiences continue? He looked at the large landmass he floated above, so many feelings even while these beings slept; some so tender and passionate, some dark and malevolent. Hopefully the light would not be too disturbing.

His vessel continued to fail. It was moments now. He concentrated with his entire mind to the core of his existence and felt his being begin to disassemble. With his last cogent assembled thought, he directed his being to seek out hospitable, open hosts. As his vessel began to disintegrate, he felt his essence break apart with it and fly downward. In a cascade of light, his being lodged again and again within the primitive open hosts lying dormant below, each programmed to join again. They would call again and again to each other until the gathering was complete.

The center chamber of his vessel shimmered and flickered dimly as it plummeted to the world below, sailing over thick groves of vegetation and slow, brown rivers. As the chamber continued to descend, it seemed pulled toward a spot that vibrated with energy, sad and desperate. A place that had hungered for some sort of resolution, some redemption. This place was dark and evil, cruel and filled with fear. It permeated the very bones of this place and pulled the being toward its core. After all, seeking these emotions was what it had been programmed to find. It plowed into the soft, muddy bank of a sluggish river, disappearing into the thick grasses and brush thickly carpeting the riparian edges with a loud boom that rattled the windows on the nearby house. The metallic edge of the chamber protruded from the silted tomb, casting its gaze on a crumbled bridge and rusted, forgotten signal on a rotted pole.

The lens on the long-dead train signal came to life and illuminated the surrounding riverside, bathing the banks in a vibrant, emerald glow.

4 Travis

Travis stood under the warm water with his eyes closed, willing himself to wake up. He felt as if he had not closed his eyes since getting back in the bed last night. His head throbbed and hurt as if giant hands were gripping it like a baseball. He gave up trying to sleep around 6:00 am and not knowing what else to do, drug himself to the bathroom and tried to drown the buzzing and thumping inside his brain with the water.

Travis never ventured into the shower on a school morning, having learned early on that with an older brother in high school and a dad headed to work, he was low man on the totem pole in regard to shower time. Long ago, the smaller bathroom had become the men's bathroom, with the larger one completely occupied by his mother and sister. No boys with their dirty feet, smelly socks, and tendency to miss-fire around the toilet were allowed in the pink tiled boutique. This meant that he and Trey and even Andy took every opportunity to secretly visit the girl's room and mark their territory with various bodily fluids and scents without getting caught. Hearing the complaints as an unwary mom walked into the eye-watering scent of a clandestine dump taken in her inner sanctum was sheer bliss. Not to mention the joy that was found in hearing that his sister had gone to the bathroom in the middle of the night expecting the seat to be down and falling inside the toilet bowl with a shriek.

But sneaking into the girls' bathroom was more than just fun, it was essential sometimes. There was an unwritten rule in the McGee household that you could not lock a door, especially the bathroom. This had all started during the Cowboys vs Redskins game a couple of years earlier. Travis's dad had made his mad dash to the bathroom only to find that Trey was locked in one and Teppy in the other. Cursing, he ran out in the backyard to pee but it was raining buckets. So he stood on the back steps under the eaves of the roof and sent and golden stream into the pouring rain only to realize Mr. and Mrs. Nallin were just returning from Sunday dinner and were just getting out of the car staring straight into our backyard and Mike McGee's johnson. Within minutes, the phone was ringing and a hysterical Mrs. Nallin was screaming at Travis's mother while Mike pounded down the hall to the bathroom and literally kicked the door open, quite surprising Trey who was trying to have a few private moments with himself and a sticky Hustler magazine.

By the next weekend, both bathroom doors had been fitted with new lockless doorknobs, much to the chagrin of Teppy and Janet (and a mortified Trey.) Mike explained that you simply had to knock on a closed door to find out if there was someone occupying the bathroom. When Trey mentioned that knocking meant actually waiting to hear if someone was busy in the bathroom, Mike backhanded him in the mouth and that was that. Unlike the rest of the men in the McGee household, Travis was already reluctant to take a dump in public bathrooms, having seen far too many boys hauled off a toilet at school and scramble to pull up their pants while mocking bullies laughed and pointed. Along with that terror was the school's decision to reduce vandalism in the boys' bathroom by removing the doors to the stalls. Hey, it's good enough for the soldiers; it ought to be okay for these slackers. Many days he had hobbled home with bowels ready to rupture, determined that at least this one humiliation was one he would not have to endure. Clearly comfortable on the throne, Travis had lost count of the times he had walked in on his dad reading the paper on the commode. Trey and Andy seemed to literally wait until Travis was in the shower to come in and sit for a while, which was incomprehensible to him. More than once he had ducked into the bathroom at his friend Eric's house on the way home. He had subtlety trained his body to wait until the most opportune moments like when his mother was cooking dinner and Teppy was on the phone or staying late for band practice to sneak into the clean, pink comfort of the girls' bathroom. For a while, he even carried a small wedge of rubber he'd found on his way home from school in his pocket that fit nicely into the crack under the bathroom door that would at least halt a rampaging brother or dad from interfering with a boy's few private moments. That ended when Mike knocked/barged into the bathroom during a commercial break on "All in the Family" while the doorstop was in place and banged his face, chipping a tooth in the process. Mike bulldozed the door open and smacked Travis in the head hard enough to send him flying off the pot.

The boys had the chore of cleaning their bathroom once a week, but since his mom rarely wanted to check it out, it often was much longer before the brothers were forced to clean it up. Most of the time, Travis ended up cleaning it himself when the smell of urine and wet towels became too much for even him to stand. Today, he felt himself rock back and forth a bit, trying to get the ringing in his ears and constant pain in his head to lighten up. He could hardly see the tiles in the small bathroom that were strangely baby blue, caked with soap scum and mildew in the corners of the shower or his dad's Old Spice Soap on a Rope that hung on the hot water handle. Travis filled his hands full of shampoo and worked it into his hair as he stood in the water wishing his head would clear when the door opened. The toilet seat clunked up against the tank, with either Trey or his dad's fire hose-like piss filling the bowl.

"You better not be using up my hot water, Nutsack," Trey barked in his low early morning voice.

"Hey, I can take a shower too." Travis answered feebly.

"Not in the morning, Beanbag. You and Andy get nights." Travis noticed he was always Nutsack or Scrote, but Andy was always Andy. Just then a new voice joined the mix.

"You boys need to get done in here, I need a shower."

"I haven't even started, this retard is messing up the . . ."

"Travis, hurry and get out – Trey get in and make it snappy."

Travis gritted his teeth and grabbed his towel, trying to find a place to dry off a bit before dashing into his room. He bent down to dry his feet and got a face full of Trey's bare ass heading into the water on one side while Mike bent over the sink shaving in his BVD's with the saggy elastic. About that time, Andy came in the bathroom and started to pee.

"God, this place is a mad house!" Travis snapped wrapping the towel around himself and stomped away, head still pounding. He made a mental note that next time he'd just go find some aspirin if he had a headache. He found some clothes that looked somewhat clean and started pulling on his underwear when Andy came back in the room.

"Are you kidding me? It's like a damn airport or something around here."

"Why are you so mad? I've seen you get dressed a million times," Andy asked pulling on an old H.R. Pufinstuf T-shirt.

"Forget it. I just have a headache," Travis said pulling on his jeans. The boys dressed the rest of the way in silence. Travis walked over and switched off the water cooler. It was early September, but the Texas heat was already making the room hotter as the air blew into the room. Travis figured he would be drenched with sweat by the time he made the walk to school. So much for the shower, he thought.

"What was that, last night?" Andy asked. "What was that light?"

"I don't know."

"I had a dream before the light came on and you were up in the air."

Travis's head snapped around to look at his little brother struggling with a knot in his tennis shoes. Travis walked over and pulled the shoe away from the boy and undid the knot. "What do you mean, I was up in the air?"

"In my dream, you were floating in the air. Isn't that weird?"

"Yeah, Weirdo, it's weird." The sparkles behind Travis's eyes flared again and another tingle of pain contracted across his head. "I got to get some aspirin."

"There's no orange ones that you chew up, just the white ones. I ate all the orange ones."

"How many did you eat?"

"Just 5 or 6, that's all there was left," Andy said grabbing his library book and heading out the door to the kitchen.

"Stop eating those things, they're not candy," Travis yelled after him half-heartedly, remembering a few months ago when he had drank an entire bottle of Creomulsion Cough Syrup for Children simply because it tasted good. He went to the kitchen and grabbed the box of Captain Crunch and sat at the table. Trey rushed into the kitchen, hair wet from his shower, a damp line of water drops down the back of his t-shirt. He pushed Andy out of the way and grabbed a package of Pop-Tarts.

"Ok Later," Trey said heading for the door.

"Can you give me and Andy a ride to school?" Travis asked knowing the answer before he asked.

"No can do, Scrote. Gotta pick up some high schoolers. No room for munchkins," he said with a full mouth heading out the door.

"Don't be late for work after school," a deep voice rumbled from the other side of the kitchen table.

"I won't," Trey said banging the screen door.

Travis looked across the table at his dad's head buried in the morning paper. The front page had a small headline in the lower left corner that caught his eye.

Bright Lights Startle Neighborhood

Travis read the short article that explained that some residents of Cowhill were awakened last night by bright lights around 1:00 AM. It is believed the lights were from a military helicopter being tested from Greenville's LTD airfield. Phone calls to the airfield director were not returned. That was it. There were was literally no details at all and it seemed like the newspaper was just making up some nonsense. Andy sat beside Travis and looked at the story as well. He leaned over to his brother.

"Didn't sound like a helicopter to me," Andy said flatly.

"Yeah, me neither," Travis agreed. "Dad, how come you are still home?" Travis asked.

"Got to head down to Kaufman for a meeting later so Bill is opening up" the voice of his dad croaked from behind the Cowhill Journal. He must have handed the paper off to Janet because

Mike went over and grabbed some more coffee from the Mr. Coffee and tore open a Sweet N Lo to add to it. Travis couldn't help but notice the back of his white jockey shorts sported a quarter-sized hole, his fuzzy crack peeking out into the bright light of the kitchen. Travis looked away trying not to lose his cereal. Andy must have noticed too.

"Dad, you got a hole in your underwear," he reported.

Mike looked around, sticking out his backside to try and see and ripped a loud fart that echoed in the tiled kitchen. "Yeah, looks like a blowout," he said smirking. Andy laughed loudly while Travis fanned the air. Janet looked around the paper with annoyance.

"It's like living with a bunch of monkeys here sometimes," she muttered. "Throw those things in the trash and could you please put some clothes on. You have a daughter you know," his wife admonished.

"Well she's off to college and besides, she might as well get used to all this," Mike said spreading his hands wide and taking a slight bow. His furry belly hanging slightly over the waistband of his briefs. "She's gonna get married to some dream stud like me one of these days and he's gonna walk around the house in his shorts too."

Janet looked daggers at Mike and muttered, "God help her if she does," she said before disappearing behind the paper again.

Teppy walked into the kitchen in her Cowboys jersey and hot rollers in her hair. "There's the man of my dreams," she said leaning over and kissing her dad on the cheek. Janet rolled her eyes and smiled. "Daddy, remember my car is still doing that shuddery thing when I put it in reverse. You said you would take a look. I don't want to deal with a broken car down in Fort Worth."

"I already took care of it darling," Mike said. "Can't let my baby have a crappy car when she's cheering for the Horn Frogs." Mike was still bragging all over town about Teppy's scholarship to TCU and even more about her making the cheerleading squad. He was proud that she was going to a more renowned college rather than the local small East Texas State school in town.

"You are wonderful, Daddy. Remember I'm gonna get you all tickets for later on this fall. I am getting ready to head out. I am going to hang out with Amy today over at ET. I don't have class this afternoon so I won't leave until tomorrow." Teppy hugged and kissed her dad again and then hugged her mom. She grabbed Andy and gave him a big hug and kiss which he promptly wiped off.

"Bye, Travie, have a good day," she said kissing him lightly on the cheek. As the two of them touched, an odd surge of electric energy seemed to pass between them. She touched her lips and looked at him with an odd expression.

Travis grabbed his books and ran out the door.

5 Jack

Jack adjusted the radio as he reluctantly headed back home after the failed fishing trip. Tim was already softly snoring in the passenger's seat of the truck, his mouth open and face pressed against the window, hand tucked into the waistband of his sweatpants. In the middle seat, Joey napped as well, pacifier hanging out the corner of his mouth, his hand slid inside his Pampers. The aspirin he had taken an hour ago were having no effect on his headache at all. He rummaged around in the glove compartment and found an old box of Midol and took a couple of those too. Now he felt like his stomach was cramping, which was ridiculous.

He eased off the gas and settled into a slow 60 mph as he headed north on Hwy 69, which always made him think of sex. It might be juvenile and immature, but it still did. And the fact he rarely got any these days didn't make it any easier. He and Tim had packed up the truck early in the morning. Tim met him at the boat ramp and they quickly loaded the small bass boat back on the trailer and took off. No one had caught a thing, except a frickin' headache that wouldn't budge. The radio began to play "Carry on Wayward Son," and he turned the dial up a bit, softly singing along with Kansas.

He had taken off work early the night before hoping for some peace and quiet and also just to escape the hell of being locked in the depressing prison home had become. The idyllic first year of marriage seemed like such a long time ago now. He could hardly remember the carefree, spontaneous lovemaking, the constant touching, that wonderful feeling of a hand sliding inside his underwear early in the morning bringing him to life in seconds. Now, a huge gulf of sheet stretched between him and Lori, that is, on the mornings when she was in the bed at all. More often than not, she was gone and when he found her, she was curled in the big chair in Joey's room. Sometimes she would be alone, other times cradling the boy in her arms protectively. Lately though, it seemed she was even distant from Joey, not responding to his cries or attempts to be held when he wanted his mother. She sleepwalked though most days, groggy from the drugs she continued to take that did not seem to improve her mood at all, but at least deadened the pain. Jack understood all this but inside he could feel his patience running out. He was sad too, devastated goddamn it. But that didn't mean he could check out and pretend he didn't still have responsibilities. He still had to work, still had to be a dad, still had to hold it together when he felt dead inside too.

Joey shifted in his car seat and sucked loudly on his pacifier. Jack knew he should be trying to get the damn thing away from him. He would probably be so buck-toothed he could eat a peanut butter sandwich through a chain-link fence, but he just didn't have the energy to worry about it. Same with potty training, forget that, he thought. Jack scratched his chin, rough as sandpaper and looked at himself in the rearview mirror. His thick brown mustache was trimmed up compared to the handlebar porn-stache Tim sported. He looked okay but damn, he thought, the mileage was taking a toll. Kansas faded out on the radio and was replaced with Barry White's "Can't Get Enough of Your Love, Babe," which used to be one of the songs that always got Lori turned on and now just brought back dim memories.

When Jack got back from Viet Nam in 1968, he was lost like so many other vets. He and Tim took off to Mexico for the better part of a year, hiding from the world and a country that didn't seem to give a shit what had happened to them or what they had endured. They tried to stay high or drunk most of the time, living on their veteran benefit check that didn't amount to much. They had made it out of that hell when plenty of their buddies did not. There were also plenty of other disillusioned vets hanging out in the bars in Carmen del Playa. The sad souls recounted battles like old men, started drinking or smoking weed by noon, and didn't stop until they couldn't stand up anymore. Part of the time, they hooked up with local prostitutes to try and feel good again, it rarely worked. More than half of the veterans they hung out with migrated to cocaine and then heroin, anything to take away the pain. Luckily, Jack and Tim didn't fall that far down the hole of depression.

One blurry day, ten months after they had made their way to the Yucatan peninsula, Jack and Tim ran into a couple of Texas girls on spring break. Lori and Candy were twenty and away from home for the first time. The girls were fresh and sweet and oh so naïve. Jack and Tim were so brown from hanging out on the beach every day the girls thought they were locals at first and were somewhat disappointed to find out they were just good ole Texas boys running away from life.

But after those first two days of flirting and getting to know each other, the girls relaxed and Jack began to feel something stir within himself for the first time in a long time. The door to his past life began to creep open and something close to happiness began to filter through. Tim and Candy began to spend some of their time alone which made Jack glad, because he wanted to be alone with Lori. He rented a boat one day and took Lori out to one of the barrier islands, their own paradise for the afternoon. After working their way through a dozen bottles of Dos Equis, Jack and Lori swam naked in the Caribbean and then made love under a palm tree on the old army blanket he had brought along. Lori cried out as Jack claimed her virginity, but was soon moaning in pleasure. By the next day, she was climbing on top of him and riding him like a rodeo superstar, head flung back in pleasure, as he unloaded his desire.

That glorious two weeks pulled Jack and Tim back from the edge and brought them back to life. The guys followed the girls back home, much to their families' delight. Lori and Candy's parents were happy to see their girls dating local war heroes. Jack and Tim were ready to try and live in the real world again as well. Tim's dad, Frank, had owned the Western Auto in downtown Cowhill for a long time and was ready to retire. He hired both guys to run the store for him and never looked back, heading off for his house on Lake of the Pines. Jack and Tim proposed to their girls the same weekend and even did the clichéd double wedding ceremony in June of 1971.

Within three months, Lori was pregnant. She miscarried two months into the pregnancy. A year later, she was pregnant again, this time she miscarried after five months. Jack was devastated but for some reason, Lori kept being positive and saying she knew everything was going to be just fine. So Jack just believed her. Finally, Lori was pregnant again in late 1975. Jack almost felt like he didn't breathe for the whole nine months until the baby was born. Then, in the early morning of July 4, 1976, Jack and Lori Tanner got their baby, a Bicentennial baby boy. They named him Joseph Colt and they were so happy. He was an easy baby. Didn't fuss, was rarely colicky, slept all through the night by three-weeks old. Jack was so proud of this boy and had never seen Lori so radiant. She was a natural mother, seemingly growing with beauty and confidence as the little boy grew as well. Three months after Joey, somehow Lori was pregnant again. Jack was dismayed by the news but Lori seemed thrilled. She had a plan and that meant getting the years of diapers and nursing and lack of sleep over with soon. She figured it was just easier to do it all at once and then move on with the rest of life. Jack had a feeling it was going to be hard work but soon warmed to the idea as he watched Joey grow into a toddler. Lori's excitement seemed to grow as did her belly, Jack noticed.

Then in July once again, just after Joey turned one, Amber arrived and she was perfect. Golden-haired like mom, small and graceful. Like big brother, little sister was peaceful and good-natured. Lori kept commenting that if raising babies was this easy, maybe they should just keep on going. Jack secretly was thinking two kids sounded about right and wondered how he could try and lower the odds that Lori would get pregnant again soon. He shook his head at the irony of all that now. Interestingly, he thought, Tim and Candy had yet to start a family. He wondered if they were the really smart ones.

Like her brother, Amber had started sleeping through the night around three weeks of age. Then on August 19 it all changed, He closed his eyes at the memory again. The shriek that ripped him from early morning sleep, the frantic minutes of trying to figure out what was going on, Lori's terrified face, Amber's limp body in her arms. He had never heard of SIDS before. She was perfect, how could something like that just happen? None of the explanations or sympathy or words of comfort or promise of prayers did any good at all. The shattered family stumbled through the next week; supported by many well-meaning friends and family, but it all did little to deaden the pain. But sometime a couple of weeks later, Jack decided Joey alone was reason to keep on going and he tried to focus on his son and not dwell on his little girl, now an angel.

But Lori was lost to him. She retreated into some other dimension that could not cope and could not deal with reality. Like The Zombies sang, "She's not there," seemed to sum up her post-Amber world. Slowly and methodically, Jack began to be more and more the sole caretaker for his little boy as Lori would shun him or simply not respond in any way. The only time she seemed to deviate from this was her middle of the night journeys to Joey's room. But even when she would hold him, it seemed more motivated by terror and despair than by love or longing. Jack had given up trying to touch and comfort his wife. She refused to respond in any way to his embrace or touch. A few weeks ago in desperation, he crawled on top of her in bed and slid himself inside, thinking maybe this would unlock her wounded heart. The sadness of that necrophilia-like coupling ended any attempt to force her to a different place.

Now a year later, the couple was in a different place, but not much. Lori had decided to go back to work as a hair stylist and Jack had to admit this had helped her catatonia, but gone were the conversations, the cuddling, the dreaming together. And her coldness and reluctance to bond with Joey was excruciating. Jack made the mistake of suggesting they try again to have another baby only once. That mistake sent Lori back into her dark place for over two weeks. They rarely kissed anymore, other than the perfunctory good-night version. It had been so long since they made love, he didn't even remember. The routine of rubbing one off in the shower was so common now, he didn't even question it anymore. Another throb of his headache radiated through his skull and Jack rummaged around for a pair of sunglasses to ease the strain on his sore eyes. He began to click through some of the list of tasks from work he needed to think about for this week, but he just couldn't concentrate. Western Auto would just have to wait for him. Today, he didn't give a damn anyway. And what the hell was that light thing last night anyway? Turning into town he began to think of Lori again. He squeezed his crotch, wishing for once he could just come home and find her happy. Wished he could slide into bed and into her again, feel like a man again. He stopped the truck and Tim sleepily opened his eyes and looked around.

Whispering, Jack said, "I'll come by later and give you your gear. Just want to get Joey home and maybe he will sleep a bit more."

"OK, buddy," Tim croaked getting out of the truck. "Thanks for a great trip," he added with thick sarcasm. "That was worth letting Crazy Ray run the store for us. We'll probably find out he started running a poker room in the back and a whorehouse upstairs."

Jack pulled away and was frankly amazed that Joey was still content to be sleeping. The little guy had almost a smile underneath the Binky. Jack wondered what he was dreaming about. He kept thinking about Lori, too. This was crazy. It was just going to be more disappointment. But this overwhelming sense of confidence and raw sensuality seemed to course through him. If Joey would just stay asleep, she had been in such a good mood lately. Maybe, just maybe, she would be into a little make out session at least. He felt he'd probably blow a load in his pants with that alone. Jack parked the truck and eased the door open. He unbuckled the car seat straps and began to lift his boy out of it. Joey gripped his dad's neck and continued sleeping. Jack quietly made his way back into the house and laid the toddler down in his bed, fully expecting his eyes to fly open and the nap to be over. But he kept on sleeping. Jack kissed his head gently and rubbed his hand across the boy's soft hair and left the room, quietly closing the door.

Jack tiptoed down the hall and saw his still sleeping wife turned away from the door, soft breathing filling the room along with the drone of the fan. Jack pulled his t-shirt up to his nose and sniffed and then lifted his arm and caught a whiff of his pits. He walked softly to the bathroom and jumped in the shower and quickly washed, intentionally avoiding his normal happy ending with the soap. He dried off and quietly walked back to the bedroom and slipped underneath the covers, scooting over behind Lori, softly kissing her neck. He didn't know why, but he knew she wouldn't recoil this time. He pressed his erection against her ass and wrapped his arms around her and there it was; her soft sigh of contentment. How long had it been? She turned her head to his and their lips met in a long, warm, hungry kiss. Her breasts swelled against the palms of his hands and she wriggled and pressed against him in a longing, languid rhythm.

6 George

The aspirin hadn't put a dent in Travis's headache by the time he had started his walk up Church Street toward the junior high school. He still felt light-headed and dazed, and floating specks of black and glittery white danced across his vision as he stepped out into the damp, hot morning. Along with the headache was that unmistakable feeling that he was forgetting something, something big. His Converse sneakers puffed up tiny clouds of dust as he absent-mindedly trudged toward school, straining to remember, trying to will his mind to conjure up its mysteries, but the brick wall continued.

"Wait up, Trav."

George Harris ran up beside Travis puffing, "Jeez, wait will ya, you turd."

Travis looked at the equally disheveled teenager and decided he wasn't the only one who had had a bad night. "Your shirt's on inside out, Spaz."

George looked down and frowned at his shirt, pulling the collar of his t-shirt out. "Damn it, this morning has been a pile of crap." He dropped his books and sack lunch onto the cracked sidewalk and ripped his shirt off and flipped it right-side out and pulled it back on, managing to miss the arm hole and running his hand out through the neck so that the shirt was hanging like a toga off one shoulder.

"Shit!"

"Hey, watch your mouth, George Harris!" Mrs. Sutton admonished as she ferociously swept her front porch. The boys took off at a slow trot, George stumbling to pick up his school things while continuing to adjust his shirt.

"Sorry, Mrs. Sutton," he yelled back over his shoulder, and then under his breath continued, "You old Harpy." The boys slowed again a couple of houses down the street and settled into a slow shuffle.

"You look like I feel," Travis said.

"My mom was riding my ass like a bull all morning. That time of the month or something, I guess. What's your excuse?"

"My head is killing me for some reason."

"Really, cause I have a headache too. When I mentioned it to my mom she said I was faking and trying to get out of going to school 'cause I hadn't studied at all for that Texas History test today."

Travis stopped dead in his tracks. "That isn't today?" he asked with weak conviction.

"Looks like I'm not the only procrastinator today." George loved finding ways to use his small assortment of big words in conversations. It was an ongoing hobby that Travis was finding more and more annoying.

"I totally forgot."

"Big deal. It's not like you ever study anyway. You always find a way to pull all the answers out of your ass just from reading or listening or telepathy or something."

"I study," Travis began but stopped when George pulled back his fist ready to pound it into his shoulder, "sometimes."

"I study . . . " George said in a mocking, baby voice. "Yeah, right. Ferle is really gonna flip her wig if you don't make another A." Ferle was in reference to Mrs. Ferle Hawksworth, the Texas History teacher that wore an unfortunate shag wig to school since the beginning of the year. In the sweltering heat of her classroom, one of the great pastimes was watching her begin to clandestinely try and sneak her pencil up the side of the wig to give her head a scratch, making the whole ratty coif shudder back and forth on her bony skull. Mrs. Hawksworth also had a habit of telling anyone in class who was being nonchalant or disrespectful to "not be so flippant....or don't be flip with me," which combined with the wig more shaggy than The Partridge Family mom, became Flip Wig and brought new meaning to the whole "Don't flip your wig" saying.

"I'm dead," George began. "I don't have a clue on all those damn explorers. LaSalle or DeScroto or that Cabeza De Goma..."

"De Vaca."

"What?"

"Cabaza de Vaca. Cabeza de Goma is like rubber-head or something."

"Why don't you just suck my cabeza, smart ass?"

The boys continued down Church Street, turned left on College Street between the fire department and the A&P. Travis winced as the sun reflected off the shiny windows on the grocery, stumbling against George as he covered his eyes.

"Watch it, retard. What's up with you today anyway?"

"I told you. I have a headache, a bad one." I didn't sleep well at all."

"So what the hell do you think that was last night?" George asked suddenly sincere.

"I don't know. For a while I thought the whole thing was a dream. But it did happen, right. The light and all that?"

"Duh. Yeah, why else do you think the whole god-dang neighborhood was standing out in the yard in their BVD's?" Was funny to see the McGee men were all sporting the tighty-whities last night. Bet Emily enjoyed seeing your johnson flopping around."

"What the hell were you wearing? Looked like a frickin' dress?" Travis snapped.

"It was a long t-shirt. Lots of guys wear them."

"You just keep telling yourself that," Travis said with a smile. The boys turned onto Pecan street and picked up the pace hearing the first bell from school ringing. First period was wood shop class and Mr. Monroe was pretty laid back as a teacher but he had a total bug up his ass regarding being tardy. The boys had heard plenty of stories from older guys about Mr. Monroe's paddle he had named White Lightning. They had already seen it in action first hand this year when Marty Minor had ambled into class just after the second bell. Just as Marty was getting to his seat, Mr. Monroe with his big smile told him to come up to the front of the class. All the air in the big workshop left through the open windows as the teacher lifted White Lightning out of the chalkboard tray and tossed it in the air a couple of times. Marty was a pretty big boy, a thick peach fuzz mustache and tufts of hair poking out from the pits of his tank top. But he visibly trembled as he stood beside the teacher's desk and gripped the corners, bending slightly forward. Mr. Monroe walked behind the boy and ran his hands across both back pockets, pulling out a wallet and a big comb, feeling his legs and backside like he was having a pat down from a cop. The teacher's face was pleasant and emotionless as the paddle rested on Marty's blue-jeaned butt cheeks. Mr. Monroe rubbed the paddle back and forth against the fabric a couple of times and then in a blinding motion, brought the paddle up and back down, cracking hard against the tightly clinched buttocks of the tardy boy. There was a gasp from the class and a groan from Marty that filled the room. Instinctively, Marty grabbed his ass, and Mr. Monroe said calmly, "Move your hands or you might lose a finger," in his low gruff voice. Marty's trembling hand moved and a blurred second lick popped against the boy's ass. Mr. Monroe laid the paddle back in the chalkboard tray and said nonchalantly, "Let's get to work fellows." Nothing else needed to be said and no one else was stupid enough to be tardy.

"My mom said that light must have been a plane or a helicopter," George said jogging slightly toward the shop building. "Yeah, my dad said the same. But I don't know. Did you hear any motor or rotors or anything?"

"Nope."

"And the light, it didn't move. It just stayed there."

"Must have been really bright or something 'cause it like made me fall down or something," George said. "Cause all of a sudden I was like laying on the ground." Travis grabbed George's arm and stopped him. "We're gonna be late if we . . ."

"I got knocked down too. That's really weird. I was having this dream before the light woke me up and it felt like I was . . ."

"Flying. Or floating." George finished his thought.

"What the hell?" Travis hissed just as the second bell sounded. They were still more than fifty yards away from the doorway and safely resting their butts into the stools around their workbench. Both boys eyes widened and they froze. "RUN," Travis yelled as both boys tore toward the shop. He kept thinking about the bell and just kept saying over and over, "Just keep ringing, just keep ringing." They exploded into the workshop, falling into their seats at the workbench, as the bell continued sounding for another 10 seconds or so as Mr. Monroe came into the room from the back office.

"Cutting it close today, gentlemen," he said with a grin, tying his nail apron around his waist. "Looks like that bell saved your butts. Ok fellows, let's get your projects out and get back to sanding today."

Running the sandpaper across the surface of the mahogany step stool he had chosen for a term project, Travis allowed his mind to wander and his eyes to almost close. This seemed to abate the thrumming that continued in the front of his head and reduce it to a manageable dull ache. Listening to the various scratching sounds echoing around the shop from a dozen or more sanding blocks being used was almost hypnotic.

Travis glanced across the workbench and saw George diligently working on his walnut gun rack, a promised Christmas present for his dad, with abandon. Whatever innate skill Travis may have had with a history test not studied for was matched by George's patient and artistic skill with a band saw and sander. In fact, George was the only boy in the entire class who had been allowed to use the lathe, and his work was finely demonstrated in the delicate turnings that he was carefully attaching to the front of the rack.

George Harris was his best friend. More than a brother, the two shared every secret and laugh possible since the day they had met in first grade. Travis hadn't even noticed the stocky, dark-headed boy until both of them had ended up in the locker area at the end of the day. This was where Miss Skipper sent all miscreants to wait in shame until she decided what to do with them. Travis had been sent to the lockers around 1:30 in the afternoon after Miss Skipper had asked why he wasn't copying the two lines from the Dick and Jane reader into his Big Chief tablet like all the other children were. When Travis explained he had already written the two lines down twice and would rather spend his time reading the book he had brought with him to class, she told him to quit being so silly as he couldn't possibly be able to read the book he was holding, "The Autobiography of a Super-Tramp," by W. H. Davies. At this apparent challenge, Travis opened the book and began to read from the chapter he was currently enjoying, recanting the tale of a lynching witnessed by the famous hobo. The children sat in rapt attention while Travis skillfully read about the condemned man being dragged from a building screaming. At the point the poor individual was jerking helplessly on the end of a rope while the mob actually fired bullets into him, Miss Skipper's red-taloned fingers closed around Travis's wrist and pulled him quickly to the back of the room into the locker area.

"That is not a book for children. How dare you? Were you just making that story up?" the teacher snapped as she flipped the book open and confirmed that indeed, Travis had been reading the story verbatim. Her eyes narrowed and she closed the book and smacked him sharply on the top of the head with it. "You can just stay back here for a while, Mr. Smarty."

Never one to continue a confrontation if it could be avoided, Travis sat in one of the empty locker cubbies and looked around the small room. His eyes spied a stack of new reading books, obviously being saved until the class was ready to handle such difficult material. He cracked the book open and began to read of the further adventures of Dick, Betty, and Sally.

The afternoon drug on and soon Travis had made his way through all four volumes of the First Grade reader set scheduled for this year's instruction. He figured the teacher had forgotten about him by now as there seemed to be a new hysteria taking place back in the classroom. An ear-piercing shriek accompanied by laughter and the sound of clipped heels, more laughter and suddenly around the corner came Miss Skipper with a wild-eyed stocky boy held by the ear. When she saw Travis sitting in the area she sucked in her breath with a start. As suspected, she had forgotten all about him. Her eyes took in the scene, with Travis sitting in a cubby surrounded by a year's worth of readers obviously finished, and her dark red lips pressed together into a line so thin and sharp, it looked like a paper cut. But the wailing from some girl was continuing back in the classroom.

"You stay here. I'll deal with you after class." The teacher disappeared back around the corner to deal with the crying girl. The boys looked at each other for a moment, then the new arrival broke into a big grin.

"What a cow."

Travis smiled and nodded. The new boy came over and sat in the cubby beside Travis. "I'm Travis. What happened?" he asked.

"Hi. I'm George. I walked in on this girl that was in the bathroom peeing. It wasn't really my fault. She hadn't turned the stop light around to red. So it was her own fault."

Now this made complete sense to Travis since Miss Skipper had spent the better part of fifteen minutes explaining that under no circumstances were the students to ever actually lock the door to the classroom bathroom because the lock would get stuck and Mr. McDaniel, the janitor, would have to be called to take the hinges off the door to get them out. Instead, she had devised the fool-proof system of a red and green traffic light to indicate whether or not the bathroom was in use. Now Travis saw immediately the folly in expecting six-year-old children to remember to look and see if the bathroom was occupied before opening the door. But to think they would remember to actually turn the sign back around to green when they left was simply ridiculous. This was further backed-up two hours later when young Susan Grant stood in front of the door and peed her pants to the shock and amusement of the class. When Miss Skipper had asked why in the world she didn't just go into the bathroom instead of standing in front of the door, the tearful girl choked out that the traffic light was red. Sure enough, some fool had already forgotten to flip the sign back around after using the bathroom and the result was a wet floor and Susan's lost dignity. Travis also remembered at this time, George had been the one who had suggested perhaps the traffic lights should be colored yellow and brown instead. And as he began to explain just why this made perfect sense, Miss Skipper had walked by him and thumped his ear sharply with her long red-nailed fingers, making a clear popping sound as George grabbed his ear in pain.

"Who did you walk in on?"

"Luann, that skinny girl with the pigtails." George whispered in a soft giggle. "You should have seen her eyes pop out. I got to see her banana split thing too."

"What'd you mean?"

George leaned closer and whispered, "You may not know this, but she didn't have a wiener. Just a banana split between her legs." It was then and there Travis decided he really liked this kid.

"That was a cool story you were reading. Heck of a better one than she was reading us. How do you already know how to read?"

"Not sure, just learned how. I think everyone gets to learn this year."

"You ought to teach us. You know how to better than Miss Stinker," he whispered.

Soon the bell was ringing and the students were piling into the locker area to grab lunch kits and book satchels. The boys gathered up their own belongings and shyly made their way up to the teacher's desk.

"You two have had quite a first day, haven't you?"

"Yes ma'am," the boys answered in unison.

The teacher looked at George. "Hold out your hand," she said sternly. George held out a trembling, sweaty hand and with a lightning quick stroke, Miss Skipper brought down a wooden ruler hard into his palm. "Next time, you be more careful with that bathroom door. How would you like it if someone walked in on you with your pants down?" George didn't say a word. He just looked down and blew cool air on his reddening palm.

Travis's eyes were huge as Miss Skipper turned her gaze to him. He began to hold out his hand when he realized the teacher was shoving a book into it, instead of a ruler. "I don't know what I'm going to do with you this year," she said dryly. "But let's start with reading this instead." Travis looked down and saw a pirate and boy on the cover and "Treasure Island" across the top. "This book still has quite a bit of adventure, but is better for you to be reading at school." Walking together on the way home, Travis learned that George had just moved to his neighborhood and lived only a half a block away. They talked excitedly the whole time, beginning to make plans to play together as soon as possible.

"Is your hand okay?" Travis asked.

"Huh? Oh yeah, that was nothing. My dad whips me way harder than that. So, do you think you can read more of that story to me when you come over to my house?"

"Sure. I can show you how to read it yourself if you want," Travis added. And that was the start of their great friendship. Over the next few weeks and months, Travis and George spent almost every day after school together. Travis never really understood the attraction the Super-Tramp book had for George other than the fact the boy had been a hobo for Halloween the year before. Travis got the idea he hadn't been read to that much in his life because he soaked up the story like a dry sponge. Before long, he was peppering his conversations with as much tramp and hobo jargon as he could, much to the dismay of his mother, Darla, and Miss Skipper. A typical conversation ended up something like this:

Mom: Do you boys want something to eat?

George: Oh yes, lady (with a British accent for some reason) Me mate and I could just go for some bullets (beans.) We're C. H. and D (cold, hungry, and dry) for sure. Been out all day carrying the banner (keeping in constant motion) and we're about to catch the westbound (die.)

Dad: What in the hell are you talking about?

George: We saw the easy mark (hobo sign indicating a good place to find food and shelter) on the gate, Mister. Be real nice to get a gump in the banjo (piece of meat in a frying pan) so we don't have to spear biscuits (raid garbage cans for food) or keep stemming (beg for food) before we go on the fly (jump a moving train.)

Mom: What does that mean?

Dad: (smacking George on the back of the head) Knock that shit off and go wash your hands.

George continued his fixation on all things tramp, bum, and hobo at school which did not go over well with Miss Skipper:

Teacher: Boys, stop talking back there and get back in your seats.

George: (To Travis in British accent again) Bull's (officer) gonna throw us in the big house (prison) if we don't get back to our flop (desk.)

Teacher: What did you say? Were you swearing?

George: No ma'am. Just padding the hoof (walking) with this road kid (young hobo)
back to our flop (place to rest) before we grease the tracks (get killed.)

Teacher: George, go stand in the hall again.

The Super-Tramp phase lasted for three months. Travis figured maybe he ought to be careful introducing George to the next book or else who knew what crazy imaginations would come out of it. He intentionally skipped sharing "Treasure Island" because even a seven-year-old could see all that pirate shtick was going to get them in big trouble. It had been just last week when both he and George had ended up in Principal Leonard's office after both boys had demonstrated their karate expertise with kicks and neck chops on David Reynolds. Their knowledge was based on steady doses of Hai Karate commercials and "Green Hornet" reruns on after school television. Travis knew he would be getting acquainted with Mr. Leonard's electric paddle that he had heard Trey describing in detail before school had started. George was his best friend, but the guy was a magnet for trouble. More than Travis had ever seen before in his life.

He and George shared so many interests: Dark Shadows and vampires, Matchbox and Hot Wheels cars, medieval torture, Batman, James Bond, blowing crap up with fireworks, and music to name a few. Back when they were in fourth grade, the Dark Shadows thing got so out of hand the boys had converted several of their G.I. Joes to vampires, complete with bloody fangs painstakingly painted on their tiny mouths. They made coffins for the action figures out of old shoe boxes and capes out of old scraps of black velvet they found in George's mother's sewing room. Eventually, the vampire dolls found their way to Teppy's Barbie collection and with the aid of a straight pin heated to red hot on the stove, delicate vampire bites were found in all their slender necks. The holes might have gone unnoticed, but the boys decided one of the newly formed vampire brides had to be destroyed. Skipper (who had no boobs since she was supposedly a teenager) was found by a hysterical Teppy in a shoebox with a nail driven through her flat chest. Travis got backhanded into the middle of next week by his dad and grounded for ten days. He and George had to buy a new Skipper doll and replace the one they had murdered. Travis had thought it was rich that Teppy flipped out so much since she was practically in high school at the time and didn't even play with dolls anymore.

After watching The Addams Family and deciding that Cousin Itt's small home guillotine was really cool, Travis had persuaded his dad to help him build a real working model. Mike used a piece of lead for the blade and the boys worked it until it had a sharp edge. At first, Travis and George were content with chopping carrots and celery with the guillotine, but that got dull and eventually their ideas turned to more exciting prospects. The toy beheader was about eighteen inches tall and the table connected to it was a perfect length for action figures and Barbie dolls. The unfortunate vampire Skipper doll was the first to feel the kiss of steel on her neck, her head tumbling gracefully into the small basket set below the device. Unfortunately, the boys had read about Marie Antoinette and decided that Teppy's Midge doll in the wedding dress had to be punished for taunting the other dolls with her "Let them eat cake" sarcasm. The boys lopped her head off a dozen times or so before they carefully replaced her in Teppy's doll case, shrewdly using some Elmer's glue to reattach the wobbly head. But sometime later, their younger cousin Sherry was staying for the weekend and she and Teppy were having a fashion show on the coffee table in the den during The Carol Burnett Show. As the girls had the dolls walk down the makeshift runway, Midge lost her head which rolled like a golf ball across the table and bounced into Andy's bowl of ice cream. Trey shouted "Hole in one!" while Sherry shrieked. Mike had taken one look at the severed head and walloped Travis with a hard smack to the back of his head. "Stop doing crazy shit," Mike said, giving the boy a Vulcan neck pinch that sent him to the floor in tears.

Mr. Moore told the boys to clean up since class was almost over. George and Travis hurriedly put their projects on the shelves and stored away the tools. Shop class first period was fun but half of the time you ended up being covered in sawdust or metal shavings or paint for the rest of the day. George took the big black comb out of his back pocket and raked it though his hair to get the sawdust out. He handed it to Travis who did the same.

The boys left with the others when the bell rang and joined the crowds in the hall. They stopped off at the bathroom and took a quick pee, watching Jimmy Earwood and Joe Cunningham terrorize poor Doug Ailes, a new student in eighth grade that had the unfortunate luck to still have a high squeaky voice, as well as a penchant for wearing outlandish, flamboyant clothes that got him exactly the kind of attention that George and Travis worked hard to avoid.

George whispered to Travis as they left, "We shouldn't let those a-holes do that to the new kid. I know he's a weirdo, but that makes me mad."

"Do you want Jimmy Earwood to sit on your head like he did back in sixth grade?"

"No," George said pushing that troubling image out of his mind. "But someone needs to kick his ass. I hate bullies."

8 Carl

Carl Washington ran into the City Council chamber only minutes before the meeting began. He was winded and sweating, his papers sticking out from the edges of a worn briefcase like a peacock's feathers. He expected to be tired after last night. He and Mary should never had stayed out so late. Then there were the lights, which had both frightened and excited them. Today was the culmination of so much work, he was smiling in spite of himself.

The mayor called the meeting to order and the commissioners took their seats. Mayor Al Moore was a thick-necked farmer masquerading as a dignitary. He had run for the open seat last year after long-time Mayor Calvin Webster had stepped down to head to his retirement getaway in Galveston. Rumor on the street was he was pushed out by JL Martin, who had then orchestrated Moore's successful election. Carl and half the town had long wondered why JL didn't just run for the mayor's position himself, but he always took the humble road of saying he wasn't made for the big chair and that just being a servant alongside his brethren from Cowhill was more than enough recognition for him. Like a crumbling, dangerous movie set sitting on a Hollywood back lot, it was best not to peel back the veneer of JL's false modesty. It looked marvelous on the screen, but up close it was hollow and empty and utterly false.

Carl had dealt with the likes of JL Martin his entire life. On the surface, they had congratulated him on his hard work in high school, his ultimate triumph of a college football scholarship, and his small-town hero return from Viet Nam along with Mike McGee. But behind the smiles and handshakes, he heard the remarks, the racial intolerance, and the clear message that he was an uppity nigger than need to watch his P's and Q's. Even when they were smiling, it was in the eyes. The loathing and hatred was deep in the bones of this place. But it was his home and he owed it to his grandfather to carry on.

The first item on the agenda the commissioners were taking up the ever-important topic of whether or not to charge a fee for garage sales in town. It was quite the heated debate with several downtown merchants feeling it was a great idea, Duskie Meyers, the bric a brac store owner right on the town square, was one of the loudest proponents. There were also those who railed against the government interfering with folks' own personal business. Frank Cooke was at the microphone:

"...And it seems to me that y'all up there need to keep your big government noses out of the regular man's business. Smattering of applause. It ain't none of your affair if I want to drag my own personal belongings out on the lawn and sell 'em. I'm a taxpayer. I have the right to make a few dollars. It's good for the town to have people out and about looking for bargains. They might just decide to go to the DQ for lunch." Then in a louder voice he finished, "Stay out of our business. Don't Tread on Me!!" Greater applause.

Carl looked through his papers again as he patiently awaited the last item on the agenda and his turn to speak. The real drama and victory had happened a month ago. He had worked for over five years to get a law firm to take up the case of Norton Community, et al VS Hi-Gro Chemical. Back in the late 1940's, Hi-Gro had been manufacturing arsenic acid for use in fertilizers used in the local cotton fields. Hi-Gro loaded the chemicals on railroad cars and shipped them to states all over the South. The company was located right on the railroad line that divided the white side of Cowhill from the Norton Community, more widely known across the tracks as "Nigger Town." At first, locating Hi-Gro in "the holler," which was what the neighborhood was called by the white citizens, and most of the black ones as well, was a boon to the local economy. A large number of black residents found work in the plant, but complaints about the company began almost at once. The air often was filled with a pungent, acrid odor that burned the eyes and nose. Some residents began to notice that their drinking water was cloudy and soon turned yellow. Hi-Gro responded to the complaints, had tests run, and assured the community that all was well. They were all safe and a bit of smell or discolored water was a small price to pay for a better economy and jobs.

But by the sixties, it was clear the reassurances from Hi-Gro were untrue. Multiple reports of cancer, birth defects, and chronic health problems began to plague the residents of Norton. An environmental legal firm did a pro-bono test that proved that holding tanks from the plant routinely overflowed into Sayles Creek, which ran from the Hi-Gro plant right through the middle of Norton Community. In addition, eyewitnesses testified they had seen the liquid arsenic dripping from railroad cars housed along the tracks near the community and even pouring from leaking valves as the cars were transported to other states by Southern Pacific Railroad and St. Louis Southwestern Railway.

Finally, in 1968, the Dallas firm of Brownlow, Curtis, and Schwartz agreed to take on the class action lawsuit that Carl and others from the community had fought for. They came to town, took depositions, and collected a huge amount of discovery. But just as soon as the wheels of justice seemed to finally be moving, they slowed down and finally ground to a halt. It appeared powers behind the scenes kept throwing up roadblocks as more and more Norton residents either sickened or died. Carl tried over and over again to restart the case, but was rebuffed every time. He finally swallowed his pride and went directly to JL Martin, who owned Hi-Gro as well as the cotton gins in town.

As he spent time with the man, he found to his surprise that he was open and welcoming. Carl didn't feel the subsurface hostilities from him that he felt from so many in the white community of Cowhill. Most of the hostilities seemed to stem from the fact that most, if not all, of the possible compensation that might come from the case would benefit Norton and the African-American residents. To many in the community, no good could come from giving the likes of Carl Washington the reason to put on more airs than he already did.

Suddenly in 1977, the case was transferred to a new law firm from Jefferson, Texas called Whidbey, Anderson, and Lowe. Almost overnight, a judge agreed to a court date and the civil trial was underway. The Norton Community et.al VS Hi-Gro and Southern Pacific case was heard before Judge Norman Randall in the Hunt County Courthouse in Greenville. The attorney for the plaintiffs was a handsome, tall man named Judson Anderson, who was originally from Natches, Louisiana. His slow, sweet drawl took the jury through the mountains of discovery documents, charts of illness, testimony from residents, not to mention expert witnesses from the EPA, the railroads, and various scientific establishments.

In the end, the jury agreed with Carl and the residents of Norton that Hi-Gro and the railroad was culpable. The day the verdict was to be delivered, Carl, Delois, Mary and Yancy sat in their Sunday finest in the front row of the courthouse. Judge Randall asked the jury if they had reached a verdict.

"Yes, Your Honor," a short man wearing a white short sleeved shirt and a red bowtie answered.

"How do you find in the matter of Norton Community VS Hi-Gro and Southern Pacific," the judge asked.

"We find in favor of the plaintiff," the small man said in a robust voice. Murmurs of excitement echoed around the stuffy courtroom. Judge Randall tapped his gavel three times and the room grew quiet.

"Have you assessed civil damages?"

"We have, your honor," bow tie man said with confidence.

"What say you?" the judge queried.

In the matter of Norton Community VS Hi-Gro Chemical, we assess special damages in the amount of $3.5 million dollars."

The courtroom erupted. Cheers filled the paneled walls of the room and echoed down the halls of the courthouse. Judge Randall banged his gavel again and again, finally splitting the wood base in half. After a minute or two, the crowd began to quiet and realized the foreman of the jury was still standing up holding his paper. At the judges urging, the crowd sat again.

"I will have order in this courtroom," Judge Randall barked. "Is this the full extent of civil penalties, Mr. Foreman?"

"No, your honor. In addition to the special damages, we rule in the plaintiffs' favor against Hi-Gro Chemical and Southern Pacific Railroad and assess punitive damages in the amount of $17 million dollars."

Faye Miller, the court reporter, looked up and stopped recording. The room sat in stunned silence. Then like a dam holding back a raging flood, the courtroom exploded in shouts, screams, and sobs. Judge Randall banged his gavel on his desk until the head broke off and flew back up into his face, striking him above the eye and giving him a nasty gash. Norton Community members and environmental activists hugged and cried. It was the largest civil penalty damages ever awarded in the county and more than in most of the counties in Texas. Sitting near the back of the room was JL Martin. Carl still remembered the look on his face; more of a pleased smirk than defeat or anger. Carl knew the verdict would be appealed, but maybe, just maybe he thought; there would be some justice after all for the people of "The Holler."

But in an even stranger turn of events, Hi-Gro did not appeal. Instead, the company declared bankruptcy and began the initial settlement payments within the next three months. The railroad had vowed to fight, but with Hi-Gro's capitulation many felt it would only be a matter of time before Southern Pacific worked out some settlement.

Many in the white community of Cowhill were furious at what this new transfer of sudden riches would mean to the status quo of the town. The newspaper had painted a bleak future for Norton in the opinion section, warning against the lure of ill-gotten gain as well as pointing out the slippery slope of instant wealth to those who had never earned it through regular business practices. But if many in the community were anxious and angry, JL Martin seemed at peace and served as the major leading voice of reason and tolerance.

Carl learned quickly that the wheels of justice run painfully slow and even though his community had won a great victory, the actual promise of recompense so far was little to none. Today the City Council meeting would decide the fate of a $127,000 portion of that money that had been actually awarded to the City of Cowhill. As would be expected, many interested parties were present to spin their own story of why their cause or constituents were the most deserving of the windfall.

The city council began the hearing on the funds. First up was Neil Tatum, the school superintendent. Clearly, the Cowhill school district was the most in need of the funding. Next the hospital administrator from Cowhill Memorial Hospital gave an impassioned plea for updates to the dated emergency room. The water department needed sewer repairs. The

Soroptimist Club wanted a new meeting hall. The high school band director asked for new uniforms and large instrument replacement. Next, it was Carl Washington's turn. He took his notes from the stack of papers in his briefcase and placed them on the lectern and breathed deeply.

"Ladies and Gentlemen of the Council. You have heard from a number of passionate, equally deserving folks today. All of them have compelling needs and arguments for the funding. I am glad I don't have the responsibility to deliberate on these and make a judgment. I am not going to spend a long time talking here today. Most of you know me; been a part of this town for my whole life. My father, Franklin Washington, began his adult life advocating for the people of Norton and Nelsonville. I have been so honored to stand for the people of Norton during this hard time. I am so grateful for those in the community that have stood with us. This money exists because of the trials and tribulations of the Norton community. The residents there have literally given their lives and are waiting to see this money come back to the community and complete the work on removing the toxic soil and restoring the water sources for the community so they are once again safe. I long to see the day when the children of the Norton community no longer have to fear going out to play or taking a drink of water. I long for the day when the families from the Norton Community are welcome everywhere. But until then, I dream of a community that is safe and clean and whole. Please help us right this wrong. As John Lennon reminded us in his great song: 'You may say that I'm a dreamer, but I'm not the only one. I hope someday you'll join us. And the world will live as one.'"

Carl thanked the council and took his seat. Normally, the council would move into executive session at this time and make deliberations behind closed doors. Today, Commissioner Martin pressed his microphone button on and spoke. His voice was choked and tearful. "Ladies and gentlemen. I have rarely been so moved by testimony before this council. I have had the distinct pleasure of spending a great deal of time observing Mr. Washington over the past few years. I know him to be a man of singular dedication and character. I would like to make a motion that the council earmark these funds for restoration of the Norton watershed and removal of the toxic materials from the land in the community. Do I have a second?"

"I'll second that," Barbara Kelly said through quiet sobs.

The council voted unanimously to support JL Martin's motion. The meeting was adjourned and the crowd began to disperse. Several of the audience members stopped by to shake Carl's hand. He noticed a number more left with angry or suspicious faces. JL Martin came down from the council desk and grinned as he shook Carl's hand.

"So glad that worked out, Carl. Certainly where those dollars should be spent. Congratulations on this new victory. You have had quite a year," JL said patting the tall man on the back as he continued to wring his hand.

"It has been the best year, for sure Mr. Martin," Carl said with a big grin. "None of this would have happened if it hadn't have been for you. Your support has made the difference. I can't tell you how grateful I am."

"Don't mention it, Carl. I can't tell you when I have enjoyed myself more. Just feels so good to set some things right. I have a feeling more and more is going to get set right before we know it," JL said enigmatically.

"I hope so, Mr. Martin."

"Now, Carl. I have been trying to get you out to my place for such a long time. Why not tonight? We are going to have a good ole fish fry. I'm sure you like some catfish and hush puppies and some coleslaw? What do you say?" JL took a Tiparillo out of his pocket as the two men walked out of the council hall. JL lit the cigar and took a puff then handed the slender tipped cigar to Carl. Carl looked curiously at the man and reluctantly accepted it. He put the plastic tip in his mouth and drew the smoke deep into his lungs. He hadn't smoked since returning from Viet Nam. The aromatic tobacco went to his head but he blew out a big smoke ring and JL chuckled. He took another from his pocket and lit it, biting on the tip like FDR as the two men walked down the street toward Mac's Café.

"So, what do you say, Carl? Can I expect you tonight?"

"Sure thing, Mr. Martin. I'll be there," Carl said grinning, holding the cigarillo on the side of his mouth as he did.

"Tremendous. See you around 6:30. We like eating early. No need to bring anything. Just yourself."

"Would it be alright if I brought my daughter, Mary, along? She would get such a thrill out of seeing that big place of yours."

"Would she? What is she now, about thirteen or so?"

"Fourteen."

"My goodness. Well sure. Why don't you bring her along too? What about the missus?"

"She would probably not be able to make it. But thank you, sir." Carl said sincerely.

"I've really got to get you to start calling me JL. Maybe after tonight you will."

9 Emily

The boys stopped by the park on their way back home that afternoon per their usual routine, but later than normal. They had just finished band practice and were wet with sweat and exhausted from all the marching. George, Travis, and Emily were currently part of the high school marching band, along with twenty or so other junior high students. Mr. Smith recruited the best of the junior high players to be part of the band. It was as prestigious as nerdy musical recognitions get, mostly because you got to leave fifth period early and ride a bus to the high school for rehearsal. They had been part of the band now since the last couple of weeks of August. Summer band rehearsals lasted from 8:00-12:00 and then back after supper for more practice from 6:30-9:00. The first few days, the boys had felt like they were back in kindergarten, sitting in the trombone section along with scruffy bearded high school juniors and seniors. Some of the junior high recruits were hopeless, like blind school kids trying to play baseball. Mr. Smith would bellow from his perch atop the director's crow's nest on the practice field a litany of choice lines like "Someone check that guy's pulse" or "Give that girl a map, she is lost." George and Travis figured most jocks would not fare that well trying to memorize music, memorize a marching drill, and then play your part while remembering all that. Left, left, left, right, left. "Left! No your other left, you nitwit!" Mr. Smith would scream.

The boys and Emily had managed to pick up marching well enough to avoid rousing the ire of the director most of the time, except for that time when they were supposed to move from the arcs near midfield to the pinwheel design into the blockbuster drill. The band was already experiencing growing pains as Mr. Smith had evolved the band from the traditional six-to-five (six steps to every five yards) military style marching style that most of the high school bands in East Texas did to the newer corps style eight to five, free-form designs of marching like the college band at East Texas State University. Travis and George were supposed to make a right flank and march eight steps, then a left flank for eight, another left for eight, and then one more left for eight to bring their block back to the main group while the other four corners of the band did their own block-busting drill. But in a moment of confusion, when they got to the break strain portion of "Alhambra Grotto March" by K.L. King, both Travis and George had made a left flank to start which caused them to crash into the rank of trumpets directly behind them. The bell of Travis's trombone had struck the bell of Mark Reilly's trumpet and split Mark's lip on his braces, with a gush of blood spraying out across the shiny brass. This caused a chain reaction of collisions and Mr. Smith was blowing his whistle like a madman and yelling into his electric megaphone.

"McGee, Did your parents have any children that lived? Harris, should I get you a white cane? Are you mental?" Obligatory laughs and catcalls echoed around the practice field as both boys' faces darkened crimson in embarrassment. They never make that mistake again, though. The marching and playing became more and more automatic and by the time school was starting, they were feeling like old-timers. They had also learned to keep their heads down and not act like show-offs like Mike Lowenstein. Mike was an accomplished saxophone player and the school's only Jewish student. Mike's grandiose personality, know-it-all lacking, and tendency to enjoy the center of attention, started rubbing the upperclassmen the wrong way from day one. Finally tired of all his antics, on the last day of summer band, Sue Nabors, who was first chair alto sax, took action. She waited until Mr. Smith halted rehearsal to align a portion of the drum line, then she took a small water balloon she had somehow hidden in her halter top, walked over to Mike, pulled his elastic waist gym shorts open and dropped the water bomb inside. Then with a swift punch, racked his balls and popped the balloon sending a big splash of water radiating across his crotch and down his legs. The dark, wet spot looked like a map of Africa as it colored the light blue shorts. Mike stood there transfixed, not believing what had just happened. "Welcome to the band, Mikey. Try not to pee your pants," Sue said with a fake smile. George figured Mike must have gotten the message because he took on a much more subdued demeanor afterwards.

The school bus dropped the teenagers off at the corner of Maple and Park Street before heading back to the junior high parking lot with the rest of the students. Emily stopped at Mack's, the neighborhood corner store with another girl. The boys headed to the park, walking past the city pool, now closed down for the season. George thought that seemed really stupid because it was still hotter than hell and a dip in the pool would feel good about now. The city park was around the corner for Travis and directly across the street from George's house. The park was about six acres of land, dotted with large pecan and sycamore trees, and complete with an open rain flow and storm drainage system that all the local kids called the sewer. The open ditch ran through the park and continued on via large culverts in both directions that went under Park Street on the north and Church Street on the south. The culverts continued through the low-income housing project known as the Durham Homes with periodic concrete vents that popped up along the way. One of the regular pastimes for kids in the area was to scamper down the culverts, legs akimbo to avoid the small river of water running through the middle, and sit on the ledges underneath the vents. This proved to be a perfect hangout for all the essential activities of junior high boys: smoking cigarettes, smoking pot, drinking warm beer, and jacking off to stolen porno magazines. Earlier in the summer, Travis and George had achieved the trifecta of smoking pot, drinking warm beer and whacking off to an old copy of Oui magazine shockingly donated to Travis by Trey in some moment of brotherly insanity. They had made a deal for the beer and pot from Cedric Purcell, a tall black boy in their class who was currently holding court in the culverts on the north side of the park. It had cost them $4, but had certainly been worth it. It was their first experience with weed and it proved more enjoyable than Travis had expected. He wasn't a fan of smoking, having choked one too many times in the back seat of the Vista Cruiser while his dad filled the vehicle with the acrid wafts from his Marlboros, especially lethal on winter days with the heater running full blast as well. Travis had dodged his dad's flailing hand more than once after he had suggested his dad crack a window or refrain from smoking. The warm beer on the other hand was mostly disgusting, flat and bitter, and he wondered secretly who in the world really could enjoy that stuff.

This afternoon, the weed had come from Cedric again, but was purchased behind the band hall, along with a line of other boys and a few girls. Cedric was quite the drug mogul these days, his large afro combed out impressively with a large fro pick buried in the side. George lit the joint and passed it to Travis as they stretched out on the ledge allowing the buzz to work its way into their heads. The concrete felt cool to their skin with damp t-shirts sticking to their backs. Light filtered through the filter grate striping the boys like zebras. A small cloud of pot smoke filled the culvert, hanging like a fog around the boys.

"So last night," George began, "how come we had the same dream about floating?"

"I'm not so sure it was just a dream."

"What do you mean?" George asked taking another drag on the weed.

"Andy told me he saw me floating, or at least he thought he did. He figured it was a dream.

But I swear to God I remember hitting the bed right when we woke up."

George passed the pot back to Travis exhaling a long cloud of smoke. "I think I was floating too. That's what woke me up, falling back to the bed when that light was everywhere. Was Andy floating too, or did he think he was?"

"I don't think so." Travis felt the weed work its way to that spot behind his eyes he liked and filled him with mellow relaxation.

"What about Trey?"

"Not sure but, I don't know, I don't think so. He seemed like he didn't care about the light or anything. Not like us. I mean, did it feel like all this stuff was just pouring down into your head?"

"It was like warm water or oil sliding down my head, and I just couldn't stand up. It, like, pressed me down onto the ground just like I was as heavy as a sack of bricks."

The boys whipped their heads around and up and saw a girl's face peering down through the rebar in the vent opening, long blonde hair pulled back in a single braid down her back. She still wore the halter top and cutoffs from band practice, Mr. Smith let the girls wear that to march since it was so dang hot. Travis thought she looked beautiful, like Marcia Brady.

"Shit, Emily, man you scared me," George said exhaling quickly. "How did you know we were in here?"

"Um, you guys are always in there and the green cloud of marijuana smoke was kind of a clue too," she said sliding her feet inside the vent, twisting slightly and slipping her thin frame down inside the culvert.

"Holy crap," George said waving his hand around trying in vain to dissipate the smoke from the small enclosure. Travis just grinned watching George, but mostly at Emily. Seeing her always made him smile. The girl pulled herself up onto the ledge between the two boys and took the joint from George's fingers and drew in a long drag of smoke, letting it slowly slide out the corner of her mouth as she handed the short joint back to Travis. "So, you guys felt it too; in the light, that weird energy thing or whatever?"

"Yeah," Travis said, feeling self-conscious at his croaky voice still higher than he wished it was. "Did you end up on the ground too?"

"Um yeah," Emily said looking up into Travis's eyes through the blond hair that covered most of her face.

"Did you feel like you were floating, before the lights woke everyone up?" Travis asked.

"Oh wow, yeah. Did you?"

"We both did," George said with some annoyance, reaching in vain for the joint smoldering in Travis's oblivious fingers. Emily reached over to take it from Travis, her hand brushing the boy's as she did so. She inhaled again. "This is helping my headache," she added looking up. "Marching was really hard today. My head was throbbing."

"Yeah, it's helping mine too."

"Well it's not doing shit for mine since you won't freakin' share," George huffed grabbing the burning stub and puffing the remaining tip, hot-boxing it to nothingness.

"Cool it, Pot-head," Emily said with a smile letting her fingers rest on Travis's hand and then intertwine with his fingers. "This day has been crap."

"Yeah, it has," Travis said. "We almost got busted in shop today for being tardy. If the bell hadn't kept ringing forever, we would have had our butts lit up by white lightning."

"You mean first period second bell? Yeah we all kept laughing that it just kept ringing forever." I swear Mrs. Peters's iron bra started vibrating in Algebra it was going on so long."

The boys broke out in loud laughter. It was widely known that Mrs. Peters had had breast cancer and was currently sporting a fetching red wig as well as the sturdiest underwire bra ever made. Her tight pink Chanel knock-off jacket stuffed to the bursting point with her massive rack. One of the pastimes of her students was to subtly flick bits of eraser toward her impressive bosom and watch it bounce off, a clear indication that the iron-bra rumor was true.

"I can hear those ta-tas ringing now, bong, bong, bong," George said in between laughs.

"You have any more weed?" Emily asked as the laughter died down.

Travis pulled a small baggie out of his pocket, a couple of half-smoked joints dangled in the sack. "They are kinda skanky but …"

"Light em up, Jimmy," Emily said with a cackle.

"Sure thing, Witchipoo," Travis said.

George rolled his eyes and added, "Before you pull out Freddy the Flute to see if someone will give it a blow, I'm gonna go. My dad will have my ass if I don't get the backyard mowed before dinner and I am dead tired already. See you later, kids," George said jumping down from the ledge and heading down the culvert to the opening.

"Later Dad," Emily answered back. Travis smiled and yelled, "Come over later if you want." George looked back and Emily waved a peace sign as a good-bye. George politely returned half of it over his head. Travis and Emily laughed and leaned back on the cool concrete wall of the drainage pipe and passed the weed back and forth. Emily shifted so she was leaning against Travis's shoulder.

"You know, something else weird happened today."

"What was that?"

"Well, in Homemaking, we had to keep making those stupid soufflés. Mine never comes out right and I am so tired of getting the evil eye from Mrs. Turner and seeing her gush and rave about Roberta. I mean, we all know she is Betty Crocker's evil twin or something, but she just goes on and on. So today, when I saw that my soufflé was going to be crap again, I just started wishing that something would happen to Roberta's. Just for once."

Grinning widely, Travis said, "Yeah, so what happened?"

"So I was standing over by the oven, looking in the glass at her perfect soufflé rising up like a cloud and I just started thinking, 'I wish you would burn, I wish you would blow up.' And it was so weird, the thing just started getting bigger and bigger and it was starting to almost glow before it started getting a bit charred. And Roberta starts yelling, 'Mrs. Turner, Mrs. Turner,' and before you know it they open the oven and reach in to grab it and the pan is like red-hot and they bring it out and the second they set it on the stove, the whole thing explodes like a bomb and bits of burning chocolate fly everywhere. Girls start screaming and a glob lands in Roberta's hair and starts smoldering." By now Travis is doubled over laughing hysterically, while Emily continued. "And Mrs. Turner, all chocolate faced, is pounding on Roberta's head with an oven mitt, trying to knock the hot bits of soufflé out of her hair."

Travis wiped his eyes and said, "Sounds like my kind of a cooking lesson." The teenagers continued to pass the weed back and forth until it was smoked up, and Travis stubbed out the remaining end.

"How did you do on that Texas History test," Travis asked.

"I don't know. Not very good. My head was hurting so bad."

"Yeah, mine too. I think I totally failed it."

"You never totally fail anything, Brainiac," Emily said jumping down off the ledge.

"I better go too. I've got some homework."

Travis hopped down and landed square in the middle of the slimy water in the culvert, splattering both teens with the green water.

"You spaz," Emily screeched whacking Travis hard on the arm. Travis blocked her hand and wrapped her up in a tight bear hug, picking her up off the ground while she squealed louder, her voice reverberating off the concrete walls. "Put me down, Travis McGee," but the boy noticed there wasn't a lot of conviction in her protest. He gripped her waist and flipped her around and over his shoulder and carried her down the pipe to giggles and wails of false complaining as her hands pounded on his back and ass cheeks. He managed to grip her backside firmly and pretended to spank her as he jogged down the pipe and out into the bright sunshine. He set Emily's feet down on the grassy bank while she pushed him away and he gripped her tightly. The two stood there momentarily, the boy looking into her bright blue eyes, crinkled up into a smile.

"You butthole," she whispered lamely pushing him away again. He pulled her close once more, his nose dangerously close to hers.

"Why Emily Moon, you should watch your mouth," he said softly. The two held this embrace for a moment; long enough to feel warm breath against each other's faces and then Emily pulled away and started running up the bank back toward her house.

"See you tomorrow," she yelled behind her. Travis sighed and crawled up the bank toward the edge of the park and walked back across the footbridge, around the swimming pool and toward his house with a grin on his face and tightness in his Levis.

10 Travis

Travis ran home and in the back door, pulling off his school clothes which reeked of pot, and into some shorts and t-shirt. He had made it all the way through math and was halfway through with his English homework before the fireworks started. As he was walking back into his bedroom with a glass of iced tea to get back to diagramming sentences with dependent clauses, in the corner of his vision Travis saw Trey out the window, crouched low, moving along the fence in the backyard. Oddly, it almost looked like he wasn't wearing any pants, which was ridiculous, he knew. He stood and parted the blinds a bit more and wide-eyed, saw his brother's bare ass disappearing around the corner of the house to the back porch. Travis ran to the door of the porch in time to see Trey red-faced and breathless tear open the screen door and race inside.

"What the hell?" Travis began smiling.

"Get out of here," Trey hissed running for his dresser. He ripped open a drawer and grabbed a pair of briefs. He had barely pulled him up over his furry ass cheeks when his dad barreled into the room belt in hand.

"Come here you little shit," Mike growled gripping Trey by the neck, pushing him down to the bed, bringing the belt down in a flash of leather and fury.

Travis looked on in horror as his dad tore into Trey with his belt. He had seen and been the recipient of plenty of his dad's punishments with the belt. The blows fell in rapid succession on the boy's backside, legs and back. Mike held him down with a vicious grip, ignoring the cries of pain and pleas for him to stop. Travis was only vaguely aware that his little brother, mom, and sister were standing in the doorway to the porch. All of them seemed to be yelling, pleading, sobbing for Mike to stop, for God's sake stop. Travis felt something inside himself building, roiling up from his belly. For a split second, he locked eyes with Andy who stood staring in horror. In that moment of connection, Travis could see and even feel the terror in his little brother's eyes. "Save him," seemed to burn inside Travis's brain and without thinking, he stepped forward and grabbed his father's arm in mid-swing, halting the strong man's blow in an instant.

"That's enough," Travis whispered through gritted teeth. His dad's eyes, mad with rage burned hot and wide and the man turned to change his attention and punishment on Travis. A combined "NO!" echoed from Andy and Travis together and with a fluid grace, the teenager gripped his father by the collar and pushed. The man flew off his feet, through the screened side of the porch and crashed into a heap on the lawn. The family stood in shock looking at Mike lying still on the grass, then all eyes moved to Travis who noticed for the first time he wasn't breathing. He exhaled slowly, feeling the rush of adrenaline release.

"What have you done?" Travis heard his mother say as she ran forward to Trey who pushed her away as he scrambled to his feet. Ugly, red welts in angry stripes rose on his back and on the back of his legs. Trey pushed past his mother and siblings and ran toward the bathroom, slamming the door. Janet ran past her children and out into the yard, shaking and prodding her husband. "Are you ok? Mike, wake up?"

Travis turned away as realization of what had just happened dawned on him. Fear and panic began to rise in his stomach, gripping him like a vise. Teppy reached out and gently touched his arm, uncharacteristically tender. He understood the message of thanks conveyed through the tears shining in her eyes.

"I don't know how you," she started then went quiet. Squeezing his hand she whispered, "Thank you," and turned back toward her room. Travis looked at Andy who was standing motionless in the middle of the bedroom, his eyes wide with fear and bewilderment.

"He just had to stop, I just wanted him to stop. I just kept thinking, Stop him, stop him! I wanted you to make him quit. And then you just . . . "

"Shh, it's ok. Come on, let's get out of here. Go to Teppy's room. Stay in there with her for now." Andy nodded slightly and ran down the hall. Travis walked to the bathroom and quietly turned the door knob, opening the door gently and quickly closing it again. Trey sat on the edge of the bathtub in his underwear, face wet with tears, looking like a small and fragile boy for the first time Travis could ever remember.

11 Trey

The tall muscular boy felt the tears stinging his eyes as he bolted into the bathroom and slammed the door shut. His mind was reeling. What the hell had just happened? One minute his dad was beating the tar out of him and the next he was flying through the screen porch and lying flat in the backyard. Trey remembered the look in Travis's face and the momentary connection he felt. For that split second, he knew that his brothers were in his head with him. They knew what he was feeling and he knew they were not going to stand for their dad whipping him anymore. The power and surge had been there. That same strange surge he had been feeling for the past day or so. He had felt it all day. Why hadn't he felt like this last week during football practice when everything was going wrong? He had missed every tackle, looked like an idiot the whole practice.

He looked in the mirror, his red-lidded eyes staring at the rising angry stripes on his back. His tanned skin looked brick red and throbbed as he craned his neck to see the damage. He looked at himself: his short-cropped black hair, wide nose, blue-green eyes, thick lips. He was an alien in this house. He didn't belong, never had. In this household of blond and red hair, he was the oddball, the mistake. He long ago stopped asking his mom why he looked so different than everyone else. When he was a little boy, he was content with the explanations of distant forgotten relatives with tan skin and dark hair. Now, it just seemed like so much bullshit. He pretty much knew what the story must be, but no one was honest. No one had the balls to just come out and say it. So he played along and pretended he was one of the family, knowing all the time he was some interloper and had been for the seventeen years he had been part of the family. Jesus, that had to be the reason his old man was just a bastard to him all the time. Nothing was ever good enough. He sniffed and tasted the tears trickle from his stubbly mustache into his mouth. He sat on the edge of the tub and felt the sobs fight to come. The bathroom door slowly opened and Travis peeked inside.

"Go away," Trey said in a low croak, his voice thick with emotion. Travis ignored him and came inside. He opened the linen closet door and searched near the back and found his precious rubber door stop and fitted it under the door with as much pressure as he could muster. He grabbed a wash cloth and ran it under cool water, rung it out, and walked over to his brother. He pressed the cool cloth against the crimson stripes on his back. Trey sucked in his breath for a moment as the rag touched his back, then relaxed and allowed Travis to bathe his injuries. Travis continued to let the cool rag tame the angry marks for some time, Trey's silent sobs and tears splashing to the bathmat making a pattern on the light blue rug.

"You want to sit in the bath for a while? It might make the marks get better," Travis asked softly.

"I don't know. Maybe," Trey mumbled back. God it is always like this, Trey thought. My little brother taking care of me again instead of the other way around. But instead of it making him mad today, Trey just soaked in the kindness. Because if truth be known, it was about the only nice thing that had happened lately. He sure as shit wouldn't get any understanding from his old man or mom.

Travis put the stopper in the tub drain and turned the water on, feeling it to make sure it was cool but not cold. Trey slipped off his shorts and gingerly sat in the tepid water, sucking in his breath as he did.

"Son of a bitch," he hissed through clenched teeth.

Travis turned and sat against the outside of the tub, reaching up to turn the water off as it filled near the top of the tub. He sat quietly with his brother not knowing what to say. Trey took the washcloth and draped it over his face, leaning back against the back of the tub. After a few minutes, Travis spoke.

"What happened? Why was he so mad?"

"Angie's dad must have called him or something."

"Why? What happened?"

With a sigh Trey began, "I found out I didn't make first team. I was mad and so I went over to Angie's after school, telling Coach I was sick. I just didn't feel like practicing today after I found out. I knew Dad would give me shit about not trying hard enough and all that, not to mention how he would ream my ass for ditching work. And I have been busting my ass at practice." The teenager winced as he repositioned himself in the tub and continued. "I saw Angie right after sixth period and she could tell I was all bummed out and she said to come over and we could watch Gilligan's Island or something and raid the fridge before her folks got home."

Trey figured Travis could see where this was headed but continued on. It felt good to say this and not instantly be judged like he was sure it would go with his mom and dad. Angie Matlock had been Trey's on-again, off-again girlfriend for over a year. She was pretty, and a cheerleader, and popular, and dumb as a post, absolutely perfect for Trey. He looked over at the door and double-checked that the doorstop was still in place. He was wondering why the pounding and cussing hadn't started already. In fact, it was eerie why no one had come to check on them yet. He was secretly glad the bathroom had a nice big window, just in case they had to make an escape.

Trey went on, "and we were just, you know, laying on the couch and making out and stuff. And she said she was ready and if I wanted to it was ok and so, you know, I thought, cool. And she took off her top and bra and stuff and her titties were so nice and soft..."

Travis bit his lip and turned pink but just sat and listened. He appreciated this new candor from this older brother but he squirmed knowing that in almost any other reality, there would be no way in hell he would be party to any of these details. The confessional went on.

"And she started giving me a hand job and I just pulled off my pants and shit, Then she laid back and I was rubbing and humping against her and she was so wet and I just got it all lined up and everything and that's when I heard the shell load and..."

"What? Travis snapped out of his intentional deafness. "You heard a what?"

"Shotgun shell, locked and loaded."

Travis's eyes widened. "Oh shit."

"Yeah. Angie's dad had the shotgun aimed right at me and said, 'You got ten seconds to run, boy.' So I just ran; I ran like hell."

"Which is why you were bare-ass naked sneaking into the house. You mean you ran all the way home like that?"

Trey grinned his sideways smile and chucked, "Yeah. That's why it took so damn long to get here. I was hiding out in every fucking bush in the neighborhood. Probably got chiggers or ticks all over my balls. I thought I could sneak back in. I guess the old shit called Dad or something."

A knock at the bathroom door startled both boys into silence. "Trey, are you in there," Teppy asked in a loud whisper. Trey rolled his eyes.

"Yeah."

"Well mom told me to tell you to hurry up and come out 'cause she wants to talk to you."

"OK," he answered, then under his breath, "Goddamn it, they are gonna kill me."

"No they won't. I'll come with you. I won't let . . ." Travis began handing a towel to his brother.

"How the hell did you do that anyway?" Trey asked standing up and wrapping the towel around himself. I mean it was like you just tossed the old man out in the yard."

"I don't know, just lucky shot or something. Leverage or . . ."

"Leverage my ass," Trey snorted. "You threw him through the wall like Fritz Von Erich or something. Shit, you may end up being in as much trouble as me, Nutsack," he added with a grin sliding his Fruit of the Looms and shirt back on. Hey numbnuts, will you go grab me a pair of shorts or something?"

Travis smirked, nice to see he was back to being Nutsack again. This excruciating bonding session with his brother was clearly over. He took the doorstop out from under the door and opened it quietly looking down the hall. The coast appeared clear. He replaced the wedge in his secret spot at the back of the linen closet figuring that Trey would be using it for some privacy insurance as well from now on out. He jogged back to Trey's dresser and pulled out a pair of old Levi cutoffs and brought them back to the bathroom.

"Not these, idiot, my dick always falls out the side 'cause they are too short."

"Tough shit, Romeo. Get your own damn shorts," Travis hissed.

The boys walked together down the hall, through the kitchen, and into the den. Janet was sitting up rigid in her recliner with a confused look of anger and panic on her face. Mike sat back in his own recliner, feet up, with an ice pack on the side of his face. Travis felt a strange mixture of fear and satisfaction flood his belly, making the hair on the back of his neck stand up, bracing himself for the explosion.

"What are you doing here?" Mike asked looking at Travis suspiciously.

"I dunno. Just thought you'd want me, too."

"No. You've done enough. This is just about your brother." Travis started to back up and leave the room when Mike continued, "I guess I got too carried away and mad. I shouldn't have." he said taking a long drink from his bottle of Bud. He looked sheepishly at Travis from a bowed head with a sideways glance. "I can understand you sticking up for your brother, but I'm still your father and you can't..," he trailed off and then added. "Go do your homework."

Travis said nothing realizing the admonition was over and frankly, he was so surprised not to be backhanded into the middle of next week, he practically ran back through the house to his bedroom. He just realized they hadn't had dinner and he was starving. The wondered if any of his secret stash of candy bars was still under his bed. He knelt down and felt up under his bed until he found the cigar box wedged on the small ledge he had secretly constructed underneath and pulled it out. There was only a Zero bar inside and a scrawled note from Trey saying "Thanks for the Baby Ruth, Dickhead." Travis opened the candy bar and shoved the entire thing into his mouth, pushing in all inside and chomping on the chocolate marshmallow bar until he could finally swallow it in one big gulp.

"I never saw you eat a whole bar at one time," Andy said from underneath the table on the other side of the bed. Surprised, Travis began to choke on the wad of candy and Andy crawled over and whacked him on the back to help it go down.

"Jeez you scared me, kid." Travis said with a gasp sitting back down on the floor.

Andy grinned and flopped down on the bed, raising his eyes and motioning with his head toward the door, "What's happening to Trey?"

"I don't know."

"You want me to find out?"

"Yeah, ok. Don't get caught."

Travis knew that Andy would be sneaking back through his parents' bedroom into the little bathroom that adjoined it with the den. If you put your head down by the vent in the door, you could pretty easily hear what was being said in the family room as well as see most of the television. The boys had used this method for years to eavesdrop on whispered conversations, ball games, TV programs on too late for them, or other illicit moments. He still shuddered when he thought of the time he and Trey had quietly crept to the door to try and catch the end of The Carol Burnett Show after being unceremoniously sent from the room only to realize they were in fact, watching and listening to their parents doing it on the couch. Travis could still remember being mesmerized and horrified by the sight of his dad pumping in and out of his mother as she straddled him, her nightgown thrown to the floor, her breasts bouncing up and down. It was certainly the first time he began to understand the whole mechanics of what "doing it" entailed and Trey relished in explaining all the various details with him later on, learning that the girl on top thing was a new one even for world-wise Trey.

Travis half-heartedly returned to his open English book, wondering what was going on in the other room, copying down the sentences to diagram from the page, but he knew he wasn't going to get them right if he didn't stop being distracted. How in the hell did that happen? In a million years I couldn't have thrown my day through the window. But for some reason, right then in that minute, I knew I could. I had to make him stop and I knew it would be easy. But that's insane, Travis thought trying to will himself to work on the assignment. In a few minutes, Trey stormed through the bedroom door and across to the back porch door, which he opened and slammed, however the vacuum of air kept the bang from being loud at all. So the boy when back to the door and opened it again and tried even harder to slam it, but once again, only a soft pfft filled the room.

"Damn it." Travis heard from the other side and he stifled a laugh listening to his brother bang around out on the porch, loudly complaining and muttering.

Travis looked up and Andy crept back into the room and leapt on the bed with him, bursting to spill the news.

"OK, Trey is like really mad. He got really busted. He is grounded for two weeks and can't see Angie any more. Whatever he was doing with her made everyone so mad they don't want him to go over to her house anymore. I didn't really get it, but Mom kept saying he was acting like a sex criminal and was going to have to go to some meeting with Brother Nelson at the church."

"Holy shit," Travis said in a whisper. "That's stupid, he's not a sex criminal, he's just a horny football player."

"What does that mean?" Andy asked.

"Never mind. What else?"

"Oh the big thing, Dad is making him give up his room on the porch and move back into this room."

"He's not gonna like that," Travis said. Of course, neither did he. It was crowded enough with he and Andy. It had been a relief to have Trey demand his own room and fix up the back porch into a pretty good space for a teenage boy. "Is that it?"

Andy thought for a moment, "Yeah, I think so. Oh yeah, and you have to move out to the porch."

"What?" Travis asked dumbfounded.

"That's what they said. Something about Trey couldn't be trusted and that you acted more mature or something. And that's when Trey really got mad and started almost crying and saying it was unfair to make him share a bed with a little kid like me and all that. But they just told him to shut up and start moving."

Travis tried to process all this information just as his mother came into the room. "Travis, um I need you to do something for me."

"Ok."

"Your brother is going to move back into this room for a while and I need you move out to the porch. I know it's not really fair to make you move when you didn't do anything wrong, but can you just go along with this for now?"

Travis sat quietly for a moment and then said quietly, "OK, I'll do it." Teppy walked in and draped her arm around her mom's shoulders.

"Thanks honey," his mom said. "Travie, how did you do that? It was like you just tossed him out the window like he was a rag doll. I just can't figure it out."

Travis looked at his mom's face, lined with concern and something else. Fear maybe? "I don't know, Mom. It just happened. Adrenaline or whatever that stuff is, maybe?"

Janet smiled weakly and tousled Travis's blond hair. "I guess so," she said unconvincingly.

Teppy leaned over and kissed him on the head. "You won't be too lonely out there, will you?"

"Um, no. It's ok. I'll be fine, I guess," he answered, hopefully containing his absolute elation with this news.

"Well good. You can start moving your things out there when Trey gets done packing up." Janet and Teppy turned to leave when Janet added, "I've got dinner going, it's just going to be a corn dog and potato salad for tonight. Oh, and a can of green beans."

"Sounds fine to me," Travis said. This just keeps getting better he thought.

Janet turned back and touched Travis lightly on his face, "I don't know how you broke that up today, but thank God you did. Your father didn't mean to get so mad. He was just embarrassed and let his temper get away from him," she added weakly.

"It's fine mom. I just wasn't going to let him hurt Trey any more. You don't half to defend him either."

She looked at him with watery eyes and smiled briefly. "Ok honey, dinner in about fifteen minutes."

Teppy grabbed him and hugged him tight. "Thanks for taking care of Trey. And don't be too mad at Daddy. He is really sorry," she said with tears in her eyes as well. They left the room and headed back to the kitchen.

Andy moved closer to Travis and looked him square in the eye. "I knew you were going to stop Dad from hurting Trey."

"Oh yeah? How come?"

"I just wanted you to. It was funny, I just thought about you stopping him and being strong and then you were. Did you feel it too?"

"Um, yeah I guess I did kind of. I did know you just wanted me to stop him. And I really wanted to."

"The way dad just flew through the air when you pushed him, you were like Bruce Banner, just not so mad."

"Or green."

"And without having to rip your pants."

Travis laughed and ruffled his little brother's hair with his hand. Come on, let's go get some corn dogs."

It took the better part of the next two hours for the boys to swap out their rooms. Trey fumed and fussed for a while but eventually his anger turned to resignation. He had only been out on the porch for six months or so, after winning a major battle with his parents over needing his own space. Travis knew good and well that all during the summer, Trey had sneaked out most nights after his parents had gone to sleep, hanging out with his football team buddies or Angie. Since half the time the kids ended up staying in the McKee's backyard, he imagined his parents probably knew he was sneaking out too, but had no reason at the time to worry much about it. He supposed that getting a phone call about a butt-naked teenager scared off from his romantic moment of triumph at the end of a shotgun brings you back to reality.

Andy seemed completely at peace with the transition. He loved hanging out with Trey and rarely got to anymore. The idea of being able to share the room and the bed with his oldest brother seemed to make him happy to the point of being hyperactive. Already Travis had heard Trey bark, "Calm down, Andy, or I am going to thump you." Travis had watched his dad wordlessly grab some thick plastic from the shed and staple it into place over the ripped screen on the porch. He even mumbled something about going to put up more plastic before it gets cold to and to keep out the rain. He kept sneaking glances at Travis but not connecting his gaze with the boy. Mike McGee was strong as an ox himself. Travis wondered when the last time was he had been pushed around by anyone. He could see it in the furtive glances that his father was totally freaked out. As if this situation couldn't get any better, Travis was secretly relishing this new humility or reticence from his Dad instead of his normal asshole self.

George had called after the big event wanting to talk, but Travis had mostly blown him off by saying he had homework to do and had to go. He managed to whisper, "Holy shit, you won't believe what happened tonight. I'll tell you about it tomorrow." Of course all that did was make George crazy to find out more right then. But Travis refused and went back to the room transfer. In the end, the boys' stuff was moved around enough for the night. Travis had decided to stop after he pulled out a shoebox from underneath the bed only to find it stuffed full of used Kleenex. It didn't take genius to figure out what that was for and he smirked thinking that was one more reason sharing a room with Andy was going to cramp his big brother's style. He figured the bathroom doorstop was going to get plenty of use with this new arrangement.

Travis lay on his single bed, feeling the warm, damp air from outside get swirled around by the box fan he had perched in the window. It was a bit warmer sleeping out here, and he had no doubt that before too long, it would be too cold. But independence has its cost and he was glad to pay it. He put a hand behind his head and closed his eyes thinking of this crazy day: the eternal first bell, smoking weed and hearing he wasn't the only kid who felt different since the light, and best of all, Emily's face so close to his. Looking up behind his head at the shelf he saw Trey's forgotten Kleenex and thought that shoebox might not be such a bad idea. But the image of his dad flying through the air pushed most of that out of his mind and he struggled to sleep. His head ached and when he closed his eyes, his mind filled with flashes of green light that throbbed and glittered like fireworks.

13 Janet

Mike was already in bed. Laying in the dark, she watched the glowing tip of his cigarette burn bright as he took a deep drag. It was obvious he was still upset or worried. He hadn't smoked in over a year. From the thick clouds in the bedroom, it seemed he had smoked half a pack in the hour he had been in bed. She hated the smell. She was so glad her clothes and hair had stopped reeking of smoke in the past year, not to mention how Mike's health had improved. But after the events of the night, she didn't feel like fighting about it. She finished washing off her make-up and rubbed her Oil of Olay into her face, brushed out her hair, and climbed into bed beside him. She cuddled close, rubbing her fingers through the ginger colored hair on his chest. Even in the dim light, she could see the tight line of his jaw as he smoked. The sides of his face appeared to be wet. She reached over and kissed him lightly on the cheek, tasting the salt of his tears. He reached up above his head to the headboard shelf and tapped the ash from his cigarette into the metal ashtray he kept on the shelf. He moved his arm and Janet nestled into his side, feeling his strong arm around her back.

"Don't be sad," she whispered. "Everyone's fine. They know you didn't mean to hurt…"

"But I did. I always lose it with that kid. I would never have been that way with Trav or Andy."

The two lay in the dark. Janet could feel the strong beat of Mike's heart against her hand as she rubbed his chest. God, she loved this man, but he didn't make it easy. It had been this way since high school. Earlier, she had watched from the kitchen as Mike opened the door to the boys' room, long after they went to bed. He walked in and knelt down beside Trey, laying his forehead on his son's head. Trey never moved as Mike's prayer or penitence continued until the end when the boy's hand went up and touched his dad's face gently. Janet couldn't hear what they said, but she felt the tears well in her eyes. Jesus, these two, she thought. Oil and water.

"None of that matters. You made it right, that's all you should think about. He always pushes all the limits, that's for sure," Janet said running her hand through Mike's soft red-blond curls. Mike took her hand and pulled it free of his hair.

"How the hell did that kid throw me out the window?" I just can't figure that out."

"I don't know, it was weird. Maybe it was just because of the moment, he was worried about Trey and all that. It doesn't matter. Everything is fine. Trey knows you love him."

"I wonder about that sometimes. Damn, he certainly has his dad's way with the ladies, wouldn't you say?" Mike said, an edge to his voice.

"That's not fair," Janet began.

"Doesn't change the facts though," Mike said. He reached up and stubbed his cigarette out in the ashtray. He roughly turned over on his side rocking the bed just enough to tip the ashtray off the headboard shelf, dumping the ash on his face and in his ear.

"Cocksucking bitch!" Mike swore spluttering through the ash. He jumped up from the bed and stumbled toward the bathroom. Janet pulled her pillow to her face and buried her mouth against it, stifling the shrieks of laughter. She heard the shower turn on and pulled herself together. She pulled the sheets off the bed and took the pillow cases off and found some new sheets in the linen closet and began changing the bed. She remembered the first time she laid eyes on this guy.

She was a new student at Cowhill High School, having moved with her family from Grapevine, Texas. She was a city girl compared with most of the students. Half of them had never hardly left the county. She had grown up spending time in downtown Fort Worth and Dallas. She had been to Dallas Cowboy games and the State Fair of Texas more times than she could remember. Her dad had even taken her on an airplane ride to visit family up in Portland, Oregon.

Her first day at school, she went to her locker only to find that the combination she had been given wasn't working. She kept trying to make it work only to spill all of her newly acquired books from her accounting and typing class on the floor.

"That lock is a real bitch," she heard from behind her. A tall, wide shouldered boy with close cropped blond hair and a varsity letter jacket stood there holding his books on his hip. "Would you like me to give it a try? I had that one last year."

"Alright, sure. Thanks," Janet had said quietly.

The boy put his books and notebook between his legs, squeezing them and holding them there while he spun the lock and then bumped the door with the side of his fist at the end and it easily opened up. "There you go," he said.

"So, I need to bump it with my fist at the end?" Janet asked bemused.

"Oh yeah. You have to show it who's boss. I'm Mike, by the way," he said holding out his hand.

"Janet Browner. I just moved here from ..."

"Big D or Fort Worth or somewhere cool," Mike finished. "God knows you aren't from around here."

"That's a good thing I hope?" Janet said placing her books on the locker shelf.

"You have no idea," he said. "There's a dance this Friday after the football game. Call it the 'Howdy Dance.' You want to go with me?"

Janet looked at his big blue-green eyes with lashes every bit as long as her own. He had the faintest hint of a mustache above his lip, just a bit of blond stubble but for some reason he looked as delectable as James Dean. "Well, I don't know. It's my first day and I might get a better offer," she teased closing the locker door and leaning back against it, holding her notebook across her chest.

Mike had looked intently at her, not really smiling but a definite twinkle in his eye. "So you want to take that chance?" he said moving close to her. She could smell his Aqua Velva and her knees felt like giving out.

"Not really," she said.

He smiled and reached out and tucked a stray curl of hair behind her ear. His slight touch was like 1000 volts. "Cool. Well should I pick you up or ...?"

"I can just meet you here after the game," she offered.

"Sounds like a plan. I'll even take a shower for you," he said leaning in even closer. Their noses were dangerously close now.

"You really know how to make a girl feel special," she said. The bell rang and she looked up. "Do you know where Mr. Scott's psychology class is?"

"Kismet, my dear. I am headed there myself." The big boy offered his arm and she hesitantly took it knowing for sure she was dreaming.

Mike came back into the bedroom toweling off his hair. She had long ago gotten used to seeing him naked but she never tired of it. He had been the first boy she had ever seen without any clothes having grown up with two sisters. She was glad to see he wasn't as mad. She looked in his drawer and handed him a pair of BVDs.

"Thanks," Mike said subdued. He stepped into the leg holes and pulled the shorts up only to find out they were on backwards. "Sonofabitch," he mumbled under his breath. Janet walked up behind him and wrapped her arms around his chest. He was a foot taller than her.

"What's all this?" he said.

"I was thinking of the first day we met. Do you remember?"

"Sure. Helped you with your locker."

She smiled. "How lucky was it that it had been your locker."

"Oh it wasn't. All the lockers on that whole hall had the same combination and were all sticky. Back then, I don't think they thought anyone would actually steal something out of a locker?"

"What? You're ruining my memories."

Mike turned around and wrapped his arms around Janet. "Are you kidding? I would have told you anything to get in your pants. You made me wait long enough, too."

"Good things come to those who wait. Though it was painfully obvious only one of us was a virgin on our wedding night," Janet teased.

"Hey, somebody needed to know what to do or we would have just laid there until someone turned on the TV," Mike said.

"God knows, you knew how to get me going," Janet said.

"Still do, Sweet Cheeks," he said kissing her. He pressed against her, rubbing his erection into her belly. She reached down and gripped him.

"Well, hello Richard," she said. "It's been a while, she said kissing him deeply.

"I think it's okay if you call him Dick. I know it's been a while but you are well acquainted. No sense being that formal," Mike said pushing her back onto the bed.

14 JL

Dinner was served under a large lattice patio, draped with yellow climbing roses that were still blooming this late in the season. It was not that different than in antebellum times when dozens of servants would have been on hand to make the affair perfect. It was a mere trifle that the servants would have also been slaves. Semantics, JL thought. Today, he had to be content with Hazel Carter and Betty Thomas from Norton Holler and they were surly and demanding. The last time he had reached around to grip Hazel's bouncing round ass, she had grabbed his wrist and almost broken his hand, giving him a look that said 'try that one more time.' That was the thing about these "enlightened" blacks. They disrupted the normal order of things here in the South. If they didn't want to stick to the status quo, then maybe it was time to move up to Detroit or some other god forsaken Northern atrocity.

Hazel was busy in the kitchen frying up mounds of crispy cornmeal drenched catfish and her hush puppies that were simply the best in the county. There would be some fresh coleslaw, cornbread, okra and fried potatoes. And for dessert, slabs of creamy cinnamon bread pudding with ice cream. Many of his church brethren, who also happened to be businessmen and local farmers, were going to be present. He had planned this night for so long, it all had to come together.

"Mr. JL," stop eatin' those hush puppies or they won't be any left for yo guests," Hazel said slapping his hand.

JL pulled this hand back and giggled. He thought a few years ago he would have slapped the shit out of this uppity bitch, but those days were gone. Caroline Martin was presiding over the kitchen, ordering the women around in her best southern belle, late summer sundress. JL had worked hard to make sure her sister, Annie, was present. He needed her out of the way tonight and the surest way for that to happen was to get the two of them together. They would be into the fourth bottle of chardonnay or continuing on the old fashioned cocktails. With any luck, by 10:00 PM they would be passed out in the same bed.

JL's son, Theo, was leaning up against one of the carved posts holding up the large lattice canopy. Theo's soft brown curls blew in the wind. He wore a starched white button oxford shirt and crisp khaki chinos and Bass cordovan loafers. The fitted shirt clung to his wide shoulders and showed off the curve of his muscles and his slender waist. A shadow of razor stubble decorated his cheeks and framed his mouth as he sipped a tall glass of iced tea that JL was sure was of the Long Island variety. Theo was JL's most prized possession. He had doted on the boy since he was born, having endured three daughters previously: Aubrey, Carlene, and Sheridan. JL loved his daughters but they were all vain, silly things that took no interest in anything JL did. He knew that most fathers enjoyed special relationships with their little girls. That had never been his experience. Caroline had dressed them in frills and bows, sent them to ballet and horseback riding lessons, and made sure each one grew up cotillioned and courted by proper southern boys who promptly bedded them, wedded them, and then forgot about them as they carried on with other random women who were richer or prettier.

They were all miserable and rich, rarely came home, and hardly had a word for JL other than to beg for more money or complain about their neglectful husbands. Aubrey lived in Austin and worked as an editor for Texas Monthly. She had two chubby girls that seemed to cry incessantly. Sheridan was newly divorced, living abroad with a friend named Suzette. JL had the distinct impression the girl was a carpet-muncher but had no direct proof. Carlene had given him a marvelous grandson, surprisingly named Josiah who looked startlingly like a young Theo. But he lived in the Houston area with Carlene and her lout of a husband J. David March. JL and Caroline had to make the effort to go down and see them since Carlene abhorred anything to do with Cowhill and its backwater ways.

Theo was prettier than the girls, smarter, more affable, and charming. He cast a spell on everyone he knew, leaving them all with the distinct impression their lives were suddenly much better for spending time with Theo Martin. When he was a younger boy, the two were inseparable. He had molded the boy into his image, but a far superior one. He was a better con artist, a better drinker, a better negotiator, and a better lover. Theo had matured early in that regard and JL saw no reason for the boy to miss out on all the joy he had as a young man waiting for the right girl. JL had quietly taken care of two stupid local girls who didn't have the sense not to get knocked up, sending them off to a clinic on Greenville Avenue in Dallas so some darkie doctor could tidy up that little hiccup and set things right again.

His son was a star linebacker on the football team. He was president of the senior class, class favorite, voted Most Likely to Succeed, Mr. CHHS, the list went on. JL watched as he worked the crowd like a magician, saying just the right things, complementing these fools and getting them on the hook before setting it and having them around his finger forever. That was his way and now it was his boy's way. A wave of admiration poured over him.

JL went out to the patio and found a quartet of his deacons standing around the punchbowl, which had already been spiked with a generous amount of rum and triple sec. It had been a convenient revelation of his that his congregation had been given special dispensation to partake of spirits. In one of his visions from the angel Azarel, he had learned that to be "in the spirit" as the Lord wanted us to be, one needed to partake of spirits from time to time, which meant daily.

"Great evening for a get-together, Brother JL," Buck Matlock said gripping JL's shoulder. He looked three sheets in the wind already, JL thought. What a redneck sack of shit. Bill Bidwell and his son, Junior were there as were Clovis and Toy Benton. The wives were off in the conservatory cackling and laying some eggs while Caroline fussed over them. Most were white trash housewives who spent their days ironing, spraying Easy Cheese on Ritz Crackers, and watching "The Edge of Night." He smirked thinking that a couple of years ago, he wouldn't have given these idiots the time of day. But they ended up being exactly the kind of sheep he needed when he split off from Living Waters Community Church. What kind of name for a church was that anyway? It wasn't that long ago that it was First Assembly of God. Then that crackpot Clyde Nelson had let the hippie college kids in and the darkies. Next there would be a row for the Spics, Chinks and Jews and a special place up on the platform for the queers.

"So is everything a go for tonight, Brother JL?" Toy Benton asked with Junior Bidwell at his side as usual.

JL smiled. At least these fools knew how to keep their voices down he thought. "Yes, boys. I think the Lord is going to bring it all together tonight. Our guest of honor should be here directly. I'm gonna be depending on both of you a bunch tonight. And there just might be a surprise in store for your peckers too," he said reaching down and casually patting Toy's crotch. Toy jumped backwards and laughed and the two went back to the punchbowl.

JL left the party and went into his office, a decidedly masculine room complete with dark oak paneling, a large twelve-point buck hung over a fireplace and a mammoth desk. He grabbed keys from his pocket and opened up the drawer and pulled out a small pouch. He then turned behind his desk and pulled the frame of his impressive reproduction of William Joseph Shayer's "Foxhunting at Cover" forward. Behind it was a safe. He grinned as he spun the dials. He had wanted a safe hidden behind a painting since he was a little boy. He heard the click and opened the safe. Stacks of cash lay neatly inside along with some of Caroline's most expensive jewelry. There was an antique Colt 45, stock certificates, savings bonds, his father's coin collection, some Dutch pornography with boys and girls that he found particularly stimulating, and his stash of Sernyl. It had been developed back in the early 1950's as an anesthetic, thus the name referring to "Serenity." Ironically for many, the drug produced exactly the opposite effects causing hallucinations, mania, delirium, and even schizophrenia. JL had a good friend at Parke-Davis who managed to secure a large amount of the discontinued drug and sold it to him a few years ago.

JL had suffered from depression, insomnia, and impotence at the time. He needed something to make a difference. He had started using it three years ago, coming up with the ingenious idea of sprinkling it on oregano or ginger leaves and smoking it. It was like his head had been opened up and his brains stirred up with an egg-beater. It woke him up from his depression. He would still sometimes stay awake for three or four days at a time, but then he would crash and have some of the best sleep of his life and his pecker was as hard as a fifteen year old boy's. But the most unexpected benefit had been the visions. JL had taken to heading down to the old barn on the back of his family property down by the river. He had made a cozy bed there of an older mattress, old sleeping bags, and blankets. He would go down to there to think and get away from Caroline. Sometimes he would meet a college student or two there as well. But mainly, he would take his Sernyl and some Wild Turkey and have a smoke. Within minutes, he would be taken out of the barn to some fantastic new place, or he would see heaven, or he would feel his brain stirred up again and he would see Azarel, an angel of impressive strength and wisdom. The celestial being had shown JL wonders and opened up scriptures and even helped him pen new testaments like the Mormons did.

It was there he had learned about the special dispensation he had been given. He was anointed by Azarel to be the leader of a new congregation of believers. This was a congregation dedicated to holy purpose, of returning to the ancient paths, and above all purity of blood. That was essential. His forbears had certainly understood this and he was determined to bring that practice back. This lovely place had been sullied of late. His church was infected and his town was infected. As for the church, it became clear in the visions that Living Water Community Church was the devil's business, watering down the gospel and traditions to reach out to the unworthy. With the new revelations he had been given while on Serynl, he forged a new plan. He gathered a flock of followers from Living Waters that felt uncomfortable with the radical worship, the racial mixing, and the relaxed morals. They split from the church and set up shop in the old Masonic Lodge out on Jernigan Street. He spent some money fixing it up and now it was a proper church. He found a pastor, Brother Oliver, who felt the same as he did. He had shared his visions and the testaments of special dispensation given to him by the Angel Azarel. The pastor opened his mind and heart to these new teachings. He loved that the congregation was held to a much stricter standard than the leadership, who clearly needed to be free to delve deeper into the spirit to lead the flock.

So from the pulpit, a strict message of no alcohol, no smoking, no drugs, no sex outside of marriage and then only for procreation was given. There was no going to movies, attending dances, listening to worldly music, playing cards or bingo, or mixed bathing. Women were expected to look like women, with longer hair, no slacks, limited makeup, and above all they were not allowed to teach or speak up in the church. Church was a place for men to do the leading. The music was traditional gospel hymns that were "good for our fathers, good for our mothers, and good enough for me." He drew the line at the handling of snakes, but speaking in tongues and being shaken in the spirit was highly encouraged. The church attracted plenty of white trash rednecks that had grown up on the kind of legalistic teachings known as Holiness. They longed for the simplicity of being told what they could not do so they didn't have to use self-control or common sense. When he revealed to his Deacon board that they, being the spiritual leadership of the church, would live by a different creed, he found the men gladly accepted this. Some of them had never had a drink in their entire lives much less imbibed in the more creative expressions of lovemaking, all of which were allowed for the leaders who would need to be open to the spirit.

To solidify his leadership, he had taken to hosting the men's fellowship meetings out in the barn. He introduced them to Sernyl by serving a rum punch laced with the drug. For the most part, the men loved it. He would see them sprawled on the barn floor which he had covered with rugs and mattresses. A few had had the lesser desirable side-effects of hysteria or mania. But that was usually taken care of with a quick injection of morphine that he also had a large supply of from his friend.

It was an inspired drug of choice for JL. He was looking for insight and clarity and he found it in Sernyl. And how fitting was it that the gateway to his visions with Azarel had been opened by a drug known on the streets as Angel Dust. As JL unzipped the pouch, he pulled out the hypodermic needles he now used to inject himself. The results from the smoked angel dust had begun to wane and he found that he had instant gratification from the properly administered injection. He used the webbed spaced between his toes or hidden spots in his groin to hide the needle marks. Azarel had laid out his next plan in vivid detain once he began to inject the drug. He saw the plan for the ceremony and offering that would pave the way back to racial purity as well as cleanse the land of toxins. It was simple and organic and ancient. What could be better? And on top of it all, Carl Washington would get what was coming to him.

The arsenic in the water of the Norton Holler was unfortunate. It had never been foreseen. It could have been the death of him but then the visions had shown him another way. He manipulated the process, stalled the litigation, put his own clandestine legal firm in place and then proceeded. He knew the settlement would be big, but goddamn, he didn't know it would have been that big. The Norton fools were so greedy for money they gladly signed up with a firm who took a cool forty percent of the settlements as payment for their services. Once things began to move in their favor, they thought it was the best deal ever. JL was now looking at picking up $8 million and dumping Hi-Gro in the process. He would even pick up all that settlement money from the railroads carrying his poison. It was brilliant.

Once he had the vision of the ceremony and knew he needed a worthy fatted calf, he latched on to Carl Washington and treated him like the son he'd never had. He had spent more than a year ingratiating himself to the fool, building him up in the community, making sure everyone fell in love with him. But he also began work on the other parts of the plan: he spread the story among part of the community that Carl was a secret violent pedophile who had been a monster in his earlier years. There was even a bogus unsolved police case from years ago that could fuel that fire. He knew the few people he shared that secret with would do a good job of spreading the news. Folks loved nothing more than learning a little dirt about a supposed man of character.

His other stroke of genius was making sure that Sherriff LeRoy Hines was part of his congregation, part of his men's fellowship, and most importantly, a gleeful recipient of part of the Hi-Gro settlement money. JL had helped LeRoy set up the Sherriff's Department Retirement Fund, which he had sole control over. The deputies knew about the fund, but it was off the books and they didn't dare rock the boat since they would be able to partake of the fund once they retired. The fact was, Hines planned to be long gone with the funds before any of the younger deputies got anywhere near retirement. He had gotten rid of all the old duffers and now had a posse of twenty-something deputies that were as dumb as a bag of hammers. Now, when questions about Carl might come up, it would be a simple bit of deflection and police incompetence and at the end of the day, just another dirty nigger that came to no good end.

JL smiled as he felt the effects of the angel dust coursing through him. He leaned his head back on the big leather chair and felt himself take flight. The shelves behind his chair sparkled in the golden hour sunset, with shafts of light playing across the ancient totems, idols, and figurines of the Earth Mother that decorated his office. Tonight was going to be a big night and now, he had the edge he needed to be the celebrant of the ceremony that would reclaim Cowhill for the true inhabitants and rid them of Carl Washington at the same time. JL put the drugs and paraphernalia away, closed the safe, and made his way back to the party. He was glad to see the tall, strapping black man in a crisp white shirt and navy slacks chatting animatedly with some of the men from the fellowship along with some of their wives now. The young girl beside him was lovely, with smooth dark brown skin, large brown eyes, full lips, and surprisingly large tits. She had a ridiculous puffy afro hairdo that made her head look about three feet wide. The hoop earrings glimmered in the setting sunlight along with her bright white teeth. He felt himself stir and decided he needed to get his mind on something else. He was glad to see Carl with a cup of punch and that he had handed Mary one as well. He assumed it was common practice for the little slut to drink alcohol even at her age. The girl seemed to stare at the cup and take small sips.

JL came up and wrapped his arm around Carl's shoulders pulling the man close to him. He could smell the soap and Old Spice and that other smell, that distinct sweaty jig-a-boo bouquet he had known his whole life.

"So glad you made it out, Carl. This must be your Mary," JL said holding out his hand to the girl.

"Yes sir," she said quietly taking his hand. JL stared unabashedly at her breasts that strained against the thin knit fabric of her dress. Theo came up beside his father and draped a heavy arm over his father's shoulders.

"Now who do we have here, Daddy?" Theo asked, his low voice melodic and smooth as aged single malt.

"This is the lovely Mary Washington and her distinguished father, Carl," JL said making the introductions. He felt Theo's grip tighten as he introduced Carl as "distinguished." Theo took Mary's hand and kissed it like it was 1878 instead of 1978. His gentility and flair put everyone at ease, JL noted.

"Lovely to have you, my dear," Theo said. "I hope you enjoy the evening. We have some extra special treats in store for both of you," Theo said with a grin.

15 George

It took Travis the entire walk to school to recount the events from the night before. George listened with rapt attention for once, not interrupting a million times as usual. Travis could tell he was genuinely moved by the whole dad flying through the air thing, but wondered if it was because his dad deserved it, or because Trey was getting the crap beat out of him. The final analysis summarized by George was succinct and funny as usual.

"I'm not sure Angie Matlock is worth losing your own room over, not to mention getting your ass whipped," George quipped. "You think it was for real, were they really gonna do it?"

"I think so. Why else would Mr. Matlock have pulled a gun?"

"Hmm, maybe it was to try and force him NOT to leave. He's gotta be pretty desperate to unload that loser."

"Yeah, right," Travis said with a half-hearted laugh. He knew the talk around town was that Angie Matlock was easy and a bit of a tramp, whatever that meant. But he secretly understood Trey's attraction. The girl was cute, had big boobs, and knew how to shake her booty as a cheerleader. The boys cut across the vacant lot behind the College Street Baptist Church and headed toward the rear entrance of the fenced school yard.

"Man, we are way early today. I don't want to just hang outside the shop." Travis wandered over the edge of the empty lot and underneath the lone white oak tree that made an umbrella of shade in the hot morning air. George joined him, dropping his backpack and lunch into a pile and bending down to pick up a branch on the ground, absent-mindedly drawing in the dusty dry ground.

"You think you just got lucky knocking Daddy out like Rocky or . . . " George trailed off wonderingly.

Travis thought for a few moments and answered, "Nah, I'm pretty sure there was more to it than that. I could feel something, and like I said, Andy knew about it too. He told me –'I wanted you to stop him, and you did.' I knew what he wanted too, I could tell he was like yelling in his mind for me to stop Dad."

"Maybe it was like Mr. Nallin, when that car ran over that baby at the corner store and he picked up the front of that car off the kid and saved him."

"I don't know. I don't think so. It was like I just knew I was going to stop him and I felt all strong. And it was almost like Andy was helping me do it even though he was just standing there."

The boys stood around a few moments longer, kicking a flattened Coke can back and forth between the two of them like a soccer ball. Finally, George stopped and looked hard into Travis's face.

"Ok, I'm just gonna say this. There is some weird shit going on since, you know, the light thing the other night; you and me and Emily and now Andy. Sorry but that is too much to just be a coincidence. Something is different, I feel wide awake, like more than ever. What happened to us?" George asked.

"Don't know but I think you are right. I know I feel different. It's like somehow down inside, I know I can do stuff better, or quicker, or harder, or smarter than I ever did before. What's that all about? And there's something else. I came into the kitchen and my dad had just been on the phone. My mom was looking all freaked out. I was trying to eat breakfast and my parents are sitting around the table both looking at the newspaper, my mom looks like she has been crying and my dad is all serious. It didn't seem to be about the night before either. So I say 'What are both of you so interested in this morning? And all my dad says is 'Oh, nothing' then they just went back to the paper. So we need to get to the library today and see what is in there."

And we better start walking again too."

The boys picked up their backpacks and lunches and headed toward the school. George reached over to Travis and gripped his arm, stopping his progress. "Ok, look, we are going to test this thing today or something, alright?"

"What do you mean?"

"Well, let's pick something and try and make something happen."

"Like what, numbnuts?"

"Don't know yet, but I'll think of something." The boys began trotting now toward the school as they heard the first bell sounding. "In third period, Ferle's class."

Travis saw Emily briefly between first and second period. She warned him, "The Duck is in rare form today, watch out," she whispered as she gathered her books out of the locker and headed off to her next class.

"OK see you in Flip Wig's class."

Emily was right. Dr. Peters was snappy and fuming when the class settled into their seats.

"Pop Quiz," she quacked before the last person was seated and the groans were quickly drowned out by her first question. "What is the greatest common factor of 256 and 120?" This was followed by the equally incomprehensible to most "What is the least common multiple of 75 and 29?"

Travis wondered what could have ruffled Dr. Peter's feathers, who seemed to be in truly "fowl" mood. He noticed her hair was different too. It was clearly a wig, but a dull brown one with less curl in it. Travis was equally struck by how his mind seemed to clearly understand the questions and as he jotted the numbers down, he quickly factored the numbers and knew the answers. He was confident. There was no doubt that he got the answers correct. Wherever this was coming from, Travis was enjoying the clarity and ease of understanding the math problems today. It was like suddenly, after sitting in a classroom taught in Mandarin for months and months, a switch had flipped and he now understood what was really being said for the first time. The Duck continued firing off questions and then ordered the class to switch papers and get out their red pens to be ready to grade them when she called out the answers. The air in the room was electric with frustration and murderous energy being directed at Dr. Peters, who clearly had gotten up on the wrong side of the nest this morning. Travis traded with a shell-shocked Belinda Bell, who was chewing on her bottom lip in great distress. Her normal teacher's pet smirk washed away by the reality of the unexpected quiz.

Dr. Peters rattled off the answers in machine-gun like fashion. Travis could feel Belinda's sideways stares the entire time as she strained to see which ones of the questions were marked wrong. He stifled a grin as he marked two, three, four, and now five of the answers wrong. He drew the X's in big red crosses over the numbers on the page, hunching over the paper to block Belinda's persistent stares. After missing question ten as well, Travis marked another X on the paper and attached the large red 40% at the top of the paper – complete with a smiley face and "well done . . . brilliant!" underneath. The teacher ordered the class to hand the papers back to their owners and Belinda stared in horror at the failing grade, certainly the first one she had ever received. Travis looked down at his paper and was both pleased and not surprised to see a 100 at the top. Belinda hastily folded the paper and slid it inside her math book hoping this ordeal was over.

"I'll be taking these grades today," Mrs. Peters said opening up her grade book with a flourish. She raised her hand when the groans from the class rose, "And let this be a lesson to all of you that you are responsible to be prepared and study for this class." And then with a clear louder voice, "Allison Andrews?" Followed by a weak "70." Next was "David Baker," followed by a loudly announced "50," which was followed by a smattering of laughter. Next "Belinda Bell?" The visibly shaking girl took the paper from her book and started up the aisle to show the teacher her score, which was normally standard procedure in this classroom. Belinda was one of the students who alternated from announcing her 100 or 94 grade with sometimes taking them up to the teacher as if she was not completely proud of her great grade like some of the less stellar students who consistently took the walk of shame with their paper to show the teacher another failing grade.

"Not today, Belinda," Dr. Peters boomed holding up her hand like a traffic cop, pointing for her to take her seat. "What's your grade, don't take all day."

"40," Belinda said in a red-faced whisper.

"What was that?"

Then in a defiant shout, Belinda said "40!" The blond girl buried her head in her arms as snickers and gasps filled the classroom.

The litany of failing or near-failing grades continued, which seemed to fill Dr. Peters with great satisfaction. Travis couldn't help but think that even for her this was really odd, and really mean. "Travis McGee," the teacher snapped.

"Hundred." Travis answered straightforwardly.

"What?" The Duck quacked in astonishment. "Bring me your paper." Travis obliged and stood beside the old cow while she lifted her cat's eye glasses on the jeweled chain off her massive iron tits and placed them on her nose. A quick glance down the paper and a short, "Tut," was all she said and then moved on to "Sam Nicholas." Travis walked back to his seat feeling all the eyes in the class on him. By the end of class, Travis wasn't sure anymore that he liked the feeling of being a know-it-all at the cost of friends or even casual schoolmates thinking you were.

He was still sorting out the strange feeling of being the top score in class when George caught up with him as they took their seats in third period Texas history. The room was stiflingly hot, no wind flowing in the wide open windows and the soft whir of the big oscillating floor fans failing to really move the moist air around the room to create a breeze.

"God, it is so hot. Mrs. Webster's room is going to be an oven this afternoon," Travis groaned, thinking of fifth period Lit class.

George leaned over and whispered, "OK, we are gonna try and make something happen together today in class."

"Like what?" Travis said in annoyance. It was too hot to cause trouble today.

"I'll tell you in a while when I figure it out."

Flip Wig began the class with a droning lecture on LaSalle and early French exploration of Texas. Travis looked across the aisle to Emily and smiled. She caught his eye and casually handed a note to him, folded like a paper football. Travis took the note and positioned himself squarely behind big Joe Cunningham, blocking the note from the teacher's eyes.

Dear Travis,

How was the Duck? I hope it wasn't too bad. I think if she was being extra quack-tacularly bitchy today it might have been my fault. I'll tell you about it at lunch. Hey, I heard a rumor that you have some big news. You know George, if he has a secret, he has to at least tell you that he has one. I feel like corn muffins and ice tea for lunch today? How about you?

PS – That was good "spinach" we had yesterday. Hope we can get some more.

Em

Travis looked over at Emily who was now drowsily resting her head on her arms, her hair blowing softly as the fans struggled to move the thick air around the room. He kept thinking how nice it would be to tuck the loose hair behind her ear. He shifted in his seat and tried to think of something else. Ferle was telling the students that she had graded their last quiz was not very impressed with them and had made notes on a few of them requiring them to be taken home and signed by a parent. Travis hoped to God his wasn't one of the ones who needed to be returned with a signature. Ferle handed the stack of tests to Lisa Glassman on the front row. Lisa had inexplicably worn a maxi dress to school that day along with some high-heeled platform shoes. The thin cotton paisley print hugged her ample backside and Travis could see the outline of her panties when she walked around the room, the patchwork design of the dress flowing down the aisle. Lisa handed Travis his test with a bright red **92** in the corner and then handed George his test with a bright red **69**. George stuffed the test into his binder and then leaned over to Travis.

"Watch this," he hissed.

Lisa continued to flow up and down the aisles, thoughtlessly moving past the big floor fans in the corners of the room, spinning in fast, pointless back and forth motions. George got up from his seat to throw away some crumpled paper. Travis watched as George casually touched the back casing of the large fan as he made his way back to his seat. As she walked past the fans, Travis noticed her skirt flow dangerously close to the blades as she continued to hand back the papers. He looked across the aisle to George who was now staring fixedly at the fan he had touched. Travis felt his belly have that same surge he felt last night with Andy once again and he instantly knew what George was up to. Travis looked back at the fan now, the blades were picking up speed, whirring around like a saw blade, filling the room with a louder buzz, the air moving, shifting papers and blowing across the classroom in an ever growing torrent of humid air. Travis's eyes widened as Lisa drew near the fan once again on her way down the aisle. As she walked past the spinning blades, the updraft of the now roaring fan blew her skirt up and into the blades. In a split second, the room was filled with a shower of patchwork cotton fabric bits that snowed down on the class as Lisa's ear-piercing shriek pulled their attention to the front of the class where she stood in her bra and panties and platform heels as the fan chewed her dress to confetti, spewing it back into the faces of the stunned students. Lisa bolted from the room running toward the nearest girls' bathroom. The laughter from the class rose hysterically as Mrs. Hawksworth grabbed hold of her wig, trying to keep it from flying off her head as she reached for the off switch on the fan that was now droning like an airplane propeller, blowing papers and books and bulletin board art all around the room. Steve Jackson ran over to the wall and jerked the electric plug out of the socket and the fan began to slow, suddenly filling the room with a rhythmic clang as one of the blades clearly was striking the metal frame around the fan, throwing off a small spark as they continued to slow their spinning.

Travis looked over at George who was sitting back in his seat with a stunned expression of mixed horror and satisfaction. Ferle was shouting at the class to calm down and told Elisabeth Worth to stand at the chalkboard and take names while she went to check on Lisa. As soon as Mrs. Hawksworth left the room, DeAundra Rutherford, a tall thin black girl with short hair held back with a dozen hair clips walked up to the chalkboard and slapped the chalk out of Elisabeth's hands

"Get your white ass back in that chair, snitch," DeAundra ordered. The class clapped its approval and settled into a low mumble of excited giggling and retelling of the last few remarkable moments. Emily looked across the aisle from Travis to George until she caught his eye. She looked at him hard.

"I know that was you," she whispered.

George gave her an incredulous, and false "Who me" shrug of the shoulders before breaking into a wide grin. A few moments later, Mrs. Hawksworth reappeared with Mr. Franklin, the school custodian. The man picked up the fan that was smoking from the motor in the rear and carried the contraption from the classroom, filling the now warmer air with the smell of ozone and burned circuits. The bell rang and George and Travis headed to Health class while Emily took off for Home Ec.

"We have to talk about this more at lunch," Emily whispered to Travis as she moved past him in the hall

The boys were happy to find that their health class was being taught by a substitute teacher who took the class to the library to avoid doing any work at all.

"This sure beats drawing our gonads again," George said under his breath. He was browsing through some magazines while Travis made his way over to the newspaper rack, bringing today's paper over to their table on the large oak rod. Travis turned the pages of the small daily paper, scanning the interior for the story that was grabbing his parent's attention this morning. But it was George's breath sucking in and grabbing for the paper that got his attention. George showed him a story on the front page underneath the headline.

No new leads in baffling missing person, assault case

Authorities have nothing new to report in the missing person case involving Cowhill resident, Carl Washington. Washington, 40, was reported missing last night, from his Norton Community home by his wife, Delois Washington.

Washington, a life-long resident of nearby Nelsonville and Cowhill, is a well-known local athlete and Viet Nam war veteran who runs Washington's Washateria in Cowhill.

Washington's disappearance coincides with another disturbing case, the abduction and sexual assault of his daughter who was found walking naked, dazed and confused, on a back road in the Scatter Branch area of the county last evening. (Continued on page 5a.)

The boys turned to the remainder of the story which outlined the search for Carl's daughter's abductor, leads in his disappearance, the conjecture that he had skipped town because the law was after him, and a juvenile case of his where he was accused of sexual misconduct with a girl three years younger than himself, even though the records were supposedly sealed when the case was dropped due to lack of evidence. There was a quote from JL Martin that Mr. Washington had left a city council meeting happy last evening due to the council ruling favorably for his recommendation to spend $100,000 of the Hi-Gro Fertilizer chemical settlement to help restore the Norton community watershed.

George kept reading the story but Travis looked up and felt his headache begin to flare up again. He sat and rubbed his head, taking in the news. He knew this had to be what his parents were reading this morning. He should pay more attention to what was going on he figured. He knew Carl Washington. He was one of dad's old school mates and a bit of a local celebrity, along with Mike McGee. Both had been fairly accomplished celebrated football stars for the local Tiger football team and the Nelsonville Colored School. His mother had known Carl well, too. He remembered they had actually had Carl, his wife Delois and young kids, Vivian, Mary, and Yancy over for barbecues sometimes, though not as much lately. He also remembered the disapproving looks from the neighbors and the burning paper sack that had ended up on their porch, stomped out my Mike. Mike had to spend the rest of the night cleaning his work shoes to get the burned dog shit off.

Cowhill, like its neighbor, Greenville, was a great place to live for whites and blacks alike, as long as the black folks knew their place and kept on their side of the tracks. Mike McGee had created a huge stink a few years back when he hired Carl as a cashier and department manager at the grocery store. Mike had taken over running the store from his father when he came back from the war. Carl was a college graduate, but his options in Cowhill were slim to none. He had tried to help a veteran and friend back from Viet Nam get back to work and back to normal. But normal had very little to do with a big black man ringing up a white housewives groceries. It seemed many white residents were content to have Joe Green pick up their trash or let Avery Thigpin pump their gas. But some drew the line at having an uppity black man touching their groceries, asking them to hand him money, and worse of all, having to place it in his outstretched hand. Travis had watched from the magazine rack as the majority of the women in the line put their cash or check on the conveyer belt so Carl had to take the time to pick it all back up, Some actually stood and reviewed their cash register receipt to make sure they hadn't been cheated. Sometimes the other checkout lines were overflowing with carts while Carl had only one customer. Carl saved and managed to buy the Washateria from Elmer Perkins with a small business loan for veterans and moved on to run his own business. Once again, most of the townsfolk didn't seem to mind a black man dry cleaning their clothes or helping them with the washing machine that ate their money.

That was a few years back and Mike had adamantly refused to curtail hiring other black workers, though Travis noticed that most had been women, with the occasional football star helping out in the back, stocking groceries, or being a sacker. Little by little, black residents of the town were finding more and more opportunities to mix with everyone else, but even if nothing was said, the negative energy surrounding such meetings was palpable. It was an unspoken rule that black patrons of the movie theater still sat more or less in their own section in the auditorium. Travis and George both noticed that most of the time, black students sat in the back of the class. They had even had some teachers that expressly designed their seating chart with all of the dark faces as far away from the front as possible.

It had only been a few years ago while Travis was in third grade that the classes in Cowhill had been integrated, resisting Brown VS the Board of Education as long as possible. Travis still remembered everyone in his third grade class turning in their seats to watch Mary Washington come up the aisle and sit in her desk, two rows behind Travis. Not exactly at the back, but certainly not at the front either. Travis made his first obvious racial blunder later that fall when coloring his Indian head for the Thanksgiving artwork project the class was working on. He had used the crayon helpfully labeled "Indian Red." But as he colored the face and added the black yarn tresses for the hair, he innocently exclaimed in a fairly loud voice, "My Indian looks more like a nigger." A number of students began to giggle and at least one sucked in their breath in surprise. Travis instantly felt his face grow even redder than his artwork and he turned his head to look back at Mary. She never looked up, never looked his way. She just quietly continued working on her project. Travis didn't even notice when Mrs. Hardin walked briskly down the aisle and proceeded to rap her knuckles hard on his head like she was cracking a coconut, while Travis yelped and saw stars.

Long before Travis was born, Carl Washington had been a friend with Mike McGee. Whether it was just the military experience or something else, Travis really didn't know. But something happened along the way that almost doomed their close friendship. And now, even thought they were clearly friends, they hadn't been close for some time. A few times Travis had walked in on his parents seemingly having a discussion, or maybe it was an argument, and he had the distinct feeling that Carl was somehow part of it. That seemed highly unlikely but he still had a funny feeling about it. Nowadays, the only contact the McGee family seemed to have with Carl Washington was taking clothes to the dry cleaner or an occasional "Hello" at church.

Bucking social mores once again, the Washingtons had started attending Living Waters Community Church, a decidedly white church in a white part of town. But Living Waters was far from a mainstream church. It was a Pentecostal nondenominational church that was rigidly conservative and fundamental about scriptures and social issues, oddly liberal in regard to demonstrative worship and progressive music. It was not one of the socially accepted churches in town like First Baptist, First Methodist, or even The Church of Christ. But due to the lively music and charismatic preacher, Brother Nelson, the congregation had grown from fifty to over two hundred in the past two years. The Washingtons had arrived like several other new families, looking for a new church experience although they still attended the Mt. Shiloh African Baptist church in the Norton community as well. On the surface, they were warmly welcomed and included as any other family. But underneath, there were angry whispers and frustrated old-timers that continued to complain to the pastor and the church board that an integrated church was probably not a good idea and most likely was sinful. Travis thought again about whispered conversations he had overheard at home and remembered something about a group that split from the church and had been meeting in some old building over toward Wolfe City or Scatter Branch and it had something to do with the Washingtons or at least black people in general. Travis remembered his dad quietly swearing that those god-dang Klan-lovers were a bunch of ass-clowns and needed a boot up their collective asses. For once, his mother had agreed without a hint of admonition to watch his language.

"I don't guess I had realized any of this had happened," George said closing the paper and sitting down beside Travis. "That's really terrible, if something like that happened to Mary."

Travis looked up blankly. His daydreaming had taken his totally away from the story in the paper and he looked in confusion at George who punched him hard on the shoulder.

"OW, damn it. Knock it off," Travis snapped in a low whisper. Rubbing his arm and looking around to see if anyone way paying attention. "It is a terrible thing. I can't imagine something like that. What do you think happened to her?"

"What do you think, dumb ass? Some pervert screwed her or something," George said. "It's going to be weird the next time we see her," George said.

"Yeah, I guess so. But it's not like we ever talk to her. She's even in band with us and we never talk. That kind of makes me feel bad," Travis said putting the paper back.

"Hey let's go see if we can get the sub to let us go to the bathroom so we can skip out early over to the Chat N Chew."

"He's not going to do that," Travis said heading toward the substitute teacher's table with George.

"Positive thinking, Sherlock," George said. "Let's tell him we just got our period or something. He looks a few bricks short of a load."

16 Emily

The three sat at their back booth in the Chat 'N Chew at lunch and were uncharacteristically quiet. The café was lightly populated for a lunch crowd today for some reason and the teens were not in the mood for some of the usual hijinks they routinely stooped to.

"You know, we were lucky that sub didn't make us stay behind after class, you idiot." Travis said with a frown. "Not all the teachers are dumb, you know? Even a sub." George just shrugged and continued eating.

Being able to walk to downtown restaurants for lunch was a real luxury, even if the selection was limited. There was Mac's, with its policy of having local students enter the rear of the café to pick up a hamburger made earlier and clear out. Mac wasn't fond of the school kids cluttering up his lunch counter but was plenty fond of their lunch money. The Chat 'N Chew was smaller, closer, and more tolerant of the loud voices and antics of the junior high crowd that filled the booths during the lunch hour. There were a few local adults that dared to continue to invade the café during lunch, like Mrs. Patterson. Adele Patterson had been coming to the Chat 'N Chew for lunch for twenty years and she was going to have her poached eggs on toast even if the place was filled with these teenage hoodlums now.

George looked over Travis and Emily's shoulders at Mrs. Patterson and said, "Have you ever noticed how Mrs. Patterson looks just like her lunch?"

"What?" Emily said with a giggle.

"No, really. I mean, she has those huge bugged-out eyes and then she eats those big poached eggs on toast that look just like her eyes."

"That is the stupidest thing I've ever heard," Travis said, though to himself he had to agree with George on this one.

"My mom says she has Grave's Disease or something, that makes her eyes pop out like that." Emily said buttering her cornbread muffins.

"Yuck, that sounds really appetizing," George said stuffing another bit of grilled cheese sandwich into his mouth.

Travis laughed and took another bite of his hamburger. He had found three cents in one of his old pants pockets that morning and with the fifty cents he normally got for his lunch, he had enough for a hamburger. He tried to explain to his dad that fifty cents didn't really cut it for lunch anymore and was promptly told that a plate lunch in the school cafeteria was fifty cents and that was all he was getting so shut up about it. So half the time, he and Emily would order two corn muffins and a sweet tea which cost 45 cents and that would save a nickel to put toward a better meal on another day or give you five cents to blow on candy at Western Auto before heading back to class. George obviously got a dollar for his lunch today since he had splurged on a grilled cheese basket for 75 cents, tax included. Travis routinely spent more of his dollar on lunch and candy when he was given that, but paid for it the next day with a paltry lunch or no lunch at all. He had learned the hard way not to ask for additional lunch money and winced at the thought of being backhanded by his dad. With a little effort, he could usually collect empty coke bottles on the way home to turn in at the corner store to make back the extra he spent. And then sometimes, Emily would help pay for his lunch, which made him feel like a bum but was also pretty great too.

"OK, we have to talk about this thing, whatever it is," Emily said after taking a long drink of the sweet tea.

The boys looked at each other and shrugged. "OK," Travis said.

"So, I mean it's obvious that ever since we saw that light or whatever, that we can make stuff happen. I wasn't completely sure but all of us have done it now. I know you made that fan eat Lisa's dress. That was really dangerous," Emily said with indignation which quickly turned to a fit of giggling, where both boys joined in loudly.

"She was just standing there in her underwear with that look of 'duh, what just happened' on her face. It was so funny," George said wiping his eyes on a napkin.

"She could have been hurt, though," Emily said, with a weak admonition.

"Nah, I didn't want that. I just thought it would be funny to see her skirt chopped off. I mean, who wears a damn maxi skirt to school when it's 100 anyway. So Trav, did you try and make the fan go faster too?"

"Yeah, I could tell when I started really concentrating on it, it went even faster. It was like I knew what you wanted and I just sort of connected with that and made it go faster."

"How is this possible," Emily said in a low whisper. "How can we just Kreskin the fan and make it turn into a buzz saw?

"It has to be that light. We all have felt it, you know, like humming inside us right? And stuff keeps happening."

"Like the bell," George said.

"And the soufflé," Emily added

"And my dad," Travis said. When Emily looked at him questioningly, he gave her the short version of the previous night's happenings.

"You think Andy can do this too?" Emily asked in wide-eyed wonder

"I think so, I felt him connected to me too. What did you mean today in your note, that it might be your fault if the Duck was in a bad mood?"

Emily sat quiet for a moment and then said, "She was being such a witch to the whole class and for some reason she was really picking on Veta Wilcox. You know she's kind of weird and all, but she's not that bad. That old cow just kept harping on her for not having her homework. Then she made her go up to the board to work some problem and she didn't know how to do it so she just kept standing there with the chalk in her hand, writing numbers on the board then erasing them. Then I heard Dr. Quack actually have the nerve to say to her that she needed to sit down and remember to take a bath tonight, too."

"What a bitch," Travis hissed.

"And I just couldn't stand it anymore. I looked at her damn wig and I just told it to shrink. And just like that, it started getting smaller and smaller. And the Duck kept pulling on it and trying to fit it back on but it just kept shrinking and shrinking until it was just this little red puff ball on top of her head."

George and Travis roared with laughter. But Emily sat quiet with a pained expression on her face.

"So what?" George said. "She deserved it."

"She was bald. You know, from the cancer treatment stuff," Emily said. "It was so horrible and pathetic and it made me feel even worse," she added in a repentant voice. "She grabbed a head scarf out of her purse and ran out of the room."

Travis reached over and cautiously gripped her hand in his, sensing George watching him as he did. "Hey, you were just trying to stick up for Veta. She had it coming."

"Really, does anybody really deserve that?"

"Yes," George said with finality. "If you are a mean bitch to people, you deserve it. You would think someone with cancer could have some compassion. Good thing she carries a spare wig, I guess. Who does that?"

"Well it made me feel like crap and I don't want to do that anymore."

The three didn't speak for a minute or so. The occasional sounds from the kitchen or other students filled the air. Travis finished his burger and downed the rest of his ice water and lemon. "You know," he said, "We don't have to just think of doing joke stuff or being mean or anything."

The other two looked at him intently letting the revolution wash over them. "That's right," Emily said. "If this thing is real for some reason, then let's use it to help someone."

"Use what? I mean do we really know what the heck we are doing," George added. "It seems to just happen when you least expect it or when stuff is really funny or bad or something. Can we just decide to do it whenever? Does it work more when we think about using it together?"

"There's only one way to find out," Travis said. "Let's try and think of someone who could really use some help and see what that's like."

"Ok, cool I'm fine with that," George answered. "But can we just do one more experiment? On the way back to class, can all three of us try to make something happen together? Something that won't hurt anybody, just show that it's real and that we have super powers now or something?"

"Like?" Emily said standing up. "Let's go to Western Auto before we have to get back."

The teenagers paid for their lunch and talked as they walked out into the blazing heat of the midday sun.

"Ok. Here you go," George started. "When we get back to Webster's class this afternoon, it's gonna be an oven in there, right?" Both Travis and Emily nodded in agreement. "So let's all three concentrate and see if we can make it get cooler."

"How?" Travis asked.

"Um, let's try and make a cloud come up and maybe rain or something"

"That seems really hard. There is like an only a 20% chance of showers or thunderstorms this afternoon," Travis said knowingly.

"God, thanks Mr. Weatherman," George snapped. "Who cares? If we have super powers it should work anyway."

Emily and Travis looked at each other with skepticism but shrugged and agreed they would give it a try. The group headed up the street past West Side Barber Shop and Clark's Clothing Store to Western Auto. The bell jangled loudly as they went inside. A small group of other kids were rummaging through the penny candy counter loading up for the afternoon classes. Strictly speaking, no candy was allowed in class but that rarely stopped anyone. The Bike banana taffies or Jolly Ranchers were easy enough to enjoy discretely during class. Travis had seen a few kids buy Charms Blo-Pops or Sweet and Sour lollipops and he wondered how they ever got away with eating those in class. They went up to the counter to pay for their candy.

Jack Tanner smiled broadly and said, "Hey kids, how's it going today?"

The three teens answered "Okay. Great. Fine," before heading out the door. Travis looked back to see Mr. Tanner staring at him intently, but still with that contented happy face.

"Jeez, he must have gotten some this morning or something," George said with a snicker. "When's the last time ole sour-puss spoke to us?"

"I know, he seemed really happy," Emily said unwrapping a watermelon Jolly Rancher and popping into her mouth.

"Yeah, something else too." Travis added.

"Like what?" George asked

"Not sure, just something else. It's weird."

"You're weird. Come on, haul ass or we are gonna be tardy."

George ran ahead and started talking to Don Edwards about something, leaving Travis and Emily alone. She casually slid her hand into his. It was sticky and hot like everything else, but Travis smiled and felt his cheeks redden.

Trying to think of something to say, Travis asked, "Have you heard about that stuff with Mary Washington and her Dad?" Emily's head snapped around and looked deep into Travis's eyes, her own blue ones shimmering with tears.

She nodded and added in a low voice, "It's so horrible. I couldn't believe it when I heard people talking about it. I mean, how can she face people and everything? I think I would just have to change schools or something."

"Do you really know her?"

"No, we aren't friends. I was in a stall in the bathroom today. I heard these two girls laughing about it. I mean, how much of a shit do you have to be to get some sick pleasure out of that? They were mocking and saying she probably liked it or wanted to fool around with her own dad or something disgusting. I came out and I saw them and I went over there and told them to get the hell out. That slut Nelda Potts started to give me some lip and I hauled back and pushed her. Funny thing, she went flying all the way across the bathroom. But I was just so mad. How could they torment that poor girl?"

"Good for you."

The upstairs classroom was baking in the hot afternoon. Dr. Edith Webster, PhD, sat on her stool at the front of her class, handkerchief in hand, slowly dabbing her forehead, face, and neck as she began to call roll for the afternoon class. Most teachers could easily take a look around the room and figure out who was present or not as most of them forced the class to sit in assigned seats. For some reason, Mrs. Webster did not enforce the seating but insisted on calling roll. A pesky mud dauber wasp circled in and out of the open window as the teacher droned on. Travis actually put his head down on the cool surface of the desk wishing he could sleep. At least the headache was better. Brandon Boone, a small, sullen black boy sat across from Travis and made no pretense of paying attention, drawing an elaborate pencil sketch in his spiral notebook.

"Angela Andrews?

"Here"

"Leanne Bailey?"

"Here"

"Danny Black?"

"Here."

"Brandon Bone?" No response.

"Brandon Bone? Is Brandon Bone here? Bone?" Mrs. Webster continued.

"My name, Boone," the boy boomed from the back row.

Travis bit his lip to keep from laughing. Most of the rest of the class, especially the other black guys sitting around Brandon hooted and mocked. Mrs. Webster had continued to call Brandon, "Bone" since the first day of school. Clearly it wasn't going to change any time soon. After the teacher had checked the homework from yesterday's assigned reading of a passage from "Paradise Lost," she began her lecture for the day's study of "Ode on a Grecian Urn," Emily turned around in her seat halfway, feigning looking in her purse for a pencil, catching Travis and George's eye.

Whispering she said, "Look at the clock. At 1:15." The boys nodded in understanding.

Emily half-heartedly began to read the poem, feeling her eyes flick back and forth to the clock every few seconds. After two minutes, she realized she had read the entire poem and had no idea about what she had just read.

> *Heard melodies are sweet,*
> * but those unheard*
> *Are sweeter: therefore, ye soft pipes,*
> * play on;*
> *Not to the sensual ear, but,*
> * more endear'd,*
> *Pipe to the spirit ditties of no tone.*

What the hell? Emily thought to herself. She might as well be reading Sanskrit. 1:10, 1:11, 1:12. The damp hot air was oppressive and made her t-shirt stick to her skin uncomfortably. She glanced at Travis and noticed trickles of sweat from this temples making meandering trails on his tanned skin. The thick peach fuzz on his upper lip was wet and she watched as he pulled his lower lip up and tasted the dampness. Through her peripheral vision, she saw George staring at the clock as well. Neither of them appeared to be reading.

> *Fair youth, beneath the trees,*
> * thou canst not leave*
> *Thy song, nor ever can those trees*
> * be bare; Bold lover, never, never*
> *   canst thou kiss,*
> *Though winning near the goal - yet,*
> * do not grieve;*
> *She cannot fade, though thou hast*
> * not thy bliss,*
> *For ever wilt thou love, and she be fair!*

Emily looked back at the clock. The second hand ticked off the final six seconds. She gripped the edge of her desk and concentrated with all her might on one singular thought. RAIN. She stared at the clock as the seconds swept around the face, focused like a laser on that thought of RAIN. For a few moments, it seemed like the rest of the room faded away and he saw nothing at all but that clock and felt the electric connection between herself, George, and Travis. A vibration started in her ears and radiated through her teeth and throughout her skull as she continued to have no thought in her mind but RAIN. Emily felt her entire head begin to move just as the room fell into shadow. A gust of cool wet air like the mouth of a cave poured into the stifling room and lifted papers and books off desks. She could not stop looking at the clock, could not stop thinking of RAIN. Her grip on the desk began to cut into her hands as her fingers locked tighter on the corners.

With an ear-shattering boom, thunder and lightning simultaneously cracked through the moist air. Students screamed and some even covered their ears or heads. Some ducked underneath desks or ran to the front of the class near the teacher's desk. The darkness became almost like twilight as the heavens opened and a torrent of rain hammered the roof and windows of the classroom. Distant cries and shouts were heard from other rooms and the rhythmic slamming of windows around the school. Rain and hail rapped a staccato tattoo on the school. The wind blew the rain in sideways, a wave of cold drops drenched the students and the room like a fire hose had been turned on. Then a roar like a freight train barreling down a lonely stretch of track pounded against her eardrums. Emily felt the tendons in her neck straining with vibrations and tension as she finally wrenched her gaze away from the clock and out the window, wide-eyed at the flash flood surrounding the school. In a second she took in the scene, dark as night over the building, yet a block away toward downtown, bright sunshine. A murky funnel cloud spout was pouring out of the roiling clouds moving toward the roof of the building. Tree branches ripped and swirled. Trash and debris flew in a swirl of litter high into the sky.

With all her might, Emily screamed "NO!"

Then like a light switched off, her vision was filled with sparkles and bright orange light. She felt herself sliding, sliding toward the floor. Travis caught sight of some odd movement out of the side of his vision. When he turned, Emily's limp body was falling to the floor of the classroom. Travis leapt forward to grab her before she struck the hard floor. He looked over at George whose face was positively green. George lurched from his seat toward the door but it was too late, as his grilled cheese basket erupted in a hot projectile over the students in the first two rows of the class. Desks and chairs overturned as the students hurled or fled away from George's fountain of vomit. Linda Baker who was sitting in the next row across from Travis and Emily pointed at both of them and began to point and yell. Mrs. Webster looked horrified backed up against the chalkboard, color drained from her face. Her constant handkerchief was mopping her face. Mrs. Simmons, the Science teacher, appeared in the doorway surveying the carnage of the room, slipping on the puddle of sick left by George as he fled the room. She was a large lady with a booming voice. She clapped her hands loudly.

"This place is a madhouse. Get quiet right now!" That summed up the situation succinctly, Travis decided. For the first time in the ringing quiet of the room, he noticed a bitter, iron-like taste in his mouth. He put his hand up to his face and stared at the bright red blood all over his fingers. By this time, Vice Principal Anderson entered the room and took one look at the situation and barked instructions to the class.

"All of you, out in the hall. This is a tornado drill. Get in positions now!"

Travis thought *this* was too *little*, too *late*, but it did serve as a good way to get thirty screaming, out of control students doing something else. For the first time, he thought those drills might actually be worth something. Emily was vaguely aware of Travis holding her and it was nice. It was always nice being close to him. His arms felt strong and somehow made her feel safe. Mr. Anderson directed Mrs. Simmons to watch the students in the hallway while he moved aside turned over desks and chairs and squatted beside Travis and Emily.

"Are you hurt? Why are you bleeding? Are you okay? Did you hit your head," he questioned in quick fire rapidity.

"I think I'm okay," Emily said with a sluggish whisper. Travis continued to wipe his face with his sleeve as blood continued to flow past his lips toward his mouth. Mr. Anderson took a handkerchief from his pocket and told Travis to try and stop his nosebleed. He patted Emily on her face a couple of times and kept saying, "Miss Moon, Miss Moon, can you hear me?" Emily's eyes finally focused and she looked up into the eyes of Mr. Anderson and then toward Travis. Her eyes grew large as she saw his bloody face. She started to try and sit up.

"Whoa there, Emily. Lie still until we get you checked out," Mr. Anderson commanded.

"I'm fine. What's wrong with Travis, why are you bleeding?"

"It's just a bloody nose or something. I'm fine. Are you okay? You passed out."

"I'm okay, just light-headed." She looked around at the empty classroom. "What about everyone else? Where's George?"

"He threw up and ran to the bathroom I guess."

The school nurse followed by three firemen entered the room and began to work on the teenagers. Travis was pulled over to one side while one of the emergency responders began to wipe off his face and removed his shirt and began to look for other signs of bleeding. Travis kept telling them he was fine as they pushed and prodded around on his belly and even down to his groin, hands unfastening his pants and palpating his belly and thighs and crotch looking for more bleeding. When they were satisfied that all this blood indeed had come from his nose, they stuffed cotton pads up his nose and told him to pinch it closed. Mortified, Travis tried to hold his nose closed while he worked to hitch his jeans back up and rebutton them. Emily was continuing to say she was fine and must have just gotten scared or something. It appeared her blood pressure and pulse must have been normal because the fireman waved off the other emergency responder with the gurney. Mrs. Kelly, the school nurse, came over and helped Emily stand and told Travis to come with her. When both Emily and Travis were a bit wobbly on their feet, Mr. Anderson scooped Emily up in his arms while one of the firemen steadied Travis by draping his arm around the boy and walked them back to the nurse's office. Mrs. Kelly commanded both of them to lie down on the cots in the room. Travis looked over in the corner and saw George slumped into a fat leather arm chair, holding his belly, his eyes closed.

"It seems like these three got the worst of it," Nurse Kelly told Mr. Anderson. "I don't think there are any other injuries or mishaps other than scrapes or bruises. I'll get hold of their parents and keep an eye on them here."

"Do you really have to call our parents?" Emily asked.

"I'm fine, it was just a bloody nose," Travis said.

"I don't have any food left to barf," George added in a tired, weak voice.

"I'm fine too. I was just too hot or maybe I just got my period or something," Emily added brazenly. She figured this would grab someone's attention. Like most girls her age, she used having a period to her advantage as often as she could, getting her out of gym class or an extra trip to the bathroom during a really dull class. She noticed Travis choked back a laugh as he saw the nurse's shocked expression.

"In my day, we kept information like that very private," she said with a hiss. Emily had a feeling the nurse was considering this might be a possibility, though.

Vice-Principal Sam Anderson looked at the teens again and said, "I'll leave this up to you, Mrs. Kelly. They look alright to me now. No sense getting the parents all excited if we don't have to."

"I'll keep them in here until the end of the day and then see if they can get home on their own," she added as Mr. Anderson left to see what other drama had not been dealt with already. The nurse rummaged around in a back room and returned to Travis handing him a bright green t-shirt with a big smiley face and the ubiquitous "Have a Nice Day" emblazoned on the front.

She ordered him to go into the bathroom and change out of his bloody shirt. Travis looked fiercely at George who silently guffawed at the shirt. Travis struggled into the t-shirt that was clearly a size 6X or something and came out of the bathroom with his own shirt wadded in a tight ball. Emily took one look at him and hid her face in her hands.

George laughed loudly, whistling, "Man, you are just poured into that shirt, hot stuff."

Travis handed his bloody shirt to the nurse who went to find a bag to put it in. Travis put his hand behind his back and stuck his middle finger up for George to see which made him laugh even more. Mrs. Kelly came back and handed Travis a bag with his shirt inside. She told them she was going to make the rounds to see if there were any other problems and she would be back directly and to not even think of leaving or moving around. As soon as the door shut, George snorted loudly again pointing at Travis.

"I can see your nipples that shirt is so tight."

"Shut up you idiot," Travis snapped. He walked across the room and sat on the cot beside Emily. The three sat quietly for a minute, listening to the rumble of students changing classes as the bell sounded for fifth period. Travis noticed Emily was wiping what appeared to be tears off her face.

"What's wrong, are you hurt again?"

"No. It's just…" She looked at Travis and then George. "We did that, you know. It was us."

"It might have just been a coincidence," George said without much conviction.

"No, Em's right. We did make it happen," Travis said.

"And look what it caused," Emily said with concern. "It did something to each one of us. I could tell it was a bigger thing than the fan or any other stuff we tried. I don't think we should try it again."

"But, that's not cool. I mean, everyone with super powers has to learn how to use them the right way," George protested.

"There aren't any other people with super powers," Travis barked. "We don't have powers. It's just some weird symptom or by-product of that damn light thing. We need to leave it alone like Em is saying."

After a minute, George responded. "I'm not going to stop. It's not that powerful when we don't try stuff together. Don't ask me to 'cause I'm not," he said with finality. The three sat in silence for the remainder of the school day. Emily slipped her hand into Travis's. George bit his fingernails and drummed on the edge of the chair, humming Fleetwood Mac's "I Don't Want to Know." Mrs. Kelly came back and actually let them leave about five minutes before the final bell so they could get an early start home. George bolted from the room and ran toward his locker. He grabbed his notebook and math book and slammed his locker shut.

"See you," he shouted over his shoulder as he ran for the door.

Travis and Emily grabbed their things and headed out into the thick, hot air. The only sign there had been a cloudburst was an almost dry mud puddle in the dusty dirt between the sidewalk and parking lot. Emily felt Travis pull her close and drape his arm around her shoulders. She wrapped her hand around his waist, sliding a hand into his back pocket as they walked slowly back toward home.

17 Jack

Jack noticed the dark bank of black clouds build and explode just a block away from downtown and wondered where that had come from. Main Street still simmered in the early afternoon heat radiating from the bricks paving the road around the square. From his vantage point, he could see all the way from the barber shop around to JC Penny and then around the corner to Eastland's 5-10 and then further down almost to Drake Furniture.

As he listened to a fly lazily buzzing in the window and half-heartedly worked on straightening some oil filters, he kept thinking of his good luck yesterday with Lori. She hadn't wanted to have sex in so long and then twice yesterday. It was strange, her mood didn't seem a lot better but when he started really thinking about wanting her, it seemed almost like she could read his mind. Before he knew it, she was moving over to the couch, crawling between his legs and kissing him before moving down and sliding off his work pants and taking him deep into her wet mouth. Jack could count on one hand how many times she had been willing to do this. As he focused on his desire she hungrily brought him to a shattering climax then headed back to the kitchen to finish dinner, leaving Jack breathless with pants around his ankles.

Later, as the two lay in bed, back to back as per normal these days, he began to wonder if it might happen again. As he lay listening to her breathing, he began to focus again on his desire, which seemed to leap to attention twice as fast as normal. He felt alive, harder than ever, pulsing with hot-blooded passion. In less than a minute, Lori was reaching for him, grasping his erection through the damp cotton. Then she ripped his BVDs down fast so his dick slapped his belly with a loud smack. Like an Olympian equestrian rider, she straddled him in one fluid motion and he buried himself within her with a groan. She rode him hard and fast, head thrown back, breasts bouncing as she skillfully gripped his shaft tight and wet until both of them exploded in a blinding orgasm. She fell asleep laying on his chest and he felt his heart hammering against her chest as he slowly slid out of her, spent once again. He dozed for a bit then slowly shifted her off to her pillow, spooning behind her. He kissed her neck and wrapped himself around her, holding her close drinking in this intimacy that was so lucky, so unexpected.

The bliss of the evening lovemaking seemed to bleed into the morning. Lori awoke happier that morning, greeting Joey with a kiss and hug as he wandered into the bed that morning, a far cry from the usual practice of bolting from the bed leaving Jack to cuddle with the little boy. Jack wondered as the three of them lay in a tangle that morning if maybe, just maybe, they had turned a corner. Could the crush of all the gloomy depression finally be lifting? It might have just been his imagination but it seemed like Joey was really turning on the charm too. His smiles and giggles seemed to be melting something frozen inside his mom and the feeling was palpable, almost electric.

Later that morning, as Jack was sitting Joey in the high chair for some breakfast, he noticed that the sad expression had returned to Lori's face. He padded barefoot to the fridge and grabbed the carton of chocolate milk. He tipped the carton up and drank a big gulp of milk, some of it dribbling out the corner of his mouth and down to his chest and belly. This normally would have elicited a snappy admonition from Lori but today she didn't notice. He watched his wife preparing the oatmeal and toast in her usual somnolent way deciding that he should thank his stars for the brief respite of loneliness when he became aware that when Lori sat the food down in front of their little boy, she brightened again. And as he laughed and giggled, she stroked his hair and sat at the table and engaged in the babbling small talk parents often make with a small child. Jack thought, *it has been ages since I've seen this* and it dawned on him that it was almost like the little guy was some magnet drawing his mother close and causing her to smile and be happy.

Lori checked her watch and yelped exclaiming that she was going to be late. Jack took over as she hurried from the kitchen to finish getting ready. Jack gazed at her white panty clad ass as she left, smiling with memories of the night before.

"Hey there Little Man, you are really making your mommy happy today."

"I make her smile today," Joey said with a mouthful of toast.

"You sure did, Sport. Hey better have some more of this oatmeal."

"No, I don't like it." The little boy played with a toy car on the high chair tray and was repeating the same song-like chant over and over.

Red light . . . yellow light . . . green light bridge

Just down the hill from Scatter Branch ridge

Devil's on the switch, change the road to red

Better be green or you'll end up dead

Jack listed to Joey repeating the chant again and again until it dawned on him what he was saying.

"Where in the world did you learn that song, buddy?" Jack asked, half-knowing the answer before he did.

"I dreamed it at the place with the green light," the little boy said driving the car up his dad's hand and arms. A chill went through Jack as the boy continued to sing the song.

"Come on, bud. Have some more breakfast." Jack picked up a spoonful of the cereal and did the airplane sound, "Here comes the plane into the hangar . . . "

"NO!" Joey shouted picking up the bowl and hurling it across the kitchen like a major league pitcher, smashing it against the refrigerator. Jack ducked as bits of oatmeal flew into the air and spattered the floor and his legs.

"What the hell?" Jack said looking at the surprised look on Joey's face. Lori ran into the kitchen and asked what happened. She took a look at the shattered bowl and mumbled something about cleaning the mess up and she fastened her skirt and went back to finish dressing. Jack tiptoed around the broken bowl and grabbed the broom and dustpan and cleaned up the bits of oatmeal and the bowl, thinking all the time that this hard plastic bowl should not have broken like this. How hard did that kid throw it?

Lori came through kitchen on her way out the door. She almost walked past Joey but then seemed to stop and turn and kissed his cheek and gave him a long hug.

"Love you, Little Man," she said with a smile as she ruffled his hair. She turned to Jack and kissed his cheek as well, though more or less like in a daze, then headed to the car. Jack looked back at Joey who seemed to be still radiating some extra happiness or something, a wicked grin across his face.

Jack looked down at the boy's diaper and exclaimed, "Oh buddy, I forgot to change your diaper from last night. Come on, I bet you are soaked." Jack carried the boy into living room and slid a finger down the front of his diaper. "Hey, you are dry. You want to go try the potty?"

"No."

"Oh come on, it will be fun. I'll give you a sucker if you pee in the potty."

Joey grinned and ripped off both tapes from the diaper and ran shrieking and naked to the bathroom. He stood on the small stool in front of the toilet, his penis hard and ready to fire.

"No, no, no, wait. You need to sit down."

"Stand like Daddy."

"I know buddy," Jack pleaded, but you really make a mess. Just sit down and I'll get the sucker." Jack eyed the boy's pecker like a grenade about to go off. He'd been pissed in the face way too many times to not be gun shy around this kid.

"Play swords, Daddy," the little boy whined.

"Yes I know, but that's just for outside remember, when we don't have to worry about all the pee-pee going everywhere." Jack gently worked the boy off the stool to straddle the toilet seat, moving slowly like he was diffusing a bomb. He got Joey settled on the seat and was just reaching in to hold his pecker down when it went off. A fat stream of piss jetted out of the boy like a fire hose blasting Jack square the face, knocking him backwards into the bathtub. Joey shrieked with joy as the arc of urine rose three, four feet in the air like Old Faithful, soaking Jack to the bone.

It had taken Jack the better part of an hour to clean up the bathroom, jump in the shower with Joey to clean them both up, then get them both dressed and Joey off to the baby-sitter before getting to work. Tim thankfully had been on time for once and opened up the store at 9:00. The two men had gone about the morning routine of opening the register, rolling outside displays to the front sidewalk and beginning to work through the evening shipment of merchandise. Tim brought Jack his mug filled with fresh coffee and looked at his boss with a puzzled grin.

"If I didn't know better, I'd say somebody got laid,"

Jack nodded thanks for the coffee and took a big sip before lifting his eyes and adding, "And you wouldn't be wrong about that...twice."

"Woo hoo, looks like your prick finally remembered how to have some fun."

"My prick's never been the problem and you know it," Jack said picking up the clipboard and checking off the shipping manifest of tools and air filters. "Guess Lori just started feeling a bit better or something."

"So you didn't just get her drunk and sleep fuck her again did you?"

"No! I never did that and you know it."

"Ok, ok, I was just joking with you. So how were you able to charm your way into a quick poke?"

"Who said it was quick or just a poke?" Jack said drinking another long gulp of coffee.

"Oh now I know you are just bullshitting. When's the last time you had more than a quick poke?"

"Duh, last night, Gomer."

"So what did lovely Lori have to say when you were making your moves?" Tim asked.

"Not so much, she's too polite to talk with her mouth full."

"Bullshit! There is no way you got a bee-jer last night." Tim was always bemoaning the lack of oral sex in his own marriage. It was often the topic of conversations at lunch while he was showing Jack dog-eared pages from his latest Hustler magazine.

"Let's just say there was no clean up needed afterwards."

"Oh you lucky bastard," Tim hissed throwing a package of steel wool at Jack's head.

A customer came in and thankfully cut the conversation short. While Tim helped them with finding the correct windshield wipers, Jack continued working on the stock and smiling to himself about his good morning, even if he got a piss shower from his boy along with it. He couldn't shake the feeling that Joey had actually caused Lori to feel happy and loving this morning. And when he thought about it, it was almost like he had willed her into wanting sex with him as well.

It was a fairly busy morning of customers for a change and that always made the day go faster and made Jack's mood lift. The store sales had been flat lately and any extra customers could make a difference. It was noon before he realized it. The first wave of school kids banging through the door making the bell ring off the hinge took him by surprise. He and Tim had to wait until after the school rush to eat their lunch. They did a very brisk business with candy sales during lunchtime, but they also had to be on the watch for the asshole kids who tried to swipe candy without paying. There was also always a crowd of boys at the magazine rack at the back.

Tim had come up with the idea after seeing how many kids hung out at the magazine counter at McGee's grocery and figured why not try and get some sales off the lunch kids. They did a brisk business with Marvel and DC comics, Eerie, Creepy, and Terror Tales as well as with Mad, Cracked, and National Lampoon magazines. Tim had insisted in also keeping a selection of porno magazines on the top row for all the farmers and businessmen who came to the store looking for spark plugs and some new jerk-off material for the spank bank. Most of the time, Jack felt the magazines were more trouble than they were worth. Tim and he were constantly having to tell the boys to put them back and not look at them, mostly half-heartedly. After all, he had sure as hell learned most of what he knew about girls from Playboy and other skin mags. Every week they caught some boy trying to sneak a magazine down his pants or inside his shirt to take home and hide under the mattress. In fact, if his count was right, clearly half of the magazines disappeared out of the store because they sure weren't being paid for. Tim usually pulled the would-be jerk off shoplifters to the back of the store and scared the shit out of them, threatening to call their mothers. Once, Jack had actually walked in on a boy in the back bathroom with a centerfold laid out on the sink, unloading his passion right on her tits. Tim had made the kid pay for the magazine and kicked him out of the store for the rest of the month as well as threatening to tell the cops he was a sex criminal.

Jack absentmindedly looked at the trio of junior high kids at the candy counter and smiled at the two blond kids holding hands. They seemed really into each other and less silly for some reason compared to most of the kids from the school. He wondered about the dark-headed boy, who seemed like a third wheel, too. The boy kept staring at the couple and Jack kept thinking this trio was actually some kind of love triangle and he chuckled remembering a couple of those dramas from his school days. Christ, that seemed so long ago. And a pang of sadness wafted over him thinking of Bill and all the great times and how all that had ended when Bill's number came up and Viet Nam took him away forever. Jack and Tim had escaped that horror, but just barely. They had made Western Auto one of the best stores on the square but it was huge drain on them. Tim had almost burned through his marriage already and was walking a tightrope with his wife, Candy.

The trio brought their candy to the counter and Jack rang them up, almost 25 cents worth today. "Hey kids. How's it going today?"

The three answered back with "Fine, Good, or OK" before looking at him bewildered and heading for the door. As they reached the door, all three turned back to look at Jack and it was then he felt it again; for a split second he was in their heads or they were in his and the green light and the humming . . . *"Red Light, Yellow light, Green Light Bridge . . ."*

Now, as he watched the freak storm create a flash flood a block away from the sweltering town square, he kept seeing those kids' faces with wide eyes, gritted teeth, like they were getting blasted with a Louisville Slugger, his headache returned with blinding force. Somewhere in the back of the store, Jack heard Tim drop a load of something and bellow "Goddamn it!"

18 JL

JL put his truck in drive and burned out of the driveway and onto Hwy 24 heading away from Cowhill. He needed to clear his head and going back to work or having any of the idiots he had to deal with up in his face was more than he could bear. His shirt was already sticking to him from the Texas heat and his pants felt too damn tight. He had taken to wearing them low slung underneath his sizable beer gut. But the thick leather belt and big buckle he used to keep his pants up was cutting into his belly and making him feel sick. His balls were all bunched up too, making the ache even worse. He stretched up and tried to pull the crotch of his pants down some to make some more room and almost swerved off the side of the road. Then he overcorrected sending the truck into the other lane, narrowly missing a horror-struck housewife with her hair up in rollers.

"Get off the road you stupid cunt," JL yelled from the open window extending his middle finger toward the woman's car. The woman's mouth fell open and she clamped a hand over her mouth as if she could block out the profanity as she slid her car to a stop on the shoulder of the road.

He wiped his balding forehead with the back of his hand and looked at himself in the rear view mirror. He looked like crap. He rubbed his eyes and noticed a dark red smudge around the cuticles on his right hand. He rubbed at them with his other hand but they stubbornly refused to wipe away. Looking at his hands, he noticed the scrapes and bruises on them and decided he was going to have to remember to use some gloves next time.

He had planned the offering so carefully. He chose the gift with great care from all the other cattle in town. He was perfect. Well-known but still humble. Talented but not haughty. Uppity, but still tolerated by the townsfolk. The offering would have been exquisite. JL had spent the better part of six months planning for last night. He had swallowed his natural revulsion and accepted the offering with open arms. He had made him a local celebrity of sorts, allowing him to be the advocate the vermin demanded. He was cocky and insistent, but still just a damn sheep like all the rest. Why shouldn't he be? Everything had been given to him on a silver platter. He was practically revered in town, and for what? Not getting to play in a bowl game? Getting himself almost killed in the war? Coming back home alive. Finding some way to ingratiate himself with half the decent people in town along with all his ilk.

JL settled back with the speedometer hovering right around 80, his typical speed when he got away from Cowhill for any time. He needed to think and decide what his next move should be. So much was dependent on him getting it done right. *The fools in town would be lost without me,* he thought with a smirk. He was hungry and wanted some fried chicken and mashed potatoes with lots of white cream gravy. Might be nice to have some fried squash and some beans and cornbread on the side too. A big sweet tea and some peach cobbler and ice cream. *That sounded wonderful* he thought.

"Goddamn it all to hail," he cried pounding the steering wheel. "So close, so frickin' close," he said. With all the troubles he had been having, the damn government up his keister, bleeding hearts looking to sign up every nimrod in town that thought he could make a nickel off his hard work, he could hardly think at all. Someone should just round them all up and nuke the place until it glows, he thought.

He turned on Hwy 69 toward Canton, might as well head for Beaufort's, one of his favorite places in the world to eat. The food was just like his momma used to make, or at least how the maid, Pearl, would make it. His mouth was watering just thinking about the food and the hot rolls. The rolls in particular were outstanding: big cat's head yeasty rolls with just a touch of sugar, bowls full of creamy butter, and honey just waiting to create a divine explosion of joy in his mouth.

His mind swept back to the failure of the celebration the previous night and he clenched his teeth to keep from screaming. The fool had never known he'd been drugged. The greedy animal had eaten so much catfish and hushpuppies, JL didn't have to worry at all other than how to move his huge bulk to the barn. Clovis and Buck proved useful there after all. Those dumb ox rednecks were good for nothing most of the time but hauling dead weight was one of their few talents.

The girl was an unexpected bonus. Why in the world the fool had brought her along was beyond JL's understanding. She was young, but her breasts were round and pressed tight against the thin cotton blouse she had worn. Like all of her kind, her ass was already full and round. She had eaten just as much as her daddy, *gluttony must run in the blood*, JL thought. Watching Junior and Toy pull her clothes off to reveal her shockingly big tits and the dark triangle of fur between her legs was unsettling. His hunger caused his flesh to rise and leak. It had been too long since he fed his need. His great-great grandfather certainly wouldn't have abstained. In the end, neither had he. Seeing her bound and stretched over that barrel was a stroke of genius, giving all the men such a feast, made it all the sweeter with her father looking on. He could see Theo's face, both shocked and pleased, drinking in the moment.

The ritual was ancient. Like his biblical namesake, Josiah, he had provided a worthy sacrifice. And like the Earth Mother before that, this spilling of blood was required to purify, to sweeten the land, to set right the order of things. It was the only way to rectify the unplanned mistakes of the past that had threatened to poison them all. Of course his son had been brilliant. All JL's acolytes had been there. They performed admirably; all but the one. He would pay for his treachery. His family had sworn allegiance to the faith and yet he had betrayed them. He could not be allowed to break the brotherhood. He would either return or pay the price.

The ceremony was magical, the chanting, the drums, the fires. Watching the offering be stripped and then strung up like a hog for slaughter fed the burning within the brothers, more than any anemic church or vain recitations of childhood prayers could ever do. This was the real God. Her spirit demanded obedience and sacrifice. Since the days of Twelve Oaks and the War of Northern Aggression, it had not been performed. Finding the journals had been the real stroke of luck. When all seemed dark and he had so idea of what to do next, the journals showed the way. Like the Angel Moroni did to Joseph Smith, Theocrates Martin's journals had outlined the ancient paths. JL had filled in the rest from the visions he had while using the drug. Satan had meant that for evil but JL had redeemed it for good. It even had that heavenly name. He knew it was right for him because when he partook, he only had visions and amazing energy. He had none of the side effects he heard lesser minded persons .

JL flipped on the radio. Glen Campbell was belting out "Country Boy." JL sang along in his clear baritone. The day was hot but the sky was clear. Billowing white clouds like those mounds of mashed potatoes he would soon be experiencing piled up on the edges of the horizon. He grabbed his Aviator sunglasses and slid them on it was so bright.

His mind filled with the images of last night. When the acolytes had seen the offering hung up by his wrists, his filthy member swollen and heavy against his stomach due the tight black band clamped tight around it and his sack, they cheered and moved forward with the rods to scourge the tainted flesh and subdue the beast for sacrifice. As the men circled the offering and scourging him, bright lights in the distance illuminated the barn sending brilliant shafts of light through the boards creating vertical rays of pale green along the back wall of the sweltering structure. JL had been distracted by that, worried it was headlights, but no headlights were ever like that. He thought it might have been lightning, maybe ball lightning like Pearl used to talk about. The kind that would boom and flash in a ball outside the house, then move through the open door and down the hall and out the back porch. She had told that story often enough. JL saw the blood from the sacrifice's beaten face trickle down on his chest, drip off his nose and ears. His eyes were swollen shut except for slits. But that was enough for him to watch as Toy Benton dropped his trousers and slid inside the bound girl's sex in one brutal push. That had woken the little bitch up. He rode her like a bull on a heifer and grunted loudly as he filled her with his seed. JL seized that perfect moment to pull out the razor sharp filet knife and slice open the man's scrotum. The man howled as his testicle slid out of the flesh, the bowl underneath capturing the precious sacrificial blood of the fatted calf. JL had been surprised at how little blood had actually flowed as he watched the bowl. Maybe that damn elastic band was a mistake. He looked at his boy, Theo, urging him to mount the bitch next. But Theo just stood there stupidly like a little scared boy. Junior Bidwell took Theo's reluctance as an opportunity. With cheering and shouts from the robed men, he dropped his Dickies to the straw covered floor, his huge penis stretching the girl wide. Then it was Lonnie Matlock's turn to breed and suddenly, all hell broke loose.

The green light had grown from a dim glow to a laser beam of kryptonite that blasted the barn in an angry display of fury. As Lonnie mounted the girl, a sonic boom explosion like the one from the night before rocked the barn. Burning debris of some kind hit the roof and punched through the ancient metal in a meteor storm of flaming carbon. The fiery bits ignited bales of hay and landed in the men's shirts and hair, causing them to shout and run around like decapitated chickens, swatting one another and trying to stamp out the growing flames. The air quickly filled with smoke and the men began to panic and run for the exit that had been barred with a heavy beam. Tim Murphy had thrown the doors open and run for his truck, the coward. He hadn't participated. JL remembered his look of horror and disgust. He wasn't worthy of the calling. His father had been a faithful acolyte but the stroke last year had sent him to the nursing home. JL had reached out to him as a favor. Now he saw what a mistake that had been.

The flames inside the barn were beginning to grow. JL hated to see it go up in smoke, after all, it was one of the oldest buildings still standing on the Martin property, part of the original plantation, and something like this might bring the sheriff and he couldn't have that. *But what about the man and the girl,* he had thought. Even if their bodies burned to a crisp, that would be hard to explain. As the acolytes ran out like frightened children, JL shouted at Theo who had the wherewithal to grab an axe and chop the heavy hemp rope that strung up the sacrifice, tumbling him to the ground like a side of beef. JL ran to the bound girl and used his filet knife to slice away the ropes. He pulled away the remains of the ropes and left them in the barn. Just another crazy, sex-crazed nigger that raped his daughter and ended up killing himself in the process somehow. He was sure Sherriff Hines would see it that way, especially with a hefty donation to the policeman's retirement fund.

It looked like the flames might be calming down, but he couldn't stay around. *The smoke alone would finish off these two,* he thought. He grabbed the bowl of blood, paltry as it seemed. It would hopefully be enough and do the trick. He tipped it into the empty thermos he had brought and ran toward his truck. He sped away up the back road through the fields behind his home. He would run inside and jump in the shower. If someone stopped by, he would just be having a relaxing night at home.

JL shook his head. He had driven for miles and didn't even remember it at all. He was lucky he was one of the few on the road since he was straddling the center line. He pulled back over to his side and was shocked to see the city limits of Canton sign. *Where had the time gone?* He moved the thermos and secured it underneath the never used seat belt. He turned onto Main Street and parked in front of Beaufort's. It was a little early, but he was ravenous. He opened the door and was greeted with the aroma of hot buttered rolls, roast beef, fried chicken and fresh pies.

"Well Mr. Martin, we ain't seen you round here in a spell. What brings you to Canton today?" a large bosomed black woman said, bright red lipstick on her full lips, a gold tooth sparkling in the side of her grinning mouth.

"You know, I was gonna say my deep desire for your rolls, Janelle. But maybe it's just this big beautiful behind of yours," JL said patting the woman's ass that bounced and jiggled underneath the floral print jersey fabric.

"Oh Mr. JL, you wicked. How 'bout some fried chicken and squash. Maybe some sweet potato pie?"

"Bring it on, sweetheart," JL said. "I've got a monstrous appetite. "

19 George

George's stomach had mostly recovered by the time his mother had called him for dinner. He made sure to get to the table on time and helped put the last few bowls from the kitchen on the table for her before his dad sat down. Duke Harris seemed positively beaming compared to his usual glower.

"I think I'm gonna be able to close that deal with LTD this week. If I do, that means I will make my nut for the whole year. We will be able to take that trip to Oregon like we've been talking about."

"Oh honey," that's great, Darla answered setting the plate of pork chops on the table and taking her seat.

Duke eyed the crumb covered chops and then lifted one up with his fork. "What the hell is this?"

Darla jumped up and grabbed the pitcher of sweet tea. With a sunny giggle she said, "Oh it's just pork chops, honey. I did them a little different this time."

Duke continued to look at the meat with confusion and distaste. "But what the hell is on it? Looks like Grape Nuts."

"No. It's Shake n Bake. I heard from Janet that it was really good on the pork chops so I thought we would give it a try." Darla nervously continued to watch Duke eyeing the chop suspended on his fork. Giggling softly again she added, "You know like on TV, Shake n Bake?"

"And I helped!" George chirped in a little girl southern accent. He ducked as the pork chop flew by his head and splatted against the wall.

"Duke, no!"

"No one pulled your chain, dummy," he growled at George wiping his hands on the napkin.

Defiantly, George got up and picked up the thrown chop and took a bite. "Dee-licious mother. You've outdone yourself again," he said sitting back down, making sure he was more than arm's length away from his father. Nothing else was said as plates were filled and sure enough, Duke ate three pork chops making not another comment about the strange aberration to his normal pan-fried preferred recipe. When he left the table, he walked by the kitchen sink long enough to pat Darla on the ass and take a last piece of cornbread with him to the living room. He sunk into his chair and turned the volume up on Barney Miller.

George brought the rest of the dishes to the sink and helped his mother fill the dishwasher. "Thanks honey," Darla said.

"Sure Mom." The two finished filling the dishwasher and George filled up the dispenser with Cascade and turned it on. He looked at his dad in the living room and then asked in a low voice, "So is there any chance Dad really is going to get his "nut" with this deal thing with LTD?"

Darla looked at him with a weary expression and weakly smiled, giving her head the barest of shakes. George gave his mother's shoulder a squeeze and headed back to his room.

Duke Harris had been on the prowl for that big deal with that would make his nut for as long as George could remember. He had sunk a good deal of money and effort into half a dozen get-rich quick schemes looking for the elusive nut he loved talking about. George had no idea how much money his nut actually amounted to, but it might as well have been $10 million because there was just no way any of his lame ideas were going to work.

Last year Duke had invested in a company that was going to be selling heated bras to women. George remembered laughing when his dad had mentioned it at the dinner table and was rewarded with a backhand that knocked him into the middle of the kitchen floor. When he had talked about it with Travis later, they had come up with so many hysterical advertisements and add-on products they had laughed themselves hoarse. Luckily they were in a tent in the backyard. There was a litany of jokes about smoked breasts, boob basting, Titty tots (like Tater Tots,) not to mention the inevitable companion products for men – heated banana warmers, wiener roasters, and nut warmers. Duke had actually brought a prototype home and forced Darla to wear it. Darla relented and wore the battery-powered bra to a high school football game because it was supposed to be cold. George watched as his mother's face began to glow bright red by half time, sweat trickling down her forehead. Janet and Mike kept asking her if she had a fever and by the time they made their way back to the car after the game, Darla was almost sprinting. The minute she was inside car, she ripped off her coat and sweater and unhooked the bra right there in the parking lot.

"Are you crazy, Darla? You are showing your tits to God and everyone," Duke had shouted trying to cover her up. Duke drove away from the stadium like he was headed to a fire. Darla sat in the front seat topless all the way home, gently covering her burned breasts with her hands, quiet tears streaming down her face. George had remembered the bra flung out in the yard as his mother ran inside sobbing. She had worn a loose t-shirt for a week around the house until the blisters had healed.

That pretty much summed up all the crazy ideas his dad had to reach the elusive nut. George actually wanted to kick his dad in the nuts and tell him to grow up and buy stocks or bonds or something like normal people did. But the fact was, George kept his distance from his dad most of the time. Things had been much more balanced at home when his brother and sister were still there. Fred and Cindy were almost twelve years older than he. By the time he was really interested in either of them, they were grown. Cindy fell in love with a boy from school and got married when she was only 17. She wasn't pregnant or anything, she just wanted out of the house and away from Duke. She seemed more like an aunt or something to George these days. She and Greg lived near Amarillo and rarely made it home for holidays or birthdays. She already had two kids and another on the way. Uncle George didn't really know his niece and nephew at all.

Fred was a year younger than Cindy but still eleven years older than George. He had shared a room with his brother for five years. Fred was patient, kind, and funny, all the things his dad was not. Duke Harris idolized Fred, who was a star wide receiver on the football team, senior class president, and prom king. He had a string of girls on his arm most of the time but never settled down with just one of them. Being such a little boy when he moved into the room with Fred, George was crazy about his big brother. During all the lightning storms that would flash across the sky on spring and summer nights, Fred patiently let George crawl into bed with him and wrapped his big arms around the boy and helped him fall back asleep. George became so used to sleeping with Fred that on nights when he was away at a friend's house or off camping, George would sneak into his parents' room and crawl in between them during the night. It was one of the only times he could remember his dad being nice and kind to him, as his dad would hug him close like Fred did and help him fall asleep again.

Fred taught George to ride a bike, to catch a ball, and tell a joke, dirty and clean. He had laughed at all George's crazy hobo talk, listened to his stories about adventures with Travis, and read aloud from school books that he had to study. He confided in George secrets about his girlfriends and love life. He listened in rapt attention as Fred recounted losing his virginity with a cheerleader at an after-game party when he was 16, not that George understood much about it. He watched Fred shave and comb his hair, practicing with an empty safety razor and some shaving cream as Fred laughed and gave him instructions on giving a good shave.

Fred graduated from high school and was headed to SMU to play football when his draft number was called. George remembered watching Fred wave from the back of the Continental Trailways bus as he headed off to basic training at Fort Sam Houston. George made a calendar and marked off the days until basic would be done and Fred would make it home for leave before heading off to Viet Nam to kill gooks.

Five weeks into basic training, an Army Chaplain and another soldier showed up at the Harris house one evening. They had come to express their condolences and gratitude on behalf of a grateful nation that Fred had given his life in service to his country. Only thing was, he hadn't. He was running an obstacle course drill when an artery to his heart had burst. It was a birth defect that had never been caught. With all the sports physicals, football practice, games, and army medical exams, none had ever discovered Fred was literally a time bomb waiting to go off.

When his mother and dad had been handed that folded flag at the cemetery six years ago, it was like they had both been buried with Fred. Darla became obsessed with going to church and going to bible studies. Duke decided that God was a heartless bastard that took the best part of you away for no reason. He descended into a state of perpetual rage that boiled over with the least provocation. The first time George had crawled into his parents' bed after Fred had died, his dad picked him up and literally threw him into his room and slammed the door. All the kindness and fatherly love his dad might have had was six feet underground with Fred and there was simply nothing left for George.

The universe had been looking down kindly on George when he found himself in the locker area with Travis that day, listening to stories of the Supertramp and developing a friendship that carried him through those dark early days, Travis was clearly his surrogate brother, but more than that, too. And even tonight, when he was pissed at Travis and Emily for trying to shut down this amazing new thing that had happened, it didn't matter. All he could think of was calling Travis or heading down to the McGee house and talking. George grabbed a spiral notebook off his desk and lay on the bed and began to think about everything that had happened since the light. He made a list of what he thought he knew:

- We can make stuff happen longer

- We can be stronger

- We can make weather change

- We can make stuff get smaller or bigger

- We can make stuff go faster

George looked at the list and rolled over on his belly and thought some more. *Ok we know we can do this stuff. So what's some other stuff we might be able to do? It seems like joining our powers together makes it happen more. But then there was that bad side effects thing too.* George tried to push the memory of projectile vomiting all over Veta Hitchcock in class out of his mind. *Damn, that girl already had enough problems with that name and being a Jehovah's Witness and all that.* George turned the radio up because "Detroit Rock City" was playing and he loved KISS.

"Focus Harris," George admonished himself. He wrote at the top of the next page:

Other Stuff We Should Try

- Can we make people give us money?

- Can we make ourselves smarter for a test?

- Can we make our eyes see farther or ears hear better?

- Can we run faster?

- Could we make our burps or farts louder or longer?

George thought for a minute and his eye landed on his stack of comics. Looking at the stack his mind began to spin even more.

- Can we fly, like make gravity less?

- Can we make ourselves luckier?

- Can we walk on water?

The song on the radio changed and Lionel Richie was extoling how he was "Easy, Like a Sunday Morning." George thought for another minute then wrote:

- Can we make someone extra happy or extra mad?

- Can we make someone fall in love with us?

"George, honey, did you get your homework done," Darla asked sticking her head in the door.

"Crap," George said, "I forgot. Thanks Mom."

"Sure honey, don't stay up too late."

George grabbed his Math book. He only had one page of problems to work on. The one upside of their afternoon storm was no homework from last period classes. He opened up the book and started working the problems. He figured this must all be review stuff because it was really easy.

$2^3 = 2 \times 2 \times 2 = $ _________. Simple: 8.
$4^4 + 9 = $ _______. Simple: 268.
$5 \times 10\ (4) = 625.$

George smiled as he quickly worked through the problems remembering Jimmy Earwood who sat by in him in class missing the boat completely with the exponents. It seemed like half the class continued to think 3^3 was 9 when of course it was 27.

He finished up the homework in a few more minutes and checked the clock: 10:30. Might as well go to bed. Maybe he could think of a few more experiments to start working on with his super powers. He brushed his teeth and tossed his dirty clothes in the hamper. He thought about taking a shower but decided it could just wait until the morning. He looked at himself in the mirror again, checking out the crop of hairs in his pits and taking a quick sniff, pulling back quickly. *Guess it was hotter in that damn school than he thought today.* George wondered why he didn't have all the muscles his brother, or Trey or Travis McGee had. Could it have something to do with the fact he never exercised? He turned his face to the side and checked out his thickening mustache. What he lacked in muscles, he made up for in hair. Travis was forever calling him Chewbacca. George was blessed with a fine covering of dark fuzz from his belly to his ankles. George knew Fred hadn't been so hairy and neither was his dad, except on his back which was really gross. He got plenty of stares and wisecracks in gym class and in the showers, although he figured most of the boys were actually a little jealous of all the hairs since most of them were as hairless as a baby. He flexed his non-existent muscles and then flipped the bird to his scrawny body and padded down the hall to his room. He stopped in the doorway to his parents' room. His mom was sitting up in bed reading her Life Magazine.

"Night, Mom."

"Good night, honey. Did you finish your homework?"

"All done. See you in the morning."

"OK, dear. Tell your father goodnight," she said returning to her magazine. George pretended not to hear that last part and shut the door to his room. He noticed it swung open again and he closed it harder, but didn't slam it. He didn't need any drama from his dad tonight. The door remained closed for a moment and then slowly opened a crack again.

"Damn it," George whispered. He grabbed an old trading card off his desk and folded it several times and made a wedge to put in the door to make it stick. *There*, he thought after placing the card. He had unsuccessfully tried to talk his parents into a lock for his door earlier that year and was promptly subjected to questions about drug use, self-abuse, pornography being the secret reasons he needed this unnecessary privacy. Of course he denied all of the above, which was pretty rich considering he was currently enjoying all three of those vices as often as possible, and just said forget it. He and Travis had lamented about the intolerable lack of privacy around their respective houses and he smiled recounting some of the stories Travis had shared about his secret door stop for the bathroom. Half the time, Travis came over after school to "drop off the kids at the pool," as he called it. *That kid had a serious phobia about school toilets.* George opened a top drawer and pulled on a big white t-shirt to sleep in. He had started sleeping in Fred's old t-shirts back when he was really small and he just kept doing it. They used to hang down like a dress. Now some of them didn't even cover his butt anymore. A few of the bigger ones did and he liked those the best. Quite a few of them had pretty big holes now, but he couldn't part with them and luckily his parents didn't try to make him stop.

He turned off the light and switched on the small lamp by his bed. He reached for his spiral notebook to continue his list of what to do with his powers, but then he saw one of his comics and grabbed it instead started reading. But as he flipped through the pages of the latest Spider-Man, something was nagging him. Something in the back of his mind was trying to get out. He kept trying to read the comic but kept stopping and thinking about the day and the rainstorm and Lisa's shredded skirt and the huge nosebleed. His mind seemed to be running a hundred miles an hour tonight.

"Man, I wish I had some weed right now," George said in a quiet voice to himself. Then he thought, always other ways to clear the cobwebs. He got out of bed and felt underneath his mattress until he found a magazine and pulled it out. He checked the door to see it was still closed and pulled his shirt off and tossed it to the bottom of the bed. A little George Time would do the trick nicely. That was what he and Travis called it; George Time or Travis Time. He turned the pages to one of his favorite photo spreads, one with two mustached hairy guys and a curvy blond girl. George never tired of all the positions, the creative angles, the close ups. They had an immediate effect on him and he laid back to enjoy the moment, pushing his shorts down to his ankles. Sometimes he wanted it to be fast, other times he liked making it last a long time. He thanked the guys at Western Auto for making these great images available to growing boys like him, even if he didn't actually buy it. He wondered what would happen if he started really concentrating. Could he use his super powers to make his George Time finale even more spectacular? He flipped the page to his all-time favorite photo and began to stare, to concentrate, to feel the light spark inside his brain. It grew and fueled his passion to some new dizzying height until it exploded, sending his pleasure all the way to a satisfying end above his head and on the Farrah Fawcett poster on the ceiling above his bed. George lay still and felt his breathing return to normal, allowing the images to dance across his mind as he drank in the warm glow of relaxation. *Holy crap.* Add one more awesome side effect to the list of super powers. *I could get a girl pregnant half way across a room* he snickered to himself. He reached up to grab a tissue out of the Kleenex box he kept on his headboard. He kept reaching around to find it, moving his hand left and right, but it didn't seem to be there.

George sat up and turned around to find the tissues and sucked in his breath. His bedroom door had come open a crack once again and his dad stood in the hall staring intently at him.

"Dad! Jeez, do you mind?" George hissed grabbing for a sheet to cover up with. George turned back and Duke Harris pushed the door open wider and continued to stare silently.

"What? Holy crap, Dad. How long were you …?"

"You looked so much like your brother. I walked in on him." George took a deep breath and willed himself not to yell every cuss word he knew.

"Yeah, ok. First, um … eww. And second, all the more reason it would be a good idea to have a door lock, Dad."

"I don't think I realized you are growing up," he said looking around the room and then back to George.

"Well, I am, Dad and it would be nice to have some privacy, you know," George said, still clutching the sheet up to his neck.

"You know it's um, normal and all that to …"

"Oh God," George said burying his face under the sheet. "Please don't, Dad.

"If you need to talk about your penis …"

"I'm begging you, please just stop. It's fine. No need to talk. Mortified enough now," George said in a muffled voice from under the sheets.

"OK, well goodnight then. And maybe I'll pick up a doorknob with a lock tomorrow," Duke added.

"Ok. Great. Thanks, Dad. Please don't tell mom. Goodnight," George said. He stayed under the covers until he heard the door close. *My face must be the color of Superman's cape right now.* Even when his dad wasn't being a mean bastard, we was just so weird. Oh God, George closed his eyes tight trying to forget the look of what: sadness, surprise, realization in his dad's creepy stare. He switched the light off and fumbled around for his shorts and pulled them on and tried to get his breathing to calm down. As he lay wide awake now, a low rumbling rolled across the sky outside. Soon bright flashes filled the sky as well as the thunder. George's heart rate skyrocketed. He buried his head under his pillow but the thunder continued to boom across the evening sky.

George threw back the covers and headed to his window. He opened the window and hopped down into the backyard. He looked around the night sky. The storm was quite a way off but rolled and boomed in the western sky. The air was still and, but the rain would probably come. The sky cracked open again and suddenly his mind was filled with another scene: a dirt road, trees and brush lining the edges, leading toward a bridge. The air was humming and the light began; a soft green glow across the bridge, like a dim traffic light floating in the air. He needed to get to the other side. He stepped on the bridge but the boards were rotten and missing in many places. He took another step and heard another loud crack and fell, down, down.

George was on the ground. The light show continued to blaze across the sky as he got to his feet and ran full out across the backyard. When he got to the fence, he tore the gate open and ran through the next yard, and the next, and into the McGee's yard. George ran up the back steps and into the back porch. He stood for a moment catching his breath. Travis was sprawled on top of the covers in the middle of the bed. George stood at the foot of the bed letting his breath slow down more.

"Whaa ...?" Travis hissed bolting upright in the bed. "Jesus, George."

George walked over and crawled into the bed beside Travis pulling the sheet up to his chin. He was trembling.

20 Travis

"What's wrong?" Travis asked laying back down. "Is it just the storm?"

George was a frequent late night guest at the McGee house. Travis had lost count how many times he had woken up to find George lying beside him in bed, usually when there was a storm blowing through the area. At first, Travis thought he might be sleepwalking but George had confessed he just didn't like sleeping alone in a storm. But over the last year, there were plenty of times he came over when the weather was fine. After the first few times of being awakened by him crawling into bed, he had gotten used to it. George and he usually stayed over at each other's house at least one night a week anyway, usually Fridays. But the midnight visits were getting more regular. George was like a cat burglar, walking into the house past Trey sleeping on the porch and climbing into Travis's big bed along with him and Andy. Luckily, George had enough sense to set the alarm on his watch and wake up early to make it back to his bed before his parents, or Travis's parents, noticed. Andy always slept like a rock so he didn't even know most of the time George had been there. Trey had woken up a couple of times and reached for his baseball bat before realizing it was just George and threw a pair of dirty underwear at his head whispering some choice curse words and falling back asleep.

Travis remembered the story George had told him from earlier in the summer. He had been at summer church camp as a counselor with Andy for a week and there had been a big storm that rolled up one night. George woke and had made a beeline for the McGee house per usual only to find Travis gone and Trey snoring away in his bed on the porch. George had stood around for a few moments, but when another loud thunderclap rocked the sky, he dashed to the bed and crawled in beside a clearly startled Trey.

"What the hell?" he had gasped waking up looking at George beside him. "Your boyfriend isn't here, Twinkletoes. No way are you sleeping with me," Trey whispered. But George didn't move and Trey must have been sleepy enough not to care. He had informed George that he slept in the raw so he better not get any ideas. Travis still laughed at George recounting the following morning, waking up with Trey's arms wrapped tight around him. George had opened his eyes to find Mike McGee standing in the door to the porch looking at the boys. Mike had a wicked smirk on his face telling George his dad had just called looking for him. He had walked over and pulled the covers off Trey.

He bellowed, "Hey Lover boy. Your little buddy needs to get home."

Trey had literally pushed George out of bed and scrambled to cover himself up while Mike roared with laughter saying "Let's go Homo, breakfast is ready." Mike had told the story at a backyard barbecue the next week further humiliating Trey. George, good natured as usual, just laughed it off but Travis had remembered Mr. Harris not looking too happy about the story at all. George told him his dad had forbid him to sneak out of the house anymore. That had lasted a week until he showed up again, next time armed with his wristwatch alarm.

"So what's up G?" Travis asked. "You were, like, shaking."

"God what a night," George said quietly. George launched into the events of the night from the flying pork chop to his dad walking in on George Time.

"Stop laughing," George hissed as Travis shook the bed with silent giggles. "It was horrible. Like Barnabas Collins just standing there watching me launch an ICBM of jizz all over Farrah's tits." Travis buried his head in the pillow and howled. The image was just too much. He wiped his eyes and whispered, "Yep, those super powers of yours are something else, Spidey. You are quite the web-slinger."

"Shut up!" George said starting to laugh himself. Soon both boys were hollering into their pillows in fits of laughter until tears streamed down their faces.

Travis recovered and said, "Don't worry about it, man. My dad walks in on Trey about once a week. He's caught me a couple of times. Serves him right since no one gets to lock a door around here."

"You didn't see my dad. It was so creepy knowing he was watching me. It would have been different if he just walked in and said, 'Oh shit,' or something.

"Yeah, okay. That's weird. You know your dad is weird, though. Forget it. He probably was just jealous watching you give ole Farrah a facial."

"Eww, sick," George said.

"So did you just come over tonight because of the storm? Sounds like it's over by the way."

"No, it was weird. Something else. Crap, what was it? George pounded his fist into his temples and then said, "Oh yeah, the bridge."

Travis sat up in bed. "What do you mean, the bridge?"

"When I started coming over here, it was like I was dreaming, but I was still awake. And I saw this road, like a dirt road. It was all creepy and plants grown-up to the edge. And then there was this light . . ."

"A green light, like a traffic light . . ." Travis added.

"How did you know?"

"And that old bridge with the broken slats and you had to go across."

"You saw that too. You mean we had the same freaking dream?" George whispered, wide-eyed in wonder.

"And I fell. Then I woke up with you just standing there like a zombie. I almost pissed myself," Travis added.

"Ok this is some seriously weird shit now," George said moving even closer to Travis.

The boys lay quietly. The rhythmic tapping of the water cooler fan and Trey's low soft snores from the next room were all they could hear. A cooler breeze stole across the porch and the screen door softly bumped against the door frame. Travis crawled down and pulled the door closed and latched the hook on the door, scrambling back under the covers.

"There's something else," George began. "When I was doing my math homework tonight I sort of started thinking about this. But now I'm sure."

"What?"

"What's happening to us? It's like exponents."

"Huh? What does that mean?"

George sat up on his elbow. "You know, like numbers with exponents. Power of ten. Take 3 and cube it. What do you get?"

"I don't know – you mean like nine?"

"No you idiot, Jeez you and Jimmy Earwood. It's 27.

"Huh?"

George sighed heavily. "It's 3 times 3, TIMES 3, you lunkhead."

"Oh yeah. So?"

"So? So?" George exclaimed in a loud whisper which caused Trey's snoring to snort like a pig and then he turned over.

"Shhhh," Travis said.

"So it's like this: when just you, or me, or Em try to make something happen, it's like double. You can jump twice as far or be twice as smart on a test maybe. But when we do it together, then it gets multiplied more or something. You and me looking at the fan, it goes four times faster than normal. And when you me and Em try to make it rain…"

"It's eight times more powerful," Travis said, the impact dawning on him.

"And if there was another person with us …"

"Sixteen times bigger or faster or whatever."

"And that's only if by ourselves we are double our regular selves. What if we are actually triple? Then joining together multiplies everything by 10 to the third power."

The boys lay in silence for a while with their hands behind their heads, thinking about what all of this could mean. Travis leaned over and sniffed George's thick pits and pushed his arm down.

"Wow, how about taking a shower, stinky? You smell like Trey's jockstrap."

"Oh that's why you were wearing it on your head when I got here."

Travis slid his hand under the cover and punched George square in the balls. George twisted and kneed Travis in the belly and the two started wrestling and trying to pin each other. Another snorting snore from Trey broke up the match as they laid back clutching their bellies and balls trying not to make any more noise.

Travis whispered, "I think you are right. We need to figure out more about these powers."

George recounted the list he was working on back in his bedroom. Travis thought about his ideas and said, "We need to be like scientific about it. Conduct experiments. Try and figure out stuff."

"I Agree. You think Emily will go along?"

"I hope so. But we're doing it anyway."

"Wow, look who just grew a set of balls?"

"That's me. Conan the Cannonballs."

"Is that your superhero name?"

"I'll have to think about that. Did you set your alarm? We better try and sleep because we still have school tomorrow," Travis said turning over on his side.

George set his wrist alarm and turned over on his side and scooted closer to Travis.

"Scoot over you, homo," Travis whispered over his shoulder, wiggling his ass against George.

"Don't start something you don't want to finish," George whispered back.

21 Emily

Emily woke with a start and sat straight up in bed. The thunder and flashes of light continued to dance across the sky outside, lighting up her room like a disco. Through the flashes, Emily could see the face of the alarm clock on her nightstand read 11:30. She went to the window that was open, with the wind whipping her curtains back and forth. She looked out to the backyard and saw a skinny boy in a long white t-shirt and underwear vaulting over the fence and continue through the backyards toward Travis's house.

There goes Steve Austin, Jr. again, the Six-Dollar Man, Emily thought then felt bad about being mean to George. She was still annoyed with him from earlier. She really was serious about forgetting about this power or whatever it was. It was just weird and made her feel bad and she didn't need anything else in her life that made her feel bad. The dream she had been having flooded back into her mind and she didn't like the feeling one bit. Scary roads, floating green lights, rickety bridges that collapse when you walk on them and then falling, falling . . . " She suddenly noticed that her nightgown was soaking wet. Oh god, had she wet the bed or . . . no, it was sweat. Good grief.

She pulled the sleep shirt over her head and stood in the window feeling the night wind dry off her skin until goose bumps began to form on her arms and chest. She went to her dresser and pulled on a t-shirt and went back to bed, wondering if she would be able to fall asleep. She thought the boys were pretty lucky to be able to just sneak out and talk or hang out in the middle of the night. Travis had told her about George's thing about storms and she felt envious thinking of him sleeping next to Travis instead of her. She wondered what they would say if she just showed up and crawled in the bed right in between them. She smiled at the thought and decided maybe soon she would do just that.

She turned on the radio and found Z-97 and listened to Rod Stewart singing that "Tonight's the Night," and snuggled her bright pink fake fur pillow closer. *Boys were so stupid,* she thought. They always want to ruin stuff instead of just enjoying what you have. The wind picked up again and she heard the wind chimes on the patio begin to tinkle and sing in the breeze.

Emily did not like being the only kid on the block, it seemed like, whose parents were divorced. Two years ago she was just like all the other kids, complaining about both parents. Now it was just her and her mother. Being an only child was always weird compared to everyone else who seemed to have a house full of siblings. Now on top of that, there were funny stares and comments about her mother being a divorcee, which made it sound like she was a prostitute or something. Her dad was the one who left. He was the one who found another woman, other kids, boys, and even had a new little boy of his own now. Emily had only seen her little half-brother once since her dad had moved to San Antonio, but it was clear her dad was crazy about him. Not that he didn't love her; she knew he did and mourned the fact that splitting with her mom meant he basically lost her, too. But it was his own fault. She heard all the excuses from him and accusations from her mom and it all sounded like nonsense. Two adults who were selfish and acted like children were never going to be able to make it.

Emily curled up on her side and listened to Rod Stewart make way for Supertramp singing "Give a Little Bit." She figured the boys were over at Travis's either laughing about today or planning the next experiment with their super powers. The thought of it made her mad. She hated the way doing that stuff had made her feel today. She admitted there was a momentary rush paying the Duck back for being so horrible to Veta and Lisa's skirt getting shredded by that fan had been pretty funny. In fact, she started giggling remembering her face as her skirt disintegrated into confetti. *Wow, her boobs are huge,* Emily thought looking down at her own mostly flat chest with a sigh. But that thing with the weather had really freaked her out. It was way more intense. It felt like all three of them were in each other's heads and she could feel the power pulsing through herself. What if some total a-hole like David Hamm or Terry Dixon had a power like this? She had watched those idiots mock and ridicule anyone the least bit different, or fat, or poor, or smart. They were bullies of the worst kind: loud and belligerent. They would hurt people, they would do terrible things. And somehow down inside, she also thought that any of them could go too far really easily. What if you could make someone give you money, or could punch someone so hard it hurt them really bad or even killed them? That seemed to be the slippery slope.

Turning on her other side she thought about how if you were careful though, you could really do something good for people. You could make life better for them somehow. *That's got to be why we have these powers. It can't be to just be selfish like her parents, she thought. I've got to make a pact with the boys.* If we are going to use the powers, then it has to be like a real super hero. They do their amazing things for the greater good. Superman doesn't rob a bank just because he could punch through the wall. But down inside, Emily had the idea the boys might not be as keen about sticking with total altruistic motives with using the power. *It's probably fine to use it just to have a bit of fun sometimes, but only if it doesn't hurt people. I wonder, can I just make the volume on the radio go up just by thinking about it?* She flipped on her stomach and stared at the soft green glow of her radio, now softly playing "More than a Feeling." *God, I love this song,* she thought. Then she stared, really stared at the radio and just kept concentrating: *get a little louder, get a little louder.* She continued to look at the radio volume knob and then she felt it, that sparkle behind the eyes, that flutter in the stomach. Sure enough, the volume dial slowly began to rise until Boston was happily crooning twice as loud as it had been before. Emily quickly grabbed the volume knob and turned it back down. Ok, she thought. *Maybe I will go along with some of this, but those idiots are not going to talk me into anything else than can hurt people.* Emily fell asleep thinking, one of those boys is a pretty cute idiot.

The following day Emily was sitting beside Travis and across the booth from George at Chat N Chew. She and Travis were sharing another corn muffin basket and sweet tea since both of them had decided to pool their money for more candy to enjoy in class that afternoon. It had been a funny morning. She and Travis had hardly spoken at all in the halls or at the lockers. But no one was mad. It just seemed that something was unspoken, the air needed to be cleared between them all but no one wanted to be the first to talk. George had barely looked at her all day, but again, not because he seemed mad. Almost like he was avoiding looking at her. Finally Emily couldn't stand it anymore.

"Ok," she said adding another pat of butter to her muffin. "What is going on with you two? You haven't said two words hardly all day. All tuckered out from your sleep over?" she added with a sarcastic grin.

"What do you mean?" George asked with a mouthful of hamburger.

"Oh I think you know, Spanky. You were positively glowing last night running toward Travis's bed in that lightning," Emily added feeling this was probably not the way to smooth things out with George but he made her so mad sometimes.

"Jeez, that's a bit harsh, Em," Travis hissed back as he saw George looking daggers at Emily not saying a word. Travis decided to try and change the conversation quickly.

"Actually, George had a, um . . . what do you call it, a . . . "

"Seizure? Brain fart? Aneurysm?"

"Epiphany," Travis said weakly.

"Oh this should be rich," Emily said wiping her mouth and sitting back in the booth. Why she was so bitchy today she couldn't say.

Travis began to recount George's revelation about the seeming exponential relation of their new powers. George spoke up and filled in the gaps and soon both boys were rattling off a diatribe about powers of ten that made Emily's head spin. But she had to admit, a lot of what they were talking about was making serious sense. In fact, it was more sense than either one of these idiots usually made.

"And George and I think maybe we ought to keep experimenting, like testing our powers, you know, scientifically and find out more about them."

Emily looked at both these wide-eyed numbskulls and had to admit they were extremely cute at this exact moment. She popped the last bite of muffin into her mouth and took a big drink of tea.

"Agreed," she said looking at both of them implacably.

"Really?" George asked incredulously.

"Really," Emily replied. "But I have one condition."

"What?" the boys asked simultaneously.

"Whatever we do, these experiments or testing, no one gets hurt. I mean it. We need to come up with a plan to test and control these powers without hurting people. And besides that, I was thinking last night that all the superheroes I know about always seem to use their powers for good, not to play practical jokes on others or hurt anybody."

The boys were quiet for a moment then Travis answered. "Yeah, we sort of thought about that too."

"But just for the science of it," George began, "We might should include a few experiments that might not just be about helping others. You know, just to see what works and doesn't."

"Okay," Emily said. "As long as we don't hurt people or do mean things just to play pranks on people."

"What if they deserve it?" George asked.

"Well, I don't think any of us should just try and pay someone back without really thinking about it first. Eventually people are going to notice funny stuff happens when we are around. If there is some reason we have to pay a bad person back for being a jerk, then let's at least decide we ought to talk about it with someone else. Don't just react because we are pissed off and want to hurt them back," Emily said emphatically.

"I think that makes sense," Travis said noticing how pink Emily's lips were today, *all that butter from the muffin was making her lips shine like lip gloss.* She would probably hate that but it looked good to him.

"Ok, since neither of you has said a word about this, I will say it," Emily began. "I know you both saw it last night."

"What?" the boys asked warily.

"That bridge, the light . . . I know you must have seen it too." Emily watched as the boys looked quickly at each other and then down at their empty plates.

"Um, yeah. I sort of dreamed that," Travis.

"Me too. " George said.

"We didn't really talk about it much. Guess we got to talking about other stuff," Travis offered.

Emily looked at the boys incredulously. "What was so important that both of you forgot to talk about having the exactly same freaking dream?"

George dug his spiral notebook out of his backpack and showed Emily what he had written down. She read the notes and was actually impressed he had thought of all this. She tended just to think of him as a flake and a pain in the butt, a third wheel, you name it. But she could tell he had really been thinking about this. She told the boys about turning up the volume on her radio last night.

"I guess we can probably check off "make stuff get louder or stronger," George said. "When should we do some of this other stuff? And it's fine to keep trying a few things on our own. I mean, that's probably a safe way to see what might happen. But we need to test this idea of our joined power being exponential."

"What about on Friday night?" Travis asked. "The football game is out of town but we could get together afterward or maybe even on Saturday. We can always tell our parents we are sleeping over at the others' house. Em you could go to a girl's sleepover thing at someone else's house That always seems to work pretty well."

"I could see if my dad's in a good enough mood he would let me take the VW," George offered.

"As long as we keep it really quiet. My mom would still freak about me riding around with you driving," Emily said

Emily was frankly astounded with the knowledge that George was permitted to drive at fourteen. With what she understood of George's difficult relationship with his dad, it was bizarre that his controlling a-holeness seemed to not come into play in regards to George using the car. In fact, she was downright jealous listening to him talk about the driving lessons his dad had given him over the past few months. She wondered if it was Mr. Harris's way of trying to connect with George and heal the rift between the two of them since Fred had died. George wasn't fifteen yet but he drove like a pro. She had ridden with him and Travis a few times late at night driving around on back roads and she had to admit, the kid was good. She smiled remembering Travis telling her about Mr. Harris encouraging George to take the car and pick up a girl from school and go to the basketball game or something like that. Mr. Harris always seemed to be working hard to find a girlfriend for George. She wondered if it was because he was used to Fred having so many girls interested in him or if he was worried George didn't care for girls all that much. From what she could tell, George was like most of the boys, silly and immature. But maybe that was unfair too, because she really didn't spend any time with just him and boys always act stupid around each other. Emily knew what her mother would say about riding around with two underage teenage boys in a car, which was why she never told her and also why it was so much fun. Supposedly, George was teaching Travis how to drive a stick. Thankfully she had not been present for any of that. She had already heard a few horror stories of near accidents they laughed about.

"One of these nights, we should go play night golf again," George offered.

"What's that?" Emily asked warily.

"You'll see," Travis said with a wry smile. "It's great. Yeah, I don't know if we could this week but let's do that soon." Travis checked his watch. "Shit, we need to scoot. We barely have enough time to get to Western Auto and back to Webster's class on time."

As the kids walked quickly across the street and down the square to the store, Emily asked, "Does that revival start this Sunday at church?"

"No, thank God. It's in a couple of weeks," George said. "That's church for a solid goddamn week. Every night."

"With that mouth of yours, it sounds like it could do you some good," Emily scolded.

"It's a great way to get out of doing homework," George added. The teacher's don't like sounding like communists about doing your homework instead of going to church. Believe me, I've used it before."

"You know, for such a smart guy, you sure do work hard to get out of doing homework, G," Emily said.

"It's the principle of the thing. If you already know how to do the shit, why should you have to prove it on paper? It's a stupid waste of time," he added opening the door of the store. "Isn't the revival going to be with that nutty evangelist who does the illustrated sermons?"

"Yeah, Brother Zane Zigler," Travis said rummaging through the rack for as much candy as his 37 cents would buy.

"He sounds like a used car salesman," Emily added.

"It will be a hoot," George said. "Better than the crud Brother Nelson usually offers."

"I would have to agree with you on that."

The kids looked up and realized Jack Tanner was talking to them

"What did you say Mr. Tanner?" George asked grabbing a Jolly Rancher Fire Stix.

"That the Brother Nelson sermons usually leave something to be desired," he added with a grin. "How are you kids doing, today? That was quite the storm the other day that hit the school wasn't it?"

All three teenagers looked at each other and then back at Mr. Tanner. Travis spoke up. "Um, yeah it was pretty weird."

"Just sort of came out of nowhere, huh?" Jack Tanner asked holding out his hand for Travis's change. When the boy's fingers touched his palm, a bolt of energy passed through Jack. In a nanosecond, he was connected, felt the power surge. The dream, the one with the bridge he'd had last night, blasted across his mind and he knew the boy was seeing exactly the same thing.

Travis pulled his hand back as if a scorpion had just struck. The two stared at each other wide-eyed while Emily and George's heads snapped back and forth between them. Jack's hands darted forward and grabbed Emily and George's offered hands holding the change for their candy. Again, the bolt of energy arced between them, even stronger this time; the blinding flash in their minds, the collective awareness and the dream images. The teens pulled their hands back, dropped the change on the counter, grabbed their candy and practically ran out the door, leaving Jack Tanner shouting for them to come back.

22 Jack

Jack stared at the trio of teenagers running across the street. *So now I know.* He had worked out that he and Joey were experiencing some sort of connection and some strange new ability or something since that night with the light. In the past few days, he had watched as Joey continued to use this new power to weave a spell of magic around Lori causing her to be happier, more energetic and attentive than he could ever remember. He himself had experienced the enhanced attraction and passion between himself and Lori. The sex had never been this good. He lasted longer, was harder and recovered faster than when he was kid.

He'd tried out this new ability on some customers as well. Twice now, he had customers, who were reluctant to purchase a new lawn mower or air conditioner, suddenly change their mind and fork over the bucks. All he had done was look at them and carefully concentrate on the one idea: you really want to buy this. Sure enough, whatever salesmanship he had seemed more powerful after that and the customers walked out of the store with their purchase feeling happy, but a little dazed.

He wanted to talk to Tim about it, but for some reason felt so foolish about bringing up his new power, or whatever the hell it was. But Jack was pretty sure he had seen Tim manifest some new mental muscle himself. Once, he was in the back where Tim was working on a lawn mower. He was trying to loosen the bolts that held the motor onto the deck and they were clearly rusted shut. Jack watched as Tim seemed to breathe deep and stare intently at the bolts and sure enough, the wrench spun around and loosened them as easily as if they were brand new. Just yesterday, that tease, Betty Whitener, had been in the store, wearing a blouse about two sizes two small over her large melons. She clearly wasn't wearing a bra and her tits were bobbing around her shirt with the buttons straining almost to the bursting point. Both men were behind the counter as she wandered the aisles, bending over in her shorts for various items, turning around with a smile to make sure she was being watched. Jack looked at Tim who was staring intently at her ass. When she came up to pay for her items, he saw Tim was continuing to stare fixedly, now at her bazooms. Jack didn't have to think twice about what Tim was thinking. Jack turned his gaze on to Betty's bosom and the buttons of her shirt. He thought, *just give up buttons, just go ahead and pop,* with all his might.

Pow! The buttons corralling her massive breasts popped off her shirt like bullets, ricocheting off the cash register and out into the store. Betty shrieked as her tits plopped out of her shirt like two water balloons.

Mrs. Clemmons who was looking at gardening gloves gasped, "Oh, Lord a Mercy."

Jimmy Earwood, who should have been in school, was so surprised he walked straight into the glass door, his head cracking against the glass like a rock, falling back into the floor with a grunt. Betty had wrapped her blouse around herself and tore from the store like a bat out of hell. Tim had looked at him wide-eyed with a grin as big as Texas.

"Talk about lucky. I guess those poor buttons just couldn't hold on any longer," he chuckled.

The men ran around the counter and helped Jimmy to his feet, asking if he was alright. Mrs. Clemmons clucked about indecent loose women and gave up on choosing some gloves and hurried out of the store. Jack thought, *that might have been funny but it sure isn't very good for business.* He was sure of one thing though: whatever this shit was, it had happened to Tim too, even if the dope didn't know it. How unaware did a person have to be to just miss all this, he wondered? Joey seemed to be dialed into the power and he was a baby. What did that say about Tim?

Later that day, Tim was up on a ladder shelving extra stock of radiator hose. He called for Jack to come hand him another box. As Jack started to hand it up, Tim lost his balance on the ladder momentarily and reached back to steady himself. Jack grabbed his hand and instantly the connection was there. His mind lit up like the fourth of July. In a second he felt like he was inside Tim's mind. The light, the energy, the dream were there. But even more. He saw Tim and Candy fighting, then fucking. He also saw Tim and another woman that looked really familiar. He saw Tim and JL Martin at some bonfire along with other familiar but faceless men.

"We gonna keep holding hands here or you gonna let me get back to work?" Tim asked giving Jack an intense, questioning look. Jack wondered what Tim had seen in his mind and his face went red imagining what it might be. Jack let go of Tim, handing him the box of hoses. He waited to see if maybe Tim would say something. Did he feel it too, he wondered? But Tim continued to stack the boxes seemingly nonplussed. Jack waited a bit longer until Tim said, "You gonna just stand there and sniff my sack all day, or are you gonna bring me some more shit?" Jack turned and grabbed another box and handed it up to Tim, making sure to shove the corner of the box hard into his balls on the way up.

"Ooof," Tim grunted. "Watch it Mr. Magoo."

The bell on the front door tinkled and the men looked across the store to see who was coming in. Jack did a double take as JL Martin sauntered over to the ladder.

"Afternoon, ladies," he said with his usual flair.

"Hey, JL," Tim hollered down. "What are you up to today?" He tried to make his voice sound casual, but behind the professional courtesy was something else. Fear?

"Just out for a couple of errands. Hey can I have a word?" JL asked Tim who was making his way down the ladder.

"Sure. Come on back to the office," Tim said. "You want an RC?"

Jack neatened up some car air fresheners that had fallen on the shelf and then made his way back to storeroom. From there, it was easy to listen in to conversations in the office since the walls didn't go all the way up to the roof of the warehouse area. It had been a point of contention for the guys for a while since more than once, Jack had overheard conversations about business or personal life Tim had never intended to share. He couldn't really say why he wanted to overhear the conversation, but he wanted to anyway. He positioned himself close to the bathroom so he could make an easy exit in there if it seemed like they were thinking someone was listening.

"You ran off the other night. Just when things were getting interesting." JL said taking a long swig of the cold pop.

"Yeah, I just decided that's probably not for me. I think it's great for all of you. I, you know, would never say anything obviously."

Jack's mind quickly ran back to a month ago when JL had cornered Tim at Graves Hardware. Jack had been there as well but JL acted like he didn't exist, which was just fine with him. JL had invited Tim out to his new church again and Tim had continued to decline. But JL didn't like taking no for an answer.

"We'd love to have you. You are just the kind of guy we always are looking for. We have several guys who don't make it to church. A few even belong to other congregations. But our men's fellowship group is open to any that we invite and brother, we sure want you. Your dad always was such a big part of our group. So sorry about him, too."

"Uh thanks, Ok. When you getting' together again?"

"Couple of weeks, out Scatter Branch way. My place between here and Greenville. Got us a good place out there on the back of my property. Our fellowship just helped repaint the sign heading into Greenville last weekend."

Jack's stomach had contracted. He knew which sign he was talking about. Greenville, Texas was notorious for its "Welcome to Greenville" sign that proudly proclaimed, "The blackest land and the whitest people." Jack remembered his dad talking about another sign that used to hang underneath that one: "Nigger, don't let the sun set on your black ass in this town." What was Tim doing talking about meeting up with JL or any of his cronies? Tim had told him that he would think about it.

J.L. cleared his throat. Nothing was said for a few moments. JL continued to drink his RC along with Tim, the awkward silence thick and uncomfortable. "You need to be careful, Tim. We come to you, you say thanks and I'm honored. We let you in ... you don't just leave in the middle of a ceremony. You don't run off. What you saw, it's private and sacred."

The hairs on the back of Jack's neck stood on end.

Tim chuckled. "Yeah, ok. Well it's all great and everything. I guess y'all had a good reason for, uh doing all that. It's just not for me. And you know Candy might not be that thrilled ..."

Tim's voice broke off as something thudded loud onto the desk with a grunt. Jack moved to the corner of the office where there was a small gap in the drywall they had put up to create the office. Focusing on the small crack, Jack's eye widened as he saw Tim's face and chest smashed down on the desk. J.L stood behind him, Tim's arm bent up behind his back in his left hand. His right hand held a 9mm pistol to his head.

"Listen you dickless piece of shit," JL hissed low in Tim's ear. "This is not a negotiation. We pick who we want. You're in or you are out, as in permanently out." JL pressed the gun tighter against Tim's temple. "Your ass is mine, and you do as you're told. We revealed ourselves to you like the Almighty revealing his face to Moses on Mt. Sinai. That is a lasting covenant. You don't get to quit just because it's not your thing. And fuck whatever Candy wants," he said rubbing his hand roughly against Tim's khaki covered rear. With a quick jerk, JL pushed Tim's pants down off his butt cheeks. He reached down and grabbed a grease gun that was sitting on edge of the cluttered metal desk and forced the nozzle hard inside Tim's ass crack. As he pulled the trigger on the grease gun JL whispered, "I'll lube you up then be like a bull up in your ass."

The door to the office flew open and Jack punched JL in the face harder and faster than he'd ever moved in his life. The redneck flew across the room and smashed into a set of metal filing cabinets and slid to the floor in a heap. Jack kicked the gun away from JL's hand and turned to Tim.

"Are you ok? Jesus Christ!"

Tim stood up weakly pulling his pants up over his ass, not looking at Jack. He stumbled toward the desk and grabbed at the corner to steady himself. "Oh God, what did you do? Oh shit, oh shit," Tim exclaimed in a hushed voice.

"What did I do? What the fuck? That piece of shit was raping you with a grease gun not to mention holding a pistol to your head," Jack said through clenched teeth. "What is going on? Why is he talking to you or trying to make you do something?"

"Not now," Tim snapped. "Jack, we gotta get him out of here or something. Is he dead?"

That question brought Jack back to earth in a sudden crash. He crossed to the crumpled man on the floor and felt his neck. "Yeah, he's alive. Unfortunately," added Jack.

Tim looked weak and wild, like a caged animal backed into a corner. He looked furtively around the office and then pleadingly back to Jack. "What are we gonna do?"

Jack felt clear-headed and sure. "He didn't even see me when I came in. He had no idea I was here until I punched him. We can load him up in the truck and take his sorry ass out on a back road and dump him. He wouldn't know how he got there or what the hell happened," Jack offered. "Or … we could try and wake this sack of shit up and pretend he slipped or something and hit his head. Personally, I'd like to … "

"Let's kill him," Tim said in a dead voice.

"What? "

"Let's take him for that ride out in the country and blow his goddamn head off."

Jack walked over to Tim and put a hand on his shoulder. Tim pulled away and backed against the wall of the office. He wrapped his arms around himself, visibly shaking. Jack walked over and stood in front of him.

"Listen to me. I got this. I know what to do. Here's what we're gonna do. We are going to make this sum-bitch forget he even came in here. Then you are going to go. And I'll wake him up and get his sorry ass away from here. We can't kill him 'cause that will just hurt you and me and our family and he's not worth that. Okay?"

Tim looked nervously around the office, back and forth to the slumped man on the floor and then up at Jack. "What do you mean, make him forget."

Jack looked intently at Tim. "We are going to touch this asshole's head and we are going to force him to forget. Together, we do it together, and it will be even better." Jack looked at Tim as he stared bewildered back at him. "You know it will work," he said grabbing Tim's hand. Their thoughts locked together and in that moment, Jack felt Tim's terror, and shame, and hate boiling all around him. He saw flickers of black robed shapes, gold grotesque faces, a hanging naked man. But he pushed beyond that to the light, to the power. In that instant, Tim's eyes flew open and understanding dawned in him. "So, okay. You got it now."

"Yeah. Oh God!"

"Come over here and squat down. Put your hand on this motherfucker's head and I want you to just think, 'Forget,' with all your might. Okay?"

Tim nodded. The men crouched over the unconscious man and laid their hands on his head. Like an Oral Robert's crusade from hell, they closed their eyes sent their own prayer straight into the rotten mind of JL Martin. "Forget." Like a blast from a car battery, Jack felt the energy surge between himself and Tim and straight into JL. *With any luck,* Jack thought, *he won't even remember his damn name.*

"I want you to go ahead and walk to the Showdown. It's almost 4:00. I'm gonna take care of this piece of crap and then join you down there in a bit. You hear me?"

Tim nodded and headed toward the door, but he stopped and walked back to JL and swung a hard kick with his boot into the man's ribs and stomach. He turned and headed out the door, reaching behind and pulling his pants and underwear out of his crack and he wobbled toward the bathroom on his way out of the store. Jack ran to the front door and looked around the aisles. *No one around thank God,* he thought. He turned the sign to "Closed" and hastily scribbled a note on a piece of paper: "Closed for Inventory" he wrote and taped the sign on the window. He locked the door and opened the cash register and pulled out the day's sales along with the register tape and ran them back to the safe in the office. JL was still out as Jack expected. He opened the safe and put the cash and checks away. He grabbed the gun and unloaded the magazine and removed the clip and set it inside the safe before he closed the door and spun the dial. He looked up and saw Tim heading out the back door of the store. Jack bent down and hefted up JL in a fireman's carry and dumped him on the Naugahyde sofa, enjoying the thunk of his head hitting the heavy wooden arm. He stood up with hands on his hips and looked around the office. A blaze of anger coursed through him and he came back to the body on the couch and ripped the trousers open and pulled them down off the man's ass. Jack grabbed the grease gun and forced the nozzle deep inside his anus and pulled the trigger again and again and again.

"You'll be shitting axel grease for a week," Jack murmured pulling the man's pants up over his buttocks. And then for good measure, Jack reached down and gripped J.L. crotch and focused: *you need to piss worse than you ever have in your whole life.* Sure enough, within moments, a dark flow of urine began to darken his groin and seeped into the fabric down the legs of his pants.

"Time to go, Asshole," Jack said and grabbed a cup of water from the water cooler and threw it in JL's face. Jack gripped the man's slick bald head roughly, pulled his head up, and thought: *wake up!*"

JL Martin's eyes began to flutter and soon they opened slowly, unfocused. In a few moments they began to slowly look around the room and then fixed wonderingly on Jack. "What the hell?"

"Hey there, JL. Wow, you had some kind of fit or something and passed out. We got you up on the couch here. Tim had to go to an appointment so I stayed to make sure you were okay."

JL groggily rose up and grabbed his head and then his side. "Holy shit, it's like I've been run over by a truck."

"Yeah, you really hit the deck pretty hard," Jack said stone faced. "Kinda looks like you pissed yourself too."

JL looked down and felt his crotch. "Damn it," he croaked. He looked up at Jack with a pained expression on his face. I can't even remember coming in here," he said obviously confused.

"Well a bender'll do that to you. You better be heading home, buddy. Go home and sleep it off, okay."

"Okay," JL said as Jack helped him to his feet.

"Just go out the back here. Less folks will see you wet yourself," Jack added with a smile.

JL stumbled through the warehouse and out the back door. The bright afternoon sun and heat blasted through the dark room and caused Jack to squint watching the wobbling redneck make his way out the door and down the alley. Jack headed back to the office and picked up the phone and quickly dialed the sheriff's office.

"Hey Sandra, this is Jack Tanner down here at Western Auto. Yeah, I'm fine sweetheart. Hey, I just saw ole JL Martin wobbling down our back alley looking like he is three sheets to the wind. Looks kind of like he pissed himself. Thought one of the deputies might want to check it out. Yeah, heading toward Bonham Street it looks like. Ok, thanks."

Jack flipped off the lights and went out the back door locking it as he looked down the alley toward the still tottery form of JL making his way toward Bonham Street. Jack smiled as he watched the man walking bowlegged from the piss on his pants and the grease up his keister. As he made his way to the opening of the alley, a patrol car with blue and red lights flashing stopped in the entrance. JL stopped in his tracks and as the deputies approached him began shouting and waving his arms about like a crazy man. Just like clockwork, the deputies had him slammed over the trunk of the patrol car, frisking him. Jack couldn't help but snicker wondering what they were going to think of his pissed, greasy ass. He turned and walked down the back of the alley toward his truck and drove away toward the Showdown.

23 Tim

Sitting in a back booth with Tim, Jack took a long drink of his draft Coors. Tim had moved on from beer to boilermakers, clunking the shot glass into his beer mug with a splash. Jack had just sat with him for near half an hour, not talking, just letting Tim be. The juke box was blaring "Freebird." Jack cracked peanuts and threw the shells on the floor along with all the others. Tim took another long drink.

"Thanks. Back there for, you know . . . shit. Stuff is so messed up," Tim said, never quite looking at Jack.

"No problem, buddy. Always got your back, you know that. Always have, always will."

It had always been that way; from grade school to high school football to getting drafted and deployed to Viet Nam. Their tour had been mercifully short. They both had only been in country two months working for the quartermaster and manning a munitions depot for 1st Cavalry Division in support of the battles raging near Khe Sahn when a freak accident got them both shipped home. Jack still had a great photo of Tim standing shirtless in the hot sun, guarding captured Viet Cong ordinates. The faded photo showed Tim hefting a three-foot long artillery shell, holding it at his crotch like a mighty cock. General Westmorland had visited the site that day. Jack remembered him grinning and saluting as Tim stood with the shell. Tim practically broke his foot dropping the shell so he could salute the general.

The supply depot went under attack and they were thrown together manning a machine gun, Tim firing while Jack held the bandolier of shells ripping through the gun. It was chaos, taking lots of enemy fire. They had already lost two guys and with the smoke and explosions and screams, it was impossible to make out anything. Finally the CO ordered both Tim and Jack to pull the machine gun and move it to a more favorable location a half-click to the south. Then the bullets seemed to fly from every direction, ripping through men and trees. Tim grabbed the gun and started running. Jack grabbed the stanchion and ammo and tore off after him, ducking as low as possible, running like scared rabbits through the jungle. As they ran, Jack felt the round or shrapnel or a bullet tear into his calf, but he just kept running. They ran fast and wild, like deer in a forest fire. Both men fell into a foxhole on top of one another as the rain began to pour hard in a torrent, making the dark forest impenetrable to the light. They huddled together, eyes closed against the rain and the inevitable attack. More explosions, more fire, a roar of rotors filled the air above the jungle canopy overhead. Jack managed to get the stanchion in place but when he reached for the gun, he saw in horror that Tim had grabbed the muzzle of the gun at some point during the run and his hands were burned red, practically melted to the metal. While Tim sat in shock, Jack eased his fingers off the hot muzzle and mounted it on the stanchion. Jack loaded the ammunition and grabbed the handles, looking for something, anything to shoot. Tim was sitting in stunned silence, staring at his ruined hands. The rain increased to a roaring flood, rivulets filling the foxhole with a shocking glut of muddy water until the men were waist deep in the soup.

They stayed in that hole for hours, freezing in the water, being eaten alive by mosquitoes.

To their right, Corporal Mark Judson and Sgt. Frank Macon hunkered down. Jack didn't dare fire into the blackness for fear of giving away their position and there was nothing to shoot at anyway. Finally, sometime in the early morning hours, they heard rotors overhead again and celebrated that recon troops were there. But as the Chinook neared, Viet Cong rockets found it, shattering the rear rotor and sending the aircraft spinning to the ground. Jack grabbed Tim and started running. As the helicopter slammed into the ground in a ball of fire and smoke, it exploded, sending rotors and metal flying through the air like an arsenal of death. A flying three foot piece of rotor caught Corporal Mark Judson under the neck, decapitating him. His head slammed into Jack knocking him to the ground just as a huge part of the landing strut impaled the ground exactly where he had been standing. Tim grabbed Jack and the two rolled over and over on top of each other until they splashed into the river as the aircraft exploded again, turning the site into hell on earth. Jack woke in the infirmary in Da Nang with stitches in his leg from where the surgeons had pulled a bullet and three pieces of shrapnel. Tim was in the next bed, both hands heavily bandaged.

After an eventful furlough in Bangkok, they were medically released from active duty and sent back to the States to finish their tour as supply clerks at Fort Hood. They had been stacking, inventorying and ordering shit together ever since then; first for Uncle Sam and now for the store.

Jack picked up one of his peanut hulls and pitched it toward Tim, bouncing it off his head. Tim looked up and then gave a weak smile, tossing another nut over the table hitting Jack on the chest.

"So you ready to tell me what all that shit was about?" Jack said raising his beer mug for the waitress to bring him another.

"Could we just let it go?" Tim said rubbing his closed eyes with his hand.

"Not likely," Jack said. "What the hell is going on? Why would that redneck be looking for your ass and packing a gun," Jack whispered.

Tim waited until the waitress had brought two new drinks and then launched into the story.

"You heard of the Black Knights of God?"

"Not really. Sounds like some stupid Klan shit," Jack added.

"More or less. I think it's guys too stupid even for the Klan."

"Why in the hell would you be mixed up with idiots like that?"

"I'm not. Or not really. It's complicated," Tim said in frustration. "JL's family started up that group back during Reconstruction or something. It was mainly Martin family but they invited some others to join. From what I just learned, I think my dad, granddad, great-grandad, way on back were part of it. It's like the fucking Rotary Club to them or something. As a kid, I remember him taking me to this bonfire and barbecue one time. It was all men and a few boys like me. I had no idea what it was about. The men just sat around drinking beer, talking about hunting and fishing mostly, while the boys ran around throwing sticks and branches into the fire. At the end of the night, the guys all got together brand stood and were reciting some pledge or creed. Three of the men donned these black robes and put on these weird gold masks with super freaky faces on them, like tribal masks or something. The masks were attached to what looked like skulls. They were rotating around the fire, but then I saw they were walking on this big star that had been scratched on the ground, which I thought was really weird. Then out of nowhere, they pull this black kid, he must have been about seventeen or so. He was bound and gagged. They pulled his clothes off and fastened a rope to him and hauled him up by his arms. By this time, I was so scared and shocked. They just left him there, they didn't do anything.

About that time, my dad and some of the others that had brought kids with them all left. But as we got back in the car and started to leave, I know I heard screams. On the way home, my dad, who was definitely drunk, pulled me over to him and put his arm around me and hugged me close, which he never did. He kept saying it was good to have me with him and that he was proud of me. I honestly did not know what was happening. I just enjoyed my dad being human and kind to me for a change instead of just a dick like normal. I asked him what happened to that boy and he just said, 'Oh nothing. He needed to be taught a lesson, that's all.'"

Tim took another big drink and continued. "I didn't know anything more about this until last year when Dad had that stroke. A lot of those guys came to the hospital and the nursing home afterwards and were talking to me about Dad and how proud he was of me and all that. Then JL took me to the side and invited me to his new church, told me I would fit right in and that I would especially like the men's group. I wasn't really interested but it seemed like they really wanted me to come over and thought it would be a nice thing to do. Even though my dad couldn't talk, I could tell he wanted me to go. But something came up and I didn't go. That was months ago. Then just last week, he came by my house and invited me again. He said it was really important meeting that he and these guys from his new church were having. You know, how he has started up that new crazy Holy Roller church over in the old Masonic Hall out on Jernigan Street."

"Yeah. He stopped in at work and invited me out there. I'd just about rather be set on fire than go to a church where he was the one in charge," Jack said.

Jack told Tim to hold on and he ran over to the payphone and made a quick call then stopped at the bar and ordered something and came back to the booth.

"Ok, called home and told Lori I'd be late. She seemed fine about it. Ordered us some barbecue and fried okra. I think you need to eat something and not just drink," Jack said smiling.

"Yeah, probably so," Tim agreed. "So you want more of this sorry tale?"

"Sure. Best tell me all of it," Jack said.

"Okay man. Well, I had promised you we'd go fishing, so we went out to the lake and boom, the crazy light shit happens. I get back home that afternoon and JL comes by yet again to say that they were meeting that night and they just had to have me come join in. I wasn't in the mood at all, hell I was still trying to figure out what had happened to us. Well, I got out there around 7:30. The old geezers were sitting around a big fire again and there were some guys our age out there this time too. Jerry Morgan, Jim Measles, Randy Hamm, Lloyd Massey. And a few younger ones too, Toy and Greg Benton, Junior Bidwell.

"Bunch of rednecks but mostly normal guys, at least they were in school," Jack said.

"That's what I thought too. So I stayed. Had some beer and some fried catfish and hush puppies and the like. It was sorta' weird 'cause it seemed like most of the guys had been there for a while before I got there. They were lit up pretty good. I couldn't figure it out cause they are supposed to be so religious, but they were downright drunk, most of them. Some guys were over doing some cane pole fishing in the pond. Some others had a game of corn-hole going. Seemed not normal though." The waitress brought over two baskets of barbecue brisket, fried okra, and some cornbread, along with a couple more beers. The men tucked into their dinner for a time, then Tim returned to his story.

"After a while, it seemed like some of the older guys went into the barn there. Then the younger guys seem to trail in after them. I was over on the far side of the pond with a fishing pole. Finally Jerry Morgan came up and said, 'Hey Tim, come on, we're getting started.' When I asked what, he just gave me a weird look and said 'Hurry up.' So I pulled up the line and followed him into the barn." Tim ate a bit more of his brisket and okra and took a big swig of beer. "I get in there and just stop right in my tracks. Here, right in front of my eyes, were these guys wearing black robes with hoods with skulls and had these gold masks on. The last couple of guys were pulling theirs on. There were some tarps or big curtain things at the back of the barn. There was a small fire in a barrel in the middle of the floor. There was all this crazy writing on the floor and a star and a goat head hanging on this pole."

"You are shitting me," Jack said.

"And Jerry came up with his robe on but not his mask and said, 'Here you go, put this on,' and handed me a robe and mask. Then a guy at the front banged a big staff on the floor and everyone got in a circle and got quiet. The guy said something like, 'Brother Murphy, this should be your initiation ceremony tonight, but extraordinary circumstances cause us to include you as a full member now. We will revisit your initiation at a later date. Please don your sacred robes.' And I don't have to tell you I was practically pissing myself by this time. I had no frickin' idea of what was going on. I honestly thought it was some elaborate practical joke."

"Did you put the stuff on?" Jack asked mesmerized.

"Yeah, I mean, I didn't know what else to do. So I put it on and got in the circle. Then the main guy started this chant that sounded like freakin' Latin or Ubangi or something and the guys kept answering back in a big grunt of some sort. None of it made sense to me for a while. Just a bunch of gibberish and crap. But then the main guy says, 'Now we will begin the purification' and these other guys pull back the tarps or curtains or whatever and I almost shit. There was two people back there. One was a big black guy, with a hood over his head. He was nekkid and strung up by his wrists about two feet off the ground. On the other side was a person bent over this contraption, like feed bags wrapped around saw horses or something. By the look of the legs, it seemed like a woman or a girl to me. She was bent over and tied to that sawhorse or barrel thing."

"Oh God."

"It felt like my heart was up in my mouth or something. The main guy started talking about how the black guy was the 'fatted calf' and how his sacrifice would bring cleansing and purity to the land and better crops and all this crap. And then he said the girl there wasn't the only seed of evil, that there was another. He said the man would have to pay for his sins and the girl would have to be cleansed by blood and seed or some crazy ass shit like that. And the other guys were saying stuff like 'Cleanse the Evil' and 'Power of the blood of white saints.' They started moving up closer to the black guy the girl. I just kept slowly walking back until I was at the back of the crowd. No one was paying attention to me anyway. Then this other guy went up to the black guy and took out this knife and carved a star into his belly. The black guy was flailing around and screaming, but something was obviously in his mouth because it was just loud grunts.

"Fuck me," Jack whispered.

"And then they all grabbed these rods or sticks like broom or hoe handles and started beating the guy like he was a piñata or something. Someone handed me a stick and I just let the crowd push me forward until I was in the middle of it. I never hit the guy but I acted like I was. I was so scared and I just didn't know what was happening or why I was there or anything. And the next thing I knew they were yelling and a couple of guys started pissing on this poor guy and he was just a mess of blood and everything. And then I saw he had a tattoo on his arm. He was army, he was from 1st Cavalry."

"Jesus Christ!"

"And then they were going around in a circle hitting, spitting, and pissing on him more. And then it got even worse," Tim said, his voice catching in his throat. "They started raping that girl.

I mean, they just went up and started doing it with her like she was an animal or something. Then this other guy went up to the black guy and made a slash with the knife and I saw a spurt of blood between his legs and I think they might have cut him around his balls or something. And then this crazy ass green light started blazing and lit up the barn and all these metal bits like tiny meteors or something started smashing through the walls and roof. It was like a ball of green fire flooding the place, with bullets going off in every direction. It was like I was back in fuckin' Nam. I just freaked out. I pushed out of the circle and took off running. I just jumped in my truck and burned out of there. I still had the fucking mask on and everything for a minute. Then I tore it off and kept trying to think of what to do. I mean, I was planning to go to the cops and everything, but then I thought, oh shit, I was there. I was guilty like all those sick fucks. I was crazy and I just kept driving. I drove all the way to Wolfe City and out on a back road and then just parked and sat there for a long time." Tim's hand was shaking as he took another drink. "I had an empty five gallon bucket in my truck bed. I took all the garb they gave me and burned the shit: robe, mask, all of it. I stayed out there for a couple of hours just listening to the radio and smoking. I smoked all the weed I had and then moved to cigarettes. I finally went home and went to bed. I swear to God the next day I half convinced myself it was a freaking dream. Then I was there at the store the next day and it was late. You had already left. I was getting ready to close up and in walks J.L. And he proceeds to be all nicey-nice and everything and then at the end says: 'What happens at the council stays there.' When I act like I don't know what he's talking about, that's when he pulls his jacket back a bit so I can see the Glock. And says, 'See you at the next meeting. We will need to get you initiated. Sorta got all bass-ackwards but that was some important council business. That's our mission, like I know your old man told you. The law can only do so much, that's why we're there. To keep darkies and other filth in their place. Been that way in this county for over a hundred years. It's your time to step up and take your place. And it goes without saying, you open your mouth about any of this and it will be the last thing you ever do.'"

Jack sat in stunned silence, the food and drink forgotten. "Did you ever go back?"

"No. And then today J.L. pays me another visit. I am in trouble, man," Tim moans.

The men were quiet for a while longer. The juke box was playing "Dream On." There were more patrons at the bar now, the volume of their conversations was a solid buzz against Jack's ears. He couldn't wrap his head around any of this. It just seemed so impossible, the stuff you see in the movies but not in real life. "That girl, did you get a look at her at all?"

"No."

"You think it could have been that Washington girl, the one who disappeared and then turned up naked and all messed up out on Hwy 14?"

"I don't know. I've thought about it. I guess it had to have been her. The girl I saw did seem to be kind of dark skinned, but the light was really dim.

"That girl was raped," Jack said in a clinched whisper. "Do you think those sick fucks did that to her?"

Tim face fell into a weary resolution. "Yeah. When I saw them start that, I just froze up. I should've done something. I know. I'm a piece of shit." Tim's watered and his lip actually trembled.

Jack looked around nervously. "And the guy, Tim there aren't that many black guys in the area that were in our division.

"Don't you think I know that?"

Jack looked around and grabbed Tim's hand underneath the table and held it tight, out of sight. Even without looking, Jack could feel the smooth, glossy healed skin that covered his palms. Unspoken realization, energy, memories flowed back and forth between them. Tim's eye's opened wide as sweat broke across his face. Both Tim and Jack's faces began to subtlety vibrate. Sweat broke out on their faces and their teeth ground against each other. A small trickle of blood began to flow from Tim's nose. Tim pulled his hand free and grabbed a napkin and wiped his nose, pinching it closed.

"Why'd you do that, asshole?" he whispered back.

"You know why. Now I really get what you were saying. I mean, I believed you and all but I needed to see it, feel like you did. You know we're connected now."

Tim pinched his nose and looked around the bar. Through the smoke and dim light, he could see no one was looking. Steve Miller was crooning "Fly like an Eagle." "What do you mean, 'We're connected?'"

"You know what I mean. I know you have felt it too. Ever since the light, that night at the lake. Something happened to us, man. It changed us and we can do stuff now. That's how I took care of JL today. That's how we took care of him. We made him forget," Jack said with urgency.

"That really happened?" Tim said weakly.

"Yes, you idiot." Jack hissed back. "I know you have felt this stuff, like with Betty's tits the other day." Realization dawned anew on Tim's face. "That's right, Einstein, we did that. And we aren't the only ones. Those kids that come in the store, you know the McGee kid and the other two? They can do it too."

"They can?"

"Yes. I didn't know until today for sure, but when I grabbed Travis's hand, that thing happened again, like when I just grabbed yours. I could see into his mind a bit and I knew what he was thinking and what he had been doing. Those kids made that storm happen the other day."

"No shit?"

"Tim, I don't know what this means, but we have to do something. I mean, we may know what happened to that girl. And if what I just saw in your mind is what I think it is, we may know what happened to Carl, too. Those sick fucks got to him and maybe they've killed him," Jack whispered so low Tim could barely hear. Tim looked wild with fear and took another drink of his warm beer. Jack continued, "Look, I don't know what we can do yet, but we need to try and think of something. I'm going to try and figure out a way to talk to those kids somehow. I'm pretty sure Joey got zapped by that ray or whatever too, which is probably why he is making Lori so happy and blasted me across the bathroom with his pee."

"What?"

"Never mind. Let's get out of here. I'll drive you home."

"My truck is outside."

"Forget it," Jack said laying down $15. "You're not driving tonight." The men left and piled into Jack's truck and he headed toward Hwy 24 and Tim's trailer house. They drove with the windows down feeling the night air smooth and moist on their skin. The radio was playing "Life in the Fast Lane," by the Eagles. Jack's beer buzz had worn off from the horrific confession Tim had made. His head was filled with shocking images from Tim's mind, his own encounter with JL, those kids, the light, and the bridge. It felt like his head was going to explode. Jack looked over and Tim had his eyes closed, head leaned over against the door frame, obligatory hand down the front of his pants. But instead of the normal placid, stupefied sleepy look, his face was a rictus of agony. His jaw was set almost like he was grining his teeth to dust. *This guy is in torment,* Jack thought.

Jack had been looking out for Tim since they were boys and it was still that way it seemed. But he was as close, damn, closer than a brother. They had been through hell together and now were part of each other's lives as much as any husband and wife. In fact, he figured they talked more than most couples. He was at a loss for what he could do for his friend, but he knew somehow he needed to help him through this. And that crazy shit, there had to be some way to get Tim away from those freaks. Jack never understood the hateful racist climate that permeated this part of Texas. It was part of the fabric of this place, like chicken fried steak and the Dallas Cowboys. It had always been there, or at least it seemed that way. White people looked down on Black people and treated them like second-class citizens without even realizing they were doing it. Blacks lived across the railroad tracks in their own portion of town. The separate water fountains may have been taken down, but the feelings were mostly the same. Only the young people of the town seemed to be able to rise above the feelings and treat everyone with more respect, but that certainly wasn't universal. Last year when the football team had voted for a black girl for homecoming queen, you would have thought they would have crowned a horse, or worse, a boy. Jack had privately been glad the black players on the team block voted for one girl while all the other players spread their votes around to the four white girls nominated. It seemed pretty smart to him.

He even knew really bad things had happened to some in the black community over the years, but it wasn't like burning crosses or white robed riders in the Christmas parade. This nutty crap Tim was involved with sounded like devil worship meets KKK. And of course, JL Martin was involved. The thought made his stomach churn again, it made him wish he had killed him like Tim suggested. Jack pulled into Tim's driveway and put the truck in park. Tim was practically snoring by this time, his legs sprawled wide, mouth open. Jack rolled his eyes and reached over and punched him square in the nuts.

"Oh God," Tim doubled over clutching his crotch, "My beanbag, I think you busted it. Why?"

"We're home, dear," Jack said coolly. "That's for keeping shit from me and being a horse's ass half the time too.

"Man, you didn't have to blow out my sack. I'm going to be limping for a week."

"Good, maybe you will pull your head out of your ass and make better decisions," Jack said in mock indignation. Tim looked up at him like a repentant child. Jack knew Tim wasn't fooled by his feigned anger. "Is everything alright between you and Candy?"

"Yeah. You know, it runs hot and cold sometimes. But we are good. She's mostly mad about no kids you know. She even had me go and have my gravy tested to see if I was shooting blanks.
"

"And?"

"I'm as fertile as Myrtle. So is she. Doctor says she is all nervous about it and it's making it not work. Told her to relax. Damn, I think you blew out a testicle."

Jack grabbed Tim's hand out of his lap and held it again, zooming once again back inside his friend's head. He blew past the events of the day and the horrible ones from the barn until he saw what he was afraid he had seen before. Tim's naked backside as he rode Neva Shedder, her legs locked around his waist. Jacks eyes flew open and Tim was staring, his eyes filled with fear.

Jack's fist shot out and slammed into Tim's gut, bending the man over gasping for breath. He hit him again, this time on the side of the head. His hand throbbed in pain. Tim grabbed the door handle and fell out of the car, scrambling to get away from Jack. Jack bolted out of the cab and headed around the truck. Tim held up his hands in surrender.

"Okay, okay. I know I'm a piece of shit. Don't hit me anymore, man."

"I ought to kick your ass until next Sunday," Jack said through clinched teeth figuring Candy was inside trying to sleep. You tell me why?"

Tim looked up in misery, his eyes glistening and nose running. "It's just been a bad couple of months. She doesn't want to do it except if it's prime time for her to conceive or something. And she's always bitchy and I was just out at the Bar G honkytonk. Candy didn't want to go. Neva was there. She's been having a lot of trouble with Troy. He's been out sleeping around with half the county. Anyway, one thing led to another and we ended up in the back seat of her car out on Hwy 14."

Jack seethed. "So things get a little tough and you go out and chase tail? Troy Shedder is a giant and probably retarded to boot. And you thought you would go screw his wife. Jesus, Tim. What if she gets pregnant? Did you use a rubber?" One look at Tim answered that question. "I am the last person to judge you most of the time. You have saved me from fucking up more times than I can remember, but you are better than this and Candy deserves better."

"I know. I fucked up, I'm sorry." Tim said now actually crying. "Should I tell her? Tell Candy I'm sorry?"

"Hell No! All that would do is make you feel better. You keep your mouth shut and your pecker in your pants. If you get horny, then jack off like all the other married guys in town do." Tim nodded wiping his nose on the back of his hand, lifting up his shirt tail to wipe off his eyes. "What was that other stuff I saw, you sitting in the doctor's office all scared out and everything?"

"Aw, nothing. I didn't want to say anything. Candy don't even know yet 'cause I know she will just freak out and everything," Tim said.

Jack felt a wave of fear grip his belly. "Tell me right now what's going on," he demanded.

Tim sighed and leaned back against the tailgate of the truck. He rubbed his eyes and looked up weary and sad. "When the doctor was examining my balls, he found a lump. He spent the next hour holding my sack in his hand and did this x-ray and everything. He did some tests and I just found out it looks like I've got ball cancer. I'm going in next week to get one of my boys cut off. Hopefully the one you just ruptured."

"Come here you idiot," Jack said pulling Tim into his arms for a long hug. Tim held on to him tight for a long time, his face pressed against his neck. He and Tim had been through so much together and the thought something like this could end his best friend was simply too much. "I am so sorry, buddy," Jack said feeling the tears sting his eyes. An electric buzz filled Jack's ears. The longer they hugged, the louder and stronger it grew until he felt like his head would explode. Tim let go and planted a wet slobbery drunk kiss on Jack's cheek.

"Love you, man." Tim said as he stumbled toward his front porch..

"You too, Turkey," Jack said getting back into the truck and putting it drive. "See you tomorrow. When you go to the doctor, I'll go with you. Make sure he only cuts off one of your tiny stones." Tim waved a middle finger over his head as he wobbled up the steps to his porch. Jack shook his head and smiled, driving away and back onto the highway.

24 Twelve Oaks ¹⁸⁶⁰
PLANTATION

Theocrates Martin rode his graceful Appaloosa mare, Lady Anne, across the lower fields of Twelve Oaks in the late afternoon golden sunlight. The meadow was full of evening primrose and Indian paintbrush and the pink and red carpet glittered like rubies and opals in the sun. In the distance the acres and acres of cotton stood green and bright, the plants just now beginning to take off. By late summer, the carpet of verdant green would be speckled with the puffs of white cotton bolls. The arc of the South Sulphur River curved around the property, its caramel colored water slow and sluggish as it flowed toward the Red River on its trip toward Louisiana.

Twelve Oaks had been a plantation in North East Texas since long before Santa Anna decided to take care of the Texas rebels at The Alamo and ultimately met his Waterloo at the Battle of San Jacinto. It was a grand Greek revival mansion, two and half stories with six massive Corinthian columns gracing the front portico. The bright green roof of the house was topped with a gilded Belvedere. The home had over ten bedrooms, two kitchens, parlors, conservatories and a ballroom. It also was graced with some of the earliest indoor plumbing in all of Texas.

The five-thousand acre plantation was small compared with some of those in Louisiana and Georgia and Maryland, but what it lacked in size, it made up for in style. Theocrates was born in Natches, Louisiana in 1833 and then moved to the Texas territory with his family when he was a small boy along with Stephen F. Austin and his followers. His mother, Anabelle Monroe Martin, had perished of scarlet fever when Theocrates was only two, leaving the boy to be raised by a series of Mammy slaves and distant relatives. The boy was close to his father, but Asa was poorly equipped to provide a young boy the attention and affection he longed for. Asa Martin died when Theocrates was seventeen and the boy had taken over running the plantation, having learned much from his father and the plantation manager, Alton Thibodaux, a Creole from Lake Charles. Thibodaux was a stern manager, though not as cruel as many. His café au lait colored skin looked stunning against the maroon velvet of his surcoat. Theocrates was a resolute bachelor for years until later in 1870 when he finally married Amanda Bell from Paris, Texas in Lamar County.

In 1860, Texas joined the Confederacy as part of the coalition of southern states that were drawn into the War of Southern Aggression. The Yanks were determined to take away the way of life of the south, and all for a bunch of farm stock. Slaves were as vital to the south and Texas as water and cornbread. Jim Bowie and William B. Travis, in addition to Stephen F. Austin, were all slave owners. In 1860, there were 182,566 African slaves in Texas, which made up thirty percent of the state's population. As the war increased in the Deep South, many plantation owners relocated their stocks of slaves to the slave friendly and dependent state of Texas. It was the perfect place, far away from the war, and was available to assist with Texas's main mission for the Confederacy, to be the supply cache for the war effort. By 1865, the numbers of slaves had risen to 250,000. About twenty-five percent of the population of Texas owned slaves, which were ninety-five percent illiterate.

Twelve Oaks owned 267 slaves. Most were men and women in their thirties and forties. There were twenty year olds and the smattering of children among the slaves as well. They chopped cotton under the watchful gaze of Alton Thibodaux. In the history of the plantation, there had only been seven runaways. All but one was caught. The six who were brought back to the plantation did not survive for long.

In general, Theocrates Martin was a genial and kind owner. He did not tolerate thievery or sexual wantonness in the slaves, nor sloth or insubordination. Otherwise, Twelve Oaks was a lovely place to be a slave. Martin kept at least six housemaids at all times in addition to cooks and kitchen help. All of these were female, young and curvaceous. He dressed them in bright cotton pinafores. Only the cooks were women of some age since most of the young women were not skilled in cooking.

In addition to the housemaids, Martin kept a cadre of footmen and squires, young black men aged twelve to twenty. These he dressed in soft, frilled silk shirts in the same shades as the pinafores of the maids. As the young men advanced in age, they were removed from house service and reassigned to the cotton fields.

The balls and cotillions held at Twelve Oaks were epic, bringing in the very best of the East Texas social upper crust. These occurred five or six times a year, often coinciding with holidays and special events. Since he was a bachelor, every eligible southern belle from South Carolina to El Paso seemed to find themselves at a Twelve Oaks ball. But even though given a host of beauties to choose from, Martin continued to live as a bachelor. Theocrates also hosted hunting weekends for the men four times a year. The five thousand acres of Twelve Oaks bordered an even larger forest along the many rivers in the area, resulting in a vibrant area in which to hunt.

The years leading up to 1860 were the pinnacle of Twelve Oaks antebellum preeminence. The plantation was vibrant, cotton prices were good, and the social events were legendary. Stories circulated among the neighboring counties regarding Martin's reluctance to take a wife. Some took the path that Martin was so devout he chose to live a life set apart from the moral weaknesses of sexual congress. Others believed him to have a wife secreted away due to madness or possibly one was so homely and disfigured, he chose to hide her from public eye. There were even some unsavory rumors that Theocrates was a secret member of "the third sex," meaning he preferred the company of men in his bed.

The answer was far simpler. Being a virile, healthy seventeen-year old when he became master of Twelve Oaks, Martin had learned early on that he absolutely loved sex. More specifically he adored sex with Negros. Theocrates had lost his virginity at the ripe old age of thirteen with one of the housemaids, Bitsy. She had been twenty six and had taught the boy well how to pleasure a woman. He impregnated her and she bore a son whom she named Theo. She was immediately relegated to the cotton fields. In an effort to curtail his son's proclivities, Asa forbade Theocrates from spending any time alone with housemaids. Unfortunately for Mr. Martin, Theocrates simply began to look for other outlets for his surging libido. He began to go off on hunting trips with a small cadre of squires that he found were more than willing to participate in his sexual explorations in exchange for favors or the threat of punishments or being sent to the fields.

But soon Master Asa was gone and the regular nightly companionship of housemaids recommenced. To keep some variety in his insatiable appetite, he continued to routinely require the company of his squires and footmen, sometimes along with the maids, sometimes with Master Theo alone. By the time he married, Theocrates had sired over twenty-seven children, all but six of them boys.

In addition to his love of pleasure with Negros, Theocrates was an ardent student of the occult and indigenous religions. He found the rituals and ceremonies of the ancient peoples far more spiritually engrossing and fulfilling than the dull Episcopal services. In fact, the only parts of the Bible he routinely studied were eschatological ones: The Book of Daniel, Revelation, and Ezekiel. He was fascinated with Aztec culture and gods, especially their penchant for human sacrifice. He studied some of the Indian tribal religions, especially those surrounding the Earth Mother. He began to attend lectures and visit museums when he traveled around the southwestern territories and Mexico. He collected Aztec relics along with Native American artifacts looted from burial sites by grave robbers looking to sell to rich collectors like Martin. He soon had a collection of effigies of earth mother idols from all over the world, many of them purchased by one of his close friends, Frederick Tunstall, who routinely visited relic sites on his behalf, as well as participated in the nighttime activities in Theocrates' bedroom with the maids and squires.

Theocrates had images of Toci from Mexico, Asherah from the Holy Land, Artemis from Greece and *Na'ashjéii Asdzáá*, The Spider Grandmother, from the Navajo. He studied the sacrificial ceremonies of the Aztec and Druidic people. He made copious journals of the practices and how the ceremonies were performed. He also learned of black magic and occult practices surrounding the Earth Mother. While doing his research, Theocrates would often use poppy tea, a sugary concoction from Bitsy that was English tea laced with laudanum.

As Texas moved toward secession along with the Deep South, the first stirrings of discontent among the slaves of Twelve Oaks reared its head. The execution of abolitionist John Brown fueled much of these feelings. Secret meetings among some of the younger men of the plantation began to take place late in the night, often including some of the house squires that shared Theocrates' bed. There was a growing quiet movement throughout plantation cultures for slaves to begin to challenge their masters and disrupt the normal running of the farms.

As Theocrates Martin rode along the lower fields of Twelve Oaks that May evening, a flash of light caught his eye. He turned back toward the house and saw flames licking up one of the columns and out of an upper floor window. He turned Lady Anne around and dug his heels into her flanks, urging her across the field back toward the mansion. He galloped down the willow lined driveway leading to the house and pulled up, the horse lathered and snorting. His mouth flew open as he saw his beloved Twelve Oaks burning. A handful of slaves had formed a human bucket brigade and were tossing water on the flames they could reach. But far above on the top floor, flames and smoke poured from an upper window. Alton Thibodaux was ordering some of the slaves from the field to grab buckets and head into the home. Theocrates watched as a handful of those who entered the home drop and spill the contents of the buckets before reaching the burning bedroom. Sensing something was very much amiss, he ran toward his library. As of yet, it was untouched by the flames and smoke. Within was one of his squires, Matthew. He was a fifteen year old slender boy today wearing a lavender silk shirt as he dusted shelves, seemingly unaware of the tumult in the rest of the house. Theocrates grabbed the boy by the collar and pushed him against one of the built-in shelves in the library. The boy's eyes flew open as wide as eggs. He pulled his head back from his master's that pressed in close, hissing through clinched teeth.

"Tell me, Matthew. Tell me and I will spare you. I will make this the best day of your life. Remain silent, and I will make you sorry you were ever born," he hissed.

"I don't know nothing, Mr. Theo," Matthew said looking at his master's mad expression.

Theocrates slapped the boy violently across the face and shook him hard enough to dislodge a row of books from the shelves above. He gripped the boy by the throat in one hand and gripped his privates in the other, squeezing until the boy howled.

"Tell me what this is, Matthew? Who started the fire? I know it wasn't an accident or some natural occurrence. This was intentional." Theocrates gripped the boy harder until his eyes began to water. "Who did this?" he whispered. He leaned close and spoke into the boy's ear, twisting his manhood violently. "Tell me and I will give you your freedom. Lie to me and I will cut off your fucking head."

Matthew looked at Theocrates. He mouthed the words but no sound came out. The master loosened his grip on the boys throat and he squeaked out, "It were Tom Crow, Joseph McNee, Henry DuBois, and Letty, Letty Sue."

Theocrates closed his eyes and winced as if he had been mortally wounded. He relaxed his grip on the boy's throat and groin. With tears streaming down his eyes, he pulled the boy close and kissed him. "Thank you, Matthew. I know that wasn't easy. No one will know that you are the one who told me. I want you to stay in this room at your work. Keep the door closed to keep out the smoke. Do you understand?"

"Yes sir, Mr. Theo," the boy said softly through his swollen throat.

Theocrates ran back out into the great hall and saw smoke everywhere. He grabbed Alton.

"How bad?" Theocrates asked.

"We might catch it in the bedroom. Otherwise, it will get into the attic and the house will be lost."

Every field slave was now manning buckets along with the house maids and valets. The men and women were drenched in sweat. Rivulets of soot and smoke stained their faces and clothes. Alton organized field hands up on ladders and even upon the roof to combat the flames. After two solid hours of attacking the flames, the battle was won, but at a mighty cost. The flames had consumed two rooms and damaged the entire top floor. A portion of the roof was ruined but the attic was spared as were the floors. None of Theocrates most precious possessions were lost, but his beautiful Twelve Oaks was spoiled. Like a virgin bride bedded before the wedding, the innocence and beauty of the home was ruined to him. In addition, a burning hatred for those that destroyed the sanctity of his home was ignited and burned bright. As soon as he found him, Theocrates pulled Alton aside and told him of the four arsonists.

"I will have them," Theocrates said with a vicious rasp.

Five hours later, the three men hung by their arms from the heavy beams in the main barn. The woman was lashed to a post that held up one of the hay lofts with a noose around her neck. Each had been beaten and pummeled as they had tried their best to escape before being hunted down by Alton and a posse of nearby landowners. Alton and Theo were joined by Fred Tunstall who happened to be visiting Twelve Oaks that week. After Fred had entered the barn, Alton barred the large doors. The only light in the dank barn came from two torches Alton had placed inside. Their smoky flames guttered as a light breeze found its way through the cracks in the barn walls.

One of the men, Henry DuBois, spoke in a hoarse whisper. "You been told wrong, Mr. Theo. We ain't had nothing to do with the fire."

"Save your breath," Theocrates said quietly removing his necktie. I saw you dump the water before you even reached the fire. I know you all planned this. I would like to know why?"

Tom Crowe spoke up defiantly. "It's for what they did to John Brown. Slaves gonna rise up, Mr. Theo. People have a right to be free."

Theocrates unbuttoned his shirt and carefully slid it off his wide shoulders and placed it on a pile of feed sacks. Alton and Fred had followed suit and removed their own ties and shirts.

"I have no doubt one day that may be true. People do deserve to be free. There is only one problem with your declaration, Tom. You are not people. You are property, bought and paid for.

I have treated you with respect and care and you have repaid that with treachery." Theocrates steadied himself against Fred and removed his shoes and socks.

"We sorry," Mr. Theo, shrieked Letty. "We didn't mean it. Please, Mr. Theo, have mercy."

Theocrates and the other two men untied their britches and let them fall to the floor. They slid down their undershorts and placed them in the piles with the rest of their clothes. Fred pulled three golden masks out of a sack and handed them to the three. The men fastened them on. The faces were tribal, hideous faces with grotesque deformed features, curved horns festooned the sides. When Letty saw them she began to shriek anew.

"You have fouled this place. The only way it can be cleansed is through a ceremony of sacrifice. You caused this damage and you will be the penitence from which it can be made new.

Alton brought in large washtubs and placed underneath each of the men. The men writhed and screamed and tried to wrench free of the ropes holding them. Letty had fainted and stood slumped in the ropes that bound her to the post. Fred took a long pole and begin to draw a large five-pointed star in the dust and chaff on the barn floor. Alton produced three large butcher knives, gleaming in the dim torchlight. Fred and Theocrates began to chant in words of Greek, Latin, and Navajo, calling on the spirit of the Earth Mother.

> Na'ashjéii Asdzáá, Lava quod est. Sana quod est. Nostras aquam. Enischytheí androprepís spóron mas; Confirma nostra virili semine. Lava a perfidia. In terram fructiferam, fac nobis. Adeptus peccatorum in infernum.

Cleanse this place. Heal our land. Purify our water. Strengthen our manly seed. Wash away this treachery. Make our land fruitful. Doom these sinners to hell.

With that, Theocrates moved toward Tom Crowe and began to cut a five-pointed star into his belly. The man, screamed and tried in vain to pull away as the other two men begged for God to save them. The blood began to stream from the cuts in the man's flesh. Theocrates continued to chant as he finished carving the symbol into the man. Alton carved the star into Joseph while Fred marked Henry. Theocrates then moved and stood in front of Joseph McNee.

"I appreciate you staying silent like Christ before Pilate. I will show you the mercy of sending you on your way swiftly. Your blood will cleanse away your treachery and return this land to fruitful purity."

With that, he slashed with the knife and opened up a smile in the man's throat that flowed red against the man's shiny black chest. The blood poured forth in a stream of crimson that spread like a curtain across the man's belly and began to drip from his member and his toes. A look of utter surprise and disbelief still registered on the man's face as his muscles relaxed and he hung heavy over the basin catching his blood.

Theocrates moved to Henry who was jerking and writhing like a hog set for slaughter. "You dared to lie and tell me I was wrong. Your end will not be so quick." With that he gripped the man's genitals and opened his scrotum with the knife, the contents spilling out along with a gout of blood. After the man hung there draining for five minutes, Alton took his knife and opened the man's throat from ear to ear, finishing him.

The three naked men stood in front of Tom Crowe, golden masks gleaming. Their hands and bodies splattered with blood. "Your time on this earth is over, Tom Crowe. Perhaps John Brown will assist you in the next." Theocrates slashed the man's belly open spilling his intestines in a foul rush of steam into the waiting washtub. As Tom began to slip away, Theocrates reached up into the gaping cavern of the man's torso and pushed stomach, liver and lungs aside until he felt the still beating heart and wrapped his hand around it. He plowed his other hand up inside the gore and used the knife to sever the heart from arteries and veins. With a sharp tug, he brought forth the heart and held it up above his head. He brought the warm flesh to his mouth and bit into it, feeling his mouth fill with blood and meat. He passed the organ to Alton who took a look at it and passed it on to Fred who mimicked Theocrates. Fred grabbed the basin from underneath Joseph and began to tip the contents to the ground along the outline of the star on the floor of the barn. Alton took the filth filling the washtub underneath and drug it to the side. Theocrates and Fred together filled jar after jar of blood from the basin underneath Henry to be carried into the fields to bless the earth and the water.

Theocrates stood like an ancient king, dripping in the blood of his enemies. He had purified the house. The evil had been cleansed through blood and sacrifice. His mouth still tasted of gore and a new darkness crept into his soul, a darkness that would consume him the rest of his days.

"What do you want me to do with them?" Alton asked.

"The hogs will think they died and went to heaven," Theocrates said. "Make sure none of the slaves feed them for two days. You might want to disassemble them to make transport a bit easier. You can keep them in the root cellar here in the barn for the next two days. It's cool down there."

"What about the girl?"

Theocrates moved toward the girl and picked up an axe. He chopped at the rope lashing her to the post and she swung free, the noose digging into her neck as she fell forward. He moved to the large peg holding the rope and began to pull it up on the pully until the woman hung high above them. He wound the rope back around the peg.

"She can join the rest," he said. "Fred would you be so kind as to get the buckets of water and the soap from the tack room. I believe we need to freshen up before heading back to the house."

Afterwards, Theocrates was never the same. His interest in the occult and ritual sacrifice became an obsession. He gathered a small cluster of novices that joined him, Alton and Fred and he created a catechism for his acolytes to study and follow that he carefully outlined in his journal. It cobbled together Druid, Aztec, and Native American rituals and ceremonies supposedly designed to honor the Earth Mother and revitalize the soil and water as well as purify the "sin" of the land. Reportedly, a slave was listed as a runaway every six months after Twelve Oaks burned with that individual never found or returned to the plantation. True to his word, the slave known as Matthew was set free by Theocrates that same year. He moved to the Missouri Territory and took the surname Washington where he stayed until he returned to the county around 1900 with his wife, Selma, and two small sons Joseph and Franklin. The family settled in the Nelsonville community not far away from the original site of Twelve Oaks.

Six years later in 1866, Twelve Oaks burned again, this time struck by lightning. The structure was a total loss with only a few of Theocrates' prized possessions saved. Luckily, he had created a new place to hide these treasures having felt the home was no longer a safe place. After the home was razed, he rebuilt a much more modest structure not far away but then only lived there a year before moving away and finally marrying the lovely Amanda Bell. They immediately began to have children and over the next seventeen years they had nine, all boys save two beautiful girls.

He took to spending as little time at home as possible, turning over the running of the farm in its entirety to Alton. He and Fred traveled to Europe, Central America, and the American Southwest continuing their search for Earth Mother treasures and furthering his study and practice of ritual sacrifice. Theocrates began creating the ritual and lore for his secret society,

The Black Knights of God. His hope was to turn his vision into a new and better KKK, but his following remained small and the plans to spread the gospel of ritual purification and sacrifice dwindled.

Two freed mixed race men turned up missing in Santa Fe, NM while Theocrates was visiting with Fred, searching for more relics in 1880. For a week he was a person of interest in the case but missing people of color were seldom made a priority by local jurisdictions and his private practices were never investigated. He and Fred continued to travel together for the next few years, rarely staying at home for more than a month. He died in 1888 in a hotel room in Guadalajara, Mexico. He was found by Fred who discovered Theocrates naked with a silk cord around his neck, leather bands tied tightly around his genitals, an apparent accidental suicide from autoerotic asphyxiation.

Theocrates' youngest son, Ashton Louis Martin married Cecilia Jane Robertson of Bonham. He ended up inheriting the land Twelve Oaks stood on as most of his older brothers and sisters had displeased their father enough to not be as fortunate in the will. Ashton was a shrewd businessman and invested in the newly forming oil companies in Texas. That along with the cotton farm proved highly successful. Ashton and Cecilia had five children: Woodrow, Albert, Cynthia, Louise, and Josiah Louis. Both Woodrow and Albert did not survive World War II, one killed in Germany, the other in the Pacific. Cynthia was killed in a car crash in West Texas in 1948. Louise got married to a Mexican man named Juan Pablo Garfais and relocated to Cartagena, Columbia. Josiah Louis and his mother lived in the old house on the Twelve Oaks property until her death in 1970. JL became the sole heir (other than Louise who had not been heard of in years) to Twelve Oaks and the Martin fortune. He rebuilt the home in 1975, recreating some of its Greek Revival Style.

The only structure remaining from the Civil War era plantation was a grand old barn, now sagging and in dire need of repair. One Saturday in October 1976, JL was in the barn moving some old boxes out of a forgotten tack room when he spied a shiny gold five pointed star made of brass affixed to a crumbling wall. When he attempted to remove the star, the wall fell away revealing a four foot long chest within. JL removed the rest of the wall and worked for over an hour, finally extricating the chest. When he opened it, it was like finding the Ark of the Covenant.

Within the velvet lined chest were dozens of relics, totems and effigies from all around the world. There were six carefully written journals, the ink still clear and legible on the brittle but smooth pages. There were shiny polished human skulls that had been cut away and had straps attached to be worn as a headdress of some kind. There were three carefully folded black robes. Shining in the dim light, JL removed the golden masks and stared at them in awe. They were the most beautiful things he had ever seen, as polished and sparkling as the day they had been entombed. And most amazing of all, a letter in a faded green envelope with a wax seal still attached. JL took out his pocketknife and carefully pulled at the wax. It crumbled into pieces and fell away. With trembling hands he opened the letter and read:

> *Within this chest, you will find some of my prized possessions along with my journals. Do not judge me too harshly for what you may find here. If you are one of my grandsons or great-grandsons reading this, I pray you use the knowledge and power you find within to secure Twelve Oaks for our family for all time.*
>
> *If you are a stranger to our family, I trust that you will return these belongings to their rightful owner. If you are a thief, be warned you will rue the day you took this chest from its resting place.*
>
> *If you look to profit from the contents here and you are not of the Martin family, you will perish in fire and pain.*

To my descendant reading this letter, use these items and the other knowledge within to keep Twelve Oaks safe and in the family.

Your Pater Familias,

Theocrates Louis Martin
1888

25 George

George lifted the needle from the album on his turntable and replaced it at the beginning of the track for the fifth time. He had been writing music all week in his free time at home. He didn't know why, but he could see the notes as he listened to the record. He had been playing around with some music arranging for a while, but his new ability had clearly accelerated his skill. As he listened to Robert Lamm singing "Mother" and the horn line from his beloved Chicago III album beginning the instrumental break, he quickly jotted down the trombone line on the manuscript paper. He had already transcribed the two trumpet parts. He wondered what Mr. Smith would say when he gave the charts to him for the jazz band to play? George had hung out after practice a few days to talk with the director. He had noticed that Mr. Smith's bluster and strictness seemed to end with dismissal. George had stayed and helped refile music or pass out new charts on music stands for the next day's rehearsal.

George had never been one to brownnose a teacher, but he actually liked Mr. Smith. Being in high school band was by far the most interesting part of his school day. Not to mention being part of high school football games and away game hijinks on the band bus. George had already experienced his first real taste of alcohol when Jim Guffy offered him a squirt of "valve oil" which was actually a boiled out bottle full of cherry vodka. Travis had mentioned it tasted a lot like Creomulsion cough syrup. The kid was addicted to that stuff, George remembered. Travis and he had also seen a quick flash of titty when Pam Anderson, one of the clarinet players, had taken off her outer shirt to change into her band uniform and managed to lift up her entire shirt. Wolf whistles and claps filled the bus along with Pam's screams of humiliation. But George saw the look on her face and it seemed more flushed with pride than embarrassment. Which was pretty funny, he thought, considering his boobs were about as big as Pam's. He and Travis had luckily remembered to wear gym shorts under their jeans so when they changed into their uniform pants, they weren't stripping down to their jockey shorts like Pete Clark. Pete had given them the intel during summer band practice that only total douches wore their entire uniform on the bus and if they were going to be in his trombone section, they better not be dickheads.

George tried not to make a big deal out of it, but being in the high school band was so cool to him. His dad didn't say much but it seemed like he was a bit proud of it too. Might be far cry from Fred's Big Man on Campus jock reputation, but at least his kid was part of the damn football game, even if it was the fairy-cakes band. Music had been part of his life forever it seemed. He loved stupid music class in elementary school singing "Sweet Betsy from Pike" or the "Erie Canal" while playing rhythm instruments. He had a decent voice and had sung in church since he was small. Travis was shyer about his voice, but it was good too. You just had to be careful about singing because you could get beat up at school for that kind of behavior. You had to walk this thin line between mocking artistic things and embracing them, especially if you were a boy. Because nothing got you branded a fag quicker than going on and on about a musical, or acting, or even a song on the radio that wasn't rock or Hee-Haw country. But the fact was, music had been George's passion since he was very small and even if he kept a low profile, using his super power to make it even better in his life was groovy. It wasn't just the fact now he could actually seethe music and notes forming in his mind that had happened either. While Emily had been busy turning her radio up and down with her mind and Travis had been pushing his dad out the window, George had been experimenting with music and hot damn, it worked. His fairly decent guitar skills suddenly leaped forward to double his former ability.

When Travis had come over to play guitar with George, which was usually not very productive because Travis never practiced, the boys began to play along with songs on the stereo like they were studio musicians. Right before they started, George grabbed Travis's head in a mock evangelist spiritual anointing and focused with all his might.

As he pressed his forehead against Travis's and held his hands on the boy's head he evoked, "Oh yes, Lord Jesus. Just release the gift of music to this sinner."

Travis's hands had been right on top of his and in a few moments, the energy, the light shimmered behind their eyes and flooded the boys with awareness. Some mini-Mozartness was birthed inside them, making them four times better, more skilled, more adept, and more creative. The first song they played was just a simple John Denver tune, "Poems, Prayers, and Promises." They liked that song, especially when John sang of passing the pipe around. But this time, when they got to the line and played the Bm7 chord, it wasn't the pussy 1, 2, 3 on the second, third, and fourth fret. It was the real chord, the bar chord that used all four fingers and all five strings, and it sounded great. They just knew how to do it and it was as natural as tying a shoe.

The next song they tried was "Nights are Forever." Travis quickly picked up the driving rhythm on the acoustic guitar while George began to play his electric guitar, actually through the amp this time, and the notes were clear and in tune. The two sang along, in harmony, as they played guitar like England Dan and John Ford Coley. Then with wide-eyed glee, George put on his Boston album and grabbed his other older electric guitar, the one that had been Fred's, and handed it to Travis, who was hopeless on electric. They spent a quick minute tuning and then put the needle on "Peace of Mind." The boys closed their eyes and listened as the multiple lead and blended harmony guitar lines of Tom Scholz and Brad Delp filled their ears. For good measure, George placed his hands on Travis's head again and concentrated his focus as hard as he could. He felt the edge of nausea begin to rumble in his belly as he broke off. He noticed Travis had a small drop of blood barely peeking from his left nostril. George reset the needle and the boys looked at each other as the music began. Their fingers found the frets and chords, harmonizing the complex line in thirds. As they continued, there were less thuds on the chords, less missed notes, until they were connected, ripping through the guitar lines with grace and power. They finished the song and just stood there, feeling the joined power and connection release somewhat. Travis noticed that George seemed to have watery eyes.

"You boys must have been practicing. That sounded really good," a voice broke the connection. It was George's dad, just home from work. His head was poked in the door and he had a puzzled look, one mixed with a bit of pride perhaps. "I don't know a lot about rock music but that sounded pretty groovy to me."

George winced. "No one says groovy anymore, Dad. But thanks. Um, we have been practicing." Where was this nice guy side of his dad coming from? He didn't know but he sure was enjoying the change. He'd been thinking lately when he saw his dad . . . "Be Nice." Maybe it was working.

"Okay. Well, just saying hi. Have fun guys. Good to see you Travis. Say hi to your folks for me."

"Sure, Mr. Harris," Travis said haltingly. Duke closed the door and disappeared. "Are you zapping your Dad cause I have never seen him so nice."

"Not intentionally, but yeah, I think I have been keeping him on the back burner. Guess it works that way too a bit."

"Hey," a voice called from the window. It was Emily. She was looking beautiful with the sunlight behind her hair. Travis noticed she had a tear sliding down the side of her face. "What's wrong," he asked going to the window.

"Nothing. I was just sitting here under the window listening to both of you sing and play. And then that Boston song…" she drifted off.

"It must have been pretty bad," George said.

"No, meathead. It was good, really good. It was like I could see it while you were playing. There were colors and all this energy and it was in my head and all through me."

Travis looked at her and then back at George. "That's why we were so good. It was all three of us." As an afterthought, he reached up and felt his nose and saw the drop of blood on his finger. "Why were you sitting under the window?" he asked Emily.

"I just couldn't stand up anymore while you were playing. It was like all the energy was gone from my legs and in the music or something," she said with her eyes closed. As she opened them, the green sparkled with new tears.

"Come here," Travis said putting down the guitar and reaching through the window, helping her climb inside. "Well, I think it's pretty clear now that if we all three use our super powers together, it's really strong and it makes us get all sick and stuff."

"It's worth it," George said flatly.

"I agree," Emily said.

"You do?" George asked.

"When it's for something that beautiful, yes. It's like I said. If we are going to use them together, it ought to be for something good. You both have to play and sing with me at church on the first Sunday night of the revival. I am supposed to sing this song for the altar call after that evangelist finishes the illustrated sermon. I want you to help me."

"I don't know," Travis said. "I don't like doing stuff up in front in church and maybe we shouldn't use our powers when we are there?"

"Why the hell not?" George said. "Who said God didn't give us the power. Maybe it's like a Holy Ghost thing like Brother Nelson is always talking about. You know, those gifts of the Spirit or whatever."

"I don't think it's that but whatever. George is right, it is a gift of some kind. Let's do something with it other than make it rain or make people fart."

"Okay but you have to agree, that was so cool," George said with a big grin. George was referring to a few days ago when they were in Texas History with Ferle again. Big-ox Joe Cunningham was being his usual ass self, sitting in the back row, flicking wads of paper into Mary Washington's hair. The girl had come back to school but was so beaten down these days. Everyone avoided her like she was a bomb or a broken china plate you carefully placed back in the cabinet so no one would know you had cracked it. Mary just sat there while her afro filled up with bits of white until a veritable snowstorm was whirling in her hair. Emily was livid, her nostrils flaring wide as she watched. She had already put her hand up and told Ferle that Joe was shooting spitwads. Ferle stopped her lecture long enough to say, "Stop it, Joe or I'll have your name on the board," before going back to her droning about Coronado and his search for Quivera. George had looked over at Travis and handed him a small note on which he had written a single word. When Travis opened the note, his eyes twinkled and he looked back at George and nodded. Ferle stopped yammering and assigned some study questions at the end of the chapter. The class began to get out paper and pen and work on the questions. Two minutes later, George felt Travis's hand on his shoulder. George reached over and gripped Joe's chubby forearm.

"Didn't you hear? Flip Wig said she needed your help with something," George said staring hard into Joe's muddy brown eyes. The boy's face went blank and then his eyes lit up with some thought. *Maybe he was getting out of class early or something*, he thought. He hoisted his bulk up out of the desk and began up the aisle, his boots creaking under his weight. He took three more steps and a blast, a neutron bomb of death, blurped out of his fat ass, ripping across the room like a machine gun; four times louder and fouler than any fart had ever been. The methane explosion literally pushed him forward into Vince Constantine's desk, rattling the glass in the classroom windows. The class sucked in its collective breath then exploded in laughter, which quickly dissolved into gags and retching noises as the fetid stink of Joe's bunghole blast hit their noses. Joe's face dissolved into a puce pudding, jowls shaking in humiliation. Ferle began to bang on the bell she kept on her desk which she used to call the class to order. Her eyes widened as the wall of scent hit her. She grabbed for a tissue to cover her nose.

"All right. Get quiet. Joe, sit down. Ronnie, go get Mr. Franklin. Quickly!"

The class had spontaneously moved to the windows for more air. Paul Blankenship actually barfed right out the window into the hydrangeas. Ferle was adjusting her wig, which seemed to be melting from the stench into a puddle of polyester goo on her head. Mercifully, the bell had sounded and the class bolted from the room with shouts of "Joe just bombed the class" "Joe cut the cheese" "Joe farted and made Ferle's wig melt." The big boy had bounded out the door and out toward the shop building on the other side of the parking lot.

Emily's lips were pursed together in a straight line of disapproval, but she knew that kid had deserved it after being so cruel to Mary.

"Okay, but remember. Let's try and do good. So anyway, this song. I think you have the album, G," Emily said running her finger across the spine of the large bookcase of albums in George's room, pulling out a pristine record jacket of Larry Norman's 'Only Visiting This Planet.' It's this track here," she said pointing at "I Wish We'd All Been Ready."

"I know this song," Travis said. "Isn't it like a rapture song or something like that?"

"Yep, well it's about getting left behind."

"Why are you supposed to sing that?" George asked taking the album out carefully, wiping it off with his dust removing cloth and easing it onto his turntable. He lifted the needle and set it in place, hovering above the third track.

"It's for the Sunday night opening meeting of the revival with Brother Zigler. He's doing an illustrated sermon on the rapture." Emily turned and dug a folded piece of paper from her big cloth purse. "I read through the sermon outline and all the dramatic bits that he uses. It's, um, a little corny to say the least."

"That will be a hoot," George said adjusting the volume. "Remember going over to Greenville and seeing the 'Thief in the Night' movie?" Travis started nodding his head, biting his lip and Emily covered her mouth with her hand giggling softly. "I hear there's a sequel coming out this year: 'A Distant Thunder,' I think. Oh and don't forget about "The Burning Hell.""

Travis guffawed. "Oh God, that was so stupid. Remember the motorcycle guy's head gets chopped off and there goes his helmet rolling along the road filled with soggy paper towels dipped in fake blood? Oh and the worms eating the guy's face?"

"And when the people dressed in bible clothes were falling into the pit of hell and the wind blew up their robes and you could see they were wearing regular street clothes, and Hush Puppies!" Emily shrieked.

George started playing the song, as Travis and Emily continued to giggle and talk about the movies.

"Wow, this is real uplifting. I forgot what a downer this song was. Why this song? I mean there's better songs than this. If you want Larry Norman, why not 'UFO?' At least it is about getting to go up instead of down," George said.

"Oh you know why," Travis said, "He's going for the big gut-punch. You know, dangling us all over hell like a wiener at a campout fire."

"This is why people don't want to go to church," George said. "That and the shitty music. And begging for money . . . "

"And sending us all to hell for smoking a bit of weed . . . "

"Or looking at some premium bazooms," George added

Emily stood with her hands on her hips, lips pursed into that thin line again. "Maybe both of you ought to knock some of that stuff off and you wouldn't be feeling so guilty."

"Look who's talking? You smoked all our weed last time yourself," George accused. "Besides, I don't feel guilty, just annoyed. Some of that stuff Brother Nelson talks about is so stupid. He only let ladies start wearing pants to church last year, and he still acts like they are wearing a G-string or something."

"That's disgusting," Emily snapped.

Travis went over to the album and reset the needle wanting to stop this argument. *What was it about these two*, he thought? "Let's just learn the dumb song. Em, do you want us to pull out George's keyboard so you can play along?" Emily had been playing piano at church for the youth group for over a year and she wasn't bad."

"No, I sort of already learned it and I might not play on this song anyway. I think it works better as just a guitar song."

The boys picked up their guitars and had the chords worked out in two tries. Emily sang along, with George picking up the harmony. Travis sang along with Emily on the melody on part of the song. As they sang and concentrated on the music, their connection seemed to increase. Voices were clear, sharp, melodic and in tune. The boys were creative with their guitar work. Near the end of the song, Travis's nose began to drip blood from one nostril again.

"You notice that only happens when we really concentrate and especially when we are all together. If we don't focus so hard, it probably won't happen," he said.

"Good 'cause I'm getting sick of this," Travis said grabbing a tissue from the box beside George's bed. "It's a good thing it doesn't happen in band or I would be gurgling a bloody nose through my trombone all the time."

Travis and George put the guitars away. Emily went over to the George's bookshelf and ran her finger along the carefully alphabetized collection. She selected The Best of Bread album and dropped the needle on "Baby I'm a Want You." Both of the boys gave her a "Really?" look.

"I like this song. I know it's sappy but it makes me feel good. Don't judge! Besides, you've got plenty of Barry Manilow records here," Emily laughed.

"Do not disparage the Manilow. He is a musical genius," George said defensively. "I've also got Zepplin, Aerosmith, and Queen if you want something more serious!"

Emily grabbed one of George's jasmine cones and sat it in the Buddha incense burner and lit it. She closed his curtains and turned on his black light and the revolving multicolor mirror ball he had on the headboard of his bed.

"It's pretty bad when your bedroom is so much cooler than mine," she said.

Emily flopped back on George's bed looking up at the poster of Farrah Fawcett on the ceiling.

"Do you think they really airbrushed this photo so that her hair would spell out SEX?" The boys were busy talking about something else and were not paying attention to her. She was used to that happening. Half of the time, she felt like she wasn't there when they were talking. As she looked up at the poster she noticed a dirty smudge on the side of Farrah's face. She stood up on the bed and reached her hand up to touch the poster.

"Did you, like, have a can of Coke explode or something in here? How did you get food or whatever all the way up here?"

Travis exploded in laughter and fell on the floor. George, blushing bright red, left the room to go get something to drink. Emily stood on the bed with her hands on her hips.

"Why was that funny?" she demanded.

Travis just continued to laugh, holding his belly as he rolled on the floor. George came back in with a tall glass of Fresca. "Damn, there was nothing to drink but Fresca or Tab. So, pretty cool about getting to help out the high school with their musical," he said. "I can't believe they are letting them do 'Godspell.'"

Emily sat up on the bed. "Miss Cantor tried to work it out to do 'West Side Story' but there was just too much dancing. She even tried to talk them into 'Hair!' She's a little naïve to think they would go for that. Too hippy and controversial."

"It's too bad, you would have looked great dancing naked around the stage on 'Where Do I Go?' at the end of Act I.

"I could say the same for you," Emily sniffed, her lips tight together. "So, that brings up an interesting thought, though?"

"George naked? I've seen it. No big deal," Travis joked. George flicked a guitar pick hard at Travis's head which flew so fast it left a big red mark on his forearm. "Ow. That hurt!"

"No, you spaz. What I wondered about is, can Trey really sing? How did they ever cast him as Jesus? I do think Miss Cantor got it right with Theo Martin as Judas though."

"Yeah, that's just type casting," Travis said. "I think she was going more for looks than voice with those guys. Also trying to get other football boys involved. I mean, I've heard Trey sing in the shower . . . he's not bad. He can carry a tune and everything."

"Since we will all be there, maybe we should plan to give him a little help," George said.

"What do you mean?" Travis asked.

"I don't know, make his voice better, his acting more real. You know, I've been wondering anyway, could we help him be a really good football player too? It would be cool to give him a little extra 'Na-Nu, Na-Nu.'"

"You are full of , 'Shazbot' Mork," Travis said, "but he could probably use a little jump start. The coach is all bummed out with him for some reason."

"Did you see Miss Cantor gave Mary Washington the "Day by Day" number? I think she will do great on that," Emily said. "I feel so bad for her. She just seems so fragile all the time. I don't know if she really should be back at school."

"Maybe it's just her way to try and get on with stuff. You either do that or just crawl in a hole and die. She does have a nice voice," George said. "I really like her hair, it seems bigger than ever. Hey, let's blow this taco stand and go down to Freeman's and get some fries or a brown topper or something."

"Brown topper always sounds like someone just took a squat on your ice cream to me," Travis said.

"That's sick," Emily said wrinkling her nose.

26 Trey

Trey scrabbled his wide shoulders through the small hole in the bottom of the tree house and hoisted himself up to the small, dark lower room. It was stiflingly hot, crisscrossed by dim orange and yellow lines of sunset striped across the walls and his tank top. He crawled over the tangle of old sleeping bags and discarded pornos and wormed his way up into the main floor of the fort.

Grunting he pulled himself up to the shag-carpeted floor that smelled like a toxic mixture of mildew, weed, and old semen.

"I can't believe we have to hide up here. This place reeks like an old rubber," he said in disgust, flopping back on the pile of old pillows and sleeping bags.

"At least it's private," Angie whispered reaching over and pulling Trey's sweaty bulk into her arms.

The two began kissing immediately, groping each other with hungry abandon. Trey could taste the saltiness of Angie's skin against his lips and tongue as he continued his deep kisses, his hand finding her sumptuous breasts. She threw her head back in a gasp, her light brown hair tossed low on her back as his fingers tweaked and twisted the thick nipples. Trey pushed the shirt up and sucked the pink flesh into his hungry mouth while the girl writhed underneath him. Angie's hand was fastened in a vice grip around the boy's rock hardness, working him into a quick erection that threatened to burst the worn out seams of his cutoff sweats.

Trey had waited exactly four days after the incident before he suggested they meet here in Pete Clark's old tree house. Trey had spent many, many nights up in the fort with friends in the past. He had learned to cuss and drink and smoke weed, not to mention the education provided by stolen copies of Oui, Penthouse, Playboy, and a few Hustlers. For some reason, there had even been a couple of Colt magazines with naked guys in them which were universally mocked and abused for being Fag Mags. But Trey noticed they were just as dog-eared and spunk-stained as the rest of the literature in the tree house. In fact, he remembered when he was a freshman being really disturbed by a series of intense dreams that included one of the hairy mustachioed models from that magazine that sent him into more than one panic attack. Those troublesome dreams had played a part in that crazy week he spent in a tent with Kevin Webb at the Boy Scout Camporee. Trey decided he would go to the grave before sharing any of that information. In a moment of insanity after a particularly manipulative sermon on personal purity at Youth Camp, he had actually confided in Tooter Turner, a senior on the football team, and a genuinely nice decent guy, about his dreams, experiences, and worries about whether or not it meant he was destined to bat for the other team.

Trey took a walk with Tooter late that evening in the woods surrounding the camp, which was a violation of the rules but one that was regularly overlooked. Like lancing the proverbial boil, Trey poured forth the poison of his soul to his teenage father confessor. The boys sat on a big log beside the silver lake lit with a bright summer moon. The smooth surface reflected the light like a mirror, the Milky Way sprayed across the glassy surface like a dropped box of glitter. Trey had struggled with his emotions, choking back tears and snot ropes that leaked from his nose.

Tooter was a young man of few words. It was doubtful the corn-fed farm boy had ever heard a personal revelation of such sexual confusion and creativity before. He listened and waited until Trey had vented his sins. The night was so still, hot and muggy like a Chinese laundry. The big boy had pulled his t-shirt off halfway through Trey's story. He absent-mindedly swatted gnats and mosquitoes away from his back with the damp shirt. He was chewing a plastic straw and the end was a macerated glob of plastic by now.

"So, do you think I'm a queer? Am I going to hell?"

"Well," he began in his sleepy, slow low croak, "I figure you ain't the only boy to have some mixed-up feelings." He bent down and picked up a smooth stone and skipped it five times across the flat water, creating bright eddies of silver on the smooth lake. He added, "Does your pecker still get hard when you think about tits and pussy?"

Trey wondered if any confession had ever included that question before. "Yeah, it does. I mean, sure all the time. I spank it all the time thinking about tits and pussy."

"Well," Tooter drawled again, "Then you cain't be too queer, you know what I mean?"

The boys continued their quiet vigil, alternating skipping stones into the darkening water. Finally Trey asked, "Are you sure, 'cause I haven't really done anything with a girl. But the stuff with Kevin…" he trailed off.

Tooter skipped another stone, six skips this time. Then with a tone of finality, the redneck Nostradamus provided the last word on the subject:

"Just 'cause you eat a few bananas, don't make you a monkey."

And that was that. Absolution was complete in Trey McGee's heart. Trey never lost another night's sleep or spent another minute doubting his heterosexuality and he was determined to never let that be an issue again. And to that end, he continued to pound his pecker as often as he could into Angie's honey pie. Today, the naked girl gripped the trunk of the pecan tree that served as the main mast of the tree house as Trey worked his magic from the back. His dark skin wet with sweat that matted the thick black fuzz that covered his muscled ass in a rhythm that matched his thrusts as he rode Angie doggie style, his favorite. Their bodies making the thwack, thwack, thwack sound as boner and balls slapped against Angie's round backside.

Sex with Angie was a new thing but in the limited time he had known her, it was always good. It seemed as natural for the teenagers as dog-paddling is to a terrier. But as Trey continued working his magic, he realized that in the past few days, this had started getting even better. It seemed like all he had to do was think about it and he was bigger, harder, and longer-lasting than he had ever been before. Two days ago, he had managed to come three times in an hour of non-stop lovemaking. The sweat had poured off both of them, but both teens seemed to have unending energy and libido. Angie's orgasms were so intense, it felt like a vise was gripping Trey's cock, *but not in a bad way*, he thought. No, this was like the best, tightest feeling he had ever experienced. Even better than that time he had tried out the shop vac. He had gotten the hose positioned just right so there was this amazing sucking taking place and this intense fluttering vibration on the tip of his Johnson. He was supposed to be vacuuming out the station wagon, but he got distracted like often happened. He had laid in the backseat with the vacuum hose attached to his boner for what seemed like twenty minutes. That constant fluttering vibration and hard suck brought him to a staggering climax without ever having to touch himself. *And even better*, he thought, no clean up. In fact, the whole experience would have been perfect except for the part where he opened his eyes and suddenly realized his dad was standing in the backdoor of the wagon with his hands on his hips and a strange look on his face, a mixture of amusement and bewilderment.

"If you two are finished, you need to get back to cleaning the car," Mike said dryly as Trey dislodged himself from the hose, scrambling to stuff his erection back inside his shorts. "You better dump the shit in that vacuum, too. I'm sure as hell not doing it," he said shaking his head heading back toward the garage.

Maybe it was the sneaking up here, Trey thought. Maybe that had made the screwing so much better. He was typically horny most of the time, but this was epic. It felt like his balls were emptying a gallon of nut inside Angie. He had abandoned trying to use condoms. He hated the way they felt now and the last two times, they had burst either through the friction or the load of semen. Besides, she had told him it was the right time of the month for her to be safe, whatever that meant. She seemed to understand it so he really didn't care. When his first orgasm came this afternoon, he thought the top of his head was going to come off. When the familiar quickening started, it just kept increasing. The intensity skyrocketed like a roman candle, jetting out fireball after fireball of passion. He had held his hand over Angie's mouth as she began to wail and moan louder than ever before, trembling inside like fast-purring engine.

The teenagers collapsed in a damp heaving heap and Trey noticed once again he needed to piss worse than ever in his whole life. And when he looked at Angie, it looked like her nose was bleeding. *That was definitely weird,* he thought. He crawled over to one of the windows in the tree house and sent a fire hose blast of urine out in a big golden arc to the ground.

"Are you ok, baby?" Trey asked flicking off the last of his pee.

"Yeah, why?"

"Your nose is sorta bleeding."

"Who cares," Angie said wiping her nose on a nearby pillowcase and pulling him into a tight embrace again. Within moments, Trey was rock hard again. He didn't care after that. He slid back inside and began to ride once more. He kept seeing that damn green light when he closed his eyes and hearing that stupid jump rope song. *"Red light, Yellow light, Green light bridge ..."* His thrusts began to mimic the rhythm of the chant. And in the middle of all this, he was thinking about running down the football field, across the middle, catching Bo's screen pass and running, running, running like hell for the end zone. *Did it get any better than this,* he thought?

27 Travis

Fridays at CHJHS were always good, but for the lucky few who were in high school band, they were the best. It might have been the only time when all the kids who joked and marginalized band members were actually jealous. On football Fridays, the students got out of all of 5th period in order to ride the bus over to the high school pep rally that took place in the gym. This was going to be the first pep rally for a home game and it promised to be exciting. Travis found himself daydreaming about the pep rally already and it was only first period shop class. He knew from what Trey had told him that there was always a competition for the "Spirit Stick," which was given to the class with the most enthusiasm, which basically meant who was willing to scream the loudest during the V-I-C-T-O-R-Y chant.

The air in the shop was mercifully cool this morning, giving the slightest hint that the oppressive Texas heat might be starting to ease its grip and give way to that brief but magical season of autumn that Travis waited for all year. He realized that most of the country was getting ready to mourn the end of summer and fear the coming deep freeze. Not Travis. He loved the cool weather, the break from the sweltering humidity, and even a chance to wear a sweater or flannel shirt to school for a change. The sounds surrounding him in the workshop this morning mixed with the sawdust and varnish smells made him feel nostalgic, even though he had no recollection of ever being around a wood shop when he was younger. It was a comforting sound, the tapping and sawing, occasional curses uttered sotto voce. The wood shop had a Welcome Back Kotter vibe to it, and Travis figured he and George were Sweathogs, at least they were Vinnie and Washington, maybe Epstein. Not Horshack.

Travis looked over at George and was astounded as usual with the skill and artistry of his work. He was currently working on a large string art creation of wood and silky gold thread wound around hundreds of tiny gold nails to create an impressive tall ship model mounted on a smoothly sanded piece of thick veneer wrapped with black velvet. The western red cedar bow, stern, and various masts and yardarms were polished to a mirror like satin finish. George had attached the boat pieces to the veneer and was now meticulously adding the rows and rows of tiny brass brads. There were a number of boys actually working on the nautical string art projects, but only George's looked like real art. David Gillespie had hurried through his project and the rough, splintery blocks of wood were haphazardly placed on some burlap backing which made the whole thing look like a boat sailing through the local feed store. To top it off, David's brass nails were tapped in at all angles and depths and the string design was a frightful disaster. It looked like a Spiro-graph when the ink pens were all skipping and in your haste, the little wheels jumped the cogs and you ripped across the page with a bright red slash in the middle of your cool design. The rigging sagged and was a chaotic mess.

Shop class was about the only time Travis ever saw George truly transfixed, completely devoted to what he was doing. Playing music was the only other close activity. Regular class lessons, homework, or tests were a jumbled mess in comparison. Travis was also noticing that Mark Montgomery, the skinny blond boy who sat across from him and George, was chattering like a chipmunk today, yakking incessantly about yesterday's Star Trek rerun. It appeared to be the one where Captain Kirk was trapped on the desolate planet and forced to battle the Gorn, a rubber lizard man. Usually this would not have been a problem but he was talking really loudly and he was also getting all the details wrong as he recounted them to Ricky Gonzales, who had a mustache that would make Burt Reynolds jealous. Travis noticed the veins in George's temples were pulsing, his mouth a thin white line. There were a few things you didn't want to do around George: one was make fun of any musical artist that he liked, which was a big list. The other was make fun of or mess up the details about Star Trek. For George, the jury was still out on Star Wars. He loved the movie, he and Travis had seen it four times already. But he wasn't convinced it would have the longevity or profundity of Star Trek.

"Yeah Captain Kirk was fighting the lizard guy, Garn, and he had to make a cannon out of bamboo and this big rock salt crystals. They could talk to each other because they had a tri-recorder that unscrambled their language. And Doctor Spock wasn't even there to help him he got put in the transporter without anyone sending him. And then he made the cannon and blew a big hole in the Garn," Mark said to a totally disinterested Ricky who just grunted and continued working on his gun rack.

Travis noticed George had stopped working. He was looking murderously at Mark who was continuing to recount the Star Trek episode, mangling every detail. Mark was absent-mindedly sanding his white pine birdhouse across the grain as he chatted like Chip and Dale. George went over to Mark and gripped his shoulder.

"You know, that would go so much faster if you used the disc sander," George whispered.

On cue, Travis added his hand to Mark's other shoulder and whispered, "Yeah, that white pine will be as smooth as a baby's bottom. Go for it."

Mark's eyes had gone slightly out of focus as he continued to rub his sandpaper across the grain of his project. Travis and George went back to their work and watched as the skinny boy picked up his project pieces and made his way to the disc sander.

Now there were plenty of rules in shop class that Mr. Monroe drilled the boys with constantly. Right up there with *"Measure twice, cut once"* was the less helpful but decidedly more ominous: *"Use white pine on the disc sander and get two from White Lightning."* Mark Montgomery made a beeline to the sander and clicked the power on, commencing to run the soft, sticky wood back and forth across the whirring gritty sander. In a few moments, white dust was clouding around the machine and Mark. Thick, sticky pitch was coating the sandpaper and gumming up the internal workings of the sander like a Big Mac clogging up your dad's arteries. Mark continued to run the wood back and forth across the sander in detached oblivion until the wood shop hammer and sanding chorus was joined by a deep bass bellow.

"Jesus, Mary, and Joseph what the heck-fire do you think you are doing!"

Mr. Monroe had noticed the cloud of white pine enveloping the sander. All over the shop machines were powered down, hammers were put away, and sanding blocks stopped their scratching. Mark Montgomery must have realized where he was and what was happening because his grip on the birdhouse loosened and in a snap, the sander flung his project across the shop like a catapult and it smashed through one of the big windows at the back of the shop. Mr. Monroe reached around Mark and snapped the power button on the sander off, the whine of the machine in stark contrast to the strange silence inside the shop. As the motor ground to a moaning halt, Mark turned around and looked at Mr. Monroe and then at the crowd of boys staring through the early morning sunlight now punctuated with clouds of white dust.

"Christ on a crutch," Mr. Monroe hissed in a rumbling whisper. He looked at the wide-eyed boy and pointed toward his desk. "You know what to do Montgomery."

Mark swallowed with an audible gulp and made his way through the shop to the teacher's desk. He shuffled around some loose papers and found White Lightning and brought it back to the teacher with visibly trembling hands. Mr. Monroe pointed toward the back of the shop to the bathroom and the two made their way inside to the chorus of low "Ooooooooooohs" that filled the room. The group of boys stood in frozen silence, like a doomed man waiting to hear the firing squad lock and load. The first crack of the paddle split the quiet air like the lightning the paddle was named after followed by a groan. The second blow must have hit prime buttocks real estate, because the shotgun like smack actually made the group of boys listening wince and grab at their butts or balls in obvious empathy. This was followed by an unsettling sob of pain that bounced around the cinderblock walls like thunder. A red-faced Mr. Monroe stormed out of the bathroom and toward the disk sander. He whirled on the group, staring at each one in turn.

"Could not one of you numbnuts have stopped that idiot, reminded him of the rules? What is rule number five up on the wall, Mr. Peterson?" the breathless teacher hissed.

"Um, Keep your eyes open and help your neighbor," Billy Peterson answered in a small voice.

"That's right. But that doesn't matter to any of you jokers, does it? No, better to watch some imbecile ruin my sander and practically put a piece of wood through someone's head. I want everything powered down. Grab a broom. We are cleaning for the rest of the period."

Walking to second period, Travis pulled George into the first boy's bathroom they passed. When he had checked that the coast was clear he unloaded on George.

"See, that is exactly the kind of shit that Emily was talking about. We can't do that; blast some guy just for the fun of it because we feel like it."

"He is a moron and he was totally screwing up that episode the way he was talking about it. Dr. Spock my ass."

Travis rounded on George and continued in a malevolent whisper.

"Just because a guy is stupid, G, does not mean we get to jerk him around and make him our little toy. That's mean. You know it is. I know it is. And yeah, I like it a little sometimes. And maybe sometimes a guy does deserve it. But it's got to be for something more than just messing up a Star Trek episode. Otherwise, we are just bullies like all the other dicks that have been around all the time. We are better than this."

Travis was breathing hard, the energy arcing between the boys was palpable. It felt like a Tesla Coil just getting ready to explode. George looked furiously at Travis, his teeth almost bared, fuming with his fists balled up ready to strike. The boys stood like that for another minute and finally, the energy dissipated and George looked away.

Travis spoke again, softly and slowly, bending his head around to make sure no one was listening once again. "I don't know why this has happened, but it's like Emily said, it has to be more a bigger reason that just to give us the chance to be a-holes, even if it feels like people deserve it sometimes." He waited a moment then added, "It needs to be for good, at least most of the time for good. If we do that, then we won't be feeling like crap all the time."

"Sometimes people deserve it. Sometimes people ought to be taught a lesson," George muttered back.

"And what happens when it's you or me that deserves to be taught a lesson? Are you going to march me up to the front of the class and made me have an intense desire to take a leak in the trash can or french Jimmy Earwood while everyone watches? My mom always talks about slippery slopes, starting something that you can't stop or getting dragged down by your own big-headedness. We can't do that."

"Okay! I know you're right but stop being such a Know-it-All. And we are going to be tardy if we don't book out of here right now." The boys tore down the hall, ignoring the call from Mrs. Hoffman to slow down. George added, "And don't go telling Emily everything. She already thinks I'm a loser."

The boys sat grimly in the trombone section of the band that afternoon, watching the stand fill up with high school students. This was when Travis both enjoyed being part of the senior band and also felt the most conspicuous. The junior class sat nearest to the band in the gymnasium bleachers. Travis spent a large amount of time watching the sixteen year old girls and their tight t-shirts and sweaters cupping a wide assortment of boner-inducing breasts; from barely there bumps to god-dang mammary mountains, like the Dolly Parton-like rack on Belinda Bonham. But he also noticed the bulging muscles and mustaches and wispy chin whiskers of the boys and that made him feel small and ridiculous.

Mr. Smith counted off the fight song and the band blasted out the familiar tune while the students clapped in rhythmic chorus. The principal introduced the football coach, Jimmy Bates, who in turn, introduced the starting lineup for the 1978 Cowhill Tigers. If the junior class boys were big, the football players were monsters. There was Trey McGee in his black number 83 uniform jersey. Travis noted Trey was relatively big compared with some of the defensive backfield and the bulldozers that made up the O-Line. After the team was introduced, the majorettes bounced onto the wooden floor and got in position for this week's routine to Johnny River's "Rockin' Pneumonia." The girls started out the routine bent over from the waist down, baton on the ground. When the drum line kicked off the song, the girls fist-pumped toward the ground which in turn made their tight uniform panties bounce back and forth like small bowls of Jell-O, especially LaMisha Williams whose bottom was full and plump and stuck out wide and proud compared to the other girls. The boys in the various classes hooted and wolf-whistles started almost at once. When the majorettes spun around later in the routine and shook their asses at the football players, the roar was loud, low, and filled with cat-calls. More than one of the players grabbed at their crotch or mimed reaching out to grip the tushes being wagged in front of them. Travis cut his eyes over to George who was bug-eyed staring at the bouncing butts. Travis noticed even Mr. Smith was not paying attention to conducting as his attention was grabbed by the routine, probably calculating how many phone calls he might be getting from upset parents who were opposed to the sexy routine.

The evening of September 15th was actually cool by Texas standards at least. The lights at the football stadium were attracting clouds and clouds of crickets to the stands, creating a nauseating stench of squashed insects mixing in with the scents of popcorn and Frito pies, served in the little packages, heaped with shredded cheese and onions. The band was located in its normal seats, between the 20 and 30 yard lines. They were not performing a pregame show tonight, opting to serenade the crowd from the stands instead. It was basically a laid-back way to practice the tunes prior to performing them for halftime. Mr. Smith was adamant about memorized music, too. Absolutely no lyres or music charts in flip books were allowed on the field. Travis and George had agreed that the memorization rule had made the band better prepared and play tighter. Members actually looked at the drum major now when he was conducting instead of being glued to the music.

Last week at the Honey Grove football game, both boys mocked in superiority as they saw the Warrior Marching Band, complete with moccasin-wearing majorettes and a war-whoop screaming Drum Major in full war paint litter the field with dropped music books from end zone to end zone. The low point of that musical mayhem had been a fire baton routine to Paul Revere and the Raiders' "Cherokee People." Travis had watched Emily standing on the sidelines waiting and watching the Warrior Band as guest bands most often did since they got to perform first. Her lips were in a thin line and her eyes blazed like incensed smoldering... Travis had seen that look quite a few times. Both boys had agreed her Evil Eye was to be avoided at all costs. Travis had also watched one of the twirlers fire baton flame grow and burn bright until it resembled a small bonfire on a stick. The wild-eyed girl managed to catch her faux buckskin skirt fringe on fire and one of the athletic trainers ended up tossing a cooler of water or Gatorade on her to extinguish the flames, which ended up dampening the big finish of the song as well as the sobbing brunette's skirt. George had asked later that night on the bus back to Cowhill if Emily knew anything about that fire baton that turned into a flame thrower. She smirked back at George and reminded him to mind his own damn beeswax.

George had grinned saying, "Ancient Chinese secret, huh?"

Tonight the director led the band through a warm-up of scales and a chorale of "Glorious Things of Thee are Spoken." Then he counted off Sousa's "King Cotton March," and the band roared to life. There was no doubt that Mr. Smith was reluctantly leaving the six-to-five military band traditions and embracing eight-to-five show band components, because after the traditional opening number, the band moved into a medley of Chicago songs: "Beginnings," "Does Anybody Really Know What Time it is?" and "Make Me Smile." The last song from the set was a rocking rendition of "Long Train Running." In the past year, this song had become the De facto new fight song for the Tigers. It wasn't a great arrangement, but it got the crowd on its feet and was significantly more interesting that the actual fight song which may have been a rousing tune in 1939, but was little more than a jaunty sea shanty now. The majorettes stood on the track – twirling and rocking to the music, along with Terri Kenner, the Tiger mascot who was wearing the cat suit and big head, which was mirrored by her considerable backside.

The band finished the pregame music then waited for the announcer to welcome the crowd. "Welcome Tiger Fans to the opening game here at Memorial Stadium between the Cooper Bulldogs and the mighty fighting Cowhill Tigers" A robust roar rose from the crowd as the starting lineup of the Tigers was announced. Then the announcer asked the fans to stand and remove their hats for the evening benediction, tonight given by Rev. Vetter of the St. Barnabas Episcopal. The microphone feedback whooped briefly as the mike was adjusted and then with the crowd quiet with heads bowed began.

"Heavenly Father, we lift this athletic contest up to you tonight and pray that your hand of safety and mercy will protect the players on both teams. We ask that the spirit of competition be strong and fair and that the players all give their utmost to win. And we ask a special blessing on our Tiger fans and visitors to enjoy this game and remember it is just a game..." Quiet murmurs and a few boos filtered into the night at this point. "And give the visiting team a safe travel home and lift their spirits as they deal with the inevitable beating they are going to receive tonight." A large cheer rose from the crowded, punctuated with a few boos and 'shut ups' from the visitors' side of the stadium. "In the name of our Lord Jesus, Amen." More cheers.

"Please remain standing and raise your voices as the band plays the national anthem," the announcer commanded. The crowd responded obediently and sang loud and proud as the band played The Star Spangled Banner with applaudable dynamics and feeling. Mr. Smith had found a great arrangement of the tune and the band actually enjoyed playing it. The band then segued into the school alma mater, an absolute funeral dirge of a song, complete with the sappy last line, "Dear Cowhill high School, we'll always love you..." As the crowed clapped, Mr. Smith started the count for the fight song and "One, two, one, two, three..." the band began the song as the Tiger Football Team ran out of the end zone and toward the large orange banner that blazed: "Muzzle the Dawgs." The boys split the breakthrough and headed toward the home bench. The fight song ended and the crowd sat briefly. But within a few moments, the team lined up with the Bulldogs winning the toss and the Tigers kicked off to a new roar from the crowd. Friday Night Football in Texas was underway and, as usual, it was sacred.

Mr. Smith began to dismiss the band members a section at a time to go to the bathroom before half time. George pointed at a beehive blonde seated in the row the boys were walking beside and Travis choked back a laugh as he saw two crickets burrowed in the middle of the hairdo.

"That's going to be fun in a few minutes," George offered. Travis looked toward the field and was annoyed to see Trey on the sidelines.

"Why are they waiting to play, Trey? He's the best player they've got," Travis offered heading down the stairs to the bathrooms. As the boys were almost to the bathroom, Emily appeared with Karen Bone, headed back to the stands. George pulled her aside along with Travis.

"What?" Emily asked slightly annoyed.

"We're going to be late," Karen started.

"Just go on, she will be right there," Travis said. Kim took another look and made her way through the crowd under the bleachers back to the band.

"What's going on?" Emily asked.

"Ok. You are always wanting to use these powers for something good, right?" George asked looking at both teens who had migrated toward each other, Emily's hand taking Travis's as she stood close.

"Sure, I mean, yeah," Emily began. "So what is your big plan?" she asked, nicer than Travis was expecting.

"Well, maybe tonight Trey McGee should have the best game of his life," George offered. "I heard one of the tuba guys saying there were a couple of scouts in the audience tonight, mostly here to watch the stupid Bulldogs. But how about they get the surprise of their lives from a certain tall, dark and handsome tight end?"

Travis looked at Emily as she processed this and was surprised when she broke into a big grin and said, "Oh why not, it's just stupid football. Yeah, I'll go along with that. How are we going to..?"

"First of all, the coach has to put him in," Travis began.

"No problem," George said. As soon as we get back, make sure you are touching each other, which shouldn't be too hard for you two, and just start looking at the coach and sending him the thought, *you really need to put Trey McGee in the game or you are a big queer ...* or something like that."

"I don't think you need to add that last part," Emily said, her lips thin with disapproval. "But sure, let's see what happens."

"Oh it will happen," George said. "And as soon as you see him in the game, just send every ounce of power and speed and perfect ball control to him that you can."

"Okay, I have to go or Smith will kill me," Emily said giving Travis a peck on the cheek as she left. "Hey what about me," George added. The girl rolled her eyes and ran back and smacked him loudly on his fuzzy cheek. The boys ran into the bathroom and stood at the urinal trough, sending loud piss against the porcelain back. The man beside them hocked up a large wad of phlegm and sent it into the urinal as he finished up, shaking a fire hose of flesh proudly to get rid of the last drops. The boys bit their lips until the man left and then both broke into a loud snort. Travis began to sing the theme song to "Mr. Ed."

"Look at you making fun of Mr. Donkey Dick," George laughed.

Travis just grinned and said, "You know, you really get this stuff don't you? The powers."

The boys started back through the milling crowd waiting in line for popcorn, chili pie, and hot dogs.

"I guess," George answered. "In the dreams, it's like I see us doing this stuff and I just know it's how it works. I mean, you see all that too in the dream right? The ones with the green light and the song and all that?"

Travis thought for a moment and then felt the certainty that George felt surge into him along with the memories of the dream. And yes, when he thought about it right now, it seemed clean that this is what they were supposed to do. But there was more. Travis felt the images of the recurring dream flash in his mind like a movie on some sort of fast forward. He had mostly ignored the continuing dreams he was having most nights, almost getting used to them, but as George mentioned it now, their proximity seemed to ramp up the memories. In the moment he could see the green light again, the bridge, the song that seemed to be calling him to cross to the other side.

"Come on, Nutsack, we better hurry back or Mr. Smith will have our ass," George said reaching over and shaking Travis's arm. "Buddy, are you ok? You sort of phased out there or something."

"Fine. Let's go give Trey a great game."

It seemed like nothing was going to happen at all for Trey in the game. As the night cooled and the pesky crickets stopped flocking around the bright lights, Travis watched his brother as he stood on the sidelines, watching the game and then turning his head back to the coach to see if there was any chance of him getting into the action. But as the clock ticked down to 5:00 left in the half and the band began to file out of the stands to line up on the opposite sideline, it was apparent nothing was going to happen. George was lined up in the company front standing behind the visiting Bulldog's bench with Travis behind him. George held his trombone in one hand and reached behind and stuck his hand out behind his back. Instinctively, Travis took a small step forward and grabbed his hand, hoping no one would pay attention because he really didn't want to explain why he was holding hands with a boy while standing ready to take the field. With the band standing so close, he figured it would be inconspicuous. Travis felt a hand grip his other hand that was holding his trombone. Emily's fingers were smooth and moist and they grabbed hold of his hand. Like a bottle rocket, the green light and familiar surge of power coursed through him. Travis looked across the field at Coach Bates and thought with all his might . . . *You are going to lose this damn game unless you start Trey McGee in the second half.* He wasn't sure what George and Emily were thinking, but the power always seemed to resonate and find some harmonic and he knew they were on the same frequency. In between his blitz of the coach, Travis looked at Trey and kept thinking one thing . . . *"on your way off the field, come right through the band and right in between all of us. You have to do it, you have to come over here . . ."*

The half ended with the Bulldogs kicking a 20 yard field goal, an oddity in the fast run, up-the-middle, style of Cooper, making the score 17 – 6. The teams broke and the Cooper band began moving to their starting positions in the north end zone. Cooper still marched a military style 6-5 counter-march heavy show and always entered from the end zone to begin their initial march down the field. The football teams headed toward their respective locker rooms. As the Tigers jogged toward the Cowhill band and then veered to the side to enter their locker room, Trey McGee continued toward the band at a fast pace. Ramona Monroe actually squealed a small cry of alarm as Trey, huge and imposing in his pads and cleats, stopped directly in front of Travis with a look of bewilderment and expectation on his face.

"Why am I here?" he asked.

"Because we love you," George whispered gripping Trey's muscled forearm. Travis and Emily did the same and were almost knocked off their feet by the reciprocal energy surge. Emily stumbled sideways, almost in a faint. Travis felt blood ooze out of his left nostril toward his lips, and George winced and literally crossed his legs to try and stave off the explosion that wanted to proceed from his bowels. The front of Trey's football pants bloomed a darkening shade of black as he clearly began to piss. He reached down and gripped his crotch and turned toward the locker room as the other teens tried to regain some composure before it was their turn to march.

The Bulldog band completed their traditional halftime show with a clunky version of "Love Will Keep Us Together" while their plus-sized majorettes did a curious routine with twirling machetes, dull knife-shaped devices that actually hooked together for some dramatic effect. But Travis had a hard time figuring out why in the hell they were twirling them to a pop song about love. Maybe if they were playing "Kung Fu Fighting" it would make more sense. Travis looked over at Emily whose face was alarmingly pale. Ahead of him, George was still clinched in a death grip with his stomach. Travis and wiped the blood off his face and he figured he looked like someone with war paint on or maybe someone who had just been popped in the mouth. He reached forward and touched George again and tried to send some message of health or calmness. The drum major called the band to attention and the group took their places on the far sideline. The drum major counted off the tempo and the band marched forward to Aaron Copeland's brass-filled "Fanfare for the Common Man," literally blowing the Bulldog band off the field.

The half-time show concluded as usual with a rousing rendition of "Long Train Running" that got the crowd on its feet and blasted the front rows of the bleachers with a Memorex tidal wave of sound. The band filed onto the track and then turned and made its way back into the stands to the clicks from the snare drums on the side of the rims, left, left, left-right-left. As the band made its way back to its place in the stands. *Thankfully,* Travis thought, *we get the third quarter off.* Typically he and George and Emily would head for the concession stand to get a Coke but tonight the three moved over to an empty part of the stands nearby and looked at each other with wide eyes.

"I thought you were going to blow chunks big time," Travis said as George continued to take deep breaths and hold his stomach.

"That was a bad one for sure, don't really know why it was even stronger."

Emily stood near Travis and slid her hand inside his again. "I've got an idea why."

"And?" George inquired.

"Trey has the power too."

Travis let that bit of information sink in and of course, it made complete sense. He had been there in that back yard the night the lights came down. Who knows what else he might have experienced? It wasn't like they chatted very much. Hell, most weeks they barely said two words.

"Whoa, maybe it starts up for kids at different times or something?" George wondered.

The announcer was telling the crowd that the Bulldogs would be kicking off to the Tigers to start the second half. Number 83, Trey McGee is back deep to return the ball for Cowhill. With that bit of information, the three turned their attention toward the field, grins stretching across their faces like horror movie clowns. The Bulldog kicker fired off a deep ball that sailed all the way to the three yard line. Normally, the players would simply let a ball like that roll into the end zone and take the touchback on the twenty But as the trio watched, hand in hand, Trey grabbed the kick and began to run straight up the middle toward the phalanx of Bulldogs on a mission to teach this idiot a lesson. The three gripped each other tighter and watched as Trey moved straight toward the first special teams player and literally hurdled over him. The next two defenders grabbed at his orange jersey and came up empty as Trey blasted past both of them in a blur. He ran toward the next crowed of players and spun once, then twice, and pulled free and broke away into the open field and ran like the wind toward the end zone. The Tiger crowd was on its feet, the cheers and screams roaring like a jet engine as the tall boy broke the endline and jogged back toward the bench, tossing the ball politely to the ref who was standing in the middle of the field still wondering what had just happened while the line judge threw his hands up to signal the touchdown.

The three friends jumped and screamed like the rest of the crowd, continuing to smile like Cheshire Cats. Emily gave both boys a new set of kisses to the cheek. Travis turned toward the press box and saw the three scouts conspicuously staring at Trey through binoculars, no doubt trying to figure out why they had come to see anyone other than this kid.

The Bulldogs went a quick three and out on their next series. Once again, Trey was deep for the Tigers. The punter wisely decided to try and kick away from him, but that caused him to shank the ball off the side of his foot for an unremarkable punt of twelve yards, giving the Tigers the ball on their own 47-yard line. The Tiger quarterback moved under center and gave the hard count. Trey ran down to the far end of the line and set just before the ball was snapped. Trey was a blur for ten yards and then as he cut back across the middle, the quarterback threw a torpedo straight into his numbers. The Bulldog safeties and corners flew toward the tight end, but he mowed them down as if he weighed three times more than he really did. The speed and grace with which he moved was breathtaking. The crowd was on its feel again but this time, instead of a huge cheer, it was like a giant vacuum as the entire 2,000 strong crowd held its breath as Trey blew past every Cooper defender and broke the plane of the end zone like The Flash. As he crossed the end line, the crowd exploded again. The kids danced up and down again with the band who had been called back early to start playing the fight song. The scoreboard now read Bulldogs 17, Tigers 22 with the touchdowns and two 2-point conversions.

The remainder of the third quarter was scoreless. The fourth quarter began with Cooper eating up the clock with a sevenminute drive that made it all the way down to their own 21-yard line. Their attempt at a field goal was blocked by none other than Trey McGee who had stepped in to the special teams play at the coach's direction. The Tigers took over on the Bulldog 21. The first two plays were runs up the middle for a four yard gain. Then a surprising run by the quarterback made a first down on the 32. Once again, the coach called conservative plays that gobbled up the clock but made almost no yardage. With 1:02 left on the clock on third down, Trey lined up on the line ready to block for a wide receiver. But as the quarterback fell back to throw, two defenders pushed past the O-line with a massive blitz. As the defenders grabbed the quarterback, he lobbed the ball forward in a pathetic attempt to get rid of it before being sacked. Like a boomerang, Trey stopped his forward progress and swung back toward the line of scrimmage with a flying leap and scooped the lame duck pass from the grasp of a Cooper defenseman, and rolled over the top of him and landed back on his feet running like mad for the sideline. As he neared the sideline, he turned toward the end zone with seven Bulldogs on his tail. The safeties and corners launched themselves at the bullet that was Trey McGee. Their hands gripped the shirttail of his jersey while another reached out and gripped the belt of Trey's pants.

The crowd let out an audible gasp as the defenders pulled back on Trey's uniform like cowboys trying to throw a calf at a rodeo. Trey momentarily tipped backward ready to be pulled to the ground. But like a slingshot pulled back to its utmost point, he suddenly shot forward with a mighty lurch. The tight end's uniform ripped apart like the veil of the temple when Jesus was crucified, tearing apart with a splintering snap. Trey McGee bolted toward the end zone, rushing for the Holy of Holies wearing nothing but his shoulder pads and a pee-stained jock strap. The explosion from the crowd was like a bomb. Trey seemed to finally realize he was standing under the goal posts bare-ass naked as he looked down at his furry legs and bare chest. He stood there for a moment looking around, then up toward the crowd, and suddenly he spiked the ball and proceed to do two running handstands, ending in a flip. By this time, the crowd had gone completely insane with students pouring over the bleacher walls wanting to rush the field. The coach roared at the students to get off the goddamn field since there were still 23 seconds left on the clock.

After the extra point, the Bulldogs grabbed the kick off and tried a hook-and-ladder play to make a miracle of their own, but they were stopped at the 40-yard line as the gun sounded and the game ended. The fans flooded the field at this point. The training staff handed Trey a towel which he wrapped around his waist. He stood on a bench and swung another towel over his head yelling at the top of his lungs as the crowd gathered around. Soon he was riding the shoulders of two O-lineman as they paraded the shirtless boy up and down the track to the strains of the fight song and the chants of TREY MA-GEE, TREY MA-GEE! Emily was in tears and George and Travis were staring in stunned amazement, not bothering to even pretend to play the fight song.

The team finally put Trey back on his feet near the 20-yard line in front of the band. Trey still in his towel and bare chest and shoulder pads, began to conduct the band as they started up Long Train once again. From the stands, a blonde blur suddenly collided with Trey, jumping up locking her legs around his waist and planting a long, deep kiss on his lips. Trey spun Angie around to the music as the two continued to kiss as the crowd hooted and clapped and danced to the song of victory.

Unnoticed by Travis, Trey or most of the crowd was a small knot of grim faced fans seated together near the top of the stands above the band. J.L. Martin, Toy Benton, and Junior Bidwell glared at the scene unfolding on the track. The three men cut a hard look toward Buck Matlock who gaped in open-mouthed horror as his daughter continued to grip the tall, towel-clad boy with her legs as she planted kiss after kiss on his face.

28 Mike

Mike looked back toward the bed as he quietly pulled the door closed. Janet was a tumble of sheets and blankets and the curves of her beautiful pink ass. Her blonde hair was a wild nest of curls, hanging down and framing a brown nipple that still stood erect on her full breast. He had taken a quick shower but realized from the straining in his shorts that he just wanted to climb back into bed and slip inside her once again.

He reluctantly closed the door and headed down the hall. He ran into Andy coming out of the bathroom. He got a sleepy, but loving hug from his youngest then he made his way outside the car. *He needed to get to work early, he could just get coffee there,* he thought. He started the Vista Cruiser wagon and backed out onto Maple and headed for the store. The morning was soft and damp, still warm. Was going to be hot again today he figured.

As he headed toward Washington Street, he thought again how strange things had been lately, not the least of which was that he had had the best sex of his married life in the past few weeks. It had surged back to life in this gradual storm that continued to build. From practical celibacy to every night, sometimes more than once; sex on the couch, in the shower, from behind on the edge of the bed, Janet on top riding him and once in his office at the store while the damn place was wide open.

She had walked into the office in a skirt quite a bit shorter than what she normally wore. He was over in the corner looking in some files when she sauntered in and hopped up on his desk, flushed cheeks and hair in provocative pony tail, looking more twenty than forty. As he looked over in cautious curiosity, she had shifted on the desk, uncrossing her legs, revealing her damp, golden thatch and pink lips, moist and swollen. She leaned back on her shoulders and spread her legs wide. Mike's eyes bulged and he tripped rushing to the door and grabbing a rubber door stop to jam under the bottom. He buried his face in her lap and found her spot, teasing and nipping with his lips and licking with a lusty tongue. He didn't remember losing his pants but when he pulled up out of her mound, his cock penetrated her in one thrust. He pumped inside her over and over while she gripped his shoulders and planted hungry kisses on his open mouth. Then he pulled out while she moaned in protest, smiling at her damp, wet face. He roughly flipped her over and bent her over the desk and drove inside her wetness, pounding deep and long, He came in loud grunts, emptying his nuts inside her pussy, slamming his body hard against hers, then collapsing on top, spent and happy.

He wondered if they had been heard. From the looks of a couple of stock boys and Frank the butcher, he figured they had been. The stock boys looked sheepish and smirking when he gave them work to do while Frank's face was a mixture of contempt and pure jealousy, he thought. *That poor wretch,* Mike thought, *been a coon's age since that guy's pecker had had any pleasure* he figured.

Mike got out of the car and headed for the back door of the grocery store. As much as he was enjoying this renaissance in his sex life, he had no idea what the hell was going on with those kids of his. Things with Trey had been tense for a while he knew. That kid was just a giant walking hormone these days. Half the time he was ready to kill him, the other half he was so proud of his performance on the football field; he thought his heart would burst. They had never had an easy time of it. He tried, not very successfully, to be a caring and decent father for him. It was pretty easy with Travis and Andy, and Teppy had always been a darling. His feelings for them were genuinely loving and kind. But with Trey, it seemed there was always drama. The boy always challenged him, hell, defied him. The few times he had tried to make a real effort and connect with him, Trey had shit on those moments in his patented smartass style. He didn't like to be hugged, didn't like to be complimented, didn't like anything that made him feel foolish or not in control. *Funny,* he thought, *he didn't like that out of control feeling himself. Maybe Trey was more like him than he realized.* But that was ridiculous.

Of course it didn't help they didn't look anything alike. Mike's red-blond hair, shaggy and curling over his ears and collar these days, was in stark contrast to Trey's dark brown, almost black tight curls. His curly hair was beautiful and when he was a boy, more than once he had been mistaken for a little girl. But once he hit puberty, which must have been when the kid was ten, he rebelled against the curls and demanded his hair stay short cropped, even though the style for most boys was longer and longer these days. He excelled at sports, not so much with his grades. He was still shockingly handsome, almost still pretty. Smooth, milky-brown skin, big hands and feet, muscles galore, and a big smile that charmed the pants off the girls it seemed. Although he refused to divulge any of his activities with the various girls he had been dating, Mike felt certain the boy was likely a stud horse these days. Since all the guys in the family shared that one bathroom, he had gotten plenty of glimpses of Trey's mighty member; one more distinct difference between him and the boy. He wasn't some tiny pencil dick guy, but damn, the kid was a little intimidating if he was honest. And now he was all mixed up with Angie Matlock of all people. He figured that girl with her big tits and pouty lips would make easy work of Trey.

"Hey boss," Kevin Montoya, the produce guy said as Mike flipped on the lights in his office. "You're in early today." Kevin was normally the first guy in each day getting a start on the morning produce delivery out on the floor before the doors opened at 7:00.

"Yeah. Thought I'd make an early start of it myself since I was already up."

"Hope you weren't having a sleepless night. I hate those myself," Kevin asked.

Mike turned the air conditioner on in his office. "Nope. Just got woke up a bit early this morning by the missus," Mike said with a grin.

"That's my very favorite kind of wake up call," Kevin said smiling, holding a banana down in front of his crotch waggling it provocatively, stroking it with his free hand.

Mike shook his head and closed the door. He pulled out the cash register receipts from yesterday and began to run the totals through his calculator and enter the amounts in the ledger, then remembered he hadn't even had his coffee yet. He got up and went back to the break room area and found Alice Davis sitting there, smoking and reading the morning paper. He poured himself a cup, added some Sweet and Low and Coffee-mate and sat down beside her.

"What's going on today, Alice?"

"Same ole shit," she added after a long drag on her Virginia Slims. "Looks like the Catholics have a new Pope. Some Polack named Karol. That's good since he already wears a dress. They killed the last one 'cause he was connected to the Kennedys. Gonna call himself John Paul."

Where does she come up with all this, wondered Mike? "You Catholic, Alice?" Mike asked taking another long sip of coffee.

"Hell no," I'm just plain ole Baptist like most of the rest of this town. I should be like you and go and join the Holy Rollers."

"Well I have invited you plenty," Mike said.

"Yeah, I know. I just don't know about holding those snakes and all that," she said with a wicked grin looking over the top of her cat's-eye glasses.

"Well we start newcomers out with a nice little garter snake. We save the copperheads and coral snakes for the truly devout," Mike added playing along. There certainly was a faction of the church congregation that would probably be fine with some snake handling. Thank God the church was beginning to move into some less legalistic crazy fundamental practices. But those old teachings died hard. The pastor had just started letting women wear pants to church services a year ago. Now the congregation was clearly divided along the lines of those who wore pants and those who still thought it was a sin. It was the stupidest thing he ever heard of and yet he understood how the older people saw it as some sort of fatal compromise where all their revered traditions and beliefs were being swept away by the modern age of long-haired hippie song-leaders and Jesus People playing tambourines and dancing in the spirit instead of waiting for the Holy Ghost to zap you into a stupor complete with speaking in tongues.

"There you go, pulling my leg again, Mike." Alice said lighting up another cigarette and blowing the smoke far up into the air where it caught on the air conditioner vent and swirled away. "Tell you the truth, I've been worried about my Yvonne."

"What's up?"

"She's just been weird lately. I went to her room the other morning and she was sitting up in bed reading this library book. But the thing is, she was turning the pages so fast, it was like a blur. When she saw me staring, she stopped and got all snippy and asked if I had a problem. I told her to watch her lip and then asked her if she was just going to flip through the pages of that book or really read it. See I knew she had a book report due the next day." Alice flicked a long snake of ash into the ashtray and continued.

"Well she told me she was reading and to mind my own business. I started to slap her silly, that's what my mother would have done. But I thought, ok I will teach you a lesson, Missy. I asked her when she had started reading the book and she looked at the clock and said, about five minutes ago. So I asked, what's the book about? She was reading "Great Expectations" which happens to be one of my favorites so I knew she couldn't bullshit her way around the story with me." Another long drag and plume of blue smoke was sent toward the air conditioner vent.

"So what did she say?" Mike asked.

"She proceeded to tell me about Pip and the graveyard and Abel Magwitch, meeting Miss Havisham, Joe, Estella, Miss Havisham setting herself on fire…everything. I couldn't believe my ears. The girl never reads, I knew she must have really read it. But how could she by just flipping through the pages? Speed reading?"

Mike's mind went back to all the crazy happenings around his house in the past few weeks and just shook his head. "Not sure, I guess she could have learned. But it doesn't seem likely."

"Lots of weird stuff like that has been happening. The other day I was sewing up this new skirt and I was trying to get her off the couch to go and grab the laundry off the clothesline and fold it up or put it in the ironing basket. She was giving me her normal sass and I was giving it right back. In fact, I went right in the living room and jerked the plug for the TV right out of the wall. She got up in my face and I just hauled off and slapped her." Alice looked over at the time clock, grabbed her time card and slid it inside until it punched her in and set back down.

"She went out in a huff and got the clothes and did the chores, yelling and slamming stuff the whole time. When she came back in, she stood behind me in the doorway of my sewing room while I was working on that skirt. All of a sudden, the motor of the machine sped up and started sewing so fast I couldn't get my fingers out of the way and I sewed my damn fingers into the skirt!"

"That's why you had them all bandaged up," Mike asked.

"That's right. And that little bitch just stood there and laughed like she was from the Village of the Damned. ." Alice stood up and put on her apron and applied some new lipstick. "Well I better get to my register. Good talking with you, Mike. You sure seem happy today, by the way."

"Uh, thanks. Had a good night," he added.

She stood in the door and looked him up and down. "I bet you did," she smirked and headed out the door.

Other employees were crowding into the break room and clocking in. Mike said good morning and headed back to his office and closed the door. He sat in his chair and thought about Alice's story. He thought back to his own family. His kids had been acting odd as well. Not the least of which was Travis throwing him through the screened back porch when he was walloping Trey. He winced when he thought of that. Not his finest hour to say the least. Why did that kid always bring out the worst in me? But he knew good and well why that was.

And then last Friday night. That kid had stepped on the football field his regular screw-up self and walked off a hero. That boy had flown like the wind, looked like Mike Ditka. Then that crazy moment when he just tore out of his uniform and was running down the field bare ass naked in his jock strap and whole town was cheering. He had been so proud when he hugged him after the game. Nothing else mattered. He was his boy and he was his dad and so proud he thought he would burst. *Why couldn't he just keep that feeling all the time*, he thought? Mike wondered what this week was going to be like on the football field. Would lightning strike twice? He had loved seeing Trey so happy and confident this week. He was less surly. He hadn't roared out of the driveway in his car in the mornings. He had been more patient with the boys at home. If he keeps this up, I'm gonna have to give him back his room, he thought.

Mike flipped the radio on. "Time in a Bottle" by Jim Croce filled the quiet in the office. Mike got back to the cash register receipts and finished adding them to the ledger. Next he turned to tackle some of the delivery manifests. His desk was a forest of paper towers, his patented filing system. But so far it was working okay and Melba the bookkeeper seemed to be able to find what she needed as well. Then she could move it all to the files and save him the trouble. A knock at the door broke his concentration and he looked up.

"Hey don't be working too hard there, big guy."

Mike forced a mask of pleasantness on his face and answered, "No chance of that. What can I do you for, JL?"

JL Martin came into the office and closed the door. "You don't mind, do you? Just thought might could use a little privacy."

Mike nodded in agreement, though his annoyance was growing by the moment. *Why the hell is this creep here, he wondered?*

"That was quite the performance by your boy last Friday night. He keeps that up and he is going to follow in his old man's footsteps and get a football scholarship."

"That would be sweet," Mike said. "If I can keep his nose in the books, maybe he can make it."

"Whole town would love to see that, I'm sure. Hey, you ever hear from Carl Washington since he supposedly run off after raping that daughter of his?" JL leered and continued to breathe through his mouth as his rattled breath filled the small room.

Mike stiffened. "No. And I doubt very seriously that Carl had anything to do with what happened to Mary. In fact, I am certain of it."

"Oh yeah, well the sheriff and District Attorney sure as shit seem to feel different. I would think you would think twice about sticking your neck out for him, seeing how he betrayed you like he did. You and that coon has always been tight, ever since you went off to be roommates at college. Plenty of folks think that's still pretty damn strange. But maybe it's true what they say, 'Once you go black, you don't go back.'"

Mike stood up so fast one of his towers of paper fell sideways and littered the floor. JL stood and backed up against the door. Mike moved in close, so close he could smell the early morning hit of Jack Daniels JL had obviously taken.

"It's none of your goddamn business what I think or feel about Carl, Mike hissed. "He's my friend and I know he didn't hurt his little girl. As to where he is, I'm wondering if you and your kind may know a lot more than you are saying. Just a few weeks ago you were ready to hand him the key to the city with all that Norton money. If you want to talk about shit that is damn strange, I'd say let's start there."

JL tried to move further away but his back was already against the door. He began to feel for the doorknob behind his vast lard ass. "Look, Mike, I just came by to say that Buck Matlock don't want that boy of yours around his girl anymore. He was going to come over here himself but I talked him out of it with him being still pretty fired up. I didn't want any real trouble breaking out."

Mike stepped closer until he ran into JL's belly. "Again, none of your fucking business, thank you just the same. I have talked to Trey and he knows not to go around that girl. If Buck Matlock has something to say to me, he can have the balls to come say it to my face. And while we are on the subject, if I find out that you or any of your freak show rednecks had anything to do with Carl disappearing or Mary, I will make you sorry you were ever born." With that, Mike reached out and gripped JL's testicles in a vice grip and twisted them hard. "Stay away from me and my family. Got it?"

JL stumbled forward groaning, clutching his crotch. Mike opened the door and let it bang against the filing cabinet. "Thanks for stopping by old friend."

JL hobbled out of the office. He turned back and spat on the floor. "You gonna be sorry you did that, you nigger-loving piece of shit."

29 Theo

Theo parked his 1979 metallic blue Trans Am across three parking spots on the front row of the parking lot in the senior rows. He grabbed his notebook and trigonometry textbook and jogged inside the school, dodging the rain that was pelting down.

Theo said good morning to dozens of students and teachers as he made his way to homeroom. He had learned from his dad that these generosities to the little people always paid off in big dividends. He saw Trey McGee standing at his locker, methodically looking for something. Right beside him, Angie Matlock stood looking into hers as well. It was painfully obvious the two were talking, but pretending not to. These amateurs, Theo thought. He decided to have some fun.

"Hey there, McGee. How's it hanging, brother?" he said in his smooth roguish southern lilt. Trey jumped a foot and spun around slamming his locker shut. Angie grabbed her purse and turned to leave as well.

"Hey, no need to run off, sweetheart. You are looking great today," Theo called after Angie as she hurriedly made her way to her class. "Man, she is looking fine. Have you seen her tits? I mean they seem bigger than ever, just these big ripe melons waiting to burst," Theo held his hands up cupping Trey's chest. Trey smiled weakly and pushed his hands down.

"I guess I didn't notice," Trey said.

"Then you must be blind, bro. Those are some bodacious ta-tas. Can you imagine sucking on those babies? Hold it, what am I saying, you have sucked on 'em." Theo smiled and leaned into Trey, pressing the boy into the locker.

"Uh, we aren't going out or anything anymore," Trey said in a quiet voice looking for a way to escape.

"Really?" Theo said disbelieving. "So I guess you would be okay if I took a turn on the Angie Wagon? From what I hear, I'm about the only guy who hasn't."

Trey's face flushed darker. "That's not true. People say that all the time, but it's not right. I mean, she may have had a couple of boyfriends, but she isn't some slut. Please don't go around spreading that shit. She is a good person."

"Looks like I struck a nerve. If you two aren't together, why the fuck should you care what I say?"

"Cause what you say seems louder than other people, cause you are super popular and everything," Trey said looking Theo in the eyes.

"Well, that's nice of you to say, buddy. Hey, why don't you and me hang out after practice today? I mean, your star is rising, Trey. After last week on the field, I may not be the big man around here for much longer."

"I doubt that," Trey said looking up as the first bell sounded. "Uh, okay, sure. Guess I'll see you then."

Sounds like a date," Theo said grinning running off to his class.

Theo went through the rest of his day as he did most of them; charming and completely useless. He was smart enough, he knew. But honestly, he just couldn't bother doing a lot of homework or showing up for every single class. That was for the kids that didn't have other chances. His future was laid out for him on a fat plush red carpet of opportunity that his dear old dad had made happen: the oil money, the fertilizer cash, the investments, the real estate. Altogether, he thought Dad was worth at least $50 million, maybe more. When you have that kind of scratch, doing civics homework was pretty pathetic, he figured.

He charmed and smarmed his way through class, promising he would get the homework in later. He often would crank out a week's worth on one night, saving the rest of the time for himself. All it took was a few hits on Daddy's precious angel dust. JL was really so naive, Theo thought, sitting in his physics class not paying attention at all. He had known the combination to Daddy's safe for over three years. He consistently borrowed cash from the stashed stacks, keeping it along with the generous allowance Pop already provided. He had started snorting the powder or lacing joints with the stuff. No wonder his old man loved it so much. It was excellent. It gave him an edge without making him listless like the weed could. He heard that lots of kids freaked out on the stuff and wanted to cut out people's hearts or try to cook a baby or something. That was probably just shit that cops shoveled out there so the regular folk didn't figure out how great the stuff really was.

Theo had taken advantage of the porn in the safe, excellent spank material he had to admit although he had never had that much of a thing for kids. Still it was fun because it was naughty and forbidden, which always made anything that much more fun. That's why he loved the crazy shit his dad was into with his sacrifices and rituals with the Black Knights. When he first discovered some of what his dad was into, JL had been nervous and worried that Theo shouldn't take part in the ceremonies. Theo had surprised him by participating in every way. The ceremonies were special, dark things that filled some deep void in his soul. Theo still had no idea where his dad came up with some of the losers that ended strung up in the barn like an October buck. He liked the pageantry of the ceremony well enough, but it was the cleanup that he was surprisingly adept at. He loved the disarticulations, the way a sharp knife would slice into flesh like butter. He had seen the inside of enough men to wonder if he might possibly think about being a doctor, but in the end, it just seemed like way too much work. He had perfected the sulfuric acid baths to make the disposals so easy and problem free. *Sometimes, he thought the State of Texas should just pay him to take care of all the convicts they executed, God knows there were enough of them.* They should just turn the criminals over to the Black Knights and save the taxpayers a lot of money and anguish.

As he walked down the hallway toward the parking lot so he could get to football practice, a bubbly redheaded girl swooped around him and grabbed him by the arms, wrapping them around her.

"I haven't seen you all day," the girl said feigning a pout. "Were you trying to avoid me?"

"That's right, darling. Guess I am losing my touch 'cause here you are," Theo said. The girl either didn't understand the sarcasm or didn't care because she slid underneath Theo's arm and hugged up close to him.

"Do you want to pick me up after practice and take me back to your place? I can do that thing with my tongue you like so like so much."

"As tempting as that sounds, honey, I think I'll pass. Now do me a favor and go fuck yourself," he said with a smile and a kiss to the side of her head. The girl stopped in her tracks, her face melting into sobs. She had given her virginity to him last Saturday. He was already bored with her. *He did enjoy that fire crotch action, however*, he thought. He loved the way his cock looked sliding inside that fiery bush, his dark pubes blending in with her orange ones. Theo hopped in his Trans Am with the big feather design on the hood and roared off to the field house across the street.

Theo walked into the locker room like a B-list celebrity. Every boy was shouting out his name, high fiving, and giving him slaps on the ass. He got undressed and made sure to make the rounds of the locker room wearing his jockstrap. That always seemed to get plenty of stares from the guys. He enjoyed being the envy of most of the pasty, chunky guys whose bellies poured over the top of their supporter or else were emaciated stick-insect guys that looked like just walked out of Auschwitz. Five years from now, all these guys would look like hell, he figured. Might as well let them enjoy all this for now. In fact, the only guy in the whole locker room that could come close to his looks was goddamn Trey McGee. And his creamy brown skin, muscles, and big round ass made an even more impressive statement as he walked around the changing room half naked. Theo followed his ass as he bent over to slip on his football pants.

"Okay ladies, let's get with it, Coach Bates bellowed. Hope you brought your rubber ducky today 'cause it's a little damp out there."

Within ten minutes, the Tiger varsity squad was drenched to the bone. The boys were covered with mud and grass as they ran plays, ran dashes, and worked on special teams. Whereas most of the guys were putting in a half-assed effort today in the inclement weather, Theo watched Trey practice again like a man possessed. He was faster than anyone avoiding tackle after tackle, getting off the line and making it twenty yard down field before anyone knew where he was. He jumped defenders like a gazelle. When a safety or corner would close in on him, he kicked on an afterburner and left them gasping. And in the middle of this, Theo noticed, it looked like he was hardly breaking a sweat. The kid was grinning, that big white toothed grin that was set off by those big lips and slight dimples in his cheeks. When it came his time to block, Trey knocked Theo out of the air and on his ass, sliding ten feet in the mud. The kid even jogged over and reached out a muddy hand to help Theo up.

"Sorry about that hit, brother. Got lucky. Hope I'm still invited over," Trey said with a shit-eating grin.

"Bring it, big guy," Theo said slapping Trey on the ass leaving a big muddy handprint on the mostly white pants.

The coach called the team together to take a knee. "Alright men. This week at Quitman, we want to make another statement like we did last week. I want to see better blocking, O-Line get off your man and make them work for it, protecting the QB. Defense, keep playing tough. I like what I am seeing out there from Theo and the rest of you. And it goes without saying but ...pardon my French boys but, that goddamn Trey McGee is an animal." The team cheered and a short round of "McGee, McGee, McGee" rose up from the soggy high schoolers. The coach told the guys to hit the showers but called Trey over for a quick word. Theo busied himself with picking up cones and yard markers, straining to hear what the coach had to say.

"I don't know what you've been smokin' or puttin' on your Wheaties ...maybe you started getting laid, I don't care. You are the reason we have a chance to win district, Trey. You are playing the best ball of your career. I've had some calls from scouts and colleges. You keep this up and you have a real shot at a scholarship. Just keep your head screwed on right and don't get to full of yourself. You have some humility out here which helps, also makes the boys like you better. Don't be a wise ass like some of these guys, you know what I mean?"

"Yes Coach."

"Okay buddy. Go clean up," Coach said smacking Trey's rear.

When Trey walked into the showers he was the last guy there. Quarterback Bo reached over to give him a high five as they passed. Trey disappeared under the water letting it wash over his head as he held on to the wall. He was exhausted on the one hand, but felt better than he ever had on the other. He grabbed some soap and began to lather up his chest and worked his way down to his feet.

"You were flying around out there today, McGee."

Trey stood up quickly and turned around, bumping into Theo Martin, standing at the next shower wearing his normal sideways grin.

"Oh shit, Theo. You scared me. I thought I was the only one in here," Trey said. "But, uh, thanks. You were hitting me pretty good. It should be a great game this week."

"That it will," Theo said.

Trey went to turn off his water when Theo stepped closer to him. Trey turned and the two were standing inches apart.

"You missed a bunch of mud back here, bro. Turn around," Theo said with his usual authority. Trey robotically turned his back to him. Theo took his soap and washed away the splats of mud that still clung to Trey's neck and back, letting his hands linger on the strong brown back and slide down to his ass.

"Whoa, hopefully not too much mud up in my crack," Trey laughed scooting away from Theo. "Thanks for catching that."

"Sure thing. Let's get out of here and go soak in my hot tub. Just the thing for sore muscles."

"Wow, you have a hot tub? Cool. Okay sure, whatever you want to do," Trey said grabbing his towel.

"That sounds like a deal," Theo answered flipping off his water and grabbing his towel, following Trey out to the locker room.

Thirty minutes later, Trey was standing in Theo's family game room playing Space Invaders. Trey was grinning like an idiot standing at the console playing game after game in turns with Theo. The room was almost as big as the McGee's entire house. Large windows stretched from floor to ceiling on one side looking out on the pool and manicured grounds of the Martin estate. The room was so spacious that the carved legs of the pool table seemed almost small and insignificant. A foosball table and an air hockey game completed the person arcade.

"I can't believe you actually have a real arcade game like this. No quarters," Trey said like a moron. The boys finished the video game and then began to play pool. Theo loved watching guys be awed by his place, knowing they were so envious. It made having all the shit sweet once again since for the most part, he was bored with all of it. When they finished the game which Trey won, thanks to Theo sinking his 8-ball, Theo showed Trey the frozen margarita machine that was spinning the frozen concoction in slow, icy circles.

"It's like the ones in Mexican restaurants. Dad got it for mom's birthday. He says she is such a lush she needed one like another hole in the head." Trey giggled though he wasn't sure why. Theo grabbed a glass and poured it full of the frozen lime drink. Trey took a sip and grinned.

"Oh man, that is awesome."

Theo grabbed one for himself and took a big swig through a straw. "Ahhh," he said. "Brain freeze," he said laughing. "Hey, I just wanted to say, you are doing really good in the dumb musical. I know we were hating the idea of it and only going along to get some cred on our transcript for college and all that, but it's been fun. I didn't know you could sing at all."

"I'm pretty sure you are just yankin' my chain, but yeah, I like it more than I thought. A lot of kids are doing good. That Mary Washington has a great voice."

"Yeah. She's got a great ass too."

"I guess. With all that shit that happened to her, it seems kinda weird to think about it.

"I don't know…she's already broke in and everything…" Trey chuckled but his face belied his amusement. Theo could tell that struck a nerve. "Sorry. Guess that was a shitty thing to say. "Come on, let's take these to the hot tub." Theo put his glass dangerously on the edge of the pool table and pulled his shirt off over his head, kicking his shoes off at the same time. He hooked his thumbs in the waistband of his sweatpants and pushed them off along with his Calvin Klein briefs. Trey looked around nervously.

"Aren't your parents home?" Trey asked.

"No, not yet. No one here but Hazel, our maid, and probably Dub, the gardener." Theo stood naked in the game room relaxed, drinking his margarita.

"You don't care if they see?" Trey said.

"Fuck no. They've seen my dick ever since I was a baby. Probably the highlight of their day. Come on, McGee. Let's go. My drink is melting."

Trey put his drink down and pulled his clothes off leaving them in a pile on the floor like Theo. Trey grabbed his margarita and nervously looked around. "Lead the way, Garcon."

"Garcon is for the help," Theo said matter of factly. He led Trey though the hallway and through the great room, a cozy fire burning in the massive rock hearth. Theo turned and headed out through the kitchen. Just before they went through the French doors to the deck a low, smoky voice spoke.

"Who's your friend there, Mr. Theo?" Hazel said coming in from the pantry with an armload of potatoes, onions, and carrots. Trey almost dropped his drink and instinctively grabbed for his crotch trying in vain to cover himself.

"This is Trey, Hazel. He's staying for dinner."

"That sound good, Mr. Theo. Don't drink too many of them margaritas or you'll spoil your dinner." Theo turned to leave along with Trey who turned back to see Hazel staring fixedly at his rear. "Ooo child. That is one fine ass you got there, Mr. Trey. Mmm, now that's what I'm talkin' about." Trey bolted out the door and sprinted after Trey.

The boys traversed the patio and settled into the steamy, foaming water looking up at the sky. The clouds had left and stars were beginning to peek out. Trey eased down into the steamy water and leaned back taking sips of the icy drink.

"Wow, I would never get tired of this. You are so lucky," he said.

Theo looked at him and sighed. "It's only fun if you have someone else around to enjoy it with. Otherwise, it's boring just like everything else." He downed the rest of his drink and set the glass on the side of the hot tub. "I always forget that this is impressive to poor people."

Trey choked on his drink, bringing tears to his eyes. "Oh man, that made me choke. I'm not poor, you know. I'm just like normal. Most everybody in the world is like me. You are the different one."

"I guess you're right," Theo answered with a big grin.

The boys floated in the water and chatted about football and classes and teachers. They laughed about coach getting knocked on his ass by Big Fred Walker today at practice getting a face full of mud in the process.

Theo laughed. "He looked like one of those big grinning niggers from the old minstrel shows. Then he looked at Trey and added, "You don't take offense to me using that word, do you?"

"Uh, no. Why should I. Plenty of people do, especially around here." Trey grabbed his neck and stretched his muscles as his sat in the water.

"Hold on there, sport." Theo said scooting over sliding in behind Trey and gripping his neck, massaging the tight trapezius muscle. Trey closed his eyes and let the fingers dig into his sore muscle and relive the tension there. He kept thinking this was so cool, so amazing to get to sit here and float in the warm water relaxing with a drink. Theo was pretty good at unkinking tight muscles too he had to admit.

"Grab hold of the edge and float up. Let me get those quads. I know they are tired after today," Theo ordered. Trey flipped over and floated up in the water as Theo moved in between his legs working the knots out of his quadriceps. Trey thought, *this is so much nicer than when the assistant coach trainers at the field house work on you.*

"You've got some real skill there, Theo. You could always become an athletic trainer," Trey said as he continued to grip the edge. Theo's hands moving up from his knees along the tops of this thighs.

"I think my Daddy has higher aspirations for me than to be a glorified janitor," Theo said. He gripped Trey's muscled thighs in his hands and slid his hands further up as he pressed on the boys muscles.

"That's a little harsh. I mean they have to be trained and all . . . whoa," Trey said as Theo's hands closed around his dick and balls. "Watch it there. Coach. You're gonna give me the wrong idea."

Theo moved closer to Trey, his nose an inch away from his. Droplets of water hung in Trey's cropped hair and on his eyelashes. Those goddamn blue-green eyes. He reached around and put a hand on Trey's neck and pulled him into long, open-mouthed kiss. Trey reached out and gripped Theo's strong shoulders and eased him away.

"Hold on, Theo. Uh, I don't know what gave you the idea . . . but I don't like you that way. I like girls, you know? I mean, don't you have a girlfriend?"

"I have several. I fornicated with one in this hot tub three nights ago," Theo said his lips and face still uncomfortably close for Trey.

"Really? Wow, well then, I guess I don't get . . . you like boys too?"

"Not particularly. I like you. You are ten times more special than any tramp I've bedded this year. You and me, we are the best things about that shitty school."

Trey tried to ease away from Theo but he kept his strong hand on the back of Trey's neck. "That's nice of you to say, but I really don't want a boyfriend or whatever. Really. It's okay if you do. I won't tell anyone."

"That's not what I heard from Kevin Webb," Theo said reaching up and running his finger across Trey's eyebrow and down the side of his face to his lips. Trey pulled his head away.

"I don't know what you heard but that was just kid stuff, you know. Horny Boy Scouts in a tent. I'm sure you had a moment like that growing up."

"Several actually." Theo leaned in to kiss Trey again. Trey gripped his wrist and his hip in a flash and hoisted the boy out of the hot tub, hurling him toward the lounge chairs like a basketball. Theo's head struck one of the metal legs and he sank to the ground in a heap.

Trey stared. He looked around and then scrambled out of the hot tub. "Oh Jesus. Please don't be really hurt," Trey whispered. Trey felt for a pulse on his neck and not knowing really what he was doing, he put his ear on Theo's chest listening for a heartbeat, which he heard loud and strong. He felt a hand reach up between his legs to grip him.

"Now that was impressive, McGee. You have to tell me where this new strength of yours comes from." Trey reached down and slid himself free of Theo's grasp. Hazel stuck her head out of the kitchen.

"Mr. Theo. Yo' daddy will be here in about ten minutes. You boys better quit playing grab ass and get dried off for dinner." Trey turned to grab for a towel from the stack of them laying neatly in the basket by the back door. Hazel looked Trey up and down again and said, "Umhmm. That look good enough to eat off of."

Trey and Theo sat beside each other at the dinner table twenty minutes later, working their way through chicken and dressing, fried okra, cornbread and buttery lima beans. Caroline Martin was into her second glass of merlot. Trey noticed she didn't have much to say at the table. But JL Martin made up for it by talking enough for two.

"Well I tell you, Trey, when I saw you flying down that field last week, ripping right out of your uniform, your brown ass shining in the bright lights, I almost pissed myself. I mean it. There were tears in my eyes it was such a thing of beauty. You know, your dad was quite the football player himself. And I got to see both him and Carl Washington play college ball. They were quite the players and great friends too, from what I understand.

"Yes sir. I hear they were pretty good too. Lucky you got to see them and all that," Trey said with a mouthful of dressing, bits of food flying out and hitting the white tablecloth. Caroline closed her eyes in disgust as she took another drink of wine. "Um, sorry," Trey said seeing the woman's face.

"Don't worry about it, Trey. You boys must be so hungry after practice. I was sitting in the car watching y'all today. You were like a maniac out there. Knocked this one on his butt, that's for sure," JL said reaching over to ruffle Theo's hair. He left his hand on the side of his son's face. Theo reached up and rubbed his dad's hand.

Trey watched them. It was pretty clear to him they had a pretty special father-son relationship. He wondered what that would be like. He remembered after the game last week, the look of pride and joy on his dad's face. That embrace and kiss, the sweetest thing he remembered with his dad. It made his heart ache just thinking about it. Theo's left leg stretched wide and pressed against Trey's. Trey started to move it away but figured the idiot would probably just stretch out even more. So he left it there feeling Theo rub his leg lightly back and forth against his. All this going on while at the dinner table was almost more than he could deal with. Part of him wanted to kick Theo's ass. The other part was what was worrying him tonight, though.

They took their dessert in the family room, seated on a large sectional sofa with suede buckskin leather covering. Caroline sat in her chair working on a needlepoint of bluebonnets, having moved on to margaritas herself. Hazel served pecan pie a la mode and coffee that was more Irish than coffee, filled with Bailey's Irish Cream. Trey had to admit it was delicious. Theo sat on his couch, his sock clad feet rubbing casually against Trey's leg as he stretched out on the couch. Trey looked up and saw that Mr. Martin was watching him but not reacting in any way. Theo ate his pie and continued to stare at Trey. Trey's eyes suddenly grew wide and he swallowed his bit and spoke.

"Oh wow, I just remembered I never called my parents. They will think I'm dead on the side of the highway or something," Trey said clearly alarmed.

Theo put his pie down on the side table and practically crawled over Trey, stretching for the phone. "What's your number," he said in that languid lilt of his. His crotch was practically in Trey's face.

"886-3322," Trey answered pulling his face back.

Theo dialed the number. Trey was racking his brain trying to think of what to say when Theo spoke. "Is that Mr. McGee? Mr. McGee, this is Theo Martin. I wanted to call and apologize to you. I had invited Trey over for dinner tonight and I told him I would call you and make sure you knew and like a total jackass, I forgot. I hope you weren't too worried." There was a short pause and Theo continued. "Well, that's spectacular, Mr. McGee. We have had a great time. Trey worked me over so hard at practice today we both came back here and took a good long soak in the hot tub. Oh yes sir, it felt amazing. Trey will be coming back home right after dessert here. Thanks again and sorry for the bother. Good night, now." Theo hung up the phone.

"Your ass is saved," he said taking a long sip of his coffee. JL chuckled.

"That's my boy. Quite the public relations master already," JL said.

They finished up the dessert and Trey said his good nights. "I better get Trey back to his car at the high school before some fool tows it away," Theo said.

"Thanks very much for the dinner and everything. Your home is so nice," Trey said genuinely.

"You are so welcome. Please come back, Trey. You know, you running on that field. More than anything else reminds me of old Carl Washington. You have moves just like him. Isn't that strange? Such a shame how it seems he has turned out; an incestuous child rapist. Probably for the best he ran off, never to be heard of again."

Trey was so stunned by this he had no response other than, "Uh huh. Well, good night and thanks again."

Theo drove out of the wide concrete driveway, through the gate that said Twelve Oaks and back onto the county road headed to Hwy 24. He clicked on his cassette player and The Eagles "Lyin' Eyes" began playing. Theo took a half smoked joint out of his ashtray and lit it, handing the blunt to Trey who took a long drag and handed it back.

"Aren't you worried you might get caught, you know just leaving your weed in the car," Trey asked.

"Nope. They wouldn't dare," Theo said resolutely. They drove and turned onto Hwy 50 and back down toward Culver Street. "Thanks for coming over, McGee," Theo said handing the joint back. "I don't get that many decent people over. Most just want something or are trying to get on my good side. You are a good guy. Way better than me. Hope that's not going to be bad for you one of these days," he said enigmatically. "'Cause I really like you." He reached over and took Trey's hand, sliding his fingers in between the tanned fingers. Theo smiled when he saw Trey didn't pull his hand away. The boys rode the rest of the way like that, Theo's thumb slowly caressing the outside of Trey's smooth hand.

Theo pulled into the parking lot and up next to Trey's 1972 Toyota pickup, shining bright yellow in the orange glow of the parking lot lights. Trey slid his hand away from Theo's and turned to leave. Theo gripped Trey by the back of the neck and pressed his face against his smooth cheek, his eyes closed, breathing in his smell. Trey reached up and held Theo's face lightly against his hand for a moment and then pulled away, giving him a weak smile that said so much.

"Our secret," Theo said. Trey nodded patting him on the leg as he climbed out of the Trans Am. Theo put the gas down, burning off into the night leaving Trey stunned standing beside his truck.

Theo lay on his side listening to the radio much later that night. He saw the door to his room open, light splashing across his open window. He felt the mattress sink down as his dad sat on the edge. His dad rubbed his hand across Theo's strong bicep and across his chest.

"Thanks for bringing the McGee boy over here tonight. I needed a bit of up close time with him. You're right. He's quite the find. If my suspicions are correct, he will be the most perfect offering we have ever had." JL's hand slid though Theo's soft curls. "You never cease to amaze me, son. I love you, Theo," JL said softly leaning down and kissing his son's cheek.

A single tear slid down Theo's nose and onto his cheek. "Love you too, Daddy."

30 Emily

The teenagers drove along highway 24 out of Cowhill toward Delta County in the light blue 1968 VW beetle, sunroof open, stars and moonlight streaming down. George drove the little car expertly along the highway, making sure to stick to the speed limit. He tried not to continue to look in the rear-view mirror at the couple tangled together in the back seat. The moonlight glinted on their faces, wet with kisses, as the two continued to try and swallow each other whole.

Emily gripped tightly around Travis's arms feeling his growing biceps beneath his t-shirt. She ignored the stares through the rear-view mirror. All she knew was she loved this boy. He was good and kind and sweet. There was something else too, she wasn't sure exactly what it was, but she wanted it. She wanted it to pour over and cover every part of her. She could feel the energy too. Whatever it was that they were experiencing, it was stronger and more powerful than ever. It took all of her control to stop and not take that next step, that big leap that seemed so right and so perfect right this minute except for the little troll that was driving them right now, looking hateful in the mirror. But since he continued to look she might as well give him a little show.

She reached down and gripped the shirt tail of Travis's t-shirt and pulled it up past his belly and then over his head before she went back to kissing him. His chest was smooth and cool, with goose bumps that she could feel like Braille against her fingers. The soft tufts of armpit hair she touched were slightly damp. She rubbed her fingers against his arms and down to his belly, feeling the trail of soft hair that disappeared into his cutoff jeans. She knew this was unfair and probably would give Travis a terrific case of blue balls, but it was just too much fun. As the *pièce de résistance*, she ripped her own shirt over her head and arched her back as she felt the night air on her skin, her bra shining pearly white in the moonlight. The Beetle veered over to the right shoulder of the road and George over-corrected slightly, causing the two teens to tumble into the cramped floorboard.

"Watch it you idiot," Emily scolded crawling back up into her seat, accidently kneeing Travis in the nuts which elicited a loud "Oh Shit" hiss from his side of the car. George looked murderously at Emily in the rear-view mirror, adjusting the growing bulge in his own shorts.

"We are almost there in case you two want to put your clothes on," George said.

"I thought the idea was to strip anyway," Emily snapped back slipping her shirt back over her slim shoulders.

Travis interjected, "Actually you are supposed to try and not strip, remember. You only have to strip if you lose."

The week at school had been mostly normal for the three with only slight deviations now and then with their powers. It seemed like they were all more easily linked together than ever now, especially after last Friday night. It also didn't seem to take quite the toll on them unless they were really concentrating. Emily remembered sitting in her Math class with the Duck and sensing Travis and George all the way out in shop class. Brenda Thomas was making a big show of going up to the electric pencil sharpener with two new pencils. She had on some new platform clogs and a short pink skirt. For some reason it was really annoying Emily. She knew she shouldn't let things like that bother her. But right as she got up to go sharpen her pencils, she stumbled a bit on the tall clogs and fell against Justin Taylor, a cute dark-haired boy that Emily had always liked. It didn't seem like a real slip to Emily and she didn't like the girl gripping Justin around the neck to steady herself. Justin had smiled and then looked at Emily who was steaming, which made him redden and look down at his book.

Brenda shook her skinny ass down the aisle and went to the pencil sharpener and placed her hot pink pencil in the machine. The sharpener roared to life and in two seconds, whittled Brenda's pencil down to a two-inch nub. The look on her face when she pulled the tiny pencil from the jaws of the sharpener was priceless. She put her next pencil in the sharpener, holding it hard to keep it from getting gobbled up. The blades took off devouring the pencil. She gripped it with two hands and the whirring gears whined so loudly that the Duck and half of the class looked up. Brenda lost hold of the pencil and the blades chomped the wood down to the eraser and kept going throwing up a cloud of rubber, metal, and wood back up into Brenda's face. She screamed.

"Stop playing with that sharpener, Miss Thomas. Sit down. I'm giving you a dot for that," Dr. Peters quacked. Dots were her special disciplinary tool. If you disrupted class, were tardy, whispered or passed notes, or took too long in the bathroom, she made a "dot" in her grade book which would lower your citizenship grade on your report card.

Brenda turned to go back to her seat, her face now smeared with pencil lead and eraser stubble. Emily rubbed her foot on the floor. *The floor is so slippery,* she thought. Brenda took another step and her clog slipped on the now slick-as-ice tile floor. She fell, sprawling on the tile, her short skirt flipping up revealing white panties stained brownish from small leaks in her maxi pad. Her clog sailed through the air and hit David Baker in the head knocking him out of his chair. The class roared, the Duck quacked, and Emily slunk low in her chair and kept working. *You are worse than the boys,* she thought.

The three teens had also tried to do some good that week instead of pranks. During one class they saw Mary Washington sitting alone in the library, she was reading an Essence magazine, but they noticed her face was wet with tears. Emily told the boys how poorly she was doing in many of her classes. She had seen more than one test paper returned with a big red F scrawled across the top. Emily and the boys walked up to her table. Emily reached out a hand to grab Mary's, asking her if she was okay. The boys walked around to the back of her chair and very lightly touched her shoulder. She flinched and looked around almost in terror. But Emily grasped her hand and said it was fine. They are just worried about you too. But in that moment, they had zapped her with a big dose of their powers. For the rest of the week, Mary was less tearful; she aced every test, and began to talk again in class.

George rolled down the long driveway to the Delta County Country Club, which was a country club in name only. It was a sad log cabin structure and a pokey 9-hole course that was hardly distinguishable from the cow pastures that surrounded it. But it was the course that Mike McGee had taken the boys out to teach them how to golf, mostly because it was a public course that had a whopping green fee of $3 per person. Cart rental was another $5. The boys were basically glorified caddies because Mike never paid the extra $5 each for them to play. But when they were on the far side of the course, he would let them play. They also had to clean the golf balls in the ball washers, keep an eye out for oncoming players while Mike took a long noisy piss in the middle of the fairway or against a tree, and look for all the balls that got lost due to Mike's impossible slice that sent the ball into the rough most of the time. Emily had heard about the last time the boy had played with Travis's dad. Mike was hogging his turn driving the cart as usual with George in the middle and Travis on the other seat. Mike and George were constantly fighting over the steering wheel. On one steep portion of the course, Mike grabbed the wheel and turned it hard left while George gripped it and pitched it back hard right which ended up catapulting Travis out of the cart like a rocket, tumbling down the hill shouting "Goddamn it!!" Travis had expected the wrath of god to descend on his head for that slip of the tongue, but when he got back, both George and Mike were laughing so hard they were practically crying.

Emily climbed out of the Beetle and looked around at the silvery grass like a shining carpet in front of them. "Are you sure it's okay to do this? Don't they have a security guard or something?"

Both boys laughed. Travis said, "My dad says we are lucky they have toilet paper in the johns, this place is really cheap. The last time we were here we just drove the bug around the course like a cart. No one came around." George reminded both of them to leave their shoes and wallet and purse in the car. Emily didn't ask why but it sounded pretty reasonable.

Emily was shocked and asked quickly, "We aren't going to do that this time, are we? I mean, we aren't going to drive a car on the golf course?"

Travis laughed. "Nah, that was probably dumb last time. We'll just walk. So you remember the rules?"

Emily walked with the boys toward the first tee, Travis lugging the small bag of clubs that George has somehow extracted from the front trunk of the bug. "It's just like regular golf. Try to have the lowest amount of strokes on the hole. The other two have to strip off something the winner of hole tells them two. And no fair using your powers"

"We'll try not to stare at your boobs when you lose in a little while, probably by Hole 7," George added with a toothy grin.

"And I will try not to laugh at your wiener when you lose by hole 6," Emily smirked then added, "Or your pasty butt, McGee."

By the time the kids were on the water hazard on Hole 3, Travis was down a shirt and shoes. Emily was down socks and her shirt. Her bra glimmered in the silvery moonlight as she teed up on Number 3. She lined up the shot and took and smooth stroke with her 5 iron and sent the ball in a clean arc over the water and landed lightly on the center of the dewy green. Both Travis and George sent their shots into the drink. Travis decided to take a drop on the far side. George tried three more times before getting on the other side. He lost the hole and his shirt to Emily's delight. She had a sneaky suspicion that at the end of the day, the boys were going to be way more intimidated by running around in their underwear in front of her than the other way round.

Emily's next drive was long and straight. Both of the boys hooked left and ended up in the weeds. Five minutes later, both Travis and George were in their jockey shorts, glowing like snow in the moonlight. Emily had opted to go for the big item and let them keep their shoes. Emily noticed George's face was ruddy in the moonlight and figured he was hot enough to fry an egg. Travis was attempting to be cool about everything, but it was obvious that the same condition that happened in the middle of algebra class when he got called up to the chalkboard to work a problem was happening right now. Emily grinned as he kept nonchalantly trying to hide his growing boner to no avail.

Emily lost her pants on Hole number 6 while George lost his socks. One more loss for either of them and it was going to get interesting, she figured. But for some reason, she was loving this whole experience. At Hole 7, the kids shared a joint that George produced from nowhere along with a lighter. She decided it was safer not to ask where the blunt had been stashed and hoped to God it wasn't in the little turd's crack. The night wind was cool and the smoke from the weed drifted high above them before it dissipated into the night. They settled back against the trunk of the huge oak that sheltered the tee box.

"That was the coolest thing ever, what we did for Trey," Emily said exhaling smoke from her nostrils.

"Yeah," Travis added looking down at his shorts. "It was so amazing watching that happen. I watched those scouts up in the press box. They were practically wetting themselves when he pulled out of his uniform. Leave it to Trey to run around naked in front of half the town and not have a problem in the world with it. Travis scooted down and felt the cool night air play over his bare chest, looking at the stars poking through the dark canopy of leaves that were already beginning to fall from the massive tree. The Indian summer was hanging on, even if the trees were giving up their leaves.

"I think we did a good job with it tonight too," George said taking the joint from Travis. "He played great again, but maybe not so crazy. He was still super-fast and those Quitman defenders were bouncing off him like he was made of rubber....and, he managed to keep his clothes on,"

The Tigers had beat Quitman 40-8 and Trey had scored three touchdowns. He had gone from zero to hero and was playing practically every down now. "Do you think he knows? I mean, he probably has the power too, right? He was out there in the light with us," George asked.

"I don't know for sure, but yeah, I'm thinking he must. I know Andy has some of it but I don't know if he understands it," Travis said.

"Well if that's true, then there could be others. I mean, we weren't the only ones outside that night," Emily added.

Travis put his hands behind his head and soon he felt Emily settle in beside him, turning on her side and wrapping an arm around his belly. Travis smiled as he felt George settle in beside him as well, laying his head on his friend's arm. Emily figured this was about as nice a feeling as she could remember: sandwiched against her two best friends. *That's weird. Do I really consider George one of my best friends now,* she thought? Emily felt Travis's heart beat strong and hard against her palm as hand lay on his warm chest. The cool breeze and the comfort of laying by her friends was soporific. Travis ran his hand lightly across Emily's hair as the three lay quietly under the spangled blanket of stars. She closed her eyes and the image of the green light flowed easily into her mind.

This time all three friends were standing on the edge of the dilapidated bridge, looking over the rotting planks toward the far side and the green light that shown in a steady, persistent emerald glow. The air was alive, pulsing and vibrating with energy. All around them the chant whispered like a scratched 78 stuck in a groove.

Red light . . . yellow light . . . green light bridge

Just down the hill from Scatter Branch ridge

Devil's on the switch, change the road to red

Better be green or you'll end up dead

The trio gripped each other's hands tightly and even though they were leaning back with all their might, some force like a giant cowcatcher was pushing them forward. Emily looked down at her feet as they plowed through dust and scraped against the old boards. The teens made the old structure crick-crack as their feet were pushed from plank to rotting plank toward the chasm looming in front of them. They held their collective breath as the toes of their sneakers met open air and still they felt themselves pushed forward. The arches of their feet passed into open and air. Only the heels of their shoes remained on the planks and then a giant hook seemed to wrap around their backbone and jerked them into the inky blackness separating them from the light.

The teenagers slammed back against the cool damp ground with a thud that knocked the breath out of them, cutting off their joint scream of terror. They lay motionless for a moment, hearts pounding like Taiko drums on Chinese New Year. Emily lifted her head and looked at the boys who were staring back, wide-eyed and frozen, goose bumps rose like a lunar landscape across their bare legs, ivory in the moonlight.

"Why the fuck does that keep happening?" George whispered through clinched teeth.

"I don't know," Travis said, "But that time was the clearest it's ever been. Probably because we are all here together, touching and everything."

"What is that place?" Emily asked sitting up and pulling her knees up to her chest, suddenly feeling vulnerable and silly for being so undressed.

"It's Green Light Bridge," George said. "Like in the song. You've heard that story before haven't you?

"Sure, but that's just some stupid camp story like 'Bloody Mary' or something."

"Well either way, we've all been seeing that place since this thing started," Travis added. "I'm pretty sure it has something to do with all of this. There is definitely something out there that has something to do with our powers. We ought to go out there and take a look."

"That sounds like a load of laughs," George added sitting up and looking around. "We're lucky no one heard us. I think we were all screaming our heads off. So, do you want to just go home?"

"Hell no, Georgie-Boy. You aren't getting out of this that easily," Emily said getting to her feet and grabbing a 3 wood.

Travis looked at his buddy and grinned, "You heard the lady. Time to put up or strip down."

Hole number 8 was a 275 yard par 4. Emily teed up her shot making sure both boys got a good look at her backside as she bent down provocatively to place the ball. She playfully looked through her legs and smiled as she watched both of them reflexively place a hand over their crotches trying to convince their libido to go away. She addressed the ball with a couple of wide wiggles and swung the club in a smooth arc. The ball smacked off the tee and sailed pretty as a picture toward the middle of the fairway. George went next and managed a decent drive but swore loudly as it hit a divot and landed right against the rough well short of Emily's shot. Travis felt the club twist in his sweaty hands as he swung toward his ball. It smacked loudly against the ball which caromed off to the right and directly into the rough.

George exploded in laughter chanting "Show us your dong, show us your dong."

Emily grabbed a 7 iron and smiled as her shot sailed straight for the green and bounced casually toward the flag. George shouted another string of obscenities making Emily smile even wider. George's stroke slammed into the ground before the head of his club struck the ball and sent it limping forward twenty feet. Emily roared along with Travis while George continued to cuss a blue streak. Travis hacked at his ball through the tall rough and managed to get it back to the fairway but woefully short of the green. The boys took turns slicing and dicing their way to the green. George's face was glowing red in the pale moonlight by the time he made it to the green.

"Looks like it's gonna be sausage time soon," Emily sang as she lined up her putt and sent the ball toward the pin. Her eyes widened as it began to veer left and she saw it turn back right and roll steadfastly toward the cup with a gurgle as it tipped inside. Emily did a little dance around the green to the sounds of George's protestations.

"Cheater. I saw you zap your shot. There is no way that was going in the hole," George griped.

"Tell you what, you can use your powers all you want on this hole," Emily said with a smirk.

"Yeah, now you say that when it's too late to catch up," George said huffing, arms folded defensively in front. Travis walked up to him and leaned close to his ear, hanging his arm around his neck.

"Buddy, there was no way we were ever gonna get out of this deal without showing our dicks. You and I are terrible at golf. Don't be a douche, just go with it. It'll be funny. Em isn't gonna make fun of our wieners."

"So you to say," George said back in a low voice and sighed. "Guess she might as well see that if she's wanting size, she's picked the wrong guy."

"In your dreams, John Holmes," Travis said reaching around and gripping George's nipple in a tight titty-twister. George swung around a punched Travis square in the nuts.

Travis groaned and hunched forward with a low "Shiiiiiit" escaping his lips.

"Come on y'all," Emily commanded. "Finish up and drop 'em."

The boys tapped out on the hole and walked over to Emily, turning their back to the girl whose grin was flashing bright in the moonlight. On cue, George and Travis began a trombone duet with their voices, sliding right into "The Stripper," one of the tunes they had recently learned in band. The boys swung their hips back and forth as they slid down their briefs in sync with the music. Their revealed butt cheeks glowed brightly in the silvery light as they moved slowly down to their knees and then dropped to the ground. Both boys kicked them wildly into the night air and spun around in a big pirouette complete with jazz hands.

Emily shrieked in laughter and put both hands up over her face. "Oh my God, it's horrible. Too many boy parts and they are like all big and everything."

"That's right baby, biggest in the county. Don't be covering up your eyes. You are the one who wanted to see all this awesome manliness," Travis said folding his arms along with George and standing with his legs spread wide saluting the giggling girl proudly. George's face still glowed red in the silvery light but a wry smirk crossed his face as well. Travis knew for a fact it was probably the first time someone other than George's family or he had ever seen the twerp naked and it was hysterical seeing him all emboldened for a change.

"Guess it's time to finish the game," George said grabbing a 2 wood and walking to the tee box. Emily continued to giggle uncontrollably, peeking through her fingers right as George bent down to tee up the ball. She exploded in a huge shriek again and ran back toward the last hole.

"Oh no, you don't," Travis said taking off after her. "We have another hole to play."

"I've just seen my last HOLE tonight," she yelled as she ran further away laughing loudly.

"Hey unfair," George said standing stupidly holding the club, trying to act nonchalant.

Emily continued to run toward the last hole when a spitting, sizzling sound filled the air and the sprinklers clicked on, soaking the trio of them with cold jets of icy water. The kids howled and ran away from the jets only to run into the next set going off. In the middle of all this, Emily unfastened her bra and pushed down her panties, holding them in her hand as she continued to run away from the water. The boys followed, laughing, chasing her shimmering ivory form skipping through the night like a Naiad dancing to the full moon around her magical water source. The laughing and chasing filled the air with musical shouts and cat-calls and George moaning loudly.

"Oh Jeez, my balls are about to snap off." Suddenly, the night was punctuated by a gruff, growling voice.

"Hey, who's out there? You kids ain't supposed to be on the course. What the hail do you think yer doing? This is sum bullshit! If I ketch you little monsters I will have yer hide. Jesus, keep me near the Cross - is you kids nekkid? Holy Ghost on Toast!"

"Run for it!" Travis shouted as the teens bolted toward the VW scrabbling to pick up clothes along the way. They tumbled into the car with the course caretaker shouting after them, waving a flashlight.

"Git back here y'all nekkid heathen!!

"Drive," Emily gasped through her breathless laughter pulling her t-shirt and panties back on.

"Shit, I don't even have my clothes on or anything," George complained.

"JUST GO!" Travis and Emily shouted in chorus.

George started the Beetle, thanking God he'd left the key in the ignition, and jammed his bare foot on the gas and tore out of the parking lot, past the caretaker who was shaking his fist and his flashlight.

"You nekkid sum-bitches, Git back here!"

The teens shouted war whoops back at the man. Emily stood up and lifted her t-shirt as she poked through the sunroof, waving like a homecoming queen at the man who now was standing still, mouth open at the fleeing Bug. Travis rolled down the back window and stuck his ass out to join with Emily's goodbye and the actual full moon that was illuminating the long driveway like a silver ribbon. George punched in his 8-Track of Fleetwood Mac's "Rumours" and the strains of "Don't Stop" boomed from the speakers as they roared out of the driveway and back on to Hwy 24.

Travis tiptoed around the corner of his house and eased the squeaky backdoor open gradually, grimacing with the moaning of the springs as he opened the door wide enough for Emily and George to get inside. Emily was still in her t-shirt and panties. Her soggy jeans were laid on the bottom step of the back porch. George had managed to grab his jeans but they were soaked as well. His underwear was somewhere back on the golf course and he had his shirt tied around his waist like a loincloth. Travis had his underwear on, but his jeans were soaked and his shirt was lost as well. Travis held his finger up to his mouth and looked in the door to his brothers' bedroom. Trey was sawing logs in a loud snore, one hairy leg out of the covers. Andy was curled up beside him unaware of anything but his dreams. Travis closed the door and looked back at the two teens standing awkwardly in the doorway of the porch. He glanced over at the digital clock radio. Almost 3:00 AM. He went over to his dresser and pulled out a pair of underwear for George to pull on. George dressed quickly and pulled his shirt on afterwards. Travis jumped into his bed and Emily crawled over him and snuggled into the spot between Travis and the wall. Travis spooned around her, pulling her tightly against himself. George stood on the outside, the frown on his face illuminated by the setting moon. He pulled the covers back and crawled into the bed as well, snuggling up closely behind Travis, wrapping his arm around Travis's waist to hold on and not fall out of the bed. Travis felt his heart rate slow its pounding against Emily's back. Her hands gripped his tightly around her. The smoothness of her skin against his legs was silky and warm. That was contrasted with the scratchy fur from George's legs that were pressed against the back of his legs. He could feel George's breath, hot and steady on his neck as his friend's hand wedged its way between Emily's back and his belly.

Morning light was filling the back porch when Andy crawled up in the middle of the bed and shook Travis awake. Travis's eyes opened blearily and focused on his younger brother, grinning widely.

"Dad is gonna whip your butt if he catches all you in the bed together," Andy said with a giggle.

From across the room a much deeper voice added, "Shit, I don't know why I'm always the one getting in trouble. I've never had a threesome," Trey added with a smirk. "But I think you need some help figuring out how this thing is supposed to work. You and idiot boy are supposed to both be banging the girl. Not her watching you bang your boyfriend."

Travis raised his head and the penny dropped. He was cuddled up spooning George who had an incomprehensible grin on his sleeping face while Emily was wedged against the wall, her face pressed against the window. She woke and half her face was dented with the waffle print of the screen. Travis pushed George away, who promptly fell out of bed with an "Oof."

"Damn, kid. That is a serious tent pole you got there, brother" Trey mocked. Travis grabbed a discarded flip-flop resting in the window and hurled it at Trey's wicked grin. The tall boy easily dodged it and turned toward George. "Bet you were having a sweet dream sitting on that thing, faggot," he said ruffling George's hair.

"Shut up!" George pulled his t-shirt down further to cover his early morning erection. Andy giggled and bounced off the bed.

"Y'all better get moving or y'all's ass will be grass."

Travis crawled out of the tangled covers and found a pair of sweatpants on the floor and pulled them on.

"He's right. Get out of here, you two. You were supposed to wake up hours ago." Emily slid out of bed gracefully and gave Travis a big kiss on the side of his face before casually skipping down the stairs and heading off toward her house through the back yard.

"Do you have any shorts I can wear?" George grumbled as he stood awkwardly, legs pressed together and his hand holding down his morning salute.

"Hey, here you go sport," Trey said lobbing a pair at George's head. The boy caught them and then realized it was a stained jock strap, with the funk of a hundred football practices cooked inside the pouch. George ripped the pouch off his face and lunged at Trey.

"You motherfu.."

"Now, now. Language!" Trey chided, laughing and easily holding George's attack at bay.

Travis grabbed George and pushed him back. "Just go. Run and no one will see you. You have to get back now." George gave Trey one more seething look and started for the door.

"Hey, no kiss?" Trey teased. "That hardly seems fair."

"Shut the fuck up, Trey," Travis hissed. "Run!" he commanded to George who was balling his fists ready to attack Trey. He watched as George crouched low and ran through the backyard and over the fence toward his own house, bare white thighs and darker brown knees flashing in the morning sun.

"So brother, did you have fun double pumping your little friends last night?"

"What does that mean?" Andy asked with rapt attention. "And you said that F word," looking back at Travis.

"Nothing. Just forget it, Andy. And Trey, unless you want Dad to know you are continuing to do plenty of double pumping with Angie Matlock yourself, shut the hell up," Travis said in a low morning growl that sounded a lot more ferocious than normal. Trey leaned against the doorway to the porch and smiled, but Travis noticed the smile was far less bright than a few moments earlier.

"You don't know shit," Trey said.

"Yeah, sure, brother," Travis said with sarcasm dripping from the corners of his mouth. He didn't bother to explain how he and George had followed him to the tree house some days before and easily overheard the loud lovemaking session. They hadn't even needed to use their power. "I hope you are wearing a rubber. Otherwise, your ass is the one going to be grass."

"What's a rubber? Is it that balloon thing you put on your wiener? How does that work and what's it for? Mike Tomlinson and me found one of those in his brother's dresser drawer. Mike calls them Trojans," Andy chattered away like a chipmunk.

"I'll leave you to explain all that, Brother," Travis said heading toward the bathroom.

When Travis got out of the shower he noticed Trey was a lot less chatty. Sitting at the kitchen table in his shorts eating a mixing bowl full of Count Chocula. He was intent reading the back of the box, no doubt trying to make his way through the maze game that was printed there.

Small rivulets of choclately milk ran down the corner of his mouth and dropped onto his chest. Travis watched the drops bead up on the scattering of hairs across his chest, drops the same color as his skin.

"So I figure Mom and Dad are up and gone already?" Travis asked getting a bowl from the cupboard. "You or Andy could have said that this morning."

"What's the fun in that?" Trey mumbled through a huge mouthful of cereal.

Travis rolled his eyes and sat down pulling the cereal box out of Trey's hands.

"Hey!"

Travis tipped the near empty box into his bowl and frowned at the pathetic amount left over. He shoved the box back over to Trey and grabbed the milk.

"You're pretty touchy today for a kid that got to screw his girlfriend last night …and Emily!"

"You're a regular Richard Pryor," Travis said with disgust. The two boys sat in silence, Trey munching his cereal like a hog at the trough. Travis tried to hear the television over the slurps and crunching. Andy was clearly watching Saturday morning cartoons. It must have been a Multiplication Rock break. "Figure 8, is double 4…" Travis looked at Trey as the song continued. *How come he is so different than me,* he thought. We have almost nothing in common. We don't even look alike. As he ate his paltry bit of cereal he kept wondering why? He and Andy seemed pretty much carbon copies of each other, and of Mike McGee for that matter. Trey stood up and belched loudly as he lifted a leg and ripped a booming fart that echoed across the kitchen tile. He bent over and wiggled his butt back and forth, the seat of the white briefs stretched far beyond their expected size.

"You had quite the night again last night," Travis said munching on his cereal. Travis ran some water in the cereal bowl and came back to the table and grabbed the newspaper folded on the side. "And don't act like that's the first time you have looked in the paper."

"Just thought you might want to check it out too, little bro," he said warm and syrupy, plopping the open paper down in front of Travis. The sports section headline blazed:

"McGee Muzzles Dogs" and underneath that "Star Tight End Makes History."

"Wow, from benchwarmer to star in just two games."

"Shut up, Scrote. I never was just a benchwarmer. I got in games all the time."

Travis wanted to bring up the fact that it was usually late in the fourth quarter of most games when the Tigers were hopelessly behind or so far in front all the second and third stringers got in. But he let it go. Trey was reading his press, probably for the third or fourth time, a subtle grin across his face.

"So why was last week so magical, you think? And last night was pretty great too. You just get lucky or are you really that good?"

Trey looked up from the paper, clearly ready to make his usual smartass reply, but he stopped short. He looked intently at Travis, back down at the paper for a moment at the large photo of himself ripping free of his jersey from last week, his face ablaze with wildness and intent. New photos of him from this week's game demolishing the Quitman defensive line with that look of wildness in his eyes beside them. He looked up again and Travis was startled to see light flashing across his watering eyes.

"It was like magic, or the power of God, or something. I never felt like that before, so strong and fast. It was like I was on fire or glowing hot inside. And the weirdest thing, none of it surprised me. I just knew I could make the plays or make the tackles or pull away from the defenders."

Travis watched his brother stretch a finger out toward the photo and trace along his outline, as if by doing so he could feel that magic once again. "What if it does just happen once or twice? What if the guy those scouts saw last week just managed to have one or two perfect nights and then goes back to being the regular fuck-up he always is?"

Travis moved around the table and stood next to his brother. He reached down and grabbed his hand and at the same time, reached up and grabbed Trey by the neck and pulled him forward until his forehead touched his brother and their minds exploded in green light. He gripped the boy tightly, not letting him pull away. In that connectedness, he saw Trey running back naked from Angie's, saw his dad and the belt, and saw him sitting on the bench waiting for the coach to give him a chance. And then he was inside the tree house and Angie was there and he was holding her, kissing her, and then was sliding inside. Trey's eyes had been closed but they flew open as the images from Travis's mind began to fill them: the bell, the disc sander, the storm, the music, the golf game, and then the football game and the three of them standing there holding hands. Suddenly, the boys were standing on the ramshackle bridge again, their feet moving imperceptibly toward the yawing chasm of black, pulled there by that green light…"better be green or you'll end up dead." The boys looked at each other, wind ripping and pulling at their hair and Travis's shirt. They were holding hands, slowly feeling that pull toward the edge of the bridge. Travis turned his head and looked directly into Trey's dawning realization.

Trey gripped Travis by the shoulders and pushed him away, falling back into the floor. With fear and confusion in his eyes, the dark boy scrambled to his feet and across the floor to the cabinets beside the stove. He held on to them and looked back up at Travis.

"All that shit is true? I just thought it was a dream," he began. "You mean you and Em and George did this? It was you?"

"No. Well, some but not all of it. It was you last night," Travis tried to explain. "We just helped."

"What do you mean, you helped? How is that possible?"

Travis began to walk Trey through the story, from the night the lights arrived until last night. He looked perplexed, his face darkening as he tried to wrap his mind around it. Every few moments, Travis saw the look of dawning realization cross his face; sometimes accompanied with a smile sometimes with a look of shock or worry.

"So together, you like zapped me and made me four times better, faster?"

"More than that. Since you were part of it, it was more like sixteen times better."

"But there's just four of us counting me."

"I know, but it's like every time you link together, it multiplies the power times itself or something. So it's more like 2 x 2 x 2 x 2, and that's not eight, it's sixteen.

"So by yourself you double stuff, and together it gets multiplied more?"

"That's pretty much what we think. And we don't know why it seems to be happening to us and not everybody. Maybe it's got something to do with us being kids and that we are still growing. Maybe it's just a few people got zapped by that light. Maybe there are a ton more people with powers but they haven't figured it out yet or maybe it takes time for them to get switched on."

"You think Angie's got it?" Trey asked with mounting worry in his voice.

"Possibly. Have you maybe felt that energy connection with her?" Travis asked almost knowing the answer before he said it.

Trey looked at his brother with a smirking realization. "Yeah. And you should know that since you were just in my head…and dick." It was Travis's turn to let the truth drop like a bowling ball into his belly. He looked up sheepishly at his brother and a frown furrowed his brow.

"Oh God, Trey."

"So if my spunk is twice as powerful just because of me. Then with her having the power too, she's like…way more likely to get pregnant, right?" Travis nodded, swallowing down the realization like a week-old hushpuppy. "Oh Lord, I am so dead," Trey moaned collapsing into a chair, burying his face in his hands. Travis sat beside him and put a hand tenderly on the big boy's muscled shoulder.

"Maybe it will be okay," Travis offered lamely. "It doesn't always work, right? I mean you don't have a baby every time you do it or anything. Just, take it easy and maybe don't do it with her anymore," but he figured that was like telling the sun not to rise tomorrow morning. "And always use a rubber," he added as if he really understood what he was talking about.

"Thanks, Dad," Trey answered with sarcasm. "I kept blowing them out so I just stopped using them."

Travis grimaced at the thought of Trey's soggy condom blow out and decided to change the subject, "Did you get to talk to mom and dad about last night? I bet they were really proud again"

Trey looked up and the tired, worry slipped away from his face as he thought about the week. Just a few moments ago it was the week of his life. Now it seemed compromised and tainted. "Last week, Mom just hugged me and cried and everything. Dad came over and grabbed me and hugged me like never before and kissed me right on the mouth."

"Wow."

"I know. Told me he loved me and everything. If only I had known I just needed to be Superboy to get him to do that, I would have done it a long time ago. All the guys at school have been high-fiving me and girls have been all flirty. The teachers have been cool and nicer and stuff." Trey walked over to the fridge and grabbed the carton of milk and tipped it up and gulped down in long, noisy swallows. A river of milk trickled out of the corner of his mouth, down Trey's chest. The cartoon in the other room must have ended and another Schoolhouse Rock song started up: "Interjections. Show excitement or emotion, generally set apart from a sentence by an exclamation point. Or by a comma when the feeling's not as strong…" Trey wiped his mouth with the back of his hand and croaked out a loud burp once again.

"So, what's this dream thing we keep having, that light and the bridge? It's like we are all there and there's others too. Like in the background too. Have you seen them too?

"Yeah," Travis said. "We've all seen them. We think those two guys right behind us might be Jack from Western Auto and Tim, his business partner."

"Why them?"

"No idea. George has probably a clearer picture of all the others than I do because he figured out the dream and more of this stuff before any of us did. Behind the Western Auto guys might be a couple of other kids, one dark, one small but lighter. George thinks they might be you and Andy. Behind you, it's much harder to guess but we've all had glimmers of who they might be."

Trey leaned back in the chair until the back tipped against the wall of the kitchen, his big feet dangling in the air. "So can we like fly or something?"

"We don't think so," Travis laughed. "George said though that technically, if you got enough people with powers together and they thought about reversing gravity hard enough, you might be able to make someone float or something. But Trey, you have to be careful. Whenever you join together to magnify the power, it stresses out your body. It gives me bad nosebleeds. Emily gets light-headed and sometimes faints. George barfs all over the place.

"So what happens to me? My clothes rip off like The Hulk?"

Travis thought back to the spreading piss bloom darkening the crotch of Trey's football pants the night of the Cooper game. "Um, do you remember any weird stuff happening when you were playing last week or last night?"

"You mean weirder than being a football god and ripping out of my uniform? I'm glad that didn't happen last night. I don't know. That was weird last week when I ended up running up to you and George in the band."

Travis smiled. "That was when we zapped you. But we think it worked a lot more than normal 'cause you had the power too so it was really multiplied.

Trey looked up toward the ceiling, closed his eyes, and concentrated. He muttered to himself as he thought. Then this eyes snapped open and he glared at Travis.

"Holy Shit, Batman. I pissed my pants. That's my thing? You get a nosebleed and I need a fucking diaper? I wet myself again last night, but just a little. Why can't I have like a giant boner or grow a beard or something?"

Travis laughed. "Yeah, that would be way better."

Andy came in from the living room. "Someone keeps saying tons of bad words today and I have a feeling it's my big brother." Andy pulled down the peanut butter and opened up the Wonder Bread, spreading a thick layer on a piece of bread and folding it in half. He looked at this brothers and said with a mouthful of sandwich, "I'm wunna ga boer." Travis and Trey looked at the small boy and laughed.

"What's that, Bubba?" Trey asked.

Andy's eyes watered as he swallowed with difficultly, sending the big bite of sandwich down. "I said, 'I'm the one that gets the boner.'"

Trey and Travis's mouths fell open and Travis fell on the floor in spasms of laughter. Trey shook his head.

"Are you shitting me?" The big boy grabbed Andy and pushed him down to the cold tile floor and began to tickle him mercilessly. "My little brother with a two-inch dink gets to have a monster hard-on and I get to piss my pants?"

An hour later, the boys were floating in the pool in the backyard. It might have been one of the above-ground kind, but it was the only pool on the block and was still a great place to relax on a hot day. Even though late October, the day was hot and summer was not relinquishing it's chokehold on northeast Texas. The mid-afternoon sun had warmed the water to bath temperature. The boys had created their own version of the Log Flume ride from Six Flags by running around the pool perimeter in a circle. After a few minutes, the water was flowing clockwise in a brisk whirlpool. The brothers counted off and on "GO" they pulled up their legs and floated around the pool like ducks down the river. Technically, the boys were not allowed to swim when their parents were not at home, but that hadn't stopped the McGee Brothers. Sometimes at night, the boys had come out with their dad for a moonlight skinny dip. But in the afternoon, it was strictly a cutoff jeans or swim suit affair. Trey pulled himself up onto a blow-up air mattress and Andy straddled him like a horse slowly spinning around the pool with Travis in an inner tube floating around behind. Travis felt the hot sun baking his face and chest, the light bright orange behind his closed eyes. He kept thinking of last night; seeing Emily's pearly skin glowing in the moon, her dancing and running around the golf course naked. Her dark nipples and her small but full breasts and that small triangle of blonde hair between her legs, just like Miss May from a stashed Playboy from 1974 that lived in the tree house along with all the others. Next his mind floated to Emily lying beside him in bed last night, his legs pressed tightly up against her backside, rubbing dangerously against her beautiful bottom. His arms pulled up against her chest, held there by her hands, maybe a few times managing to do a bit exploring on their own. He concentrated on the feeling of his heartbeat thumping against her back as his face lay so close to hers; the heartbeats that seemed to echo all around him front and back. *That's funny,* he thought. Feeling heartbeats in front and back. The water continued to lazily carry Travis around the pool and he smiled thinking of how close he had been to Em, his arms around her, touching her face and arms and tits. And the hands rubbing his chest and sliding down to his underwear and groping him there. But, that was weird too because Emily was facing away from him and ...

Travis's eyes flew open. "George!" he hissed.

"Yeah, what?"

Travis turned around and there he was, like a little puppy that wants to ride with you on the school bus. George. His puppy. Suddenly a big splash of water hit him in the face. Travis sputtered and turned the other way to see Emily standing beside him, her black and white bikini top looking beautiful in the bright sunshine.

"Wow, that must have been some dream you were having, Trav," she said. Travis looked down and groaned and flipped himself out of the tube.

"I didn't even hear you guys get in."

"Seemed like you wanted to be alone," George said with a smirk. Trey said we could join you. Trey was smiling like a mental patient with Andy riding along giggling as well.

"Figured we could have a talk with the whole gang, little brother, Trey added.

"Talk about what?" George asked suspiciously.

"Oh not much, just your help last week and again last night turning me into the Six Million Dollar man in front of the scouts and everything." George and Emily unconsciously drifted to the other side of the pool away from Trey and Andy. "Yeah, Dickhead here told me the whole thing. And although I really appreciate you thinking of me and giving me the best nights of my life, exactly what do you think is going to happen the next time we have a game and everyone expects the same kind of performance? Or what if were to get a college scholarship? Are you all going to come along and think your happy thoughts or lay your Jesus hands on me make me Superboy again?"

None of the others said anything for quite a while. Finally Emily spoke in a soft voice.

"We just wanted you to be great. We wanted you to have the best night ever. And you did. You were amazing again last night too."

Trey leaned back on his air mattress, hands behind his head. "Maybe y'all can zap me for this stupid musical. I still can't remember the words to that fast song. I just don't want to look like an id-jit. It's hard enough to be up on the stage prancing about like Tinkerbell."

"I don't know, in practice you seem to be doing okay already. I know you don't want to admit it big guy, but you are pretty much a big pressed ham already." George said. "As for the football stuff, um, no one would expect you to be that great every game. Even the best football players aren't perfect every game. And part of that was you. Shit, it was really all you. All we did was just magnify what you already could do."

Trey looked at them all with his most withering stare until he couldn't hold it anymore and then burst out laughing. "Ah, man I'm just shitting all you. I'm not mad. I mean, it did steal some of my thunder when Travis told me how this stuff works. But, hell, it's still been the best weeks ever.

"My Dad even kissed Trey on the mouth," Andy said to be helpful.

"Well then, that was a special night for you," George added with a smile.

"You can have your turn now if you want, G-Man," Trey answered tipping out of the air mattress and pinning George to the side of the pool. George tried to escape, but 200 pounds of solid Texas tight end was more than he could hope to fend off, even with twice his normal strength. Trey pinned George's arms to the edge of the pool and planted a big, wet, sloppy kiss on the boy's mouth, ending with a loud smack.

"Bet you been dreaming of that for a long time, Fairy cakes."

Suddenly, Trey flew through the air and landed with an oomph on the Saint Augustine lawn. Emily, Travis, and Andy stood together, their hands still outstretched.

"God, can't anybody take a joke anymore?" Trey groaned as he clambered back to his feet. He looked back at them as he held his side and walked toward the back porch. "A-Holes!" he muttered as he went flipping the bird over his head as he climbed the stairs to the back porch.

George looked at all of the kids left in the pool, sending each one a wordless thank you that they all understood. "So kiddo, how long have you known about the power?"

Andy grinned. "I knew after that day when we made dad fly through the screen porch window. That night, Dad was watching football and he was being real dumb and he kept turning the sound up louder and louder because mom was on the phone with somebody yakking real loud. I was sitting at the kitchen table trying to do my homework and I just couldn't stand all the racket any longer. So, I just started thinking: *I wish the TV volume would turn down.* Nothing happened at first, but then I noticed that it slowly got quieter where you could barely hear it. Dad kept getting up and turning the volume up, but it was already at the top. He was pounding on the set and going crazy, but finally he just gave up and moved real close so he could hear at all." The three teenagers laughed and nodded their understanding. They had all experienced that before.

"And then, I thought, I should try it with Mom because she was being just as stupid. She asked me to fill up her coffee, like I was her slave. So when I got up to get it from the Mr. Coffee, I just thought, *what if the coffee was so hot she couldn't drink it or something and she would get mad and hang up.* So I thought really hard when I filled it up and I could tell it was really hot. I took it to her and I even said, 'Watch out it's really hot.' But she was too busy talking and she never pays attention to me anyway and took a pretty big gulp."

"Oh no," Travis said with a grimace. "Was that the night she threw the coffee cup across the kitchen and cussed?"

Andy nodded. "I didn't know it would be that hot. I tried to tell her. I never heard her use that word before. Dad does all the time. So does Trey and Travis."

George roared. "High Five, Little Mac," he said. Little Mac was his pet name for Andy. Emily crossed her arms and gave him a withering look.

"She could have been really hurt. It's not funny."

"I didn't know it would work," Andy answered clearly upset with what Emily was saying.

"I know, Andy. It's not you. You couldn't have known. Unlike this dim-bulb who thinks people getting hurt is funny.

"There she goes. Sister Mary Elephant trying to make us all behave." He looked at Travis who momentarily lost his mind and joined in the chorus of "Claaaass. Claaaass. Claaaasss. SHUUUUUUT UP! Thank you." Andy giggled but all three boys were now the recipient of Emily's death ray stare.

"You know, it's a miracle the two of you haven't killed someone yet."

"Hey, that's a little harsh, don't you think, Em?" Travis said gently reaching out for her hand. Emily pulled it away with a snap.

She climbed out of the pool and wrapped a towel around herself taking off for the back porch and into Travis's room. Travis shrugged and the other two boys got out as well following her into the house. The boys followed her into the kitchen where she stood with the refrigerator door open looking for something to drink. She looked up with her disappointed pout, wet hair trailing into her eyes. Beads of water still glistening on her bare shoulders and down her cleavage. Her lips were parted and the light from the fridge illuminated her features in a flattering way. She closed the door and grabbed Travis by the face and planted a hard, long open kiss on his mouth. The boys all looked in wonder as she continued the kiss long and hungry on his face ending with a resounding smack.

"And next time we sleep together and make out, it would be cool if it was just you and me."

From the living room, Trey's voiced boomed. "Busted!" Emily turned and left again with Travis dazed, Andy grinning, and George's face bright red.

32 Green Light Bridge

Cowhill, Texas was little more than a squatty village of a few cotton farmers and a local cotton gin until the Teacher's College relocated to "the hill" that made Cowhill in 1898. Cowhill Normal College was a teacher prep school that prided itself on its graduates that were sent forth to educate the children of counties all around northeast Texas. Its founder, William L Mayo, had relocated the college from its original home in Cooper when the building had burned. It was a widely held belief that the Delta County residents had never quite forgiven Mayo for relocating to Cowhill instead of rebuilding. But Cowhill's proximity to the railroad was key in getting students from the Dallas-Fort Worth area to the school as well as cotton to the market. Over the years the college grew, the name changed to East Texas State University. Cowhill continued to thrive and Cooper remained a moribund backwater town in the second smallest county in Texas.

Greenville was the county seat for Hunt County, replete with its friendly sign of greeting to all that visited about "The Blackest Land and the Whitest People." There were also several "unofficial" welcome signs that had been erected by well-meaning citizens who were firm believers in the status quo. Both Greenville and Cowhill had been designed with "community" in mind by city planners in the early 1900's. There were the regular business district and residential areas. In Cowhill, there was the university district as well. There were industrial areas near the railroads in both towns. And there was also a residential area "across the tracks" in both towns. In Cowhill, this residential area was officially called the "Norton Community," named after one of the first black leaders to reside in the county. Unofficially it was unabashedly called Niggertown by all the residents of the white areas of Cowhill and even by some of the Norton residents.

Integration was brought kicking and screaming into the area around 1967 thanks to the Johnson administration's civil rights legislation. Students were bussed to school from the small community of Nelsonville between Greenville and Cowhill. Nelsonville was almost one-hundred percent populated with blacks looking for newer housing than the dilapidated "colored community areas" in Cowhill or Greenville could afford. The Cowhill School District turned the Norton School into a one-grade intermediate school for sixth graders between elementary and junior high. Every day, a hundred students were bussed from gleaming white Cowhill, across the tracks, through the rundown, potholed streets of the Norton Community to the former colored children's school.

Hwy 224 that connected Greenville with Cowhill bisected Nelsonville. The highway also ran through a small unincorporated township called Scatter Branch, which was a flat, rural floodplain rife with cotton fields and a pecan plantation. A thick ribbon of hardwood forest ran perpendicular north to south across the west end of the Scatter Branch community following the snaking path of the South Sulphur River. The river was a sluggish, grey, meandering cesspool most of the time. But in those days of flash floods which North East Texas is famous for, the sluggish swamp became a roaring cauldron of death for cows and the occasional recreationist that was stupid enough to try floating in the normally still water. The gravel road that ran off of Scatter Branch cemetery road ran along the property lines of several large cotton farms or cattle ranches, dotted with stock tanks and ponds that glistened in the sunlight like dirty pearls in an open oyster. Along this gravel road that took a sharp turn north at the three mile mark there was a road that continued on due west. The ruts barely showed through the tall grass and the path was blocked by a rusted gate whose lock had long ago been cut through. It would swing limply on rusted hinges in the hot afternoon sun. Down that faded road a mile and a quarter, one came to the edges of a dilapidated bridge that used to be the main thoroughfare for cotton wagons from Greenville to the gin in Cowhill. The river crossing was always sketchy. The old pony truss bridge had been built ancient from the start out of old barn siding and rafters. It sufficed when the wagons were horse drawn, slowly lumbering carts. But things got interesting once tractors and eventually trucks began to pull loads over the river. The clap-trap bridge would groan and flap a rhythmic protest as the vehicles would travel across, echoing the shoddy engineering.

The area was unusual in another way as well. The slow moving fetid water mixing with the moist humid air, almost non-existent wind, and swampy surroundings created a fog zone that hung over the bridge from November through April, especially in the evening and early morning hours. The fog blanketed the road in the middle of the night as well but no fool would dare make the passage in the dark if they could possibly avoid it. With short guard rails and the often present fog, it was like driving your truck off the edge of a cliff, trusting that the clouds would ferry you across to the other side. The rickety bridge remained virtually unchanged from the early 1900's until 1920 with steady traffic using the bridge mostly during cotton harvest time. The local farmers in the Scatter Branch area would also use the bridge as a shortcut between the regular farm to market roads and Hwy 224.

The Cotton Belt railroad company decided they could help the situation by selling one of their old banjo style signals to the county to install at the bridge. The railroad even put up the money to run the electric connection from the highway to the bridge believing that a better managed bridge would get even more cotton to the railroad station in Cowhill quickly and safely. The concept was simple: before moving out on the bridge, a vehicle would stop and punch the button. This set the light to red on the opposite side, warning any vehicle or pedestrian using the bridge that they needed to wait until the light changed to green in order to proceed. With the ever-persistent fog, this allowed vehicle to use the dangerous bridge with a modicum of safety. It was welcomed by the local farmers and residents as a great advance in technology and cut down the travel by avoiding the dangerous bridge by several miles.

Of course this was long before the advent of worst case scenario types of planning. The light was there, everyone knew how to use it. No one would forget to stop and set the light before venturing out on the bridge, would they? Luckily most traffic on the bridge moved at a crawl, so when invariably some fool forgot or simply decided not to stop and change the light from green to red, it meant one of the two had to back up and let the other vehicle pass, which was no small feat. Backing up usually required a spotter because of the infernal fog during the early morning or evening hauls. As clunky and prone to failure as it was, the signal was still deemed a great leap forward and traffic on the road continued to increase.

At some point in the late 1920s, school busses began to take the bridge as a way to shorten route times. Supposed improvements to the infrastructure of the bridge were made, though local folk were hard pressed to remember a time when the bridge was closed for more than a day. With the increased traffic, the old crick-crack boards groaned and swayed more and more. The local residents of Scatter Branch and Nelsonville took to calling the bridge, Green Light Bridge, after the hoped-for green light to speed you along the way across the river.

In November of 1927, two brothers, Harold and Lenny Hatcher, stayed home from school on a cold and stormy day on the pretense of having the flu. Actually, they simply were looking to skip a geography test neither had a chance of passing. Both parents loaded up some calves in a trailer and headed off to an auction in Winnsboro, warning the boys to stay in bed or face a licking. The fear of corporal punishment lasted for an hour before the boys were outside exploring the edge of the swollen South Sulphur River. They floated makeshift boats down the caramel water, threw rocks and horse apples into the eddies, and splashed in puddles until they were soaked to the skin.

They made their way to Green Light Bridge and were astonished to see the torrent of the river crashing against the shoddy pilings that held the bridge in place. The light on this side of the bridge glowed bright red. The boys walked across the bridge and stood watching the water rush past, the roar of the water filling up their ears. They continued to the other side of the river and saw the light was glowing red here as well. They looked and it appeared someone had placed a piece of bailing wire on the switch and wired it on *Stop*. Harold walked over to the switch and fiddled with the wire.

"Guess they ain't gonna let the bus drive over during the storm," he said.

"Looks like it. That's too bad for the niggers. They gonna get soaked in this mess," Lenny observed.

Harold's face broke into a wide grin. He reached up started wiggling the wire until he pulled it free and slid the switch back up into the green Go position. "Don't never let it be said the Hatcher boys aren't kind to the coloreds," he said with a chuckle. "Come on brother, you can take the wire off the other side." Lenny stretched on tiptoes to reach the switch and finally Harold slid his head between his brother's legs and hoisted him up on his shoulders so he had an easy reach to the switch box. The boys giggled and scrabbled away from the bridge and back to the house to dry off, reminding themselves to get back out here before 3:45 when the bus should be making its way down the road.

The boys peeled off their sodden clothes and threw them in the washtub. Lenny came up with the idea they had needed to run outside in the rain to shut up a cow that got out of the fence, which is why they got so wet. Harold stoked up the fire in the kitchen stove and the boys grabbed some dry underwear and sat in the warm kitchen eating some tomato soup and toast and played checkers, watching the wind and rain outside lash against the windows. They turned the radio on and lay on the living room floor in their shorts flipping through the Sears catalog looking at the models in their underwear.

Just before 3:00 pm, the rain and wind abruptly stopped and a thick, dense fog began to form around the soggy, now warming ground. The boys grabbed some of their work clothes from the mud room at the back of the house along with some rubber boots and some oilskin ponchos and headed out to see the bus make its way across the creaky, flood compromised bridge. The boys figured the kids would start yelling and it would be quite the carnival ride as they slowly crept across the rocking bridge. They found a good hiding place on this side of the bridge where they could watch the excitement. With any luck, all the kids would have to get off the bus and slip and slide in the mud all the way to Nelsonville.

At 3:30, the Route 3 bus pulled out of the parking lot from the Norton Colored Students' School and rumbled down the rough road toward the stops in Scatter Branch and Nelsonville. The bus was loud and filled with the laughs and shouts of students glad to be out of school and close to home. The Thanksgiving holiday was ahead and Christmas just around the corner. The bus leaned deep into muddy ruts in the poorly maintained roads that ribboned their way across cow pastures to the black community. Tom Jenson, the bus driver didn't like the look of the weather and figured the bridge would not be a good choice with all this rain. But as he got down the road closer to the turn off, he saw a truck transporting chickens had overturned and was blocking the road. Chickens squawked and ran around everywhere and a number of motorists were trying to help out. Jenson just wanted to get home and start the weekend himself. Since he was going to have to wait anyway, he decided he might as well try out the Scatter Branch road and see if he could get across the bridge because it looked like it would take half the afternoon to clear Hwy 224.

Tom carefully backed the bus into a gravel driveway and turned around and headed to the Scatter Branch cutoff road. The wipers were old and sticky, leaving big smears of mud and grime on the windshield. The lights were so poor it hardly made any difference to have them off or on. One of the high school boys, Joe Washington, noted the bus was turning on to the Scatter Branch road and spoke up.

"Hey there, Mr. Tom, you ain't gonna take us crossed the bridge today, is you?"

Jenson looked up in the mirror hanging high on the windshield that gave him a view of the seats in the bus. "Well y'all ain't getting home on 224 today so I'm gonna go take a look. Probably have to turn back but we were just sittin' there anyway. Never you mind, though. Don't be asking me what I'm doing."

Joe looked at his younger brother, Franklin, and muttered low out of the corner of his mouth, "This fool gonna git us all killed." Franklin gripped the seat in front of his and nodded his head in understanding.

Back on Hwy 224, Billy Thigpin was hauling a load of hay bales from Greenville back to his cattle on his farm in Pecan Gap. He had picked the worst day to do this, he kept thinking. He had tried to cover the hay with tarps but he knew it was getting soaked. And now he saw the whole road was shut down with the overturned chicken truck. He just didn't have time for this. He made a big U-Turn in the road and headed back to Nelsonville. He would drive through the colored town and take the bridge and get around this horse hockey and save an hour of soaked hay. He pushed his truck up to its top speed of sixty and crashed along the rutted road through Nelsonville toward the bridge. He knew no one else would be crazy enough to be using it today anyway so it was sure to be clear.

The conversations and chatter filling the bus quieted down as it neared the sharp turn and moved toward the bridge road. The rain had mostly stopped but the fog had moved in thick and dark. But glowing in the distance, the green light shimmered in the fog, welcoming the bus forward.

Billy squinted in the gloomy fog as he barreled toward the bridge. If he didn't get this hay put up soon it would be ruined and his old man would chew his ass all week. With the back of his hand, he wiped off the windshield and smiled to see the green light shimmering in the foggy mist. *At least one damn thing had gone right today* he thought.

Tom Jensen saw the green glow of the signal and shifted into low and rolled the bus onto the bridge. The timbers creaked and groaned as usual. The load of schoolchildren were completely silent as the bus rumbled across the bridge.

Billy Thigpin pressed down the gas hard. He wanted across this god-dang bridge and out of this soup fast.   His eyes flew open in horror as the blurred edges of the yellow school bus came rushing out of the gloom toward his truck.

"Holy God," was all the had time to say as the front of his pickup slammed into the giant grill of the bus, catapulting Billy out of his seat and through the front windshield. Tom Jensen shrieked like a stuck pig as the bus collided with the pickup, exploding the front glass in a fireball. Involuntarily, Tom slammed on the brakes and pulled the wheel hard to the left in a shuddering squeal of rubber and shattered glass. Students went flying forward as the bus careened against the old trusses breaking them free, sliding to the edge of the bridge. Loretta Jimson, sitting directly behind the driver slammed into the metal partition and as she flopped back into her seat, Billy Thigpin's decapitated head landed like a bowling ball in her lap. His ruined torso blasted through the windshield and slammed into the two rows of boys sitting beside Loretta.

The screams from the school children rose to a deafening roar as the bus teetered on the edge of the bridge, the front tires dropped over the edge causing the chassis to scrape in a shriek against the thick planks. Then with a shudder, the center truss of the bridge broke with a splintering crack and the bus plummeted to the roiling cauldron of mud below. The horror-filled wails of the children were swallowed up in the thick torrent. The bus quickly filled with the rushing river water, tipped on its side and slammed into the river bed below.

On the edge of the river, Harold and Lenny Hatcher watched in mute terror as the bus disappeared along with the children. Lenny took a couple of steps toward the center of the bridge but Harold pulled him back. The boys ran and slipped in the mud back to their house. Lenny was sobbing so hard Harold slapped him in the face.

"You shut up. Get out of your clothes and stuff now. We were never there," Harold ordered. The boys stripped down and splashed freezing cold water from the pump outside on their faces and legs until the muddy remains were washed away. Harold took the oilskins and soaked clothing into the house. He made Lenny stay in the back porch area until he had dried him off and the boys had rinsed off their clothes and ran them through the wringer. He hung them by the kitchen stove with the others. He would stick with the story of the cows, that the dang things had gotten out again and the boys got wet putting it back in the fence. Harold ordered Lenny into his union suit and told him to go get in the bed, he was sick. Lenny obediently crawled into the bed he shared with his brother and cried for the images burned into his vision to go away. They never did.

Harold went to the telephone and picked up the receiver. Two neighbor ladies were on the party line discussing a failed apple crisp recipe.

Harold interrupted the ladies. "Scuse me ma'am's," he said.

"Hold on, Ruby. Sounds like Mr. Ears is listening in on our conversation. Is that you Harold Hatcher?" Mayvois Little snapped.

"Yes ma'am. Sorry but I think something bad just happened on the bridge."

"What do you mean?" Ruby and Mayvois asked in unison.

"Well it sounded like there was some kind of wreck or something maybe on the bridge and it's all broke down. It sounded bad like maybe it was the school bus or something."

"Oh my God," Mayvois screamed. "Ruby, hang up. Hang up child. I will call the sheriff's office. Oh dear God!"

Harold decided maybe getting back in the bed wasn't the worst idea. They would already be in for it probably for not staying there all day. He struggled into his old union suit that was almost six inches too short in the legs and about that much on the arms. He pulled the covers up and scooted over closer to his brother who was still quietly sobbing. A moment later, Harold was sobbing too.

On the freezing, muddy banks of the South Sulphur River, Joe and Franklin Washington pulled a small girl from the submerged bus and dropped her on the grass and went back yet again. There had been a small air pocket in the bus that the boys had navigated toward along with a few other children. Most were hopelessly tangled in the legs of the crushed seats and trapped in the churning water. One by one, the Washington boys swam their way into the freezing water and pulled six other children to safety. Twenty-five others were lost including their two sisters, Claudia and Corinne.

The sorrowful aftermath of the school bus tragedy was a defining moment for the black community of Cowhill and Nelsonville. Quiet and unnoticed by many, a slow and steady wave of activism began to grow within the communities that gradually fought for improvements for their communities and schools. The open sewers, lack of police presence, failures in the electric grid, and out of date textbooks slowly began to change, much in part to the hard work of two brothers who had lost so much that chilly November day. The brothers married local girls and started families, both of them working as janitors for the Cowhill School District. In particular, Joe's first son was born in 1938. He named him Carl. Across the county in Cowhill another little boy, Mike McGee was born. The Washington brothers' community work continued until their deaths fifteen years later. The brothers were discovered in the small home they shared, both shot in the head. The local sheriff deemed it a murder-suicide, even claiming there was a note discovered. The note was never made available to community leaders although repeated requests were made. Among the members of the black community, it was also quietly mentioned that both brothers had thick bruising on their necks, scratches cut deep into the flesh, along with the petechial hemorrhaging normally found in strangulation victims. It wasn't too hard for most to piece together what had happened. Sadly, it was far too common.

The mothers remained in the area, raising their children and staying under the radar of the local groups that were well-known to the colored community but seemingly nonexistent to the majority of Cowhill. Franklin Washington's son, Carl, became a sensation on the local black high school football field, which ultimately lead to him receiving a scholarship to the University of Buffalo along with another local boy, Mike McGee.

The green light was deactivated on the Scatter Branch bridge. The road was closed for over two years before it was opened back up to the local farmers in the area. The county withdrew any maintenance from the bridge by the 1940's and the structure began to fall into disrepair. Local residents continued to maintain the bridge in some respects, but by the 1950's the bridge was no longer used. The landowner installed a cattle gate to block the road from outsiders and the curious, which did little to stem the curious from visiting the area.

In the next few months, a new jump rope song began to be heard in the school yards of Cowhill and Greenville. It chronicled the faithful day in a way no other lasting memorial had. The children of the area knew it by heart, it was part of the tapestry of their lives.

After the initial curiosity seekers stopped visiting the bridge to witness the site of the fatal bus crash, the bridge dropped off the radar and returned to its normal use as a dangerous, but sometimes necessary means to get around in the Scatter Branch community. Sometime in the 1940's though, a local couple, Albert Jones and Betty McDonald, were parked on the road in front of the bridge. The bridge was falling into ruin and local high schoolers frequented the road as a Lover's Lane of sorts, much to the chagrin of the landowner. Albert and Betty were seniors at Cowhill High School and had been dating for almost a year. Betty had been slapping Albert's hand as he slid it up her skirt for about the same amount of time. He had mastered the art of unfastening her iron bra with one hand, freeing her melons for his kisses and fondling. Betty had been sliding her hand inside Albert's trousers for a few months, stroking him and releasing him into his underwear with a sticky happy ending. But the special night had finally arrived. After months and months of promises and rebukes, Betty had agreed to be Mrs. Albert Jones, even though her father had forbidden her from getting married before she was out of high school. Albert had even bought her a $15 ring which she kept secret except for their dates.

It was May 2 and the evening was warm. After the beer Albert had provided, Betty stood up on her knees in the bed of Albert's truck on the mattress Albert had managed to put in the back and tossed her blouse at Albert's head. She continued her strip tease as The King Cole Trio crooned "Nature Boy." Emboldened by the beer, Betty unhooked her bra and flipped it at Albert. She stood in the moonlight shaking her tits like Betty Boop. It took Albert all of five seconds to shed his clothes as he sat up against the cab of the truck, feeling the night air on his dick that stood at attention. Transfixed, he watched Betty slide her shorts down to her ankles and step out of them with a little dance. To his surprise and delight, there were no undies, just a fiery red triangle of curls matching the red curls on her head. Trying not to take his eyes off the prize he had waited so long for, Albert tore open the Trojan package and fumbled with the rubber until he finally slid it on, glad he had wasted half the box practicing putting one on for just this moment. Albert rose to his knees and took Betty's hand like she was a princess and lowered her to the mattress. The two wrapped themselves in each other's arms, kissing deeply and exploring each other's bodies. Betty guided Albert's hand down to her crotch and the farm boy's fingers nervously parted the pink lips and slid inside the velvety moist walls. Betty's head arched back as Albert slid his finger deep within her. He turned and climbed in between her legs as she pulled them up, resting them on his strong back. Concentrating with all his might not to blow his load before he even started, Albert finally lost his cherry along with Betty in a glorious thirty seconds of glory.

Betty gripped Albert's back, locked her heels around his meaty ass and pulled him deeper and deeper inside her. It had hurt a bit, but now, she found the sensation wonderful and wondered why he wasn't continuing to make it feel good. Little did she know, Albert's thirty second performance would prove to be his modus operandi for most of his life. As he felt himself slide out of Betty, Albert turned over on his back and lay against the cab of the truck holding Betty in his arms, a wide grin of success spread across his face. He looked out across the river to the far side, barely making out the crumbled ruins of the bridge in the moonlight.

At first, Albert simply thought it was the post-coital bliss. But as he continued to stare, his eyes opened wider as he saw in the far distance, a dim green light eerily wink on across the river. Albert sat up in the truck in a flash, startling Betty into thinking they had been discovered. She covered her breasts and sat up with Albert looking around frantically. When she saw the light, she gripped Albert's hand and froze. The teens sat mutely staring at the emerald glow from the light. It seemed to pulse and throb along with their pulses. In a soft whisper, Betty began to chant.

"Red light, yellow light, green light bridge."

Albert joined in, "Just down the hill from Scatter Branch ridge"

Together they finished the chant staring unmoving at the light.

The glow of the light now flooded over the couple, bathing their naked bodies in that verdant neon hue. As they stared, their warm sensual afterglow was replaced with a growing unease. Later, both Albert and Betty would describe the cries of the lost children filling their ears and swallowing them with such a horror they clamped their hands over their ears to drown the wailing. Betty began to sob and Albert leapt out of the bed of the truck without his clothes and jumped in the cab and roared off away from the bridge.

Within a matter of days, other high schoolers were making regular treks out to Scatter Branch to sit vigil at the bridge. The stories continued to be told from lovers, hunters, young men and old alike of the random appearance of the light. Science students from the college would regularly make efforts to capture the light phenomenon in some way to study it, but it was capricious. Over time, many began to think the entire story was simply a rural myth that grew up around the tragedy. But the story persisted, especially among the youth of the area. Even in 1978, kids and adults alike would sometimes visit the overgrown road and wade through the waist high weeds to stand on the edge of the muddy river and look at the ruins of the bridge, sing the chant, or maybe, just maybe see the light. Regardless of belief, there was no denying it was a tragic place and the sadness and horror of the lost souls was part of the bones of the crumbling structure.

The sun had not yet risen but Jack Tanner was wide awake. That damn dream had come again last night. The light, the crowd, the broken bridge, the chant, the fall into the blackness. He had woken with a start, opening his eyes a bit only to find Joey standing a foot away in the darkness staring right at him. He had sucked in his breath and sat bolt upright and only just contained a scream.

"I had a dream and peed," Joey said in a loud whisper. Jack scooped him up and took him into the bathroom. Lori was still sleeping. She had been sleeping so much better lately. In fact, things were so good, Jack didn't even want to breathe sometimes. It was like he had gotten his old life back.

Joey had already pulled his wet clothes off and was standing expectantly in the bathroom.

"Guess you want to get in the tub," Jack said quietly. Joey nodded gathering up toys from the cabinet in the corner of the bathroom. Jack stoppered the tub and got the water warm and threw in some Mr. Bubble and watched the foam build up in the tub. Joey threw the toys into the tub and climbed in.

"Come on, Daddy," he said.

Jack slid off his underwear and climbed in the tub and leaned against the back. He was still sleepy and almost fell asleep again before remembering to turn off the water. By the time he did, the water was only an inch from the edge of the tub. Joey was in heaven.

"It's like the pool," he said sliding around.

"Don't scoot around too much, sport. Or we will soak the floor and mommy might get sad."

"Mommy won't be sad anymore. I made her happy all the time," Joey said floating a boat across the tub toward Jack.

"You think so, huh buddy? When did you start talking so much like a big boy?"

"Since the lights. Can we go to church today, Daddy?"

"Church? Why do you want to go to church?" Jack had to smile. They had only ever taken him once and he was so squirmy and unhappy they had left early. *What the hell was that about the lights?*

"I dreamed it. Like the green light and the bridge song."

Even in the steamy water, Jack suddenly felt cold. He pulled the boy closer to him. "You have been dreaming about the green light and the bridge and all of that."

"Uh huh. It would be good to go to church tonight. I seen it,"

"You saw it," Jack said. He rubbed his fingers though Joey's curls and stared at the boy. "Okay, let's hope mom will be up to it."

"She will be," he said with finality.

"I will be what?" Lori said squinting in the bright light of the bathroom as she came in to pee. She sat on the toilet and brushed her hair out of her eyes. You boys are up very early for a Sunday," she said. "So what will I be, Jo-Jo?" she asked.

"I want to go to church today and Daddy said we could."

Lori laughed right out loud as she flushed the toilet. "That is really hard to believe, buddy."

"I know but he can be surprising." Joey said with a straight face.

Jack just looked up at her and shrugged.

"Okay big guy, if you want to go, I guess we can but it is way too early right now." She picked the boy up in a towel and began to dry him off. "If we go, will you try and go back to sleep for now?"

"Sure thing, Mommy."

Lori laughed. "When did you start talking so grown up?"

"Ever since the lights."

"What does that mean? Oh never mind. Come on, Jo-Jo and let's get a bit more sleep." She took Joey into the bedroom and wrapped him up in her arms and hugged him close. Jack climbed out of the tub and dried off. He came back in and spooned up behind Lori and reached his arms around to hold on to his little boy as well. The three of them quickly drifted back to sleep. As he slept, the green light returned but this time instead of just the chant and the bridge, he noticed a crowed of faces around him, like a group huddle almost. He saw Lori and Tim. He saw the McGee kids again and Emily Moon and George Harris. There was some other face there as well and in the far distance, other faces that seemed to loom menacingly over the scene. But here in this small crowd, there was peace and safety. There was music playing and he had to admit, it did almost seem like he was in a church, but maybe that was just the power of Joey's suggestion.

He opened his eyes again as he realized he was very close to coming. He looked over at Joey who was on his side and sleeping deep and hard. He felt Lori's mouth continuing to bring him close to climax. He lifted up the covers to see her smiling face looking back at him.

"Surprise," she mouthed.

He pulled her up and she straddled his waist, planting warm wet kisses on his mouth. She reached behind herself and slid him inside her. He froze as he did, looking over again at Joey. Lori grabbed his face and held it straight looking at her.

"He's not going to wake up. Fuck me, mister," she whispered.

Jack slowly slid his hips up and down with Lori riding him gently, the mattress barely moving. She did that thing with her hips and pelvis that gripped him and thrust him deeper and deeper inside her without him having to do anything. A minute later, he threw his head back and silently exhaled as he came in three long blasts inside her. Lori continued to rock her clitoris against Jack's erection until she shuddered and came, collapsing on top of him. They kissed deeply and help each other until Jack slipped out of Lori. He shifted her to lay beside him, both looking at their sleeping boy.

"Ok that was a little crazy," Jack said smiling. "Not complaining, just glad the boy sleeps like a brick."

"Oh I bet parents did it in the bed all the time with kids in the olden days. Probably how half of us got here."

Jack stroked her hair. "It's so wonderful to see you so happy."

She smiled back. "It's wonderful to feel that way again. I love my boys. Life is good." She scooted her butt back against Jack's soft penis and wiggled it again. "Want to try for round two?"

"You are really being greedy and naughty," he said stroking her breasts. "I like it."

Five minutes later, Jack lay back on the bed, sweaty and spent. Lori climbed over him and went to take a shower. Jack heard Joey turn over and the little boy's eyes crinkled into a smile. He crawled over and Jack hugged him tight.

"Can I get up now?" he asked

"Sure. Go put some clothes on, you jaybird."

"You're a jaybird too. It's good you have this big bed," he said climbing over his dad and touching the floor.

"Why's that, kiddo?"

"More room for the baby," he said running away toward his room.

Jack laid back in stunned silence. He really hadn't thought of this very much. What would happen to Lori's happiness if she got pregnant? Part of him relished the idea, but would she. He got up and jumped in the shower himself out of habit before realizing he had just taken a bath a short time ago. He laughed to himself and plunged his head under the water. It was still wet and steamy from Lori's shower before. As he stood under the water Jack found himself thinking of all that had gone on lately, especially for Tim and him. He had managed to convince Tim to go ahead and tell Candy about the testicular cancer diagnosis. He thought the two of them had a refreshing response to the whole scare. Candy had called Jack and said Tim would not be coming to work for the next couple of days. Instead, she and Tim had spent the days naked in bed, making love so often Tim finally had no more sperm left.

"She was like Nancy the Salt Monster on 'Star Trek,'" Tim had told Jack describing how Candy had drained him of all his Murphy essence. "She even made me go to that sperm bank up in Dallas and dump off some loads, which was pretty weird and fun at the same time. They did have some good titty mags, though," Jack had said.

Jack had accompanied Tim to the hospital for his surgery. It was actually very quick and straightforward. The doctor acted like it was successful and explained that if the cancer hadn't spread in any way, Tim might not have to go through chemotherapy and radiation to complete the treatment. Tim kept his sense of humor and told Candy if he had to do the chemo, she would finally get all that hair off him she'd been complaining about. She just cried and said she didn't care. A week later, Tim had pushed his pants down and shown Jack his surgery scar.

"Looks like a goddamn deflated balloon," he said. "I keep finding myself walking leaning to the right, my missing nut makes me off balanced," he had said. But all in all, Jack thought he seemed okay and maybe relieved, though clearly worried about doing the other part of the treatment. Jack finished up in the shower, dried off and pulled on some shorts and went out to grab the paper.

"You want pancakes?" Lori asked.

"Sounds great. Getting the paper," Jack said stopping by the stove to plant a kiss on Lori's forehead.

Jack opened the door and almost screamed. Hanging from a noose tied to the porch light fixture was Smokey. The cat's belly had been split open and his intestines hung like Christmas garland from the lattice beside the front door where the remnants of last summer's climbing rose still stood, withered and dead. A crudely written sign hung around the cat's neck that read "Next time, we gut the brat." A five-pointed star had been hastily scrawled in blood on the threshold steps of the porch. Jack recoiled in horror but then thought, Joey and Lori can't see this. Jack reached down and picked up the paper, ripping off the corner of the front page that had drops of blood on it.

Coming back in, trying to be nonchalant, Jack sat the paper down and said, "I think I left the garage light on. I'll be right back."

"Hurry up. The sausage is almost done and I'm gonna start the pancakes," Lori said.

Jack slipped on some shoes by the door and a jacket over his bare chest. He grabbed a pair of gardening gloves on the edge of porch he had forgotten to put away and undid the noose and took the cat and his scattered organs to the garage. He found an old liquor store box and old towel and laid the cat inside and covered him up. He would have to deal with this later on he told himself. He grabbed a brush and bucket and went back to the porch. He poured some water in the bucket from the hydrant and poured water on the step and furiously washed away the bloody sign. He tossed the water and left the bucket and brush on the porch and went back inside. His hands were shaking.

"Okay. Let's come get it fellas."

"Be right there," Jack said. He ducked into the bathroom and washed his hands hoping there was no clue of what he'd just done. His heart was pounding, his hands were shaking so bad he put them under his armpits to try and keep them still.

"Oh God, oh holy shit," Jack whispered to himself. A million thoughts were rushing through Jack's mind. He knew he should have left the cat and everything and called the cops, but he just couldn't let his little boy see that, or Lori for that matter. He would go by the Sherriff's office tomorrow and tell them. But what would he tell them? This had to be JL or some of his crazy group. What had he really done to deserve this? Throw a guy across the room. He was holding a goddamn gun to Tim's head. Hell, he raped him with a grease gun. All because Tim didn't want to join his fucking Klan devil worship group? *This can't be happening*, he thought.

"Daddy, momma says to come now 'cause your pancakes are cold," Joey said pulling on his shorts.

"She's right, little man. Sorry, Let's go." Jack took Joey's hand so he could lead him to the kitchen. The little boy took three steps and stopped. He turned around, his eyes full of tears. He looked at Jack and said in a quiet voice, "They hurt Smokey. They shouldn't have done that. They will be sorry they did that."

A powerful blast filled Jack's mind. A horror show of fire, pain, and shrieking. Great gouts of blood flowed, faces melted, and green light showered over the scene. He shook the image free of his mind and looked back at Joey. The boy had a defiant, hard look on his face.

"See Daddy. They'll be sorry. Come on, pancakes are cold."

Jack sat down and ate his breakfast, but it tasted like sawdust in his mouth. He kept looking over at Joey who seemed his normal young self. He noticed though that the toddler was holding his fork with confidence and drinking his milk with steady hands, not even needing the sipper top on the Tupperware cup. Jack's mind was a whirlwind of images and emotions. Whatever had happened to him and Joey, it seemed like Joey was flourishing and handling it better than his dad.

"Jack!" Lori called.

Jack snapped back to attention. "Wha?"

"Phone, honey. It's Tim. Good Lord, you are dozy today," Lori said holding the receiver for him. Jack shook his head and smiled a forced smile and took the phone.

"Hello?"

"Christ. Thank God you're okay."

"Yeah, sure. What's up buddy," Jack said with feigned restraint.

"They killed two of my steers. I went out this morning to feed the cows and they were there right in the front yard. My young steers. They had chopped off their heads and stuck them on these metal fence posts looking right at my front door. My whole porch was ankle deep in organs and shit. And they cut off their dicks and nailed them to my front door."

Jack closed his eyes and tried to keep his voice quiet, moving around the corner of the kitchen with the long phone cord. "Did they leave a note?"

"Yeah. How did you know?"

"Cause they hung our cat on our front porch and gutted him."

"Fuck me," Tim said.

"Let's talk about this a little later today, okay. Meet me at the store like at 2:00 this afternoon," Jack said.

"Why don't we just meet now?" Tim asked.

"Cause we are going to church this morning?"

"Holy shit, I didn't think things were that bad."

34 University of Buffalo ¹⁹⁵⁷

Mike McGee hitched his duffle back up on his back and grabbed his suitcase and stepped off the train in Buffalo on a sweltering day in early August 1957. His white shirt was stuck to his back. His muscles were still and sore from sleeping in his train seat for the past three days. But he stretched and smiled, he had done it. He had made it out of Cowhill and away from his dad. He was a college student on a scholarship to play football for the Buffalo Bulls all the way in upstate New York. It seemed like he had stepped off the train into another country.

One of the assistant coaches, Richard Holder, known to the team as Coach Dick, met Mike at the station. He gave him a big handshake, clapping him on the back, commenting on how much bigger he seemed even since last year. The coach showed him the sites of town as they drove toward the campus. He helped Mike with some paperwork and got him settled in McDonald Hall on the top floor with the other freshmen. Most of them athletes. Mike noticed his roommate had not yet arrived and wondered who he would be spending this term living with.

Coach Dick told him his roommate should be arriving the next day, interesting he was also a Texas boy. He was recruited by Coach Offenbach as well and they put the guys together thinking they could look out for each other, being Texans up here in Yankee country. Mike thanked the coach and tried to move his spare belongings into the drawers and closets before taking off to find a payphone to let his mom know he had arrived safely. Mike met a few of the other team members that evening. Most were guys from the upper Midwest and Atlantic states or even New England. He was the only southern boy on the team it seemed; him and his yet unseen roommate.

Two of the upper classmen took Mike out to one of the local student watering holes for a beer or five. Joe Oliver was the quarterback and one of the team captains. He told Mike he was going to work harder than he ever had in his life but he was going to love it in Buffalo. Big Jack Ramsey, a defensive tackle towered over Mike who stood 6-2. Ramsey, who could drink more than anyone Mike had ever seen, gave him a rib-cracking bear hug at the end of the night telling him he'd heard that the only two things that came out of Texas were "steers and queers" so he would probably be wanting the big guy to spend the night. Mike thanked Jack and pushed him out into the hall and back toward his own room.

As he turned to leave, Mike asked, "Hey Jack, is Coach's name really Dick Holder?"

"You betcha, Red Ryder," Jack said with a wink and finger point like a pistol.

Mike got up early and went out to take a run around the campus to get his bearings, running along busy streets and on quiet early morning sidewalks. Even the air here seemed so different than East Texas. He noticed there were students here from so many different countries. He had seen Orientals; some dark skinned guys that he thought might be from India. He even saw a black girl and a white boy sitting in a coffee shop talking together. It was like he had jumped into a time machine and went forward in time. He ran back to the dorm and took a quick shower, finding a clearly hung-over Jack Ramsey propping himself against the shower walls, trying to wash away all those beers from the night before.

"Hey there, Tex. How's it hanging today? My head is singing pretty good this morning."

"I bet. You can really put the beer away."

"Shit, that was nothing. Just wait 'til we start winning ball games this year." Jack turned around and bent back, his hair under the water, soaping up his hair and pits. Mike couldn't help but be distracted by the heavy penis that flopped between his legs, hanging low and covered with a thick fleshy foreskin, Mike had seen exactly zero uncircumcised men or boys in his entire life, as strange as that sounded. It was like showering with an alien from another planet.

Mike found the cafeteria and had a large breakfast before looking for the locker room over in Clark Gym which sat near Rotary Field, the stadium for the Bulls. He met Coach Dick there and got his locker assignment and got fitted for his uniform and checked out the workout clothes he would need. By the middle of the morning, he along with Jack, Joe and other members of the team. Gene, Phil and Nick were hard at work in the weight room. They guys were affable and welcoming. Mike looked around hearing someone enter the weight room and spied a small, muscular black athlete in shorts and t-shirt walking in and picking up some free weights and getting busy on his bicep curls. Mike started to say something, like maybe that the guy had accidentally come to the wrong gym. But all that melted away when QB Joe yelled over at the guy and said, "Hey Tommy. Got another new teammate for you here. This is Mike McGee all the way from Texas." Tommy smiled a big smile and walked over extending his hand to Mike. Too stunned to think, Mike took his hand and shook it, making that the first time in his life he could remember touching a black person. Mike knew then and there he really had gotten off that train in a different time in history.

The teammates worked out until lunch and headed over to a smaller room next door to the gym which had been set up as a small lunch room for the athletes. Jack Ramsey explained the school had done this so the sweaty players didn't make the regular students lose their lunch sitting with them all sweaty and stinky. "It's just too much damn trouble to take that many showers, you know?" he had said. The air in the small room was thick and ripe, but Mike just soaked it in, part of the camaraderie of the team, he figured. And there was Black Tommy, just as bold as brass, sitting at the white players table, sharing food with them, talking and laughing just like he was one of the regular guys. It was unsettling and completely eye-opening.

That afternoon, the team had introduced Mike to "The Log," a broken off telephone pole covered in old carpets hanging on an A-Frame, used for blocking practice. It felt like hitting a block of concrete. The first time Mike hit it, he bounced off and onto his ass. The guys howled. Black Tommy hit the log and it swung wide. He was 5-6 of solid muscle.

Later that afternoon, he stood in the showers with the other teammates and sure enough, Black Tommy came in and just like it was an everyday occurrence, dropped his towel and stood there beside Kenny and Gene washing his black ass. No one seemed to notice or care in the least. Mike was literally shaken to the core and finished up as quickly as he could, and headed back to the locker room. As he left the shower room, Black Tommy called out, "See you later, Tex McGee," in a genuinely friendly voice. Mike had raised his hand in a weak acknowledgement and tore out of the tiled shower listening to several loud laughs behind him.

"Look like he just seen a black ghost," Black Tommy joked.

After dinner, Mike was sitting at his desk writing a letter back home to Janet when there was a knock at the door and a large black man about Mike's age stuck his head in the room.

"Can I help you?" Mike said.

"Are you Mike? Mike McGee?" the large man said coming in the room with a large suitcase. "I'm Carl Washington. Coach says I'm your new roommate."

Mike laughed. "Yeah, right. Those guys must have set you up with this. You are probably looking for Tommy. Not sure what his last name is. Y'all are probably roommates."

Carl set his suitcase down and dragged his sleeve over his shiny face, the room was warm and little air was moving through the open window. "Yeah I just met Tommy. He's rooming with Paul. Coach Dick said you and me is roommates. Thought us both being from Texas and all ..."

Mike stood in the room feeling like he was going insane. This was just too unexpected and just wasn't the way things were. He understood it was different up here. Students from all over were here on campus together. But surely, white and black boys were not expected to live and sleep in the same room. That was crazy. Just then, Coach Dick stuck his head in the door.

"Oh good, you boys found each other. That's great. Hey, Carl why don't you get settled while I borrow Mike here for a bit. He'll be back and you guys can get to know one another. Mike, can you help me?"

Mike left the room like a zombie and followed Coach Dick down the stairs to the benches out in front of McDonald Hall looking at the quadrangle of other buildings. Michael Hall, the girl's dorm directly to the east.

"Take a seat, Mike. Let's chat." Mike sat beside the coach and watched the cars drive past on Hayes Road. "So Mike, I take it we have thrown you for a loop assigning you Carl as your roommate. He told me as much when I was driving him here from the train station. I'm afraid us New Yorkers are just not as sensitive to these things as you boys from the south. To us, it's all just the same. He's a freshman football player and so are you. You both are from East Texas, basically the same town. Same age, all of that. Other than the fact his skin is dark brown and yours is very light brown, you are pretty much the same to me."

"I can appreciate that, Coach Dick. But it's just not like that back home. I mean, I just saw a black guy's bare ass a few hours ago for the first time in my life. We aren't even allowed to be in the same school much less take a shower together. It's just pretty uncomfortable. I don't know how to act or talk. I've never had a conversation with a black guy in my whole life."

"I can see that is a big adjustment for you, Mike. But I'm going to need you to suck it up and deal with it. We just don't tolerate any bigotry or racism here. We have stuck our necks out showing the NCAA that white and black athletes can live and work together with no problem. They are always looking for ways to tell us it is too soon for all this. That's horse hockey to us. You boys are both valued and talented athletes. All teammates. We are a family, all colors and shades of us. So, I need you to grow a pair of balls and learn to live with Carl. Believe it or not, yours will be the first white ass he's ever seen. Be a man, be a Bull. We are gonna beat the heck out of you boys so much at practice, the last thing on your mind is going to be the color of your roommate's ass." Coach Dick patted Mike on the leg and took off for the field house. Mike felt like he'd just been kicked in the balls, but he went back up to his room and walked in just as Carl was pulling off his white dress shirt and hanging it in the closet. He smiled a huge, white toothed grin and sat on the bed facing Mike as he sat on the other.

"I told Coach this was gonna be a stretch for us, maybe harder for you. But, we ain't in Texas no more. Guess we might as well try and fit in with these crazy Yanks. Shit, they wouldn't last a day down in Cowhill or Nelsonville, would they?"

"No. They'd be run out of town on a rail," Mike said. "You're gonna need to be patient with me, Carl. I will probably be acting like you're a Martian or something sometimes. I literally know nothing about black guys at all."

"'Cept we be liking fried chicken and watermelon and cane pole fishin'." Carl said leaning back and laughing a deep hearty laugh. Mike laughed along with him. "Let me ask you something. They really want us to take a bath together and everything?" Mike nodded reluctantly. "Damn!"

"I know. They don't know they you and me would be chased out of town for even sharing a room back home."

"I just might be swinging by my neck from a Bois d' Arc tree for getting' nekkid in the bath with white folks," Carl said with a mixture of amusement and stark reality.

"I know. And I guess we both know that's crazy. Just some of that shit dies hard, don't it? Well I tell you, you and me are here representing the great state of Texas. No sense in these Yanks knowing how fucked up some of our shit is, so I'll try my hardest to just be your roommate and not some redneck jerk," Mike said extending his hand.

Carl reached out and grabbed Mike's hand and pulled him up into a quick hug which surprised Mike so much he practically fell over. "I like you, McGee. Just you and me, roommates from Texas, all cosmopolitan and hip like these northern motherfuckers."

Mike grinned. He had literally never heard that word before but it sounded so audacious and nasty, he had to laugh.

"White boy ain't never heard a colored brother ever say 'motherfucker' in his presence before, has he?"

"Nope, I kind of like the way it rolls off the tongue.

"My mom would skin me if she heard me. Hell, I can't say so much as *shit* back home. Hey, I been sitting in that bus for three solid days. You want to go take a run with me? Make these Yanks think we are already bosom buddies?"

"Sure, that sounds pretty good. But let's keep it kinda short. These crazy Yanks done wore my ass out today.

Mike and Carl ran along Hayes Road out to Niagara Falls Boulevard. They didn't really chat, just ran and waved at students and residents alike who seemed to take absolutely no notice of a white and black man in shorts running around the neighborhood. Mike actually smiled just thinking how pissed off his old man would be. That thought alone make this experiment worth trying.

That night after dinner, Mike had taken Carl to the Buffalo Bar Fly and introduced him to Jack, Joe, Nick and several other teammates, including Black Tommy. Mike enjoyed seeing the two of them laugh and hit it off, sharing several whispered conversations that Mike figured were either at his or the other white teammates' expense. The team was impressed with Carl's size and strength, already figuring out he was going to be a potent asset to their defense. Mike and Carl called it an early night, he was still weary from that long train ride.

Walking back to the dorm, Carl laughed. "Never in a million years did I see this night ended with me and a bunch of white boys sitting in a bar having a beer together."

"Same for me, unless you were serving us the beer wearing a white coat," the boys laughed loudly.

The two brushed their teeth and hit the toilet before heading back to the room. Mike began to get undressed and noticed Carl was trying to busy himself with unpacking and not pay too much attention. The night was still and close, no breeze creeping inside the window. Mike stripped down to his BVD's and took the box fan he had and propped it in the window to bring in a breeze. Mike fell back on his bed, grabbing a book from the stack he had picked up at the bookstore and thumbed through one.

"White boys walk around in they draws and sleep in um too? Shit, I always thought you wore them pajamas like on 'Ozzy and Harriet.'" Carl pulled his shirt and pants off folding them carefully and lay back on his bed, his boxer shorts gleaming against his dark brown skin. His long six foot five frame filled the bed, his feet sticking off the end. He had his hands behind his head, staring up at the ceiling, feeling the cool breeze from the fan on his skin.

"Hey, Carl. Can I ask you a personal question?"

"'spose so."

"Well, several of the guys on the team have that skin on their pecker. And I guess I thought maybe all black guys were like that too. But your dick looks like mine. So, do all black guys get circumcised or what?"

Carl rose up on his shoulder and propped his head on his hand. "Fool, you did not just ask me if all colored boys get clipped."

"Sorry, I didn't ..."

Carl laughed loud. "Shit, I never seen any of that elephant trunk shit on a dick in my life 'til I seen some of these guys up here. Most black folks get their boys' dick clipped down in Texas just like white folks, I think. And as for your dick looking like mine, well add 3-4 inches and maybe you be right," Carl howled.

"Yeah, that thing you got is downright scary. Like the Black Mamba," Carl said.

"Black Mamba. What that?"

"I saw it in my World Book encyclopedia. It's this huge black snake from Africa that's fast and deadly."

"Now that's what I'm talking about. I like the sound of that. Check out my Black Mamba, sweetheart," Carl said hauling out his huge penis and gripping it like a sword.

"Jesus Christ," Mike said staring. You're hung like a horse."

"No. Black Mamba, here, Tex McGee," Carl said with a wicked laugh.

The boys continued talking about home, people they both knew, and local spots they had both visited. Mike found out Carl's family was the Washington's from Nelsonville he had heard much about. His father, Franklin, had been quite the activist, helping colored families and schools for some time. He was one of the reasons the Nelsonville Colored School football games had been visited by athletic scouts from colleges. He had done that work years ago and even though he had been dead for a few years now, his legacy in the communities was still felt. Carl even talked about his family way back in the Civil War times that had worked as slaves in the area and then went north before returning back in the early 1900's.

"Do you wish you had just got to stay up North?"

"I don't know. Cowhill is home, you know. Even when they's folks that make you feel like you shouldn't be there, it's still home."

Mike changed the subject. "So Carl, you got a girl back home?"

"Nah, no girl to speak of? How 'bout you Mike?"

"Yeah. Pretty serious girl. She may come up here to school herself. She is going to graduate this year."

Carl rolled over on his belly and hugged his pillow. "So Tex, you mind if I ask you something personal?"

"No. Go ahead."

"So white boys like you . . . you already had some pussy?"

Mike laughed, taken by surprise by Carl's frank talk. "Uh, yeah. I've had some pussy. I mean, a bit. Two girls. That's all. How about you? I bet the girls are crazy for that black mamba of yours."

"Yeah you'd think so. Nah, I ain't been with no girl yet. Still a virgin. That's pretty embarrassing to say."

Mike scrambled for something to say, since he was totally surprised by this revelation. "No, I think there's plenty of guys our age that haven't...you know..."

"Fucked some pussy?" Carl offered.

Mike burst out laughing. "Yeah, fucked some pussy."

"I had a few chances, but they were all pretty skanky 'hos.' Some of them already knocked up and just looking for a baby daddy too. So, I just kept the black mamba in his cage and wait for a nice girl. What was that white girl pussy like for you?"

"Um, well it was good. I mean, the first girl I was with was like older. I was only 16 and she was like 30."

"Day-um."

"I mowed her yard, you know. And this one day I was mowing at it was so hot, you know how it gets back home . . . a cool 105 or something."

"I do know all about that."

"Anyway, she asked if I wanted a drink and said she was worried about me. So I went in and was sitting in her kitchen having a Coke and I kind of almost started to pass out from the sun, you know. So she insisted I go and get in the shower to try and cool down. She goes in with me and turns the water on and gets it cool. Then she says to get in. I mean, I am just waiting for her to leave but she doesn't. She says she better stay in case I slip or faint. So, I just finally pulled off my clothes and jump in the water that was practically freezing. But it did feel good and I stood under the water until I felt all cool. I turned off the water and pulled the curtain back and she was standing there bare ass naked. Her hair was down, her tits were so big and all pink and swollen. Between her legs, this light brown triangle of fur. I had never seen a naked woman before."

"Holy shit," Carl says sliding his hand inside his shorts.

"And I get out and she starts toweling me off until I'm dry. She is like down on her knees drying off my legs and feet and butt and then her face is just right there, you know in front of me..."

"Oh no she didn't..." Cark said, his eyes popping out of his head.

"She did. I didn't even know people did that you know. And I was just standing there while she worked me over good."

"Oh man," Carl said with a groan.

"And then she led me by the hand to her bed and lay down and spread her legs all open. She pulled me down and I crawled in between her legs and then I was pumping in and out like a jackrabbit in heat on a hot summer day."

"Shit!" Carl exclaimed. "You get your cherry popped by a lonely housewife and a blow job to boot. You the luckiest son of a bitch I ever heard. You shoot your nut in her and everything?"

"Well yeah. I didn't even know what a rubber was much less what to do with it. I would've probably put it on my head instead of my dick." Carl hooted.

"Here I am a damn virgin and you out boning bored housewives."

"The crazy thing, a few months later, that lady is walking around out in the yard and I see she is fucking pregnant."

Carl began to pound the mattress he was laughing so hard.

"Oh good Lawd, a white boy done knocked up the neighbor lady. Her old man ever figure it out?"

"I don't know. I mean I saw her and I just stopped there and stared, feeling my life kind of end right in front of my eyes. She saw me and I could tell she was nervous but she looked around and motioned for me to come over. She took me into the back yard where other neighbors couldn't see. She told me that she and her husband had been trying to have a baby for six years and it had never worked. She said she thought he was shooting blanks, which I didn't even understand then. Then she leaned over and kissed me right on the mouth and told me I had given her the greatest gift of her whole life. She kind of got all teary eyed and begged me not to tell anyone, told me he thought the baby was his. Then she went as far as to say if I wanted another blow job, she would be glad to give me one!"

"Okay, I want to meet a lonely lady like that. You lucky duck. You ever see this baby?"

"I did. I mean I see him all the time. He's just a cute little blond haired two-year old boy named Cory. Funny thing is his mom and dad are pretty dark-complected and he's this sandy haired little guy."

"Just like his daddy. Lord a mercy, you had quite the story there. And no one else knows?"

"No one. You are literally the only person I have ever told, which is so strange when I think of it. I barely know you and here I am telling you my big dark secret.

"Well, no need to worry. Black folks know how to keep they mouth shut. Well, I ain't got no fun stories with lonely housewives like that. I only had a few hand jobs and two blow jobs in my life and I still ain't slid it up inside a girl. You said you done it with two girls. So is the other one this girlfriend of yours that might come up here?"

"Oh God no. That's Janet, and she and I haven't done it, though we have come so close, I'm really surprised we didn't slip up and just do it."

"Why you waitin'? Black folks don't be waiting on that. If you loving someone, then you be banging."

"Sounds more reasonable to me. She is determined to be a virgin when we get married. I already told her I'm not, which she said doesn't matter. It's only for the girl. The other was a girl named Cheryl Arnold. She was a cheerleader at school. We dated for about three months. One night, we were making out in the backseat of my old man's Buick. She leans back and throws her legs up in the air and I see she doesn't have on any panties."

"Goddamn," Carl said with his hand sliding back inside his shorts.

She actually reached in her purse and handed me a Trojan. I'd never even put one on before. By the time I got the damn thing on and slid inside her, I lasted all of fifteen seconds and shot my wad. She seemed totally bored with the whole thing and I found out later, she was mad at her real boyfriend who was a senior and wanted to make him jealous. I'm lucky the guy was basically a coward otherwise he could have kicked my ass big time."

"Hell, then you almost as much a virgin as me. At least you had the one nice time but with a lady that old and you a boy, that's some bullshit, too." Carl said sagely. "Woo, man. I am one tired nigga'. I think I'm just gonna rub one off and go to sleep."

Mike's eyes flew open. "You're just gonna masturbate right here in the room with me?"

"I ain't got no other room to masturbate in."

"Yeah, I was kind of wondering about that myself. I wondered if black guys even, you know…"

"Choked the chicken?"

"Beat your meat?"

"Jack yo' junk?"

"Mangle your mamba!"

Carl cackled. "That the one, my new brother."

Mike reached behind him and clicked off the desk lamp. The air was cool now and the hum of the fan was hypnotic. Mike lay still wondering if Carl was just a very quiet jerker compared to him or if he'd been pulling his leg.

"Hey Carl. Last question?"

"Better be good," the sleepy voice replied.

"So when you mangle your mamba, is the sperm white like mine?"

"White boy, you did not just ask me if my nut is white like yours. I tell you what, I'll blow my nut in a minute all over yo' face and then you will know firsthand."

"Jeez. Okay, just wondered."

But a new friendship was born that night. Mike and Carl grew utterly inseparable. Mike wrote Janet and told her all about his Negro roommate and she thought it was brilliant and progressive. On the other hand, he did not mention it to his mother. He and Carl took almost every class together. Neither of them had a mind for the hard science courses that many of the students at Buffalo took. They both settled for a business degree, hoping that would help them with jobs after college and football ended. They trained together, built up muscles, and drank a lot of beer along with Jack and the other guys at the Bar Fly.

Carl was so friendly and personable, he instantly became well known on campus. He was invited to parties and even offered memberships in two fraternities, but he declined them both saying he was just too busy this year with football, maybe would look into it in the spring. Carl also worked on campus, but not in the cafeteria or sanitation crew or cleaning bathrooms. He got a job as a front desk assistant in one of the dean's offices. Mike had settled on being part of the grounds landscaping crew. But he enjoyed the outdoor work, even in the snow, which Mike and Carl both thought was the most amazing thing they had ever seen, especially when the drifts around campus became taller than they were.

Carl was also a sought-after date from many of the college girls, both black and white. Sometime after the first football game against Carnegie Melon, which they won 14-9, Mike came back to the room to find Carl bare-ass naked driving it home hot and heavy with a voluptuous black coed named Monique who had the biggest breasts Mike had ever seen outside of titty magazines. He stood stunned in the doorway for a moment, while other guys from the team were walking by as well. Jack and Nick stuck their heads in and Jack wolf whistled saying "Go Bulls!" Carl's head practically broke off as he swiveled around but he smiled wicked grin before waving the guys to get out. Monique never seemed to realize they were there, she was too busy with the mamba.

After that, the guys devised the signal that a bright blue rubber band on the door handle meant a party was going on inside. This worked for about three weeks until Mike demanded Carl cut back on the sex because he was spending half his time cuddled up with Jack or Joe or one of the other teammates because Carl was holding court with half the school.

Janet came up for homecoming with an aunt who had family in the nearby Niagara Falls area. The Bulls played a Michigan school, Wayne State, and manhandled them 37 – 7. Carl had four tackles and two sacks. Mike caught a 20 yard pass across the middle and ran it in for a touchdown, his first points as a Bull.

Mike had shelled out $17 of his precious dollars for a nice motel room for the two of them, even though Janet had told her aunt she was staying with a girl named Charlotte that was a freshman at the school. It was an agonizing, ecstasy-filled weekend. Janet adamantly refused to let Mike penetrate her with his penis, but she was pleasantly open to just about everything else. Mike had his first truly toe-curling sixty-nine experience that blew his mind. He honestly had never understood the term until Janet explained it before they began to practice it in earnest, three times in a row. He used his tongue and fingers in every place he could, with Janet following suit, surprising the hell out of him at every turn. They spent the entire Sunday in the motel room naked, ordering room service, and having more sex than Mike ever thought possible without actually fornicating.

Carl surprised the shit out of Mike one Sunday soon after this. They had beaten Temple 13-6 in Philadelphia to finish out the season 5-6, not great, but remarkably better than in recent years. There was real reason to believe next year could be an amazing one. The team had gotten off the bus late and were having a well-deserved sleep in on Sunday morning. When Mike woke up, a towel clad Carl was sitting on his bed staring at him.

"Ahh, Jesus!" Mike shouted sitting straight up in bed.

Carl smiled and put a hand on Mike's shoulder. "Damn, Tex. You'd a thunk you never been woke up with a smiling nigga' two inches from your face before."

"What's wrong with you," Mike said annoyed from being woken. "I was still sleeping."

"Yeah, well. You can sleep when yo' dead. I gots some news and I need your help tonight."

Mike leaned up against the wall and reached over and picked up a half-smoked marijuana blunt from the ashtray. One of Carl's true revelations as his roommate along with picking up more girls than he ever thought possible. Mike lit the spliff and handed it over to Carl.

"Alright. I have a lady coming over tonight."

"Carl, I don't want to have to go sleep at Jack's. He snores and he tends to grope me while I sleep and Nick is always there too. It's too many guys in one room."

"No man. You don't understand. See this lady, she's um, a white girl." Carl said with some trepidation.

Mike had seen Carl hump black girls, yellow girls, a red one, and maybe a brown one or two. It was like a chorus of "Jesus loves the little children" in their room.

Mike eyed him hard. Even with all the progressive growth he had felt in his belly concerning his ability to treat blacks like everyone else, this was pushing hard against his own boundaries. A black man having sex with a white girl was as bad as it got in regards to racial pitfalls. In the south, you would be better to just take a gun and shoot someone. Black men and boys were routinely hunted down and lynched for simply speaking or flirting with a white woman. This was not only stepping over the sleeping tiger. This was hitting it in the nose with your dick and pissing in its face. Carl had confessed to him that he had already secretly bedded two white coeds who clearly had a goal in life to be with a black man. They had not returned nor did they try and date Carl or anything like that. They just wanted to ride the black mamba. Mike had kept his judgment to himself but felt pretty sure that Carl could tell this was pushing at the limits of decency as far as Mike was concerned.

"Look man, I know you got feelings about this. Believe me, I do too. That first time, it took me twenty minutes to get hard. It usually take about twenty seconds. I spent my whole life afraid to even look at a white girl much less touch one. But this is a different world up here. I might never get this chance again in life. I go back to Texas, I will never be able to even have a white woman say hello to me."

"All the more reason why maybe it's not the best idea for you to get used to being so forward with a white girl. What if you go back down there and forget you are supposed to look the other way? You don't get a second chance for all that down there."

Mike sat beside him a while. "It's cool, man. I don't want to make you feel bad or lose your friendship, so I will just tell her you're not interested."

"What do you mean, 'I'm not interested?' What are you trying to cook up?"

"See, it's a package deal man. She wants to see what it's like with a brother, but she won't do it with me unless there is a white guy in the mix too. She wants one of those ménage a trois things…and she wants it to be you. She thinks you are far out." Carl stared earnestly at Mike.

Mike was almost lightheaded from the weed and now with this news. "Carl, I have a girlfriend. I'm not going to help you molest some poor girl…"

"Now wait a minute. This a grown-ass woman. She is twenty-six. She's a grad student here. She knows what she wants. She's the one asking me, and you for that matter. I'm not chasing after her. If you don't do it, she will probably just pick someone else. Someone like Jack or Paul or someone"

"I'm supposed to be true to my girl, you know that," Mike said trying to ignore the swelling he felt in his shorts.

"You been plenty true to her. You waitin' for her to be ready and all that. Whatever you do up here is just still waitin'. It's not like she here and you messin' around with her around the corner. You not engaged yet. You just taking the edge off once in a while, you know. Then when you settle down, you be all into her forever and all that. You need to play the field a bit, Mike, or one day you might be tempted to mess around once your married and all that."

Mike figured this was quite a load of bullshit, but there was one nugget of truth: he had hardly been with anyone. He did wonder a bit what it would be like to experiment with a few different girls before settling down with one. At least he was up here and Janet wouldn't have to be concerned with it.

"Tell me about this girl," he said.

Later that night, Genvieve Poirot, a French graduate student took two redneck boys from

Texas to school, sex school that is. Mike and Carl experienced positions and sensations they never had imagined. Some of the things, Mike didn't even know you could do and was pretty sure they would get you arrested or worse in Texas. But in their dorm room, they played a dangerous and erotic game with Miss Poirot, who wove a magical dance with her body, hands, lips and tongue. By the end of the evening, the three students lay in a naked heap, sharing a joint, and soaking in the sexual fantasy come true. Mike tried to actually count off the new and forbidden experiences he just had and gave up. Some of them he would literally never forget, a few he might spend quite a long time trying to.

The roommates stood in the shower an hour later, not really talking or looking at one another. As fun as it had been, it had walked a dangerous line close to where it's hard to look at your friend the same way. Back in the room, both sat at their desk reading or working on some assignment. At midnight, Mike turned off his desk lamp and climbed into bed. Carl did the same five minutes later.

"You okay, Tex?" Carl finally said into the darkness.

"Yeah. I'm good. How about you?"

"I'm good. That was . . .uh, kinda wild, huh?"

"Yeah. Pretty wild." The alarm clock on Mike desk sounded like a jackhammer it was so loud.

"I didn't expect some of that tonight. But damn, you quite a stud, Tex."

"Pretty sure neither of us expected some of that. She had a way of talking you into anything."

"Yeah. Well, guess we better try and sleep," Carl said. "Thanks, Mike. I mean it. That was out of sight."

Mike smiled in the darkness and reached his hand across the small gulf between their two beds. Carl grabbed his hand and slapped him some skin. "I'm gonna have some nightmares of that damn black mamba."

35 Mary

Mary ran the pick through her hair until it was fluffy and full. She was working on her eye shadow when her mother came in the bathroom looking for some more Darvocet.

"You done taken all of it, Mama. Maybe the doctor will write you a prescription for some more," Mary said adding some blue mascara to her lashes. She was wearing an orange cardigan and white blouse and her Calvin jeans that hugged her body. Delois Washington sat on the lid of the toilet and stared at Mary.

"You keep dressin' like that and you gonna end up in a bad way again," she said morosely.

"I hope you do not mean that, Mama. There is nothing wrong with these clothes. You act like I am strutin' around like some whore."

"Don't you talk like that to me, girl. I can still whoop your ass."

Mary stared at her mother and thought, *I'd like to see you try it.* She looked down at her brown lipstick that was so low the gold case was sticking up higher than the makeup. She needed some more but no chance of that right now. She focused on the lipstick and turned the bottom and watched it grow a half inch. She smiled and added the color to her lips.

"Who you dressin' up for anyway? Ain't nobody gonna take a look at you in this town now that they know you used goods." Delois leaned over the shower to turn on the water. It came on so fast and with so much pressure it blasted her head and soaked her hair in two seconds. She screamed and stumbled away from the water.

"Damn that thing. Practically drowned me," she said.

Mary smiled and picked up her makeup and handed her mother a towel. "Here you go, Mama. Is Yancey ready? He better be or I will leave his ass behind today," she said leaving the bathroom.

"Don't forget your lunch money," Delois said wringing out her hair.

Mary yelled for Yancey and picked up the fifty cents off the table. Yancy's Jackson 5 lunchbox was packed and waiting for him. The boy came running out and grabbed his lunch and told his mom goodbye and ran out the door ahead of Mary.

They walked to the bus stop where the school bus picked up the children from the Norton Community and delivered them to the various schools around town. Integration may have come to Cowhill, but no one seemed to make it easy for the students that needed to be bussed into the schools. There was no cover at the bus stop, so often the students would huddle in the edge of a nearby small grocery store and make a dash for the bus when it stopped. You had to be quick as well. The bus driver didn't wait for students late for the bus. More than once Mr. Daniels had blown the horn in triumph as one or two students ran after the bus yelling for him to stop. Once across the tracks, the rules changed and he suddenly became patient and accommodating. He was in his less-than-helpful mood today. As Mary got on the bus, she looked behind and Yancey had stopped to tie his shoelace. Mr. Daniels closed the door as soon as Mary boarded, not waiting for her to be seated.

"Mr. Moore, Yancey is right there. He had to tie his shoe," Mary explained trying not to fall as the bus roared out of first gear. The driver paid no mind. Mary sat down and stared at Mr. Moore and suddenly the man jammed on the brake so hard half the students fell off their seats. Then he opened up the door and a breathless Yancey climbed on. He sat with Mary and grinned.

"I bet that was you," he whispered.

"Shush," Mary said.

Things had definitely improved in her life in one way since the night with the lights and then the horrible night when she and her dad had been drugged and taken to that barn. She wouldn't dare let her mind go to that place anymore. At first, she was so paralyzed with fear she thought she would die. Her mother was still a mess. She never left the house, hardly ate or slept, and never cooked. It had been up to Mary to pick up the slack. Her older sister Vivian was at college at Prairieview A&M and couldn't make it home although she called almost every night.

Mary and her father, Carl had always shared a close bond. They just understood one another. She had taken to helping out so much at the washateria that she practically knew how to run the place herself. Now that the family was opening a second laundry in nearby Cooper, she actually thought she might get to run it for her dad, especially in the summers.

The day after that horrible night, Mary had almost cut her wrists and just faded away. She couldn't stand the humiliation and pointed looks. She struggled with inferiority half the time anyway, it was hard not to in Cowhill. But when she saw what they did to her dad, how dead he looked, and how they had used her, it was too much. Mary had sat in the living room and heard the horror stories from her Grandmother Beulah, how her grandfather had been lynched, and how it had been covered up. She heard tales of so many more, especially in the old days. But the hate ran deep as an oil well in these parts and Mary had seen her own share.

But in the middle of her grief and shame, whatever the lights had done glowed within her. She woke in the middle of the night listening to the whispers of her father. Faint and weak, but it was him, she just knew it. "Believe" it had said and "Hope" and later…"I'm still here." That brought her back from the brink. She began to be less afraid and felt the presence of her dad somehow throbbing in the energy she felt.

She also began to realize she was different too. Her mother, who had practically shut down, didn't seem to notice any of these changes. She had toyed with things: turning the television off and on, making the burners on the stove raise and lower. Yancey had picked up on things right away. One night, not long after she discovered she could do things, she had sat on the bed in his room and taken one of his model airplanes and flew it all around the room to Yancey's delight. She had used the powers or whatever it was to protect herself and Yancey as well, like with the bus driver today. Two girls began to harass her in the bathroom last week, calling her a whore and talking about how she loved getting used by dirty men. She felt her anger flair just as one of the girls was putting a nickel in the Modess dispenser. Suddenly, the sanitary pads were cascading out like a slot machine, flying across the room and hitting the girls in the face and body like shrapnel from a bomb. They ended up with a number of cuts on their faces which Mary was a bit sorry about, but not too much. Emily Moon had been in the bathroom too and for a brief moment, it was almost like she and Emily were sharing the same thoughts. A moment later, the machine had gone crazy.

Mary spent the next few weeks at school watching Emily and her friends, Travis and George. They were in band with her. It seemed to her that there was something there, something like the energy she felt. She also remembered that some of the strange things that had happened around the school always seem to take place when one of them was around. But then, the same might be said for her. All she knew was this: whatever this presence or energy was, it had saved her life, maybe more than once. Remembering back to the night, she recalled the green light, the beams that seemed to penetrate the barn and stopped the men somehow. Whatever it was filled up her soul with the will to get up and get out of that place. She didn't ever remember walking out or stumbling down Hwy 24. She was grateful for the elderly couple that stopped and helped her. The man had taken off his own shirt so she could slide it on to cover up. She didn't even know their names or how to thank them, but she had spoken a prayer of thankfulness every day since.

Her weekends were full with football games and helping out at the washateria. Her father's friend, Malcom, had stepped up and helped Delois with running the place since Carl had been gone. The police had only come around the first couple of days and then just stopped. No one seemed to care that Carl was missing, or kidnapped, or dead. To this town, he was just another missing colored man, nothing to get excited about. She had heard the ridiculous rumors about him being the one that raped her. She had practically set Colleen Murphy's hair on fire for saying so in the gym locker room. The cow had been using a curling iron on her hair after she took a shower and Mary caused the thing to glow so hot her bangs simply melted away, gluing themselves to the iron in a cloud of burned hair. She had worn a bandana on her head for a month after that. *So many hateful people*, she thought. She and her mama had been watching an old movie on TV the other night, a Broadway musical, "South Pacific." The soldier on the screen wanted to love an island girl and everyone was giving him grief about it just because she was a little browner than him. He sang a song about those feelings, she tried to remember what it was. Something like "You've Got To be Carefully Taught." God knows, residents of Cowhill, Texas had been born and bred to hate, but more and more of them seemed to be crawling out from under that cancer. But it was so slow and so wearying to always be on the butt-end of people's prejudice. Sometimes, she felt like turning on the sprinklers and sending the electrical wires into the puddles and just being done with the whole place. Watching it burn while comfortable wearing the pig's blood.

For some reason, she woke up from a deep sleep last night and had the distinct feeling she needed to go back to the white church her dad had visited some with the family a few months back. Her mom had never felt accepted there even though they really liked what the youth group was like. The rest of it seemed stuck in the past and incredibly white compared to Mt. Shiloh African Baptist. *Thank God for the musical,* Mary thought. When Miss Cantor had first asked her to try out, she thought she was just being nice, trying to include the unfortunate colored girl. She had always loved singing but never had sung for anyone outside of church. It had been the most freeing part of this fall. The white kids in band still didn't talk to her much but she had started to get to know Emily Moon who she liked quite a bit. Those two boys she always hung out with were pretty okay too. That George was one weird dude, but he made her smile with all his funny jokes. For some reason, she just felt connected to them.

The bus pulled up in front of the junior high and Mary got off and headed to her locker since the first bell was just sounding. She grabbed her math book and added it to her notebook and headed for first period math with Dr. Duck. She was a mean old thing, but recently she had taken a chill pill and been much nicer. Mary had the distinct idea that Emily, Travis or George had something to do with it as well. Mary heard about the day when the old bat's wig had shrunk so small it fell off her head. For the first time ever, Mary had high grades in Math too. Whatever was going on, it was great for her grades. Mary took her seat and watched Emily come in the room and sit in the chair ahead of her in the next row. Out of nowhere, Emily turned around.

"Hi Mary. Hey would you be interested in coming to Living Waters this weekend, we are having this revival with this preacher that does these illustrated sermons? It might be really good."

Mary smiled slightly. "Yeah, that sounds pretty cool. Maybe I'll come check it out. Thanks."

"By the way, your solo in 'Godspell' is just about the best thing in the show. I bet your family must be really proud."

Mary smiled, forcing the tears pricking at her eyes to dissipate. "Yeah, they real proud."

"Hi Mary. Hey would you be interested in coming to Living Waters this weekend, we are having this revival with this preacher that does these illustrated sermons? It might be really good."

36 Janet

Sitting in Miranda Moon's living room, Janet pressed her foot on the sewing machine pedal and ran a seam in the vest she was creating. Janet, Miranda, and Darla Harris had taken on the responsibility for the costumes for the high school musical, not realizing what a chore it actually was. Naomi Cantor, the high school drama teacher, was young and ambitious. She had chosen to create all new and original costumes for the production of "Godspell" that premiered in a few days for a three day run. The teacher had decided on a hybrid sort of look somewhere between "Hair" and "Carousel." The result was an eclectic nightmare as far as the seamstresses were concerned, but the young drama teacher seemed positively thrilled. She stood in the room and modeled the long fringed vest that Theo Martin was to wear as the John the Baptist/Judas character. She spun in a circle sending the fringes in a wide flurry of copper fake suede.

"Oh that's perfect. Just what I imaged," she said.

How she had ever recruited some of the boys for the musical was a mystery to Janet other than the fact the teacher wore tight shirts and no bra much of the time. Such a thing would have been a firing type offense only a few years ago. God, when she was a girl, you could get detention for not wearing a bra while in gym class. Janet watched the boys stare as she went through the choreography, bouncing merrily along the way, half the time with her nipples hard as erasers under her thin shirt. *Good for her*, she thought. *Shake it if you can, sister.* The young teacher thanked them again for all their hard work and left to get rehearsal started.

Naomi had first wanted to do Jesus Christ Superstar, but the only way the school board would approve it was if she changed the show and put in an alternant ending that showed the resurrection. Naomi absolutely refused to make those concessions and just changed the whole show. 'Godspell' was a better choice anyway. Easier songs and no real controversy, although Janet was sure some of the die-hard fundamentals in the community would have plenty to complain about.

"You know," Darla Harris said, "I was listening the other evening while the kids were practicing. Trey is pretty good. I didn't know he could really sing like that at all."

"That makes two of us. He won't open his mouth and sing at church at all. Travis has always been the singer in the family. Trey never seemed to be interested in music at all. I was amazed that Naomi got all those football players to sing and dance. They are actually good now," Janet said finishing another seam and holding the shirt up. "I'm still not sure she's going to get Trey into those shorts. The Superman shirt will be fine, it will go great with his big head."

Miranda laughed. "I heard the kids the other night too, working with the stage band. Even the chorus kids are good. And that Mary Washington, she is a wonder. I have to admit, our Emily isn't bad on her solo either," she said. "And George and Travis, out there with those high schoolers, we have some talented kids for sure."

Janet agreed with the others. To be honest, she was thinking lately that the kids were amazingly talented, almost to the place it made you wonder. Travis's grades had never been this good. Andy was settled down in class more. Even Trey was doing his homework, the play, and practicing harder than ever in football. She wondered what was in the water that had made the kids so productive. Now she was hearing that Emily, Travis and George were doing some worship leading in the youth group too. That made her so happy. It had always been a struggle to keep the kids interested in church, especially as they got older. That Cory was special too. The last youth leader they had was over sixty and had as much in common with the kids as Methuselah. There was something so familiar about Cory. She loved talking with him. When he would sit with them after church having lunch or supper, he just felt like one of the family. He looked so much like Mike, she called him his long-lost little brother. Mike always dismissed that as silly.

"So Janet. How have things been for you and Mike lately," Darla asked? "I know earlier this year you said it had been pretty tense."

"Well things were rough at the store. And then the horrible stuff with Carl. It just took a toll, you know. He was smoking a lot, grumpy, just sitting and watching television with a beer. That was about it."

"Hmm. Sounds like every night for Duke," Darla added with a sigh. She pinned up the hem of a pair of striped pants and began working on finishing them off. "But I'll admit, it has been a bit better lately. Duke and George never get along. They are like oil and water most of the time. I don't know why, but Duke seems more patient with him now. A little more interested in his things too. I know he is way too indulgent about the car. George is a good driver though."

"Well that sounds wonderful," Miranda said smiling. "Emily just seems so engaged with school and friends. Well, with Travis and George. Those three are like Moe, Larry, and Curly."

"I think there's more to it than just palling around the boys," Janet said. "I've been watching them. Travis is crazy about her. In fact, I've been a little concerned about the impromptu sleepovers sometimes. I mean, they've hung out like that for years but they're getting older and I don't know…"

"I ask Emily about it all the time. She insists they are just being friendly and having fun together," Miranda said. "The other day, though, I did think she smelled a little bit like pot when she came home"

"Hmm, that's every week for Travis. Oh well, I would rather have them play around with some weed than drink or use hard drugs. You all probably think we are way too permissive. We are like the worst church-going folks. I just had so much of that legalistic crap growing up. I still wonder sometimes. They aren't little anymore, that's for sure. God, if we can just keep Trey's pants zipped up it will be a miracle. That kid is one raging hormone," Janet said.

"I know what you mean. After we lost Fred, so much of that stuff just seemed like so much horse-shit to me. Sometimes the more you fight it, the more the kids want to do it," Darla added biting her thread and smoothing the pants, folding them up and placing them in a box.

"You were asking about me and Mike. Well, I will tell you one thing that has definitely improved as of late," Janet said with a twinkle in her eye.

"Oh?" Darla said with a grin, putting her scissors down. "Spill the dirt, sister."

"Well…let's just say that something got ahold of his interest and turned the dial WAY up."

Miranda laughed. "You are going to have to give us a bit more than that. Hold on," she rose and went over to the kitchen and brought back the pitcher of mai tais she had made and poured new drinks for them all. "Let's hear some details. I am only living vicariously through y'all these days so give a girl a break."

Janet began, recalling how she and Mike had turned a new leaf in their sex life. In particular she recounted going down to the store wearing the short skirt. She recalled the freedom of walking into the store without any panties, feeling the cold air from the freezer section blow around her legs, hardening her nipples. Then she told of sitting on Mike's desk, spreading her legs, and watching his mouth drop open and his erection swell.

"Oh my!" Darla said taking a big drink.

"And I have never been all that crazy about, you know, going down there with him," Janet said with a knowing raise of her eyebrows.

"I used to hate that with Charlie. It just made me gag 'cause he would go so fast. Plus he also expected me to…"

"How rude. Ugh. I mean it's pretty amazing we let them put that thing in our mouth at all. Could you imagine what our mothers would have said?" They all laughed.

"But for some reason in the last few weeks, I can't get enough of it. I have just been the BJ Queen." The women hooted and laughed wildly. "Just call me Holly the Hoover." More loud giggles.

"Well, I don't know if I can top that," Darla said. "I mean, it's been like the Sahara around our place for so long. But last week I was doing some laundry pretty late at night. I had taken all the wet things out and put them in the dryer. But there's always that one sock or whatever that is stuck to the side. I was leaning way over trying to reach it. I am pretty short and everything…"

"Go on," Janet said taking a big swig of her drink.

"So I feel these hands move around my waist. Scared the bejesus out of me. I turn around and there is Duke with a look on his face like he was ready to eat me like the Big Bad Wolf. Then I look down and he is buck naked, standing up at attention like I haven't seen in years. He pushed my panties down and when I felt his thing brush my pony, I almost fainted. He just kept rubbing the lips down there and when he slid inside, it was so big and hard. It stretched me so far, like on our wedding night practically. He put my leg up on the washer and just starts drilling into me over and over, gripping my boobs, kissing me as I turned my head back. He yelled so loud when he finished I just knew George was going to come out and find us. He just kept pumping inside me."

"Holy shit," Miranda said with a whisper, adjusting on her chair.

And then he pulled me into the bedroom and pushed me back and went between my legs with his face and, you know, finished me off with his tongue. He never does that."

"Wow," Janet said fanning her face.

"And then he climbed around and put it in my mouth, which we have not done for ten years or more, and I just went for it. Since then, we have been doing it about three times a week. It's like a miracle." Darla's eyes sparkled, clearly enjoying sharing this bit of news.

"What about you Miranda? Anyone special in your life, yet?" Janet asked.

"Well…"

"Oh dear. Here we are bragging about things and it's not like that for you," Darla said.

"No. But let me tell you, there is nothing worse than having the wrong guy in your bed. My current fellow is strong, solid, smooth, and never, ever fails to make me come more than once."

"Really?" Darla said. "Who? What's his name?"

"Vinnie. Vinnie the Vibrator. And he never lets me down unless I forget to change his D-batteries!"

The ladies shrieked in laughter.

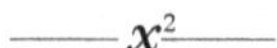

$$x^2$$

The high school musical almost collapsed when the students found out that dress rehearsal was set for October 31. The high school and junior high had their one joint dance of the year scheduled for that night. Luckily for Miss Cantor, the students were more prepared than she had ever dreamed. They began rehearsal early, after a lengthy negotiation with Coach Bates, at 4:30 and practiced hard, running straight through the show twice before dismissing the cast before 8:00. She practically held her breath during the run-throughs trying to find much to offer in the way of notes for the cast. For her first real production, it was more like working with college students than squirrelly teenagers. She just kept saying thank you over and over to the Almighty. Maybe doing a religious themed play was making the Man upstairs happy.

Janet had offered to help chaperone the dance along with Miranda. Mike refused at first and then unexpectedly changed his mind and said he would go ahead and come along. Miss Cantor was one of the faculty there along with Coach Bates, Mr. Smith, and Arlene Johnson, the Home Economics teacher from the high school. Mrs. Simmons and Mr. Monroe from the junior high were present along with a few other parents. This was Janet and Mike's first-ever duty as chaperones. Trey was furious that his parents would be present and threatened not to come. In the end, he was there wearing a Fred Flintstone costume that was way too short. His big hairy legs and bare feet, along with a big plastic club made him look more like teen Bam-Bam. Although not officially together as a date, Janet noticed that Angie Matlock was dressed as a very provocative Wilma Flintstone, with an off-the-shoulder white dress and a red rinse in her ponytailed hair. A shiny white bone fit in the knot of her hairdo.

George had insisted on being Luke Skywalker and twisted Emily and Travis's arms to be Leia and Han. Travis actually made a pretty convincing Han Solo. He had the smirk and smile of Harrison Ford in a young teenage way and his hair was close enough. George on the other hand wore a curly blond wig over his dark hair that unfortunately made him look more Harpo Marx than Mark Hammel. Emily at least got into the fun of the costume by wearing a dark wig with actual sweet rolls fastened to the sides. Janet had to admit though, the kids had a lot of fun with their friends. Mike and Janet saw Mary Washington, Carl's daughter and made a point to say hello with big hugs. She didn't have much to say and kept to herself mostly and with another young black girl, Mattie, who also played clarinet in the band. Mary had her hair teased out to its fullest afro extent with huge bell bottom pants and a low cut top and scarf around her neck. She carried a toy gun in her belt.

"You look just like 'Get Christy Love,'" Mike said grinning.

Mary smiled back. "Daddy always loved that show."

Theo Martin came as Mork, complete with a mop-top wig and tall white boots. His one-piece coverall was shockingly tight leaving absolutely nothing to the imagination. His Mindy date was forgotten the minute he arrived.

"Where does he keep his car keys?" Janet asked as Theo bent over to pick up a napkin from the refreshment table he had dropped. The tight pants disappeared up his backside a good three inches it seemed.

"Don't know," Mike said. "If you ever wanted to know whether ole Theo was circumcised or not, just take a look. Jeez! My eyes!" Janet giggled.

Mike asked Janet to dance about thirty minutes into the dance when the music slowed down. They moved around the floor to "Colour My Word" and Paul Davis's "I Go Crazy." Trey and Angie were barely moving at all, mostly they just hung on each other rocking back and forth. Trey and Emily left the floor after the fast dances, but Janet smiled when they came back to dance to the second number, Emily's hands locked around Travis's shoulders, his hands around her waist. George was holding court near the snack table showing off his homemade light sabre, holding it in front of his pants like a big wiener.

"These kids are going to dead tomorrow and it's their big opening night."

"Ah, they're young. They'll do fine. How about you and me take a little break," Mike said.

"But we're on duty," Janet teased.

"These kids are just fine. Let's give them a little space," he took her by the hand and led her off the floor and out the doors of the cafeteria down the hall of the school. Mike tried several classroom doors before finding an open one. When he did, he led Janet to the back of the room far away from the door. He took her in his arms and kissed her long and deep, their tongues dancing around one another's mouths. He gripped her breast, running his thumb along her nipple until it responded the way it always did. Janet's hand disappeared inside Mike's trousers and gripped his thick shaft, feeling the leaking tip slick against her finger. She sank to her knees and unfastened his pants. They fell around his ankles as she took him into her mouth, pulling all the way off before she let him fill her mouth again. Mike pulled her up and laid her back on the teacher's desk, reaching up to press his fingers into the damp fold of her panties. He gripped the elastic and slid them down until they hit the floor and he buried his face and tongue into her wet sex. He found her spot and teased it with his lips and tongue until she shuddered and came in quiet gasps, gripping his head in her hands. He stood up and faced her. She pulled his face to hers and tasted herself on his lips as he parted her lips and sank fully within her. Mike pumped hard and deep until he drove his release within her quivering body, his soft grunts filling the room along with the slapping of his balls against Janet's ass. They lay on the desk for a moment still coupled before Mike slid out and kissed Janet once again.

"I think the teacher is going to have a new stain or two on the desk blotter tomorrow," Mike whispered. Janet hit him softly on the shoulders and stifled a laugh into his neck.

"I think this is where they do detentions. If only I had known they were this much fun back in school," she said. "I love what is happening to us, Mike," Janet said softly stroking the side of her husband's face, feeling his member still pressed against her. She spread her legs again and felt him enter her again. She lay back as he held her legs wide apart, watching the sweat build on his lip and forehead as he thrust again and again, this time groaning loudly as he reach another climax and filled her again.

"God, I love fucking you," Mike whispered. "It's like brand new or something lately."

"I know. I feel the same." Janet sat up on the desk and slid her skirt down. She gripped Mike's penis playfully and tucked it back inside his jockey shorts. "We better go, darling," she said kissing him again. He bent down and handed Janet her panties. She smiled and put them in her purse. His eyes went wide.

"I am gonna ride you good when we get home, my little slutty seamstress."

"Promises, promises," Janet said.

The Cowhill High School production of Stephen Swartz's Tony Award winning play, "Godspell" opened on November 1. Janet smiled as she watched Travis and the other kids walk around to the band and the acting company, touching each one almost in a blessing of sorts, telling them to break a leg. The energy in the green room before the show was electric. The auditorium at the high school was packed. The small orchestra tuned and warmed up, the house lights dimmed, and the show began. The band played a short overture and the lights went to blackout. From the back of the house, the shofar horn sounded loud and foreign. The spotlight came on illuminating Theo Martin in his John the Baptist costume that looked remarkably like something Tito Jackson might wear right down to the floppy baseball cap. Theo opened his mouth and began to sing "Prepare Ye the Way" in a clear tenor a cappella that was startling. He strode down the aisle singing the clarion call as the cast wandered in from all parts of the auditorium. As they came closeer, he baptized them with a handful of colorful confetti and glitter causing them to join in the song. After the first number ended, the crowd applauded robustly. The stage was a series of platforms and multicolored boards and sawhorses that the company could move and reset in a moment to create other staging. The backdrop was a large cargo net strung into the stage fly that allowed the cast to even climb on it.

Andy leaned over to his dad. "Travis and George said that guy was a dick. But at least he can sing," he whispered. Mike elbowed him in the side. "Ow!"

The play moved on. When Trey walked out wearing his costume, there were a few giggles. He wore a baseball style shirt with a Superman logo on the front with big wide suspenders holding up the shortest shorts you can imagine. His outfit was finished off with knee high athletic socks and tennis shoes. It should have been so ridiculous the audience would be unforgiveable. Mike put his hand over his mouth and stared. The shorts were so tight they looked like underwear.

Mike leaned over to Janet and whispered. "Who knew Jesus was hung like a mule?"

"Shush," Janet whispered looking around to see if others heard. No one had but Andy who had fallen over in the chair in silent giggles.

But when Trey opened his mouth and began to sing, "Save the People" no one laughed. His rich tenor wasn't halting or tentative. He sang like a Broadway veteran, moving through the company as they sang along in background with his solo. Janet felt her heart swell watching Trey so full of confidence and artistry. It was a revelation, like seeing a flower for the very first time. As she watched the company on stage, seeing Travis, Emily, Mary and George along with the other high schoolers, she was struck by how grown up they all seemed. The crowd applauded loudly again as the song ended. No one giggled anymore at the shorts or the clown eye makeup with the teardrop on one side.

The play continued and moved into the most anticipated number of the show. After spending a number of weeks on the pop charts back in 1972, "Day by Day" was by far the most known and singable song in the musical. The stage lights dimmed to a soft orange and the spotlight hit Mary Washington, her hair big and full, big hoop earrings, a tight fitting white long-sleeved top and a flowing patchwork maxi skirt. Her rich alto voice began the familiar tune with gorgeous clarity, like warm honey poured over the crowd. Janet watched as the audience began to pat their feet and sing along with the song. By the time the company ran out into the aisles to dance and clap along with the song, Mary had the audience in the palm of her hand. She hauled off and sang like Tina Turner, ripping off runs in the vocal that were a wonder. The house began to clap and sing along with the company in a joyful celebration. The band rocked loud and hard through the number. Lights and music worked together to create a magical moment. When the song ended, the crowd leapt to its feet and cheered for a good minute. Janet's smile widened as she watched Mary touch her chest, obviously moved by so much love and adoration.

Emily's solo on "O Bless the Lord" was fun and full of energy. She danced and interacted with the company with such confidence and expertise, she looked like she had been on stage for years. The next big moment in the play was "All for the Best." Trey began the vaudeville number with an actual soft-shoe dance complete with cane and top hat. Mike was awed.

"Where in the hell did the kid learn to do that?" he whispered.

Then Theo joined in for the fast tongue-twisting counterpoint to the song. He ripped through the fast clipped words and then he and Trey joined in for the finale doing an actual tap dance, hoofing it like vaudeville veterans. They tapped up the boards on the sawhorse and actually down the other side like a see-saw. It was simply remarkable. A second standing ovation brought the show to a halt again with Theo and Trey actually making a small curtain call of their own, bowing slightly to the adoring crowd.

Before the intermission, the company sang "All Good Things." George and Travis took turns on the solo, standing the middle of the stage with blue lights filling the space. The company danced in a circle, performing an almost Hebrew-looking dance as the boys sang the soulful melody, hauling off and hitting the high notes perfectly. The sweetness and devotion of the song permeated the hall and Janet looked around to see dozens of audience members wipe tears from their eyes. By the time the cast closed the first Act with "Light of the World," the crowd was enraptured.

During the interval, Mike and Janet received congratulations from a large number of highly impressed townsfolk. Darla and Duke Harris came over, Darla's face wet with tears.

"I never thought he could do that," she said with a blubber. Others came up echoing the same sentiments over and over, "Your boys are amazing. Who knew?"

The second Act began with "Turn Back, O Man," a campy, vampy number a la Mae West meets Carole King. The surprise here was Angie Matlock, strutting her stuff in fishnet stockings and heels, with a top cut so low Miss Cantor even suggested she use some adhesive to keep her tits from falling out. But instead of coming across as slutty, she was a strong, in-charge, liberated woman who knew what she wanted. Her dance and flirtations with Trey as Jesus were both hilarious and provocative. Janet looked over in the audience to see Buck Matlock and his family with decidedly less-than-excited faces, which was totally the opposite of the rest of the crowd that simply loved it. At the end of the song, the company joined up in a long chorus line and did a kick step that would make the Rockettes jealous. The crowd went wild.

Right before the lovely "On the Willows," a Last Supper moment in the play, Judas/Theo is forced to make his big decision: to betray or believe. Theo played the part to the fullest, pantomiming a man whose every possible choice and path is taken away from him only to lead him to Jesus and his ultimate destiny. As the music stopped and the two young men faced each other, the excruciating decision facing Judas held the audience breathless. Judas fell at Jesus's feet in supplication and Trey stretched out a shaking hand and touched the side of Theo's head in a gesture of the most tender forgiveness imaginable. When Theo stood and grabbed Trey and planted an uncomfortably long full-mouth kiss on the Savior, Janet heard audible gasps and sniffs from the audience. From the look on Trey's face, he was as unprepared for that as the audience.

"Damn," Mike whispered, "Is that in the play?"

"I don't know. It wasn't in rehearsal, that's for sure."

During the "Finale" the disciples took the part of the mad crowd, beating and pummeling Jesus with such viciousness, it looked completely real. As the mob attached Trey to the cargo net, hanged above the rest of the company, the blood capsules he had concealed in his wrists and forehead exploded and crimson flowed over his face and hands eliciting actual cries of shock and horror from the crowd. The band played the guitar licks loud and rocking. The lights strobed and flashed while the disciples grieved and collapsed in emotional dances. The band quieted and Trey hung dead on the net. Quiet sobs and sniffs punctuated the quiet auditorium. The disciples continued to sing "Long Live God" as they took Trey's dead form off the net and held him high above their heads and walked around the stage, laying Jesus in his tomb on the stage floor. The counterpoint of "Prepare Ye the Way" reprised along with "Long Live God" as billows of smoke from a dry-ice machine flowed over the stage and built a wall of mist behind the high schoolers standing across the stage. As the chorus grew and then built to a last loud note, Trey emerged from the mist, now wearing a solid white tight-fitting jumpsuit and a circle of gold on his head. The crowd gasped and awed and began to clap while the company transitioned into the reprise of "Day by Day." They danced in the aisles and grabbed audience members up on the stage. A startled Miranda Moon and Principal Charlie Jones did their best to rock along with the students. Streamers were tossed, the spotlights moved in drunken circles around the auditorium. On the final note of the show, the audience roared, standing and giving a three minute ovation as one by one, the disciples from the company came out and created a line. Lastly, Theo entered to a new roar of cheers from the crowd. Trey jumped up on the back platform and bowed as actual screams and whistles filled the air. He walked over and embraced Theo and then the entire company took a long bow.

It was the most amazing performance Cowhill High had ever had. Last year's production of "Annie Get Your Gun" was so horrific, the show opened and closed the same night, Charlie Jones adamantly saying he had never seen anything so terrible in his entire life. The drama teacher's contract had not been renewed. Needless to say, Naomi Cantor was floating on Cloud Nine, her damp face shining as the class presented her with a large bouquet of yellow roses, courtesy of JL Martin who seemed so proud of Theo he was ready to burst.

The remainder of the performances were strong and well attended just like the first, but the magic of that opening night was unique. Late that night, long after 2:00 am when the kids should have long been in bed, Trey and Travis walked back into the house and to their parents' bedroom.

"Sorry, folks. The party went on a little long. Charlie Jones was pretty mad we were still up in the choir room that late. So, what did you think?" Trey asked flopping down on the bed accidently sitting on Mike's feet.

"Oh boys, you were so amazing," Janet said reaching for them. "I have never been more proud. I, I just kept reminding myself that you were mine. So many people came up to say how great you were. It was the best show the school has ever done."

Trey beamed. Travis looked a bit embarrassed, but still grinned and seemed very happy.

"Guys, I did not know you had it in you. I guess you got more of your mom's creative talent than I ever realized. I almost busted the buttons off my shirt I was so proud," Mike said grabbing the boys in big rough hugs. "And wow, your first big stage kiss too," Mike said with a wink and smile.

"Yeah, I almost peed my pants when Theo did that. But I guess it worked. Miss Cantor already told us to do it that way the next time too."

The boys got up to head to bed. Mike caught Trey by the hand and held him back. "You've had a great few weeks, buddy. Remember this. It's not always going to be so great. But when you have a crap week, remember this one. Between this and the football...damn, Trey."

As Travis lay in bed thirty minutes later, Trey came into the porch and sat on the bed. "I know a lot of that tonight was the alien magic, but dang, it was so fun. Thanks, Trav."

"Hey, you must have real talent Trey or it wouldn't have mattered if we zapped each other or not. But yeah, that was super cool to say the least."

Trey reached over and rubbed Travis's hair, messing it up and patting the side of his head. "Have to hand it to you bro, you and your friends...I owe you."

JL reached into his desk drawer and opened his bottle of Percodan and took three with a swallow of Hires Root Beer. He rubbed his temple, his head was throbbing today. He clearly needed to spend some quality time with his friend *Sernyl* and see if the angel had anything new to say to him. He was feeling antsy all the time and had to balance the high the *Sernyl* could bring with the morphine or Percodan to keep him level headed.

He was working on some of the damn Norton trial paperwork that was needed by one of his financial guys as well as making some plans to move forward with another ceremony as soon as he felt like he had received the vision he needed in order to proceed. He had been unsuccessful lately bringing any new revelations to himself through the drugs, studying his great-grandfather's journals, or even inviting his college student diversions over. In fact, the last time that LaFonda and Joe Wilson came over, he was so distracted and disinterested, he couldn't even get it up, which absolutely never happened to him.

He grabbed his reading glasses and tried to make sense of some of the numbers on the ledger sheets he was reviewing when the front door creaked and the bell on the handle tinkled. JL looked up perturbed, which grew even greater as he saw it was Dr. Hillman heading in to see him. He hated ambushes and this had the stink of a big one. Caroline no doubt had something to do with it.

"Hey there, Doc. How's it going for you today?"

"I'm fine, JL. Thank you. Um, I have been leaving messages for you. Some of the tests I ran for you recently came back and there is some real concern. I wanted to talk with you about your CT scan you had done at Baylor Hospital."

"Okay. Doc. Well you got a captive audience here so, shoot."

"Well, the scan came back with some concerning anomalies. It appears your headaches are most likely caused by a shocking number of vacuoles, like big bubbles, that have appeared in your brain. JL, I have to tell you this is very serious. I am not aware of anything we can do to repair this kind of damage. And I must also say, I feel it's clearly related to your continued use of the Phencyclidine. I told you more than once it was a dangerous drug and I am afraid that it is mostly likely the contributing source of this brain damage," Doctor Hillman said in a grave, authoritative voice.

"Well, alright then, Doc. You've told me. I will cut back on the use of the *Sernyl*. But honestly, there must be another reason because the stuff makes me feel better, not worse. Without it, I think this Swiss cheese brain of mine would really be hard to manage."

"No, that is not it at all JL. It is the cause of the problems. If you stop using it, it's possible that you will at least not get any worse. If you continue, I am afraid you will very soon reach a toxic situation that could even kill you," the doctor said impassioned.

JL smiled and stood up. "I hear what you are saying, Doc. I will try and stop using the medicine. But right now, I am very busy so if you will excuse me…" JL held the front door to his office open. The sounds of Main Street and the city square filtered into the small office. Dr. Hillman hesitated and finally shrugged his shoulders and left.

"Damn, that is one pesterly doctor," JL mused. "Junior, Toy, y'all back there?" JL hollered toward the back rooms of the offices he held on the corner of Square across the street from the Palace Theater.

Junior Bidwell came around the corner with his mouth full holding a crispy piece of meat in his hand.

"Yeah, Boss," he said chewing. "Sorry, it's steak finger basket day at the DQ. Only $1.79."

Toy Benton sauntered out with his cup of gravy, dipping in the Texas Toast before putting half the bread in his mouth at once. JL looked at the men with disgust. Junior held the half-eaten steak finger behind his back. "What can I do for you, Boss?"

"How many times have I told you to stop calling me that? You aren't on a fucking chain gang, though I'm sure you have had that experience before and most certainly will again. Never mind. I want you to get a word around to the deacons and other important church members. I have heard about this ridiculous illustrated sermon charlatan preacher that is blowing into town at that infernal Living Waters travesty of a church. They are inviting half the town and I don't like it one bit. They will have a pew for coons, spics, and homos if I know that idiot preacher. We are going to crash that service and make a statement for real religion."

"Yessir, Boss," Junior answered. "Sorry, not boss."

"Jesus, keep me near the cross," JL snapped. "By the way, any word at all, anything turn up on our dark friend we lost track of out at the barn that night? It's been six weeks or more. If he's dead he should have been found. If he was hiding out, someone should have seen him."

"No sir. I think that ship has already left the barn."

"What?"

"He up and disappeared like a rabbit wearing a magician's top hat."

"That is the stupidest thing I have ever heard. I am literally surrounded by idiots."

38 Travis

Sunday mornings around the McGee home were usually more chaotic than school days. Everyone trying to get in and out of the bathroom and dressed for church and out the door to get to Sunday School by 9:45. With Teppy now at college most of the time, Janet had relented and allowed Mike back into her bathroom which made the crush in the boy's bathroom less hectic than normal.

Since explaining to Trey what was happening with the powers, Travis and Andy had endured plenty of his own attempts to flex his mental muscles. Trey had already managed to burn Travis's Eggo to a crisp setting off the smoke alarm in the process, which was always a great way to get Mike bent out of shape. Then for more shits and giggles, Trey zapped the elastic in Andy's underwear somehow, making it stretch out twice as far as normal, so when the little guy crawled up on the kitchen stool reaching up to grab the Capt'n Crunch, his Spiderman Underroos lost their spidey senses and dropped to his ankles which surprised him so much, he lost his balance and fell off the stool sprawling in the middle of the kitchen floor. Trey's booming laughs could be heard through the entire house, making Mike run to the kitchen with shaving cream still on his face, slipping on Andy's spilled cereal and slamming into the boy causing even more chaos in the house.

Andy and Travis managed to pay Trey back by causing his Polo men's cologne to spray four times more than normal, exploding in a cloud of mist, drenching him in sickening scent. He was so pungent; Mike made him go take another shower before the family could leave. Needless to say, by the time the family got in the station wagon, the stress level was off the Richter scale.

It only took about five minutes to drive to the church from the McGee house on Maple Street. Mike and Janet got out of the car and headed to the church sanctuary and their bible study class. The boys headed toward the church annex building but Travis grabbed Trey's arm and pulled him back.

"What?" Trey said in his typical pushy loud voice.

Travis leaned and said in a quiet voice, "Quit using your powers on us like that."

"Screw you, Scrote," Trey said turning to leave.

Andy and Travis grabbed the tall boy and literally pulled him off his feet and pushed him up against the wall of the church. Andy leaned close and whispered, "Knock that shit off, big brother." Travis smiled wondering if they were all going to get struck by lightning.

"Jeez, okay, okay, little dickweed," Trey said back looking around to see if anyone had seen him get manhandled by his two little brothers. "I was just having some fun."

"It's not funny when you just do stupid crap like that all the time," Travis added. "Look, we've all done it before but it's just not cool to keep making that stuff happen to each other. Like Emily is always saying, use your powers to help people instead of just be a super jerk."

"Sure thing, Gandhi," Trey said with sarcasm. Trey waved to Sam Miller from the football team and headed over to talk with him. Andy headed to his Sunday school class. Travis followed Trey into the youth hall. Trey and Sam headed over to some chairs at the back of the room. Travis slid into a chair closer to the front room beside George and Emily.

"You're cutting it close today," Emily said smiling. She had her hair curled and a tailored navy blue pant suit on that made her look ready for the office.

"It's been one of those days," Travis whispered back. "Trey decided to play with his new discoveries, if you know what I mean. What an idiot. You look nice by the way."

"Don't sound so surprised," Emily said.

"She decided to risk the wrath of God with the pantsuit today," George teased. "And then there's Maude," he sang.

Emily punched him in the arm, bending George over in pain. "Man," he complained, "Not so hard, Ali."

Emily looked at George with her stern school teacher look. "And I still can't believe you told Cory that we would help lead worship in here today. I thought we weren't going to do that."

"Hey, you were the one who keeps saying use our stuff for good. Singing for Jesus sounds like a pretty good thing to do," George answered rubbing his arm. "I will need to have prayer for my injured arm when they take prayer requests. Besides, after our great triumph at the musical, we might as well continue our tradition of being the next new thing."

"Would you two knock it off? Could we just concentrate on doing this and doing a good job? I don't want to bleed all over the place," Travis said.

"That hasn't been happening anymore, has it? Remember, don't try too much. With the three of us together, it flows easy. Think how easy it felt for 'Godspell.' Just think about it, pull from each other, let it flow," George said like a guru leading a group meditation. "Like we practiced at home. And here," he handed a wad of Kleenex to Travis. "I'm sure you won't need this, but just in case."

Judy Stevens, one of the youth group leaders, came in and following her was a nervous black girl with a large afro hairdo and a bright African print maxi dress. The teenagers in the room all stopped talking when the girl walked in, but she smiled at them all and looked around for a seat.

"Come sit over here," George said scooting over to make room. Emily and Travis moved over as well. The girl joined them.

"Thanks," she said in a quiet voice.

"Sure thing. Nice to see you, Mary." George said. "It's cool you came and everything. How have you been?" George's face instantly turned red as he realized what he had just asked and began to sputter like a motorboat.

Mary smiled and actually reached over and grabbed his hand. "I'm okay, thanks for asking. Everybody treats me like I'm a ticking bomb or something these days."

Emily reached over and took Mary's other hand. "We are so sorry for all that's happened. Any word on your dad?"

Mary's eyes were tearful but she maintained her composure and even managed a small smile. "Not yet. But I just know he's okay. He's hiding or something. Those monsters didn't finish him. I can just feel it."

None of the three had anything to say to that, so they just patted her arm and squeezed her hand and sat back. Travis noticed that most of the other kids in the classroom kept looking back at them. Most just seemed curious or even a little nervous. But he noticed a few of them, seemed irritated or even angry. One of ones looking the maddest, Henry Manning, was leaning his chair back against the wall, shooting evil glances with his eyes. Travis reached over and grabbed Emily's hand. Two seconds later, Henry's chair slid out from under him and he clunked his head hard on the wood floor. Travis looked over at George who extended his hand out behind their chair and offered a quiet high five.

"Okay, Henry stop messing around and let's settled in," Cory said. Cory was the youth leader and most of the girls were secretly in love with him. His shoulder length hair was frowned on by the adults, but it made the girls long for him and the guys respect him for not bowing to the pressure to conform, especially here at church. It might be the norm at school to see guys with long flowing hair, but here at Living Waters, the conservative haircuts of the 1960's still ruled for the most part, with hair beginning to creep down on collars and ears along with big sideburns and facial hair. He had a gentle demeanor and smile that was charming and welcoming.

"Have you ever noticed when Cory smiles, his eyes do that same thing your dad's do?"

"What?" Travis said. "No, I don't see that."

"Okay, let's move in closer and let's spend some time in worship this morning. George, if you and Travis and Emily would come up and help me out," Cory said picking up his guitar and adjusting the strap. The three stood up and momentarily gripped each other's hands and then walked to the front of the youth hall. George picked up another acoustic guitar and Travis picked up George's electric. Emily sat beside Cory and adjusted the microphone.

"I'm so glad these guys have come up to help out. I knew there were plenty of talented teens in this church, but I am really impressed with these three. Thanks again for helping lead with me today," Cory said with a gentle smile nodding at each of the kids. The three nodded in return, reddening in embarrassment as they did. Living Waters Community Church was mostly still stuck in the past it seemed, but the youth group had been willingly led into the new age by some free thinking Jesus People from the West Coast that had moved to Texas to try and make a difference for teen groups in traditionally fundamental churches that offered very little relative spiritual life for young people. Their parents were mired in traditions. "Give me that old time religion," was still sung by the congregation. Old gospel hymns from "Heavenly Highways" were still part of the song service. But once a month, the youth was allowed to lead a Sunday night service. Interestingly, more youth attended church on that night than any other.

Cory counted the band off and they kicked off the worship time with "Joy is the Flag."

The group sang loudly with hands waving above their heads. The band played the guitars and piano loud and exuberantly, smiling at one another as they felt the energy circle between them. Cory transitioned to "This is the day that the Lord hath made," and the other three followed along keeping the accompaniment going fresh and lively. The kids clapped and joined in with joy and Travis couldn't help but compare this to the way the youth of the church normally interacted in the main service. Out there, they barely sang and half of them would pass the time writing notes or doing the crossword puzzle from the Sunday school newsletter. Here, the teens joined in, felt connected, and there was a real sense of spirituality that seemed fresh and genuine. He also continued to wonder if all of these kids had the new power like they did. Did they just not know it? Did they think they were the only one and so they just kept quiet?

Cory counted off the next song slowly and George took the lead, picking out the melody to "Open our eyes" along with Emily. Travis closed his eyes and it was almost like he could see the music and notes floating in his mind as he played.

Travis looked out over the youth group and saw silly girls and sullen boys with their eyes closed and faces turned to the sky. Many of them had their hands lifted in supplication to the heavens as the power and sweetness of the music poured over them. *This was real power,* Travis thought. But a part of him also wondered if it was even greater than usual because of the three of them channeling the special abilities. He looked over at George whose eyes were closed as he played. He looked at Emily who was quietly weeping as she played the piano softly. He felt his own heart expand and fill with a wonderful gratefulness and hope. He noticed even Trey had his eyes closed and singing. Whatever this was, he thought, I wish it would always be like this.

As the song ended, George and Emily continued to quietly play. Cory began to speak.

"There is a very sweet spirit here today and I just want us to continue to let it pour over us. Is there anyone here today that has a special need that you want us to pray about as we continue to worship?"

Karen Allen slid her hand up and in a quiet voice asked if we could all pray for her grandmother who was very ill after suffering a stroke. Cory began to pray, leading the youth in a prayer of intercession and healing for Karen's grandmother that seemed like one of those from an evangelistic faith healer from days gone by. Several of the nearby girls and boys had reached out to touch Karen as they prayed. Cory then asked if there was anyone else who needed prayer. From the back, Mary Washington's hand rose.

"I have an unspoken request," she said barely more than a whisper.

Cory smiled and asked those standing near Mary to reach out and lay their hands on her as we prayed. Tears flowed down her face and as they prayed. George began to sing "Cares Chorus." Kelly Willard's words seemed to pour out like a healing potion and the whole youth group turned toward Mary and began to sing and lay their hands on each other as they circled around the trembling girl who stood with her hands lifted high above her head. As the song continued, Travis could literally feel the energy rocket around the group and ignite a fire of intense comfort and peace in this small band of teenagers. Several others were weeping now and the teens stood together in solidarity of spirit as they shared in Mary's sorrow but also together wrapped arms of blessing around her. For these special moments, Mary's story, the fact she was a black girl in an almost all white church, none of that seemed to matter.

The music came to a close and the youth, almost embarrassed, wandered back to their seats not sure what had just happened. Cory began to speak, explaining that the Holy Spirit was right there with them and how precious of a moment this was. He continued to speak and encourage the kids to continue to care and stand with one another in the coming days and weeks like they had today. Travis couldn't help but notice some of the kids seemed positively shocked at what they had just participated in and he felt it was unlikely many of them would be planning to reach out to comfort the likes of Mary Washington again anytime soon. But for these moments, it was wonderful to see how amazing it could be "for men to dwell together in peace" the way it said in the Bible.

Cory spent a bit longer sharing some encouraging words from the Bible and reminded the group that the revival was going to start tonight and that Brother Zigler's illustrated sermons should be a great opportunity for them to invite another school friend to church as well. He looked at his watch and said it was about time to close the youth group service and head to the sanctuary for the Sunday morning congregational gathering. The group stood and George and Cory began strumming their guitars again. The group formed a circle and held hands and sang "Pass it on." As the words flowed forth, it felt like a real spark of love and connection burned brightly within the teenagers.

Together in the back part of the sanctuary, Emily and Travis held hands sitting with George on the other side of them again with Mary. George had insisted she sit with them in the service.

Travis was amused to see how protective and kind George was with Mary since he rarely seemed to care that much about anyone else beyond their small group. Trey and a couple of his football buddies sat two pews back, talking quietly with each other. Travis looked at Trey who looked up at him. For a moment, they locked eyes and it seemed like Trey's hostility and anxiousness was gone and Travis was seeing a new kind of Trey. A moment later Trey looked away and began to rub his nose with his middle finger sending a clear message to Travis. *That didn't last long,* Travis thought as he shook his head.

Emily twined her fingers through Travis's hand and reached over and softly stroked the fuzz on his knuckles. Travis watched the mood ring on her cool hand quickly shift from amber to teal and then deep blue. As he watched the ring warm and settle on passionate colors, he felt himself rise and stiffen in his polyester double knit trousers that left absolutely nothing to the imagination. Emily smiled and took her crocheted shawl from beside her and laid it in Travis's lap.

"Thanks," he whispered clutching the shawl to his lap.

"Just think of Ferle or Coach Beadles naked on a bear skin rug."

"Yep, that should do it," Travis said with a chuckle. He rubbed Emily's fingers with his thumb and smiled at her. "That youth service today…"

"Was so beautiful. See, what I was saying. We can use these powers for all sorts of good stuff too."

"You think that was just us?"

"What else? Emily asked.

"Not sure. But I have a sneaking suspicion more kids than just us got zapped by that light," Travis answered.

"And they might not even know what's going on," Emily said contemplatively.

"That's what I was thinking. But when we were all together like that, singing and being all worshippy, it sort of turned on a switch."

Emily's eyes widened and she started to speak but Pastor Nelson began to call the congregation to stand and sing the call to worship. Travis and Emily stood along with the rest of the crowd and began to sing.

Jesus has the table spread where the
   saints of God are fed

He invites his chosen people,
   "Come and Dine."

With his manna he doth feed
And supplies our every need
Oh, 'tis sweet to sup with Jesus
   all the time

"Come and dine," the Master calleth,
   "Come and dine";

You may feast at Jesus' table all the time;
He Who fed the multitude, turned
   the water into wine,

To the hungry calleth now,
   "Come and dine."

George leaned close, "This song just makes me hungry. Where are you parents taking us for lunch after church? And if Jesus was okay with the wine . . ."

Next, the crowd launched into "Power in the Blood."

Would you be free from your
*   burden of sin?*

There's power in the blood,
*   Power in the blood*

Sin stains are washed in the
*   life-giving flood*

There's wonderful power in the blood.

"They should let Cory do all the worship for the church," Emily said. "This stuff is so dumb to me. My grandma is into all these old songs but that's about all. I'm going to the bathroom." She scooted by Travis, her backside rubbing against his crotch as she did. He lowered the hymnal to waist level. The last song of the morning was the mournful, "Farther Along."

Farther along we'll know all about it
Farther along we'll understand why

Cheer up my brother, live in the sunshine
We'll understand it all bye and bye.

As terrible as Travis thought the songs were, there was no doubt that Mary was enjoying them. Singing along, clapping, and even lifting her hands on the chorus of "Farther Along." No doubt she had more reason to identify with these songs of wishing life was a lot better now and hoping for a day when it would be better. When Travis thought about that, he figured the songs made more sense.

After the song service concluded, Brother Nelson encouraged everyone to find a hand to shake or a neck to hug, men hug men and women hug women. With Emily still in the bathroom, George moved closer to Travis and locked him in a big hug pressing himself tightly against his friend. George looked up slyly at Travis.

"Um, is that a hymnal in your pocket or are you just happy to see me?"

Travis narrowed his eyes and pushed George away. "Eat me," Travis mouthed.

"You wish," George mouthed back. Travis elbowed George in the stomach which sent the boy flying back into the pew with a crack, knocking the wind out of him. Mary turned around staring and tried to help George up.

"Are you okay," she asked.

"Yep, just lost my balance," he said looking with narrowed, dangerous eyes at Travis.

The man in front of Travis turned around and held out his hand. Travis suddenly realized it was Jack Tanner from Western Auto. He hadn't seen him at church ever before that he could remember. Jack pulled Travis toward himself and hugged him in the "brotherly way" that the pastor admonished the crowd to use. As he held Travis's hand and pulled him close, their minds locked together again and Travis saw Jack and Joey along with Tim Murphy in the tent, saw them at the store, saw that mean Mr. Martin holding Tim down on the desk with a gun, Tim's pants down around his ankles. He saw Mr. Martin fly across the room. He saw Jack in bed with Joey and his wife. And then he saw the cat. He pushed away from Jack staring.

Jack leaned forward with a hand on Travis's shoulder. "I need to talk to you and your friends.

Come by the store tomorrow at lunch, okay?" He pulled away and then said, "Hey Travis, this is my wife, Lori and that's Joey." Travis nodded hello both of them.

Travis stared in shock but nodded in agreement. Emily returned and settled in beside Travis. She dug out some paper from her purse and the two of them played dots for the rest of the service. Brother Nelson's riveting sermon on wives being submissive to their husbands being almost more than they could stand. Travis kept staring at Jack during the service and noticed that Joey kept turning around and staring back at him, studying him deeply.

By the time Brother Nelson was asking the congregation to stand and calling those couples down to the front that wanted to rededicate themselves to living godly lives, Travis was exhausted. He watched as one after the other, most of the married couples in the service went down to the front. He wondered how many of them wanted to rededicate themselves and how many got peer-pressured into following the crowd? He saw his own parents down at the front, along with Duke and Darla Harris. He looked across the church and saw Emily's mother sitting quietly alone. Finally, Emily leaned over.

"I'm going to get mom and get the hell out of here. This is just so mean to someone like my mom. What is she supposed to do? What about the old ladies here whose husbands are dead. Oooo,"she said in frustration.

"I need to talk to you," Travis began.

"I'll come over after lunch." She leaned over and kissed him very close to his mouth and he felt himself instantly blush. She crawled over him and George and Mary and made her way to her mother and grabbed her hand to lead her out of the church. Travis saw Lori Tanner get up and extend her hand to Jack who took it and rose to his feet. He started to reach for Joey, but the little boy pulled back.

"I'll stay here. I'll be good," he said.

"I can watch him for you," Travis leaned forward and said. Joey looked up and grinned, climbing over the bench and into Travis's lap.

Jack smiled. "Thanks," he said while Lori pulled him up toward the front. It looked like Jack was going to get rededicated whether he wanted it or not. George scooted over closer to Travis.

"Who's this big guy?" George said extending his hand.

"I'm Joey Tanner. You and this boy see the green light too. You are at the bridge in my dreams. You need to be careful," he said then stared hard at Travis. "The bad man wants to hurt your brother and my daddy. And that black girl too."

George froze and turned to look at Travis who was staring in disbelief at the small boy. He reached out and took George's hand in his. He leaned forward and touched his forehead to Travis and blasted both of them with his vision. They were instantly with Joey along with his dad, his business partner, Tim, Emily, and Mary Washington at the edge of the ruined bridge.

> Red light, yellow light, green light bridge;
> Just down the hill from Scatter Branch ridge ...

The familiar pulling toward the edge by the unseen hook in their belly began and as Travis looked around, he saw more faces. One of them now seemed clear. The red, puffy face of JL Martin came into view, except it was wrong. He had horns and was all in black, like some Halloween costume of a devil. Others crowded in close to him and Travis felt for sure he knew more of them. The musicians at the front of the church were playing "Turn your eyes upon Jesus" as the vision continued. Travis felt anxiety creep up his neck like a cold sweat. Something was wrong. He could feel it too. Someone was definitely hurt or in danger.

> *Turn your eyes upon Jesus*
> *Look full in His wonderful face*
> *And the things of earth will grow*
>   *strangely dim*
> *In the light of His glory and grace*

The vision vanished leaving the boys breathless and sweating.

"I need to go pee," the little boy said gripping himself through his pants.

George spoke up, "Okay, buddy. Um, hold it. We'll take you. Let's go, man or this kid's gonna blow," George said pushing Travis to get up. Travis looked up at the front but Jack and Lori were still up with the other couples. He stood up and Joey followed still holding himself while holding George's outstretched hand. The boys walked quickly down the side aisle and back to the men's bathroom. They went inside and locked the door. Joey ran to the toilet and stood on his tiptoes.

"It's too tall," he said.

George looked panicked at Travis with a 'what do we do now' look. Travis pushed him out of the way and grabbed the little boy and stood him up on the rim of the toilet bowl and helped him balance as Joey pushed his pants down and peed, managing to get most of it in the toilet bowl. Travis put him on the floor after he was finished and helped him get his pants back up.

"See, these are all the things I missed out on by not having a little brother," George said clearly impressed.

"You want to wash your hands?" Travis asked.

"No, I didn't pee on them," Joey answered matter of fact.

"That's what I say. Why should you need to wash your hands after you pee? I mean, unless your Johnson is filthy or something. I mean, maybe it makes more sense to wash your hands before you hold your dick . . . "

"Would you knock it off," Travis said. "Come on before Jack thinks we kidnapped his kid."

The boys came back into the sanctuary just as the dismissal prayer was being said. The pastor reminded the crowd that the revival started tonight with Rev. Zigler and that they wouldn't want to miss the illustrated sermon entitled "Destination: Heaven or Hell." As the couples walked back to their seats to grab their purses and bibles, Joey ran toward Jack and Lori and launched himself into his dad's arms. Jack walked up to their seat to let Lori grab her purse.

"Thanks for watching him. Maybe I'll keep you in mind if we need a sitter," Jack said.

"They helped me go potty. Travis held me up on the potty like you do, Daddy."

"How nice of them," Lori said. "Thanks boys. He's doing pretty well with the potty training these days and it would have been bad for him to have an accident right here in church.

"Sure, no problem. He's really good at peeing for such a little boy," Travis said stupidly feeling instantly embarrassed. "He really talks well too. Kind of wild for such a little guy."

Lori laughed. "I know. You should have seen us a month or so ago. It's like night and day."

Travis looked up at Jack and wordlessly communicated. He figured Joey learned how to control his bladder right after September 12. Somehow, this little kid figured into all of this, just like Mary Washington and her missing dad. And Travis had a suspicion Jack was thinking the same thing. Lori picked up Joey and headed for the back door.

"See you later guys." The boys waved good-bye to Lori and Joey who waved like a crazy man as he left.

"Um, guess we'll see you at the store. Getting more candy, you know," Travis said.

"Sure thing. Guess we might see you tonight. Joey wants to come back and see this illustrated sermon thing tonight."

"Oh cool. It won't scare him or anything will it?" Travis asked.

"Not sure. He's the one that said we need to come tonight. And I am pretty reluctant these days not to go along with what he says like that, if you know what I mean?" Jack added.

"Yeah, we are picking up on that," Travis said. There was so much more he wanted to ask about but just let it go for now. "Okay, then see you soon." With that, George and Travis left and headed out to the parking lot. Trey was already fuming that all the tables at the Charcoal Broiler would be taken since Travis was so slow in dragging his dead ass out of the church. Mike McGee smacked Trey in the back of the head, not hard, but to get the point across. Andy laughed and was thumped on the ear by his dad as well which made the young boy grab his ear and holler loudly.

"Hey, that hurts!" Andy yelled.

Travis rolled his eyes and climbed in the back of the station wagon with George.

"My dad gave me $5 bucks, Mr. McGee so I won't be such a bum for you today," George announced from the back.

"My lucky day," Mike answered, "Now if I could just get a few of these other deadbeats to pony up some scratch."

39 George

The boys sat at the back of Charcoal Broiler while Mike and Janet enjoyed a quiet lunch alone for a change. The boys had ordered chicken fried steak with a baked potato and fried okra. Tons of creamy white gravy was served over the crunchy steak. Rivers of butter flowed from the baked potato along with sour cream. The okra was crunchy and salty like popcorn. The large chunk of Texas toast barely fit on the plate. And of course, the obligatory green salad drowned in Thousand Island dressing completed the lunch, all for the affordable price of $3.25.

Travis told the other boys what he had seen when Joey was in his lap and what he had said. They sat and listened, working their way through the okra and potatoes. George was aware that for once, Trey didn't have one obnoxious joke or a-hole comment to make. He asked a couple of questions, but seemed subdued and actually paying attention, especially to the parts where the kid had said he was in danger.

"So, one more time," Trey asked. "The kid said he saw me in trouble or hurt, or he just said he thought someone wanted to hurt me?"

"This is true," George said, "Cause if they just wanted to hurt Trey, then that could be half the town."

Trey put down his fork and leaned down to pick up his napkin. He punched George hard in the sack on the way up, causing him to double over and groan. Andy started laughing hard with a mouthful of food which got stuck, and Travis had to whack him on the back to help him cough it up.

George gripped his testicles and groaned, "My nutbag. Damn, there goes my future children."

Trey took a big gulp of sweet tea and resumed his questioning. "So was it just me, or was it me and this Mary girl? Or was it someone else too?"

Travis shook his head. "Trey, I don't know all that. He's a little kid, okay? But he knew stuff. He's been having the same dream as the rest of us. And he's not normal either, okay? He talks way too good for a little boy his age."

"And don't forget he taught himself how to be potty trained by himself in like a couple of days it sounds like," George said still groaning.

"Knock it off," G, it sounds like you have to take a dump or something," Travis said scanning the restaurant to see if others were paying attention. They weren't.

"Excuse me, Travis. Just because you don't have any balls doesn't mean you can yell at those of us that do, Right Trey?" George asked.

Trey balled up his fist and aimed for George's groin again but didn't hit this time. "Made you flinch, butt munch," Trey said socking the smaller boy in the arm instead.

"Mother ..." George groaned falling over in the booth.

"You guys are gonna get our asses kicked," Travis said.

Andy spoke up. "So we've all had this dream for a long time, right? And when we get together and join our powers together, we can do stuff way bigger, right? So maybe if we like all got together and tried to sleep together we might have a bigger, more real-er dream?"

"That sounds like a load of laughs, sleeping with all you ass wipes, holding each other's dicks so we can have sweet dreams together," Trey said.

George opened his mouth to interject one of his patented bon mots, but Trey held up his fist which shut George's mouth as he clamped his hand over his lap. Trey looked at him daring him to say something else, but the boy turned a key on his mouth and kept eating.

"Irregardless," Trey began, "The munchkin does have a point. We might get somewhere if we did try and link up for this dream."

"We could invite Jack and Tim over and Joey too for a big sleep over," Andy offered.

"Yeah, that's not going to happen, idiot brother. Two grown men are not going to come over for a slumber party with a bunch of boys so we can have a big circle jerk together while we listen to Stevie Nick's sing "Dreams," Trey snapped.

"What's a circle jerk?" Andy asked.

"What does Stevie Nicks have to do with any of this?" George added.

Travis put his hands up. "All of you shut up. Andy's had a good idea and we just need to plan a time to get together and try and make it happen. Where should we try and get together for the experiment? Our house?"

"I think the parental units will smell a bad egg like Hamlet did, we should go somewhere else?" Trey said with superiority.

The boys sat and stared at Trey bewildered. George asked, "Do you mean they would know something is rotten in the state of Denmark?"

Trey's lips pressed together. "Yeah, fine, whatever Brainiac. Why don't we just go out to the bridge? Make it a campout or something. We can probably make that work next Friday since we have a bye. No football."

"What bridge?" the boys asked in chorus.

Trey took another long drink of tea and swallowed. "Green Light Bridge," he said with a small burp.

"That's just in the song. There isn't a real place called that," Andy said.

"Wrong you are little brother," Trey said in a funny, cartoonish voice. "Been there before I have." Two years later, Trey would swear he had invented Yoda's voice and his predilection for rearranging sentence syntax. People would roll their eyes then as Travis and George did now.

"I thought that place was long gone," Travis said.

"Well there's not much left of the bridge, but it is still there. I went out there with a couple of the guys last summer just chillin'. It's a creepy place for sure. Never did see the light though."

"I don't want to go out there," Andy said adamantly.

"Hey, I would take care of you, munchkin," Trey said ruffling Andy's hair.

"And who's gonna take care of you if we go out there and something happens, like Joey says? Like we all kind of know about?" George asked.

"Look, nothing is going to happen if we just go out there and camp out for the night. I could borrow Pete Clark's van. He owes me any way and he already said me and Angie could use it if we wanted sometime."

"Are you still dating her?" George asked. "Trey, you know you better not be…"

"Let's keep your big Jew nose out of my business," Trey added.

"I'm not Jewish, you moron," George said.

"Maybe not. But your big schnoz sure is," Trey said. "So is it a plan? All of us that have been having the dream in one way or another should get together and see if we can make it happen. Fill in some of the blanks."

"We can get Emily to come. Should we get Mary?" Travis asked.

"Hmm, no. Would seem too weird to get a black chick out there with us," Trey added.

"But probably makes sense to bring Angie out there, right," George asked suspiciously.

"Well yeah. She knows about all this stuff," Trey added meekly.

"I still think we should at least ask Mary if she wants to come," George insisted.

"Fine. She can be your Lt. Uhura. Maybe she could get that confused cock of yours to get hard thinking about her fine black ass instead of me or Trav here," Trey said wiping his mouth. "I'm going to talk a piss, rejects." The tall teenager scooted out of the booth and headed for the bathroom.

"Just ignore him," Travis said. "He just says that shit to get you all worked up." George had a blank expression on his face and didn't respond to Travis or Trey for that matter. "Are you okay?"

"Yes. Just thinking that Trey really needs to wash his hands before he comes back to the table. And the water pressure in that bathroom is pretty strong. Shall we pray, brothers?" George said holding up his hands with a grin. Andy smiled and gripped his hand. Travis shook his head but gripped hands with George and Andy. George choked back a small wave of nausea but continued to hold hands. As he opened his eyes, Travis was dabbing at his nose with a napkin. Andy was busy readjusting himself down in his lap. George held up his iced tea and waited for the other boys to do the same.

"To Trey's clean hands and wet pants. Cheers," George said. The boys clinked their glasses together.

Three minutes later, Mike McGee came over to the boy's booth. "Where's Trey? We need to go."

"He went in the bathroom a long time ago," Andy said.

Mike turned a dark shade of red and turned toward the bathroom. "That kid better not be rubbing one out in the men's room," he muttered under his breath.

The three boys in the booth fell over themselves laughing. "We better get out of here," Travis added as the tumbled out of the booth and ran to the car. Mike came out the door a minute later with a mortified Trey following him. The crotch of his pants were soaked to the skin. He held his hands in front of his lap. The boys in the car began to laugh hysterically.

"Oh my God," Janet said as Trey got in the car and slammed the door. "What happened to you? Did you have an accident?"

Trey looked at the boys with a steely murderous look. "No, the water in the sink just splashed on my pants."

"It looks like you took a bath in there," Janet said.

"Thanks, mother. That is very helpful," Trey said steaming.

"Don't be a smart ass," Mike said driving out of the parking lot and heading for home.

George pulled off his church clothes as soon as he got home and found some old soft jeans and a stretched-out old sweatshirt of Fred's that threatened to swallow him whole. His parents had announced they were going to take a nap which sounded suspiciously like code for old people sex in the middle of the afternoon. He tried not to think about that. He put his ELO "New World Record: album on and listened as "Telephone Line" poured from the speakers.

He was a little sleepy himself, probably from the massive size of his lunch. He thought about grabbing one of his magazines and spending some time with his good friend, Big G and some quality George time, but he really wasn't in the mood. He lay back on the bed and grabbed his copy of "The Catcher in the Rye" and picked up where his bookmark was. A couple of minutes later his bedroom door opened scaring the bejesus out of him. Travis grinned as he walked in.

"Shit, Trav I almost wet myself," George said. "Just walk right in, why don't you?" I could have been busy you know."

"Oh right. I've seen you busy more than once I'm sorry to say. Never mind that. Em called and wants to meet us down at the park. Wants to talk about something and she wants you to bring some…"

"Miss Moon needs to start to pony up some moolah if I am going to continue to supply her addictions," George said. He went over to his dresser and pulled out a jock strap and grabbed his stash from the cup pouch. "I'm getting a little low. Maybe I'll run into Cedric down at the park."

"Don't tell Em she is smoking weed you hide in your jock. Do you really use that thing? The cup is huge."

"It's one of Fred's. You think she'll be okay smoking Fred's dick-flavored pot?" George said pocketing the baggie full of rolled joints and grabbing a lighter. "You and I have sure smoked plenty. I think his old sweat gives the ganja that special something, don't you?

Travis laughed. "You're an idiot. But yeah, no complaints from me. Still think you better keep your hiding place to yourself. Come on, she's probably waiting by now. You need to tell your folks?"

"Hell no. They are having their Sunday afternoon nap," George said making quote signs in the air when he said nap. About that time, a rhythmic squeaking began from down the hall and some low moaning as well. George closed his eyes.

Travis's eyes grew large. "Oh my God, let's get out of here. That is happing at my house right now too. Sunday afternoon must be prime time for forty-year-olds. I left Trey at home sitting in his underwear in the middle of his bed actually working on homework."

George laughed as they continued on down Pecan Street to the back of the park. The day was clear with almost no clouds, but the wind had picked up and it showered them with leaves copper and gold as they walked down around the footbridge to the sewer pipe opening. They jumped the water in the middle of the concrete drainage and straddled the insides of the huge pipe with their feet making hollow clapping sounds with their Converse tennis shoes as they padded toward the first bend and their hang out place.

Emily was sitting up on the ledge but she wasn't alone. Mary Washington was sitting beside her. The girls were sitting cross-legged on the ledge, their platform shoes off and sitting beside them. The bottoms of their bellbottom jeans were worn and frayed. The boys froze in their tracks as they saw the girls. Finally Travis spoke.

"Um, Hi. You didn't mention anyone else was going to be here." And then because he felt rude, "Nice to see you, Mary."

"Yeah, great to see you," George added lamely.

Mary hopped down nimbly onto the concrete curve of the pipe avoiding the water. "I got something for you," she said to George reaching into her big purse sitting beside her shoes. She pulled out a baggie full of weed and held it up like she was offering a baby a sucker. "Ced told me if I saw you to give this to you. Said you could pay him tomorrow at school. Just drop off the cash in his locker or whatever y'all do."

George's eyes bugged out when he saw the marijuana. "Oh wow. But that's so much. I'm not sure I can pay…"

"He said, just pay your regular price. He had some extra or something this month so you get a bonus or some shit like that. That fool is gonna get caught but he does all right selling weed to white folks," she said laughing. George took the baggie and opened it up to inspect the herb.

"This is nice stuff, thanks Mary."

"Just doing him the favor since I was coming over here anyway. Emily was nice and let me stay for the afternoon so I didn't have to walk all the way back to Norton since I wanted to come back to church tonight," Mary said with a big smile. The large hoop earrings jangled on her ears. Her large hairdo filled up the dark void in the large culvert and blended in so much that you could only make out her eyes and jewelry and teeth when she leaned back in the shadows.

"That's great you are coming back tonight," George said. The short boy leaped up on the platform and Mary easily pushed herself up to sit beside him. Travis hopped up and the four teens wiggled around so they could all fit on the concrete wall. The light from the vent in the park lawn slanted down and lit the floor of the culvert, sparkling in the flowing water, making the pebbles glitter like scattered coins. George fished out a joint from his stash and flicked the lighter. He lit the blunt and took a drag and then handed it cautiously to Mary. She took the joint and inhaled deeply, passing the weed back to Emily. She turned her head up and let the long stream of smoke flow up toward the vent.

"I didn't think white kids like y'all smoked weed," she said chuckling.

Emily handed the joint to Travis who took a drag and bent forward to hand it back to George. "It's all George's fault here. He has corrupted us."

"I can see that. I knew you were trouble," she said teasing and accepting the pot for another hit. She expertly took another long drag and held the smoke a long time before letting it escape through her nose.

"I can't ever do that," Emily said. She took a drag and held it in her mouth trying to let the smoke pour out of her nose, but she started coughing and ended up almost falling off the wall.

"Girl, you gonna get sick. Just stick with hot-boxing that blunt," Mary said.

George lit up another joint and the teens continued to pass it around until they were definitely feeling buzzed. Travis turned and straddled the wall and Emily leaned back in his lap, laying her head on his chest. Mary turned around and spread George's legs on either side of the ledge and reclined with her back resting against George's chest and lap. She grabbed his arms and wrapped them around her. George was practically paralyzed and staring dumbstruck, but gripped Mary's arms and held her while she rested against him.

"You probably never held on to a white girl, much less a sister," Mary said smiling. "Well you're doing just fine. Your hands feel nice on my arms like that." George's face was stuck in a witless grin that made both Emily and Travis snicker. "Feels good," Mary said again. "I been real scared lately to let anyone get close to me. You feel safe, George. I like that," she said quietly. George reached up and began to lightly touch Mary's face and trace the edges of her ears and lips.

Emily smiled as she watched Mary close her eyes and drink in the soft, gentle attention. "Do you want to talk about anything? If you do, I just want you to know we will keep it just between us. It's fine if you don't, but I just want you to know you can trust us."

Mary's teeth glowed bright white in the low light as she grinned. "Oh I know I can trust y'all. I could feel that today when you were praying for me. I might want to talk, but right now, I think I just want to feel safe and a little happy for a change."

Travis and Emily watched as George continued to stroke Mary's face and hair and arms. George felt the tiny electricity begin in his fingers as he stroked Mary's smooth skin. He could feel his heart speed up and his jeans grew tight as his erection swelled. The girl felt like she was melting into him. There were walls of darkness still looming up all around them as he touched her, but more and more light seemed to pour into those dark corners. She sank back into his chest and turned her face up to look at the short boy, reaching up and running her fingers through his short curls. Then she turned a bit more and gripped his shoulder and her lips found his. The kiss was barely a touch at first; their noses hovering right above each other's. Then Mary opened her mouth and George pressed his lips close to her and she spun around and climbed into his lap, locking her arms around his neck and the two began to kiss deeply. Wave after wave of gratitude and longing crashed against the shores of their minds. As they kissed, George knew she wanted to let him in to her pain. But he held back, not sure she was ready and not sure he wanted to know. Like the door opened just a crack in "The Tell-Tale Heart," George peeked inside. In the midst of the sweetness of the caress and kisses, he felt the pain and fear and sadness hiding in the dark of Mary's mind seep into his.

As she pressed her lips hard against his, she slipped her tongue inside the boy's mouth. George's mind exploded with image after image. Darkness and then then fear, rocked him. Bound and bent, stripped and spread-eagled, George's mind reeled at the images. The nausea of sour, unwashed flesh in his mouth, humiliation, then the pain deep and hard, again and again. He felt the stink and weight pressing against him, the grunts and howls, over and over until his spread and aching legs trembled. He was suffocating, his lungs aching for breath until he knew he would not survive.

As he pushed away, the bond with Mary was broken and he became aware of Travis and Emily yelling. He was sobbing as was Mary, the two in a wet, broken heap on the other side of the ledge where they had fallen onto a tangle of weeds and soft earth. Travis pushed Mary away from him and George felt Travis literally pick him up and carry him out of the concrete culvert. Travis jogged toward the footbridge and bent down underneath it to lay George on the grass, out of sight of any onlookers in the park that might be around. He rubbed his hands over George's eyes and held his face in his hands.

"Are you okay?" Travis asked, panic in his voice.

George nodded. "Go get Mary. Don't leave her in there."

Travis tore back into the culvert and met the girls, Emily gripping Mary's shoulders and guiding her toward the opening. Travis scooped her up and ran toward daylight with Emily following behind with two ridiculous pairs of platform shoes. Travis brought Mary to the bridge and laid her down on the grass underneath. Her face was wet like George's. The two lay in the shadows under the bridge, breathing heavy. George reached over and found Mary's hand and gripped it lightly.

"I'm so sorry. I'm so sorry. I'm so sorry," he kept repeating. Mary wept.

Travis looked alarmed at Emily. "What the hell just happened?"

"I don't know but it's terrible. I think Mary just told George what happened to her, you know when she got abducted and ..."

The reality of that sunk into Travis like a boulder. "Oh God." He looked to Emily for some remedy, something that could make this sadness better, but there was nothing.

George sat up and looked around, his face stricken. He turned to the side and vomited. Emily reached out and touched him on the arm. He waved that he was okay as he retched again. When he sat back up he said, "Let's get out of here. We can go back to my house."

"Are you sure?" Emily asked.

"Yeah, it will be fine. My folks will be all asleep now after their Sunday afternoon screw."

"What?" Emily said shocked.

"Don't worry about it," Travis said. "Come on, let's get out of here." Travis turned to help George up but he was already helping Mary up and steadying her as they climbed up the embankment and down toward the ball fields and then to home. George slipped his hand into Mary's as they walked. She didn't pull away. Travis noticed a family sitting at a picnic table, enjoying the fall sunshine. They had made a fire in one of the BBQ grills and were cooking burgers and hot dogs. They stared at George and the black girl with the somewhat squashed afro holding hands in plain sight like that was an ordinary thing to do. It didn't take a mind reader to see the judgment and disapproval on their faces. Travis gripped Emily's hand as they walked past and Travis reached out to touch the edge of the BBQ. The fire roared and shot into the air over eight feet high and belched out a huge wave of heat that singed the eyebrows off the mom and dad and caused the kids to tumble off the picnic bench to the ground.

"What the hail ..." the sputtering man started.

"I told you not to use so much lighter fluid, you jackass!" the wife said slapping the man around the shoulders.

The teenagers didn't turn around. They just continued back to George's house down the block. They all quietly went inside and into George's room. He disappeared briefly and then came back with four tumblers of ice filled with Coke. He handed them around to the group as they sat on George's bed. He turned on the radio and interestingly it was the same ELO song that had been playing on his stereo when Travis showed up. Travis took a drink of his cola and sputtered as he swallowed.

"Did you put something in this Coke?"

"Yeah. Just a little rum. I thought we might could use it," George said walking to his desk and lighting a stick of patchouli incense. "We all stink like weed, so I figured we might better add some more fragrance to the mix."

Travis waved his hand away. "Smells like the Chimerlix," he said. The Chimerlix was a local head shop on the college campus near some of the other Bohemian shops that had sprung up around the place and stuck out like a sore thumb in the conservative town. Local teenagers had taken to visiting the shops and the Sweet Cream Deli beside it, looking for some way to escape the deep fried meals and JC Penny styles that filled up most of the town.

Mary had curled up beside George and was holding him tightly. He had his arms protectively around her as well. Travis and Emily didn't know quite what to do and the small group sat in silence as they listened to Jeff Lynn sing about the "Telephone Line."

Emily crawled over and sat close to Travis, slipping her hand into his. They sat and watched George and Mary lying there, gripping each other tightly. Travis looked over at the clock on the night stand. It was almost 4:00. They would have to get back home and get ready for church before too long. The song on the radio changed to Gordon Lightfoot wondering "If You Could Read My Mind?"

Emily took Travis's hand and the two got up and went around the other side of the bed. As George and Mary held each other, Emily put out a trembling hand and lightly touched Mary's back. Travis followed suit and touched the girl's back, feeling her breath and heartbeat tattoo against his fingers. Emily moved her head down and touched the girl's back with her forehead. Like a leak in an earthen dike, thoughts began to pour out. Slowly at first and then in a torrent. Emily and Travis felt the dark and fear grip them, the horror of the brutal attack seize their minds. They saw Carl Washington there beside Mary, but he wasn't her attacker. And even deeper, they sensed more. Images of Mike and Janet McGee and then just Janet and Carl.

"No!" Mary said and both Emily and Travis flew back and banged against the wall of the bedroom. The two shook their heads to clear the stars from in front of their eyes and Mary and George were both looking at them with a crazed expression, hands stretched out toward them.

"You two don't need to see that. It's too bad," George said. "And Mary doesn't want you to either."

Travis helped Emily up and the two joined Mary and George on the bed. Emily had tears in her eyes. Travis was too shocked to know what to feel. They may have only had a glimpse, but it was enough. They knew what had happened.

"We're sorry. We just wanted to see if there was anything…" Emily began.

"I know but you can't. At least not right now," George said. He reached over and gripped Travis's hand and in that moment conveyed "I'll tell you later." Travis nodded and squeezed his friend's hand.

The light in the bedroom was dim and as the late fall afternoon sun began to set. The teenagers curled up as couples and drifted off to sleep to the radio. The songs wove in and out of their dreams as they slept. The bedroom grew warm and George was only somewhat aware of pulling off his shoes and pants along with the others as they lay back down together, now more comfortable. The room changed from gold to shadowy grey as the sun disappeared.

A gentle hand rubbing his hair and face woke George. He opened his eyes to see his dad standing over him, puzzled but somehow kind and caring. It took a few seconds for George to wake up enough to realize his dad was watching him lay in bed in his underwear hugging a strange black girl in her t-shirt and panties. A wave of dread and fear coursed through him as he lifted his head up to see Mary along with Travis and Emily still sacked out, their bare legs entwined with each other.

Whispering, Duke Harris gripped his son's shoulder lightly and said, "We are going to need to leave to get back to church in about thirty minutes. Um, you probably want to wake up your friends and get ready." He stared at Mary and then back at George and smiled. "You never cease to surprise me kiddo," he said. He turned to leave and looked back but took the time to give George one of his customary thumbs up before opening the door and going out.

George scrambled up shaking Travis roughly. "Get up. You need to go home. Holy shit! We fell asleep. My dad was just in here!"

Travis and the girls bolted upright. No one said anything but the group quickly grabbed for shoes and pants and struggled to get them on. Mary seemed to be lost, not knowing what she should do next. Emily grabbed her by the hand.

"Come with me. I can let you wear something of mine. Travis, move your ass and get home. We are all going to die," Emily said terrified.

George reached over and grabbed both girls by the arm. "My dad wasn't mad. I don't get it but he was fine. It was weird; it was like he thought it was cool or something. I can't tell with him. Anyway, just go. See you all at church in a few."

The three teenagers quietly strode down the hall and out into the dark early evening. George headed to the bathroom and pulled his shirt and underwear off and climbed in the shower. The hot water cleared away some of the cobwebs, but his mind was a churning whirlpool of emotion. He washed himself but wave after wave of sadness and fear and pain crashed over him and soon he was holding himself against the wall of the shower as the images burned through him again and the tears flowed. He didn't hear his dad come into the bathroom or speak his name. Duke had pulled the shower curtain back to find his boy curled in a ball on the floor of the bathtub. He turned the water off and picked his son up off the floor and held him in his arms as the teenager trembled and buried his head in his dad's neck like he hadn't done since his big brother had died.

Duke carried George to his bedroom and sat on the bed with him cradled in his lap until the boy stopped trembling. He stroked his hair and rocked him back and forth, his wet skin soaking into his church clothes. After his tears subsided and he regained his composure, George hugged his dad, feeling exhausted and out of sorts.

"What happened, Georgie Boy? Why are you so sad?" Duke asked.

"It's no big deal, Dad. I just…" George began not knowing how much to say. "That girl that was here. That's Mary Washington, you know the one who got kidnapped and assaulted and all that."

"Really?" Duke asked genuinely surprised.

"Yeah. Well she just kind of told us a little about her story, you know all the stuff they did to her, and it kind of got to me."

"I can understand that. That's terrible for all you kids. Sorry that happened to her and sorry it upset you so much. Um, maybe you ought to just stay home tonight," Duke offered.

"Thanks but I want to go, Dad. I'll be fine now. Uh, I better get dressed," George said feeling excruciatingly naked. Duke let George up and the boy made a beeline for his dresser and pulled on some underwear. George noticed Duke was not getting up to leave.

"I'm really okay, Dad. You don't have to worry. It was just a bad moment for me, that's all," George said trying to will his Dad out the door.

Duke obediently stood to leave. He stopped once he got to the door and came back and placed a big warm hand on George's shoulder.

"I think it's great for you to be friends with Mary. I just hope you kids are being careful. If need me to get you some Trojans …"

"Oh God, Dad. Please. It's not like that at all," George said mortified. "We all just got too warm in the room and we took our pants off to sleep better. Just don't worry about it, okay?"

Duke Harris had a far-away expression in his eyes. "You know, when I was over in Korea, I slept with some beautiful black girl. She was an amazing kisser. And you know, when the lights were off, it felt just the same when I was inside her than it did with a white girl."

"For the love of God, stop Dad. Just go get ready for church. Don't talk about this again, okay?"

Duke looked at him confused, then shook his head. "You better put some pants on buster, it's time to head out for church."

"Sure thing, Dad."

George pulled on some slacks and found an Izod polo shirt and put it on. He found his belt and socks and slid the brown loafers on his feet. A tsunami of nausea flowed over him and he dashed to the bathroom and vomited. He hovered over the toilet, ropes of snot and mucus dripping from his nose and mouth. He grabbed a washcloth and wiped his face. He looked in the mirror and tried to push the memories out of his mind, but it was no good. He wondered how much Travis had seen? If he could put two and two together…"

40 Emily

Emily took Mary into her room and closed the door. She looked at herself in the mirror and thought getting ready in this short amount of time was probably hopeless. She looked at Mary who was just standing in the middle of the floor, hugging herself.

"Um, why don't you come look in the closet and see if there is something you could wear. I know my clothes are so boring but maybe you can find something."

"Thanks," Mary said in a whisper.

A few minutes later, both girls were dressed. Emily in a bright horizontal stripe sweater and a pair of black slacks. Mary in a longer black skirt and a bright yellow double breasted jacket that Emily had never wanted to wear. The color looked wonderful on Mary. Mary grabbed a large tooth comb and began to pick out her hair while Emily made quick work of the curling iron. The girls slapped on some eye makeup and lipsticks.

"That will have to be good enough. We have to leave," Emily said. There were a thousand things in Emily's mind she wanted to talk with Mary about but she knew now was not the time. She grabbed her purse and headed out the carport where her mother was already in the car.

"Sorry we are late, Mom," Emily said watching her mother's head spin around staring at Mary. "You remember Mary Washington, Mom. She came over this afternoon and I told her we could take her home after church tonight, okay?"

"Sure, of course. Nice to see you again, Mary," Miranda Moon said. "You were so great in 'Godspell.'"

"Thanks," Mary said.

Emily noticed her mother kept checking the rear view mirror the whole drive to church. The girls sat in the back seat in silence. Mary reached up and placed her hand against the back of her mother's seat and Miranda turned the cassette player on so Abba's "Dancing Queen" filled the car. Mary reached over and let her fingers lightly touch Emily. Quietly she said, "You and the boys, you saw the light, didn't you? You can do stuff now too."

Emily gave Mary a nervous smile. "Yes. I'm taking it you can too."

"A little. But I've watched the three of you. You can really do it. Why is it happening?"

"We don't know. We've figured a couple of things out but mostly we don't know. The green light and bridge, all that. We are still wondering."

Mary gripped Emily's fingers and nodded slowly. "Do you know where they took you?"

"Not really. When I sort of woke up afterwards, I was walking down Highway 24, buck ass naked."

"But nothing before that?"

"No. The cops think I am making it up that I can't remember, but I really can't."

"Have you been having a dream about the green light?" Emily asked

Mary's eyes grew large. "And the song, and that bridge…"

"We are all having it. Next Friday, we are going to go out to this place that Trey says is like where that song came from, a long time ago. We are going to go out there and see if all together we can have an even stronger, clearer dream and maybe we can figure out what is going on. Do you want to come with us?"

Mary looked scared. "I don't know. It worries me when I think about that, but I do want to know. My mother is so messed up since dad disappeared, she don't give a shit what I go and do. I think she had a nervous breakdown. Most of the time I have to make dinner for us or nobody eats."

"Well, together we are pretty strong with these abilities or whatever. I don't think anyone could hurt us if we are together."

Mary sat quietly then said, "Okay. I will come. I need to know more too."

Not able to help herself, Emily asked, "Do you like George?"

"That scrawny white boy?" Mary said then broke into a smile. "My dad would probably tan my hide if he saw me with him, but he's kinda cute. I just need to be around someone sweet and safe. I hardly even talk to anyone anymore. And most boys just look at me like I am a piece of trash, like I wanted that shit to happen to me…"

"And he's not like that, is he?" Emily said.

"Naw. He's good. I don't think he's ever thought much about girls before to be honest," Mary added.

"Pretty sure you are right about that. He is a good guy. He can even drive. His dad lets him take out their VW Beetle sometimes so it's fun for us."

"Y'all sure it's okay for me to hang out? It's pretty white around here and even more, town looks at me as damaged goods."

Emily leaned close to Mary and whispered, "Fuck the town and the Klan horse they rode in on."

Mary laughed. "Girl, you crazy. Good thing we're headed to church, you and that dirty mouth."

"I know. I give the boys grief all the time about their cussing and here I am the same," Emily said contritely.

"Well I'm no expert, but I think the good Lord is way more interested in how clean your heart is than with the occasional cuss word. My granny always says, 'The Lord knows how tell fertilizer from bullshit.' When I try and explain that bullshit is fertilizer, she just looks at me like I have two heads and says, 'This is sum bullshit you is sayin.'" Both girls laughed. Emily's mother pulled up in front of the church and had to drive further down the block since the parking lot was completely full.

"Oh dear, I wonder if we will even find a seat," she said.

"You can always sit with me and the guys, Mom. Travis will have places for us," Emily said closing the car door and trying to push the wrinkles out of her slacks.

"That would be wonderful," Miranda said.

The auditorium was nearly packed. Emily found Travis and George near the front along with the McGee's and Harris's. Trey was reluctantly sitting with the family, but Emily noticed he was turned so he had a view across the aisle to where Angie Matlock sat with two other girls. Emily had to feel a bit sorry for Trey. *The big lug did seem to really care for Angie and what was so bad about that,* she thought. Her stupid white trash family could only hope for her to have a boyfriend that was a local football star. With any luck, Trey would get a scholarship to college like his dad had and make something of himself. Emily was keenly aware of the stares they were receiving with Mary sitting with them as well. She was completely taken aback when Mike McGee rose to wrap her in a big bear hug, whispering in her ear. Janet hugged her as well. When Mary sat down, tears were streaming from her eyes.

"We have to go up and help do the worship service. Are you okay to stay here with Andy and the McGee's?"

Mary nodded and gripped Emily's hand quickly. Emily got Travis and George's attention and the three went up on the podium along with Cory and his ponytail. Miraculously, the worship for this first night of the revival was being handed over to the youth. So instead of "I'll Fly Away" and "Jesus on the Mainline," there would some true worship songs, Emily was glad.

Brother Nelson got to his feet and began to welcome the crowd to the first night of the week-long revival. He went through the obligatory introductions and made a special point to welcome the visiting congregation from the Trinity Church. Emily saw the surly group occupying the back three pews on the left side of the sanctuary. The stony-faced rednecks waved and nodded their heads to the crowd. It was easy for many to forget that less than two years earlier, all of these visitors were regular members of the church. JL Martin and his group had left after Brother Nelson had refused to bar Carl Washington and his family along with other black families, long-haired college students, and some local Latinos from attending. The Washington family had started coming to Living Waters Community after Mike McGee had encouraged them to visit. Emily had heard that the Washington's had been looking for another church fellowship after the pastor in the Mt. Moriah African Baptist church had left and was replaced with a simpering Uncle Tom pastor that preached the black folk in the community should keep a low profile and stick to their own kind and not rock the boat for any change. That flew in the face of everything that Carl Washington was about ever since his dad had pulled those drowned kids from the doomed bus that crashed on Green Light Bridge.

Emily wondered exactly why the defectors had bothered to come to the revival, but figured even they were curious about the illustrated sermons for which Brother Zigler was renown. She smiled as Cory took the microphone and invited the congregation to stand and join in worship. This flew in the face of the time-honored practice of a three-hymn set for the song service where you sang the first, second and last verses and only stood up on the final hymn.

Cody was leading the worship with his acoustic guitar. George was on his bright blue finish Les Paul. Travis was on bass tonight. Randy Moore from the high school band was on the drum set and Emily was playing the Fender Rhodes electric piano. Cory began the worship set with "This is the day the Lord hath made" played fast and raucous, with nice loud drums and bass runs. The crowd clapped and moved around, seemingly ready for the brighter, faster worship time. All of them except for the back three rows that adamantly stayed seated for the songs, arms folded across big barrel chests as they sat beside their beehive hairdo wives.

Cory transitioned into "Rejoice in the Lord Always" and then into "I will enter His gates with thanksgiving in my heart." As the congregation got to the chorus, a group of college-aged students on the front row began to skip up and down in a joyful dance as they clapped. The back row of observers seemed to glare even harder. *This was especially rich,* Emily thought, since these were the same men and women who would whoop and holler and stomp around under the influence of the Holy Spirit, practically getting ready to handle snakes, but sat in judgment over the young people who joyfully danced in worship now.

The guys slowed the tempo down on the "He hath made me glad" chorus and the crowd began to lift hands as they sang. George began to play the melody on his guitar of the next song. He leaned into the microphone and began to sing:

For thou O Lord, art high above
  all the earth,
Thou art exalted far above all gods.

The crowd sang along with lifted hands and closed eyes. Emily played the chorus along with the guitars and felt a surge of true joy and gratitude well up around the auditorium. The church had songs and worship all the time, but tonight, it seemed richer and more palpable. Is it because the three of us are up here, she wondered. *Maybe God really can use these powers to help make people more spiritual* she thought. The song began to slow and Emily modulated the key to G and then began the intro. She moved closer to the microphone and this time she wasn't afraid or worried. She lifted her voice and began to sing Don Moen's anthem, "Give Thanks."

The congregation continued to sing along with the worship band. The college students in the front swayed and put their arms around one another and sang. Tears streamed down faces. Emily looked across the auditorium and a glorious spirit of unity and devotion seemed to hover over the place. It truly was tangible and the crowd was reveling in the specialness of this moment. Part of her didn't want there to be any illustrated sermon or any altar call or any manipulative appeals to come to Jesus. Jesus was already here and it was beautiful.

The music began to grow quiet and Cory exhorted the crowd to continue to stay in this attitude of worship. Emily and George continued to play softly as people in the crowd prayed and worshipped. Then, like the backfire of an old jalopy on a quiet afternoon, the auditorium quiet was split with the loud, bark-like voice of Jerry Morgan from the back of the church. The man began to speak in tongues, a clacking, coughing cadence that sounded like a mixture of Chinese and Klingon.

Oh kianda a dita pho ascha a pliow. Woo stola da-chees to-ma-hundaaa. Shon-dai ree-kee-kee, rush-tai!

Though certainly not unusual in the church to have a message in tongues proclaimed, something about this one cut through the sensitive and tender moment of worship like a knife and the congregation seemed to hold its collective breath. As the harsh, undecipherable message came to a close, another loud braying voice filled the quiet church hall. This time, JL Martin spoke with authority and warning:

And I say unto thee, woe be unto those who abandon the true faith, the teachings of old to follow after teachers and minstrels who heap to themselves false teaching and those with itching ears, lusting to find succor for their sin and folly. I am the true God, I am Jehovah. Will you not return to me? Forsake your wantonness. Repent of being the harlot and polluting yourselves with those low and base born. Cling to the purity of my holiness where those whiter than snow and purer than gold will be the only ones worthy to enter my kingdom.

The room was filled with silence. The two hundred or so souls standing together were seized in the fear and harshness of the interpretation of the Pentecostal message. No one seemed to know what to do next. Brother Nelson took the microphone from Cory and spoke to the congregation in the form of a prayer.

"Lord, we acknowledge that we are in Your presence. We want to have ears to hear your message. Thank you for blessing us with Your sweet spirit tonight. Help us to always long for

Your ways. Speak to our hearts as we continue on together here tonight as Your people. Open up our understanding and challenge us with your Word tonight, Oh Lord we pray in Jesus name. Amen." The pastor looked across the congregation and continued, "You can all be seated."

Emily finally took a breath again. *Whatever that was from those men on the back row, it seemed to be the exact opposite of what was happening up here at the front of the church,* she thought. She had to hand it to the pastor, he took control of a very volatile situation and steered it back toward the comfortable waters that the church normally paddled around in. Pastor Nelson called for the ushers to come up to the front and the offering plates were handed around, most heaped with dollar bills by the time they got to the back. Emily noticed none of the men on the back row placed any offering in the plate. *That sounds about right,* she thought.

A few other announcements were made, mostly about the series of sermons that would be given that week. Cory put his guitar down and the rest of the worship band moved off the platform and walked to the back of the auditorium. They had been tasked with helping get the lights off and the actors that were being used in the illustrated sermon given a cue to come out of the meeting rooms in the back of the church and get ready to take their places. Emily also hoped it would give them a chance for a quick bathroom break. From the looks of it, Travis and George had the same idea because as soon as the boys got to the back of the sanctuary, they ran inside the men's room. Emily decided she would do the same and ran into Angie Matlock coming out of one of the stalls. Angie had clearly been crying and seemed particularly upset.

"Is everything alright?" Emily asked.

Angie quickly dried her eyes. "Yes, I just was really enjoying that worship I guess," she said quietly as she washed her hands and tried to smooth her mascara leaking down her face.

Emily finished up in the bathroom and went into the back vestibule of the church and found George and Travis in deep conversation.

"Why are they even here?" George hissed in a snarling whisper. "They don't belong here anymore."

"It doesn't matter right now," Travis said. He turned and saw Emily. He reached out and took her hand. "Was that Angie I just saw leaving the bathroom?"

"Yes and she was crying about something. She said it was nothing but I didn't buy it."

The pastor was introducing Brother Zigler, the evangelist. The man stood with a big car-salesman grin. He was wearing a shiny polyester three-piece dark blue suit with a crisp dark red Van Heusen shirt with a sparkling white color. His Jimmy Swaggart hair was combed straight back and welded in place with an entire can of Consort hairspray. As he moved to the front of the stage, a cloud of Jovan Musk for Men wafted over the crowd like an incense censer or waved by the Pope. The crowd seemed restless. The beautiful atmosphere that had been in the auditorium was gone. Now it just seemed anxious and restless. George gathered Emily and Travis around.

"You ready to make this illustrated sermon something to write home about? These folks came for a show, let's make sure they get a good one." George grabbed Travis and Emily's hands. They closed their eyes and focused. They squeezed each other's hands and broke the circle. "Let's go tell these folks to break a leg. They just might!"

The teenagers went around and made sure all the actors were lined up and knew their entrance according to the script that Brother Zigler had given them. They made sure to touch each one, sending an extra jolt of energy into them, like Stanislavski and Strasberg veterans. George manned the small light board, turned down the house lights. Tony Andrews was on the spotlight, now with a soft pink gel on the light surrounding the preacher. The evangelist took the microphone and began his sermon entitled "Destination: Heaven or Hell."

"Tonight we will follow the journey of two dear sisters: Sister Ruby and Sister Pearl." These girls had a lot in common and were the best of friends growing up. They came to church together and learned the stories in Sunday School. They even both responded to the same altar call one Sunday night and gave their hearts to Jesus."

Bev Franklin and Connie Wyngarden were playing the title roles. This was clearly the high point of their young lives, Emily figured. Both of these girls were stuck twenty years in the past, still controlled by the fundamental Pentecostal dress codes. Both of them still only wore skirts or dresses to school and Connie still wore her long hair piled up in a beehive on her head with long side ringlets. Neither usually wore makeup, but tonight must be extra special for them because both had a thick layer of pancake on and bright red lips. The girls walked down the aisle hand in hand, *more like preschoolers than teenagers*, Emily thought. They adlibbed kneeling at the altar and saying the Sinner's Prayer.

Brother Zigler went on with his sermon. At times it drifted off into just quoting scriptures or rambling on about living the life of holiness or something. When that happened, the crowd got restless and shuffled around. But when the actors came back on, they were enthralled. Emily had to admit, as corny as Zigler was, he was smart to add this to his sermons. Normally a congregation would have tuned out already.

The sermon now began to chronicle how the girl's pathways began to diverge. Bev the Pious continued to pray and help the poor, she married a perfectly handsome boy played by Danny Golden, one of the current high school football stars. But Connie the Slut wasn't content with any of this. Connie appeared from the back room and began her next journey down the middle aisle of the church. Emily smiled as she saw Connie emerge, now wearing a super short mini skirt and another pound of makeup. She had gone all out with thick emerald eye shadow capped off with a Persian eye curl at the corner. Her lipstick was vibrant red and painted well outside the outline of her lips so it looked more like she had been drinking a Big Red instead of looking seductive. She rocked her hips, waving her big behind back and forth as she paraded in her sky high platform shoes that Gene Simmons would have been proud of.

Up on the stage, Ruby was in a sensible June Cleaver dress complete with pearls and apron. Her upstanding husband sat at the card table dinette with two perfect little children and they all held hands and prayed and pantomimed eating Eggo waffles. Connie as the wanton fallen woman, pranced about letting her inner prostitute shine. George worked miracles with lights as Connie discoed and gyrated with a handful of other boys from the youth group who danced around with silk shirts open to the waist and gold chains on their hairless chests. She did the bump and grind with the boys while George played Ohio Players "Love Roller Coaster" through the speakers.

Emily couldn't help but notice that the kids on the hell side of the stage seemed to be having a lot more fun than the dull family on the heaven side. As Ruby and her family gathered around the table for a rousing game of Parcheesi, Pearl and her posse of young studs poured large glasses of ice tea whiskey from a big bottle of Jack Daniels someone had procured for the sermon. Soon the group was smoking pot, popping pills, and shooting up heroin all over the stage. The sinners continued to get bolder and more outlandish in their adlibbing. It seemed as George intensified the green lights alternating flashing them with the orange, the kids became more and more uninhibited and provocative.

Brother Zigler was describing Pearl's descent in debauchery in ominous tones, but the crowd wasn't listening. They were transfixed by the youngsters acting out the high life and the highway to hell. In fact, Emily wondered, how many other teenagers in the audience were going to sign up for the Road to Perdition instead of the Road to Glory based on how much fun the bad boys and girl were having in the drama.

Now the sermon moved into Act III. From the happy family, Ruby went on a visitation to a now clearly slum-dwelling Pearl. Her hair was a mess. Her makeup was melting, her eyes now looked like two burned holes in a blanket. Her short skirt was twisted. Her pantyhose were torn to shreds. Her sparkly blouse was drooping off one shoulder now revealing a shocking hot pink bra that Emily was pretty sure was not in the original script. Sincere Ruby tried to share her faith, waved her bible about and tried to give her lemon sponge cake as a goodwill gesture. Pearl grabbed the cake and smashed it into Ruby's face. The crowd gasped but then began to laugh. Ruby stood there stunned, clearly this had not been in the dress rehearsal. Before she could move out of the way, Pearl hauled off and slapped her right across the face knocking her backwards. The crowd clapped. Pearl attempted to grab one of the prop hypodermic needles and jab them into Ruby's rear end but Bev managed to scramble away while some of Pearl's posse of lost boys pulled her back toward the middle of the stage. Pearl grabbed hold of one of the boys and began to kiss him deeply, pulling and tugging at his shirt until it ripped off. The other boys just stood there in stunned horror as Pearl continued to maul Ben Edwards, one of the youth group boys who seemed to be gripped by the same insanity. He pushed Pearl down on the tiny love seat that was on the stage representing Pearl's shabby apartment. Pearl pulled the boy down on top of her in between her legs that were lifted high and wrapped around the boy's waist.

The crowd sucked in its collective breath and George had the good sense to kill the lights and turn the hot spot back on Brother Zigler who was standing on the side of the stage, his mouth open in complete shock. Ever the showman, though, he continued with the story, gladly transitioning back to Ruby's godly family. But when the lights came up on Ruby's kitchen table, the family was nowhere in sight. Only their clothes were left, lying in the chairs around the table. Ruby's neighbor came back to return the eggs she had borrowed only to find she had been left behind. She shrieked and dropped the eggs as the lights dimmed. Emily wondered how many of the congregation, like her, just kept thinking that Ruby and her family were stark naked up on the streets of gold now.

Almost at the finale now, Brother Zigler turned his attention back to Pearl. Left behind and clearly lost, the lights rose on Pearl, in a drug-crazed stupor. With nothing left to live for, the script called for her to actually kill her group of admirers. This was one of Zigler's most famous dramatic conventions, as he loved using his theater training to rig up the actors with some fake blood packets to drive home the realism and gravitas of their sinful ways. In the dim orange light, the stage was now a shambles. Fans hidden behind the prop walls were blowing with red and orange crepe paper making it appear the place was on fire. Pearl staggered to her feet from behind the couch. Her blouse was off now and she was clad only in the hot pink bra and her mini skirt that had now ridden up so high it showed off the matching hot pink panties. Nervous laughter rippled through the audience. Emily noticed that the faces of the crowd ranged from delight to shock to fury, especially from the rows of defectors on the back row.

Pearl took another hit on the big bottle of Jack and grabbed a huge prop butcher knife that was practically a sword. As her boyfriends came into the scene, Pearl screamed and began to attack each one. The stabs and jabs of the knife hit the packs and virtual geysers of crimson blood sprayed high into the air, drenching the boys and Pearl in fountains of blood, all set to the driving sounds of The Beatles' "Helter Skelter. Pearl wheeled about on the stage like a ninja grabbing one boy and slicing open his throat with remarkable authenticity, spraying the front row of the crowd with a thick gout of blood. The college girls screamed and Lisa Anderson fell from her seat in a dead faint. As Pearl skewered the final boy and he staggered back, she took the knife and slashed at his neck. His prop head tumbled down to the floor and rolled toward the altars at the front of the church. The congregation screamed and covered their mouths in horror. Harriet MacDonald leapt from her seat with handkerchief clapped over and mouth and sprinted for the bathroom. As the stage went to blackout and the spotlight came up on Brother Ziglar, his face was a mask of disbelief. None of his sermons had ever reached this zenith of theatrical success, albeit this one had gotten a bit out of hand but there was no denying the congregation had been mightily moved.

For the denouement of the evening, the two girls would face the Great White Throne Judgment. The lights came up, harsh and brilliant. First, Ruby came forward in a plain white gown as she bowed before the bright light, Carlene Samples in a truly impressive angel costume came forward and took her by the hand and led her to the side of the stage. A door opened into a corridor clearly lined with crumpled aluminum foil. A dry ice fog machine rolled out a carpet of mist into the front row of the church. A Christmas tree revolving light sparkled somewhere inside lighting Ruby's way to the Holy City with a lovely sparkly tableau of changing colors. The angel placed a small circlet of gold on her head and Ruby walked slowly into the beauty, with hands lifted speaking in tongues as George cued up the Mormon Tabernacle Choir singing "Holy, Holy, Holy." Emily had to admit, it kind of gave you chills and the crowd forgot about the bloody final act, lifting their own hands to worship, others applauding and cheering for the saintly girl.

But the glory was soon dimmed and a dark brooding gloom filled the stage. As the red and orange light came up, poor Pearl was led before the bright light throne in chains and a burlap sack dress. Her long hair had been quickly replaced with a short Carol Brady shag wig. Brother Zigler put on his most dramatic deep voice and pronounced judgment on Pearl.

"Depart from me you wicked of heart. I never knew you."

A gut-wrenching wail of sorrow echoed around the church as Pearl fell to her knees. Bud Davis, clad in a terrifying black robe and black wings with a thick stainless steel belt stretching from his shoulder to hip, pulled out a long silver sword and pointed toward the left side of the stage. A door opened, again with the crumpled aluminum foil. But this time, the smoke machine belched out a wave of smoke, tinted blood red. Crepe paper flames stretched out of the maw of the hellmouth. Two black clad, faceless demons gripped Pearl by the arms and pulled her shrieking and wailing toward the bottomless pit. George turned the volume up on the stage mikes to the level where it seemed like Pam's screams were reverberating within their heads. Emily saw half a dozen children clap their hands to their ears or turn to mothers to hide their faces. Faces of terror stricken parishioners glowed red as the door to hell was shut along with Pam's screams. As the building went silent, a score of sobs and wails filled the emptiness. Emily had made her way to the piano sitting on the side of the sanctuary and she began to softly play "Just As I Am."

Brother Zigler, standing in the soft glow of the pink spotlight, was speechless. Clearly, his instruction to the actors had helped them perform to a new height, even if they had gotten a bit over zealous. His ears still rung with the hopeless shrieks of that poor girl. Now if he could convey the right altar call, he would see a great result for this first night of the revival.

But as Zigler began to speak, members of the audience began to file out of their seats and crowded to the front of the church, falling to their knees in repentance and to cry out for God's mercy. Soon the front was full of weeping, prayerful congregants. There wasn't anything else to say. He encouraged any from the crowd that had not already done so to join around the front. The only part of the audience that remained seated was the back three rows of visitors from First Church of the Trinity.

Emily motioned for Cory to come up to the piano. She whispered to him and he sat on the piano bench and seamlessly began to take over playing the music. Emily patted him on the back and moved through the masses of people praying around the front of the church and found a sobbing Mary, doubled over in sorrow. Emily got Travis's attention and saw George moving up the aisle toward the front and waved him over as well. The three gathered behind Mary and laid their hands on her back and began to pray. Emily was afraid the second they touched Mary again they would be blasted back into her horrors, but for now, that wasn't happening. They were clearly filled with the sadness and fear that was part of her life now, but also a glimmer of hope in her heart as well. Interestingly, more and more people began to come nearer and many reached out to touch the grieving girl. Emily looked over and saw Jack and Lori Tanner come and kneel beside them and reach their hands out and touch them in prayer along with Jack's friend, Tim.

As this sweet and caring moment was playing out with the gathered crowd praying with and for one another, Joey Tanner made his way up toward the front. As he reached the cluster around Mary Washington, he stretched his small hands out and placed them on her head. A blast of energy arced through the web of hands connected and surged through them like 50,000 volts.

In that moment, the groups standing around Mary and Joey felt the energy flow through them and instantly they were mentally connected. Emily's mind reeled from the torrent of images flowing through her mind. Snatches of the light, the bridge, the chant from more than a dozen sources bubbled in her mind. Then *blam*, she was running down the football field and in the tree house, then she was in a back room and there was a gun and someone flying across the office. She saw Mike McGee in his office with JL Martin's face so close. She saw kids from school at home in their room. Joey Tanner on his tricycle in front of his house and in the bathtub. Emily saw Victor Landon and Katie Johnson in the back seat of his car fumbling with each other's clothes. She saw Mr. Carpenter from the variety store downtown in the bathroom with his hand up the skirt of Rachel Swenson, pressing against her. She saw Jill Bartlett and Samantha Payne in a fitting room hiding clothes underneath their dresses and walking out of Freezia and Steiger's dress shop. She saw husbands and wives making love. Boys playing baseball, girls at Girl Scouts. Mr. Baker from the high school dressed in black leather on his hands and knees. She saw Bo Williams and Greg Benton from the football team in the showers after practice when no one else was around. She saw Janet McGee wrapped in the big strong arms of Carl Washington as he slid inside her, her head thrown back in ecstasy. She saw Janet's stunned face as the nurse handed her a baby, dark and brown. She saw Mike McGee screaming at Carl and punching him in the face. And she saw Carl Washington trussed up like a piece of meat while hooded men beat him with sticks and cut him with knives. The voices of those men were familiar. She saw tattoos on forearms she didn't recognize but on the other hand, they seemed familiar. And then she saw those hooded men come toward Mary and take her over and over and over.

In a flash of bright light, the men and women and teenagers and children that were connected flew back and collapsed against one another. Later, Brother Zigler would claim it was the largest group ever to be "slain in the Spirit," attributing the phenomenon to the mighty work of the illustrated sermon. As the crowd began to regain their own awareness, they rose like stunned frightened animals, warily looking around the room trying to process what they had seen and experienced. Emily saw more than one husband or wife, pull away from their partner as they looked suspiciously at one another, hurt or angry. Emily saw teenage boys with red faces make a beeline for the back of the church, looking to get out of the building as soon as they could. Girls looked around with dismay or wonder, trying to figure out what had just happened. Jack and Tim from the Western Auto stood and looked at the men at the back of the church who had finally decided their welcome had worn thin. They exited in a hurry, looking back over their shoulders at the dispersing crowd.

And then she saw Travis and Trey still on their knees looking in shock at their parents. Janet was sobbing inconsolably. Mike's face was rigid, his eyes darting back and forth between his boys and Janet. With tears in his eyes, Trey got up and ran out of the church leaving Travis and Andy standing in the middle of the thinning crowd like little boys lost at the State Fair. Emily went over to Travis and took his hand. George was there as well, the look he gave Emily was fearful and concerned. He grabbed Andy by the hand and motioned for Emily to come. He went over and helped Mary to her feet and stumbling, she followed. Emily pulled Travis along with her and the teens walked quickly out of the church and toward the parking lot.

Emily's mother was at her car, dabbing her eyes with a handkerchief. "I don't even know what just happened in there. It was ... just weird."

"I know, Mom. Can you just take us all home, please?" Emily pressed her hand on her mother's shoulder.

Miranda Moon looked at the small crowded but just shrugged and said, "Sure. You want to go to the Dairy Queen first?"

"Yes," Andy said with enthusiasm. Emily and George laughed.

As they loaded into the car, George saw Mike McGee come out of the church looking around. George ran over to the man.

"Um, Emily's mom is giving us a ride home after we stop at the DQ. Okay?" George said gripping Mike's forearm in a tight grip. Mike nodded his head and turned back into the church.

When they got to the Dairy Queen, Emily's mother saw Madge Bell who had also been at the church and went over to talk with her. The kids ordered some ice cream and French fries, allowing George to pay. They crowded into a booth at the back of the restaurant and sat in silence as they ate. Never one to be able to deal with silence for very long, George finally spoke.

"Well, that was quite the service," he said. "Wonder what Brother Zigler will do to top that one?"

Emily added a bit of salt to her fries. "Hmm, something tells me the other nights of the revival might not quite measure up to tonight. In fact, I have a feeling there won't be many there tomorrow night."

"Why do you think that?" Mary asked.

Emily looked around. Travis was still sitting quietly beside her, not talking. Andy seemed fine, but was still saying nothing. "Whatever happened tonight when we were praying, I think most of the people there will be freaked out by it. Not to mention it stirred up quite a few issues to say the least."

"You think I caused that?" Mary asked worried.

"I think it was more likely that Joey kid. Something is definitely up with him," George said. He looked at Emily and leaned close. "Did you see the thing with Bo and Greg Benton?"

"Yes. I think everyone did."

"I didn't get it," Andy said. "Did that mean they were doing it or something? How does that even work?"

"I'll explain it later," George said.

Andy finished his milkshake and made a loud gurgling sound with his straw. "I didn't get lots of that. Some of it was dumb stuff. It was all so fast. And why was my mom kissing Mary's dad?"

"You idiot!" Travis said punching Andy in the balls. As Andy fell over in the booth groaning, Travis got up and headed for the bathroom. Emily looked at George and nodded for him to go after Travis. George scooted out of the booth and headed to the bathroom. It was locked and so he lightly knocked on the metal door.

"Trav, buddy. It's George," he said stupidly. "Let me in." No sound came from the bathroom. George placed his hand on the door and concentrated with all his might. "Travis, let me in."

The locked clicked and George turned the handle. "Stop trying to mind meld me, G," Travis said threateningly.

"Okay. I just wanted to make sure you're alright," George said in apology.

"Well I'm not. You saw that shit just like I did. My parents are big fat liars. Now everyone knows what she did. I think Trey might run away," Travis said obviously trying not to cry.

George walked close to his friend and wrapped his arm around him and pulled him close. Travis just stood there at first, but then relaxed. Neither said anything, there wasn't much that needed saying. Travis had been the one helping George with his emotions for a long time. George could tell he was sad and angry and confused. For some reason, seeing all that tonight hadn't come as a huge surprise, but it wasn't his family.

The bathroom door opened and Buzz Baker, one of Trey's friends from high school, started inside. He was the fry cook and was wearing a hair net and a white apron. "Whoa, sorry," he said startled. Then as he took in what he was seeing, he grinned and said. "Jeez, ladies. You waiting for your boyfriends to come join you in here so you can blow them?"

In sync, the boys punched Buzz in the belly sending him flying back into the hallway, doubled over gasping to catch his breath. George looked back over his shoulder as they stepped over the groaning teen. "Bathroom's all yours, Buzz," he said.

41 Trey

He kept running. It felt like his lungs were on fire but he just ran. He burned down Chestnut Street past the elementary school and kept going. He got on Live Oak Street and turned on the speed. It was raining even harder now and he was soaked to the bone. His pale blue dress shirt clung to his chest revealing his defined arms and abs. His chest heaved and he breathed in huge gasps, but he kept running. When he crossed Monroe Street, a car turning left almost plowed into him, blasting a loud blare on the horn. He ran down hill past Wheeler Elementary and out toward Hwy 50. He ran past the Hickory Shack BBQ and Walmart and the All Sports Inn, which sounded like a hotel but was just a burger joint.

Trey turned on a gravel road a mile up Hwy 50 and ran toward the farm house in the distance. There was a light on and he was grateful. He didn't know where else to go right now. His mind was frozen. The images from that prayer meeting kept repeating over and over. He saw all the people, their secrets and hidden moments played on the movie screen in their minds, like the Cow Hill Drive-In. A year ago, the run-down drive-in started showing XXX movies on the weekends and immediately their attendance tripled. Trey and Pete Clark found a spot on the road that ran behind the drive-in where you could park and see the movie in all its Technicolor filthiness. Not having any sound didn't really cause them any trouble. If you had heard one porno soundtrack, you had heard them all. They would sit in the truck, rubbing one off until they couldn't wait any more, using napkins from the Sonic to clean up the mess. It was his second favorite thing to do after boning a girl.

But tonight, it wasn't "Chewy, Chewy, Chewy" playing on the screen. It was Carl Washington sliding inside his mother, her startlingly white legs wrapped around his dark back and gripping his muscled brown ass, her hands gripping his broad shoulders as he plowed inside of her harder and harder, grunting and moaning as he emptied his nuts inside her. The nausea had already cause him to vomit as he left the church and now it threatened again. He kept closing his eyes but the images would not stop. Along with Carl and his mother's tryst, the other secrets kept flashing across his mind as well. He saw the local banker rummaging through safety deposit boxes. He saw Tim Murphy bent over a desk, his pants around his ankles and JL Martin ramming a grease gun up his asshole. He saw Jack Tanner knock Martin across his office. He saw Mary Washington bent over the oak whiskey barrel, hands and feet tied, as man after man violated her. He saw Carl hanging in a barn, hands above his head, a rope cutting into his neck as a sharp blade sliced his scrotum open, one testicle pouring out like a stewed prune. By this time he was sobbing. His mind was going to explode and he didn't know what to do.

Trey leaped the porch steps and leaned against the screen door, trying to catch his breath. He walked over to the railing and threw up again, all over some rotting chrysanthemums. He wiped his mouth with the back of his hand and knocked on the door. A moment later, the porch light flicked on and Tooter Turner stood in the doorway, barefoot in a pair of old Cow Hill Tigers sweatpants. His eyes grew wide as he saw Trey and he looked around to see if someone was actually chasing him.

"Jesus Christ, McGee! What the hell?" He said.

"Can I just come in? Please, I didn't know where else to go?" Trey implored.

"Yeah, sure. Come on, buddy. Shit, you are soaked," Tooter said steadying the teenager and closing the door behind him. Trey had already made a large puddle to grow on the hardwood floor as he stood shivering in the front hall. Tooter put his arm around Trey and guided him to the bathroom and helped him out of his soaked clothes and dropped them in the tub as he handed him a couple of towels.

"Go back in the living room. I've got a fire going in there," he ordered as he picked up the sodden clothes and disappeared. Trey walked back to the living room and sat on the couch, draping one of the towels around his shoulders. The orange and yellow flames licked up and down the oak firewood creating feathery lace on the blackened surfaces. Trey looked around the room paneled in honey colored birch. The walls were covered with old family photos, some of Tooter when he was in little league, on the Tiger football team, him graduating. Trey had never realized he must be an only child. A big German clock sat on the mantle. The dial read 10:30. The far wall opposite the big window had an impressive gun rack, two shotguns and a rifle set proudly on display. A picture of Jesus praying in the garden was beside it. As Trey looked around the room, a set of headlights flashed by out on the road, but when Trey looked up they were gone. *It must have been another truck heading home,* he thought. Tooter came back into the room with a thick blanket under one arm, two long neck Lone Star's in his hand and a shot glass and a bottle of Southern Comfort in the other.

"What's all this? You were gone long enough," Trey mumbled.

"Yeah, well eat me. I called your Dad. Put the blanket on," he commanded while he sat the drinks on the coffee table. He reached over and helped wrap the blanket around the boy's shoulders. Tooter looked out the front window. "Did someone just drive up? He asked. Trey shook his head. Tooter poured a full shot of the liquor and handed it to Trey. "The only hard stuff I could find. Down the hatch, McGee."

Trey looked up in fear. "You called my Dad? Why? That's why I came over here," he said, his chin trembling.

"No worry, buddy. I was pretty sure they were wondering where you were. I told him you were okay and were gonna stay over here tonight. That is, if you want to. He seemed fine with it. Asked me to call him if you needed a ride back home."

Trey nodded and tipped the sweet amber liquid down his throat and gasped as it burned his gullet.

"Damn, I'm not crazy about that," he said then handed the glass back to Tooter who filled it again and Trey downed another shot.

"Ack," Trey said shuddering. Tooter poured himself a glass and downed it making a face. He picked up the Lone Stars and handed one to Trey, reaching out to clink the necks together in a toast.

"Cheers," Tooter said. "Now, you want to tell me what the hell you are doing running around town in the middle of the night in the rain?"

The big guy leaned forward and draped a heavy arm around Trey's shoulders. For some reason, that made the knot in Trey's stomach tighten again and tears stung his eyes again. Tooter pulled his head close and gave him a tight squeeze. They sat that way for several minutes, drinking their beers and not saying anything. Trey figured if he was at home, his parents wouldn't be willing to just sit and wait; they would be pestering him for some answers.

Right now, he didn't care what the hell they wanted. The breeze picked up outside and the bamboo wind chimes played a haunting song. The boards on the front porch creaked softy. When Trey looked up, Tooter said, "Probably a coon or the dog." Trey heaved a big sigh.

"You remember, back in early September; the night the lights showed up over Cowhill," Trey asked.

Tooter thought for a moment. "Yeah. I mean, I heard some fellas talking about it. I didn't see them myself. Why?"

"They turned on, shone right down in our backyard. We all went outside and looked at them. It did something to us," Trey said.

"What do you mean?"

"It's hard to explain, but somehow a few of us, or maybe a lot, I don't really know, got changed by that light or whatever it was. My brother and his friends found out about it first. Whatever the light was, it gave us all like a power or an ability or something. It made us stronger, faster, smarter," Trey explained.

Tooter took another drink and grinned. "Sounds far out but I think you are yanking my chain."

Trey shifted back on the couch. "I'm not." He sat his beer down on the coffee table. "You think I could beat you arm wrestling?"

"Well, you know, I'm keeping up with my training pretty good. His arms were cut with thick muscles. He held up his arm and flexed a big rounded bicep showing the thick red fur under his armpit. "Figure I could still take you like I used to."

Trey slid down on the floor and set his arm on the coffee table holding up his hand. Tooter smiled and knelt down and gripped his hard. His large hand dwarfed Trey's and his grip was like iron. Trey held on with his other hand steadying their grip. "One, two, three," he said and Tooter set his weight and muscles into his forearm to take down this high school boy. In one second, Trey's grip tightened and he slammed Tooter's arm down to the coffee table like a dad might do with this six-year-old son. Tooter's eyes widened and he grabbed his arm back and rubbed his arm and shoulder.

"Fuck me sideways," he groaned. "How did you do that?"

"I wasn't really even trying," Trey said climbing back up on the couch. His towel slipped off and Tooter pulled his face back.

"Thanks anyway, McGee. I've already had dinner," Tooter said backing away. Trey pulled the blanket back around himself.

"I need to take a piss," Trey said moving quickly down to the hall bathroom, blue blanket trailing behind him like a king's robe.

"Best we can tell, the light or whatever it was made us all about twice as strong or fast or smart as we were before. But my brother and his friends found out we can also link up our abilities and quadruple it or sextuple it or whatever it is. We have to really concentrate, or at least I do. That's what happened the other night at the football game. That's why I was so unstoppable," Trey explained.

"You were Bruce Jenner the other night because of some alien force, like with Luke Skywalker," Tooter asked.

"Yeah, kind of. But when we link it up, it really makes weird stuff happen to you too sometimes. Like my brother, Travis gets a nosebleed. George feels like throwing up, Em faints.

And my little brother, um, gets a boner."

Tooter laughed. "Sounds like he got the best side effect. What about you?"

Trey rolled his eyes. "I have to piss really bad."

Tooter howled. "Now that's sum bullshit for sure. I'd be talking to Mr. Spock and asking him for a new kind of power."

"Tell me about it. What makes you think it's an alien power?"

Tooter shrugged his shoulders. "I dunno. Lights from the sky and all that. Sounds like Close Encounters to me."

Trey took a long drink from his beer. "Yeah, it kind of does to me too.

"So why you all bent out of shape tonight about your new super powers, Bruce Wayne?" Tooter asked. He got up and used the poker to stoke up the fire and threw another log on top making long orange shadows dance across the walls and Trey's blue-green eyes. Trey stared at the big country guy, his red mustache fiery in the flickering light. Hundreds of freckles dotted Tooters shoulders. A patch of copper fuzz grew on the small of his back looking like the world's smallest bath mat.

"It wasn't the power or the ability in the same way tonight," he began. "See, we can do some other stuff too. We can sometimes make people do stuff, especially when we link up. But even on my own, I can sometimes make guys do stuff." With that Trey closed his eyes and concentrated, gripping Tooter's hand. Tooter was still standing in front of the fire. He suddenly wheeled around and grabbed the waistband of his sweatpants and pulled on it hard, bringing the pants almost up to his chin. His eyes looked glazed, a bit out of focus. Just as suddenly, he stopped and looked down at his pants now hiked up on his chest.

"Jeezus!" he crowed, laughing. Pushing his pants down and reaching around to pull them out of his crack. "You mean you made me just do that?"

Trey smiled weakly. "Yeah, I mean, unless you just wanted to give yourself an atomic wedgie. Hold on I need to piss again," he said disappearing into the bathroom. He came back and sat on the couch, tucking the towel around his waist. "Kind of getting warm in here now. What happened to my clothes?"

"I threw them in the dryer. They probably ain't dry. They were soaked. My mom would kick my ass for throwing shit that wet in her dryer."

"Where are your parents?"

"Up in Texarkana visiting some of my mom's family. I am trying to get out of here, but need a bit more scratch before I can launch out on my own. I am so ready to get away from this place," Tooter said sitting down beside Trey again.

Trey tipped the beer up and finished it off. Tooter jumped up like he sat on the hot poker and ran off down the hall. He jogged back in with a Dutch Masters cigar box and sat down. "Figured me might as well make this a party," Tooter said. "I don't get much fun these days unless it's just on my own."

"You use or right or left hand for that?" Trey asked.

"Har har, a comedian. A real Flip Wilson," Tooter said. He opened the lid of the cigar box and pulled out a couple of fat joints. A baggie full of weed, a lighter, and even a grinder was in there. He handed one of the joints to Trey and flicked the lighter. Trey lit the joint and took a big drag. He coughed when he held the smoke which made Tooter laugh. "Bet you haven't smoked in a while since you are in football right now."

Trey coughed and blinked in the haze of smoke. "Not since early last summer. Wow, this kind of goes right to your head."

"Pretty good shit," Tooter said letting the smoke exit his nostrils in two fat streams of grey. "So, there has to be some more to this story, not that turning into Spiderman isn't pretty cool."

"Yeah, there's more," Trey said inhaling again sending the smoke up toward the ceiling. "Tonight, at our church. There was this revival service starting. The preacher guy had done this big sermon with actors and everything, it was kind of crazy. But at the end, a lot of people went down to the front to pray. A lot of us were laying our hands on each other, kind of connected, you know, praying for each other. A group of us were praying for this girl, Mary. You probably remember her being in the paper. A young girl found walking on Hwy 24 after she had been kidnapped and raped?"

"I remember. That was a terrible thing," Tooter said.

"Well we were praying for her and this little kid came up and put his hands on her head, like he was praying too. Only, when he touched her, it was like all of us were blasted with some extra juju and we started seeing into each other's minds or something. All this stuff, regular life stuff and secret stuff was pouring into our minds like from a giant movie screen or something," Trey said.

"I don't really get what you are saying," Tooter said.

"Come here," Trey said. Trey leaned over and placed his joint in an ashtray on the coffee table. He scooted over and reached up to Tooter and grabbed his head. Tooter pulled his head back but Trey held on.

"I'm not going to kiss you," Trey said. With that he closed his eyes and touched his forehead against Tooter's. The dormant images and emotions flooded out of Trey and into Tooter's mind, running fast like a flash flood into the farm boy's brain. A few moments later, Trey pulled away leaving Tooter dazed and blinking his eyes. The big man leaned back against the couch and rubbed his hands into his eyes, shaking his head.

"Holy shit, what the hell was all of that? It was like you just put a whole movie projector in my head or something. What was all of that?"

"It's stuff from other people's lives. Stuff that really happened to them."

"I saw you at the football game, like looking through your eyes running down the field. I saw you and a girl and y'all were doing it. I saw your little brother and his friends in school with all this crazy stuff blowing around and all. I saw these guys in an office and one was bent over a desk and a guy had a gun to his head and then that guy was flying across the room," Tooter said taking another long draw on his blunt. "I saw the lights up in the sky and an old bridge. I saw your dad and JL Martin. I saw someone that looked like your mom. But it couldn't have been your mom," Tooter began. He started to say more, but looked up at Trey and then back down at the floor.

"Because she was getting fucked by this big black guy?" Trey said with an edge in his voice.

"Um, yeah. Something like that. But maybe that's just a fantasy or dream or something. I've had some pretty messed up dreams before that I sure wouldn't like anyone knowing about." Tooter sat for a moment and then his head snapped up, "Holy fuckin' shit. Carl Washington. Your mom did it with Carl Washington?"

"That's not the half of it," Trey said wearily, tears stinging his eyes again. "He's my fucking dad."

"Oh my God," Tooter said.

"Once I saw that, I didn't know what to do anymore. I just had to get out of there. I mean, my parents have lied to me my entire life. They've let me believe that I am somebody I'm not. And not only that, a secret like this…I know what everybody is going to say. I'm never going to be able to go anywhere or do anything without someone rubbing this in my face. I will face shit for the rest of my life because of this."

"So what are you going to do?" Tooter asked.

"I don't know," Trey said breaking down, sobbing in big heaving sobs into his hands while Tooter rubbed his back and neck and tried to think of something to say. The fire bounced on the amber color of the beer bottles making them almost blaze. The clock on the mantle struck 11:00.

"Look. This is a shitty thing. It's a big secret. It's a big thing for your parents to keep from you all this time. But don't you think they must have had a pretty good reason for keeping it. How would you have dealt with it otherwise?"

Trey looked up defiantly, wet cheeks glistening in the light. "I would have known who I was. I could have figured out my place in the world a little bit better instead of always feeling like I was a mistake or something."

"Do you think you would have shared it with people? Would you have just walked into the locker room at school and said to the brothers, 'Hey man, ain't no thang, I got's a colored dad so we are soul brothers?'"

"You know I wouldn't have."

Tooter sighed and leaned back on the couch. The minute passed with nothing but the ticking of the clock to fill the silence before he spoke again. "I know this is a huge thing. I'm not saying it's easy. This is a hard thing. Probably the hardest thing that you have ever had to face. And you are right, I'm sure there are people that are going to throw some shit in your face if the word gets out, and I suppose it's bound to. Folks love to gossip about crap like this. There are going to be assholes that try and make you feel small because of something you had absolutely no control over at all. But I know this: you still get to have a choice. You can run away, you can hide, you can turn your back on your family because of this secret they kept. You can say that it's justified. And you will end up lonely and miserable and angry. Is that what you want?"

"I don't know. I just want people to not lie. I want to know the truth," Trey answered in a pained and pleading voice.

"Okay. So this is your big moment of truth. Right now, you get to find out what living with the truth is like. Now you know. Your daddy is a big black man. You know your mom and this guy did the deed. And for some reason, your dad stuck with your mom and raised you as his own. I get the idea it was pretty clear from the minute you were born that something was up and you weren't his boy. I mean, God, you don't look anything like the rest of your strawberry blond family. You always had this nice tan skin and dark black hair and those crazy blue eyes. Your nose is wide, your lips are full…"

"I just always thought I was adopted. I figured my parents just didn't want to tell me. My dad has always acted so, I don't know…distant. He's hard on me all the time, especially compared to my other brothers."

Tooter rubbed the back of Trey's neck. "I get it. Sounds like your dad has been a real dick sometimes. I'm sure some it has to do with the fact that every time he looks at you, he thinks of Carl Washington humping his wife. And that's got to be really hard. But you know what? Use it."

"What do you mean? Use it."

"Use this. If this makes you mad, if this makes you determined, if this makes you feel at risk, then use it. Let that be the fuel that gets into your belly and makes the difference in your life; that turns you into something bigger than this. You're more than just some scared little kid who doesn't know where he came from. Hold on, I'll be right back." Tooter disappeared into the kitchen and came back with two hastily thrown together bologna and cheese sandwiches and two more beers. "That weed is making me hungry," he said putting the food and beers on the coffee table. The guys took big bites of their sandwiches. Tooter opened up a bag of Fritos and dumped some on their plates along with some Oreos. "I love eating cookies with a sandwich and chips," he said with a mouth revoltingly full.

Tooter took a drink of beer to wash down the mouthful. "Carl Washington is a good man. Your dad is friends with him. They've stayed friends all these years even though Carl screwed your mom. That's got to be worth something. Now you get a chance to not only know your dad and figure out why in the hell he would have been willing to do this, but you also get to know another man who's responsible for you being here. And you know good and well that just because you slide your dick in a girl and drop off some nut, does not make you a father. That's just a sperm donor. I mean, they have those places now where a girl can go buy some come and shove it up her cooter and get pregnant."

"They do not," Trey said.

"They seriously do. I saw it on Donahue. They're called sperm banks and guys go there and jack off and they freeze your jizz and a girl comes and buys some and uses it to get preggers. They pay you to wax your dolphin and give them the spunk."

"If that's true, I could be a millionaire," Trey said taking a bite of his sandwich.

"Me too," Tooter said laughing. He picked up some chips and tossed them into his mouth, crunching loudly. "Your dad is a good guy. Carl Washington is a good guy. You have two times more in some ways than I have. 'Cause I just have one dad he is a sorry son of a bitch. All he wants to do is hang out with that idiot, JL Martin, and his band of Klan-loving cronies and go to that fucked-up church, finding ways to hurt or humiliate blacks, Jews, Chinamen, and wetbacks. They're just racist idiots, full of hate. My dad tried to shame me the whole time I was on the football team, telling me I was nigger-lovin' fag for taking showers with the black guys. And that made me happy, actually. To know that I was pissing him off every time I would be in the locker room with them. That's one of the reasons I stayed here in town and took the scholarship at ET so I could keep playing football and hanging with guys my dad doesn't approve of along with getting a college degree so I can get out of this shithole town and make something of my life."

Trey and Tooter clinked their beer bottle necks together again and took long drinks. Both of them belched in stereo afterwards and grinned. Tooter picked up his half-smoked joint and relit it, passing the joint to Trey.

"I tell you what," Tooter began, "The way you deal with this shit is going to speak louder than the fact that you will now be known as Carl Washington's half-nig bastard. There will be fools and idiots that make you feel bad, but you and I both know being colored isn't any big deal. We talk and play with these guys all the time. They put their pants on one leg at a time just like white guys do. You are the same guy you were before you found this out tonight, exactly the same. You are Trey Fuckin' McGee, a great football player with a big ole' horse cock, and a family that loves you. And you are going to make something out of your life."

"You make it sound so cool," Trey said sarcastically sending a cloud of smoke high into the air. "Aren't your parents going to smell all this pot when they get home?" he asked.

"Nah. I'll forget some shit on the stove and the place will smell like burned chicken pot pie or something instead," Tooter said. "Buddy, I am pretty tired, been a long day for me. I know it has been for you. You want me to get you set up in a guest bedroom upstairs?"

"No, I'll just camp out here, it that's okay.

"Yeah, that's cool. I'll go get you a pillow and another blanket." Tooter came back from the back of the house with a bright colored quilt, a thick pillow, and Trey's underwear on his head. Trey laughed and shook his head.

"The rest of your clothes are still damp but your shorts are good. Didn't want your big colored boy balls rubbing around on my grandma's quilt," Tooter said tossing the Fruit of the Loom briefs at Trey's face. Trey grabbed the briefs and slid them on and took the quilt from Tooter along with the pillow.

"Thanks for letting me stay, Toot. And for saying what you said. I still don't know how to feel about all this but at least I'm way better than I was," Trey said.

Tooter wrapped Trey in his arms and kissed the boy on the top of his head. "Don't mention it, McGee. I love you, you idjit. And besides, now I have another Negro friend." Tooter gave Trey a Dutch rub on his short hair. Trey pushed him away, smiling.

"That's African-American friend to you." Tooter laughed and hugged him again.

"Night, brother," he said. He walked down the hall and disappeared into the bathroom. Trey watched as Tooter's bright white briefs glowed in the dim light as his friend went into his bedroom. The springs on his mattress groaned as the big man lay down. Trey lay back on his pillow and pulled the quilt around him, his arm behind his head as he looked at the embers in the fire. Trey didn't notice the shape on the front porch quietly move from the shadows back towards a truck parked down the driveway. The eavesdropper eased the door open and slid his foot on the clutch and let the truck roll down the drive silently before turning on the engine and driving away without lights.

Trey woke with a start, checking the clock to see it was 3:05. The fire had died and it was cold in the living room, a howling wind blowing outside along with the rain. He pulled the quilt up to his chin, but he felt so awake, all the images and feelings of the night before pounding inside his brain along with the green light bridge dream. Trey got up and peed and walked into Tooter's room to find him on his side, snoring softly. Trey climbed in beside him and spooned back against him until Tooter woke up and threw a heavy arm around him.

"You ain't gonna use your alien witchcraft to make me blow you or take a ride on that black boner of yours, are you?" Tooter said with a deep, low growl.

"Now that you mention it…" Trey said with a laugh. "Nah, your ass is safe tonight, big guy. Maybe next time I'll make your fantasy come true." He soaked in the warmth of the bed and closed his eyes thinking how nice it would be to see Angie again. He even did his best to send out some mental message to her to meet him at the tree house tomorrow. He just had to see her.

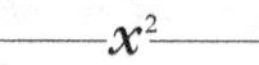

$$-x^2-$$

Trey opened his eyes and looked out the window. A slate grey sky stared back, lighting Tooter's bedroom with a dull silvery glow. He sat up in bed and noticed a note laying on the end table, scrawled in Tooter's loopy cursive:

> *"Had early class. Don't make a mess, I cleaned up. Tried to take it easy on your cornhole. The stories are true…once you go black!"*

Trey smiled. His clothes were lying on the foot of the bed. He pulled them on and turned around and made up the sheets and blankets on Tooter's bed and smoothed the bedspread. He put on his socks and shoes and headed into the bathroom. He took a long morning piss and made sure to flush. He walked into the living room and smelled the heady concoction of pot and burned toast. He looked out the window and saw the rain had mostly stopped for now but it was cold and blowing. He pulled on his letterman jacket and found a stocking cap in his pocket and put it on. It was almost 9:00, so he was already late for school. There is no way I can face that today, he told himself. He figured it was about two miles between Tooter's house and the Pete Clark's where the tree house was. He carefully closed the front door behind him and leaped off the porch and began to jog down the driveway toward Live Oak street. As he got to the gravel, he turned on the speed. He felt his strength and muscles grow warm as he flew up the road. He turned behind the businesses on the edge of Live Oak and ran through the alleys, leaping over big puddles and trash cans. He stayed off the main streets burning through the neighborhoods until he got to Pete's house. He leaped over the backyard fence like an Olympic hurdler and sprang up the ladder hammered into the trunk of the big oak and shimmied through the opening at the bottom.

Angie was asleep, wrapped in an old sleeping bag. She had the small electric heater on and it was almost hot in the small room. The boys had run an extension cord up the tree two summers ago so they could have light at night to keep looking at the pornos after dark and not have to deal with flashlights and candles. Pete had put the heater up here last year when he and Amy Edward had taken to using it as their "Fuck Fortress of Solitude," as he called it. There was a large nail on one of the walls. Like a trophy wall, all the used rubbers were impaled on the spike as an informal way of keeping track of all their conquests. Several of Trey's blown out condoms hung along with Pete's, dried loads in the tips. Pete's dad, Dr. Clark, kept him well supplied with prophylactics, and Pete in turn made sure he passed around the rubbers at school like a one-man Planned Parenthood clinic.

He took off his jacket and shoes and slid in beside Angie and wrapped his arms around her. She turned toward him and sleepily smiled, turning on her side and spooning against him like he had done with Tooter the night before. He smelled her hair, it was full of the Herbal Essence grassy smell he liked so much. He slid his hands around and cupped a breast and rubbed his thumb across her nipple, feeling it grow hard against his skin. He ground his crotch against Angie's bottom and she wiggled her round cheeks against his groin until his belly ached from the pressure in his nuts.

"Make love to me," she whispered. It was all the urging he needed. He raised up and tore his shirt off his back and pushed his jeans and underwear down in one movement. His dick smacked up on his belly with a loud thwack. He turned and saw Angie laying back against the pillows naked, her legs spread wide as her fingers rubbed her glistening lips. Trey dove between her legs and began to tease and lick her, pressing his face hard against her sex. Angie's head was thrown back in ecstasy as Trey pleasured her bringing her to a throbbing climax in short order. She pushed his head away briefly and crawled down and took his erection in her mouth, working hard to take the entire shaft into her mouth until her nose was buried in Trey's pubic bush. Trey groaned and warned her he was close. She pulled off and gripped the tip of his penis holding it tight until the urge subsided. Trey wondered where she had learned that. She pushed him back on the pillows and climbed on top of him, reaching behind and fitting him inside, sliding all the way down. Then, Angie gripped one of the branches at the top of the tree house and held on as she rode Trey's cock like a bucking bronc. Trey gripped her tits and drove himself as far inside as possible until he sucked in his breath and slammed hard against her sex and unloaded blast after blast inside her.

The two lay quietly in each other's arms afterward until they begin to cool down. She reached up and took his face in hers, his eyes were closed, tears in the corners of his eyes. She pulled his face close and kissed the corner of his eyes. As she did, the explosion from the night before returned, this time even clearer. The images flashed quickly across her mind. As the image got to the white lady getting laid by the black guy, her eyes flew open. In a split second she saw who the people were and the meaning of all this blasted through her mind. She looked at Trey who was staring, sweat on his brow and on his upper lip, his soft mustache wet. He was shaking, trembling, and a moan of pain seemed to escape his lips and reverberate through the tree house. She locked her legs around him and pulled him closer, rocking him back and forth.

"It's okay, baby. It's okay, baby," she kept saying as she rocked him.

Five minutes later, the two were cuddled in a heap, Trey's soft brown skin in stark contrast to Angie's pink flesh. She rubbed her fingers across his strong back as he touched her face and ran his hands down against her warm skin. Angie finally broke the silence.

"I didn't really understand what I was seeing last night," she said. "Maybe it was that way for a lot of people. Do you think they could even see it if they don't have the power like we do?"

"I think they can. I was able to zap Tooter with it last night so he could see it and he wasn't even at church. Maybe they won't get what they were seeing. But I figure even if one could tell what was going on, it'll be enough to blow the lid off it. This time tomorrow, the whole town will know," Trey said morosely.

"I don't care. To hell with all of them. You are perfect to me just like you are."

"That is sweet, baby. I doubt your dad will feel the same. He hates me already. Can't wait until he figures out his little girl is banging a coon."

"Half-coon," she said which made them both laugh. "Don't say that. You are exactly the same as you were yesterday."

"You sound like Tooter."

"Well he's right. I'm glad you went there last night. Sounds like he had some good things to say to you and I know you weren't ready to go to home," Angie said softly.

"Still not ready. Let's just stay here and fuck," Trey said hugging Angie closer. "I meant to put on a rubber before..."

"You always say that," she chided. "Probably doesn't matter anyway."

"What do you mean by that?"

"Oh nothing. Just probably not the time of the month when you get knocked up, that's all. Do you know what you are going to say when you get home?"

"Not really."

"Well try not to lose your temper. Just tell them how this made you feel and listen to why they did it."

"Can't wait to hear why my mom wanted to spread he legs for Carl Washington. Or why the hell my dad didn't just tell her to get out."

Angie ran her fingers along Trey's arms to his big hands and slid her fingers in between his. "No doubt there is way more to the story than you think. And as for why your dad stayed, would it be so bad if it was because he loved her?"

"If you love someone you don't go and fuck someone else."

"It might not be so black and white."

Trey looked at Angie as it dawned on her what she had just said and they both burst out laughing. Trey ran his hand across Angie's belly and felt a tiny fluttering across his palm. "You must be really hungry, I can feel your belly moving under my hand."

Angie tried to chuckle but the sound died in her throat. "Yeah, I need to eat something for sure. I'll get something in a bit. What time is it?"

Trey sat up and crawled over to the edge of the tree house and looked at the clock on the wall. About 1:00 I think."

"We should go. I want to be home before my dad or mom gets back. I told them I was sick with PMS today and couldn't go to school."

"You girls have so many things like that you can use to get out of school and stuff."

"Yes we do," Angie said "And don't you forget it. Hand me my sweatshirt."

The two dressed and climbed down the ladder and walked hand and hand down the sidewalk, daring the onlookers to say anything. There didn't appear to be any today, however. The air was cold and blustery, threatening more rain. When they reached the corner of Church Street and Maple, Trey kissed Angie softly on the lips and turned toward home. His heart was thumping so loud he was sure it would burst right out of his chest at any minute.

He climbed the stairs to the front porch and walked into the living room, relieved there wasn't someone waiting inside. He walked around the hall and into the kitchen and then into the den. Mike was sitting in his La-Z-Boy, watching The Addams Family. Janet was sitting on the couch folding laundry. The floorboards creaked and the two of them looked up. Janet's eyes flew open and she jumped off the couch, laundry basket spilling on the floor. Mike catapulted himself out of his recliner and the two slammed into Trey, locking him into a deep embrace. Janet was weeping; Mike was gripping Trey so tightly he thought his ribs were going to crack. His dad's face was pressed against the side of his head. He could feel the warm trickle of tears from his dad's face slide down his cheek. He could taste the saltiness as they flowed to his lips.

"You're back," Janet whispered through her sobs.

"Yeah," Trey says not looking at either of them, feeling the lump grow in his throat.

"Can you please come and sit with us," Janet pleaded. She took him by the hand and kicked aside the strewn laundry and gently took his hand and pulled him down on the couch. Her face was stricken, with swollen eyes that hadn't slept. Trey looked at his dad who sat beside him on the other end of the couch. His face was ashen, like someone on board a ship rocked by stormy seas. Mike reached out tentatively and wrapped an arm around Trey.

"Tooter called us a little while ago. Said you had left to come home but figured you would need a little time. So we just stayed home today," Mike said explaining why they weren't at work.

"Okay," Trey said adding one more thing to the list he ought to thank Tooter for.

"Oh honey, I am just so sorry," Janet began. "A hundred times, a thousand, I wanted to figure out some way to tell you. But how do you tell someone that? I'm sorry. I'm sorry more than you can know." The tears leaked out of her eyes and dotted the cotton blouse she was wearing with splashes. "Carl is sorry," she said trailing off.

Mike's hand gripped Trey's shoulder as Janet mentioned Carl. "All I can tell you is he's about as proud of you as you could ever imagine. He practically busts a gut every time you have a great moment on the football field or do something special. He never lets me forget, especially when you do something great, that he's half the reason." Mike tenderly rubbed his hand over Trey's back in uncharacteristic affection. "And I never let him forget that when you screw up, he's half the reason for that too."

"Guess you've had plenty of opportunity to rub that in," Trey said defensively.

"Not so much," Mike said meekly. "Uh, we want to talk to you about all this, but before we get going, if there's anything you want to say; something you need to get off your chest, you just go right ahead. You've got a right to say whatever you want to say."

Trey sighed and slumped against the big frame of his dad who gripped him tighter. Janet held his hand and set back, expectantly, waiting for Trey to lower the boom.

"I have known my whole life I was different. I mean, it doesn't take a genius. I always figured y'all had adopted me or found me in a garbage can or something and thought you wouldn't tell me for some reason. I just didn't fit, except for the blue eyes. I guess I'm grateful for them."

"Your eyes are lovely, honey," Janet said.

"They're your eyes," Trey said squeezing his mother's hand as more tears coursed down her splotched face. He took another deep breath. "I, I can handle this. I can take finding out that this happened. That I'm not who I thought I was."

"But you are, honey," Janet began.

"Not really, Mom." Trey answered. "Last night, Tooter said a lot of cool things to me and one of the things he said that was really true was that just because someone was a sperm donor doesn't make them a father." Janet began to sob anew. Trey looked up at Mike, his blue eyes glimmering with tears. "You have always been my real dad. I don't know how you did it. I don't know how you got over it. I don't know why you wanted me," Trey said watching Mike's chin quiver as he held in his emotions. "But I know I'm lucky you did." Mike closed his eyes and laid his head against Trey's. Trey took his hand and patted the side of Mike's face. Trey looked at Janet. "I don't know why you did it, or even if it wasn't your fault. But right now, that's not the hard part even though I can't figure out how to feel about it. The hard part is everybody else knowing. The hard part is all those people that were there. They are going to tell."

"Honey, no one knows what happened last night at church. That was the strangest thing any of us had ever experienced. It was like the power of God that no one had seen before. There was so much. We all were overloaded with all that."

"I don't know, Ma," Trey said apprehensively.

"Look. Whatever people saw, or thought they saw, it's going to go back and forth with folks trying to make sense of it. It's going to get debated and one person is going to say this and other is going to say that. I'm sure there might be some that think they know something about what they saw and they will be cruel and horrible. But the fact is they don't. There are only three people in the world who really know what happened: me, your dad, and Carl. I don't even know if Carl's wife knows. It was not like that back then. And you're right. It almost killed all of us. And your dad and Carl, I think they almost killed each other. But at the end of the day, they're friends. They have been through a lot. Growing up and heading to school and going to officer training together, not to mention Camp Holliwell and Viet Nam. It changed them."

"Trey, I can try to explain to you why I wanted to be your father even in the middle of all this. And I can tell you right now, I have never been sorry. It was always the smartest decision I made in my whole life, right up there with sticking with your mom. And that isn't to say that Carl wouldn't have been a great father. Of course he would have. But the fact is, back then, even if your mother and I had split and gone our separate ways, I don't know that the world would have let your mom and Carl be together. It wasn't like that back then. Hell, it's not much different now, especially around here. I know I haven't been fair to you."

"Sometimes when you look at me, I think that all you see is him and mom together."

"I'm afraid that's true to a certain extent. It's been a long time though now. I don't feel that way anymore. Carl and I are well past that. But...old habits die hard. And I know I have been unfair to you and it probably all comes back to what you saw in that vision thing. Damn, you do look like him, buddy, along with a lot of your mom. But there's none of me. And yeah, that's a little hard. But it's not because I don't want to love you. It's more that I know that half of you isn't me, it's someone else and we have always been a little bit strangers to each other."

"Well, now that the truth has come out, maybe it won't seem so strange," Trey said sliding his hand into his dad's. They all sat quietly for a while, the muffled sounds from outside casually making their way into the still room.

"I want to get to know him," Trey said. "I want to see how he fits into my life too."

"We want that too," Janet said. "We just keep praying to God that he is okay. We keep hoping that the reason we haven't heard from him is that he is hiding, laying low. We just keep trying to believe he got away from those bastards."

"Is it those men? That JL Martin and his church that took him and Mary?"

"Yes, it's him." Mike began. "But he is protected by quite a few powerful people, not the least of which is the sheriff. They aren't going to look at him as long as he owns them the way he does. There would have to be more evidence from someone else."

"The only evidence seems to be the whole town that knows what that dick has done. But nobody gives a damn."

"I think they give a damn. They just don't know what to do," Mike said.

"Oh honey, I am so sorry the way all of this played out," Janet began again. "But I will say that it is like the biggest weight of my whole life has slipped off my shoulders. It was killing me. The older you got the more you seemed like Carl. And I knew that you were going to find out there was more than just me and your dad."

Trey let his mom hug him tight. "Um, do the other kids know? I mean, Trav and Andy . . .and George?"

Mike cleared his throat. "I talked with the boys this morning on the way to school. They figured it all out last night, at least Travis and George did. I tried to explain it to Andy today. They don't care, Trey. You are still their brother…"

"Step-brother," Trey said with a bit of anger in his voice.

"Brothers, plain and simple. They love you, they want to be like you, especially Andy. The people in town will get over it. Half of them will say they knew it all along, even though they didn't. But I know you will get teased and probably worse. I am really sorry about it and I wish I could make it not happen."

"I know."

There was a loud clatter in the hallway and Andy ran inside and jumped into Trey's lap. He didn't say anything he just hugged his brother tightly. Trey looked up and Travis was standing in the doorway, smiling.

"Made it back?" Travis said.

"Yeah," Trey said hugging Andy tight.

Mike rubbed Trey's shoulder. "Is it okay if we keep talking about all this later? We want to tell you the whole story."

"Yeah, it's fine. I want to hear it all. But maybe when the munchkins aren't here."

"Hey!" Andy said.

Dinner was a subdued affair that night of fish sticks, scalloped potatoes, and green peas. Small talk was light and the boys finished eating quickly and made their way back to the bedroom. George walked in the back door almost as soon as they came into the room. They sat on the bed while Trey told them what he had done and about what Tooter had said to him. Trey told them what he had heard so far from mom and dad. They listened closely, Andy still sitting in Trey's lap.

"Does this mean you're going to start saying Dy-No-Myte or 'What you talking 'bout, Willis?" Andy asked. They all burst out laughing.

"And 'Afro-Sheen' in the medicine cabinet," Travis said."

"And fried chicken and watermelon for supper," George said.

The boys laughed again and Trey tickled Andy so hard he jumped off the bed and headed to the bathroom to pee. Travis spoke up.

"We had our own interesting day," he said. "We talked with Jack and Tim at Western Auto. This stuff is getting crazy."

42 University of Buffalo 1958
Fort Hood, Texas 1961

Mike and Carl traveled home on the train together for Christmas break after finals in December. Both of them had done well in their first term of classes managing B's and C's, not bad at all considering how much time they had spent practicing football, hanging out at the Bar Fly, and negotiating the tricky relationships of college.

But the harsh realities of real life came blasting back to life as soon as the train crossed the border from Missouri into Kansas. The conductor made his way through the carriage Mike and Carl sat in playing Rummy to ask Carl to please go ahead and move to the last car in the train. Carl picked up his things and began to move when Mike put a hand on his arm.

"What are you doing? You don't need to move."

"Yes I do, Tex. We're back in the South now."

Mike stared out the window at the bleak winter landscape the rest of the trip finding himself angry and furious at the utter ridiculousness of making a grown man move to the back of train simply because he happened to have more pigment in his skin than others did. When the bus pulled into the station in Paris, Texas, Mike disembarked from his car and saw Carl do the same seven cars back at the rear of the train. Carl waved a big good-bye and walked toward a small black woman in an extravagant hat jumping up and down in welcome for her son. Mike on the other hand found his father out in the car listening to the radio, following a ball game of his own. He barely looked up as Mike got into the car.

"Hi Pops," Mike said.

Patrick McGee raised his eyes and looked Mike up and down. "Your hair's so long I thought you were a girl," he said putting the car in drive.

Mike had scribbled down his home phone number to Carl on the train and Carl had promised to try and call once he spent a few days with his family. Five days later the phone rang and Mary McGee, Mike's mother answered.

"McGee residence."

"Yes, hello," a short clipped British accent filled the receiver. "I hate to trouble you, but is Michael McGee available? "

Mary was taken aback by the distinguished voice. "Well yes he is. Can I tell him who's calling?"

"G. Wilburforth Kumquat the IV," the voice informed her.

"Oh my. Well, hold on, please Mr. Kumquat." Mary's hand was over the speaking end of the receiver. "It sounds like a very distinguished man."

"Thanks, Ma," Mike said with a huge grin.

"Hello, this is Mike."

"Tex! You had some of that sweet tail of yours yet?" Carl said in his blackest voice possible.

"Once. But I think we will get together again soon," he answered nonchalantly.

"So you want to go up to Dallas and hear some real music?"

"Yeah, sure."

"Okay. Meet me over on Hwy 50 in about an hour. Park at the college in Berry Hall parking lot, okay? Nobody be noticing us there tonight. But park in the back."

An hour later, the men were driving south on Highway 67 toward Dallas. Carl reached over and gripped Mike's hand as he drove. "I missed you, Man. My mama really wants to meet you. Would you come over for dinner tomorrow night?"

"Sure. That would be great." Mike felt instantly awkward that he couldn't return the favor but Carl didn't seem bothered at all.

"Just wait 'til you hear the music at RG's tonight. Ray Charles, Etta James, Sam Cooke, Hank Ballard. This cover band they have there is great. Sounds almost like the real thing."

Mike had a wonderful night. He danced with almost every girl at the club, both white and black girls. It was like a secret place on Greenville Avenue where the 1950's suddenly stopped and became something else. The men and women enjoyed one another and there was no drama or stink eye because a black man danced with a white one. Mike got propositioned by two flamboyant black women that unabashedly groped his crotch as they sat beside him having Bloody Marys. Carl was talking and visiting with half of the crowd that seemed to know all about his success all the way up in New York. One of painted women finally found another fish and took off after him. But Juanita, the smoky voiced, big bosomed woman sitting by him now seemed to only have eyes for him. She worked her magic on his crotch through his pants until his dick was straining at the zipper of his dress slacks. She stood and wiggled her long taloned finger for him to come with her and for some reason, Mike did. A few moments later, the two occupied one of the stalls in the bathroom. Juanita sat on the stall with Mike in front of her. Mike felt his eyes roll back in his head as the woman's skilled mouth worked her magic on his manhood and drained him dry. At the end, she stood up and fixed her skirt and leaned forward to plant a sticky kiss on his lips, sliding a tongue inside that tasted of cigarettes and semen. Mike wiped his mouth as she left the bathroom and he stuck his head under the tap to rinse his mouth out, laughing at himself the whole time.

Carl drove carefully up Hwy 67 back toward Greenville, rain pouring down in a torrent. He had a wicked grin on his face for fifteen minutes before Mike couldn't stand it anymore.

"Okay, what is so goddamn funny, Rock?" Rock was a nickname given to Carl by Jack Ramsey who was his tackle partner during training and said hitting Carl was just like hitting a rock.

"You get your sausage swallowed back there at RG's by Juanita?"

"Yeah," Mike said smiling. "She just seemed so eager, I didn't want to disappoint her."

"I bet. You're the only sausage she got tonight I imagine."

"I don't know, she seemed pretty talented. I bet she could get as much as she wanted," Mike said.

"Yeah, it's just most of the guys there ain't too down to get blown by the likes of Juanita. That ain't her real name either."

"So? Plenty of girls in her line of work probably use a different name."

"There ain't no girls like her in that line of work, 'cause she ain't no girl. Juanita is Johnny Price. You done got your dick sucked by a drag queen." Carl laughed so hard he veered into the middle lane and had to correct back to the regular lane. Mike's face was burning so red it was on fire. Suddenly, flashing red and blue lights appeared in the rear window. "Oh fuck me. John Law done got me," Carl said pulling over to the side of the road. His hands literally trembling as he reached into his back pocket to get his wallet. Mike took a look at the situation and grabbed Carl's shoulder.

"Get over here now, he said." Mike scooted underneath Carl as the man raised up underneath the wheel then slid over into the passenger seat as the cop came to the window, shining his flashlight in the window."

"Good evening, officer. Did I do something wrong?" Mike said in all sincerity.

The officer stared at Mike and leaned down to see Carl sitting in the passenger seat. Carl bent down and waved at the officer. "Evening, sir," he said in his most subservient black voice."

Evening," the cop grunted, the rain pouring off his hat encased in a plastic bonnet. "You boys were weaving around back there pretty good. You been drinking?"

"Oh no, sir," Mike said. "I just needed to take a piss really bad and Carl here was holding this paper cup for me to use when I sort of missed and peed on the both of us, which made me jerk the wheel." Carl looked down and almost pissed himself when he saw Mike had his fly down and his undershorts sticking out.

"Well, why in the hell didn't you just pull over and take a leak like everyone else does?"

"It was just raining so hard, you know. I thought it would work. I see now that it wasn't a good plan."

The cop looked at Mike and then bent down looking at Carl again. "You just hold his pecker while he takes a piss driving 70 mph down the highway?"

"Yes sir, I mean, I was tryin,'" Carl said lowering his eyes.

"Christ almighty. You idiots get on down the road and if you feel like having your boyfriend play with your old man, get a hotel next time. There's laws about sodomy in this state. God, I am getting soaked out here talking with you fools. I don't care if you piss yourself, you get back to wherever you came from before you stop again. Hear me?"

"Yessir," both men said. Mike rolled up his window and signaled and pulled back on the road. They turned around and watched the cop make a U-Turn and both of them exhaled then broke into hysterical laughter. When they finally gained their composure again, Carl punched Mike hard on the shoulder.

"What in the fuck caused you to make up a crazy ass story like that? Did you see that man trying to figure out if I was in here holding your dick in my hand?"

Mike pounded the steering wheel. "That's what you get for letting me get blown by some old pervert tonight. My pecker is probably gonna fall off." Carl roared again.

In a few moments, Carl was wiping tears of laughter from his eyes. "Thanks, though, for jumping in back there, even if it was with the stupidest story ever told. It's never fun to get pulled over by the law when you are black and in Texas."

"And we had been drinking," Mike said.

"And orally sodomized by a drag queen," Carl added bursting out anew into fits of giggles.

"I can tell your college education is giving you a new vocabulary," Mike said sarcastically. He rubbed his face with his hand as he drove. "That ain't even the worst of it."

Carl stared. "Oh shit. Don't tell me you slid your dick up that nasty man's keister."

"Oh God, no. Shit, I'm going to vomit," Mike said.

"What then?"

"She, or he…it kissed me!"

Carl screamed so loud Mike almost went into the left lane again.

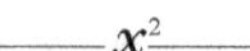

$$x^2$$

The next night, Mike drove to the Norton Community that he had never seen in his entire life and parked on Patterson Street in front of Carl's home. This part of town over the tracks was The Holler and white people simply didn't go across the tracks at all unless it was to go to the cemetery which had been built halfway between the white part of Cowhill and the Norton Community. Mike got out of his car and ran in the rain that was still falling hard and up on the porch. He knocked on the door and Carl dressed in a red shirt and black pants answered the door. Mike came inside and Carl wrapped him up in a hug finished off with a peck on the cheek. Mike was smiling when he stepped away and saw Carl's mother, Beulah. She was a tiny thing with blue hair and a radiant smile. She reached out and grabbed Mike and hugged him for all the world, tears poured from her eyes as she kissed Mike's cheek over and over.

"I cain't tell you how happy I am to meet you. Carl has written and told me all about you, Mike. He's told me to call you Mike and not Mr. McGee."

"That's right. Mike is good. I'm so glad to meet you Mrs. Washington."

"Just call me Mama, that's what the others do. Come on in Mike, we are just ready to eat," Mama made her way back into the small dining room just off the kitchen. The smells were intoxicating.

"So Mike, here's my little brother, Otho, and my sister, Diamond." Otho a thin boy of 14 stuck out his hand and shook Mike's. Diamond, a small girl of 9 or 10 waved from behind a chair. Mike couldn't help but wonder if either had ever seen a white man in their home before.

The meal was glorious. A big pot roast that was perfectly cooked with mashed potatoes, carrots, snap beans from last year's garden and some fried dill pickles. There were homemade rolls and butter and sweet tea to drink. After the meal, Mama served big slabs of chocolate pie with meringues a foot tall. The children went off to their bedrooms after dinner while Mike and Carl talked with Mama about the first term of school and football. She dabbed at her eyes with an embroidered handkerchief over and over, but grinned the entire time, a gold tooth shining like a star in her smile.

"When Carl here wrote and told me a white boy from Cowhill was his roommate, I almost had a spell. Then the next thing I hear is how you both have become the best of friends. The idea of you two being like brothers and sleeping in the same room when we can't even live on the same side of the tracks around here was almost more than I could handle. Carl tells me how so many students from all over the country and world are there and all of them get along and can be friends. He said sometimes, they even go out on dates and the like. Sounded like a different world to me."

"It's really different for me too, Mama. But it's shown me that so many of the rules and traditions we have down here make no sense at all. I'm glad that Carl and I are getting a chance to see the world in a better light up there. Maybe one day, it can be that way down here."

"Lord knows, that would be fine. I've seen some real heartache, Mike. But I know down deep inside, all of us are God's children. I think that day will come too. I hope I live to see it," she said with her smile bright and wide. "I sleep so much better at night knowing my boy is up there with a good man like you. You probably don't know it, but you might be the first white man ever come into this house."

"Well, I am honored to be here, Mama. Your son means the world to me. We have seen some wonderful things up there, learning lots too."

"Oh my Lawd, to think you boys are friends. Who could have ever thought it? Tell me, Mike. Carl won't say much, but is he making some lady friends up there too?" Carl shot Mike a threatening look.

"Oh yes, Ma'am. He is quite the Don Juan up there in Buffalo. A number of pretty girls are always making eyes at him and flirting. I think he's had quite a few kisses as well," Mike said, proud of his gentle fairy tale.

For the first time, Mama looked a bit less than pleased. She sat back in her chair with her lips in a tight line. Mike looked at Carl who closed his eyes, preparing for the storm.

"Uh hum, that sound a bit too good to be true. I think you probably said it right when you said Don Juan for sure. Tell me, does this fool keep his pants zipped up and study and make something of himself or is he humping girls like a buck in rut?" The change in this little woman was so profound Mike was simply too stunned to talk.

"I told you it's not like that Mama," Carl said in a low voice but his mother put her hand up in a 'shut the hell up' motion that did the trick. Carl sat back mutely.

Mike tried again, hoping he would do better this time. "Now Mama, Carl here is a respectful and diligent student. He has got good grades and has been dynamic on the football team. He's had a few dates and yes, he's a bit of a ladies' man, but his school and football always come first, along with his job too. You can count on me for that."

Mama looked at Mike with that withering expression of hers then finally relaxed and smiled again. "See I have to be extra careful with him since his daddy gone. He is a handsome boy and the girls are always trying to sink they claws into him. I can't believe I have a boy in college. It's a dream come true. I just don't want to see him mess it up by letting that head on his pecker be in charge of his life instead of the one on his shoulders."

"Dang, Mama," Carl said like a ten year old receiving a scolding. Mama reached over and patted Carl's big leg with her small hands.

"I know you are trying hard, son. And I'm glad you have Mike here to keep you remembering what's important. I know you boys going to be dipping your dicks into a pretty pussy now and again, but I better not hear of you getting someone in the family way or getting into some trouble. You up there to get your diploma and make a new life for yourself and family. Don't be letting a few moments of passion ruin what you have worked your whole life for. You feel me."

"We feel you, Mama," both Carl and Mike said in unison.

On Friday night before Christmas, Mike and Carl headed back to RG's in Dallas, but this time, Mike brought Janet along. He had told her all about the place and how it was so open and free with great music. He left off the part about Juanita and threatened Carl with his life if he started joking about it. Janet smiled and laughed and danced with Mike and then with Carl. She was absolutely smitten with her. Mike actually loved seeing the petite blond in his big dark arms as he swept her around the dance floor. But he had to admit, he also felt a twinge of possessiveness, a dark part inside him that didn't like his virginal girl being up so close against Carl's body. Old hate dies hard and the racism in him was in the bone, an obdurate cancer than was unyielding and clearly terminal. Up in Buffalo, he felt free of it. Down here, he was up to his neck in the stuff.

Mike danced with several pretty black girls who looked like they were part of the Supremes in big hair and big skirts. Carl twirled Janet around the floor and only let her out of his arms twice with friendly, smaller young black men in sharp white jackets and bow ties. By the end of the evening, Janet was red faced and sweaty and having the time of her life. She rode back to Cowhill in the front seat in between the two college students, listening to stories from the games, the classes, and hanging with the team after hours.

Janet giggled. "So you mean you locked him out on the balcony and he was just standing there…"

"Bare-ass naked, yep," Mike joked. Janet grabbed her mouth and shrieked.

"And he ain't the kind of guy you be wanting to see bare-ass naked," Carl added.

Mike and Janet said their good-nights as Carl pulled his car in behind Mike's in the back parking lot of Berry Hall, their rendezvous spot. Janet leaned over and gave Carl a quick kiss on the cheek.

"Thanks so much, Carl. I had such a time tonight. Thanks for making my world a little bit bigger." Mike slid out of the car and helped Janet out and she ran to the car to get out of the sleet that had started to fall. Mike leaned in and stretched his palm out to Carl who slid his hand across with a narrowed-eye expression.

"Oh my God, Tex. That little firecracker is a gas," he said waving his hand in front of his face. "I would be all over that sweet little…"

"Careful, Rock," Mike said with a fixed grin that did little to mask his annoyance.

Carl put his hands up in surrender. "Just sayin', she's a great girl."

"'Night, buddy. If I don't see you before, have a wonderful Christmas. Tell Mama and the kids I said, Hi."

Mike didn't sleep that well that night. His mind was full of images of Janet and Carl swirling around the dance floor. He also had a knot in his belly worried that Janet would tell girlfriends or even her mother about her adventure at the Dallas club. Her dad would come after Mike and him with a goddamn mob and torches. But by the morning, Mike felt pretty bad about all that and drove to Janet's and picked her up and the two of them drove over to Greenville and went through the shops on Lee Street looking for last minute Christmas presents. It was clear and frosty and both of them were in the holiday spirit. Mike made the suggestion that they might want to look for something for Carl's family and Janet became a woman possessed. They shopped all day and returned home with a backseat filled with presents.

Mike and Janet drove over on Christmas Eve morning and knocked on the Washington's door. Young Diamond answered the door and it was hard to see what surprised her most, the arms full of presents or two white people on her front porch. Mama Washington greeted them with open arms and insisted they stay for lunch, which was a lighter fare of egg-salad sandwiches on fresh baked bread and a tasty beef stew. After lunch, Otho and Diamond carefully peeled the wrapping paper off their gifts: for Diamond, a just off the shelf Barbie with a case and several outfits and for Otho, a transistor radio. Mama got a new silk scarf and a pair of bedroom slippers that were plush pink quilted velvet with ostrich feathers. She was delighted and did an impromptu fashion show for Mike and Janet. Carl sat in a chair with his new dress shirt and two neckties, thin and modern with a frozen grin on his face.

Mike helped Carl clear away the dishes from the table while Mama chatted with Janet. Carl stood at the sink with his shirt sleeves rolled up and a bright red apron around his waist washing the dishes. He was oddly silent and when Mike reached to take a plate from his hand, he could tell Carl was practically shaking with rage. Mike leaned closed and whispered.

"What's going on with you today?"

"Nothin,'" came the clipped response.

"If you say so," Mike said. They continued to wash and dry the dishes from the lunch. At the end, Carl turned around and leaned back against the sink with his arms folded. "Thank you for the presents, but you don't need to be doing that. We ain't in need of your charity."

Mike was stunned. "There's no charity here. We just wanted to buy some presents for our new friends. That's it."

"That's it, huh? Well, fine then," Carl turned back to the sink. Mike touched his arm and the man brushed his hand away.

"Hey, Rock, buddy. What is it? You know I didn't mean any disrespect or anything."

"That just his pride," Mama said walking into the kitchen to put on the kettle. "Just like his daddy that way. Plenty of folks shamed to accept gifts from white folks like it mean they still beholden to them." Mama came over to Carl and wrapped her small frame around his waist. "Don't let that pride of yours make you bitter when folks just try to be nice. Just be gracious, honey. This boy loves you too much to cause you grief."

Carl wrapped his arms around Mama and hugged her tight. He looked up at Mike and grabbed him by the neck and pulled him close as well.

The day after Christmas, Janet gave Mike his present. With her parents gone to other family for two days, she and Mike spent the next two days playing house. She worked her magic of non-consummated sex in every room of the house. They ate and played naked all day and night, trying to pack as much loving into these days as possible for Mike boarded the train back up to Buffalo. As they lay in front of the fire, sweaty and naked, stroking each other's skin lightly with their fingers, Janet asked a question.

"Do you ever date other girls up there," Janet asked watching her long hair sweep across her pink nipples.

"Why would you ask that?" Mike said with a smile.

"I know I'm making you wait a long time. All my friends tell me I'm crazy and that a big football player like you can't be expected to go that long without doing it. So, I just want you to know; until we get married, you're a free agent. You can fool around if you have the need, get it out of your system. Because once you are mine, once I let you inside me, that's it, Buster."

Mike had no response to this and just kept silent as he stroked his fingers from her blond pubic bush up to her breasts and back down. "Can I ask you something?" Mike said.

"Sure."

"Would you ever do it with a black guy?"

"What? Why in the world…" she said then hugged close to him. "I suppose if I was up in Buffalo and all modern and free, I might see what it's like. Part out of curiosity and part just because down here, it's like the worst thing you could ever do and that makes me mad. But honestly, I don't think about that. I just think about you." Mike hugged her closer to him.

"Can I ask you something?" Janet said. Mike nodded. "So is it true what they say about black guys down there," she said tickling Mike's soft penis.

"You gotta remember, I've seen exactly two black guys without their pants on. But I would have to say, yeah it's pretty true. In Carl's case, it's very true. I call him the black mamba." Janet covered her mouth with a gasp and giggled.

Mike and Carl returned to Buffalo the first week of January. They rode through a frozen winter wonderland, pointing out the sites as soon as they crossed the Kansas line and Carl was allowed to move about the train again. When they pulled into the station in Buffalo, the temperature was -26° F, colder than either of them thought possible. Their dorm room was so cold the inside of the windows was a sheet of ice, even with the radiator blazing orange in the corner. The men resolved to study hard and bring up their grades and end up their freshman year in good standing. Both of them had been approached by a local contractor that was looking for laborers for the summer offering a ridiculous $2 an hour. Carl and Mike talked it over and decided a summer spent up on a roof or ladder in Upstate New York beat a Texas summer by a mile, even though it would mean not seeing their families for a longer time. But hopefully, they would earn enough that traveling back home would be easier and more frequent. Mike knew he was going to head back to Texas briefly in May for Janet's graduation and Carl hoped to go along.

The guys did make strong gains in their classes and managed to bring home B's and an A for the winter term. Carl had taken some of his Mama's words to heart and cut back on his sexual explorations. Carl stuck mostly to black girls, with the occasional Asian or other exotic beauty riding the black mamba, filling the hallway of the dorm with moans and shrieks of pleasure. After a month of spending most weekends with Jack Dempsey wrapped around him on his tiny single bed while Nick Alagna snored in the bed across the room, Mike told Carl he was done with the sleep-overs.

"You can bone as many girls as you want, but come midnight, I'm coming back in the room. If you guys want to keep fucking, then I'll watch. I am sick of getting fondled by Jack or having to look for some other bed to camp out in like a bum." Carl gave him a big smile and said that was fine, he was always welcome to watch.

Mike also took Janet at her word. He found a collection of Tau Beta Sigma girls, all with steady boyfriends or fiancés back home who were not content like Janet to wait until they got married to start enjoying the joys of sex. So Mike bought a big box of Trojans and spent most of his weekends practicing his technique of sliding on a rubber and bringing the girls to earth-shattering climaxes, sometimes in the bed across from Carl doing the same. Some of the Tau Beta girls were curious about Carl as well and on two occasions they replayed their infamous night with the French grad student, albeit with certain modifications.

The guys worked out along with the team during offseason, lifting weights, enduring the "Bull in the Ring" drill, which consisted of standing in a circle and taking every hit and jab and slap the other teammates could send your way without running for cover. Sometimes it hurt your own hands as much as the guy you were hitting, but after a while, the Bulls gained a solidarity and toughness they had never had before. That along with hours hitting the log turned a good team into a great team, with more strength and endurance. The team was already feeling like champions during spring practice.

Mike and Carl finished up their spring term with all A's and one B. They had buckled down and studied harder than ever. They smoked less weed, went to the Bar Fly less, worked out harder, and even brought the girls back to the room less than ever. They both lost some of the freshman fifteen of flab and replaced it with twenty of muscle. Mike paid for Carl's train ticket back to Texas after spring finals, this time receiving just a 'thanks, Tex' from him. Mike dropped in to see Mama and the kids who seemed to have grown several inches. He sat in the grandstand at East Texas State Memorial Stadium watching Janet's salutatorian speech along with her mom and dad. Carl attended as well, sitting with a contingent of other black visitors in the far upper rows of the stadium.

That night, Janet shared with Mike she had been accepted to three schools: Baylor University, Ole Miss, and Carnegie-Mellon in Pittsburgh. She danced around telling Mike she was headed up north like him, only an hour or so ride away on the train or bus. Mike hugged her tight and said with his job this summer, he would be buying a car and they would be able to go ahead and get married. She was so overjoyed, Mike was pretty sure she would have thrown her virginity out the window, but he played the gallant and settled for mutual oral pleasure in the backseat of his mother's car.

The guys went back to Buffalo and spent a summer in the hot sun, working their muscles on construction jobs. Learning to swing a hammer, hang drywall, run wiring, and paint. Their muscles stayed tight and nimble. Mike's back, chest, and legs tanned to a light nut brown eliciting hoots from Carl in the room or showers as he said he needed to "grab his shades" when Mike's startlingly white backside came into view, looking like a snowman against his newly browned skin.

Fall football practice started and the team was more unified and cohesive than ever. They ran through their drills like men possessed, hitting one another so hard, there was no way an opposing team would present a problem. The team opened up against Harvard in Boston on September 27th. The trip was unique in that the boys got to fly on Mohawk Airlines to Boston and arrive two days early so they could do some actual sight-seeing along with practice. Mike and Carl walked around the Old North Church and other Boston landmarks with the open-mouthed incredulity of country bumpkins just off the hay wagon. The Bulls opened strong against a talented Harvard team. Carl and his defense, holding strong and blowing through the offensive line of the Crimson and John Harvard in his Pilgrim outfit, held the Ivy Leaguers to three points. The Bulls managed one touchdown, a screen pass into the end zone to Mike McGee. Kenny the placekicker missed the extra point. On the way back to Buffalo, the airplane struck such terrifying turbulence over Lake Erie that the pilot actually came over the loudspeaker and led the passengers in the Lord's Prayer asking for a safe landing. Mike and Carl held hands with eyes shut tight repeating, "Our Father, which art in heaven, hallowed be Thy name…" That night back in the dorm room, Mike climbed into bed with Carl and held the big man in his arms as Carl shook and wept like a baby, he was so shaken from the airplane ride.

The team rolled for the next two weeks defeating Cortland 7-6 and Western Reserve in Cleveland 19-6. The highlight of the week was the game film which showed Kenny the kicker doing a quick-kick fake hard into the wide-ass of his blocker, Jack Ramsey. The coach ran the play back and forth in the projector until the team had tears streaming down their faces. The next week was homecoming against a middle-of-the-road Baldwin-Wallace, a Methodist college in Berea, Ohio. From the opening kickoff to Baldwin that was run back for a touchdown, the team was in trouble. No one had an answer; the team literally ran into one another on the field searching for some way to get on track. The homecoming crowd left before the fourth quarter as the Bulls lost 0-26.

The speech that Coach Offenbach delivered after the game was so vile and profanity laced, it melted the sickly green paint off the walls and hovered like a Hiroshima mushroom cloud over the field house. The coach berated a "piss-poor effort by a bunch of pussy-drunk cocksucking commie-loving cunts" and "Shit-eating losers and dickless fuck-faces that didn't deserve to wear a Bulls uniform." Tactless and entirely inappropriate, the tirade must have worked. The team never trailed again that season. The Bulls wiped out Columbia the following Saturday 34-14. They demolished Temple 54-6 the week after that. The week of the game at Wayne State in Detroit, the team was part of a ribbon cutting ceremony dedicating one of the new dorms presided over by none other than Elizabeth Taylor. The violet-eyed starlet stood incomprehensibly alongside several football players including Carl and Mike, holding an actual bull that her publicist had bought from some local farm. The team got on the bus to Detroit afterwards and kicked Wayne State in the balls 44-14.

The Bulls had their only other scare the following week at Lehigh down in Bethlehem, PA. They were tied with the Mountain Hawks at 26 with only three minutes left in the game and Lehigh on the 10 yard line ready to score. Carl blasted through the O-Line like a freight train and sacked the quarterback who lost the ball. Big Jack Ramsey picked the ball up and ran 50 yards before he fell down from lack of oxygen, luckily holding on to the ball. The next play, Bulls QB Joe Oliver hit Mike McGee with a 12 yard pass across the middle and the big tight end fell into the end zone pulling three Lehigh players with him. Coach Offenbach went for two and got it. The Bulls won 34-26.

The final home game of the year was on November 22. It was snowing like mad and the play had to be stopped almost every five minutes for boys with shovels to try and clear away the yard lines. In the end, visiting Bucknell had no answer to the Bulls who stampeded to a 38-0 victory and became the recipients of the 1958 Lambert Cup, naming the Buffalo Bulls the best small college team in the Eastern USA.

That night, the team gathered at the Moonglow, a new student bar in town, and toasted one another, the coaches, the fans, and the Tangerine Bowl. After all the years, the football team from Buffalo was headed to a big bowl game. Mike drank so much that night, Carl, Jack, and Joe Oliver helped get him back to bed. Mike woke up the next morning and stumbled to the bathroom to take a piss, almost screaming as he did. He stared down at his penis now adorned with a blue magic marker Bulls football helmet drawn on the tip with a smiling face, the tiny lips of his dick painted in red and GO BULLS – LAMBERT CHAMPIONS scrawled on the shaft of his dick and in a semi-circle on his belly surrounding his pubes. Carl, Jack and two or three other teammates rolled on the floor laughing as Mike stood there with his dick in his hand, staring at his little football player. The permanent marker hung around on his penis for the next week despite repeated scrubbings, much to Carl's delight.

The joy lasted for two weeks on campus. Joe Oliver and Lou Reese actually got to travel to New York City and receive the trophy on the Ed Sullivan Show in front of a cheering audience, the rest of the team watching on Coach Dick's television in his living room in suburban Buffalo. The team learned of the confirmation they would be heading to the Tangerine Bowl in Orlando at the end of December to face, of all teams, the Lions from East Texas State in Cowhill Texas; Carl and Mike's hometown. The boys were measured for new sports jackets to be provided by one of the local haberdashers in Buffalo. For the first time in its history, the Bulls would be bowling.

Two days later, the Coach sent for team captains Joe Oliver and Lou Reese. Coach Offenbach told the players that the Orlando High School Athletic Association, the leaseholder for the Tangerine Bowl, had informed Buffalo University that the football team would be invited to play in the bowl game only if Carl Washington and Tom Williams did not attend. Florida did not allow integrated teams and white and black players were not allowed to mix on the field. The coach told the team captains that he was under a lot of pressure from local business leaders and city fathers to leave the black players at home and send the team to the bowl.

"I don't need to tell you how I feel about this. But at the end of the day, it's your team. You get the guys together and take a vote. We'll go along with what the team decides," Coach told them sober faced and angry.

Joe and Lou left the coach's office like someone had just hit them across the head with a Louisville Slugger. Neither talked, they just went back to the dorms and began to spread the word that the team had an emergency meeting that evening in Clark Gym. Mike and Carl laughed that maybe they were going to be fitted for swim suits as well as sports coats for their trip down to sunny Florida. When the team filed into the room later that evening around 7:00, the grim faces on Joe and Lou made it clear this was not a laughing matter.

Joe cleared his throat and explained what the Coach had said: the team could only go to the Tangerine Bowl if they left Carl and Tommy behind. Lou began to pass out slips of paper and pencils. Jack stood up.

"This is some fuckin' bullshit. I'm not voting. Either the whole team goes, or we tell them to shove it up their ass."

Every team member echoed the sentiment. Tommy and Carl hung in a back corner, either of them speaking. There was a bit of additional discussion about whether or not there was so legal remedy to compel them to let the whole team play, getting some politician to take up their cause, or going on television. But in the end, there just didn't seem to be anything to do. So without taking a vote, the team unanimously agreed to decline the offer to attend the 1958 Tangerine Bowl if they couldn't send their entire team. The Bulls would not make it to another bowl game for another fifty years.

The teammates gathered at the Moonglow after the vote, most sat quietly drinking or playing pool. Once or twice, loud condemnations of fucking racist redneck Klansmen were raised, but most of the team just felt like the wind was knocked out of their sails, evil bigotry chomping down on victory in the jaws of defeat. East Texas State ended up meeting Missouri Valley, defeating them 26-7, making the Lions back to back Tangerine Bowl champs. Mike saw a photo of the Lions quarterback holding up the trophy along with local businessman and university donor, JL Martin. Martin was quoted as saying the Lions were glad to be associated with the Tangerine Bowl who supported the traditional Southern values of separate but equal opportunities for sporting events. He praised the bowl committee for making the clearly correct decision to disinvite Buffalo to the bowl, along with their ill-conceived mixed race team. Mike vowed then and there to punch JL Martin in the face the next time he saw him.

The next few months were very rough on Carl. He felt personally responsible for the team missing out on the bowl game and withdrew from most activities. He stopped working out, stopped dating, and missed some classes as well. Mike finally enlisted several of the guys from the team to kidnap him for a weekend getaway to Niagara Falls that was a frozen wonderland in the winter and the hotel rooms were dirt cheap. The guys spent all weekend talking to Carl, drinking a lot of beer and vodka, and smoking a bale of weed, trying to get him out of his funk. He finally came around and rejoined the world and got back to business.

Mike and Janet got engaged in September of '58. She settled in at Carnegie-Mellon and began her freshman term with great expectations. She traveled up to most of the Buffalo games and she and Mike spent time planning their wedding for the following June. But the longer they waited, the more desperate she felt. Every time she left Buffalo and headed back to Pittsburgh, she cried the whole way back. On the train with Mike and Carl headed back to Texas for Christmas, she told Mike she was tired of waiting and wanted to move the wedding up to Valentine's Day. She talked with her mother and dad, who were not thrilled with this decision, but they both liked Mike a great deal and wanted Janet to be happy. Janet decided not to return to college for the winter term, but stay home and work on the wedding with her mom. Mike finally got her to negotiate and they settled Saturday, March 21st. Mike's term would be over and he would have a week off for Spring Break they could use as a honeymoon. Janet intended to go back to Buffalo and transfer her college credits from Carnegie-Mellon.

Janet and Mike had a huge fight over the best man choice. Mike flatly refused to make any decision other than Carl, which posed a problem since the country club they were going to get married at did not allow blacks on the premises. Finally, Mike negotiated a new venue, a lovely new private wedding chapel that was just starting up on Lake Ray Hubbard and did not have any racial restrictions. Janet's parents were not pleased with Carl being in the wedding but remained calm and in the end, grew to care for Carl a great deal.

Mike and Carl finished up their winter term in Buffalo and actually flew home, using part of their summer earnings to do so. The wedding was a beautiful affair with pastel colors of yellow, pink and green marking the spring theme of the decorations. Janet came down the aisle in a skirt bigger than Scarlett O'Hara wore in "Gone with the Wind." Carl joked with Mike that he looked the part of his servant or squire in his white jacket. Mike and Janet took off for Galveston on their honeymoon, but they never made it out of the reception hall before Mike had claimed his long-awaited prize. He bent Janet over a floral print sofa in the bride's room while they were supposed to be changing into their honeymoon wardrobe. Janet wore her tiara and veil, high heels and stockings, and nothing else as Mike bent her over and slid his fingers up inside her velvety flesh until she was wet and moaning. He gripped his cock and felt the folds of flesh envelop him as he slid all the way inside nice and easy. But a minute later, Mike McGee was pounding his new bride like a cheap $2 whore, and Janet loved every minute of it. They moaned and gasped as they orgasmed, rattling the windows of the chapel. When they emerged thirty minutes later, Janet was flushed, her wedding coiffure falling down on her neck. Carl came over to congratulate Mike.

"Damn, stud. We heard you all the way back in the holler," he joked. Mike noticed Janet's parents were red-faced and stammering. He wanted to get on the microphone and announce, 'at least we waited 'til we were married!" Mike and Janet made love non-stop for the next five days until Mike felt drained and sore. But it was a glorious time and he treasured every minute of it. Mike had gotten permission to start his spring classes late. Carl went back up on the train and Mike and Janet packed up their new shiny black 1959 Buick Electra and made the long trip back to Buffalo. Mike and Janet moved into a small apartment on Niagara Falls Blvd. They offered to let Carl stay in the extra bedroom, but he declined saying he felt better about staying in the dorm. Tommy Williams became his new roommate and Carl said the two of them spent as much time entertaining ladies as they did anything else, especially since Tommy had spent the better part of his time at Buffalo so far as a sexless monk. Carl said he was making up for lost time practically every night.

It turned out to be fortuitous that Carl didn't take the extra room since Janet discovered she was pregnant at the end of April. All that honeymoon sex had paid off with getting Janet knocked up almost immediately. Janet continued taking classes through the spring and even started in the fall term. Stephanie Renee McGee showed up on November 7, 1959 and Mike fell in love with the blond angel immediately. Teppy was an easy baby for the most part and Mike and Janet fell into the role of new parents with little drama. Carl doted on the little girl and came over to play with her often.

Mike and Carl played their last football game with the Bulls on November 21, 1959 beating Marshall 37-12. The Bulls put up another 8-1 season, tied with Delaware for best in the East. Curiously, it was the Delaware Blue Hens, an all-white team, who was selected to be awarded the Lambert Cup. The hard fought battles and a return to their victorious ways from the year before were overlooked by the NCAA and Buffalo was left out of the post-season picture.

Mike and Carl graduated with a Bachelor of Arts in Business in December of 1959. Mama Washington was there along with Otho and Diamond, who looked as proud as anyone could be. They had grown up and now were serious looking teenagers, but proud as they could be of their big brother. Mama Washington wept the entire ceremony. She was so overcome when Carl took his diploma she collapsed into her chair, Janet patting her hand. Mike's parents had come up as well. Mary was thrilled and so proud of her boy, the first college graduate in the family. Patrick, in a rare show of emotion, grabbed Mike by the neck and kissed him, telling him he always knew he would turn out to be great.

The army came calling for both Mike and Carl in early 1960. Things were heating up in Viet Nam, John Kennedy was president, and a new age seemed to be ready to dawn. Both Mike and Carl were recruited and being college graduates, they headed straight for officer training at Fort Benning, Georgia. Even the strenuous, demanding boot camp was little different than most of the football training Mike and Carl had experienced at BU. They both sailed through boot camp in one of the first integrated officers' training classes. Both men graduated from training as 2nd Lieutenants.

Mike and Carl returned to Cowhill as college graduates and military officers, but little else had changed. Carl still lived in the holler and still drew evil stares and judging looks from the white citizenry of the town, especially if he happened to come to a picnic or backyard function at Mike and Janet's new home they briefly rented on Bonham Street. Soon, Mike and Carl were stationed at Fort Hood in Killeen, TX in the spring of 1960 and joined the staff there as instructors. Janet was less than excited about the life of a military wife on a base. She hated the housing and the other frustrated southern belles that she met at the market and traded false pleasantries with. She urged Mike to give up his commission or find some way out, mostly because she was deathly afraid of him ending up in Viet Nam.

On the other hand, Mike and Carl were having a great time. They took to military life as easily as anyone could. They made new friends and found that life at Foot Hood wasn't that much different than college had been. There were new integrated military units, young strong men looking for adventure, others scared shitless to be there at all. Mike seemed to be especially effective at helping the new recruits that were terrified of combat. Even though he had yet to see any, he had the gift of gab and his superior officers were pleased to let him manage the mama's boys.

With Teppy at the "terrible two's" stage now and Janet fractious and unhappy as well, Mike took to staying out later and later, coming home drunk if at all, normally insisting on sex whether or not Janet was in the mood. One particularly bad night, Mike came home late, reeking of beer. He peeled his clothes off and climbed into bed on top of Janet who had just been through a terrible day with Teppy and was in no mood for sex. She pushed him off and got up heading for the living room. He caught her halfway down the hall and swung her around so hard her head collided with the wall, denting in the drywall. She was dazed, holding on to the door frame when he grabbed her hips and penetrated her roughly in one hard thrust, pressing her face up against the wall. He gripped her there and continued fucking her harder and harder until he came, leaving her lying on the floor crying. Mike, so disgusted with himself he didn't know what to do, left the house again and didn't come home for two days.

Janet took to calling Carl, pouring out her hurt and misery to him. He was patient and listened, not wanting to get in-between his best friend and his wife that he also cared for dearly. He finally convinced her to give Mike another chance, chalked it up to pressure at work and the uncertainty of going to Viet Nam. Janet agreed and got a sitter and fixed her hair, put on her sexiest dress, and took off for the base to surprise Mike and try and make things better. Janet arrived around 1800 hours and went through security and made her way to the barracks to Mike's office. Most of the day shift had left and many of the other soldiers were at evening mess. She tiptoed down the hall and got to Mike's office, surprised the door was closed and lights off. She quietly turned the handle and started to step inside when her eyes flew open. Mike sat on a couch in the corner, his trousers around his ankles, a secretary-type female soldier between his legs, her head bobbing up and down.

Janet turned and ran from the building, her tears blinding her. She drove over to the other side of the base and knocked on Carl's door. He answered wearing an undershirt and some old khaki slacks. He had just gotten out of the shower and still had droplets of water on his face. Janet fell into his arms when she saw him, pouring out her misery, anger, and betrayal. When Carl heard the story, he was furious and tried to figure out the best way to kick Mike's ass. He offered to get Janet a drink, she gladly accepted. They made their way halfway through a brand new bottle of Tanqueray and grapefruit juice, mixing the drinks and downing them one after the other. Carl came back from the bathroom with a couple of tablets.

"Here, take a couple of these. They will relax you. I'll take a couple myself, I've had a hell of a day too." He placed the tablets in her hand.

"What are they?" she asked trying to focus her eyes.

"Quaaludes. They're new. Good stuff," Carl said throwing a couple back and swallowing them with a drink of the Salty Dog.

Fifteen minutes later, the two were stretched out on the couch. Janet was wrapped close to Carl, holding his face as she kissed him tenderly. He rubbed his hands lightly over her breasts and slid a hand between her legs, pushing her panties to the side, feeling the wetness within. Every alarm bell in his head was clanging, but Carl pushed the thoughts away as his fingers slipped inside his best friend's wife. Carl scooted down and buried his head in Janet's lap and worked his tongue in and around her sex until she was heaving against him. She suddenly sat up and grabbed his belt and unbuckled it.

"I want to see the mamba," she slurred. She fumbled with his zipper and pushed his pants and shorts down off his ass. When his erection popped out, Janet squealed like a kid on Christmas. She gripped the mighty thing and lowered her head, playing out the scene she had just interrupted in Mike office. Carl finally pulled away and scooped her up off the couch and carried her to his bed. He pulled her dress off. He climbed in between her legs and leaned down and kissed her deeply as he slid inside. She moaned loud and gripped his ass as he plowed her deep and slow. He exploded inside her quickly, his hips grinding hard against her mound. He pulled off and began to stroke and tease her sex until she came in a throbbing climax. Five minutes later, she climbed on his belly, reaching down to slide him inside. She rode the mamba and Carl gripped her breasts as she bucked and bounced on his shaft until he released inside her again.

When Carl woke up, Janet was gone and he wondered for a time if it had been a dream but saw the two sets of glasses on the table and realized what he had done. Dread and regret flooded through him and he ran for the toilet and vomited.

Janet returned home after picking up Teppy. She drew a bath and climbed in with the little girl and tried to wash away the memories of the night before, but it was hopeless. She was caught in a never-ending purgatory of fury and hurt with Mike and horror and ecstasy with Carl. She knew part of her had wanted to do that for years. God knows, Mike and Carl certainly had sowed their wild oats. She had heard them chatting after a few beers many nights and gleaned that they had screwed their way through half the college it sounded, sometimes with the same girl at the same time. She let the tears splash into the water as she bathed Teppy and watched her play with her rubber duck. She wrapped a towel around her head and body as she dried off Teppy and put a new diaper on her, setting her in the middle of the floor with a few toys when a shadow in the doorway startled her.

Mike stood there, pathetic and disheveled. He was holding a bouquet of roses limply in one hand. His face was a wreck, puffy and swollen. Clearly, he had not had a good night either. He came in and fell on his knees grabbing Janet's legs, sobbing into her towel. Part of her was disgusted, part of her was overwhelmed. In the end, she pulled him up and hugged him as he gripped her in a crushing bear hug, vowing to change, to never do that again. Janet tried to feel his pain, his regret, but every time she closed her eyes she saw two things: that girl on her knees in Mike's office and Carl hovering above her. Was one worse than the other? If so, she had the terrible feeling it was what she and Carl had done.

Finally she took Mike's face in her hands and looked deep into his aquamarine eyes. "You are going to have to try harder, Honey. I can't do all this on my own. I'm scared all the time. I know you are busy, I know you like the work and helping these guys, but you have to be here for us too. I'm not even going to ask how many others because I don't want to know. But you are going to have to choose. If you want that, you can have it. Or you can have me and Teppy. But you can't have both. I'm not sharing. I waited for you and now you're mine. If you keep doing this, if you keep fucking up, then one day you are going to turn around and we will be gone."

Mike's eyes filled with tears again. He sobbed into her lap. She laid her hands on his head and felt his heart break and she was glad. *If this is what it took, then I am so glad,* she thought. That night, as Mike crawled into bed and slid his big body close to hers, she turned around and looked at him. "Not tonight. We are going to take a break for a bit. I need you to show me you are serious. No sex with me and positively none with any more skanks from the base. Do you understand me?"

Mikes eyes went wide. "But, what I am supposed to do until you're ready?"

She grabbed his hand and shoved it under the covers and into his shorts. "Knock yourself out, Tex."

Over the next two months, Mike and Janet fell back in love. He came home after work, he was attentive, he wooed and courted her, being sweet and playful but never pushing her to go farther. Mike didn't mention Carl or work hardly at all and Janet made sure to not ask. No news was good news as far as Carl was concerned. Finally, one night in March, two months after the moratorium, Mike was sitting up in bed reading a National Geographic when he looked up and saw Janet standing in front of him naked except for a long strand of beads that hung between her full breasts. Mike turned toward her and stared.

"Hey Hot Stuff, you up for a tumble?"

Mike threw the magazine away, dug his heels into the mattress lifting his ass, and ripped his skivvies off. Janet climbed in between his legs and kissed him passionately. He let her take the lead and she slid him inside her as she sat in his lap. He thrust again and again as she threw her head back, feeling the touch of his hands on her nipples as he drove deep within her to release himself.

Three weeks later at dinner, Janet placed a little package on Mike's plate for him to open. He undid the bow and pulled out a tiny doll baby bottle. He looked up at Janet and his eyes grew wide.

"Really?" Mike said with a huge smile.

"Really," Janet said hugging him.

"So how far along are you?"

"Just barely," she said. "That mighty McGee seed I guess," she said.

Janet went into labor ironically on September 4th, 1961, Labor Day. Mike picked her up and took her to the base hospital. She was already having hard contractions when she arrived. She delivered two hours later. Mike came into the room and found her cradling a small bundle, tears pouring from her eyes. Mike instantly became alarmed.

"What is it? The nurse said everything was fine," Mike's face was a mask of worry.

"Everything is fine. I'm just emotional, you know how it goes. Come over here and meet your son," she said, her face an exotic mixture of relief, love, and maybe worry? Mike couldn't tell. He looked down at the baby and fell instantly in love. His face was round and perfect, not squashed and pointed like Teppy's had been. His long fingers gripped Mike's little finger tightly. His long lashes lay on surprisingly tanned cheeks. He had a full head of hair, dark brown and maybe even curly. His lips were beautiful, full and dark. His nose was a wide little button. He was so long too.

"He seems perfect. Clearly takes after your side of the family though with this dark hair. Janet's father had dark brown hair as did several relatives. "Look at those hands? He'll be a quarterback for sure. Have you seen his eyes yet? I guess they're brown?"

"No. They're blue, almost blue-green."

"Oh honey, you did so good," Mike said. Janet sobbed anew.

By the following spring, the little boy had grown and changed even more. Trey Michael McGee was long, lean, beautiful, and utterly alien to Mike. Mike had lost track of how many people had asked if he was adopted. Even more that he was the most beautiful child and where did he get this lovely skin? Mike and Janet took it all in stride. Finally, in the summer of 1962, just before Trey's first birthday. Mike had invited Carl over. They had not seen much of Carl outside of work lately. He had finally found a steady girlfriend and it appeared they would be getting married. Delois Rayburn was a feisty girl from Chicago, perfect cinnamon colored skin with hair only slightly darker. She was instantly liked by Janet and Mike, who loved the idea of Carl settling down with someone who seemed to be very much her own person and not mired in the bigotry of the Cowhill area.

Carl brought some beer and was helping watch Trey as Mike grilled steaks. Mike loved seeing the two of them together. Carl was helping Trey walk around the backyard, holding his little hands with his fingers. Then he picked the little boy up and tossed him into the air and sat him on his shoulders. In that instant, Mike felt his world tilt, shift, and then disappear from his life. He looked at his son and then down into Carl's face. The resemblance was complete, other than the blue-green eyes and the considerably lighter skin. Mike stood and watched the two them feeling the bile rise in his throat.

"Hey Tex. You better watch them steaks, I think you are about to burn 'em up," Carl said. Mike came up to the man and took Trey from his shoulders and handed him to Janet who was watching the scene like someone who just came up on a terrible car crash. In the next second, Mike hauled off and hit Carl viciously in the nose, exploding it in a wave of blood. Carl fell back with Mike climbing on top of him pounding him on his face, his gut, his balls, and any place he could reach. Janet was screaming, Trey was hysterical. Teppy stood in the middle of the yard sobbing and Mike just continued to pummel Carl who put up very little resistance. Finally, Rob Winter from next door leaped the fence and pulled Mike off Carl. Mike's fists were bloody pulp like Carl's face. Janet came close to him but he held his bloody hands up like tokens of war, warning her to stay away.

Carl went to the emergency room on base telling the doctor's there he had run afoul of some young delinquents at a local bar. At Janet's tearful insistence, Rob Winter kept his mouth closed, chalking the dust-up to a big misunderstanding. Mike did not come home that night. In fact, he did not come home for three days. When he finally did, it was simply to begin packing his bags, informing Janet he had just been called up to duty in Viet Nam and was leaving the next day. He refused to have anything to do with Trey, leaving the little boy crying for him from his crib or playpen. Janet was on the verge of a nervous breakdown. When Mike kissed her cheek the next morning and hugged Teppy without so much as a look at Trey, she collapsed in the floor shrieking.

Carl came over later that night, finding Janet practically catatonic, sitting in the dark with both children in hysterics. He and Delois moved in for a few days and took care of the children while Janet simply sat in the dark in her room. It had taken Delois more than a little convincing not to hit the road herself once she learned the truth about Carl and Janet. Finally, three days later, Janet came out of her room and asked to speak to Carl alone. Once in her bedroom, Janet spoke in a hoarse quiet voice.

"This is our fault, you know that." Carl nodded. "Go get him. You are going to have to fix this," Janet said.

43 Travis

"Mom and Dad freaked out pretty big when you ran off last night," Travis began. The whole church was all stirred up. Dad told us a bunch of people were trying to go up to that Brother Zigler and get him to explain all the images. Of course, he didn't have a clue what the hell was going on. He kept babbling about not having the gift of interpretation of dreams and visions. And then he started going off on how this was a sign of the End Times. By that time, some of the people were starting to get scared and even brought up the lights and supposedly Dad heard Mark Newman talking about having dreams about bridges," Travis said.

"We didn't know about any of this until your dad told us this morning before we headed to school. Your parents were like, so worried, Trey," George said.

"I was afraid you had runned off and were not gonna come back," Andy said. "Travis let me sleep with him last night."

"That was good. Sorry about taking off. I just needed to have some space and a little time. All that pretty much blew my mind, last night. I am still pretty fucked up," Trey said.

"I hate to be the one to tell you, Trey. But that was true even before you found out you're going to have to start watching Soul Train," George said. He ducked as Trey reached out a big hand and tried to knock off his head.

"Quit being a jackass and tell me what happened," Trey said annoyed.

Travis began to tell of their day. The three of them had walked to school together and Travis and George caught Emily up on what had happened.

"He just never came home?" she asked. "I can't say I blame him. That was a real shock to me. I can't imagine what it would be for him," Emily said hugging her Trapper Keeper to her chest as they walked in the cold grey morning. It had stopped raining for now but as the three walked up Church Street toward Pecan Street, they jumped puddles and walked around mud on the sidewalk.

"I know. That was a shit way to find out that your mom let a giant black dude bang her and oh, by the way, he's also your birth father," George began.

"Don't say it like that again or I'm gonna punch you," Travis said determined.

"I'm sorry. It's just so crazy. Don't you think most people won't believe it," Emily said.

"I don't know," George said. "I mean, we all have wondered if Trey was dropped off in a basket on your front porch before. It's not like folks haven't talked about how different he looked."

Travis kicked a pine cone lying on the sidewalk into the middle of the street. "Some people will believe anything. And if they think Trey has a black dad and that my mom is a whore, then they will start up a bunch of shit with me too."

Emily walked close to Travis and slid her hand into his. "They might and if they do, we will be there to make sure you keep it together. But remember, this is way harder for Trey than you."

"Did Mary say anything last night when your mom took her home?" George asked. He was wearing a navy blue pea jacket and a Russian style fur hat that made him look like a Soviet sailor."

"Not much," Emily began. "She really thanked me for having her over and for us being friendly with her. She really wanted to say thank you to you, G. I guess those kisses were for real after all," she said with a grin.

"You mean we were thinking they weren't?"

Getting back on subject, Travis interrupted, "Did she say the cops have any leads at all on Carl? I mean, I was concerned about him before but it's way more important now. When y'all have the dream, do you ever see new flashes of him? I was thinking about that last night and I don't know that I have seen anything more than him hanging up there all bloody and everything," Travis said.

"Mary is certain he is still alive. I don't know why she feels so certain? Mary says her mother is practically in a walking coma. She thinks he's dead and that that she and the children are still targets. I can't imagine what Mary is feeling, how horrible that must have been. I think I would just curl up in a ball and die of shame and fear," Emily said. Travis squeezed her hand as they walked.

"So, let's get some lunch quick today and head up to Western Auto to see Jack and Tim. He really wanted to talk to us. And I want to talk to him more about his kid. That boy seems to know even more than we do," Travis said.

The guys began pulling out their shop projects as soon as they got in the door along with several others. It was a quiet Monday morning and you could hear Mr. Moore's radio playing "Luckenbach Texas" in the background even though it was usually covered up with all the sounds of hammers, sanding, and power tools. About the time that Wayon, and Willie, and the Boys were getting back to the basics of love, Don Edwards came up to George and Travis and stood looking like he wanted to talk to them.

Finally George said, "Can we help you, Don?"

Don looked around at the others in the shop. It was clear no one was paying them any attention. "I just wanted to say that thing at church last night was weird, wasn't it? I mean. Could you believe Connie last night in that sermon, walking around on stage with just her pink bra? You could even see her nipples sticking out."

"Yeah, that was pretty crazy," Travis said relieved that was what Don wanted to talk about. He pulled his leather wallet kit out from underneath the bench and got his shaping tools and mallet out. Since Don was still standing around, he figured he had something else to say. "What else is up, Don?"

"Um, you know all that stuff at the end of the service when people were praying. When we were all up there and everything, it kind of felt like we were connected into each other's heads. All those pictures in our minds," Don said. Travis felt his blood run cold and steeled himself for what was inevitable. Don continued, "I didn't know until last night, but y'all have seen the green light and the bridge and everything too haven't you?"

George froze along with Travis and looked at the sincere nerdy guy in the sweater vest standing in front of them. "Uh, yeah. We've had the dream for a while," Travis said. "Is that all you've noticed lately that's, um, *different*," he asked.

"Yeah, pretty much. I mean, other than having the secret powers now," he said matter of factly.

Travis grabbed Don by the arm and he and George marched him into the main shop room and then back to the bathroom. When they were inside, Travis whispered, "How long have you known about the powers?"

Don seemed to be having a great morning, since he normally was fairly alone and shunned by most of the boys in the class. "Ever since the lights, or right after. I figured you guys must know about them too since we live so close to each other. And I remember that day with the storm at school, I kept watching all of you and it seemed like you knew what was going on more than anyone else. So after that, I started trying stuff at home in my bedroom and now it's a lot easier." He reached in his pocket and pulled out a Bic lighter and flicked the wheel. The flame popped up but as Don held it, it suddenly grew twice as bright and tall. The boy smiled as the flame flickered on his glasses. Travis reached out and placed his hand on Don's and the flame brightened and became a big candle of flame. Don's eyes widened and he pulled away from the flame. When George added his hand to the mix, the lighter became a veritable blow torch with a flame four feet tall that almost singed the eyebrows off of them. Don yelped and dropped the lighter which clunked into the brown-stained toilet bowl splashing water up on the wall leaving droplets on the graffiti that adorned the walls.

Don't look here, the joke is in your hand

Underneath in Magic Marker someone had added:

If it takes two hands, it's no joke

"How did you do that?" Don asked clearly impressed.

"We don't have time to explain it all, but basically when you have the power, you can link up with others and make them exponentially greater," George said.

"So like in algebra you mean. Two times two times two, you guys just made it eight times bigger," Don said. Travis was more impressed to see not everyone was an idiot.

"That's about it. We better get back before we get licks and my ass is not up for that today," George began. "Let's talk later, Don. Okay?"

"Sure. Do you want me to bring Vince Constantine? He has them too, but we didn't know about joining them up. Sarah Ramirez has them too."

Travis and George stared at him with mouths agape. "We definitely want to talk to them too, so maybe after school you should come over or something. We all get done with band by 5:00. Can you come over to my house around 5:30?"

Don grinned. "Sure. That would be swell. I'll try and get Vince and Sarah to come over too." Don unlocked the bathroom door and ran into Terry Dixon who was standing right outside the door.

"What are you three freaks doing going to the bathroom together? You measuring each other's dicks?"

"Yes. But we needed to get a longer tape measure," George said. He gripped Terry's arm along with Travis and then Don. "You stay in here and measure yours until Mr. Moore comes to find you, okay?" Don reached over to the window sill out in the hall and found a forgotten tape measure. He handed it to Terry.

"Remember, measure twice, cut once," he said. Terry's eyes continued to look glazed as he started fumbling with his zipper. Travis reached out and pulled the door closed.

"We need to get out of here," he said.

The tardy bell rang as the boys came back in the main shop and Mr. Moore started class with the roll call. When he got to Terry Dixon's name, he waited for an answer but he was clearly missing.

"Where is Dixon? I saw him in here just a few minutes ago."

"He might have gone back to the bathroom. Looked like he was heading back there," Don spoke up clearly enjoying himself. It was the best morning he had ever had in wood shop.

Mr. Moore finished the roll call and headed back to the bathroom. "You all know, wait until I take roll before you go to the bathroom or get busy with your projects," he said walking back down the hall. The door to the bathroom was jerked open and Mr. Moore exploded, "What in the hell do you think you're doing? Why are your pants off? Holy mother of God, stop!"

George, Travis, and Don all had the good sense to keep quiet while most of the other boys roared with laughter. Mr. Moore brought a clearly stunned Terry back into the room, who was still struggling to get his pants zipped. Mr. Moore bent him over the teacher's desk and grabbed White Lightning.

"Let me make this clear to you, Mr. Dixon. You do not hang out in the bathroom before roll call and you certainly do not take tools or tape measures into the bathroom to use while you masturbate!" With that, he swung the paddle and lifted Terry off the floor with three hard swings. No one said a word even though a number of boys were bursting to laugh. By the time the last of the blows were delivered though, most were just clearly glad they had not been on the receiving end of the corporal punishment. Travis looked back at Don who was looking down, clearly upset at what had just transpired.

The boys made it through shop class and took off for their second period classes. In third period Texas history, the guys were oddly quiet as Ferle started the lesson and droned on and on about Stephen F. Austin and his settlement on the Brazos River. Finally, Emily handed a folded note to Travis.

What is up with you two?

Travis grabbed his four-color Bic and clicked on green and wrote back:

Nothing. Will tell you at lunch. New development!

The class drug on and Emily practically attacked Travis as they exited the classroom to tell her the news. He shook his head though and said it would wait until they got to the Chat and Chew. An hour later, the three of them were seated in a booth eating grilled cheese baskets and sweet tea. George squirted some ketchup into his basket and dipped the corner of his grilled cheese into the sauce. Travis had finished telling Emily the story from the morning class and she sat dumbfounded, her sandwich halfway to her mouth.

"You mean he's known about the power all this time. And there are others? Oh my God, this is huge," she said.

"Yep. Kind of changes everything. Just like with Jack and Tim. I'm thinking they are going to be telling us the same thing and God knows their kid has the mojo," Travis said.

"I can't believe that kid told us it would be "swell" to come over to my house. Gorsh, Wally, can you bring the Beav too?" George said mocking.

The three finished their lunch and took off up the street, past the bank and then West Side Barber Shop and The Collegiate Shoppe, bohemian fashions for young ladies. They passed Jim Clark's men's and ladies wear, Russell's shoes, and Duskie Meyers, a cluttered, eclectic mix of babies and toddler clothes and miscellaneous bric-a-brac, all with a half-inch of dust on top. Next up was Western Auto. Travis pushed the door open, clanging the bell on the door as they entered. Their tennis shoes made a soft scuff on the old hardwood floor as they walked up to the front candy counter, looking around for Jack or Tim. Bob Welch's "Ebony Eyes" was playing on a radio somewhere from the back.

"Hey kids," Jack said from behind the trio, making them jump. Jack smiled. "Kinda high strung today, huh?" he said. He walked to the front door and turned the lock and flipped the closed sign over. He taped up a hastily scrawled note saying Out to Lunch, back at 1 PM. "One of the great parts of owning your own business," he said grinning. "It's actually the only great part. Come on back."

Travis, George, and Emily followed the tall man back through the shelves of air filters and windshield wipers and vacuum cleaners to the back office. The three stopped in their tracks as they entered the room. Looking around, they all had exactly the same feeling: we have been here before.

"Guess this place looks familiar to all y'all," Tim Murphy said walking in the office. The three teens nodded mutely and looked around not knowing quite why they were here or what to do next. When Tim closed the door, the hairs stood up on the back of Travis's neck. Jack motioned for the kids to sit on the couch. They sat on the edge of the worn cushions, small puffs of dust wafting up as they did.

"Uh relax, guys," Jack said. "We're the good guys, remember."

"Now that you mention it, are you sure about that? We've all seen some stuff going on in this room," Travis said boldly.

"Sounds like Mike McGee to me," Tim said. "Yeah, and we've seen some pretty interesting shit with you kids too. That golf game was definitely an inspired idea. Not to mention calling down a tornado in your school room."

"Why was JL Martin in here with a gun to your head?" Emily said louder than she meant.

"Forget that," George started, "Why was he sticking a grease gun up your butt?"

The men looked at each other and held their hands up in a gesture of truce. Jack began, "We didn't invite you today to get into everybody's private business. We just wanted to hear what you kids have learned about all this. It seems like you have it figured out a bit. See if you know what some of the dream is about and see what you thought about that church meeting last night."

Travis cleared his throat. "We only know some stuff. All this started with the lights. Whatever that was, it changed all of us. For some reason we are more powerful or stronger than we were before."

"Did y'all make that storm hit the school," Tim asked. It was less of an accusation than genuinely wanting to know.

"Yes," Emily whispered. "We didn't know it would be like that."

Jack spoke up. "So, do you join your abilities or powers or whatever together and it makes them magnified?"

"Yeah," George said. "It works like exponents."

Jack thought for a minute. "Power of ten. So have you figured out about the dream yet?"

"We are pretty sure it is Green Light Bridge and we think whatever caused this to happen wants us all to go there, or maybe it's out there and we are supposed to find it," Travis said. "Mary Washington said that she was out there when she got kidnapped."

George broke in. "We are planning to go out there this Friday in Trey's friend's van and see if maybe being closer to the place we could figure out more. We thought we could try and sleep and see if our dreams would like connect or something and we could learn what is really going on."

Jack and Tim looked at each other nodding in confirmation. "Do y'all know who owns the land out in Scatter Branch where that old bridge is," Jack asked. The kids shook their heads but just as Jack opened his mouth to speak, all three of them in concert with Jack said, "JL Martin." An ice cold wave of dread poured over them like a plunge in a dunk tank at the Fall Carnival.

"I think y'all have figured out that guy is a bad man, and a dangerous one to boot. I think it's pretty clear he and his group of a-holes are behind what happened to that Washington girl and Carl too. We think they might not even be the only ones that have gone missing that Martin has had a hand in."

The teens looked worried and Jack continued. "I understand why you want to go out to that place. Maybe it's even a good idea, but you probably should stay away. If you do go out there, you probably better let me and Tim come along."

"That would be wonderful," Emily said. "Funny but Travis's little brother even suggested we try and get you come along with us."

"But Trey said you wouldn't want to," George said.

Tim poured himself a cup of coffee and moved around the edge of the desk and sat on the top. "So how many of you kids are there that can do the power stuff?"

The kids looked around at each other trying to count up who they knew. Travis began. "Well, us three. My brothers, Trey and Andy."

"Mary Washington," Emily added, "And both of you I guess."

"And your boy, Joey," George said. "Today, I found out three other kids at school can too. And that's just what we know. It makes sense there are some others too. We wonder why most the people with the power seem to be kids? You two are the only old people that seem to know about it."

"Old people, huh?" Jack said with a smirk. "We just turned 30!"

Emily spoke up, "Why do you think Joey seems to be so … powerful or insightful or something? You saw what he did at church. When he touched Mary, it linked everyone together. It seemed like he knew what he was doing too."

"I don't know. Joey was with me and Jack in a tent on the edge of Lake Tawakoni on September 12th. Maybe the light really blasted him and since we were all there together in that small place, we sort of picked up some residual power. I don't know if we can do what you kids can do," Jack said.

"Does he go around the house like baby Superman or something," George asked.

"That's just it. He doesn't. With him, it seems to be more about maturing more and almost knowing the future or something."

"Precognition," George said.

"Say what, Sherlock?" Tim asked.

"It means knowing the future. It's what it's called. Like telepathy is sending mental messages to each other or telekinesis is moving stuff with your mind."

"Okay, when I was a kid, saying stuff like that would just get your ass kicked," Tim said with a frown.

"Oh it still does," Travis said.

"Should we go to the police with all this? I mean, if there is a chance that Carl Washington was hurt or even killed by those men, shouldn't we do something?" Emily asked.

"Normally I would say yes," Jack said. "But the Sherriff's office is full of men put there by Martin or others he has in his pocket. I just don't think they would listen or do anything. And then there's the very real threat that we could bring a bunch of crap down on us and our families." With that, Jack quickly described what had happened to Joey's cat and Tim's steers. Emily gasped and put her hands over her mouth. Travis felt the icy wave pour over his neck and back again.

"So if we say or do something, he might try and hurt us or our families," Travis asked.

"Possibly. It's probably better if you kids try and keep a low profile. Maybe no more tornados in school or turning into the Incredible Hulk at football games," Jack said. "And if that stuff we saw last night is true, then your family in particular needs to keep out of the spotlight," Jack added looking at Travis.

"So you figured all that out?"

"Didn't take a lot of "precogitation" to figure that out, buddy. Your brother has always been the black sheep of your family," Tim said.

Travis frowned and reached over and touched Tim's coffee mug. It began to boil and exploded in a shower of coffee and coffee mug shards, drenching Tim's lap. He jumped up, yelping, dancing around, pulling his trousers down to get the burning to stop. Emily covered her eyes.

"You little shit," Tim snarled. "You could have burned my dick off. That is exactly what Jack was talking about." Tim slammed the door open and headed to the bathroom.

"I didn't mean that to happen," Travis said in a low voice.

"Well he shouldn't have been a tool talking about Trey," George said defiantly. "You don't have to worry about us too much. We can pretty much take care of ourselves these days."

"If you pull a lot of shit like that at school, someone is going to lock you up or send you to a laboratory so they can do experiments on you. Don't you kids ever watch TV or movies? That's what always happens to freaks of nature and that is what we are right now. And I can't let anything like that happen to Joey and I don't want it happen to you either."

Emily stood up. "We have to go," Mr. Tanner. We will keep it quiet at school and we won't try and draw attention to ourselves. We do get that part. If you want to come out to Scatter Branch with us, we will stop in on Friday at lunch and see if you can make it."

"Okay. I am going to go out there with you. I don't like the idea of you kids out there alone. So do your parents have any idea any of this is going on?"

The three teens shook their heads. "See you on Friday, Jack," Travis said. "Tell Tim I'm sorry about his nuts."

When they arrived in English class, they saw they had a substitute teacher which made it far easier for the three to carry on a quiet conversation in the back of the classroom. They moved their desks to a corner of the room and pretended to work on their vocabulary assignment. The substitute was a college aged boy who seemed far too young to be a teacher, especially compared to the sepulchral Dr. Webster.

"Do you really think we should go out there this Friday? I mean, Jack made it sound pretty dangerous," Emily whispered.

"Grownups always do that," George said. "Look, we are just going to drive out there and build a fire and sit by the van and roast a wiener or something. The land on the edge of the river there is public land. It isn't owned by anyone so it's not like anyone can tell us to get lost. And it's been so damn wet, it's not like we would start a big wildfire or something."

"I think we have to go. We need to find out some more. I think we should invite these new kids too, Don the nerd and the other kids," Travis said.

"At least the nerd knew what exponents are," George added defensively. George looked up at the clock. "I might try using some mojo on Coach Beadles today. I am not in the mood to do any Phys-Ed bullshit at all."

"How else do you expect to keep that girlish figure of yours if you don't exercise," Emily said with a wink. She had some lip gloss out applying it in class, a big no-no when Dr. Webster was present. George casually touched the sleeve of her sweater and she took the lip gloss and proceeded to smear it thick and wild around her lips until she looked like the Joker. Travis reached up to pull her hand away from her lips which broke her concentration. She looked in her compact mirror and yelped.

"I'll get you for this, George Harris," she said digging for a tissue to try and take the lipstick off her face. George sat back with his arms folded in satisfaction.

"Would you two knock it off?" Travis hissed. "We have a lot more to deal with than pulling pranks on each other."

The bell rang and Emily ran off to the girls' room still looking back murderously at George. The boys threw their books into their lockers, grabbed out the ones for their homework and headed to the gym. The way the schedule was set up, the guys only had PE every other day. Travis put up with it more than anything else. He wasn't remotely interested like Trey in achieving great success in sports. He liked playing the occasional game of football or baseball, he was a fast runner and was strong enough to at least do a few chin ups and crawl up the infernal rope in gym class, but he would rather hang out in the band hall ten times more. George on the other hand despised the class. He was just that much smaller than most of the other boys that he routinely ended up being the butt of jokes or was picked last for the stupid teams. But even George wasn't at the bottom of the heap. That place was reserved for the fat boys, the nerds, and a couple of guys who were pretty femmy to say the least. Doug Ailes often sat on bleachers during class in a giant wool overcoat or wrapped himself in what could only be described as a poncho. He wore fancy leather shoes, often with huge platforms. His pants were impossibly tight leaving little to the imagination. Some days it actually looked like he was wearing makeup. He was very fair skinned, with soft flowing brown hair that fell to his shoulders. He tended to float across the floor and talk in a girlish high pitch even by junior high standards. He almost always had a note from his mother that he couldn't participate in gym. Most days, Coach Beadles just told him to "sit on the bleachers and knit a set of balls." Today was not one of those days.

The coach came into the locker room like a bull from a rodeo chute, snorting and pawing the ground. Whatever had gone wrong must have gone very wrong and it was going to be fifth period gym class that paid the price.

"Hurry up, Ladies. Full dress out and line up on the center line of the gym. You have one minute," he barked. Doug came up with his note which Coach Beadles snatched out of his hand and proceeded to rub it up the crack of his polyester gym shorts. "Not today, Dougie. Get dressed and hit the line."

"But, my mom wrote a note. I can't..."

The coach cut him off. "Listen Darling, sorry you're on the rag again, but I don't give a tinker's damn. Dress out and hit the line or I'll flunk your sweet cheeks and it will be detention with me for a month." Doug's mouth was a thin line of fury as he whirled around and tried to find his locker that he surely had not opened up in a month.

Three minutes later the group of boys were kitted out in bright orange shorts and a grey tank top that was emblazoned with a Cowhill Tiger and CHJHS. With a blast of his whistle, Coach Beadles shouted for jumping jacks to 100. The boys began to jump and clap with their hands above their heads. Coach stood staring up and down the lines of thirty boys with a frown. Travis felt his heart rate begin to speed up but as he concentrated, he found that it slowed down and the exercises were little more than a gentle stroll. He looked over and saw George was actually participating today as well. By the look of concentration on his face, he was enjoying the benefits of a doubly-fit cardiovascular system as well. He wasn't even breaking a sweat. The coach blasted the whistle again and the group stopped the jumping jacks even though they were only up to seventy-eight.

"There is more jiggling and bouncing going on here today than at a Jell-O convention. What is this, burn your bra day, boys? I said full dress out, which includes supporters. Drop em' gentlemen. Anyone without a jock runs the bleachers."

There was a chorus of grumbling and the coach blasted his whistle again. "You do not want to be on the wrong side of me today. Now, DROP 'EM!"

Boys to the right and left of Travis hooked their thumbs into the waistband of their orange shorts and soon the floor of the gym looked like a field of deflated pumpkins. More than half of the boys stood there with their regular underwear on. Miraculously, Travis had slid his crusty jock strap on when he put on his shorts, mostly because they were already inside his shorts when he pulled them on. George must have done the same because Travis saw his bare ass strapped up beside him. A smattering of laughs were coming from the far side where Don Edwards, a big Neanderthal boy named Joe Cunningham, and a muscular black boy named Dwight Franklin stood completely bottomless, their hands attempting to cover up their privates.

"For the love of Pete," Coach Beadles brayed. "How many times have I told you geniuses about the supporters? Now you're just a bunch of fools standing around with your pecker in your hand. Pull 'em up. You three and all the Einsteins wearing their underwear can hit the bleachers. Run 'till you hear the whistle."

But right before the boys took off the coach spied Doug standing defiantly with his shorts still up on his slim hips. The beefy man steeled his eyes and the rest of the boys instantly looked around to see what had caught his attention. The coach walked up to Doug and stood in front of him with his hands on his hips. His orange polyester golf shirt stretched far out over his waist. With a voice barely above a whisper he said, "You heard me, Darling. Drop your shorts."

"No," Doug said in a high wheeze.

"Am I losing my mind? Do you think you can stand there and tell me no? This is your last chance, sweetheart. Either you drop them or you can take a ride on Big Bertha." Big Bertha was the coach's formidable paddle. It was oak and solid as a baseball bat."

Doug's face turned crimson. He grabbed the waistband of his shorts and began to slide them down an inch at a time shaking his hips as he did, gyrating provocatively as they slid ever lower down. Soon the class was all staring and for some reason, Kyle Walters started humming "The Stripper." Other boys took up the song as Doug peeled his shorts lower and lower until his pubic hair began to show over the top of the shorts. He then dropped them further revealing a half-erect penis that hung halfway to his knees. He hopped and did a little dance and flicked his shorts up into the coach's face. Then he wheeled around and bent over and spread his legs mooning the cadre of boys and looking back between his legs.

"Is this want you wanted to see, Coach? See, I finished knitting my set of balls. You like them, you pervert?

It was like all the air was sucked out of the room, a vacuum of tension. When somewhere from the back of the group a deep voice boomed, "Where'd you get that dick? We all thought you still had a pussy!"

Doug pulled his shirt down to cover himself. Don and the other half naked boys pulled their shorts back up. Don grabbed Doug's shorts off the floor and ran over to the tall, skinny boy and handed them back just as the coach descended on him reaching out to grab his t-shirt by the neck and haul him bare-assed back to the gym office. But when the coach gripped the boy, Doug reached up and gripped his wrist and twisted. The snap of Coach Beadles' radius and ulna sounded like a gunshot. The coach shrieked and grabbed his arm as he sunk to the floor. Kyle Walters, Will Hughes, and Terry Dixon rushed from the back of the group of boys and grabbed Doug who bent down and touched the floor of the gym and the trio skidded and slipped, banging head first into the hardwood.

Travis looked at George who was staring at the entire scene wide eyed and mesmerized. Travis touched George on the shirt as he pulled his shorts back up. He nodded his head and the two of them began to head toward the front of the group where Doug was standing with Don. Steve Jones and Kevin Riley knelt down and began to try and help the coach, Steve ordering Sam Weaver to go to the office and tell someone. Travis and George moved up beside Doug. George touched him on the sleeve.

"Come on, Doug. Let's go," he said and started leading the boy back toward the locker room. Don began to follow them as did Vince Constantine. They turned their heads when the heard a noise and saw Vice Principal Anderson jogging to the coach along with Mr. Franklin the custodian. The men helped the coach up to his feet. Mr. Franklin pulled off his jacket and made a makeshift sling for the coach and immobilized his arm, helping lead him out of the gym.

Principal stood holding on to Rex Monday's shoulder, trying to catch his breath. As soon as he could talk again he said, "Okay. Everyone back into the locker room. I want you in the showers and then dressed and sitting on the bleachers for the rest of the period."

Steve Jones attemped to tell the vice principal they had barely broken a sweat and didn't need a shower when Mr. Anderson turned on him and shouted, "I said get in the showers, NOW. If I see one boy trying to get out of taking a shower, you'll be suspended. Now go. You smell like a bunch of monkeys anyway."

Travis had heard enough and herded the other boys with him into the lockers and they pulled off their clothes and grabbed their towels and ran to the showers. Travis figured the quicker they got wet and got out of there, the better. Doug still appeared to be in a daze and George grabbed him by the arm and ushered him into the shower room and twisted the handles and started the showers flowing. Don and Vince were lathering up as fast as possible. Travis threw his head under the water to make it look like he had showered. George turned Doug around in a circle while he rubbed a bit of soap under his arms and rinsed off. The group of four grabbed their towels and were headed out of the shower room when a wall of boys appeared in the doorway. Some had towels around their waists, others were just standing naked with towels in their hands. But when they saw Doug, something snapped and they rushed at him howling. The four boys turned and ran toward the other end of the shower room. Most of the other boys were standing along the walls staring, but Terry Dixon and Joe Cunningham ran headlong toward Doug.

"Get that faggot," Terry shouted. The bigger boys pounced on Travis and George and threw them to the side and gripped Doug. Kyle Walters headed toward the boys hauling the water hose the coach used to rinse down the showers after class.

"Bend that freak over. Let's see if he likes taking it up the ass the way we all know he does. Terry and Joe struggled and pulled Doug down, pushing his head and neck until he was bent over. Kyle twisted the hose nozzle and moved toward Doug, pushing the brass fitting toward Doug's rectum.

Moving faster than any of them normally did, Travis, George, Don, and Vince rushed forward, gripped the bullies and threw them across the shower room until their backsides smacked into the tile wall on the opposite side. Steve Jones and Rex Monday rushed toward the four. George reached over and touched one of the shower heads while he gripped Vince who was holding on to the other three. The twenty heads in the shower room blasted out a torrent of water greater than a fire hose, slamming into the boys and spiraling them across the tile like a dozen bars of Irish Spring. The water beat against the tiles on the wall and ripped them loose until the room was filled with flying ceramic shrapnel, knocking boys in the head and slamming into their bodies. The teenagers screamed and covered their heads and tried to run out of the waterlogged room. The shower heads began to vibrate and one by one, shower heads blew off the pipes and ricocheted around the walls like cannonballs. Vice Principal Anderson appeared in the doorway to the shower and froze until a decapitated shower head slammed into his balls and bent him over in a loud groan.

Joe Cunningham began to haul his naked 250 pounds of teenage beef out of the shower bellowing, "We're all gonna die!" The remaining boys slid and dodged their way toward the locker room. Travis grabbed Doug and pushed him toward the opening. Vince practically carried Don and George out of the blasting spray and skidded into a set of lockers.

"Come on," Travis said pulling the boys away from the flood of water. They pulled on their clothes over their soaking bodies and gripped their shoes, socks, and books and ran out of the locker room. It was apparent that none of the boys were following the instructions to sit in the bleachers until the bell rang. Like drowned rats, they stood around on the gym floor in puddles of water trying to struggle into shirts and pants.

As soon as the five boys were dressed, George looked at Travis who said, "Remember the bell in shop class?"

The two of them gripped their friends' shoulders and closed their eyes and the bell rang, twenty minutes early. The bell rang for a good two minutes until students began filing out of the main building holding their ears from the cacophony. The boys made a beeline to the waiting school bus that ferried the students to the high school for band. They pushed the door open and ran toward the back of the bus, sides heaving as they collapsed into the seats.

Vince spoke up. "Are we just going to hide here until we get to band?"

"Do you have a better idea? It doesn't matter, Travis said. "Just stay back here and we maybe no one will figure out where we are until it's too late. I don't think we should hang around the parking lot or in the halls, do you?"

"Probably not," Vince said. "What the fuck just happened?"

George narrowed his eyes. "You know good and well what just happened. We all used our powers to destroy the locker room. Talk about a shit-storm."

"We had to do something. They were gonna rape Doug with that hose," Don said.

"You know, it just dawned on me, all of us with these powers are in band. Even Emily and Sarah Ramirez and Mary Washington. That's weird," George said.

"But Trey and Angie and Jack, Tim, and Joey aren't so I don't think that matters," Travis added.

The boys looked at each other. Their hair was plastered against their faces. Their shirts were glued to their backs with the water from the shower. George had no idea where his socks were.

"I don't even have on any underwear," Vince said. "I almost zipped my sack into these damn jeans."

In a soft, whispery voice, Doug spoke. "Thank you," he said. "It's all my fault."

"No it's not. It's that fucking asshole Coach Beadles fault," Don barked. The other boys stared at him in amazement. None of them had ever heard Don say so much as darn.

"It certainly isn't your fault, Doug. The coach was wrong to do that and for the rest of it, they all just sort of turned into a mob. But the cat's out of the bag now," Travis said. "We all need to get together and talk. Can you get away right after dinner tonight and come over to George's house?

Just tell your parents it's a group project or something and you don't have any choice. None of you live that far away and it's not raining tonight. You can ride a bike if you have to. George's house is right beside mine. It's 913 Maple."

The boys looked at one another and nodded in quiet solidarity. Students began to walk toward the bus and board. They were busy talking about the crazy bell at first and then saw the soaked group at the back. Nancy Rambeau rushed up to the group.

"Oh my God, you guys are soaked. So did the showers really explode? That's what everyone is saying. Someone else says Coach Beadles tried to give a boy licks with the paddle and when he hit the guy's butt, it broke his arm. Is that what happened?"

"Yeah. It was crazy," George said. "We could have all drowned."

"You should sue the school. Crappy World War I plumbing," Nancy said.

"Right on," Don said holding up a clenched fist. "Power to the People." Nancy looked at him with annoyance.

"Weirdo," she said.

Emily came up the aisle, eyes narrowed as she looked at the soaked group of boys. She slid in beside Travis and reached up and touched his plastered hair.

"Do I even want to know?" she asked.

"Not really," Travis said. "Meet the rest of the gang," he nodded to the dripping group of boys behind him.

"All of them?"

"Yep. We're having a summit meeting at G's after band. This thing is getting out of control and fast," Travis said. "Can you get Sarah to come over, she sits near you in band. And Mary if she can?"

"Sure." Emily slid her fingers into Travis's hand and interlocked them. His hand was cold and wet, the complete opposite of how it normally was. He knew he looked worried and that was putting it mildly. She put her head on his shoulder, which was cool to her cheek due to the damp shirt. He unlaced his fingers and put his arm around her and pulled her close, rubbing her hair with his hand. She turned her face toward his and kissed him lightly on the lips."

"Lucky," Vince whispered from behind them.

Travis looked at him and smiled, shrugging his shoulders. George sat beside him looking out the window as the bus crawled toward Culver Street and the high school. Don and Doug were sitting together. Doug looked small and shrunken somehow, not his usual flamboyant self. Travis thought to himself, *I never see that kid or Don or Vince for that matter.* They sit on this bus and play in the band and are in my classes and I hardly ever speak to them.

That seemed stupid to him now. They had always had things in common, now it was undeniable. He started trying to list off what he did know about them: not much he was forced to say. Vince had been in his class since first grade. He played drums in band and was pretty good too. He was a big athletic guy who probably could make it on the baseball or even football team and here he was heading to band instead. Don had been in his class since about fifth grade. He was smart. Both his parents were professors. He had older brothers and sisters he thought and he loved Star Trek and Star Wars.

That was about it. Doug was a real enigma. He had joined Travis's class late in the term last year. He dressed fancy, wore makeup, high heels, read GQ magazine in class, and surprisingly had the biggest dick in the class. Who could have guessed that?

44 George

"From the top, let's go," Mr. Smith said through the megaphone loudspeaker hanging from his hip. The band jogged back to their first positions in the long diagonals stretched across the field from 20 yard line to the other 20. The band had come a long way since August when summer band started. The group was well accustomed to the new corps style of marching and the creativity on the field had soared. Mr. Smith had recruited a number of college band students to come in the afternoons as interns. The drum line was magnificent now, a choreographed group that mostly moved about in the middle of the field while the other instruments and the color guard of flags and rifles created shapes around them. The color guard had been working night and day and now flew across the field, spinning flags and rifles, doing intricate spins and dance steps. The band now moved in smooth steps instead of high step marching or stiff military precision. The glide step kept the body smooth from head to waist while allowing the hips and legs and feet to move and pivot to the different positions required for the drill. It created a smoother, louder sound than the jangling, bouncing of horns and mouthpieces in the more military styles of marching.

The college students had convinced Mr. Smith to move towards a more modern repertoire of music as well. Gone were the obligatory marches and corny pop tunes. Even the majorettes were given flags or rifles and blended in with the rest of the corps, although they did still get to twirl and perform their own numbers at pep rallies and halftime shows. But the band was preparing for University Interscholastic League competition and there was no room for twirlers in that setting. Instead, with the help of the college students, the band was now performing a show entitled "Land of Make Believe," featuring the music of Chuck Mangione with a big kick off piece, the fanfare from the Olympics, first made famous at the 1972 Summer Games in Munich.

The drum major counted off and the band marched forward silently for eight counts with Vince Constantine on tympani on the sidelines pounding out the well-known rhythm before the brass blasted "Ta — Ta — Ti-ta-ta-ta-ta, Ta- ta-ti-ta-ti-ta-ta tat a-ti-ta tat tah, TAH…" The low brass and trumpets made a thick, rich wall of brass sound like a junior version of the Madison Scouts. After that opening, the band moved into a row of expanding arcs and began with Mangione's "Legend of the One-Eyed Sailor," the rippling brass line beginning with the sousaphones and moving to the middle brass and then the trumpets as the band moved in and out the arcs across the field, the flags and rifles crisply spinning in time with the syncopated rhythm. Next was a beautiful lyrical Spanish ballad, "Bellavia," with the band moving into a series of concentric circles that expanded and shrank on the field as the melody rose and soared. For the finale, the band created a long, swirling shape on the field with Monty Malone as solo trumpet in one and Bruce Richardson, solo mellophone in the other to begin the echoing first strains of "Land of Make Believe." The song began slow and tender, built to a thrumming frenzy in the middle, and ended with the sweet theme repeated by the soloists. The band had debuted the entire show last Friday night in Quitman and the crowd went wild. With any luck, all the hard work and creativity would pay off this next week when the band traveled to Longview for UIL competition. It had been three years since the band had earned a 1st Division ranking and it would be hard to push against the glass ceiling of military band prejudice, *but they just might be able to do it,* George thought.

George and Travis stood listening to Mr. Smith give notes and corrections to several of the squads of band members. Their faces were sweaty and their hearts were beating out of their chests. Whoever said marching band was for pussies clearly had never been in this kind of a band, he thought. George looked over in the smaller woodwind section of the band and saw Emily with her alto sax around her neck standing beside Don Edwards. Across the way he saw Sarah Ramirez standing with her mellophone and near the back, Doug Ailes with his flute, of course it was a flute, George thought. Why was this the first time he was really seeing these kids. In the past few hours he had learned all of them were just like him and Travis and Emily. It freaked him out and shamed him at the same time. They had been so busy in their own world of these powers and all that, they hadn't really considered there were others just like them right in front of them. As he looked across the field he spied Mary Washington's big hair and realized there was another one too. Mary in the clarinet section was also a mutant just like him.

The band ran through the show twice more, stopping once or twice to work out spacing problems or listen to Mr. Smith rail against the saxophones that were clearly out of tune and playing flat.

"God Almighty, would someone give those honky saxophones a tuning note. They are flatter than a Middle Ages globe."

The band dismissed a bit before 5:00 PM and the kids headed to the building to put away their instruments and go home. A few kids walked but most either grabbed rides with other high schoolers or waited for parents to pick them up. George had made friends with one of the high school trombone players, Damon Reed, who had a ridiculous 1948 Ford that he was planning to restore. It looked more like a hearse than a car, but it was huge and could seat about ten kids. Damon was a kind, pudgy guy; an Eagle Scout with a love for Civil War recreations and the Navy. George, Travis and Emily piled in the car along with Bruce Bonner and Anna Green. George had managed to touch base with the rest of the new "group" and all planned to try and come over after dinner. The old car smelled like an old sweatshirt that had been left in a locker far too long. As the kids rode along, Damon turned on his AM radio and found KISS singing "Calling Dr. Love." George looked down and saw the pavement rolling along beneath his feet, holes the size of Eisenhower dollars sprinkled over the crumbling floorboards.

"You know, Damon, pretty soon we can just put our feet down and help your power this boat like Fred Flintstone," George said over the roar of the unmuffled car.

"Or you could just walk," Damon snapped back looking hard through the rear view mirror that hung at a crazy 45 degree angle from the roof of the car. *Clearly he was tired as well* George thought. The car ground to a halt near the park and the three climbed out, thanking Damon for the lift. He reached over and smacked George on the butt and flipped him off before putting his foot down on the gas and lumbering off.

"See you after dinner? Emily said walking away with Travis, his hand wrapped around her and fitted into the tight pocket of her flared jeans.

"Yeah, see you," he said.

George went inside and smelled something bubbling away in the crock pot. His mom was on a crock pot kick lately. Everything seemed to go in there these days for dinner. The other night when George suggested some crock pot pizza, his Dad had cuffed him on the back of the head and reminded him not to be such a wise guy. George had rewarded his dad with a light touch that had cause him to squeeze the ketchup so hard, it exploded across his crock pot meat loaf and filled his plate like a bowl of soup. All in all though, George had to admit, things with Duke had been much better. Like Pavlov's dogs, Duke Harris responded well to some sharp behavior modification.

"Um, Mom, Dad? I was going to have a few friends over tonight. It's for a class project so we kind of need to work on it. They won't stay very late and we'll keep it down."

"Sounds fine," Duke said cutting into his chicken. "This stuff is so tender, you can just pull it apart. Great job again, Darla."

George took another bite of his chicken that was so overcooked it was practically liquid. It tasted fine but he was tired of every meal being another amorphous mass of indistinguishable protein with some glop on the top. He'd just as soon have a Swanson TV Dinner. But he kept his mouth shut and ate the food and took off to his room.

"Thanks, Dad," he said leaning over and kissing him on the top of his head.

Duke Harris laughed. "What a nice kid," he said.

George took a quick shower to rinse off the sweat from band. It suddenly dawned on him all that had happened today. Learning about the other kids, Terry Dixon getting licks, and then that shit storm in the gym. Things were happening really fast it seemed. He grabbed some clean clothes, jeans and his Boston T-shirt. He slid his hand along his row of albums and selected "Frampton Comes Alive" and put it on the turntable. When "Show Me the Way" came on, George picked up his electric guitar and began to play along with Frampton, doing a passable job when there was a knock on his open door and Mary Washington leaned in smiling.

"Okay to come in?"

"Sure," George said. He started to put the guitar down. "Oh, don't stop playing please. You sound like George Benson there."

"There is no way I am even close to that good."

Mary sat beside him and slid her hand onto his leg and squeezed slightly. "How about now?" she asked. George picked up the guitar licks again and this time, he was much better, playing right along with Frampton.

"I love this power or whatever it is. It's the best thing that ever happened to me. I hope we can use it help find out what happened to my dad," she said.

"Me too," George said. As the song stopped and the clapping on the live album died he asked, "You want me to put on a different record. I've got some Earth, Wind and Fire and Stevie Wonder?"

Mary looked at him with a skeptical face. "Oh I hope I didn't just hear you say that. You think a sister girl can't like Peter Frampton? Why don't we just break out some James Brown or George Clinton."

"Sorry," George said meekly, clearly embarrassed.

Mary keeled over laughing, this high sweet cackle that George had never heard. "Ooo, I got you there, George. Mm-hmm, I just cracked your face you are so red. I'm just playing with you. You aren't used to being around black folks, are you?"

"No. You're my only black friend."

"Well, you're my only white friend, so there you go!" she said leaning over and giving him a quick kiss on the cheek. Travis and Emily walked in.

"There you two go making out again," Travis said with a laugh.

"You got that right," Mary said. "G here is my main man." Emily laughed and hugged Mary.

"I'm glad you got to come over."

"Shit, these days my mama don't give a hoot what I do. She's given up the will to live. She shipped my little brother off to my aunt Diamond in Dallas."

"Have you gotten any more memories of what might have happened to your Dad?" Travis asked.

"I don't like thinking about it, but yeah, I pretty much know what happened."

The door opened and Vince and Sarah Ramirez came in. They all said hello and looked around George's room and then Don came in followed by Doug. Doug was wearing a Blondie T-shirt that was festooned with tiny rhinestones outlining the Blondie logo. He had reapplied his eye makeup. His low slung jeans were as tight as ever and the bellbottoms on the Jordache jeans hovered above his platform shoes

"Oh my God, this place is crazy," Doug said taking in George's room with the black light posters, flashing lights by the stereo, mirror ball on the dresser, Buddha incense burner, and Farrah on the ceiling. The teens stared at Doug wide-eyed. "Oh, baby. You all are going to need to chill out. Ms. Thang here knows what I'm talking about," Doug said motioning to Mary.

"You know I do," she giggled. "These white kids don't know what to do with the likes of us."

Sarah Ramirez spoke up, "I'm not white," she said flatly.

"You just go on believing that, honey," Doug said. "Good for you. So you got any food or drinks or weed or something, Georgie? What kind of a par-tay is this?"

George rose, stunned and clearly impressed by this guy's audacity. He and Travis and Emily disappeared and came back with two bags of chips, some Frito bean dip, and some cans of Coke and Sprite. The kids crowded around the makeshift buffet on George's desk and cranked up the music which had been changed to one of George's mix tapes curiously labeled "For Mary." Stevie Wonder's "Sir Duke" was blaring. After that, the group jumped up and danced like crazy along with Earth, Wind, and Fire's "September." The next song was "Dance with Me" by Orleans. Travis grabbed Emily and began to slow dance to the tune. Vince and Sarah followed suit. Mary pulled George up off the bed and wrapped his arms around her. That left Don and Doug sitting on the bed watching. But in the middle of the song, Don stood up and pulled Doug up and the two of them began a grand swaying dance together that ended up making everyone laugh so hard they all fell over in hysterics.

After that song, George lowered the volume a bit and turned off his lamps except for the black light and the spinning multicolored mirror ball. He lit some incense in the Buddha and put his newly acquired lock in the locked position. He pulled out a couple of joints and asked the group if they were interested. Everyone except Sarah and Don said yes. George lit the joints and began to pass them around. George noticed the first time around, Sarah and Don passed the weed on to the next person in the circle. But the next time around, both of them took tentative small hits on the blunt.

Five minutes later, the kids were lying back on the floor or on the bed listening to more of George's mix tape, now playing Foreigner's "Feels like the First Time." Vince and Sarah were on the bed, on their sides kissing. Emily was sitting between Travis's legs, leaning against his chest. Mary and George were sitting together on his black bean bag chair, George's arm awkwardly around Mary's back. Don and Doug were talking animatedly. George looked over and saw Vince try and slide his hand up underneath Sarah's peasant blouse. She grabbed his hand and pushed it back down. The song came to an end replaced by the less romantic "Killer Queen." Sarah was looking up at Farrah and actually stood up on the bed and touched the poster.

"Why is there food or whatever on this poster?" she asked.

Vince took one look at the smudge and began to cackle. "Great shot, Harris," he said, rolling on his side in laughter. Doug and Don pointed and laughed. George's face was so red it could be seen from space. Sarah looked around bewildered.

"I don't get it," she said.

Emily narrowed her eyes. "Believe me, you don't want to know."

Travis came to the rescue. "Uh why don't we kind of start talking about the elephant in the room," he began.

"Excuse me, I have been on a grapefruit diet for a month," Doug said comically offended. The group laughed. George had to admit, this kid was a riot.

Travis began recounting his experience with the lights and the emergence of the powers. Travis and Emily added their own stories. The kids were fascinated, especially when they described the storm at the school.

"I thought that had to be something weird," Vince said. "It just came out of nowhere."

The kids described what they had learned about the dream and Green Light Bridge, about Trey and Andy, and finally the guys at Western Auto and Joey. Vince, Sarah, and Doug were very interested to hear more about the events at the church when the large group of them shared so many images, many of them private and unknown. Finally, Travis just suggested they see if the images were still up in their heads. The group moved to the floor and grasped hands. Travis, Emily, Don, and George began to concentrate on those images. Like a jolt of lightning, the images began to roll again, this time more vivid and detailed than ever. When they opened their mouths, the teens looked around the circle stunned and embarrassed.

"Did you see…Bo Williams and Greg Benton?" Vince said open-mouthed.

"I'd like to know a bit more about that," Doug said.

"All that stuff. I kind of feel dirty," Sarah said. "All those people, the stuff they did…"

"Look," George said. "Every one of us has stuff we don't want people to know about. If you think about it long enough, you can see things from every one of us, embarrassing stuff and cool stuff. But it can also kind of drive you crazy. It's not that good to dwell on it. Let's try and focus on the stuff with the bridge and maybe we can help Mary here find out more about her dad. And if not that, then maybe what did this to us."

"I don't care what did it to us," Vince said. "It's the best thing that ever happened to me and I don't want to screw around with shit and make it go away," he said adamantly.

"I kind of feel the same," Sarah agreed, sliding her hand into Vince's.

"Hey, no one loves these powers any more than me," George said. "We just think we should keep learning about them. Get better with them. See what all they can do and yeah, maybe see why we keep dreaming about that bridge."

The kids thought about this and they started nodding in agreement in a few moments. George began to outline the plan to go out to the river where the old bridge was and have a bonfire that Friday night since there wasn't a football game. George told about Trey getting a van that can hold quite a few and about the guys from Western Auto that were going to join them.

"I kind of like the idea of a grown up being out there," Don said. "Those guys are like army vets. They aren't scared of stuff and if there's any trouble…"

"There's not going to be any trouble," Travis said flatly.

"How would you guys feel about a little group experimentation," George said.

"Oooo. I like the sound of that," Doug said.

Vince agreed. "Do we need to get naked or…?"

George looked puzzled. "Who are you?" he said.

"A total pervert," Sarah said flatly, but she slid her hand back inside Vince's anyway.

"I just thought we could test our group strength or something. You know, see if it's really greater and all that."

"It might be a little dangerous," Mary said.

"That's why I just thought we'd try something really easy." George grabbed his Buddha incense burner and placed it into the middle of the circle. It was about five inches tall and weighed about two pounds.

"So, let's just touch this. Concentrate on making it lighter. Just that. I think we have all learned that the simpler the command or idea, the easier it is to make something happen." The group nodded in agreement. They stretched out their hands and touched the statue. For a half-minute, nothing seemed to happen. Then the statue began to slowly lift away from the carpet, floating about three inches above. The kids removed their hands and stared at the figurine. It rose about a foot more in the air, hovered, and then took off like a shot and blasted through the drywall ceiling of George's room, leaving a Buddha-shaped hole.

"Holy shit," the kids said in unison, looking around the circle.

"Okay, one more thing," George said. "Let's try it on one of us. Any volunteers?"

"Did you not just see your satanic idol blast through the ceiling?" Vince said.

"Fine. I'll do it," Travis said. Emily grabbed his arm. "Look, just don't concentrate too hard. If I go through the ceiling, well … " He got up and lay in the middle of the circle. The kids gathered around and place their hands on his head, his shoulders, belly, legs. Travis felt one hand dangerously close to his dick. He grabbed Doug's hand and moved it up on his belly.

Doug shrugged. "Sorry," he said, not sorry at all.

The teenagers grew quiet as The Eagles sang about a "New Kid in Town." Moments later, Travis floated two feel above the floor. They moved their hands away and he quickly zoomed up toward the ceiling. Travis closed his eyes and raised his hands up and concentrated on stopping. He opened his eyes as he was three inches away from the popcorn ceiling. He turned around and looked down on the shocked faces all holding their hands up toward him. They began to lower their hands in concert and Travis gently floated back to the carpet until he felt the shag underneath his back.

That was fucking awesome," Vince said.

"Jesus," Don said.

"I think that happened to me the night the lights came," Mary said.

"Me too," Travis said.

"Me too," the rest of the group echoed.

"Hey, what time is it?" Vince asked.

"A little after 9:30," George said.

"Oh damn, I think we better go soon."

The group gathered up coats and shoes and began to filter out into the Harris's hallway toward the front door. Mary Washington leaned in and said, "Thanks for letting us come over,

Mr. Harris," as she belted her red patent leather coat.

"So how was the Love-In?" he asked with an insane grin on his face. George groaned while the rest of the kids giggled and waved, closing the door behind them.

45 Mike

The windshield wipers needed to be changed. They skipped across the windshield like a rock tossed at a lake. The freezing rain was light but still enough to cause the road to be slippery and freeze up the wipers and windows. Mike reached up and rubbed the inside of the windshield with his jacket sleeve. Trey sat on the other side of the truck, hands in his pockets, trying to stay warm. The heater in the reefer van was a piss-poor crapper and the sub-freezing temperatures were proving too much for it. Mike had grabbed Trey after school and persuaded him to accompany him down to Rockwall to pick up a produce delivery that had gotten stuck on the highway. Luckily, the driver was going to meet them and do all the transferring into the new truck. Mike tempted Trey with a double Whataburger with cheese and onion rings, one of his favorite foods.

As they drove along the highway, Mike had told the long and involved story of his college days up in Buffalo with Carl, the way they had met and roomed together and became best friends. He told the whole story of the 1958 football season, even though Trey had heard it at least four times before. Then he launched into officer training and Fort Hood, his terrible decision and choices, and ultimately, Carl and Janet's brief but very fruitful affair.

"And I just left. I packed up and headed to the base to climb on a C130 and fly to Saigon."

Trey sat still for a while. The AM radio was scratchy and WBAP was the only station it could really get, though neither Mike nor Trey were fans. Willie and Waylon were urging "Mammas, Don't Let Your Babies Grow Up To Be Cowboys.

"That was a real dick thing to do, Dad," he finally said.

"I totally agree," Mike said making no apology.

"But at the same time, if my best friend screwed my girlfriend and got her pregnant, I think I'd go a little crazy too."

"It was the biggest surprise of my life, that's for sure," Mike said.

"And to top it off, your boy ends up being a half-nigger."

"Please don't say that. I hate that word," Mike said. "God knows, you actually have the right to say it, but…"

"I was just being a jackass, Dad. Hey, I think I see a Whataburger."

"Copy," Mike said turning the truck into the parking lot.

Five minutes later, father and son were opening wide for a huge hamburger, rings, and milk shakes; vanilla for Mike, strawberry for Trey. "So I guess I need to tell you the rest of the story," Mike said with a mouth full of burger.

"Yeah. You don't ever talk about the war stuff much," Trey said. Mike nodded and swallowed. His Viet Nam experience might be mild compared to some, but it was still nightmare fodder for him.

Mike arrived in Saigon in September 1962. He was stationed at Long Bing Army Base and given the assignment of liaison officer with the airmen stationed at Tan Son Nhut Air Base. These corpsmen included dental students whose main function was identifying remains of soldiers. Although not the massive onslaught of bodies that would overwhelm the facility in 1968 after the Tet Offensive, it was nonetheless a shockingly chilling assignment that Mike still struggled with. Most of his work was administrative, but at times, he was called on to assist within the mortuary area. The large area contained twenty embalming tables. The perimeter of the mortuary was concealed from the regular base by eight-foot wooden walls.

Mike's very first day, he was taken on a tour of the facility. Airman Norm Van Houser served as tour guide.

"The guys come in here in the bags. We first go through all their property. Have to check and make sure nothing goes home that could embarrass families or the military.

"Like what?" Mike asked.

"Letters to lovers, photos of Bui Doi, you know, half-gook children. Sometimes there are porno mags or even naked photos of themselves they planned to send home. Drugs, lots of drugs," Van Houser said.

Mike was taken to the embalming tables. Norm unzipped one of the bags and a 20-year old soldier was inside with a massive chest wound. His left hand was also missing. Norm pulled the zipper down further and a huge gout of blood rested in the cavity where his genitals used to be, Mike's head began to swim. The next bag he opened contained a body with no head at all. A neck with ragged flesh was all that appeared as the zipper was lowered. Then as Norm unzipped further, half a head, mostly skull was propped between the soldier's legs, maggots squirmed it the open mouth. Mike ran for the nearest bucket and vomited.

Now a first lieutenant, Mike effectively ran the administrative portion of the camp mortuary, managing the corpsman dental students as well as some air force personnel in joint command. He settled into his work.

"That sounds both horrible and boring," Trey said.

"Pretty much sums it up. The days when I had to be involved in any of the mortuary work was terrible. It just kept getting worse too because eventually…"

"Someone was going to turn up that you knew?" Trey asked.

"Exactly.

"It took Carl about three months to show up. It was after a long shift and I was at a local bar called "We Try Harder." There were lots of Vietnamese girls there, hookers mostly. They would sit and drink with the GI's and the bartender would serve them this stuff called Saigon Tea. It was basically Kool-Aid but it kept the girls from getting drunk so they could control the shots better. The MP's liked it too because there was a lot less trouble that way. But still, plenty of guys hooked up with the whores and lots of them fathered children there. Anyway, I'm sitting there having a drink and reading a week-old newspaper when I hear this British accent speaking to me.

'Lieutenant Wilberforth Kumquat reporting for duty, Sir,' he says. I look up and Carl is standing in front of me with that huge grin of his acting like I would be so happy to see him. I took one look at him and lunged for his neck. Luckily, there were some MPs in the bar and they held me back. I was so furious, I just turned around and left even though I didn't know what to do. I jumped in a jeep and as I took off, this duffel bag sails into the back seat and Carl leaps onto the speeding jeep. I throw on the brake but he just looks at me saying, 'Sooner or later, you and me are gonna talk.' So I ended up driving to another bar a mile away and went inside with him.

"Did y'all fight more," Trey said.

"No. I think I called him about every cuss word in the book, as nasty as I could think of, but it just all seemed pointless. The truth was, I was lonely and scared and seeing him was the best thing that had happened to me since I arrived. He brought me a ton of photos of your mom and sister. And then he pulled out these photos of you walking and I just broke down and bawled. They were color photos and your eyes just sparkled so blue in them, I just fell apart. It finally started dawning on me what I had left behind."

"What did he say? I mean, did he try and explain what happened," Trey asked.

"He did. I mean, he cried and said he was so sorry like a million times. I tried to pick more fights with him, saying how he had always wanted to fuck…sorry, sleep with your mom.

"Dad, it's okay. I'm old enough to know about 'fuck.'"

"Yeah, I suppose you are. Well, he admitted he had always had a boner for your mom, at least somewhat. And that the moment she acted the least little bit like she wanted him, he just jumped at the chance. Of course, me being such a fucking asshole to your mom with the girl giving me the … um …"

"Bee-Jer?" Trey offered.

"Yeah," Mike laughed.

"So we spent the night talking and crying. By the time the bar closed a couple other MP's brought us back to the barracks. Since I was an officer, I had my own quarters with a real bed. We just crashed there like back in college days. The next day, my head was pounding but my heart was a little lighter. I wanted to get hold of you mother, but calling home back then was hard and a telegram, I was afraid if she saw one of those she would think I was dead."

"Whoa, that's right"

"So I just started writing letters. It was kind of therapeutic and eventually we made it through all the shit and it was okay. I mean, I was still really pissed at what they had done and frustrated that my first son wasn't technically biologically my boy. But being away from you and sorting out my feelings, I came around to understand that it really didn't matter if it was my sperm or Carl's that kick-started you. I was still going to be your father no matter what."

Trey looked at his dad and smiled. Mike reached out and grabbed his hand. "And that has never changed, buddy. I know I have been a bastard with you sometimes, way too hard and quick to judge. I know it's all wound up in all the hurt and crap that surrounded how you got here. But at the end of the day, your mom was so hurt and damaged by what I did, she went to find comfort from someone else she really loved and cared for."

"Did Carl ever act like he wanted me to be his?" Trey asked.

"Not like that. I mean, he made it clear from the get-go that your mom and I would always be your parents, that he couldn't do it nor did he feel like he should. But that being said, Oh my God, Trey, he has been watching you and caring about you your whole life. It has bound us all together in this inseparable bond, which is why this whole disappearance, kidnapping, or worse thing is about to kill me."

Mike turned off Hwy 67 and found the broke-down produce truck. The driver was in a big hurry and took no time at all transferring all the boxes, especially with Mike and Trey helping. Soon, they were back on the road and headed back to the grocery store. The roads seemed less slippery now as Mike started the truck. He looked over at Trey and asked, "You think you can handle the stick? Get us back in one piece?"

The boy smiled and nodded. "Sure I can." Mike stepped into the middle of the van and let Trey scoot over into the driver's seat. He popped the truck into first gear and eased off the clutch and they moved out onto the highway. Mike smiled and rubbed the back of Trey's neck. The kid had always been a fast learner with things like this, just like football. He remembered how he had tried to teach Teppy, finally just giving up.

"So Dad, tell me some more about the real war, not just taking care of the gross dead soldiers."

Mike smiled. "Sure, well, let's see. First in November, President Kennedy was assassinated. That was devastating to all of us over there, especially Carl. He broke down and cried like a baby, we all kind of did. He was this great hope for a new world, especially to young guys like us. We saw in him all the hopes for a future without all this hate like Cowhill has. But all that seemed to just disappear when he died. About a year later, Carl and I got reassigned to a new base, Camp Holloway. It was this helicopter base up in the mountains near a place called Pleku. It got built after the North Vietnamese Navy torpedoed these boats in the Gulf of Tonkin. President Johnson was furious and wanted to start kicking ass right away, but there was the election in 1964. He had become president when Kennedy was shot but this was his chance to be elected to the office for real. It was a pussy thing to do, but every president has acted like that during elections."

"What was the camp like?" Trey asked doing the windshield wipe off with the sleeve of his coat.

"It was actually good. New construction, the land we were on was flat and pretty. Not jungle like you saw on TV. It was more like the Great Plains, wide open skies, not nearly as hot and sticky. We had USO shows all the time. Ann Margaret came once. The guys went crazy over her. General Westmorland came too. In our down time we played baseball. There was a great bar on base called the Dragon Den Bar, the whole side of the Quonset building was a big dragon head that you walked inside the mouth to get in. Carl and I were in charge of the inventory for the munitions. We were together night and day. Sometimes, it seemed like we were almost a married couple. We fought and made up and laughed just like your mom and I did."

"You guys have as much sex?" Trey said with his wicked sideways grin.

"Smart ass," Mike said. "Even that was a little easier with someone around you could commiserate with. And we saw so many guys with the Clap or Syphilis, there was no way in hell I was going to hook up with one of those girls. Rosie Palm and her five brothers was just fine," Mike said making a jerk-off motion with his hand.

"So somewhere along the way, the North Vietnamese and the Russians tried to patch their problems up and made this secret plan to hit a US Base and make a statement. The VC had been carrying out small raids at places and no one was doing jack shit. So there we were, about 400 guys in the US Army 52nd Combat Aviation Battalion, just taking it easy, doing our job and thinking we were all fine. We were surrounded by a mile of this concertina wire. You know what that is?"

"Yeah, that slinky looking wire on top of fences like on Hogan's Heroes," Trey said.

"Jesus, what a terrible comparison. Hold it buddy, I am about to piss my pants."

"I know, me too."

"Should we just pull over?" Mike asked.

"It's pouring now. We'll get soaked. Look, I think that Gulf Station is open." Trey signaled and pulled into the service station. The guys ran for the bathroom, thankful it was open, filthy as it was.

"It's just a one-holer, Dad," Travis said with his pants already opened up.

"Go for it," Mike said turning to the sink in front of him and pulling his dick out and exhaling.

"That looks more like something me or Travis would do," Trey grinned finishing up.

"Hey, don't forget to wash your hands," Mike said still pissing into the grimy sink offering to rinse Trey's hands.

"Oo sick, Dad," Travis said laughing. They ran back to the van and took off again with Trey still at the wheel. Mike continued.

"Anyway, on February 6, the Viet Cong soldiers, about 300 of them, split into two divisions. One went for the wire, slowly crawling through it at night cutting it and making a way for the soldiers to come in. The other set up a perimeter to keep reinforcements out and to take out any soldiers that made a run for it. Basically, they set a mousetrap and waited for it to snap. Then a little before 2:00 AM, Oh God, all hell broke loose. The VC opened fire with their AK-47's and just began to light the place up. Me and Carl were sleeping and suddenly, the air is just whizzing with bullets. Windows are shattering and glass was cutting us to ribbons. We run out of the barracks in our skivvies like everyone else. Guys in boots and underwear and guns trying to figure out what the hell was going on."

"Holy shit," Trey said.

"Then as we are getting ripped up by the guns, the other division set off these mortars on the airfield, blowing the helicopters and other aircraft all to shit. It was like the middle of hell. Gasoline and oil were on fire and raining down on us. Buildings were in flames. Guys were wounded left and right, bullets ripping through everyone. Carl and I started running around the mess hall following two of our good buddies and right in front of us, their heads just exploded, the brains and blood just covering our faces, going up our noses and in our mouths. Carl grabbed me and we took of another direction. We could feel the bullets hitting the ground near our feet or whizzing overhead. Finally we ran back toward some of the burning buildings looking for some cover and ran headlong into this VC boy. He couldn't have been more than sixteen I think. He took one look at Carl and fired hitting him in the shoulder, knocking him down. And just like the hand of God came down, his firearm jammed. I was totally out of bullets and had left my weapon behind, hoping to find another one as we ran by fallen guys. I had kept my bayonet though. When I saw Carl fall, I just went crazy. I ran straight at the boy and I knocked him down. We started fighting. He was really strong for this little guy, but in the end, I was just bigger. I pinned him down with my knees and put the bayonet at his throat and I just pushed it in. I pushed it in slow so that the blood pooled up in his neck at first and then I laid into it and stuck him all the way through, nailing him to the ground. He was still alive, the blood bubbling up in his mouth, his eyes wide, flailing all around. I saw Mitch Carlson laying nearby, half his face blown away. I grabbed his side arm and came back and stuck the gun in the guy's mouth and fired. I must have put a dozen bullets in him. Carl pulled me back and took the gun away from me. That was when I noticed that I had two bullets in me as well; one in my thigh and one in my bicep."

"I've always seen your scars. You never told us about them," Trey said soberly.

"Who wants to remember that shit?" Mike said. "I can still see that kid in my dreams today. It doesn't really go away." It was Trey's turn to reach over and grip the back of his dad's neck.

"I'm so glad you made it out, Dad. You and Carl both."

Mike patted his hand and smiled. "We got sent to an army hospital in Japan. Luckily for us, the real bad part of the war hadn't started and we got discharged. Got the Purple Heart and all that. All in all it was a small battle. Only eight US soldiers died, probably more than 175 were wounded. It was such a cluster fuck for the army. They really got caught with their pants down. Johnson ordered an immediate attack and did this Operation Flaming Dart campaign that started bombing the North."

"So how many enemy guys died?" Trey asked.

Mike looked down in his lap. "Just one. That boy I killed."

"He was still a soldier, Dad. You had to defend yourself and Carl."

"Oh I know. But it really doesn't make it that much easier when you are sliding a blade into a boy's throat.

The van turned into Cowhill and made the way to the grocery store. They were met there by Kevin Montoya who helped them unload in a hurry and wished them goodnight. Mike and Trey got back in the Vista Cruiser, Mike tossing Trey the keys as he did. Trey turned out of the parking lot and up Pecan Street back toward home. The rain had stopped and the trip was fast back to Maple Street. As the got out of the car, Trey handed the keys back and stopped on the bottom step of the front porch.

"You know what's funny, Dad?" Trey asked.

"What's that?"

"I find out that my Dad isn't my dad. This other guy is. None of your, DNA, or whatever it's called, is in me. And yet I feel closer to you now than ever."

Mike pulled the big boy into his arms and gripped him tight.

"You have always been my son, Trey. Now that all this is out in the open, maybe I can really be your Dad.

46 Angie

Angie stood in front of the full length mirror on the back of her bedroom door and stared at her reflection. The floor was full of clothes she had tried on and then took off. The radio was playing Pablo Cruise "Love will find a way." Through the tears in her eyes, she wasn't so sure that was going to be true. She looked out the window and saw the wind blowing the last of the leaves off the pecan and sycamore trees in the neighborhood. It might have been late November but it felt like the middle of summer in her room. She was so hot.

She unfastened her bra that wasn't fitting anyway and threw it on the pile of clothes. She looked at her breasts, round and swollen. She rubbed her hands against them and stiffened at the soreness and pain. She ran her hands down to her belly, rounded and now protruding noticeably from her black bikini briefs. As she held her hands on her stomach, the quickening came again and she felt the fluttering and moving even more now.

So far, she had managed to conceal everything from her family and even from Trey. For some reason he had been more understanding and kept more of a distance. In fact, they had only made love once since that day up in the tree house. It had been a few days after Trey's big ball game. She was supposed to be staying over at Susan Yoder's house, but she had left around 10:00 PM telling Susan she wasn't feeling good, which was true, and was going to walk home. She had climbed up into the tree house and was not surprised to find Trey there. She had mentioned she might be able to stop by since she was going to be out for the night. Her daddy had been watching her like a hawk lately.

She and Trey had kissed and made out for so long, her lips and face felt swollen. They tugged each other's clothes off and she remembered she had winced as Trey had kissed and fondled her breasts. She had been surprised to see Trey fish out a Trojan from his discarded jeans pocket and slide it on before sliding inside her. He had given up on those before, but he seemed noticeably restrained, almost gentle. Their orgasm was still a shattering event and afterwards, Trey cursed throwing the ruined condom against the wall of the tree house.

"Those things suck ass," he muttered.

"Don't worry," she had told him. "I don't mind."

Trey had flopped back down beside her and took her in his arms. With an oddly deep and worried look, Trey began to recount the story that he and his brothers and Emily had shared; about the light and all the strange things that had happened since. He patiently answered her questions, especially about the exponential increase to the powers when the kids joined together. She wasn't real sure she understood all he was saying but she did know this: sex with Trey was the best thing she had ever felt. So much better than the stupid, brief, unsatisfying first attempts she had had with that boy from Farmersville. She hadn't even liked him. She was just tired of pretending with other, older girls she knew what they were talking about so she just found a boy and got the whole first time thing out of the way. She knew it was a slutty thing to do, but isn't that what a redneck girl like her was expected to do? The fool was hopeless and had lasted all of fifteen seconds once he was inside. It had been uncomfortable and emotionless, but it did what she wanted it to do.

And then that night when her uncle surprised her out in the shed behind the house. She had gone out there to put away her bicycle and he came up behind her. He grabbed her, spun her around and clamped his mouth to hers, forcing his tongue inside her mouth. She pushed at him, clawed at his face but he weighed almost 300 pounds and was six foot five. She could still taste the sour whiskey breath in her mouth. He had forced her down on the feed sacks thrown in a corner, ripping at her shorts and panties until they were torn off. His weight on her was excruciating, like an elephant had sat on her chest. He spit into his hand and then forced his monstrous cock inside her. He pumped and pumped. Then he pulled out and forced himself back in again, this time not in her vagina. She cried out but his hand was like a vice around her mouth, cutting off her breath with her screams. Luckily, he was too excited to last long and soon was hauling his bulk up off of her, muttering all the while what a nasty whore she was.

After that, she wondered if she would ever let someone near her again. But then she saw Trey and she knew he was special. She loved his smooth tan skin, his big arms and hands, those blue-green eyes that looked so strange in his dark face, like electric eyes. But it was his touch, so gentle and kind; his soft kisses and sweet words. It healed her heart in a way she didn't think possible. And when she saw him naked for the first time, she had become wet instantly as she saw all of him; so large and manly.

"So you see, since we didn't use the rubber, it could mean you might get pregnant. And since we are sort of both all juiced up on this weird power, it might happen easier than normal or something." Trey had explained. Even as he told her then, she knew. She had known by the next morning something was different in her body. She hadn't had a period since then and now as she looked in the mirror, the tears streamed down her cheeks.

She wasn't scared of being pregnant. The idea that she was carrying Trey's baby was actually wonderful to her. She didn't want to lose him for any reason although she had always feared he would see her for all her redneck commonness and send her packing. No, her fear was her daddy. Her mother might get mad and even call her a common whore, which was pretty funny considering she had been all of fourteen when she had her older brother, Jerry. Noreen and Buck Matlock had a shotgun wedding like half of the white trash in Cowhill. But sometimes, even white trash had dreams their children would rise above their humble beginnings.

Angie had first learned how much trouble being with Trey could be when she thought back to the day her daddy had caught them on the couch. Her dad had chased her through the house with a belt, slapping at her, hitting her everywhere he could. Her mother had actually intervened and threw herself in front of the belt, getting a thick welt across the face in the process.

"Stop it Buck, you are gonna kill her," Noreen had warned holding him off.

"I don't care. The little whore done gone too far this time, hooking up with a nigger half-breed bastard to boot. You filthy little bitch," he had screeched at her. "My brother, Lonnie had the right size-up of you."

Now as she thought about the realities of what it would mean to be discovered pregnant with Trey's baby, she almost felt faint. Everything was just so confused and happening so fast. How could she already be showing like this, she wondered? Unless there was more than one baby? The thought was so chilling she wrapped her arms around herself. She found a dress near the back of her closet, a high-waisted peasant dress that hugged her breasts tight and gave her plenty of room in the belly. It was far too cold now for this dress she figured, but she thought she might be able to wear a turtleneck underneath it. Maybe it would work. She was going to try and stop in at the local Salvation Army store and see if she could find some other loose tops and maybe some pants with more room.

She squeezed into her largest jeans using the dress as a top. She was able to zip the jeans up halfway and tuck them inside the waistband. With the skirt of the dress, no one can tell. Maybe I will just start a new fashion she thought foolishly. She began to brush out her hair and then braided into two ponytails.

Angie looked down the hall and saw that the coast was clear. She picked up the phone and called. She waited for the phone call to be answered and whispered a thank you when Trey answered.

"I really need to talk to you today" she said.

"Okay, you mean at school. We can probably duck into an empty classroom. Is that alright?"

School was the last place in the world she wanted to be but it seemed far easier than trying to work out some other plan. "Sure. I'll see you there. Second period. Meet you in the Home Ec sewing lab."

As she finished dressing, Toy Benton stood behind the large hedge and continued to gaze in Angie's window. He had seen her standing naked in front of her mirror and even he could tell the girl was knocked-up. He had pulled out and pleasured himself against the faded grey siding of the house as he watched the girl stroke her breasts in the mirror. A sly smirk crept across his face as he shook his dick off and zipped up. He couldn't wait to tell the guys about this.

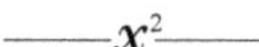

Trey and Angie sat in the dark in the sewing lab on an old sofa in the back of the room. They held hands, not talking. Angie's face was wet and swollen. Her eyes so puffy she could barely see out of them. Trey sat stunned, the blood drained from his face as he saw his future and his life leak out of the rip that just had been torn in his plans. He wiped his nose on his sleeve but the tears kept welling in his eyes.

He leaned over and put his forehead against Angie's letting the images and emotions wash over them both. He poured his thoughts into her like a thirsty man grabbing for a water bucket. Angie saw it all once again. The lights Trey had seen. The day her father had found them on the couch. Mike McGee flying through the screen porch. She saw random flashes of Trey being a classic dick with his brothers and his parents. She saw Trey on the football field. She saw them making love in the tree house. She saw the images of Carl Washington and Trey's mom again. She watched Trey and Theo in the hot tub. She saw Trey and Mr. McGee driving to Rockwall, Mike opening up to Trey in a way he never had before. He held nothing back, he poured it all into her and pulled back looking at her with pained eyes, apprehension and fear.

"I just want you to know what you are getting with me. I am a fucking mess. But I won't leave you on your own." He placed his hand on Angie's belly and felt the baby roll and kick as he did. His eyes grew wide and he smiled. "Holy shit," he said. "I will do whatever you want. If this is too much for you, we can go find a clinic to deal with it."

"It's way too late for that, Trey. And I wouldn't do it anyway," Angie said.

"Good. I don't want you to," Trey said hugging her close. She laid her head on his shoulder as he gripped her tightly to his side. "I know it sounds like a bad idea, but we are going to have to tell someone about this and soon. I don't know how you have kept it secret for so long, but that time is pretty much over. Do you think you could trust your mom?"

Angie looked at him and shook her head, Trey knew she was right. "I hate to say it, but we probably are stuck with telling your parents. Either that or just running away and that doesn't sound like a good plan."

"No. If we were older with jobs and all that, it would be different. We are just too young. It's so fucked up. Just when my dad and I are finally connecting with each other, I go and do this. He's going to hate me."

Angie kissed Trey softly on the lips. "If there's one thing for sure I know, it's that your dad loves you like crazy. Both of your dads for that matter. You are so lucky to have that kind of family. I'd do anything for that," she said, tears leaking from her eyes again.

Trey hugged Angie close again. "It's so unfair. You like have this stupid reputation of being some slut and you've hardly done anything. Half the girls in the school have screwed around a bunch more. I've seen what all happened to you. One of these days, I'm going to kill your uncle, I swear to God."

Trey checked his watch. They only had ten minutes left of their off period. Like a bolt from above, he sat up, dried off his face and turned to face Angie, holding her by the shoulders. He looked intently into her eyes. *Please have a plan*, she thought.

"Alright. This is a hard thing for us, but it's also a great thing. I love you, Angie. I am not going to let this baby derail our whole life. Plenty of people our age have had kids. I am going to get a scholarship and go to college to play football. You can come with me and we can live in married student housing with the baby. I can work some on the side. You can go to school too if you want. I know we will have to tell my parents and I bet they will help us too, however they can. As long as we stick together, we will be okay." Angie hugged him tightly.

"The hardest part of this is how to keep you safe and away from your crazy-ass dad. Now that the word is out about Carl being my real dad, he is going to be madder than ever for us to be together. So, let's go hang out with the group out at the bridge this weekend. Maybe this power we have, maybe we will get an answer out there. If not, then we go tell my parents and we get some help. Okay?"

"Okay. I trust you, Trey," Angie said. "God, my face must look like a nightmare."

He looked at her and smiled. "Maybe not your best look," he said smiling. She hit him and dug around in her purse for some makeup.

"Go ahead and go. I will be fine. Just going to try and fix my face a bit. See you later, Trey. I love you," she said touching his face.

He held her hand on his face and kissed her swollen cheek. "Backatcha, baby."

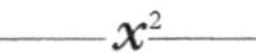

Trey left the sewing lab and stopped by his locker. He spun the lock and opened it. A foul stench filled his nose. A sack full of cat shit fell out and onto his shoes before he could hop out of the way. There were two new additions to his locker as well: a color centerfold from some magazine of an older black man being orally serviced by a younger black guy with a caption written in black marker that read "Daddy feeds Trey his night time snack." The other was a pencil drawing of a lynched Negro man with the caption "Trey McGee Washington's Senior Portrait.

The bell rang and the halls were crowded with students who instantly began to gasp and retch at the stink. Greg Benton and Cal Matlock pointed at Trey and began hooting and laughing.

"Smells like Norton Holler to me," Greg said.

Claudia Davis, one of the black girls on the basketball team who stood about six foot hauled off and slapped the shit out of Greg Benton. Marvin Jones, one of the Tiger defensive stars punched Cal Matlock so hard in the stomach he banged his head against the lockers. More punches were thrown. Trey tried to push Marvin away from the crowd of redneck white boys that had thrown down their books and began to shove and kick the boy. Mr. Baker and Mr. Scott flew out of the Teacher's Lounge and began to try and pull the boys and girls apart. In the melee, someone punched Mr. Baker, breaking his glasses.

Ten minutes later, Trey was sitting in the principal's office being grilled as to what happened. Mr. Jones had to open his window to try and make the stink of the cat shit on Trey's shoes less disgusting. Mike McGee sat on the window ledge, his arms folded tightly against his chest.

"I know you didn't have anything to do with this, Trey. But you are going to probably have some rough days here in the near future. These kids come from very narrow-minded families that can't deal with things like a multiracial student. It probably doesn't make it any easier that you also happen to be pretty popular with the kids. I know it's not fair, and I will do my best to keep this stuff from happening, but you have to be prepared to deal with a little bit of this."

Trey looked up, his jaw set in a rigid line. "I can handle people making fun of me. I can handle the practical jokes too. But if they throw a punch at me or try to hurt me, I will fight back and I don't need to tell you, I won't hold back either."

"Well, you need to be careful about that kind of talk," Mr. Jones began.

"Actually, they need to be careful. And next time, maybe some of those fools that caused the trouble need to be in here, not just me."

"I will be talking to them too."

Mike McGee stood up and came close to the principal's desk. "If I hear that Marvin or Claudia or any of the black kids are getting in more trouble than any of those redneck idiots, I will come down on you like a ton of bricks. You hear me?"

"Are you threatening me?" Charlie Jones said standing up and leaning in toward Mike.

"It's not a threat. You can count on it. Come on Trey, let's get out of here. This place smells worse than that cat shit."

Mike McGee marched Trey out of the school and told him to get in the car, but before he did, Mike reached down and grabbed Trey's leather Converse and pulled them off and threw them on the front porch of the school, smacking the glass and leaving a big size 13 foot print of cat shit on the window. Mike roared off away from the school. Trey was sitting in his seat, not quite knowing what to do or say. Mike drove down to Park Street and turned toward home. He reached over and gripped Trey's arm. "I'm really sorry, buddy. Kids can be little shits sometimes."

"I'm okay, Dad. Those guys are just redneck assholes like their parents. They don't know better, not that it's an excuse."

"Those are the same fools that will stand up a cheer and act like they had something to do with a football victory on Friday night. They will be just fine with you then." Mike said.

"Exactly. It's okay, Dad. All of the people at school that I care about don't give a crap about any of this. And the ones that do mean nothing to me. I'll be damned if I'm going to let them beat me down." Mike pulled Trey's head over and kissed the top of it. "I am so damn proud of you, Trey," he said. "I know. Thanks, Dad." Trey couldn't help but wonder if he would feel the same once he told them about Angie and the baby. Part of him was pretty sure he wouldn't be getting kisses on the head that day. "Um, my car is back at school."

"Goddamn it," Mike muttered closing his eyes in exasperation. "Can we just get it tomorrow or later tonight?" Troy nodded yes.

47 George

George and the other eighth graders piled into Pete Clark's van that Trey had parked over on Caddo Street. It had taken some diplomacy worthy of Jimmy Carter to pull this off. For the most part, George, Emily and Travis had been able to be straight with their parents about a band "bonfire." Mike smelled a rat when the kids said that Trey was taking them until they explained other members of the high school football team were invited too.

What they couldn't come up with a convincing story for was why in the heck Andy was invited. So finally, they resorted to the tried and true "divide and conquer" storyline. Andy tells his parents he is going to this friend Justin's house for the night. Andy tells Justin that he will let him borrow his Atari 'Night Driver' game for the next month if he will cover for him and tell his parents he is going over to Seth's house because Seth invited Andy over and they are all going to hang out. Travis told his parents he would walk Andy over to Justin's house, but actually they headed to Pete Clark's and climbed in the big van. Andy officially thought this was the best night of his life getting to hang with older kids and finally be included in something.

Trey maneuvered the big GMC van through the streets of Cowhill. It was a big conversion van with a big bench seat up front, two bucket seats behind that, and a big water bed in the back where most of the kids crowded in. Trey made all the kids take off their shoes before they crawled on the bed per Pete's instructions. Paul had carpeted the floor, sides, and ceiling of the van in lime green shag carpet. It was the coolest van in town.

Trey pushed in the cassette tape and "Come Sail Away" by Styx blared through the impressive speakers. The kids chatted and laughed as they rode through town and out Hwy 24 toward Scatter Branch. They drove past the old drive-in where Trey and Paul had watched XXX movies, on toward Greenville. The Scatter Branch area was only about ten minutes from downtown Cowhill but it seemed much farther away. It had rained earlier in the week but they had gotten lucky and tonight was cold but clear. Trey kept talking about how weird it seemed to not be at a football game. George was just enjoying the break. They had been working like dogs. But all the chances, hard work, and help from the college students had paid off. Yesterday in Longview, CHS had received straight 1st division rankings from the judges, bringing home the first trophy for the band in four years. The performance had been spectacular, and since it not only was vastly different from the military bands but also expertly performed, with dynamic modern music, the crowd went wild. When the scores were announced, many of the girls in band started bawling and the guys were high fiving and hugging. The bus ride home had been wonderful as well since there was plenty of time to make out.

George officially popped his cherry in regards to kissing in public. The fact that it was with Mary was utterly scandalous, but in a dark bus filled with dozens and dozens of couples sucking face, it didn't seem to garner the attention he thought it might. Mary had been shy at first, which was funny considering she had always been the one who started everything. But then George remembered all that she had just been through and was amazed she would let a boy touch her at all. But like she said, George was different. She said he felt safe and she longed for someone to touch her these days to try and take away the other memories. She had been to some counseling sessions where the woman leading her session basically told her all men were potential rapists and she would probably never be free from her memories. She even suggested she might want to explore the possibility of a lesbian relationship. That made Mary so mad she told her mother she would not go back. She figured some girls might be ruined for life, but she wasn't going to be one of them. In fact, since going to church with the other kids and having them lay their hands on her, she had started to feel so much better. Her memories were healing and she felt more happy and positive. She was hoping the big group getting together this weekend might heal her even more and she had even talked with George on the phone about it.

Her kisses had been intoxicating to George. *She knew what she was doing,* he thought, and he loved the feeling of her lips and tongue on and in his mouth. George imagined what it would be like to slide his hand on her breasts or in between her legs. At one point, they were kissing and rubbing against each other and as Mary's hand had grazed his erection, he blew his nut in his shorts. He managed to keep that bit of information to himself for now. But these days, could anything really remain secret for long? He wondered.

In the middle of the make out sessions, for some inexplicable reason, Don and Doug had started chanting the 'Ooga-Chaka' line from Blue Suede's "Hooked on a Feeling." Soon, the entire band was chanting along and then Damon Reed started singing the verse and the bus reverberated with the band members singing along full voice. It was one of those magical, team-building moments that went along with the amazing season the band had.

Angie sat on the bench seat beside Trey. George noticed she was wearing his odd poncho that looked more like a tent. He normally didn't pay attention to what girls wore unless it showed off their body. But that big top was definitely strange, especially when Angie usually enjoyed showing off her curves. Travis and Emily were curled up on the water bed along with Vince and Sarah. Doug and Don sat in the bucket seats behind Trey talking about Fantasy Island. Andy was sitting in the front beside Angie and turned around to scream, "Da plane, da plane."

"Knock it off, Tattoo, or I'll kick your ass," Trey said.

Trey had convinced all the group that a bonfire on the edge of the Sulphur River was 100 percent legal and safe. He was certain that the public had a right to stay within 200 feet of the river and since the road leading to it was still a public road, they were within their perfect right to go see the remnants of Green Light Bridge. George wasn't as convinced as some of the others. His Dad had told horror stories about JL Martin for years. The man was notoriously difficult and certainly would think that was his land, but he hoped Trey was right. They needed to get out there and see the place and see what would happen when they did.

Trey turned off on McLeod Road and navigated the tight curves and drove slowly toward the rusted gate that now lay in two pieces on either side of the overgrown brushy road. Trey switched off the lights which made everyone instantly get quiet and look out the windows. The moon was out and soon the bits of white gravel glowed in a speckled path in front of them hidden in places by grass, branches, and leaves. Trey eased the van forward and drove down the decrepit road very slowly. Twice, he stopped and got out to move branches that had fallen on the road. He turned the dome light off in the van so the light wouldn't flash when he got out. George had to admire Trey's leadership, strength, and cool head. This was the Trey that was a football star, not the one who dunked him in the pool or sat on his head and farted.

Trey finally rolled to a stop about two miles down the back road. There was a fairly large flattened down area, probably made by dozens of other vehicles that had made the trip out to the bridge. He cut the motor and the group still sat in silence.

"Damn, you all are way too serious or something. Look, try not to use your flashlights or anything. Let's just get out and let our eyes get used to the moonlight. We will make sure the coast is clear and all and then we can build our fire. Stick together and watch where you step 'cause I really don't want one of you douche bags falling in the river tonight, Trey said.

The kids climbed out of the van and followed Trey and Angie a bit further down a rutted path. They all began to pull gloves and stocking caps out of their pockets as the wind picked up. The sky was ablaze with stars even on a night with the full moon. Every branch they stepped on sounded like a gunshot to George. It was like a herd of cows moving along in the night they were so loud. They heard sharp snap of a car door behind them and wheeled around.

"Who's there," Vince said stupidly.

"Hey kids, it's just me and Tim," Jack Tanner said in his low voice moving quietly through the brush, unlike the way the kids had sounded. Tim pulled up beside him pulling his jacket on and pulling a ball cap lower down on his head.

"It's colder than a witch's…" Tim began before remembering he was with a bunch of kids.

"Shit?" Doug offered. Nervous giggles filled the air.

"Yeah," Tim said. "Got us a comedian here I see."

Jack and Tim moved to the front of the line and the kids followed in single file toward the slow, gurgling sound of the sluggish river. George could feel his heart beating so loud he knew it would leap out of his chest. In a hushed voice, Mary Washington began the chant.

> Red light … yellow light …
>   Green Light Bridge
> Just down the hill from
>   Scatter Branch ridge
> Devil's on the switch, change
>   the road to red
> Better be green or you'll end up dead

The party pulled up on the edge of the river. In front of them stretched rotting boards and large buttresses that stretched out toward the darkness and disappeared into a light mist that hung heavy in the air. On the far side of the river, a tall pole stood like a sentinel. The remains of the long forgotten signal light hung loose and twisted in the wind.

"My God," Emily whispered.

The group made a line on the edge of the bridge and continued to stare across. No one spoke. The kids reached out for one another, grasping hands. George took Mary's hand and then slid his other into Jack Tanner's large, calloused hand and felt the man grip it firmly. Tim standing on the other side of Mary held her hand. Andy was standing in between Trey and Travis, his mouth open, his face of mask of fear. After they stood there for a good two minutes, Travis took Emily's hand and moved it to his shoulder. Andy looked at him and Travis moved his small hand to his shoulder as well. Without knowing why, he knelt down and placed his palm on the rotted wooden bridge span.

A low hum and throbbing began to percolate through Travis's hand and into the chain of hands along the opening of the bridge. On the far side of the bridge, the sagging signal creaked again in the wind and then began to glow emerald until the line of men and teenagers perched on the edge of the river glowed phosphorescent green in the dark night air. Travis stood back up and took Emily and Andy's hands again as he took a step forward toward the bridge. When his foot hit the bridge, an arc of power shot through the line, throwing their heads back in a trembling rictus.

The line of people on the edge of the river began to shake in tiny waves, their hands gripped in vise locked clamps. With their eyes closed, they began a shared vision. An unseen hand flipped a switch and a projector of images began to play across their minds. A cold, grey November day came to life. Green light from an electric signal light glowing bright in the foggy day. An ancient Blue Bird school bus lumbering down a muddy road toward the bridge. A 1925 Ford pickup flying up the road on the other side. A slow-motion skid and deafening impact as the two vehicles slammed together. Screams of terror echoed in their heads as the bus full of Nelsonville students slid off the bridge and into the raging torrent of brown water below. The image jumped an even older scene filled their minds. The glow of burning torches filled the darkness of the barn. Three men wearing only golden masks and horns stood before three naked black men, strung up by their arms. A sobbing woman was lashed to a beam on the side. Events of horror played out in front of them ending in blood and gore.

The group on the edge of the river began to rise until their feet no longer touched the edge of the ruined bridge, but hovered several inches above it. As had happened in their dreams again and again, they were pulled by an imperceptible force forward into the dark abyss. Inside George's mind, he screamed 'NO, NO, NO!' The group was pulled forward now dangling over the flowing water far below. As they passed over the yawing chasm, bits of wood, metal and rock flew upward from the river bottom, the river bank, and fields surrounding the river, flying forward fitting together like a primal jigsaw puzzle. Rivets, steel bands, long-ago crumbled timbers, and masonry fitted themselves together under the row of tennis shoes and boots that hovered above as the line of teens and men passed by above.

Even as the group hovered above the reassembling bridge, more images filled their minds. Now Carl Washington hung in the old barn, bleeding and beaten. Black clad men in golden masks, forced themselves inside Mary, tied immobilized over an oak barrel. Chanting, torches, pentagrams on the floor of the barn and carved into Carl's belly. The flash of a blade opening him up, his blood spilling into the basin below. The shaking and green laser lights in the barn, men scattering. Carl and Mary left in a heap of flesh on the barn floor. Mary on her feet walking out of the barn in a daze. Carl somehow crawling, then standing out of the smoke and into the fog of the night, disappearing into the emerald glow of the signal light. From the smoky green haze a voice boomed…"I'm still here, I'm still here. I LIVE!"

Like a projector bulb that popped, the images stopped. The group opened their eyes and saw they were gliding across the river, now two-thirds of the way across the muddy expanse, the ruined bridge somehow reassembling underneath their feet. No one dared to loosen grip as they continued to be pulled to the far side. As they cleared the river bank, their feet touched the soft grass on the far side and they finally began to release each other's hands and tentatively look backwards.

Across the slow moving river, the slivery ribbon of Green Light Bridge lay before them, glowing in the moonlight. The van and pickup rested in the weeds on the far side. The group looked around and saw the dark and cold visage of a great barn over the rise of the next hill and in the further distance, the glow from the large windows of JL Martin's home.

"Son of a bitch," George whispered. Mary moved close to him and he slid his arm around her waist. She was shaking.

"I can't believe I am back here," she whispered. "I don't want to be here."

Jack Tanner came close on the other side of Mary and slid his arm around her shoulders, gripping George's neck in the process. "We're here. Nothing is going to hurt you again, Sweetheart. You're going to be safe."

"I felt my dad. I know he's alive," she said

"We all heard it," George said."

"And saw what those fuckers did to him and you," Tim growled.

Emily spoke. "As amazing as it is to know your dad is alive somewhere…" she began then pointed back toward the newly formed bridge across the expanse."

"And we just floated across the goddamn river," Vince said.

"That was so cool," Don said. "Just like in our dream," clearly enjoying all of this. Doug gripped the boy in a tight embrace, hugging him tight.

"Why are we over here?" Trey asked. "I mean, is there something else we are supposed to find or do? I don't remember anything else from the dream."

Travis looked around at the group. "I think we are just supposed to all be here. I think we will know what to do next when it happens. Should we go up to that barn?"

"We all saw what happened in there. Why don't we just tell the sheriff?" Sarah asked.

"Cause LeRoy Hines is owned by JL. In any other town, the cops would be all over something like this," Jack said with obvious disgust.

George looked up at the sparkling carpet of stars spangled across the cold sky. He could feel the thrum and energy of the place humming in his head making his teeth rattle.

"I think this place wanted us to know Carl is still alive. I don't know where he is but something or someone is telling us he is alive. Whatever made us have these powers is here around this place. I can feel it and I think you all can too; something with this light, this bridge. We all saw the bus and all those kids. This place is so sad, like a concentration camp or something. Whatever it was that was in the lights that night, it ended up here and it has brought us all back together."

"But why?" Emily asked.

Jack spoke. "I don't know that but George is right. The fact that we all aren't here shitting ourselves after floating over a river or watching a bridge just rebuild itself in front of us tells me there is way more to this place than we know. It clearly was a place of tragedy in the past and again just a few weeks ago. I don't know that we are going to find out all the answers tonight, but we were supposed to be here tonight. Whatever this is has brought us all together with the dream and the powers. So I think we just have to be patient and keep in touch and we will figure it out. Maybe we will get a new dream. Maybe we can help find Carl."

"Maybe we get to kick some racist redneck ass," Tim said through clenched teeth. Vince and Trey muttered their assent.

Jack shook his head. "I think before this is all over, that may be exactly what happens. I know we came out here to do a bonfire or something, kids. But I'm thinking this totally unbelievable thing that just happened is kind of hard to top. Maybe we should go back. Y'all could come over to my place and we can make a fire and talk some more about all this. Be pretty comfortable there." Jack turned and looked toward the Martin home still glowing in the darkness. "I don't know if JL would be particularly happy to see all of us down here on his property, especially when he sees that bridge."

"He's going to drop his front teeth," Trey said. "And lose his shit something terrible."

"I don't want to be here when that happens," Angie said quietly.

"Me either," Andy said.

"Okay. We should go back then," Jack said. Part of him wondered when they stepped on the bridge to head back, was it going to disappear or fall apart when they were halfway across. He tried to get that thought out of his mind. He had the distinct feeling the rest of the group was already thinking the same thing. "But right before we go, I was wondering. I know you guys told us about the circle thing the other night when Travis was floating up to the ceiling. And we just saw more of that when we floated across the creek. This place is special; it's like a magnifier for all this power. So, would you all be okay if we just tried on more thing before we left?"

The group of kids looked around at each other and nodded, clearly interested in what Jack was talking about."

"If you need someone else to fly, I'll do it," Andy volunteered.

"Thanks buddy," Jack said rubbing Andy's head and smiling. "But I was wondering if we could make a circle around Tim here and see what happens for him. He could use a little of this alien power and out here, maybe it would make a difference for him."

The group of kids looked puzzled, wondering what all this was about. Finally Vince asked the question on everyone's mind, "What's wrong with Mr. Murphy? Why does he need to get zapped by our powers?"

Jack didn't answer trying to figure out the best way to put it. Instead Tim spoke.

"I've got the ball cancer. They already cut off one of my nuts." Some of the girls gasped and several of the boys involuntarily reached for their crotch, pressing their legs together. "I think Jack here thinks the alien mojo could maybe make the cancer better so I don't have to do all that chemo and crap."

"They cut off one of your balls?" Andy asked before Travis elbowed him hard. "Ow!"

"Yeah. I mean I was asleep in surgery and all that. But it still sucked. I was kind of attached to the guy." The kids giggled.

Jack spoke. "Look, I'm not saying this power is the hand of God or a healing miracle or anything like that. But, I figured, what the hell? If we can use this power to cause a storm or pay back a bully, I thought we might could use it to help someone not be sick."

Emily reached over and grabbed Travis's hand. Travis said, "This is what Emily always said we should do. Let's do it. I believe it can make you better," he said matter of factly.

"So do I. I know it can," George said.

"Me too," Trey said right along with Mary who took George's hand.

The group had soon joined hands with Tim Murphy in the middle standing with his hands in his coat pockets, his eyes closed. The kids stood so one hand was on the shoulder of the person in front of them while their other hand reached toward Tim, making a wheel with spokes that almost connected as they stood around.

George cleared his throat. "Just like we did the other night. Keep it simple. Think "Heal Tim" as clear and hard as you can."

In a soft voice, Andy said, "Can we ask for his ball to grow back?" Several kids chuckled.

"Yeah, Sport. You can," Tim said grinning.

George counted to three and the group touched Tim. The electricity was immediate, surging, arcing through all of them. The group chorus of 'Heal Tim' reverberated around the circle and George could feel the thrum and vibration course through his hands and legs in and through Tim and around the circle. As they continued to touch, the power within them grew immeasurably, ricocheting back and forth around the wheel. George peeked though his closed eyelids and saw that not only had Tim risen up in the air, but the entire group had. They were suspended in midair about five feet above the ground. Tim was floating even higher. His hands were outstretched to the sky, the group now gripping his ankles and feet.

In a blast of light, the mind's eye of the group exploded into a tapestry of galaxies and nebulae. They soared and rocketed through the heavens past stars and fiery worlds and gas giants. They zoomed beside the rings of Saturn and through the moons of Jupiter. They dodged asteroids in the belt between Mars and the blue glimmering earth that shown bright and jewel-like in the inky sky. Past the moon, the group flew over the earth, seeing the continents below them shining golden in the impossibly blue oceans. They flew lower and lower over the land until they soon soared above the county and Cowhill itself came into view. And in a blinding flash of light, far below, they saw themselves out in the backyards, and parks, and lakes staring up into the brilliance.

Then in an instant, the light was gone and George felt a searing pain in his leg as a strong hand was gripping his ankle, pulling him back to earth. He fell to the ground with an oof, the breath knocked out of him. He looked around and the group of kids along with Jack and Tim were lying on the ground surrounded by men, several of them armed. The clear sound of a shotgun shell being locked and loaded cracked the still night air.

"Would someone like to tell me what the hell you are doing on my land doing your devil worship?" JL Martin's gruff voice barked.

The kids scrabbled to their feet and they ran toward Jack and Tim. The men reached out their hands and pushed the kids behind them as they stood between JL and his men and the bank of the river.

"We just came out to see Green Light Bridge," Andy said in a strong voice.

"Is that so? Well Green Light Bridge is on my land and little piss-ants like you aren't welcome. Piss-ants, hippies, queers, half-breeds and nigger lovers."

"Hey, you shut up," George found himself saying.

"You're a racist sack of shit," Jack said

Emily added, "And we know what you did. And you aren't going to get away with it,"

JL fired his shotgun into the night sky and the kids screamed, cowering behind Tim and Jack. "I'm going to politely ask all you scum to shut the fuck up," JL said. "You made a grave error coming out here. This is private property and I have every right to defend myself and my land. Especially from a bunch of faggots, sluts, and darkie renegades. I don't know what kind of satanic cult you are all part of but this is sacred ground. I have every right to make sure your devil kind does not pollute it."

"He's crazy," Vince said with wild eyes bulging out of his head.

JL pointed his shotgun at Vince and fired at his feet, kicking the dirt up three feet in the air. The boy screamed and fell back.

Travis turned to help Vince up and JL fired again, this time even closer to both of the boys' feet.

Trey pushed Angie to the side and lunged at JL. "I'll kill you, you cocksucker," he yelled.

"NOO!" Mary shrieked lifting her hands. A bright green beam of light shot out of the ground somewhere near the edge of the river and caught JL in the chest and hurled him backwards. As the rest of his group turned their shotguns and rifles on the kids, they flung their hands outward toward the men, the ground underneath them crumbled and they fell into a twelve foot deep crater that opened in the earth, dirt and roots, and rocks tumbling in on them.

The group stood stunned looking at the hole and JL Martin slumped to the ground. Finally George shouted, "Let's get the hell out of here!" The group turned and ran full speed back across the newly formed bridge to their vehicles. They loaded up and started the motors, roaring back down the overgrown road and turning north back into Cowhill.

48 Lori

It took the better part of an hour to calm the kids down after they arrived back at Jack's house. Sarah and Vince in particular were inconsolable. They wanted to go home, they wanted their parents, and they wanted to call the police. In the end, George and Travis had gripped them tight and laid their heads against them muttering, "Calm Down," before they finally settled down enough.

Lori was panicked once she saw the state of the kids and demanded that Jack explain what was going on. She threatened to call the police herself if she didn't get some answers. In the end, Jack took a page out of George and Travis's playbook. He took Lori into his arms, laying his head against hers. Tim came over and wrapped up both of his friends into this arms and added his powers to the mix. A few minutes later, Lori stepped back and staggered, falling onto the couch. The group of kids stared at her and she stared back. She looked at Jack and Tim again, clearly overwhelmed. Joey had appeared unnoticed from his bed in teddy bear pajamas and climbed into Lori's lap. As he laid his head against his mother's chest, she hugged him tight and a tear slid down her face as Joey ministered his special kind of grace and sweetness into her. In the end, she looked up and smiled weakly at Jack and around at the group.

"That is the most ridiculous thing I have ever heard of in my whole life. I even know it's true and I don't really believe it." She looked hard at Jack and Tim. "Though this does explain a lot," she said silently evaluating her life and all the strange happenings of the past few months. "Does Candy know?" Tim shook his head. "Well you are going to have to tell her. Just like you did to me," she said flatly. She looked around at the kids. "How many of your parents know?" The group collectively shook their heads no.

"Look, Lori, sweetheart. It's tough for them to tell their parents. It's not the same with us. Let's just let them figure all this out on their own. Honestly, you would be amazed at how great they have been. I mean, they didn't go around using these powers to hurt people or get popular or rich or anything."

George spoke up. "We were saving that for closer to Christmas," he said with his usual snark. Several kids laughed and Lori had to smile.

"Do any of your parents even know where you are?"

The kids all looked at one another sheepishly. "Um, they all sort of know where we are, but not really. It was kind of a bait and switch thing," George finally said.

Lori looked around with pursed lips. "Yeah I remember those little games when I was growing up too. At least you all are here now and safe. I can't believe you took these kids out to that bridge in the middle of the night. And those bastards shot at you!" she said indignantly.

"Well, these kids buried them, literally," Tim said. "It's going to take them a while to dig out and maybe they will think twice about bothering any of us again."

"Do you really think that?" Jack said and Tim had to shake his head.

Lori sighed. "Well, is anybody hungry?" Hands shot into the air and she laughed. "I guess I better get busy."

Thirty minutes later with the help of Angie, Emily, and Doug, the group was sitting around a fire eating crunchy grilled cheese sandwiches, tomato soup and popcorn followed up with some hot cocoa and chocolate peanut butter oatmeal drop cookies.

"You're a great cook, Mrs. Tanner. At least way better than my mom," Vince said with his mouth full.

"That's nice, Vince. I'll make sure to tell her you said so when she comes in for her shampoo and set next week." Vince gulped so hard Sarah had to whack him on the back.

Lori looked around at this group of kids and was overwhelmed at what she felt. There was a palpable care and concern for each other. It extended to Jack and Tim as well. She and Joey were part of this too in their own way. As insane as this whole revelation was, it explained a lot. She involuntarily moved her hand to her belly and felt a quickening there that should be weeks away. But she knew enough about being pregnant to know some things for certain. This baby was a reality and it was strangely farther along than she would have thought possible. With what she had just learned, she wondered how much of this event had spilled over into her life as well?

George and Travis found a couple of guitars over the corner of the room and spent a few minutes tuning the loose strings. Lori tried to remember the last time Jack had picked one up. The group of kids seemed to gather around these two like they were almost leaders of some group. George began the opening guitar line to "Hotel California" and the kids clapped. Soon the group was singing along. Lori was impressed with these boys' guitar skills. When they got to the guitar solos at the end, it was uncanny. In harmony they walked through Joe Walsh's riffs flawlessly. Even on acoustic guitar, it was spectacular. The thought entered her mind that these kids are using these powers to do this. In the end, she thought it was just wonderful no matter what. The boys changed keys and began to play Fleetwood Mac's "Dreams." Emily Moon did her best Stevie Nicks impersonation singing the haunting melody. The group sang along and Lori had the distinct feeling that this song about dreams had taken on some special meaning to this group. Even if these kids were using some of these new found powers, they were still talented. *Maybe that's what this did,* she thought. It took what you were naturally good at and made it that much better. *God knows,* she thought. She and Jack had always been good at making love. Nowadays, they were Olympians and she was loving it more than she could say. Even her ruminative thoughts of Amber were better, filled more with happiness to have known her sweet little girl even for a short time than the hollow emptiness she had lived with for so long.

After the song was over, some of the kids began to talk about school and in particular, ways their school experience or home life had changed since the powers had shown up. Vince had talked about making A's in English class for the first time in his life and how he could read so fast know he actually enjoyed picking up a book. Several of the kids nodded in agreement. Don talked about touching his mom and suddenly, her desire to spend every evening going through a couple of bottles of wine had disappeared. Sarah had a younger sister who couldn't figure out how to ride a bike, but now with a little help from Sarah and her power, the girl was a skilled cyclist.

The kids also laughed and chatted about using their powers to shut down bullies that were picking on kids, encouraged teachers to forego homework, run faster, jump farther, or eavesdrop on parents or friends through walls. Don had also shared how by doing this he learned that his dad was seriously contemplating leaving his family and that he had been having an affair with his secretary for months. The boy had been devastated by the news and decided then and there knowing things like that was not fun like he thought it would be. Several of the kids nodded in agreement, with knowing looks. They began to share more tales from school and home where using the powers had been a mixed bag of good and bad. Lori thought these kids had learned more about life in the past few weeks than she had learned in thirty years.

The group grew a bit quiet and George spoke up. Lori was beginning to like this kid, she thought to herself.

"Um, I'm not trying to be all youth group leader or anything but I was wondering something. Listening to all of us, it's pretty clear that all of our lives have changed because of September 12. I think it's cool that we have used our powers to help people. I also think it's great that we have used them to help ourselves: to get a better grade, or help our parents get along better, or be better at sports. And honestly, I am okay that we also have used them to put bullies in their place, 'cause God, I just hate bullies. I was thinking the other day of this thing my dad always says." George sighed and looked around. "It's probably not that big of a secret that my dad and I have not been very good for a while. Anyway, whenever my dad is watching the news and is mad at the president or government or big business, he always says 'Power corrupts and absolute power corrupts absolutely.' I always just thought that was some bullshit, but lately, I think it's probably true." Several of the group began to nod in agreement.

"All of us have used our powers to either get a bully back or make ourselves look better, only to realize there were some that get hurt along the way, our own version of collateral damage. I really don't like that very much."

In a meek voice, Mary spoke and said, "I think for the most part, we all have tried hard to do good things. But even I have accidently hurt some folks or made them get in trouble when I didn't mean to."

George reached over and held Mary's hand with surprising tenderness that took Lori by surprise. "You know, it's almost Thanksgiving. Back a few years ago, when I was pretty small, we would have to sit at the table for dinner and everyone had to say something they were thankful for before we ate. Back then, I thought it was dumb. Now, I don't," George said looking around the circle of kids, his eyes sparkling as the firelight danced across them. "Most of you know my brother, Fred, died a few years ago. He was always the best at saying what he was really grateful for. With him gone, we don't ever do that anymore in my house. There's just this big hole in our family, this emptiness that never gets filled up..." he trailed off. The fire crackled as the log settled and sent up orange glitter into the chimney. George sighed and continued.

"My granddad gave me these books a few years ago: The Chronicles of Narnia. In the front of the first book he wrote this quote from some old German guy named Meister Eckhart. It said, 'If the only prayer you ever say in your entire life is thank you, it will be enough.' I didn't really get that back then. I think I do now."

"Preach it, brother," Tim said sincerely.

"So I was thinking, maybe tonight would be a good night to go around and say some stuff we are thankful for, 'cause these powers are a gift like we never had before. I guess I'll start since I'm a blabbermouth anyway...I am really grateful for this guy here, my best friend, Travis. He and I have been friends since kindergarten and I can't hardly think of a day I didn't see him or talk to him. He was there for me in a huge way when I lost my brother. He has put up with a lot sometimes to be my friend. He's about the only person who really calls me out on my bullshit and keeps me real. He's the kind of guy who will talk to you on the phone until you fall asleep or let you climb into bed with him when you're afraid and not bust your balls about it. So anyway, I just wanted to say. You are my best friend, Trav and I love you." George reached his hand out and slid his palm across Travis's with a tickle of fingers at the end.

Travis's face was red and his eyes were moist. Lori noticed a couple of other kids brush away a tear from their face. The kids went around the circle saying what they were grateful for and Lori kept smiling and feeling like these kids were more in touch with life and their emotions than she had ever thought about being in junior high school. Sarah Ramirez mentioned how thankful she was for music and the joy it brought to her life. Emily mentioned her mother and how close they were and how she was always there for her.

The boy sitting over by Don Edwards spoke next. Lori had noticed him all night. He was a character for sure. But he seemed sweet and clearly was thriving in this group of kids she had noticed.

"Well, I am thankful for all of you," Doug said. "I know I'm not the easiest person to be around. I have been told even by my own dad that I make it hard for people to like me. God knows he doesn't know what to do with me," the boy began. He was smiling but there was real pain behind his eyes and a sense of true gratitude flowed from his face. "I know I am a bit ridiculous sometimes, part of that is probably to keep people at a distance because I have gotten beaten up pretty bad before, both for real and sometimes just with words." Lori felt her heart practically break for this boy. She wondered how many kids had she been cruel to when she was growing up just because they were different? "Anyway," he continued in his high girlish voice with a bit of attitude and sass, "I just wanted to say thank you for not being judgy like most other people. People always think they know everything about me when in truth almost no one does. So thanks for being the coolest friends I've ever had, especially this guy," with that he leaned over and hugged Don closer. Don just leaned into the boy, seemingly comfortable with this display of affection.

It was Don's turn next. He continued on with what Doug had begun. "Like Doug, I'm just so grateful to be part of a group like this. I have been an outsider most of my life. It's what happens when you wear thick glasses, make good grades, and like watching Star Trek and Star Wars." The group laughed. "But now, for the first time, when I walk down the hall, I see some of you and you smile. I go into the bathroom and I'm not afraid anymore than I'll just end up with my head in the toilet. And when I go to lunch and there's this whole table of us that sit together now, I feel like my heart will explode sometimes."

Travis spoke up next. "Kind of like these guys, I am so grateful that because of our powers, I found out that I have more friends than I ever thought I did. These two here," he said rubbing George's neck and Emily's back, "are like the greatest friends a guy could ever have and I love them more than I can ever say. But now, I see all of you and I feel connected to you. It's like my world got bigger and even if we didn't have our powers, I think we would still be friends."

Mary Washington looked around the circle, "I think I'm just grateful to be alive. I know bad stuff happened to me and my dad, but after tonight, I just know he's alive. When you go through something like this, even getting to do dumb stuff like homework or washing the dishes is pretty great because you almost weren't here to do anything at all."

Several of the kids reached over to touch or hug Mary, whose tears streamed down her face in quiet trails. Lori noticed George scoot closer and slide his arm around the girl. *Those kids really care about one another* she thought. When Trey and Angie reached over and hugged Mary, she stared, tilting her head staring deep into his blue-green eyes.

"I have wanted a big brother my whole life," she said in a near whisper. "I'm glad it's someone like you."

Trey gripped her and pressed a kiss to the side of her face. Angie quietly wept.

Jack cleared his throat. "I'm sitting here listening to you kids realizing you are probably more aware of stuff than I was when I went to Viet Nam when I was eighteen. Tim and I saw some horrible things there, felt so grateful to get out alive, and even more thankful to meet wonderful ladies that are now our partners. I have a great life, this amazing lady here and my little boy that should be asleep but is so good to just sit and listen," Jack said ruffling Joey's hair. The little boy reached up to hug his dad's neck. "Most of you know we lost a baby not long ago and it was so hard," he started. "It took us a long time to come back from that dark place, kind of like what George was talking about. And then this amazing thing happened. I'm so grateful for these powers or lights or whatever this alien did to us, and I think it's pretty safe to say after what we saw tonight that it was like an alien." The kids smiled knowingly and nodded.

"This power brought me back to life and it helped Lori come alive again too. It has made us whole," he reached over and took Lori's hand and she leaned over and kissed his fingers. And now, I think it's even helped us more because we just found out that Lori is going to have another baby."

The girls cried "Ooooh," and the boys said "Cool," though it seemed each one might have already known or suspected this, which probably had something to do with all this inter-connectedness they shared. Tim dovetailed into Jack's conversation. "And believe it or not, it looks like I'm going to be a dad too," he said. Lori's head snapped around as her mouth fell open and she grabbed Tim's neck and screamed in joy. "Just found out ourselves, pretty great timing too…" he said trailing off.

Lori brought in some marshmallows and the kids toasted them in the fire. Someone produced a couple of joints and Lori started to protest, but then remembered what it was like when she was a teenager and figured if the kids wanted to get a little buzzed, this was probably the safest place in the world to do it. She looked over at Jack who just shrugged with a stupid grin on his face and took the joint from Trey and passed it over to Tim who had magically pulled a ridiculously fatty from somewhere and lit it and passed it around too. Lori noticed the kids were careful to pass Andy by who kept trying to take a turn. Lori noticed Angie passed the joint by as well, which surprised her since she figured the cheerleader had certainly tried weed a few times before. George grabbed his guitar and began to play John Denver's "Poems, Prayers, and Promises. When they got the part about passing a pipe around the fire, the group laughed heartily. Lori shook her head seeing these kids more like college students in the 1969 than as fifteen year olds in 1979. Lori began to see why Jack and Tim felt so connected and protective of these kids. She didn't even know some of them and yet in his cocoon of happiness, it seemed like the nicest place in the world to be. She had spent the night watching the various groups of kids and it seemed like most of them were paired off in one way or another. She couldn't help but wonder what Darla Harris would say about George and Mary Washington being a couple? *But times were changing* she thought. Maybe these kids could love who they wanted. God knows it wasn't that way even ten years ago. Of all the kids today, it seemed that Trey McGee and Angie Matlock were the quietest and most withdrawn. She didn't have super powers like these kids or her husband or little boy, but it didn't take a psychic to tell those kids were in some trouble. The energy around them was filled with fear and apprehension compared to the rest of these kids.

Lori looked at the clock. It was almost 1:30 and she was tired although nowhere as worn out as she normally would be after a full day of work on her feet and then a surprise teen lock-in for the night. She looked at Jack and noted the clock. His eyes flew open, she could tell he had no idea it was that late.

"Hey kids," he said. "It's getting pretty late. I guess you all are going to crash here for the night. Just a couple of things. You better know for sure that your parents are okay with you being out tonight. Lori and I don't want to get a call from the sheriff in the middle of the night like we are kidnappers." Several of the kids laughed. "Second, it probably goes without saying. But be respectful of each other and our house. No, um …uh.."

"Fornicating?" Travis said which elicited howls of laughter.

"Exactly," Jack said with a smile. "No more weed, no raiding the fridge looking for beer or anything. And try just sleeping tonight and save your exploring with one another for some other time."

"Well what's the fun in that?" Doug said.

Lori felt pretty sure Jack had made his point and she touched his arm. "These kids are going to be fine, hon," she whispered. She began to clear a few plates and bowls away and the kids jumped up to help move the dishes. Jack brought in pillows, sleeping bags, and blankets for the kids. Some of the kids disappeared to use the bathroom or use their finger to help brush the crud off their teeth before going to bed. Lori saw that Vince was already curled up in a big chair sawing logs, with Sarah trying to squeeze in beside him. The rest of the group settled down on pillows, curled up on the couch, or wrapped up in each other's arms.

"Okay kids, this was quite a night," Jack said. "I know we didn't talk about it much and your parents would die if they knew you all were in danger like we all were tonight. I don't know if people like JL Martin can hurt you all if you stick together. But you all need to be really careful. Don't do anything that makes you stand out too much. Keep away from any of kids of any of those men that were out there tonight. Watch out for each other and keep safe. I have the same feeling most of you do: something big is coming. I don't think that will be the last time those guys try and cover up their crimes. Eventually the truth is going to come out. Maybe let's get together next week just to make sure everyone is okay. How about Thursday night? Maybe tell your folks you have a school project or something. We will make some dinner and just check in and make sure everyone is safe and sound. How does that sound?"

"Sounds good to me," Don said. "Me too," others said.

Jack and Lori turned to leave but out of the blue, Angie spoke out. "Um, if you don't mind. Can you stay for just a minute longer? Trey and I have something to talk about if it's okay."

Jack and Lori looked at one another. "Sure, what's up sweetie," Lori said moving closer to the teens. Angie was visibly shaking. Trey looked positively green. Travis must have noticed because he moved over toward the couple.

"What's wrong, Trey?" Travis asked.

Trey looked around the group. "I didn't really say anything tonight when everyone was saying what they were grateful for. But I did want to say…" the boy swallowed hard looking around the group with weary, sad eyes. "That I'm grateful for my dad, Mike McGee who has looked out for me my whole life. He has fought for me and made sure my life was good. He didn't have to be my dad, but he chose to be. Not everyone gets to know something like that. And, since all of you know anyway…I'm thankful for my other dad, Carl Washington. I don't know him much, but I know he has been brave and has worked so hard for people in our town. I know he is a good man and I'm proud to be his son," Trey said with watering eyes and a trembling chin. Travis and several other kids hugged him or patted him on the back or head and let him know how much he meant to each of them. But as the kids held him close, one at a time, they pulled away and looked at him and Angie with fearful eyes.

"Oh God, Trey," Travis said.

Angie slid in beside Trey and hugged him close. "There's no doubt that Trey is what I am the most grateful for in my life," she said quietly. "He has loved me and treated me with kindness when no one else in my life really has. I guess most of you have figured it out. It seems like there's no way to keep a secret very long in this group," she said smiling. Angie reached down and pulled off the large poncho she had worn most of the night. Emily sucked in her breath and held her hand to her mouth. Vince let out an audible, "Whoa." Angie's large expectant belly stuck out surprisingly beyond the waist of her pants that were barely staying up.

Lori went immediately to the girl and wrapped her arms around her and she collapsed into the woman's arms sobbing. Trey looked like a little lost boy. Jack put an arm around him and they set both of the teens on the couch, the severity of their situation washing over the group. Jack looked over at Tim whose face was set in a hard grim line. The teens reached out and tried to be part of consoling Angie, but they honestly didn't know what to do or say. Surprisingly Tim of all people spoke up.

"Okay I don't think I need to tell all you that this is some serious shit. First off, don't talk about this at all. I know the truth will come out pretty soon 'cause you can't keep it hidden forever, but Trey and Angie don't need more rumors and Nosy Parkers in their lives right now. And kids," he said looking directly at Trey and Angie, "You are going to have to share this with your parents, Trey. I know you probably can't Angie, at least not right now. But you need some help with all this. It's more than we as a group can do. Mike and Janet love you so much. I know it will be tough but you have to trust them to take care of you." Trey was looking down at the carpet, big tears splashed on his jeans. Angie seemed practically catatonic.

Lori looked at Jack and Tim, desperate for something to say or some plan of action. "Tim's right, kids. You will need some help. If you need a place to stay for a bit Angie, you can stay here. Maybe we can figure more out in a couple of days. But you will need to think of some way to stay out of your parents' way for a bit that they will understand."

Angie spoke in a soft whisper. "I'll come up with something. Thanks for the offer to let me stay. That will help."

Lori looked at Angie and placed her hand softly on Angie's large stomach. "I get the idea things are moving super-fast for you too. Since both of you have the power, God knows how fast this little one is growing. I will take you to Greenville or Paris or somewhere tomorrow and we will get you seen by a doctor." Angie nodded her head in relief. Trey still sat on the couch his head in his hands. Travis and Andy were literally hanging on him, arms around his big shoulders, like a small human shield. Jack stood up.

"Okay now. It's super late. Everybody settle in and try to get some sleep," he said with some false authority, but the kids began to move away and settle back down on the pillows and blankets. Tim walked over and hugged Jack briefly.

"Dude, you sure know how to throw a party," he said in a low voice. Jack chuckled. "I'm going to hit the head and then go home. Candy will be pissed if I stay for a sleep over without her knowing ahead of time. She might be pissed anyway." Jack patted his back and wished him goodnight.

Tim felt so tired as he stood in front of the toilet he didn't hear the door open until a small voice behind him spoke.

"So?"

Tim turned around and saw Andy McGee in the open door. The boy walked in and stood right beside him. Tim didn't really know what to do so he continued to drain his bladder. "Um, kind of busy here, Andy."

"Did it grow back yet?" Andy asked.

The question took Tim by surprise. But he looked down in his hands and almost screamed as he saw two big healthy testicles hanging down where they always had been before. Andy peered around the man's waist and when he saw, he tore out of the bathroom yelling, "It grew back! It grew back. Mr. Murphy has two balls again!"

49 JL

It took the men over two hours to dig out of the debris and figure a way out of the hole they were in. In the end, they had to wait for JL to wake up from his stupor and make his way to the barn and haul back an extension ladder and lower it into the gaping hole. Toy Benton and Junior Bidwell wanted to leave immediately and take care of those kids once and for all.

"They know about us. They know about us and that Washington bitch and about their shit-ass father," Toy complained. "We need to take them out and do it quick. That cow won't hunt!"

"What? And how exactly do you propose to drive into town and massacre a dozen teenagers and get away with it?" JL asked annoyed.

"LeRoy will figure something out. He can blame it on Charles Manson or something," Junior Bidwell offered.

JL winced. He was surrounded by morons and pinheads. His head was killing him ever since that bitch blasted him with that damn green light. He needed some angel dust in the worst way. It was the only way for him to think his way through this new turn of events. Most of the morons just stood around digging dirt out of their ears or picking their butts. Lloyd Massey and Jim Measles came up to JL and mumbled something about it being late and needing to get home. JL waved them off with his hand.

"Fine. Do not say a word about anything from tonight," he ordered as they left. He knew they would not talk and no one would believe them if they did.

"What in the ever-loving fuck was that tonight, Boss," Randy Hamm asked. JL stared at the fool. How many times had he told this idiot and the others to stop calling him boss?

"I don't know, Randy. What would you say it was," JL asked.

"Well, it might sound a little crazy, but I kind of thought it was like something you would see on the movies. You know, like with aliens and shit like that."

JL stared. It was the first lucid thought that came out of this vegetable of a man's mouth and it was totally indefensible and stupid. And yet, JL knew he was on to something."

"Well you might want to keep that to yourself, Randy. But maybe you are on to something," JL offered. Randy glowed with pride. It was the first time JL hadn't told him to shut the hell up in years. JL rubbed his eyes. His head was really killing him now. Whatever that green beam was had jacked up his vision. He was struggling to see without getting a double image of everything. The words of that quack doctor echoed in his ears but he rejected that summation completely. He knew good and well he was fine and just needed some rest and some more dust. He needed to spend some time with Azarel. He needed some counsel.

"Listen boys. Let's get together tomorrow or the day after in my office. Don't worry about those kids or Jack Tanner or Tim. They are no threat to any of us. We will take care of them in good time."

"But JL. Those fucking kids were floating up in the goddang air," Junior said. "I mean, that ain't natural. You said it was devil worship. Is that what is was? We should take care of them now. A stitch in time saves wine."

"And what about that bridge? I mean, the whole cocksucking bridge is there. It wasn't there before and now it is. What coulda caused that?" Toy insisted.

"I don't know, Toy. Why don't you tell us?" JL snapped. That shut the idiot up, JL noticed. There was no way he was going to offer an explanation. JL took a deep breath. He had to get these guys out of here so he could settle down with some *Sernyl*.

"Look fellas. This has been a strange night. Not sure what all went on here tonight. Maybe it is devil worship, maybe its swamp gas, hell, maybe it's like Randy here says and its aliens." Several of the men chortled at that and Randy felt his face grow red. "We will figure it out. For now, just know those kids and fucking spark plug jockeys can't hurt any of us. Just go home. We will figure out a plan and take care of all their sorry asses soon enough"

The men nodded in agreement and began to walk back to their trucks and cars and left in a cloud of dust. JL noticed when Buck Matlock was leaving, he turned and gave JL an uncertain look. JL hadn't mentioned it, but one of the kids out here tonight was his slut of a daughter and right along with her, that half-nig bastard of Mike McGee. It seemed like all the stories he had ever heard about McGee, Carl Washington and that whore of a wife of Mike's were true. JL knew Buck was embarrassed to see that tramp of his out here with her coon boyfriend, but it was more than that.

Soon JL was soaking in a hot bath trying to coax his headache away. Thankfully Caroline had drunk herself into a stupor shortly after 8:00 PM. He eased the hypodermic needle of *Sernyl* into his vein in the webbing of his toes. It sent the soothing jolt of clarity to his brain and a spike of hardness to his prick. He wondered if he could get LaFonda and Joe back out here tonight. It might be a bit tricky but Caroline would never know. As the drug worked its magic, Azarel appeared, sitting in the soapy warmth of the tub at the other end. His dark hair glistened in the steamy bathroom, his golden circlet beading with droplets of water. His thick muscled legs pressed in on either side of JL.

"You saw inside the boy's mind tonight," the angel asked in his deep melodious voice.

"Yes."

"The sacrifice has presented itself."

"Yes. It is exquisite," JL said.

"The daughter must be offered as well. Remember Jephthah," the angel reminded.

"I thought as much. Is it true the whore is with child?"

"You know she is." The angel replied.

JL closed his eyes as the image of the girl filled his mind. He would rip the spawn from her and devour it in front of her eyes along with the half-breed's heart. The sacrifice was so perfect, sprung from the loins of Carl Washington. It would be like sacrificing him all over again. The perfection was stunning.

"It will be done," JL affirmed.

"Make sure that it is," the angel said. The being gripped JL with his large hands and entered him in one movement.

50 Travis

The digital clock on the dresser said 5:15 AM when Travis was shaken awake.

"Hey Scrote. Wake up, will you," Trey said.

Travis opened his eyes. Trey was standing over him, holding his arms around himself. He looked at the clock and turned over. "Go away, Trey it's too early."

"Damn, how do you stand it out here? It's colder than shit," Trey said. He ripped back the covers and climbed in the bed. Travis yelled, ripping the covers back.

"Your feet are like ice, you jackass." Trey scooted over close, smashing Travis into the screen wall. "God, you oaf. Do you mind? What the hell are you doing?" Trey punched the pillow and pulled the covers up to his chin.

"I couldn't sleep."

"Well that makes two of us now. You just left Andy in there?"

Trey raised his head up and looked into the next room. "That kid is dead to the world. I've been awake for an hour and he never quit snoring." Travis shoved Trey over a bit and laid his head on the edge of the pillow.

"So what's up, big brother? Unless you just felt like a cuddle I have an idea there is something on your mind," Travis said. He looked out the plastic covered window and could tell it was blowing and raining outside. *It actually felt like it could snow,* he thought.

"Have you or any of your little pinhead friends said anything about Angie yet?" Trey asked looking over at Travis in the darkness.

"No. God, you know we wouldn't. But, haven't you told mom and dad already?"

"Not yet," Trey answered.

"Why not? I mean, what are you waiting for?" Travis asked. Trey put his arm behind his head, almost elbowing Travis in the eye in the process. The teenager sighed heavily and rubbed his face with his other hand, almost moaning in the process.

"The time's just not right yet. I can't say exactly why but it's not. Right after Thanksgiving and the next football game. That's when I'll tell them," Trey said.

"Is there something special about waiting that long? I mean, isn't it going to be harder for Angie?"

"She told her mom she was going to see her cousin Annie that is getting married right around Christmas time. Said there was bridesmaid stuff they had to do. She's really just going to stay with the Tanners."

"What if her mom calls the cousin?"

"She won't. They don't like each other," Trey answered.

"She's just going to cut school to go do wedding stuff? Her mom let's her do that."

"She lets her do whatever she wants mostly 'cause she doesn't give two shits about her."

"I am going to tell Mom and Dad that right after the ball game, a few of us are going over to Bo's house for a celebration or something, going to be an overnight thing. I'm really going to take Angie over to Tooter's lake house. Just the two of us for a day or so. We really need to do it. I mean, we are going to be parents soon and we hardly know each other. So, I'm just telling you that so you will know, but just keep your mouth closed about it. Okay?"

Travis looked over at Trey. He knew it was ridiculous, but he almost looked older these last couple of weeks. Worry and concern furrowed his smooth brow. Travis reached his hand up and gripped his hard muscled bicep.

"If that's what you want. Whatever you need, bro. I mean, no problem covering for you or whatever. But you really have to be careful. I still wish you would tell Dad, but I'll keep quiet."

"Thanks, kiddo," Trey said rubbing the top of Travis's head. For Trey, it was practically a kiss. The boys laid quietly listening to the wind until they fell asleep again. They woke again as Mike's loud voice broke the early morning quiet.

"You have a perfectly good bedroom and nice cozy bed and the three of you monkeys curl up out here on the freezing porch. You don't have the sense God gave a goose." Come on, fellas. Up and at 'em. Let's get the showers going."

Travis sat up and saw Andy was curled up in a ball between him and Trey. "Hey, what are you doing out here," Travis asked climbing over the two dead to the world boys.

"Trey left me. I was scared and cold."

"Well don't wake him up for five minutes and let me get in the shower," Travis said grabbing a fresh pair of underwear. "Jeez it is freezing out here. Dad is going to have to get that heater going."

Travis was toweling off when Trey stumbled into the bathroom. "What day is it," he asked turning the water back on and climbing in the shower.

"It's Tuesday. Just today and half a day tomorrow and we are out for Thanksgiving."

Okay, thanks Trav."

Travis stared at the rippling shower curtain with the clouds of steam rising up. Who was this guy, he wondered. Displays of affection and no Scrote or Dickhead. What the hell was happening? Travis was glad Trey seemed certain of his plan, but his gut told him it was a bit foolhardy to say the least. Trey got plenty of things right, but matters of the heart seemed hard for him. He could understand the two of them wanting to have a day or two together before all hell broke loose, but he still wondered with all the craziness from the bridge, the lights, those guys that actually shot at them…it probably was not a great time to be on your own for very long.

Travis got dressed, actually putting on a pullover sweater today. If this cold snap kept up, he would be the one crawling into bed with Trey and Andy tonight he figured. Janet had made oatmeal and toast for breakfast which actually wasn't bad, especially with as much sugar, butter, and cream as Travis poured on. Trey and Andy joined him at the table, the kitchen was quiet enough to hear the news continuing to analyze what would have caused all those people down in South America to drink poison Kool-Aid just because that asshole Jim Jones told them too. After what he had seen in the past few days though, Travis was beginning to see how easily simple people could be led astray by a charismatic shyster.

Travis told his mom goodbye. His dad had already left for the store. He was just pulling on his Army surplus jacket when Trey came around the corner. "Come on and I'll drive you to school." Travis almost dropped his books and notebook. Had he just fallen in the Twilight Zone? What the hell?

"Um, okay. Thanks."

They were getting into the truck when Andy came running up to the window. "Can you take me to school too?"

"No, it's the wrong direction," Trey said. "Not enough time."

"Hey that's not fair," Andy said annoyed.

"Yeah, well. Get used to that," Trey said with a grin.

As Trey began to back up, Andy flipped Trey off and shouted, "Suck my dick, Trey!" The little boy gripped his crotch and waved his middle finger high in the air.

"Andrew Michael, get yourself back in this house right now!" Travis heard his mom yell from the front door. Janet was bundled up in her pajama bottoms and big cardigan sweater and her frown let Travis knew Andy was going to be in for it. He and Trey roared with laughter. Travis figured somehow this would end up being his fault later on, but for now, it was pretty great seeing little mister perfect get in trouble for a change.

"Whoa, wonder what got into little man today?" Trey asked. "Someone's gonna get grounded," he added.

"Wonder where he heard stuff like that?" Travis asked raising his eyebrows.

"I have no idea what you're talking about," Trey said.

Trey turned onto Pecan Street and toward the junior high. He turned the heater on high. The temperature was a balmy 29 this morning. Z97was playing "One of These Nights" by the Eagles. Trey reached over and rubbed Travis's knee. "Looking forward to marching at Texas Stadium this Friday?"

Travis looked at Trey narrowing his eyes. Small talk from Trey was always highly suspicious. "Yeah, I guess. Probably not as much as you are looking forward to playing on the field."

"I know. Pretty cool to get to use the same locker room and showers Roger Staubach and Tony Dorsett use. Gives me a woody just thinking about it," Trey said, dopy insane grin still on his face.

Travis turned toward him. "Okay, I don't know what you are smoking today but you are weirding me out. What's up? You offer to take me to school. You clearly wanted to tell me something."

"Can't a big brother just want to spend some...?"

"Seriously, cut the bullshit, Trey."

"Jeez. Fine. Look, me and Angie . . .on Saturday when we go to the lake, um, we're probably going to go ahead and get married too," Trey said nonchalantly.

"What? Are you kidding?" Stop. Stop the truck now." Travis demanded. Trey looked at him and pulled over to the parking lot in front of the A&P.

"Why are you acting so crazy? Are you on the rag?" Trey said frowning.

"Am I..? Holy shit you've got some balls. Why in the world are you doing this? Aren't you in enough of a mess right now?"

"Well, yeah. But this is fixing part of it. When you knock someone up, you get married. Isn't that what people do? I figure Mom and Dad will be a little more comfortable if we are married. Not as much people can say about having a kid and everything," Trey said earnestly.

Travis shook his head. "I'm sure I am not the one who ought to be having this conversation with you. But even a dumb kid like me can figure out in no way will getting married make this bad situation better. In fact, probably the only good thing about the whole thing is you NOT being married. Seriously, big brother, I really don't think it's a good idea. Who would marry you two anyway? Aren't you too young to do it?"

"Not in Rockwall County. You only have to be sixteen. Angie's aunt is cousins with the Justice of the Peace. He said he would do it for $20."

"Oh, this can't be good," Travis said rubbing his head.

"Look. I am freaking out, okay. I find out my parents lied to me my whole life. My real dad's a big Negro man who boned my mom while my dad is out of town. So that means I'm a half-afro kid too. The school is laughing and mocking me behind my back and to my face. My stupid alien jizz not only knocked up my girlfriend but made my unborn baby some kind of fast growing mutant. And there are college scouts coming to the game on Friday that might decide my future." By this time Trey is shaking, his eyes wide like a madman.

Travis reached over and grabbed Trey's head and pressed his forehead against his brother. "Calm down. Think clearly," he spoke in authority into Trey's mind. Trey gripped Travis's hands and held his head against him for almost a minute before he let go.

"Thanks, I needed that," Trey said looking up from his lowered head with a wry smile. "At least you didn't slap me like on the Skin Bracer commercial."

"I would have if I would have thought it would do any good. Just wait another week or so, Trey. Wait until you talk to mom and dad. If they think it's the best solution, then great. We can have a wedding. But don't just go off half-cocked and think this is a solution."

"Heh. You said cocked. That's what got me in this mess."

"You jackhole," Travis said slumping back in the seat. Trey started the pickup and headed back toward the school.

"I'll think about what you said. Not promising anything 'cause Angie and me had sort of decided. But what you said make sense too." Trey turned toward the school parking lot. "Why are you smarter than me about shit like this?"

"Probably because I wasn't dropped on my head as a child."

"Huh?"

"Never mind. Go to school, brother of mine. Try not to start any riots today," Travis said.

"I'll try," Trey said.

Travis waited until lunch was over and he and Emily were walking with George over to Western Auto. He just didn't feel like involving the whole new group of kids that sat with them at the café in his family drama along with everything else. He gave George and Emily a fast recap of the morning as they crossed the street and passed the barber shop.

"And he thinks getting married will make it all better?" George said dumbfounded.

"Oh God," Emily said. "Thank goodness you tried to talk some sense into him."

"For all the good it will do. He is so messed up right now, I thought he was going to crack up right there in the truck. Part of me is tempted to just go ahead and tell dad, but Trey would probably never speak to me again. It's been really cool lately with him not being his usual a-hole self. Oh yeah, and I think Andy is probably going to get grounded." Travis quickly explained the other event of the morning. George howled with laughter. Emily narrowed her eyes and pressed her lips tight together. Travis pushed the door open to Western Auto, the bell ringing above their heads. Tim Murphy was at the front counter.

"Hey look who it is. How's the day going, kids?"

"Good," they all answered. Mary Washington came around the corner. She smiled when she saw George. Emily went over and grabbed Mary's hand and took her down the aisle to whisper something to her.

"Um, how are you feeling and everything," Travis asked.

Tim grinned and grabbed his groin. "All present and accounted for. You know, I really missed Mr. Lefty. Everything seems to work again just fine too," he said providing way too much information.

"Cool," George said. "Did you like not even notice you were regrowing a whole nut?"

"Nah, never knew a thing 'til little McGee took a peek at my privates and counted to two."

"What?" Travis said.

"Ah, never mind. He just asked if I had grown a new ball and sure enough, poof. There it was. That should have been the most amazing shit that ever happened to me in my whole life and now it just seems to be all in a day's work or something. I went to the doctor yesterday and he almost pissed himself. He literally sat there for a half an hour playing with my gonads. He called in half the nurses and another doctor. They all had a good stare at my nuggets and no one knew what to say. He is going to send me for another scan and everything, but I know what they will find. A whole bunch of nothing. Look at me, cancer free!" he said with a chuckle.

Jack came around the corner with a box of AA batteries. "Are you hearing all about his long lost ball that decided to come back home?"

The boys nodded putting their candy purchases on the counter.

"I got this today, kids." Tim said. He reached over and put another two dozen pieces of candy on the counter; hot tamales, Chick-o-Stix, Charm's Sweet and Sour pops, Blow pops, Pixie Stix, Snickers and Zagnut bars. "On the house, little buddies. I love you kids." Tim sacked up the candy and handed it to a stunned George.

"Thanks, Mr. Murphy," he said staring into the sack like a kid on Halloween.

"Now enough with the Mr. Murphy. I think you better start calling me Tim, especially with you knowing all about my testicles and all that." Jack rolled his eyes.

"Everything going okay for you kids? How is Trey?" Jack lowered his voice to a whisper. "Angie is still staying with us."

Travis nodded. "He's good. Just a little freaked out. Stuff at school has been hard. Kids are making fun of him a lot, busting his balls for being a half-colored guy. There was some trouble the other day. He's worrying me a little bit. I wish he would talk to you. You both are the only grown-ups that know what he's really going through. He's scared to talk to my parents."

"I guess I get that. I will see if I can get him to talk to me. He comes by after school to see Angie. He's not planning to do something stupid, is he?" Jack asked.

Travis thought about telling but instead just said. "Ask him. I don't want to, you know…"

"I hear you. Brother stuff, no sense rocking the boat. Leave it to me, Travis."

"Gotta run. Bye, Mr. Tanner. Bye Tim," Travis said opening the door. "Hold it, where's Emily?"

"We're here," Emily said coming around the corner with Mary. "We better hurry or the Webster will have our heads and make us write another stupid sonnet." The kids ran across the street to the Collegiate Shoppe and then around the corner to the school. Travis strained his ears to listen in Mary and George. He smiled because now his ears were like radar even though they walked ten steps behind him and Emily. Don and Doug waved at Travis. They had come out of T&O Auto Parts, another favorite candy pit stop for the junior high kids. As they walked across the street, a beat up truck slowed down. Toy Benton stuck his head out the window.

"Hey faggot. I got a big dick here for you, you queer," Toy bellowed from the truck, making a gross blow-job motion with his hand and tongue.

With a loud *blam*, the front tires of Toy's pickup exploded sending his truck sideways into a parked BelAir. The teenagers continued walking down the street. Don turned around to see Toy and Junior Bidwell standing in front of the truck, hands on their hips. Toy hauled off and kicked the front bumper of the truck.

"Goddamnit!" he shouted. "Them tires were brand new used ones!" he yelled.

The group smiled and turned on Sycamore Street toward the school. Travis held his hand up to Don for a high five. Doug looked back over his shoulder.

"Sucks to be them," he said with a flip of his hair. The group laughed. George and Mary held back at the rear of the group.

"I didn't know where you were after third period. You can always come to lunch with us." George said.

"I know. I just wanted a little time alone," Mary said. "You bought a lot of candy."

"Tim just gave it to us. He's still pretty happy, you know, with the happy reunion with his testicle and everything."

Mary giggled. "This stuff is so crazy. I'm glad he's going to be all better. I like both of those men."

"Me too. A lot of adults are dorks. They are cool." Travis watched in the windows of the stores and business and could see George reach out for Mary's hand. She let him take it, but looked around to see if others were watching.

"I'm not sure this is a good idea," she said quietly.

"Why not? I'm not afraid of what people say. I've got superpowers, remember?"

"That's right, Boy Wonder, you're a real bad ass," Mary said laughing.

"Robin is totally bogus. I'm more Spider-Man or Captain America," George said.

"That right? Hmm, I'm not sure. Half the time I think you're the Joker."

George took a more serious tone, speaking even lower. "I really don't care if people say something. I like you. Why shouldn't I get to hold your hand?"

"Only reason I know is we live in a redneck racist backwater town that don't cotton to boys like you liking girls like me. So, if it's all the same to you, let's keep our hand holding a bit more on the down low. It's not that I'm ashamed of you or don't like you. I just got about all I can handle right now to be gettin' on with. You feel me?" Mary said.

George let her hand slide out of his. "I feel you, Christie Love," he said.

"Oh, you did not just call me Christie Love, Horshack," Mary giggled.

51 Andy

Andy's face was still burning hot as he walked up Live Oak Street toward Wheeler School. Trey had managed to get him in trouble yet again. There was no reason why he couldn't take him to school as well. His walk was twice as long as Travis's. It happened all the time. Those two got away with murder and he got dumped on. Now on top of it all, grounded for a week for using bad language. *What a joke around our house*, he thought. I'm the only one not cussing all the time, goddamn it, he thought to himself kicking a rotten horse apple across the street, splatting on the parking lot of the car wash.

Jessie Allen walked across the street and ran ahead to walk with Andy. He wasn't in the mood today but Jessie didn't bother him as much as most of the girls. At least she liked Star Wars and rock music and wasn't a teacher pleaser. Not that Andy was some sort of rebel, he just didn't like brown-nosers. Karen Short's head was so far up Mrs. Green's ass she knew what she had for dinner last night he imagined.

"Hi Andy. You seem mad today," Jessie said.

"Just one of those mornings. My dumb older brothers got me grounded."

"Oh no. What did you do?"

"Told my brother to su … never mind." The two crossed Monroe Street and then continued on toward the school. *It was way too cold to be walking today,* Andy thought. He saw another horse apple in the edge of the curb. He picked the sticky green fruit up and threw it, it sailed high above a house on the other side of the street and disappeared into some large willow trees, their bare branches hanging limp like dirty hair.

"You can really throw far. I used to be terrible but I can really throw far now too." With that Jessie picked up another horse apple and hurled it almost as far as Andy's. It landed with a thump into someone's back yard and a loud, "Hey!" echoed. The kids stared and ran down the street, laughing hysterically. Andy slowed to a walk by the day care center so they could catch their breath.

"Hey, you live pretty close to me. Did you see the lights back on September 12th? Did they wake you up?"

"Yes. No one else in my house even woke up, but I did. I went outside and stood there for a long time just staring. It was like I could see into space or something it was so beautiful. Ever since then, I've kind of felt different too."

"Different how?"

"You'll just make fun of me if I tell you," she said.

"I promise I won't. Tell me."

So Jessie began to take Andy though the events in her life over the last few months that sounded remarkably like his. She found out she could do things: move them, run faster, make stuff lighter or heavier, make people agree with her or change their mind…the list went on and on. She talked about her dreams and the green lights and the bridge. They stopped before they got to the school and sat on a bench near Sweetie's Donut Shoppe.

"All that stuff has happened to me too, and my brothers and even some grownups we know. We think it was from an alien spacecraft. It made us mutants and we now have superpowers."

"It's so great. I have made my mom be so much nicer to me. She has given me more allowance, let me wear a little makeup, and bought me this awesome pair of tall wedge heels I wanted. I can even wear panty hose if I want now."

Andy thought that was the stupidest waste of superpowers he had ever heard, but the idea that Jessie understood what he was going through was amazing. "We can get inside people's heads or make them see stuff we have seen. At this church thing when people were praying, a whole bunch of stuff got shared and we even found out that my oldest brother is really a half-colored boy because my mom did it with a black guy. We never knew it before. It's been pretty stressful."

Jessie stared at this news mutely, having no response to such a strange and shocking revelation but then she added. "I know some about that. I was listening to my sister talk on the phone and I could hear all the conversation on the other end. Her boyfriend was talking to her about her coming over with his parents being gone for the weekend and they were going to do it too. And then I was helping my mom roll her hair and while I was doing it, I could tell she was all mad at my dad and she was thinking about maybe telling him to get out of the house unless he quit doing stuff with his secretary. She's in college."

"Eww. What's wrong with people?" Andy said.

"My mom says he's going through a second-childhood and she is going to get a frying pan and knock him back to the first one," Jessie said quite to the point.

The kids heard the first bell and took off running. Being tardy to Mrs. Green's class was never a good idea. By the time they flopped into their seats, they were red-faced and sweaty. But Jessie looked back and smiled at Andy. She even reached her hand back and handed him a watermelon Jolly Rancher. When his fingers touched her hand, a blast of images and energy surged through him. He felt it all the way from the hairs that stood up on his head to his toes and deep in his belly. Andy unwrapped the candy and popped it in his mouth.

Mrs. Green began calling roll. When she got to Andy McGee, he said, "Present," instead of "Here" which always annoyed the teacher.

"Andy, do you have something in your mouth?" Mrs. Green inquired over her cat's eye glasses.

"Mumpf," Andy answered.

"Come spit that out and write your name on the board. You just lost first recess," the teacher snapped, frowning in her permanent scowl. Several low muttered "Yah's" or "Hah's" were heard before she rang the bell on her desk for quiet. "If I hear more of that, the whole class will be writing lines during recess." The room went deathly silent. Andy was steaming once again and longed for Mrs. Wilson, his teacher from last year that was kind and helpful.

The loudspeaker buzzed and Principal Hollingsworth spoke. "Good Morning Wheeler Students. I hope all of have plans for a great Thanksgiving. Congratulations to our Cowhill Tigers heading to the State Football Championship!" Echoes of cheers ran up and down the hall for a few moments. "Please stand and place your hand over your heart as we say the pledge." The students recited the Pledge of Allegiance and continued to stand. "Now let's continue our citizenship by placing your hand over your heart as we pledge allegiance to the Texas fag…FLAG!"

Shrieks of laughter boomed down the hallways this time. Mrs. Green grabbed her bell and began banging on it with all her might. But after the first clang, the bell went silent. No matter how hard she banged on it, there was only a dull thud. This made the students laughter intensify to the point of hilarity. So as the pledge was being poorly recited in the other classrooms, Mrs. Green was shouting, "Stop it, stop it, stop it." She finally grabbed a stack of Fifth grade readers that had just been turned in and dropped them hard to make a loud slap to get control of the class. However, the books slowly floated to the ground instead, barely making a quiet poof. This had the exact effect she was looking for because the class instantly got quiet, now replaced by a growing "Oohhhh." Mrs. Green was dumbfounded and rattled. Her full slip had shifted and now a full three inches of sexy black lace showed from underneath her Act III pleated skirt. She started to walk to the door, clearly prepared to blast the class with a gigantic detention when her slip fell all the way to the floor, tripping her sending her sprawled to the floor. A couple of boys at the back laughed, but more gasped and several students ran forward to help her up. Andy looked up at Jessie who turned around with bulging eyes mouthing, "I'm sorry." Andy smirked and gave her a thumb's up even though he didn't like seeing a person get hurt.

Right before recess, Andy raised his hand and asked to go to the bathroom. Mrs. Green looked at the clock and said, "It's almost recess. You can wait until then." Andy shook his head.

"I really need to go. It's going to be a photo finish, Mrs. Green," which caused Jason McCoy to laugh like a maniac, resulting in his name going on the board. Mrs. Green put a big check mark by Andy's with a dramatic flourish.

"So go, Mr. McGee," she said through gritted teeth.

Andy ran out of the room with several chuckles following him. He turned around to the closed door and, after checking that the coast was clear, flipped Mrs. Green a double boner with his middle fingers like he had seen Travis and Trey do to their parents dozens of times. He finished up in the bathroom, washed his hands and dried them on his pants. He turned into the main hallway and saw the very creepy portrait of Mr. H. J. Wheeler himself. It was a gothic portrait with glowing pale candles in the background that looked more like it belonged on Dark Shadows or an Edgar Allen Poe story than a school hallway. The kids were always acting like the eyes on the portrait followed them. Andy approached the photo and touched the glass near the eyes and smiled, running back to the classroom just when the recess bell sounded. He slid into the line of kids waiting to go out and for some interesting reason; Mrs. Green didn't seem to realize he needed to stay inside. The teacher dismissed the class and they walked in an orderly line down the hallway to wait at the front door until dismissed to run out to the playground.

As they stood in the gloomy hallway, cold and dark on this late fall morning, one of the girls at the front of the line suddenly gasped and pointed. The class followed her finger pointing at the portrait which now looked directly back at them with shocking red eyes that moved and bulged. The class screamed and scattered like rabbits, running past the evil portrait and headed out to the frosty playground. As other groups of students came out of their classes, the scene replayed with gasps and shrieks of horror as the portrait sneered down at the children. Andy had grabbed Jessie as she ran out the door and pulled her back, hiding beside a trophy case. More than one teacher had shouted out. Mr. Parker had actually let out a loud "Oh shit," before running out the door with the students. Jessie took Andy's hand and the two of them ran out just as Mr. Hollingsworth came out of his office, stopping in his tracks as the portrait glared down at him.

Andy and Jessie ran to the back of the playground near the chain link fence.

"You did that, didn't you," Jessie said grinning. "That was a great prank. That picture is so creepy anyway. You are good with the powers."

"I've had some practice. And my brother and his friends are really good. They made a tornado hit the Junior High."

"Wow."

The rest of the day was more or less normal. Andy noticed that Bart Rivers that sat beside him was farting over and over again during Math. It was quiet but he just kept doing it. Andy got up to sharpen a pencil and touched Bart on the shoulder as he walked by. When he sat down again, he reached forward and Jessie touched his hand. As the two held hands, Andy leaned over and tapped Bart on the shoulder like he wanted to ask him a question. An explosion of gas hammered against the wood seat of his desk chair like a machine gun. The class instantly descended into chaos again and Mrs. Green pounded on her bell, again to no avail. She finally picked the thing up and threw it hard into the trash can. It bounced in the metal can and ricocheted out and struck one of the classroom lights exploding the fluorescent tube into a shower of glass shards that fell like deadly snowflakes on top of Starla Evans and Rory Mitchell. Even more screams and chaos ensued until Mr. Hollingsworth flung the door open and shouted for quiet. Then, to the delight of the entire class added, "Mrs. Green. I expect you to keep this class under control!"

Even though they wrote lines the rest of the day, it was worth it. "I will not act like a sideshow monkey" was scribbled with delight on every tablet and piece of notebook paper with smiles of delight and satisfaction on every student's face. Jessie had given Andy a stack of her Love Notes notebook paper, hot pink colored, and he gleefully filled every line with his punishment. As the class was dismissed, Andy and Jessie were almost the last two out of the room. They watched as Mrs. Green slid open her drawer and poured a large dollop of some liquid from a silver flask into her afternoon coffee. They fled the room giggling silently and talked all the way home.

52 JL

Junior Bidwell adjusted the binoculars as he followed the teenagers up the street toward the junior high, focusing long and hard on Mary Washington's tight Calvin Klein jeans.

"Aw man, look at that ass. Slidin' into that was like butter it was so soft. That girl was so wet that night. I think we need to pick her up and take another ride on that booty."

"Shut the hell up, Junior," JL said looking up from his paper. "Is she with that Harris boy or not?"

"Looks like they were holding hands for a bit, but not no more. She can do a lot better than that little Jew boy. Now that she's had a taste of a real man, that little boy dong isn't gonna cut it."

"Junior, your depravity has no bounds. George Harris is no more a Jew than you or me. He is a nigger-lover, however, and his open display of affection in the middle of town is just one more reason this has to be stopped."

JL sat thinking through all he knew. The Carl Washington sacrifice, as perfect as it seemed, was somehow flawed and it was rejected. When he had taken the blood to the Norton Community and performed the ceremony at Sales Creek, adding the sacrificial blood, the contaminants should have been cleansed. But the test showed it was still half poison. There just hadn't been enough blood. *Besides*, he thought, *there was more wrong with this town than just tainted water.* This village needed to be renewed. The old ways needed to be restored. So many progressive atrocities came to the town with the college. Now it was like a dam of evil that was ready to burst. The sewage of interracial marriage, miscegenation, foreign diseases, animalistic sexual appetites, wantonness, lasciviousness, perversions, now abounded. The only way to cleanse the place was with a truly worthy offering. Carl Washington's bastard and his unnatural offspring along with the Matlock girl would be exactly the right offering.

JL had been unable sleep for days since the incident near his home. It was unfathomable that bridge had just reconstructed itself. That was a kind of power and magic he knew had to be dark and evil. There was no explanation. He could call all the science professors from the college and none of them would have the faintest idea of what had happened. He could just hear the fools tripping over themselves to find some explanation of something that was either divine or diabolical. The only other explanations were all of them had some shared hallucination, but the fact was...the damn bridge was there. He had walked on it. It was sturdy and real. It was fitted together like those fucking Inca stones that you can't even put a knife blade in between. Hell, maybe that's who build the thing.

When he saw those kids floating in the air, though, that's when he knew. There was only one explanation for that: witchcraft. Some sort of sorcery that allowed a person to levitate was definitely not from any God he knew. And then there was this strange strength that some of them seemed to have. Why were most of them children as well? He saw those two idiots from Western Auto there, but that probably had more to do with them being pedophiles or something. They probably just enjoyed the pleasures of the boys and girls. He understood that attraction but those men weren't holy men. They had no business with those children other than satiating their carnal desires.

When he touched that Harris boy's leg, the images that blasted across his mind were almost more than he could absorb, He saw lights, stars, scenes from school and homes. He saw himself and Theo with that Washington girl. He saw all the way back to the bus crash and the slaves hung in the barn as his great-great grandfather slaughtered them. He saw Carl Washington mating with that whore married to Mike McGee. And he saw the McGee boy breeding the Matlock tramp and of course, their unnatural fornication had resulted in another welfare mouth to feed. How could that be? But more importantly, what did those delinquents know? Worse than them, what did those perverts from Western Auto know? Especially the traitor.

"Hey Dad."

JL looked up and smiled. Theo walked in followed by a tall red-haired young man. He rose and gave his boy a quick hug.

"Theo. What brings you here in the middle of the day? James, how are you?"

"Fine," the red-haired young man answered. He was clearly nervous and agitated, JL could see.

"Got out of class early. Thought I would make your day. Got a bit of information here you just might be interested in, Pops," Theo said sitting in a side chair and propping his boots up on the edge of his dad's desk. JL moved over to him and carefully moved the boots off and back to the floor.

"Is that so? Well, James. What sort of information do you have and what do you want for it? I am correct in thinking it is for sale?" JL said.

The redheaded young man shuffled from one foot to another, looking about the office toward Junior Bidwell. "It's private," he said barely above a whisper.

"Oh you don't have to worry about Junior, he's too thick to put two and two together, isn't that right Junior?"

"What's that, boss?" Junior asked looking up from his comic book.

JL winced. He smiled at the young man as if to say, as I told you. But he could tell it was no good.

"Junior, you go on now. See you back at the house later tonight. Go ahead and gather everyone up. Say about 8:00 tonight, alright?"

"You got it, boss," Junior said picking up his baseball cap putting it tightly on his auburn curls. "See you later."

JL invited the young man to sit. He offered him a cold pop, but the man declined. He was sweating profusely JL could tell. His face was slick with sweat. "There now. Why don't you tell me what you were thinking?"

"I've got some information that Theo here says would be helpful to you."

"Well I would need to hear it to know for sure," JL said sweetly beginning to get annoyed. His headache was coming back and he desperately needed some *Sernyl* or some morphine, preferably both. Maybe he could get his college students back tonight as well. It had been over a week and he was due a good riding.

"It's good stuff, Dad. I told him you would pay," Theo said cleaning his fingernails with his pocketknife.

JL mashed his lips together and smiled. He hated when Theo did shit like this. "That so, son? Well, what exactly is it you were wanting."

"I want to move away and finish up my college down at A&M. I talked to the coach down there and he was interested in me. I might have to redshirt, have to work my way onto the team. But I need to get out of this place, sir. I have other dreams. I know you know my dad pretty well. He's a good man but he doesn't have the same dreams as me. He doesn't think much about football or me getting a college degree. Most people think I'm just a dumb redneck, but I'm more than that." The boy had tears in his eyes now and JL was keenly intrigued.

"So I take it you need some help getting into the school, having some scholarship to take care of you, maybe a few choice introductions to some important types down College Station way?" JL asked.

"Yes sir. I know I can make it down there. I just need some help to get my foot in the door… that and some financial help too," the young man said looking down at his hands.

"Well I love seeing local boys like you make good. You were a great Tiger footballer, James. I tell you what, you tell me what you know and I give you my word I will take care of you."

The young man's blue eyes shone in the light, rimmed with red. He sighed deeply like the words were costing him everything he had. "Trey McGee is the half-colored bastard son of Carl Washington."

JL looked at the young man, narrowing his eyes. "I know that, son."

The young man seemed taken aback but he continued. "He has been banging Angie Matlock and he's gotten her pregnant with his half-black baby."

"I know this as well," JL said. *This is a waste of time* he thought to himself.

Now the young man was desperate. "Well he called and asked to use our lake house this weekend. He's going to take Angie Matlock down there for a romantic weekend or something. So if you, you know, wanted to go and talk to him. You could find him there without his parents being around and all that. Oh and, um, he also has some special alien powers or something. When those lights came over town back in the summer or whenever, they zapped him and made him like Superman. It happed to his brothers and other kids too."

"Is that so," JL said more intrigued than he let on.

"Yes sir. That's why he's turned into the shit as far as football goes. His magic powers help him be better than anyone else. He showed me into his brain and I saw lots of stuff."

"Really?" JL knew about the mental images and was pretty clear he was not that happy that even more local fools had seen things they had no business knowing about. This was getting out of control he could tell.

"Yes sir. And I just wanted you to know…just like my dad all these years. I will always keep your secrets. I would never say anything about your ceremonies or the barn or anything like that. You can trust me," the young man said boldly.

"Of course. I wouldn't expect anything else. Well that's fine, James. That is some very helpful information. I will look forward to reaching out to friends of mine down in Aggieland to let them know about you. Don't worry about the finances. You won't have to worry about a thing." JL stood and looked out on the street. He walked to the door and turned the sign in the window to CLOSED. "Theo, I am going to go grab something for James and I will meet you at the back door in just a moment. If it's alright with you, James. I'm going to let you leave through the back door. With everything going on right now, it might be best if you and I were not seen to be in each other's company, if you know what I mean."

The young man stood. "Sure thing, Mr. Martin. That makes sense to me. I can't tell you how much this means to me. It's been such a dream and I had no way to make it come true. I really like Trey, but this was a chance to make a new start for myself…I just had to take it."

"Nothing ventured, nothing gained. Besides, that young man is very disturbed and clearly is going to need some real help. You've made sure that can happen now. This way, if you would." JL disappeared into the back of the store. Theo and the red-haired young man stood in the opening of the door looking at the large inventory of boxes, a small kitchenette, and various old pieces of furniture. Tooter took a step forward but Theo caught his arm and held him back. His face looked flushed, his eyes were wild.

"Hold on, Tooter. Let my dad get the door opened and all that. Um, I told you it was going to work out. Must have been pretty hard to squeal on your buddy like that. I don't know if I could have done it," Theo said enigmatically.

"Don't make me feel worse than I already do. Your dad isn't going to hurt him or anything, right?"

"I wouldn't worry about that. Trey is way too important to my dad to hurt him. Okay, probably got the door open now. Good seeing you again, Toot."

"You too, Theo. Thanks for listening."

JL's voice echoed from beyond a large stack of boxes on the other side of the room. "Well, thank you again, James for coming by. You have made my day. I hope you won't regret coming to me with this news," JL said. "Now, what was it again they called you back in the football days at Cowhill High?"

"Tooter," the young man said in a loud voice straining his neck to find where JL's voice came from.

"That's right. Tooter."

In a flash of speed surprising from a man of his age, JL came around from one of the large stacks of boxes at a run and slammed into James "Tooter" Turner with a long black samurai that caught him at the navel and penetrated him, exiting right below his shoulder blades. Tooter stood in the middle of the floor motionless, gripping the hilt of the sword as lacy blood frothed from the corners of his mouth. His red-lidded eyes turned to JL in an open-mouthed expression of dawning realization and utter finality.

"You're still just going to be a dumb redneck, Tooter," JL said.

JL grabbed the sword hilt and pulled from the young man's sagging body. As he fell to his knees, JL swung the sword with both hands beheading him, sending Tooter's head spiraling into the middle of a Number 3 washtub full of rags and paint drop-cloths, his blue eyes still wide with shock.

JL whistled. "Hole in one, son. I've been practicing."

53 George

The 1978 AA State Football championship was played in Texas Stadium on Saturday night, November 25th. It was a brisk 34° at kickoff, but the stormy weather from Thanksgiving had broken up and the night was clear and frosty. The Cowhill Tigers were playing the defending State Champion Wylie Pirates. Wylie was a suburban school, close to the Dallas metro area. Along with having a successful football program, Wylie was known for a definitive stylized marching band that patterned itself after the Grambling Marching Band or Prairie View A&M. The bands played R&B music, had twirlers with fairly suggestive costumes and provocative routines. The band wore spats and shako hats, but danced around like they were on Soul Train more than at a marching band halftime. But the crowds ate it up usually, even if the quality of the music suffered due to all the jumping around. It was made all the more perplexing that most of the band was decidedly rich and white.

The Wylie Band performed pregame and got the crowd going in the Pirates favor from the start playing a medley of Earth, Wind, and Fire tunes and then ending up with George Clinton's "We Want the Funk." They played a horrendous version of the "Star Spangled Banner" that George thought was the most out-of-tune rendition ever played.

The Tigers played defense after the kickoff and ended up giving up a touchdown just 33 seconds into the game. Theo Martin missed a huge tackle that ended up allowing the running back from Wylie to run 72 yards for the touchdown. George watched Coach Morris grab Theo's face mask and yell at him good after that play. The CHHS band magical eight that consisted of Travis, George, Emily, Vince, Sarah, Don, Doug, and Mary watched Trey take the field and the powers were unleashed. The only problem was, the coach seemed to not be using Trey at all, choosing instead to allow Bo to hand off to the running back or make long pass attempts to one of the wide receivers. He didn't use the tight end at all in the first two possessions.

By the time Trey got into the game, the Tigers were down 12 – 0. But as Bo faded back on the next snap, Trey blasted past a defender and went across the middle and grabbed a screen pass and literally hurdled two Pirate backfield players and made a 52 yard gain. On the next play, Trey blocked a defender so hard he flew into the air and landed five yards away while Bo faked a handoff and ran the ball into the end zone. After the two-point conversion, it was 12 – 8.

The Pirates marched down the field eighty yards with a possession that took up most of the second quarter. Wylie 20 – 8. Right before halftime, Bo fell back and threw a 40-yard bomb to Trey who had lined up as a wide receiver. Trey caught the ball, stiff-armed three defenders, and walked into the end zone making the halftime score. 20 – 16. George watched his parents, along with Travis's cheer like crazy as the team ran off the field. There was little doubt that the space alien mojo worked even from the long-distances of Texas Stadium.

The Cowhill band stood on the sidelines and waited for the announcer to introduce them. They were met with cheers and even a smattering of boos from some of the Wylie fans. The magical eight had gripped hands briefly before they lined up and did their best to summon as much alien musical inspiration as possible. They kicked off with the Fanfare from Rocky,

"

blasting through the syncopated triple-tongued notes at the end like the Blue Devils. The crowd applauded with gusto as they transitioned into a new arrangement, just for the Wylie fans, of Earth, Wind, and Fire's "Fantasy, complete with a spinning spaceship design in the middle of the field with rifles and flags doing amazing work. The crowd cheered even louder. Going for the mass appeal of the movies rather than the jazzy instrumentation of Chuck Mangione, the band ended with an amazing medley from "Star Wars," opening with the "Imperial March," then a percussion arrangement of the, "Cantina Band" song. Then the band moved to a soaring "Princess Leia's Theme," and ended with the main theme. The final piece featured fast moving and shifting parallelograms rotating around the field while the flags did a fifty-yard-line exchange drill that included a head-chop maneuver, where the rifles tossed high in the air while jumping over the flags and then catching the toss on the last note.

The crowd went wild, cheering with a standing ovation. Even the Wylie band was clapping. The band members were hugging and high-fiving each other the minute they walked into the tunnel. The Tiger Football team was there clapping as well as they made their way back to the field. Trey reached out and touched the hand of as many of the eight friends as he could. As he touched George's hand, a powerful jolt of energy surged through them both.

As the band settled back in the stands before being dismissed for third quarter break, George leaned over to Travis.

"I wonder if Trey got to rub his balls on Charlie Water's locker the way he hoped he could."

"Knowing him, he probably did that and more," Travis said.

Normally, band members left the stands and headed to the concessions during the third quarter. Tonight, hardly any did. There was so much electricity in the air after the halftime. Travis, Emily and George made a quick detour into the stands beside the band and found their parents who had also made the trip. Travis sat beside his dad and sister, Teppy, who had come up from Fort Worth for the game. When she hugged Travis, she whispered in his ear. Travis whispered back and she hugged him again with a big grin on her face. George wondered what that was about and made a mental note to ask later.

The Tigers got the ball first and got to work right away, in three plays, Trey blasted through the Pirate defense and ran twenty yards for a touchdown. On the next series, Theo Martin sacked the Pirate quarterback and recovered the fumble. Two plays later, Bo Williams ran the ball in for another Tiger touchdown, made possible by a crushing block from none other than Trey McGee. The score was now Pirates 20, Tigers 32. The play settled down for the rest of the quarter with no additional scoring. Since it was third quarter, the band members got to sit with other sections. The Green Light eight sat together, laughing and cheering. Travis and Emily's hands were glued together. Mary sat close to George, her normal afro hairdo pulled back into a tight braid. Vince had his arm around Sarah's waist and he kept letting his hand drift south to end up on her ass. She kept moving his hand but in the end just gave up. George also noticed out of the corner of his eye, Don and Doug's knees pressed tight against one another, their hands a mere millimeter apart. He smiled at Don who grinned back, shrugging his shoulders.

By the middle of the fourth quarter, the game was won. On the first possession, the Tigers marched down the field eating up the clock and on fourth down, lined up to kick a 42-yard field goal, which might as well have been a 100 yard try because Blake Monroe had not completed a field goal all year. But as the snap was made, the eight focused with all their collective might and Blake hit the best kick of his life, clearing the upright with ten yards to spare. The Pirates launched another last-ditch effort to get back in the game, but fumbled the ball two yards shy of the end zone. With 1:30 seconds left on the clock, Bo took the snap and flipped a shovel pass to Trey, mostly to get out of the end zone and not give up a safety. Trey hit the oncoming defenders and knocked them over, right and left, like bowling pins. The crowd flew to its feet cheering and screaming as Trey ran 98 yards for the final touchdown of the game. As he crossed the end line and turned back around, he looked straight up in the stands at the band and blew kisses to the Green Light Eight who were going completely nuts. The Tigers made the ensuing two-point conversion and a minute later, the game ended. The Cowhill Tigers were the State AA Champions and Trey McGee was named Player of the Game. The Tiger team had him up on their shoulders parading him around in front of the home crowd while the band blasted "Long Train Running." It was the best night of Trey's life.

Trey had his photo taken so many times his eyes were dazzled. He was congratulated by dignitaries from the UIL, City of Irving, and even Tom Landry. Dozens of Cowhill residents shook his hand or hugged him, including Tim and Candy Murphy and all three of the Tanner Clan. JL Martin wrapped Theo and Trey in a tight hug and had his photo taken. George saw that as the celebrations continued for the team, Theo Martin grabbed Trey by the head and planted a deep and long kiss right on the boy's lips. Trey didn't seem to mind and just pounded on his teammate's shoulder pads and hugged him back along with many others.

Travis leaned over to George, shouting to be heard over the crowd. "Did Trey just get kissed by Theo Martin?"

"Um, it sure looked like it."

"Weird!"

"No duh!"

The band stopped at Pancho's Mexican Buffet on the way home and raised so much hell (along with the little Mexican flags on the tables to order more sopapillas) that the owner threatened to call the cops. But in true Mr. Smith style, he calmed the group down after that and there was no other incident.

"Hey, what was Teppy whispering to you about tonight?" George asked.

"Oh, yeah. I should tell you all. Well, she just mentioned that she has been using her powers at college all term long. Made the best grades, got picked to be in a play in the drama department, and this boy that was mean to her and called her a hillbilly, well his light case of acne turned into 'the heartbreak of psoriasis' all over his face and arms."

"Oh, wow," George said. Emily looked judgmental but didn't say anything.

"But she also said it really didn't start happening until just a few weeks ago. Wonder why the older you are sometimes, the longer it takes to figure it out?"

"Beats me," George said.

The bus ride back was a laid back affair since most of the students were exhausted from the entire day. Vince, Damon Reed, and Bruce Richardson had managed to smuggle a generous amount of cherry vodka and Everclear in non-descript bottles on the bus so by the time the band was on the north side of Dallas, half the bus was discretely looped. Mr. Smith might have known there was something technically rule-breaking going on in the bus, but he stayed up near the front of the bus most of the trip after one walk up the aisles congratulating the members and telling them over and over how proud he was of all of them.

By the time the bus was close to Rockwall, part of the band was asleep and the other part was deep into making out. Hands fumbled around underneath shirts and even into pants beneath blankets covering couples. In the darkness of the bus, Mary Washington leaned close and her cherry vodka flavored breath poured over George as her tongue slipped inside his mouth. George slid a tentative hand up underneath her sweatshirt and she didn't flinch or move. She responded only by sliding her own hand between George's legs and rubbing his erection until he practically blew his load in his shorts. Mary broke off the make out session as she noticed Anna Green two rows in front of them looking back with a pinched, disapproving look. George noticed as well when Mary pulled away and settled back against the window.

George leaned forward and whispered, "Take a picture, it'll last longer, spaz," punctuated by a flipped middle finger. Anna turned back around looking scandalized.

"You are just going to get us in more shit if you keep doing that," Mary whispered moving her hand back into his under the blanket.

"I don't care. She's a nosy bitch."

"Um hum. But she a rich nosy bitch with an important family. Just keep it easy, Young Skywalker."

"So, would you like to come over tomorrow? Maybe go out on a real date and everything?" George asked eagerly.

"A real date, huh? It's Sunday. Your parents okay with you going out on a Sunday night with school the next day? "

"Well normally, it would take some extra superpower work, but remember, they said if we won the game we all get the day off on Monday. There's going to be the parade so I guess the band will play and all that."

Mary smiled. "That's right. I forgot about that. So, where you taking this Ms. Thang?"

"Um, how about Butch's Barn? I'm kind of tired of Thanksgiving food."

"I don't know about eating in a barn." Mary said with an alarmed expression. George's face turned dark red.

"Oh Jeez. I didn't think. I meant, I didn't mean…"

Mary closed her eyes and laughed. "You are so easy to get worked up, G. I'm just messing with you. Yeah, I never been to that place. Sounds like it's only for white folks, though."

"No, it's on the campus. All kinds of people go there. It's really good," George said. "I'm pretty sure my dad will let me drive. He kind of does all the time."

"Okay then. So I figure Em and Travis are coming too?"

"Well yeah. I mean, if that's okay and all."

"Sure. Maybe I can stay over at her place. Make it easier and all that," Mary suggested. She moved her hand back to George's belly and down again toward his crotch. George closed his eyes and laid his head back on the seat.

"Yeah. Easier."

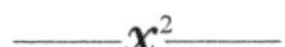

George walked into the kitchen on Sunday morning humming "When I Need You," by Leo Sayer. He grabbed some Aunt Jemima's pancake and waffle mix and stirred up a mixing bowl full of batter. He threw some Jimmy Dean sausage in the pan and let it cook slowly and sizzle. He heated up the griddle and added a bit of oil and then poured the pancakes on, watching them bubble up. The coffee was finished in the Mr. Coffee. He wore a pair of sweatpants and a "Dreamboat Annie" Heart t-shirt. Hank Harris walked bleary eyed into the kitchen in his underwear, his hair sticking up in the back.

"What's all this kiddo? Man, I figured you'd be dead this morning."

"Just felt like some pancakes and sausage. It was a great night though. Grab some coffee, Dad. You want me to get you some pants," George offered.

"Yeah. Sure son." Duke said grabbing his Dallas Cowboys mug. George took the pancakes off the griddle and set a stack in front of his dad with some sausage. He ran down the hall and grabbed a pair of pajama bottoms from the foot of his dad's bed. His mom looked up from her pillow.

"Do I smell breakfast?" she said with a smile.

"Yep. Just now ready."

"What a sweet boy," she said.

Normally, Sunday mornings were tense, especially if Darla was pushing Hank to go to church. Half the time, George just went with Travis while the Harris' stayed home. And after the big revival night, both Darla and Hank had said they were going to wait a while before going back. Even the McGee's hadn't been back yet, the emotions and discomfort of having their dirty laundry aired in front of the crowed had made them reluctant to face everyone there. In a rare display of true pastoral insight and care, Brother Nelson had even stopped by the McGee's to check on them and tell them to take their time in coming back and to assure them everyone still loved them.

This morning, the Harris family was having a normal, all-American breakfast with no drama or tears. Since the lights, George had skillfully modified his father's behavior, making him a virtual Ward Cleaver or Mike Brady. Duke flipped through the paper looking for the story on last night's game, Trey McGee resting on his teammate's shoulders as he waved to the crowd. George wondered if there was a photo of Theo Martin kissing him.

"The band was just spectacular last night, honey." Darla said. "And these pancakes are wonderful. When did you learn to cook so well? These are twice as good as the last time you tried to make them, I swear."

"Oh just more grown up I guess, Mom."

"You have plans tonight, honey?"

"Um, now that you mention it. We were hoping to go out to dinner. Maybe to Butch's Barn. If it's okay with you?"

Duke looked up over the top of his glasses. "You need to use the VW?" He offered.

"That would be great dad," George said with a smile. *Yahtzee* he thought to himself.

George was getting ready to call Travis when his dad came into his room later that morning with something behind his back. "Got something here for you, buddy." Duke handed over a sack from Ward's Drug Store. George pulled out a box of Sheik condoms. His mouth fell open.

"I got the kind ribbed for her pleasure. The black girl I slept with in Korea really liked those kind. They are flavored too, like bubble gum I think."

George's mortification left him completely speechless, his face burning red as he held the box with a shaking hand.

"Do you need a little lesson on how to slide one on" Duke asked helpfully.

"I think I've got it, Dad," George said embarrassed beyond reason.

"Don't try to push all the way up into that tip thing, it's supposed to stay loose so you have room for your sperm."

"I am going to beg you to stop now." George said reaching out and gripping his dad's neck, staring hard into his eyes. "Please don't ever talk to me about condoms anymore, okay?"

Duke Harris stared back at George and then smiled. "Hope you and that black girl have fun tonight. Did I tell you I slept with a black girl in Korea? George closed his eyes and took a deep breath. He grabbed the receiver off the wall phone and dialed Travis.

"Hullo?" a deep voice answered.

"Oh Trey. Thought you might be gone already. Um, can I talk to Travis?"

Trey leaned away from the phone and bellowed, "Hey Scrote, your boyfriend's on the phone. Not the one with the flat boobs, the other one with the little mustache." George could hear a scuffle and an "Ow! That's my sack, you dumb-ass."

"I'm here," Travis said sounding annoyed.

"Thought he would be gone."

"He's leaving in a few minutes. Jerk."

"Hey, we're on for tonight. Come over in a bit 'cause we've got some preparation to do."

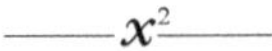
$$x^2$$

George and Travis picked up Emily and Mary at 7:00 pm and headed over to Monroe Street. They turned up Lee and then found a parking place near the Field House and walked over to Butch's Barn. Interestingly, quite a lot of people must have been tired of Thanksgiving food because the place was full. Candles flickered on the tables and red and white checked cloths decorated the tables. They got seated in a back room with only two other college-aged couples which was exactly what George had planned, sending that message strongly to the host as he touched his arm once they walked into the restaurant.

"You've got that Jedi mind trick down pretty good," Travis said holding Emily's chair out for her as she scooted into her seat. She had put her hair up in some high pony tail with ringlets of golden curls around her face. She was wearing makeup and light teal eye shadow. Her lips were glistening with pink lip gloss. She had on a pair of large dangling earrings and a pretty pendant. Her neckline plunged down further than normal and her breasts looked bigger for sure. Travis couldn't take his eyes off her.

"Yeah, it's pretty useful. Especially for my dad," George said staring at Mary. She had somehow straightened her hair and was wearing in a high bun on top of her head. Her eyelids were sparkling with gold eye shadow. Her lips were shining eggplant purple. She had on even larger gold hoop earrings. She was wearing a black cardigan sweater but the dress underneath was dangerously low cut and pressed hard against the fabric, her nipples standing out in the cool air.

"You look amazing," George said.

"Thanks. You look pretty fly yourself, Skywalker."

George was wearing grey flannel slacks and a button down white shirt with a navy V-neck sweater. Travis had a pair of khakis and a black dress shirt with an actual grey suede sports jacket.

"You know, if you boys keep this up, you just might get lucky tonight," Emily said enigmatically. Travis's eyes bulged out of his head. George was fairly sure her idea of lucky was a bit different than what the boys were thinking.

The waiter came and took their orders. Very boldly, George ordered a bottle of Chianti for the table and the waiter didn't blink. He also didn't see the four of them holding hands underneath the table as they ordered. When the food came, the portions were huge: ravioli, veal parmesan, lasagna, and baked ziti. The waiter poured the Chianti and even got a second bottle for the kids after the first was finished. The four laughed and talked about the football game, the band performance, and all the fun on the bus driving back.

"Mr. Smith probably could get in trouble for not stopping some of that," Emily said.

"Yeah, but he won't," George said confidently. Most of the kids won't even remember, right Trav?"

"Right on," Travis said, his cheeks bright red, his blue eyes sparkling mischievously in the candlelight.

"Keep on Truckin'," Emily mocked. "You sound like your dad tonight."

"He's drinking like him too," George said. "May the Force be with you, brother."

"That's a spicy meatball!" Travis yelled. Emily rolled her eyes.

"So what are we going to do after dessert?" Mary asked.

"It's a bit of a surprise. But I think you will like it. I worked on it this afternoon with my main man, Travster here."

"You're gonna love it. It's far out. It's bitchin'."

"Are you on LSD or something?" Emily said suspiciously.

The waiter was soon bringing out big slabs of Tiramisu and cannoli and even more wine.

"You better knock it off if you intend to drive us somewhere," Emily said eating a mouthful of Tiramisu. "Did we even order this?"

"It's on the house," George said. Travis spit out his water laughing at that.

"I can't believe I ate the whooooole thing," he said, his cheeks flushed, eyes sparkling in the candlelight. The other three laughed.

Thirty minutes later, the blue VW was cruising down Park Street toward Hwy 24. The night was cold but Mary unrolled the sunroof and actually stood up in the crisp late autumn air. They rolled down Hwy 24 across the bridge over the South Sulphur River. George turned left at the junction and motored toward Ladonia.

"I like this little car," she said.

George had the Saturday Night Fever soundtrack playing. "If I can't have you" blared through the open sunroof.

"It's freezing back here," Emily complained.

George turned off to the right three miles down the road. The gravel road was dark and totally abandoned at that hour of the night. He drove slowly down the road and turned in alongside a dark building. An expanse of blacktop shone like a black ribbon in the wintery air.

"Where the hell are we?" Emily said turning her head back and forth. "It looks like the airport or something."

"Welcome to Cowhill International Airport, Ladies," Travis said louder than was necessary. "George got the key for this hangar from his dad. There won't be any people out here tonight. So it's all ours."

Mary and Emily climbed out of the VW and walked with the boys to the door while George fumbled with the lock. He opened the door with a flare and flipped on a light. The room glowed with string after string of colored Christmas lights. There were cozy blankets thrown over the dilapidated couches in the hanger. Bob Seeger was singing "We've Got Tonight" on the radio.

"This is beautiful," Mary said pulling George into an embrace and kissing him deeply.

Travis looked at the two kissing before looking over at Emily. "And I halped!" he said in his most twangy Southern accent.

Emily smiled. "Come here you idiot before you fall down."

An hour later, George's face felt wet and swollen from all the kissing. His lips were chapped and he had a huge ache in his belly, and he couldn't have been happier. Mary was a passionate, sweet girl who knew how to kiss better than George could have imagined. His tongue literally ached from all the kissing. And that wasn't all. He laid back holding Mary in his arms smiling. He looked over at the floor and saw a pile of their clothes. He hadn't needed his dad's misguided gift, but just about.

"I told you there was plenty of fun to be had without doing the nasty," Mary said. In the dim light, George was transfixed by her beautiful tits as he laid on his side beside the girl. They were the most beautiful things he had ever seen. He leaned over and grabbed his small stash from his pants pocket along with his lighter and lit the blunt. The orange glow mixing with the Christmas lights in the warm, almost sweaty room.

"Hey, G …how about sharing the bud, bud?" Travis said with a giggle. *Clearly the kid was still loaded,* George thought. He got up holding his hand over his privates and finally just thought, forget it. He came over and handed Travis the other joint, flicking the lighter. In the flame, Emily shrieked and hid her face, giggling hysterically. George grinned noticing the other couples' clothes strewn on the floor as well. Emily's pearly bare shoulders glowing in the dim light along with Travis's bare chest.

George hopped back over to the couch and crawled in beside Mary, her hand sliding back around him. He passed the joint to Mary and she took a long puff and sent the smoke high in the air. "I never knew white folks smoked this much weed, either."

"They don't. Just these two," Emily said from the dark corner where she and Travis's couch lay in the shadows. She must have kissed Travis again because her giggles were suddenly stifled.

George laid there feeling grown up and luckier than he ever had. So much had happened since September 12th. He would have never guessed he be lying beside a girl like this back then. He looked at Mary's face illuminated by the Christmas lights and the glow of the joint. He could feel her happiness, but also that underlying sadness and fear. He slid down close to her face.

Mary looked at him and raised her hand to hold the side of his face. "You are a sweet boy, George Harris." She sighed, a single tear sliding out of the corner of her large brown eyes. "You have brought me back to life. I didn't think I would ever let a boy touch me again. But you are so gentle and kind, I'm never afraid. I don't even think you needed space magic either. I didn't think a boy would want to touch me with a ten foot pole…after, you know."

George kissed Mary and stared hard into her face. "You are perfect to me."

"Used goods as my grandmother and mom tell me," Mary said.

George sat up. "If there is one thing I know for sure, whatever happened, whatever they did, when we touched you and the power flowed through you, it made you brand new again. You never have to worry about that, not that I would have cared anyway. But you have a new start. And you know, I'm pretty sure that if you want us to, we can make you forget the whole thing."

Mary smiled, brushing away another tear. "I know and I have thought about it. But for right now, I think I need to remember it…all of it. It's important and it's part of me. Maybe soon

I won't feel that way and you all can just erase it for me. But for now, I'm good," she said touching George's face. "Hey honey, what time is it?"

George absentmindedly looked at his watch. It was 1:05. "Fuck me; it's after 1:00. We were supposed to be back at midnight!"

Emily squealed and jumped up knocking Travis to the floor with a loud bump on his ass. Everyone began to scramble for clothes in the dim light. The girls were giggling and the boys were trying to hop around on one foot to put on their pants. George scooped up the remnants of the joint and put into his baggie. His dad knew about coming out here and with a bit of alien persuasion, he was all for it. George just found his sock when Travis screamed in terror, gripping his head like it was going to burst, falling to his knees. Before George could react, he was blinded by an atomic blast of fear, pain, and horror, ripping at his mind like a blender through ripe peaches. The girls were sobbing, holding their heads. Emily was wailing. And then, like a pair of snips on a bomb wire, it stopped.

Travis stood up and looked around like he was insane. "They have Trey. They have him and Angie and they are hurting them. Oh Jesus, Oh holy God, they have them."

54 Theo

Driving toward the lake, Theo and Junior sat in the front seat of the Bronco while Toy and Greg Benton sat in the back. Junior had his 9mm out and lying on his leg, humming along with "Bennie and the Jets." He kept repeating, "ba, ba, ba, Benny, Benny…" over and over until Theo reached over and slapped the back of his head.

"Knock that shit off, Junior," Theo said in his low melodic voice, this time clipped and annoyed.

"Ow. That hurt. You're gonna make me shoot my dick off."

"Why do you even have that gun? There is no way in hell Daddy told you to bring it. You might as well put it away. The idea is to surprise them, not shoot them." The Bronco tore along the highway toward Lake Tawakoni. Theo rubbed his eyes. *Shit, there had been so much going on since the ball game,* he thought.

It had been a perfect night. State Champions, so great, he thought. His perfect guy, Trey McGee, had been a star. He had never seen a player move so gracefully, jump so high, and hit so hard. He felt tears sting his eyes and he wiped them away. But at least, no one else was going to have him either.

His daddy had called a special deacon's meeting for the morning. There were mimosas around the pool in celebration of Theo's and the Tigers great victory. He said Caroline had stayed up in Dallas with one of her girlfriends so they could go shopping at Northpark, her favorite mall. She would spend enough at Neiman-Marcus to balance the federal budget.

There was electricity in the air. The Bentons were there, Junior, Cal and Buck Matlock along with Jerry Morgan, Randy Hamm, Lloyd Massey, and Jim Measles. Most of the men kept looking at the orange juice and champagne concoction like it was poison but still downed them one after the other. Sherriff Hines and two deputies were there as well. He noticed that Cal and Buck Matlock were the only men present that weren't having a great morning. In fact, if he didn't know better, he would have said Buck had been crying.

JL cleared his throat and began the gathering. "Thank you brethren for coming out today. First off, let's raise our glasses to Theo who just played the game of his life." The men raised their glasses and cheered. JL reached over and grabbed Theo's head and gave him a big smack on the side of the head.

"Today is a propitious day. We have waited so long for the signs and wonders to come, tarried long and hard to know exactly what offering we need to make to cleanse our land and people of the evil and sinfulness that has taken hold here in our lovely town of Cowhill. We moved forward with the last offering and it was a special one. But I see now that it was just a precursor to the real divine offering that has presented itself to us. Last night I was visited by the angel Azarel again who confirmed that this sacrifice will be pleasing to the Lord and will rid us of this evil that has besieged us for so long. It will take all our might, not only to perform the ceremony, but to hold off those who will resist it. Brother Hines here will do all he can from a law enforcement perspective. I've made as many calls as I know to other agencies to alert them they may be hearing from people from the area who are suffering from some mass hysteria and to ignore them; that local law enforcement is taking care of the city business."

"This is not a time for timidity but for vigilance. We must stand strong and follow through with the teachings of Azarel brought to us through my great-great grandfather, Theocrates Martin and handed down to me. This is the true New Testament for us. This is a revelation given to only a handful but we will be the leaders in a new wave of truth, a return to the good ole days, to the old time religion that even preceded our parents. The cost will be great, but the results will be life-changing."

With that pronouncement, Buck Matlock actually sobbed out loud and Theo had watched the group of men step away from him and Cal who stood with his head down as well. JL went over to the man and wrapped his arms around him and comforted him while Buck literally broke down in weeping. JL hugged the man for a minute and then pulled away to continue to address the men.

"Brother Matlock is sorrowful today because the offering that I speak of involves his very own, Angie." Several of the men in the group actually shouted, "No!" JL held his hands up and called for quiet. His grave and remorseful face did not quite hide the utter delight behind his eyes that flashed bright in the morning sunrise. "I need to share some important words with all of you that came to me last night in a vision." The men gathered in closer, some of them sitting on patio chairs, others standing around the pool and hot tub with arms folded, serious faces focused on JL.

"The angel Azarel appeared to me last night after I had been praying for some time about the sacrifice that I had felt was presented to me in the past few days, both from the interlopers on my property and information that came from other respected sources. As you all know now, Trey McGee is not the son of Mike McGee but is in fact, the bastard son of Carl Washington, created through the unnatural and certainly forced fornication with Janet McGee. They have kept this secret for seventeen years. His unnatural talents of late seem to be related to some satanic interaction a group of young people have had along with the reprobates from Western Auto, Jack Tanner and Tim Murphy. It may be that these men have unnaturally seduced these boys and a few girls, most likely through fornication, sodomy, and devil worship and have turned them into acolytes of evil. They appear to even have some manifestation of power that comes from the mouth of hell itself. I am saddened to also say that Brother Matlock's daughter, Angie, has been seduced by the Washington bastard and this infernal group and is now with child, a hellish congress that has produced the spawn of Satan. Brothers, this is the mark of the Beast. I have just discovered that Trey McGee ran for a grand total of 666 yards in the State Championship. Need I say more?"

The murmuring of the men rose as they became more and more incensed and agitated. Randy Hamm, shook his fist in the air and declared, "They all need to die!"

"The angel has confirmed to me that the sacrifice of the Washington bastard along with his seed and bride will rid our town of the influence of Satan, fornication, queers, unsavory types like Negros, Orientals, and Mexicans. The true purity of the place will be restored. These other groups will flee the town and never return and a new age of peace and harmony among white brethren will be ushered in. It is a mighty price, but the angel reminded me of the word of the Lord that has decreed this before." JL picked up his large bible and flipped to the Old Testament book of 2 Kings, Chapter 23.

> [19] *"Josiah also removed all the houses of the high places which were in the cities of Samaria, which the kings of Israel had made provoking the LORD; and he did to them just as he had done in Bethel.* [20] *All the priests of the high places who were there he slaughtered on the altars and burned human bones on them; then he returned to Jerusalem."*

As you can tell, God Almighty is a vengeful God when his laws and ways are ignored. That's what we will do tonight, gentlemen. These high priests of evil will be slaughtered and their bones will be burned on the altars. And for those of you who may be still distraught over the inclusion of sweet Angie Matlock, I must also remind of the story of Jephthah. JL began to read again.

> *29 Then the Spirit of the LORD came upon Jephthah… 30 And Jephthah made a vow to the LORD: "If you give the Ammonites into my hands, 31 whatever comes out of the door of my house to meet me when I return in triumph from the Ammonites will be the LORD's, and I will sacrifice it as a burnt offering." 32 Then Jephthah went over to fight the Ammonites, and the LORD gave them into his hands… 34 When Jephthah returned to his home in Mizpah, who should come out to meet him but his daughter, dancing to the sound of tambourines! She was his only child. Except for her he had neither son nor daughter. 35 When he saw her, he tore his clothes and cried, "Oh! My daughter! You have made me miserable and wretched, because I have made a vow to the LORD that I cannot break."*

> *36"My father," she replied, "you have given your word to the LORD. Do to me just as you promised, now that the LORD has avenged you of your enemies, the Ammonites." 37 So she said to her father, "Let this thing be done for me: leave me alone two months, that I may go up and down on the mountains and weep for my virginity, I and my companions."*

> *38 So he said, "Go." Then he sent her away for two months, and she departed, she and her companions, and wept for her virginity on the mountains. 39 And at the end of two months, she returned to her father, who did with her according to his vow that he had made. (Judges 11:29-39)*

"I realize this seems harsh. What kind of father would do this to his only daughter? Surely God did not really mean for him to keep such a vow? Such is always the way of the devil. But I tell you, Jephthah honored God by keeping his vow. His sacrifice was accepted by the Lord. And his daughter willingly gave herself. Tonight, we will witness the same and begin the sacrificial process to purify our people and our land," JL's jowls were shaking, sweat dripped from his face, as he spit the words out to the men. Many fell to their knees and began to cry out to God, hands lifted in supplication. Buck and Cal Matlock gripped each other and sobbed.

Theo had slid back into the shadows by this time, turning away from the revival meeting being conducted around the pool by his dad. He went to his room and sat on his bed, his hands shaking so violently he had to put them under his legs to quiet them. His heart was beating so fast, so hard he was sure it would burst. He opened up a drawer on his desk and slid out the box inside. He opened up the lid and took out the clippings and photos and reverently touched each one. The images were blurred through his tears as he handled the pictures. Some he had clipped from the paper, others he had taken at school for the yearbook. Some he had even snapped in the locker room or shower, unbeknownst to Trey. That was one of the great things about being editor of the yearbook, he always had a camera and no one minded. And since he had a key to the darkroom, he developed the film and enlarged the photos himself.

The close up of Trey's face, outlined his lips and smile in such sharp contrast, catching the curves of his mouth, the dimples to the sides, the way his nose flared, and then of course, those eyes. Theo ran his finger along the outline of Trey's face and lips. He thumbed through the stack of photos of Trey undressing or putting on his uniform. A few even showed him smiling with other boys as they showered, his telephoto lens bringing all of Trey's beauty into sharp clarity. The photos were dog-eared and creased, but they were Theo's most precious possessions. He had looked at them all a thousand times. He knew every shadow and curve.

Trey signaled to turn off toward the lake. He put his head into his hand, weary and sad, while the other gripped the steering wheel. He still kept trying to come up with some way Trey could be saved. Getting rid of the bitch and the brat; that had to be. But if he could save Trey, then maybe his friend would change and realize just what he meant to him. There had to be some way. For all of his dad's certainty, it did not compare with his own resolute comprehension: it was truly evil to destroy something as perfect as Trey McGee.

Tonight would be the start of something deadly. But maybe, just maybe, it would also be the moment he had waited for.

Andy's screams woke Mike and Janet from a deep sleep. Mike tore into the boy's bedroom and found the boy curled in a fetal position on the floor, holding his head and yelling, "No, No, No!!" again and again. Mike finally picked the boy up and shook him to break him out of whatever dream he was having.

"Hey…hey," Mike said soothingly cradling the boy in his arms. "It's alright, buddy. You are fine. It was just a dream. Just a dream," Mike said rocking the boy back and forth. Janet came over and wrapped an arm around Andy taking him from Mike, handing her husband a pair of pajama bottoms to put on.

"Here, for God's sake, Mike," Janet said. Mike stepped into them and pulled them up over his naked ass. "Honey, what's wrong, Andy? Everything is okay. You just had a bad dream." The boy continued to hold his head and moan. "Dear Jesus, Mike. What is wrong with him?"

"I don't know. What time is it?

"A little after 1:00. Why?"

"Not sure. But I just have a funny feeling. My head was pounding right before Andy woke up and I was having a terrible dream about Trey."

"It's not a dream, Daddy," Andy said barely above a whisper.

"What do you mean, honey? Daddy isn't talking about your dream. He had a bad dream too."

"NO! Andy said insistently. "It's the same dream. But it's not a dream. Someone is hurting Trey and Angie. They are hurting them right now. Aaahhhh!" Andy screamed and went stiff in his mother's arms. At the same time, Mike bent over and gasped.

"Son of a bitch," he moaned. He looked up with eyes wild with fear. "Andy's right. Someone has grabbed Trey and Angie. Something has happened to them." Mike took Andy in his arms. "Listen buddy. You need to tell me what the hell is going on. I know you and your brothers have been holding something back from me for a while now. Can you just tell me what is going on? It's important, especially if Trey is in trouble. TELL ME!" Mike shouted.

Andy's eyes filled with tears. His chin quivered along with his lips. Finally, the boy gripped Mike's big hands and placed them on either side of his face and laid his forehead against his Dad's like Travis had done with him and Trey. A flash of green light enveloped their heads as Mike's hands tightened around Andy's head. Mike sank to his knees as he stayed connected to the boy, panting harder and harder as the knowledge, events, and dangers of the past week transferred to his mind. He finally sat drained and overwhelmed in the middle of the boys' bedroom, eyes wet, his fury building. He looked up as heard a stampede of feet in the hallway. His eyes widened as he saw Travis and George standing in the doorway with Emily and Mary behind them in nice dresses with disheveled hair and smeared lipstick. Mike rose up as fast as an attacking Tiger and grabbed Travis by the arms, lifting him into the air.

"What have you done? What the fuck have you kids done? All this time you knew he was going to run off. You went out to that place. They shot at you …"

"What?" Janet shouted grabbing her face.

Mike hauled off and slapped Travis hard on the face knocking the boy halfway across the room in a huge crash. Emily and Mary screamed.

Andy shouted "Daddy, Stop!"

Janet ran for Mike and tried to grab his arm but he already gripped Travis by the shoulders and threw him toward the wall. But halfway across the floor, Travis stopped in midair and hovered, before landing easily on his feet. Mike tore after him like a madman and Travis and the other kids put their hands out and lifted Mike off his feet and slammed him hard up against the ceiling. The man crashed to the floor in a crumpled heap.

"Mr. McGee, please stop," George said standing between Travis and his father, holding his hands up. "We don't have time for this. You can yell at all of us later, kick our asses all across town but right now, Trey and Angie are in big trouble. We have to help them!"

Janet stood in the middle of the floor stunned. "What is going on? What have you all done? How did you just do that? How do you know Trey is in trouble? Will someone tell me what the HELL is going on?" Mary Washington walked over to Janet and took her hands in hers and lifted them up to her face, leaning her forehead against Janet's. Two minutes later, Janet collapsed sobbing to the floor gripping at Mary's hands. Travis ran over to her and wrapped his arms around her.

"I'm sorry, Mommy. I'm sorry, Mommy," he kept repeating, more like he was five instead of fifteen.

George looked around the devastated family and up at Emily with a 'what are we supposed to do now' look. Emily moved forward and bravely grabbed Mike McGee's hand and got him to look into her eyes. "Mr. McGee, listen to me," George moved over and grabbed Mike's other hand. "You need to calm down. Don't freak out any more. Just concentrate on helping Trey. Trey needs you now. You can feel the strength of all of us. We can help. I think you are strong too. Help us!"

Mike McGee blinked several times and looked his grieving boys and his wife and reached out to them, pulling them into his arms. Mary moved over closer to George and slid her hand into his. Emily came over to them and George put his arm around her. She hugged him close.

"Thanks for what you did. He could have killed Travis," Emily whispered.

"I honestly think it could have gone the other way, George whispered with trepidation.

Mike McGee turned around and looked at the kids and stood up. "So I got a lot of all this from that mental thing you did. But I think you better tell me the whole story."

"Dad, we don't have time. Trey…"

"We don't know where he is, do we?"

"He's at Tooter Turner's lake house," Travis said. "He and Angie wanted a couple of days alone. Um, they…they might have gotten married."

"Son of a cocksucking whore," Mike said under his breath but clearly loud enough for everyone to hear.

"Mike. Little pictures…" Janet began but then broke off. She knew the kids had heard that and worse."

"So do you have any 'telepathy' or anything to know if they did or didn't? Do you think they were still at the lake when whatever happened, happened?"

Travis looked around the small group, urging anyone else to take a stab at the questions. Finally George spoke up.

"I don't think they did. And yes, they were at the lake when they took them," he said definitely.

Mike stared at him like he had two heads. "What about now?"

It was George's turn to look around for help.

"We can't really feel them now," Emily said with a small voice.

"What does that mean? Mike demanded.

"It might just mean they are knocked out or asleep or something. Whatever, I think they are still okay," Travis said.

Mike ran his hands through his hair like a man on the verge of a breakdown. "And all this started with those lights? And you all have been like supercharged or something."

"We're mutants now," Andy said. "Like X-Men."

"Could someone just tell me what is going on?" Mike said wearily. He sat on the edge of the bed like a man defeated. Andy climbed up in his lap and hugged him tight. Travis sat beside him and laid and hand on his dad's arm.

"This really is faster than telling you everything, Dad. Come here, Mom," Travis said. Janet sat down beside them. The kids gathered round and touched the McGee parents and they were instantly locked in an electric surge of power and understanding that flowed deep and completely through them all. It took five minutes, but in the end, the adults sat still and tried to cope with everything they had just seen and felt.

"So, you kind of know it all, now Dad. And I'm sure you have powers too, Dad. It just feels like you do. Don't know about you Mom," Travis said softly. "You get it, right? I mean, you know everything, don't you?"

Mike rubbed his head. "Yeah. I don't know how, but I seem to know all things that have happened. I just don't see how this all happened. Some of this just can't be real."

"It's real, Dad. We are super heroes now," Andy said. Mike smiled a very weak smile and rubbed Andy's head.

The phone extension by Trey and Andy's bed rang and everyone jumped. Emily actually screamed and then clamped her hand over her mouth. Travis reached for the receiver but pulled his hand away when he saw his father's face. Mike picked up the phone and gulped. "Hello?"

"Hey, is this Mike? Mike McGee?"

"Yes."

"This is Jack Tanner. Jack from Western Auto, you know?"

"I know you, Jack. It's late and I'm kind of…"

"I know you're awake and know about your boy and everything. In fact, I have a feeling you know about all this shit now. Is everyone else alright?"

Mike stared at the receiver like it was a cobra. He put it cautiously back to his ear. "Everyone else seems fine. What do you..?"

"I'm going to come over. Okay? I just wanted to see if you were all there and awake like I figured you were. Tim and I will be right over."

"Tim? What? Alright, I guess. Look, it might not be the best time…"

"See you in a few." The line went dead. Mike stared at it uncomprehending.

"It appears Jack Tanner and Tim are coming over."

George sighed. "Good. They are grownups and know about all this. Maybe he will know what to do."

"Should these kids call their parents?" Janet asked hesitantly.

"It's okay, Mom. None of them know about all this but you. They think we are just spending the night with each other. No real reason to worry them tonight," Travis said trying to be helpful but when he saw his dad's angry face, he just shut up.

"I'm going to put on some coffee," Janet said. "And find some bourbon," she added.

Five minutes later, there was a light knock at the door and Travis answered it. Jack came inside and hugged the boy, who instantly felt the calmness and strength of Jack move through him. Tim patted him on the back as well and Travis led them into the den where the group had moved. The girls were sitting forlornly in their dresses on the couch with George.

"Hi, Mike, Janet," Jack said softy. "Really sorry about all this. I figured you're pretty pissed right now. But if you can just hold off on punching me in the face until we get your boy back, it might be best," Jack said holding up his hands defensively. "So, whoever grabbed Trey and Angie, knew they were at the lake house. Guys, do you have any idea who all knew Trey and Angie were going out there?"

"I really got the idea no one else but Tooter knew. But, you don't think he would tell, do you?" Travis said softly.

"No idea. I mean, this smells like JL Martin to me. But why would he grab Trey?" Jack asked.

"Why aren't we calling the sheriff," Janet asked. "This is crazy. We need to call the police or the FBI or someone."

"I don't think calling the sheriff will do any good," Tim said. "LeRoy Hines is bought and paid for by JL. He wouldn't help us at all when someone slaughtered the animals around our houses."

"What? Oh my God," Janet said holding a hand to her mouth.

"I know it sounds farfetched, but I have some feeling that whatever is motivating JL has something to do with the whole Carl Washington thing, especially now that it has come out that he is Trey's biological father," Jack said, then looked at Mike and added. "Sorry."

"That feels right to me too," Tim added.

The phone rang startling the group in the kitchen. Mike lifted the receiver and held it to his ear. "Hello?"

"Daddy? What's wrong? Something happened, I know it. Is Trey hurt? What is going on?" Teppy asked breathing hard into the phone.

Mike shook his head trying to figure out again how she could have known. She's mixed up in all this too, he thought. He went over the basics, tried to calm her down and convince her to just stay in Fort Worth and wait until they knew more. She told him fat chance."

Hanging up, he looked at Janet and shrugged. "Teppy's on her way."

"Good," Janet said weakly.

The phone shattered the quiet again, sending the group into a brief panic. Mike walked to the wall phone in the kitchen and picked it up.

"Hello," he said much more forcefully this time.

A muffled, garbled voice on the other end spoke. "This McGee?"

"Yes. What have you done with my son?" Mike said practically shouting.

"You better calm the fuck down and listen," the voice said. Jack came over and leaned his head close to the receiver where he could hear the conversation as well. "Yeah, we have your bastard and his tramp whore. The bitch is knocked up with your bastard's bastard too." Mike's eyes closed as the confirmation of what he had seen in Travis and Andy's mind became reality.

"What do you want?"

"Oh it's easy. Money. Lots of it."

"I don't have a lot of money. You must know that." Mike said.

"Well there is a bunch of money at that grocery store of yours. We can start with that. We want $100,000 by sundown tomorrow, or this half-nigger spawn of Carl Washington's is gonna get gutted."

Mike started to scream but Jack put his hand on Mike's head and he calmed down again. "So I bring this money to you and you give me back my son?"

"Yep. Pretty simple. Oh just in case you were wondering…we are Wylie Pirates. They should have won that state championship. Your weird mutant nigger freak was some sort of ringer. If you call the cops or the sheriff or the fucking FBI, we will slit his throat. We will cut the bitch's belly and pull that freak show baby out and cook it for dinner. You comprende?"

"Yes," Mike said through clinched teeth. His knuckles on the phone were white.

"We will call tomorrow morning at 10:00 am with instructions. Tell no one, or your nigger boy dies." The line hummed.

Mike's hand shook and the receiver crumbled in his fist, falling to the floor in pieces. Tim bent down to gather up the shattered phone while Jack put a steadying hand on Mike's shoulder.

"Someone called looking for ransom. They want $100 thousand by tomorrow," Jack said. "Supposedly, they are criminals from Wylie, mad about the football game."

"Utter horseshit," Tim said.

"Why would they call and say that if it wasn't true?" Janet whined. "That doesn't make any sense."

"It's possible," Jack said grimly, "But I still say this has the stink of JL Martin all over it. I think this was just one of his jackass lackeys trying to control the situation and keep you from going to the Feds. I honestly doubt they care much about the money, but right now, I don't know if you have the luxury of not planning like you are going to pay it. Do you have any way to come up with that kind of money?"

"If I rob the payroll and drain accounts, not pay any bills, I can probably cover it. But it will ruin me," Mike said looking like a drowning man that's just been thrown an anchor. "But whatever it takes, no problem," he finished resolutely. Janet hugged him, tears pouring off her nose. She disengaged from him and began to fill coffee mugs. She brought in Cremora and sugar and a big bottle of Jim Beam. Tim and Jack took their coffee black but added generous amounts of the bourbon. Mike poured straight JB into his cup and collapsed into his La-Z Boy. The kids doctored up their coffee with plenty of the creamer and sugar. George caught no one looking and poured a shot of the bourbon into everyone's cup. When Emily gave him a scandalized look, he just shrugged and took a drink and smiled. The girls sipped the Irish coffee and made a sour face, but kept drinking. Travis looked over at his dad, slumped in his chair, his face in his hands, tears leaking out from between his fingers and his heart broke. He put the coffee down and went to his dad. The other kids followed suit and soon they were all reaching out, laying hands of healing on Mike. Tim came over and wrapped his big arms around Mike and several of the kids, closing his eyes and concentrating with all his might. In a moment, Mike was wiping away the tears and patting Tim on the arm, hugging the kids and managing even a small smile.

"Guess you all know how to make this alien juice work," he said. "I can't believe how much better I feel right now." He looked at Travis and brought him close. "I'm so sorry for hitting you like that. My dad used to haul off and hit me and my brother like that all the time. I promised myself my whole life I wouldn't do that. I, I can't stand that I…"

"It's fine, Daddy. I probably deserved it," Travis said. "You're not like Grandpa at all." Mike hugged him again.

"I don't mean to be the voice of worry and fear here," Janet said. "But what are we going to do? How can we just sit around? We need to tell someone."

Jack came over and put his arm around Janet. "I do know you must need to do something. How about this: as soon as the school district opens, we will call and talk to the superintendent or someone. Ask if he has heard of any malcontents who might be bent on taking revenge on Trey. We can say he has received some threatening phone calls. Maybe there is a chance that's the case here. In the meantime, I think the rest of us need to be ready to head back out to the bridge and JL's place. I can't imagine him going anywhere else with those kids. That place is like a fortress normally. Having that bridge restored puts a new back door into his land. That might be very helpful to us."

"But won't he have like a lot of men with him, maybe with guns again? You all have already been shot at. It's too dangerous for the kids. I won't let them go out there," Janet said adamantly.

"But Mom," Andy began.

"No way in hell you are going back out there," she said flatly.

Mike got out of his chair and went over to where Janet was standing and held her arms. "I know how you feel, sweetheart. But these kids, they are part of this. I can see it and feel it now. Honestly, I think they are probably safer all together going out there than staying back at home where one of those assholes could grab one of them. Together, you won't believe how strong these kids are."

"And there's even more of us, Mom." Travis said. "Vince and Sarah, Doug, and Don…"

"And Jessie?"

"Who?" Travis and George said together,

"A girl in my class. She's a mutant too," Andy said.

"Please don't call yourselves that," Janet said pained.

"No mom, you don't understand. It's what makes us special. The mutations are our powers. I love it. I never felt so smart or not afraid," he said. Janet patted his arm and looked down at the floor, lost in her sadness.

"Well, nothing else is going to happen tonight. You kids need to sleep. We all do," knowing there was little chance of him sleeping. "Obviously tomorrow is going to be a huge day. I don't know how yet, but we are going to get our Trey back. And Angie," Mike choked out.

"She's really nice," Dad," Andy said. "All that stuff about her being a skanky 'ho' is just lies." Even Mike had to chuckle at that.

Janet leaned her head against Mike's chest. "A baby. Oh I am way too young to be a grandma!"

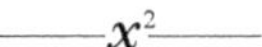 x^2

Travis let Mary and Emily have the bed in Trey's bedroom while he and Andy and George crashed on the back porch after phone calls home to tell parents they were okay just tired and staying over at the McGees. Generous thoughts of understanding were sent along the line and both Duke Harris and Miranda Moon simply agreed. Luckily, Mike had added a heater out there which made the area much more tolerable. Jack called back home to tell Lori he and Tim were staying at the McGee's. Candy was staying with Lori and was confident her sawed-off shotgun would help them be completely safe.

"I wouldn't mess with her," Tim said. "And now with all these hormones, hell she'd just love to shoot somebody."

The men leaned back in the recliners in the den, covered up with blankets, already snoring away. Mike lay in bed holding Janet, but sleep did not come. His emotions were on an endless roller coaster tonight, vacillating from rage to utter despair. For all his turmoil with Trey, he could not imagine a life that did not include him. The thought was beyond contemplation. He played the images the kids had shared back in his mind. He could not believe all the shit they had been up to, though he had to admit if he had mutant powers when he was a kid, he would have been an absolute terror. These kids had actually had some morality for the most part. They had helped people in need, protected each other, and even healed Tim. The few hurtful things they had caused seemed to be pretty deserved for the most part.

It seemed clear to him that whatever this thing was, it contributed to Trey's amazing athletic performance and must have given him, and from the sound of it, Jack and Tim, the world's most potent sperm. The idea that Trey had impregnated that Matlock girl made him almost cringe, and yet he remembered what he had felt like in high school. From the moment he laid eyes on Janet, he knew they were going to be together. He didn't even know Angie Matlock other than the fact she was a cheerleader and seemed a bit on the flirty side. But what pretty cheerleader wasn't? From what Tim and Jack said, their unborn babies were growing at an alarming rate and Trey's baby was even older it seemed. The thought of them being in peril was almost unbearable; worse than his darkest night in Viet Nam, worse than being wounded, worse than killing that Viet Cong soldier.

"You're still awake too," Janet whispered.

"Yeah. Sorry if I am keeping you awake."

"Part of me feels like I won't ever sleep again. All this stuff, what the kids showed us? It's boiling around in my brain," Janet said. She sighed and hugged Mike closer. "So, do you think it could be true? These kids sure seem to feel Carl is out there alive somewhere."

"I can't tell you why, but yeah, I think he is."

"This is all my fault," Janet began. "If I hadn't…"

"I wouldn't trade my life, wouldn't give up having Trey for anything. However he came to be, he's our boy. You know I feel this way. I love him more now than I ever have."

"I know," Janet said sniffing back her tears. Her wet face found Mike's and she kissed him deeply, their tongues touching and caressing. Janet gripped Mike's shoulders pulling him tight, not wanting to release him. Just hold me, honey."

Mike pulled Janet close and felt her wet eyelashes brush against his face. His mind was racked with guilt and sorry. He was desperate to try and fix this fucked up mess, but he didn't even know where to begin. Mike held Janet until he heard her slow breathing began and then he eased his arm out from around her and lay back on his pillow, watching the light from the windows change from black, to grey, to silvery white. Finally, the early light of morning began to peek through the blinds in their room.

Mike saw it was already 6:30. He smelled coffee brewing and maybe even some bacon. He disentangled himself from Janet and stumbled to the bathroom. He turned on the shower and let the water pour over his face, grabbing the soap and lathering his body before he felt Janet slide in behind him, her arms wrapped around him. She had already begun to cry again and Mike held her in his arms, feeling the sadness and grief shudder through them both.

They dressed quickly and went out to the kitchen. Tim was cooking eggs to go with the bacon. Jack was reading the paper. The kids were up as well, all sitting at the small table in the den. They all waved slightly and mumbled good mornings. Jack got up to grab cups for the coffee, telling Janet to just sit down and relax. Mike went over to grab some plates out of the cupboard. Tim greeting him with an awkward smile.

"Morning, Mike" Tim said in a voice louder than Mike needed this morning. Jack was busy with the coffee. He looked over and noticed the kids at the other table were sitting still, just eating, trying to blend in with the furniture. He took a deep breath and tried to be nonchalant.

"So when do you kids need to leave for school this morning?" like it would be any different from other mornings he said stupidly.

"No school, Daddy," Andy said coming over to give Mike a big hug. "It's a holiday because Trey won the championship. There's the parade today."

A solid lump formed in Mike's throat. Trey's big day, his moment of glory, taken away by these bastards. "That's right. So, you still think they will have it if the star is temporarily not available?"

"I don't guess anyone else will know until it's too late to call the thing off. Besides, the rest of the guys will be there. I think we should go down there today, show everyone we aren't afraid of them. We might figure a few things out," Jack said. "Other than waiting for the damn phone to ring, I don't know what else to do."

There was a brief hard knock at the front door. Andy jumped up, "I'll get it." Mike started to protest but just didn't have the energy. It was probably some neighbor for Janet. Andy walked back into the kitchen carrying a Styrofoam cooler with a note attached to the top. Andy put the cooler on the kitchen table.

"It's sort of heavy. Wonder what it is?" He said handing the note to his dad. He began to unfasten the tape on the lid. The group from the den came into the kitchen to see what was delivered. Mike looked down at the note.

In case you think we aren't serious ... next time, it will be your half-nigger boy

Mike stared at the note and then screamed, "No, don't!" as Andy pulled the lid off the cooler. The boy's gaze froze in a terrified stare and he jumped back in horror. The lifeless blue eyes of Tooter Turner looked up from the icy bed the severed head rested on. Janet and Emily began shrieking as they looked within, stumbling backward into Travis and George. Jack rushed forward and slammed the lid back down on the cooler and ran into the back of the house with it as the weeping and shouts continued to echo in the kitchen.

56 Trey

Trey opened his eyes to total darkness, save dim light filtering in through some wooden slats above his head. He was chained to the wall, thick bands around his ankles and wrists. The chain on his wrists was fastened to a rusted iron ring mounted to the wall of this place, wherever it was. He listened and heard soft breathing somewhere to his left.

"Angie," he whispered. "Is that you?"

"Yes," the soft voice answered. "Where are we?"

"I don't know. Are you hurt?"

"I don't think so. I'm all tied up with something. I'm sitting on the ground. Where are you?"

"I'm chained to the goddamn wall."

Angie began to wail. "What are they gonna do to us. Why are they doing this?"

"Don't cry, baby. They want you to be afraid. Don't let them get to you," Trey said looking in the girl's direction. "Hey, try and scoot over more this way. You think there's any way we can actually touch?"

"I don't know. I'll try. I need to pee so bad." Trey could hear scuffled feet and scooting and soon he felt Angie's head against his leg.

"Good. I know what you mean about needing to pee. So listen. Keep touching me and I want you to concentrate with all your might on breaking those ropes or cords or whatever, okay?"

"They are too tight, Trey."

"Baby, you are super strong, especially when you are linked up with me. Just close your eyes and think. Those ropes are as weak as spaghetti. You can break them." Trey could hear Angie grunt and felt her flex and then the ropes unraveled and her hands broke free. Soon, she was wrapped around his neck, her tears wetting his face as she kissed him over and over.

"Can we do the same thing with these damn chains?"

"I don't think so. It would take some more of us for these. But maybe we can try in a few minutes. Look around this place, Angie. See what you can find out. And if you need to pee, just go over to a corner and take a squat."

Trey listed as Angie made her way around the space. Bumping into a few things that caused her to quietly swear. Angie came back and held up an indistinguishable something in front of his face. "I found this old coffee can. You could pee in here," she offered.

"Alright. You'll have to give me a hand, baby. Did you find anything else in here that we can use in some way?"

"I'll keep looking around."

———x^2———

Trey and Angie had arrived at the lake house soon after lunch on Sunday. They had spent the first two hours having sex in most of the rooms: Bent over the kitchen counter, on the big king sized bed, in the twin bunk beds, on the front porch looking out at the still water of the lake, wrapped in a big quilt and finally in a big claw foot bathtub in the bathroom. They had talked and laughed, made plans, and forgot about all their troubles. Trey made a big fire in the fireplace and the house was so warm they didn't need to wear clothes. Angie made do with Trey's football t-shirt that hugged her expanding belly and breasts and showed off her baby blue panties. Trey wore a pair of gym shorts as he cooked some bacon and eggs in a cast iron fry pan for their dinner. Angie came over to the stove and slid her hands around his waist and down into the waistband of his shorts.

"Even superpower alien Trey needs a breather, baby," he said with a laugh. But a minute later Trey pushed the skillet off the burner and laid down on the rug in front of the fire with Angie. Trey moaned in ecstasy as he climaxed wondering how many times it had been today?

Suddenly, Angie was lifted off him in one sweeping motion and a boot slammed into his balls and then his belly, doubling him over in the worst pain of his life. Trey felt strong hands grabbing at his arms, legs, and neck. Men in ski masks filled the room. They held Angie beside him. Two men grabbed his arms and twisted him behind him bending him over the back of the frayed couch in front of the fire. Trey felt a pair of jeans press against his backside as the men held his arms and head down.

"Let's give you a taste of your own medicine," a rough, slightly familiar voice said as he fumbled with his belt, letting his jeans slide to the floor. The man positioned himself against Trey's butt. Instantly, the entire room glowed in a green flash and the man, flew across the room and smashed into the wall so hard a large German clock fell to the floor and exploded in a shower of springs and gears. The other men that had been holding Trey's arms looked at their hands that appeared to be blistered and red as if they had just been held over the fire.

"Get away from us. I'll kill you," Trey shouted grasping for Angie. From behind him, a hand flashed out and suddenly a stinging sensation filled his ass. He wheeled around to see a thick, portly man in a ski mask standing in front of him holding a hypodermic needle. Trey felt a sparkle of gold and warmth begin to throb behind his eyes, his knees weakening. A strong arm wrapped around him as he started to lose his balance.

"I've got you, buddy," a very familiar voice whispered in his ear as the world dissolved into darkness.

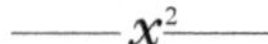

Angie came back into view, her shadow moving through the slatted lights filtering into the room. "There's not much here. I found a couple more cans, a broken chair, a shovel handle, and an old broken hacksaw and a hammer head, but no handle."

"That's pretty good, though. Let's try to use some of this. Remember you are way stronger than you think, especially with me. So let's see if we can use this stuff to help you get me out of these chains."

"Just tell me what to do," Angie answered.

"Grab that saw and see if you can make a dent in this chain right here."

Angie grabbed the saw blade and began to slide it back and forth. She concentrated and began to saw faster and faster until finally her hand was flying back and forth like a piston engine. In thirty seconds, the chain link clunked to the dirt floor and she slid the chain out of the ring on the wall allowing Trey's hands to fall down at his sides.

"Oh God, that feels good. My arms were aching," Trey said rubbing his muscles. His hands were still connected to lengths of chair but he could at least move now. Angie dropped to her knees and began to saw through the chains holding Trey's feet. In another minute, he was able to move away from the wall. He hugged Angie and tried to think of what to do next.

"Where do you think we are," she whispered.

"I don't know but probably somewhere back at Theo's house I bet."

"Why do you think so?"

"Because he was there last night. I recognized his voice. Trey bent down and looked at the few discarded items Angie had found, trying to devise some kind of plan. In the distance, he and Angie heard voices that began to move closer toward them.

"They're coming back. Quick, move back to where we were and pretend we are still locked up. When they get close, follow my lead and let's try and hit them with some of this stuff." Trey could literally hear Angie's heart hammering in her chest.

Two men, clad in flannel shirts and the ski masks, unlocked some door and the small chamber flooded with light from outside. They moved into the room carrying a bucket and a brown paper sack. They set the things down and moved closer to Trey and Angie.

"Morning, Glories," one of them said in a muffled voice though the mask. "Sleep well? Moving toward Angie one of the men reached out and stroked her face. "You probably didn't since you didn't have a big nigger cock in your mouth." With that Angie's hand flashed out and slammed the broken hammer head into the side of the man's head, dropping him to the dirt like a steer at the slaughter house. Trey gripped the broken chair and swung it, breaking it into shards over the other man's back, causing him to stumble backward.

"What the fuck?" He groaned stumbling around trying to get his feet under himself. He reached behind him and pulled out a gun pointing it at Trey's head and fired. The bullet slammed into the dirt walls of the underground room three inches from Trey's ear, spitting bits of rock and dirt into Trey's face. Trey gripped the shovel handle and hurled it like a javelin. It hit the man square in the belly, punching through his gut and exiting the back. The man sunk to his knees and gripped the handle poking from his belly before falling over.

Trey reached back and grabbed Angie's hand and they climbed over the fallen men and moved toward the light. There were some ramshackle stairs leading out of the cellar that they lightly tested and moved up in their bare feet. He turned to her, gripping her hand.

"Try and think. Send a message with all your might to Travis and Andy's brains. Just tell them to come. Tell them we are at JL Martin's. Tell them we are still okay. Tell them to bring help, bring all the kids and Jack and Tim." The two stood still and forced their minds to telegraph the message to the others. A wave of warm power flowed through them both and they glowed in a soft green hue. "Come on," Trey said leading Angie up the stairs.

They peered out of the entrance and saw they were in a vast building, a barn with high lofts and a center open area that soared upwards twenty-five feet or more. A platform of some kind was built at the end with an X-shaped cross at the back, heavy chains and shackles on its ends. A low altar of stones and wood stood beside it, chains lay there as well. Trey heard a sound behind him and he wheeled around only to see emerging from the shadows, a large black cloaked figure wearing a grotesque golden mask festooned with animal horns and a human skull. The cloak was open and the man was naked beneath, his large belly covered with hair poking from the opening. He held a wicked blade in one hand and a torch in the other. Angie took one look at the apparition and screamed. Trey felt strong arms grip his wrists and another sharp poke in his thigh this time.

Trey felt himself sliding away into darkness again. This time, Theo Martin moved close, holding him up in his arms. "You might as well relax, Trey. No getting away from me this time. Go find out what happened to those other idiots." Trey felt his legs buckle and Theo gently cradled him in his arms. Trey could see Angie slumped to the ground in front of him.

"What did you do to her?" he whispered.

"She's fine. Just taking another nap. Just like you." Theo said. As Trey's eyes closed, he felt Theo's lips press against his own.

It took Mike and Jack a half hour to get everyone settled down after the grisly package was discovered. Andy was curled in his mother's lap like a five-year old. He was sucking his thumb with his eyes tightly closed. Janet adamantly insisted they call the authorities.

"This is a murder. We can't do nothing. That poor boy. Why would they do this? We know him…knew him. Oh my God!" she wailed.

Mike, Jack and Tim conferred in the kitchen. It was finally decided to leave the "package" in a discrete location and anonymously call the sheriff's office. They debated whether or not to try and get some help, but with the threat becoming this real, Mike didn't want to take the chance of pissing them off. Tim drove over to downtown and left the cooler behind a dumpster in the alley. He went inside the store (which they had closed for the day) and called the sheriff reporting a suspicious package was in the back alley behind Main Street businesses and then hung up. He waited in his truck, watching with his hunting binoculars, until he saw a patrol car drive up the alley. It looked like Dick Sparks, one of the deputies. He looked around and found the cooler behind the dumpster. Tim watched him lift the lid open with his nightstick and the man jumped back and fell on his ass, crab-walking back to the patrol car. He got on the radio and Tim prepared for the onslaught of police presence everywhere. But curiously, Sparks put on some gloves and retrieved the cooler and carefully placed it in the trunk of the car and he drove away. When Tim saw that, he pulled away and returned to the McGee's home. His hands were shaking as he held a coffee mug and told the story he had just seen.

The teenagers sat at the breakfast table trying to eat the breakfast Jack and Tim had made, but no one got very far with it. The grownups were in the kitchen. Emily felt stupid still in her dress from last night. It was still pretty early and she didn't want to show up at home too soon or her mom would ask a bunch of questions. Mary nibbled on her bacon, but she seemed as nervous and worried as Emily did. Travis was a ghost. She had never seen him so beaten down and despondent. George was subdued for once. Finally he leaned over to whisper to the girls.

"We need to get out of here pretty soon. Go get some new clothes and get ready to go downtown. We are supposed to meet up with the band if we are still going to do the marching band / rock band thing."

"I can't believe we have to do that today. I just want to put the whole thing on hold until we find Trey and Angie," Emily whispered back wiping her leaking eyes. "I hate all this."

"I know. It's so stupid," George whispered back. "But let's just do it 'cause maybe then we can all go look for them. Everything is so twisted and messed up. You know they have to be out at that horrible barn or somewhere out at that sicko's house." George looked around, Travis was just sitting at the table pushing food around his plate. George got up and went over to him, laying a hand on his shoulder. "Hey buddy, we are going to go clean up and get some fresh clothes and everything. We will be back pretty soon. Um, do you want to get out of here for a while or anything?"

Travis didn't respond or move so George patted him on the back and started to leave.

"Yeah, I need to get out of here." Travis went over to his mom. "I'm going to go with George and clean up and get ready for this dumb parade, then I'll come back. Okay?" Janet looked at him through unfocused eyes and nodded. He went over to his Dad who just rubbed his head.

"Sounds good."

The four went out the back door after Travis grabbed some fresh clothes. Emily took his hand and he held hers and then wrapped his arm around her shoulders. She leaned her over as they walked, resting against his arm.

"I'm so sorry, Trav," she said softly.

"Yeah I know. Let's just change the subject for an hour or so then we'll go back to worrying about it. Alright? Anything but about Trey or that horrible shit we just saw."

George spoke up. "I know, we could talk about our parents and the other grown-ups as well as Trey and Angie's impressive sex lives that we are all getting a peek at with this mind-meld stuff. Damn."

"Mmmhmm," Mary said. "I didn't know old white folks got all busy with it like that."

The four of them laughed. Travis groaned. "So embarrassing, Jeez. Most people their age would just take a nap or something. My parents seem ready to start up a frickin' orgy these days."

"I think it's kind of cool they still like each other enough to want to do it," Emily said.

The guys said goodbye to Emily and Mary and walked over to George's door and disappeared within. Travis wordlessly conveyed the message to not discuss what just happened and Emily squeezed his hand. The girls went inside the house. It was still dark and quiet within. "My mom is usually awake by now," Emily said heading down the hallway. When she got to her mom's door, she looked inside and her mother was kneeling beside the bed praying. The girls backed out of the room and went into Emily's room.

"Is she having a prayer meeting or something in there?" Mary said.

"Not sure. That's a little weird. Oh well, go ahead and take a shower first. I'll go next. You can wear any of my stuff that works for you."

"Well I know my butt's not going to fit into any of your skinny ass jeans."

"Try those Chic ones. I bet they will work."

"Alright.

Emily went back to her mother's room and stood in the doorway. Miranda Moon looked up as Emily moved closer to the bed. Her face was damp from tears. Emily sank onto the bed beside her mom.

"Are you alright, Mom? You weren't worried about me were you? I know I called late last night but I just wanted you to know I was okay."

"No, honey. I've been praying for the McGee boy, um Trey? Been up praying for him for hours."

"How did you know…?"

"I just woke up last night feeling it. It was like the most vivid dream I've ever had. I saw at boy and some girl. They were in some trouble. I was really shaken by it and then I realized I knew the kids. And something in me just said to start praying. So I did. But you already knew all that didn't you?"

"Yes. It's terrible, Mom. These really bad men seem to have them. We don't know what it's about but they called and want money. So that's why the McGee's haven't called the cops or anything. They are supposed to get some more information this morning. We just hope that's all it is and we can get them back with no problem."

"I don't think they want money. They want that boy for something else and it's not good," Miranda said. "It's like I can see that they want to hurt him bad. They think it will do something for them, like some horrible sacrifice thing."

"How can you know that, Mom? We don't…"

"You aren't the only one around here who can do special things, sweetie."

Emily's mouth fell open. "You know about the powers?"

"Yes, honey. I've known for weeks although I really only figured things out last week. Something happened to me that night with the lights too. I guess it just took longer for me to work it out than you kids."

Emily and her mother talked and shared their separate journeys over the past few months. Miranda had noticed Emily was acting different, but just chalked it up to teenage hormones. Mary walked into the room, her hair up in a towel. She was wearing Emily's bathrobe.

"I hope this is okay," she said.

"Sure. I'm just talking with mom here. Looks like she has known more about our super powers than she let on for a while."

Mary sat down on the bed and listened as Emily caught her up with the conversation. Mary began to share some of her own story and experiences. In the end, the three of them were laughing at some of the wilder situations, with Miranda holding her hand over her mouth when they talked about the night at the bridge. Her eyes practically popped out when she heard about the bridge rebuilding itself and Tim's healing. But when she heard about the men and the guns, her face changed to a fierce scowl.

"I know that man. The whole town does. He has been a bully his whole life. How dare they actually aim a gun at a bunch of kids? I will tell you right now, this will not end well for him. I just seem to know, in the end, you all are going to be good. Not so much for him."

"I'm not sure, but it seems like you have some extra foreknowledge thing, Mom. She remembered what George had said then added, "Maybe that's your power. Precognition. You have a better chance of predicting the future than most people."

"You could get a crystal ball and do readings for people," Mary joked.

"A big sign in front of the house with a palm and a seeing eye on it. 'Miranda the Medium.'" The girls laughed more.

"What if we do that link-up thing? Maybe your moms could see clearer. You think it's worth a chance?" Mary asked.

"It sure might be. Let's wait 'til the boys get over here and we'll give it a try."

Emily left Mary with her mom and went to take her shower. She wet her hair and poured a big handful of Clairol Herbal Essence into her palm and worked it into her long blond curls. Her mind easily went back to the airport and laying on the couch with Travis. She had wanted to touch him like that for so long. His hands touching her had been so magical. She had never felt like that before. It was a slow and steady climb that began between her legs and radiated through her whole body in a shattering glorious finale that was better than any piece of music or happy ending in a movie. And then the part with him. It was both unsettling and unbelievable.

What was that thing that the girls were always saying on "Love American Style" about taking things too fast? She had a feeling this is what they meant. She knew some other girls at school who had already jumped into the deep end in regard to boys and sex. She knew she wasn't ready for that at all. But wading around in the shallow end, she didn't expect it to be that much fun.

Travis and George showed up ten minutes later, clean and with fresh clothes. Their hair was still wet. All Emily wanted to do was run her hands through Travis's blond hair and feel the cool curls against her hand. Instead, she just touched him on the shoulder and asked, "You okay?" He nodded and actually kissed her on the cheek right there in front of her mother. Her face reddened but her mom didn't act freaked out or anything. Emily briefed the boys on what she and her mom and Mary had shared. They agreed it made sense to see if Mrs. Moon could come up with any more details. So she sat in a kitchen chair as the teens surrounded her and touched her on the back and shoulders. A faint green glow surrounded the group. Miranda Moon's head jerked back slightly and suddenly all of them were in her mind.

They saw a large number of people running across Green Light Bridge. On the other side, men, some dressed in long black robes with strange gold masks stood waiting. They were armed with shotguns, rifles, and handguns. They were shouting something. Then the scene changed and they saw Trey fastened to a giant wooden X in the middle of a dark barn, torches burning and shimmering in the darkness. He was hurt and bleeding. Angie was chained to some raised table. Her pregnant belly was large and uncovered. A big form moved into the scene with a long black robe. His face was covered with an elaborate golden mask with a face twisted into a horrific grimace. Large horns protruded from the mask and a human skull rested on top. He had a deadly looking long knife, almost a sword. Then in the distance, another figure, glowing bright with emerald light rays emanating from his body.

The group fell back. The vision or whatever it was ended, leaving them exhausted and sweating. They looked at one another and were gripped with the fear and seriousness of what they had seen.

"We need to go talk to my Dad and Jack." Travis said.

58 George

George relayed the images they all had seen when connected with Emily's mom to the McGee household. A dozen different scenarios were discussed, but at the end of it all there was one constant: they have already killed someone and they will do it again if we don't cooperate. The phone call with the directions on delivering the money was short and sweet.

"Drive out to the lake, to the guy's place where we found your boy. You know the one. If you need directions, ask the guy in the cooler. Be there at 7:00 PM tonight. Put the money in the oven in the kitchen then get the hell out. If you screw around…we have more coolers."

Mike had already been to the store and emptied the safe. He talked to Ralph King at Security State Bank into getting him the remaining cash he needed. Ralph asked plenty of questions, but in the end, Jack and Mike had gripped the man's hand and told him to give them the money and remember 'this was planned months ago. It's that business transaction where the seller only wanted to deal with cash.' The duffel bag full of cash sat on the kitchen table. The others sat in chairs or stood around saying nothing. Teppy had arrived sometime after George and the others had left. She sat with red moist eyes staring into her unfinished coffee. Finally George spoke in a very quiet voice.

"Um, we sort of need to go. We need to get set up downtown. Is there anything you want us to do before we leave?"

The adults looked around and shook their heads. Mike spoke, "Just watch out for each other. I mean it, you see anything funny, y'all turn on the power like you never have before. Maybe tonight, this will all be over and they'll just hand Trey back."

"Won't it be really obvious today when the do this parade that the star of the football team isn't there?" Emily asked.

"Yeah, I'm pretty sure it will be. I think we all just have to act surprised that he's not there. It's the safest thing to do. I'm sure JL Martin and his cronies will be around watching. Just keep it cool. We can't risk doing anything that could cause them to freak out and hurt anyone," Jack said. George nodded and left along with Mary, Emily and Travis, who hugged his parents long and hard before he left.

"I'm sure Trey and Angie are still alright. It's like he's talking inside my head. Says he's in some cellar or something at JL Martins he thinks," Travis said with certainty. Andy nodded in agreement.

"I know. He's sending me the same signal."

George actually drove the group downtown, not even worrying about his lack of license or what anyone else would say. He was driving his mother's station wagon so he could haul all the music and sound equipment downtown. The plan from Mr. Smith was for George and the other small band combo to play for the crowd until the parade started. Then when the band marched down the street, they were going to stop in front of the square and play several tunes with the rock band. On another day, it would have been joyful. Today, it was just annoying.

Vince and Sarah met them downtown, along with Bruce Richardson, Damon Reed, and Anna Green. The high schoolers helped set up the drum set, microphones, amps and speakers. George and Travis tuned the guitars. Emily made sure the keyboard was functioning and balanced. The brass section was led by Bruce. He took them through a quick tune up and rehearsal. Vince worked through fills and cadences on the drum set. Crowds had begun to gather in the square. There were vendors selling State Champion football t-shirts. A couple of the vendors from the county fair had pulled in their mobile kitchen trailers offering elephant ears, cotton candy, corn dogs, and hot chocolate. There were orange and black flags flying, the school colors of the Cowhill Tigers. A platform had been put up for the stage band and the dignitaries from the town. George wondered if JL Martin and any of his sicko lackeys would be there on the platform, because it might just be the last thing they ever did. Travis still looked like someone had hit him over the head with a hammer. He was just going through the motions, not really there. Some of the cast from the high school's production of "Godspell" would be performing first. Mary was around to reprise her heartfelt rendition of "Day by Day." She sat on the platform behind the band for now, hugging herself, trying to stay warm in the late November wind.

Duskie Meyers had brought out a huge arch of helium filled balloons that she and the rest of the downtown merchants had bought that stretched across the stage. Some older residents were bringing in lawn chairs and setting them around the square and bundling up with blankets and quilts. The sheriff had already diverted people away from parking on the square so there was a steady stream of foot traffic meandering through the quickly set up booths and stalls, munching on snacks and enjoying the impromptu city holiday. George saw his mom and dad filter in with the all the McGees and Jack and Tim. He wondered where Lori and Joey were but remembered Jack said the little guy had a bit of an ear infection and the wind probably would be bad for him. Since Candy Murphy wasn't around either, he figured she might have stayed with Lori and the toddler. Gordon Carpenter from Eastland's had set up a quick winter themed sidewalk sale in front of his store. George could still see the image of his hand sliding up in between Rachel Swenson's skirt in the back office of the store, her arm thrown around his neck as he fondled her breasts while groping between her thighs. He had to think: this is the curse of the powers. I always liked going in his store, thinking he was such a happy, kind man. Who knew he was also an old letch that liked to fondle his young employees?

He wasn't the only one either. He saw some of the high school faculty filing in to sit along the high curb and sidewalk in front of the West Side Barber Shop, including Jed Baker, the Agriculture teacher. George shook his head to try and etch-a-sketch his brain from remembering Mr. Baker dressed in leather on his knees in some dark club, wearing assless chaps and servicing some other leather man wearing crossed leather harness across his chest along with a studded jockstrap. There were plenty of good things to remember too like Mrs. Simmons caring for her elderly mother with such care and love or Mr. Franklin, the janitor tenderly comforting his son after a bad dream, but it was hard for them to compete with the shocking ones.

A breathless Mr. Smith climbed up on the podium and went over the set list with the students. The band would start out playing "Day by Day" then move to a couple of Chicago charts. Then the parade would begin and they would wait around until the stupid square dance club arrived and play a shockingly bad arrangement of "Cotton Eyed Joe" for them to strut around on the brick pavement with their big pink and yellow poufy skirts on the women and silk shirts on the men. There would be some Shriners driving around in those small little cars wearing fez hats. Then a float with the cheerleaders would come by and some open cars with the superintendent and principal in them. Then finally, a bigger float with the football team on it followed by the band. The band would then be performing a concert of a few tunes before the presentation of the State Championship trophy.

Mary came up behind George and clandestinely slipped her hand into his. "I'm scared today, George," she said. "I just have a real bad feeling about today."

"I know. So do I. But don't say anything to Trav or Emily. He is barely holding it together anyway," George said. "Hey, let's walk around to the other stage band members and put some mojo on them. Let's make this a kick-ass show." Mary nodded. They went around to the various members of the band and patted them on the back or gave them a brief hug. Emily and Travis saw what they were doing and followed suit. When they got over to Vince and Sarah, both of them grinned and gripped their hands, feeling the surge of energy pulse between them. When George patted Damon on the back, the boy wheeled around.

"Jeez, homo. Why are you feeling me up?" Mary's hand shot out and gripped him by the arm.

"You are going to play brilliantly and you are going to enjoy yourself and you are never going to be pissy and rude to George again," Mary said with authority. Damon stared at her and then looked over at George. He grabbed him in a big bear hug and held him close.

"I love you, man," Damon said before letting a clearly squashed George go.

"Thanks, Damon. I, uh, love you back," George said before glaring at Mary. "Take it easy, will you. He'll ask me to prom if you aren't careful."

The street was filled now with townspeople and students, bundled up in hats, scarves, and jackets. It was a happy, electric atmosphere and the crowd was ready for the show to begin. In the distance, the wail of police sirens broke the clear, cold air signaling the beginning of the parade. Mayor Al Moore came up on the platform and made a brief speech, welcoming the crowd and encouraging them to enjoy the parade. He introduced the singers from the high school production of "Godspell." The stage band counted off and began "Day by Day." Mary's loud, clear alto voice carried above the crowd noise as she began the song. George saw Mary's mother, Delois out in the crowd. For once, she almost seemed happy watching her daughter sing along with the cast. Soon they reached the chorus and the singers moved and danced on the stage, clapping their hands to the music and encouraging the crowd to do the same. Before too long, the entire square was filled with people singing along on the chorus of the song. An infectious wave of happiness and joy seemed to permeate the air. The band played flawlessly, with the brass picking up on the background melodies with sharp, clear notes. Vince was amazing on the drums. George and Travis's guitar work was the best ever. When the song was over, the crowd clapped and cheered. Mary and the singers took a bow.

With no plan, George looked over at Emily and the two of them began to play "Don't Stop." Even though they had never practiced it or even knew the song, the band played along. The singers began to echo Fleetwood Mac's words and soon the crowd was once again singing along as the police cars and fire engines got closer to the square with lights flashing. The crowd seemed to have forgotten about the parade while the police and fire department moved through along with the square dancers. The group stood and kept waiting for their song to be played. But finally, they simply began to go through their routine to the driving sounds of the band. The square dancers' faces went from confused and annoyed to joyful as they danced around in front of the platform to the music. By this time the cheerleader's float had moved in, but with the dancers still in the street, the float just stopped. The cheerleaders jumped off the float and began to dance alongside the square dancers.

As the song winded down, Travis stepped up with his bass guitar and began the licks to "25 or 6 to 4." The crowd began to cheer and soon the square sounded more like a rock concert than a backwater hometown parade. In the effervescent joy of the moment, the square dancers began a complicated and surprisingly provocative dance to the driving rock song along with the cheerleaders, weaving in and out and gyrating around as if they had practiced for months.

The grandmas in their big skirts lifted them high to show their sparkly panties as they twirled around, held in the place by the grandpas whose buttoned up shirts were suddenly pulled out of their pants and unbuttoned to the waist, revealing shocking amounts of chest hair and beer guts. But the crowd cheered and applauded like this was totally expected and completely wonderful. The football team's float had stopped as well now and the team was jumping off the float to move into the mass of dancing. The boys jumped and spun and grabbed ladies and men from the crowd and soon there was a giant jumping, shouting band of students and senior citizens alike dancing along with the band. Without missing a beat, the high school band members began to crowd into the square along with the throng of people and with Vince's count off on the drums launched into "Long Train Running," the unofficial fight song of the Cowhill Tigers. When the band started, a roar went up from the crowd and now the entire square was filled with jumping, dancing people. The joy and elation was palpable. The Shriners zoomed around the square in their little cars in elaborate figure-eights. George looked around the stage and saw the band willing the crowd to join in and be part of this moment of celebration with an otherworldly electricity.

As the song reached its ending, a confused but clearly effected JL Martin came to the microphone on the stage. The band played the last notes, the crowd cheered jubilantly and clapped in appreciation. As the tumult died down, JL reached for the microphone and spoke.

"My, my, my. Let's hear it for this amazing band." The crowd erupted into cheers again as JL waved his hand back to indicate the band and singers on the stage along with the marching band standing in front. George noticed some of the square dance grannies seemed to be looking around, wondering what in the hell had just happened. The grandpas grabbed their shirts and began to button them up quickly.

"On behalf of the downtown merchants, I want to welcome all of you to this amazing celebration." Al Moore walked up to the microphone to take it from JL, but he was pushed aside as JL grabbed the mike and began to walk around the stage like a camp meeting evangelist.

Come on up, boys. Ladies and Gentlemen, the State Champion Cowhill Tigers!" JL announced in a booming voice. The crowd cheered louder than ever as the band struck up the actual school fight song. JL Martin's face was red and blotched. His shirt was stained with something that looked like dirt or possibly blood. He was sweating profusely even though the temperature was in the high thirties.

George leaned over to Travis. "There is something wrong with that asshole. I mean, more than usual. He looks crazy." Travis nodded staring at the man. "Let's get Coach Bates up here too," JL continued.

The football players were standing proud on the platform, some of them with raised arms in victory out to the crowd. The mayor retrieved the large trophy from its safekeeping area at the back of the platform and moved to the front of the stage, clearly annoyed that JL Martin was not sticking to the script. Coach Bates was moved to the front of the stage and the players crowded around him, slapping him on the back. Coach was grinning like an insane man, loving every minute of this victorious celebration.

OK, Coach. Come on up and give us a speech," JL blasted into the microphone. By now, he sounded almost drunk. Mayor Moore reached for the mike again. This time, JL pushed him so hard the man stumbled and fell back on his rear on the platform. Several gasps and even more laughs erupted from the audience. Coach Bates stepped forward and took the mike, looking somewhat uncertain at JL Martin as he did so.

"Well folks. This is the culmination of the greatest year ever for Tiger football. Each one of you out there own a piece of this trophy with all your fan support and donations and belief in us. We couldn't have done this without your great support, coming to the games and being the families and friends of these young men up here. They are special, dynamic boys that I am so proud of. Ladies and Gentlemen, I present to you, the 1978 State AA Football Champions!"

The crowd cheered loud and clapped, whistles and cowbells rang along the street. The band kicked up another short chorus of the fight song and Theo Martin and Bo Williams held the trophy aloft toward the adoring crowd. The band finished the song and for an awkward moment, the team didn't seem to know what to do next. From somewhere back against the storefronts a booming voice yelled out, "Where's Trey McGee?" George looked and saw Tim Murphy cupping his hands around his mouth. He said it again. "Where is Trey McGee."

The crowd looked up at the stage and began to take a quick inventory and discovered sure enough, the star of the game was not among the boys on the stage. A loud murmur began to grow in the crowd. Echoes of "Where's Trey McGee" began to roll up and down the square until finally, the crowd began to chant in concert. "Where's Trey McGee? Where's Trey McGee? Where's Trey McGee?"

Coach Bates began to speak into the microphone. "I am sorry to say Trey isn't with us today. He's a bit under the weather but ..."

Boos from the crowd began to roll up and down the throng of people. More choruses of "Where's Trey McGee" began along with "This is some bullshit!" and "Bogus!" JL Martin pushed his way past the coach and ripped the mike from his hand.

"Now y'all need to calm down. It's clear that McGee boy didn't want to be here today. It appears he has run off with one of the local cheerleaders he has knocked up. He was embarrassed enough to be found to be a half-Nigra colored and now it appears he is a sex criminal as well. It's best he is not part of this celebratio..."

A coke bottle flew from the audience and struck JL on the side of his head causing him to stagger back. "Liar!" someone screamed from the crowd. The townspeople erupted with shouts of "No" "Shut Up" and "Get off the stage!" Theo ran forward and steadied his father and began to help him to the stairs of the platform. The crowd surged forward toward him and Theo grabbed his father and pushed him toward the back of the platform and down the steps there and along the other side of the street. A shower of bottles, elephant ears, corn dogs, and hot chocolate followed them.

"We want Trey. We want Trey. We want Trey," the crowd chanted up and down the street. George looked around to Travis and Emily, all staring in disbelief. Suddenly a crash filled the air as windows up and down Main Street shattered sending shards of glass rocketing into the crowd. Shrieks filled the air as bloodied people ran forward into the streets to escape the glass. The cheerleaders float began to move forward, its tissue paper over the framework of chicken wire now smeared with blood from the cut crowd members. Several high school students jumped on the float which was now racing forward, mowing down people in the street. The back of the float exploded into flames and the students screamed and flung themselves off the burning hulk that lumbered down the street. Some of the crowd began climbing into the stores, carrying out clothes, shoes, pots and pans. One man was actually struggling with an air conditioner. George stared as Yvonne Davis held her hands in front of her and slammed into a cluster of girls and knocked them halfway across the street. Three junior high boys grabbed a parking meter and wrenched it free of the ground. Then one of them swung it around in a vast circle and smashed the windshield out of the police car. The other two boys stood behind the fire engine and pushed on it. The boy who had smashed the windshield of the police car ran over to join them. George could now see that it was Jimmy Earwood, Terry Dixon, and David Baker. With confused but exultant faces, they pushed on the fire truck sending it crashing into the police car, grinding the trunk of the cop car to a twisted hulk. One of the firefighters ran forward to pull the boys back. Jimmy Earwood balled up his fist and smashed the man in the face. His nose exploded in blood and he went flying backwards, landing on Drusilla and Patsy Holland sitting in lawn chairs watching the spectacle.

Gasoline from the police car ignited. The resulting explosion blew away the West Side Barber Shop along with the barber, Dale Maguire. Pieces of him rained down on the square dancers who screamed and ran backward toward the burning cheerleader float that was still barreling toward the podium. From the corner of his eye, George spied two of the football players fondling a cheerleader who looked unconscious. He dropped his guitar and ran toward the girl along with Travis and Vince who shoved their hands forward in a synchronized push that sent the boys hurling backwards into the air twenty feet. Emily rushed forward to try and help the girl. Travis looked up.

"What the fuck is going on?"

"I have a feeling we just saw a bunch of other kids' powers switch on and they don't know what the hell is going on either."

"That float is headed right for the stage," Emily shouted.

The teenagers ran to the front of the stage and shoved the air with their hands again, slowing the float. They concentrated with all their might and the flames began to die and then extinguish, leaving the twisted wire frame of the float belching out clouds of acrid smoke.

"We have to get out of here. Now!"

George looked up and Jack Tanner was standing on the edge of the stage with Travis's dad right behind him. The kids abandoned the stage just as a riding lawnmower from Western Auto crashed into the middle of the platform. Several of the Shriner's cars began to rocket around the square and drive up on part of the debris littering the brick-paved street, launching themselves like Evil Knievel across the road and crashed into scurrying members of the community in a ball of smoke and fire. George looked around and chaos flowed up and down Main Street. Men were fighting, punching one another. Women were clawing at each other's faces or pulling hair. Small children were tossed like footballs to the side. Blood flowed down most of the faces that were set in a wild grimace. There were others flowing into the melee. George saw an unconscious Gordon Carpenter bent over the front of a Chevy citation, his pants around his knees, a broken off shovel handle protruding from his ass. Rachel Swenson stood on the hood of the car, her shirt open and breasts exposed as she screamed to the wind. Two high school boys ran down the street with armloads of cash, bills fluttering in the wind as they passed.

Jack pushed the kids along with Mike McGee around the burning barber shop and into the alley behind Main Street. They climbed into Jack's pickup and he roared down the alley. barely missing two men who were trying to smash in the back door of Ward's Drug store. The kids in the bed of the truck huddled together, freezing in the cold air of the afternoon. George looked back toward downtown and saw another big mushroom cloud explosion billow above the roofs of the stores, an accompanying scream filling the air. Emily and Sarah were crying. Vince looked catatonic. Tim Murphy crowded into the bed of the truck with the kids. Travis was holding Emily. Mary pressed close to George and lowered her head to his shoulder. Janet gripped Andy tight inside the cab of the truck, sitting next to Mike while Jack drove wildly toward the grocery store where Mike had parked the station wagon. George looked at his watch. Almost 5:00.

Jack skidded to a stop in the McGee's driveway and got out of the truck, helping the kids in the back climb out. The group went inside the house. George kept wondering about his parents. They had been downtown too along with Emily's mom. Mary slid her hand into George's.

"I know. My mom is there too. But I can feel her. She's fine. I think your parents are too. They are just figuring out how to get back home." George squeezed her hand, knowing she was right.

Janet wiped tears from her face as the group gathered in the kitchen. "I am sick of this shit. We need to get busy finding Trey. I'm not just going to stand around and wring my hands. I am ready to kick some ass and end some goddamn rednecks," she shouted. "Why did everything blow up like that downtown?"

"Not sure but I think a bunch more people just figured out they had powers and when all of them were together like that, it just became a mob or something," Jack said.

"Too bad one of those bottles or burning cars didn't take out JL Martin," Tim said.

"There was something seriously wrong with him today," George said. "He was like high or something."

Mike looked at the kitchen Kit-Kat Clock, its tail swinging back and forth along with its eyes. It was 5:30. "Okay. We need to leave here in thirty minutes to get the money to the lake house. Who all should go besides me?"

"I'll go with you," Travis, George, and Tim Murphy all said together.

"Thanks guys, but you better stay here for now," Mike said. "Together, I'm not too worried about you. Tim, you good to come along?"

"Yep."

Mike disappeared into his bedroom and came back out with two handguns: old .44 Smith and Wesson specials. He handed one to Tim. The men checked the cylinders and clicked them closed, fitting them into the back of their jeans' waistbands.

"Where's mine?" Janet asked dangerously.

"I don't think you are going to need those. I seriously doubt anyone is going to be around when you drop off that cash. I still think it's a wild goose chase," Jack said.

"Probably so. But it still makes me feel better," Tim answered. Mike went over to the fridge and grabbed a few beers, passing them around to the adults. George motioned to Travis and they went back into his room along with Emily and Mary, Vince and Sara followed out as well. They sat on the steps in the backyard. Travis emerged from his room with a small Prince Albert tin with three joints inside. He lit two of them and passed them to the others.

"Aren't you worried about..?" Emily began.

"No," Travis said flatly. The teens smoked without speaking, their hands still shaking from the events downtown. A minute later, Mike McGee and Teppy emerged from the doorway. Travis and George automatically hid their hand behind their back, both still holding in a big draw of smoke. Teppy laughed.

"Busted, little brother," she joked.

"Can I get a hit on one of those," Mike said.

George exhaled a long column of smoke, his eyes watering and handed the blunt over to Mike who took it and drew in a deep drag and handed the joint to Teppy. "You kids shouldn't be doing this, but I'm pretty glad about it today," he said. Both Tim and Jack came out and looked at each other smiling.

"Damn, I need to find these kids connection," Tim said. Travis handed him the joint and he took a hit and handed it off to Jack. The group just stood in a circle, quiet in solidarity of the moment, trying to prepare to face what was next.

"No matter what happens today, kids. Stick together. You are safer that way. I have this feeling we are all going to end up out at Martin's tonight. Whatever he is after, this money is not it. He wipes his ass with this kind of money. But we'll do the drop and then see what's next. I can't believe I'm involving you in all this, but like Jack said, you're all in it whether I want you to be or not," Mike said. Janet walked down the steps and stepped close to Mike, he put his arm around her and hugged her tight. Andy walked over to Travis who put a protective arm around his brother. Teppy stood behind them both and hugged them tight. Andy reached for the joint and Travis handed it off to Tim, giving the little boy a playful kick in the seat of the pants with his shoe.

Then, like a sledgehammer to the brain, the group shouted and grabbed their heads. Jack staggered back and fell to the ground holding his head, screaming "NO!" Tim rushed to his side but Jack pushed him away, scrabbling to his feet.

"Joey. Something's happened to my boy!"

The group assembled in the McGee's backyard looked around at one another with a sober certainty. Something bad had just happened to young Joey Tanner. Jack tore up the stairs and through the house toward his truck. Tim caught up with him.

"I'm going with you. Scoot over, I'm driving," he commanded. Jack obeyed, scooting over to the passenger side. Mike rushed over.

"Take some of these kids with you. You might need them. I'll take Travis and Andy with me. We will go to the lake and then head back. We'll just go to the bridge on the far side of the Martins and wait for you there." Tim nodded.

George, Mary, Emily, Vince and Sarah loaded up in the bed of the truck as Tim roared away. The wind was bitter as the teens huddled together to try and stay warm in the back. Tim looked across at Jack whose face was stricken and colorless.

"It's gonna be okay, big guy," he said gripping his friend's hand.

"I can't feel him. I can't feel him," Jack kept saying. "Something's happened to Lori too."

"Don't say that. Candy's there. She's a tough little bitch. She wouldn't let anyone mess with them."

"Unless she couldn't."

"Stop saying that shit," Tim demanded, punching down on the gas.

The roads and houses flew by in a blur as the truck barreled toward Jack's house. Jack's mind was a cyclone of emotion and it kept whirling back to the note he'd found on Smokey the Cat.

Next time we gut the kid.

Jack was still holding on to Tim's hand as he turned into the long driveway and burned up the gravel toward the house. The door was standing open.

"Oh God!" Jack yelled jumping from the truck before Tim had stopped. He tripped and fell down but clambered back to his feet and ran for the house, Tim on his heels. The kids jumped out of the back of the truck and hurried forward as well.

Jack ran into the living room and found Lori lying in the floor. Her face was bloody from a gash in her forehead near the hairline. Jack dropped to his knees and grabbed her, pressing his ear to her chest. She was alive. His hand moved protectively to her belly, now swollen in pregnancy and felt the life inside her move to his touch. Tim ran into the kitchen and found Candy crumpled to the floor, her shotgun by her side. A blast had shot into the back door and speckles of blood peppered the wall. Tim felt for her pulse and listened for her heart as well.

"She's still here," Tim's voice broke as he spoke. Much as Jack had done, he felt her growing belly and smiled in relief as it moved underneath his touch. "My boy's okay too."

Emily's scream shattered the momentary peace. Both men bolted down the hall toward Joey's room, pushing the teenagers out of the way. Jack burst into the room and saw Emily standing by the bed, her hands covering her mouth. Jack looked down on the bed and saw Joey laying there. His head was covered in a plastic bag that stuck to his now blue face. Duct tape fastened the bag to his small neck.

"NO!" Jack screamed rushing to his son. He ripped at the tape but it wouldn't budge at first. Then he gripped again and it tore away. He pulled the plastic bag from the small boy's face, frozen in a shocked, surprised look. His hair was wet and stuck to his head. Jack pulled the boy to him and hugged him tight.

"My boy! My little boy! Oh God, what have they done?" he said rocking the small frame back and forth. Tim pushed forward and took the boy from his arms and laid him on the floor and began to administer CPR and rescue breaths. Jack slumped against the bed, utterly defeated. Emily and Mary clung to each other weeping. George came back in the room.

"I called 911," he said. For the ladies in there," he said quietly. "And for the little boy," he added weakly. "But they said it might be awhile 'cause there's so much shit going on downtown."

Tim listened for a heartbeat and breath, but soon he stopped. He looked up at Jack with red eyes. "He's gone."

Jack wailed and gripped the boy, pulling him up into his arms again, rocking him back and forth while he sobbed in anguish. Mary spoke up.

"We need to go. We need to get him out to the bridge now," she said.

Tim looked up, shaking his head as if trying to clear away the grief that filled the small room. He crawled over to Jack.

"She's right. There's nothing we can do. But that place…with all of us. Maybe we can help him there. The ambulance will get here for the girls. They are okay, I can feel it. But we need to go now!"

"I'll stay here with the ladies," Sarah said. "I don't want to go back out to that place." Tim reached over and gripped her hand.

"Thanks, Sarah."

Tim helped Jack to his feel, still cradling the limp boy in his arms. Emily grabbed a quilt off the bed and Jack wrapped it around the small boy and the group ran out to the truck and burned off toward Scatter Branch.

Travis and his family sailed along Hwy 47 trying to keep the speed under 70 mph. His dad and mom sat in the front holding hands. Mike had attempted to talk Janet into staying home, telling her she would be safer and if anything happened to him, she needed to be there for the kids. She had smiled and told him to shut the fuck up.

"I'm going. Are you kidding me? You've got Andy in the car for Chrissake."

Travis sat in the backseat with his little brother's head in his lap. Andy had reverted back to sucking his thumb again. Travis stroked the boy's head and looked at the window. Teppy sat beside him and absentmindedly patted Andy's legs. Travis tried to remember the last time the three of them had ridden together in the car. The dark evening was cold and stars were sparkled across the sky as they rounded the southern end of Lake Tawakoni toward the late Tooter Turner's vacation house. Travis closed his eyes and tried to make the image of the severed head in the cooler disappear. It wouldn't leave. So, instead he tried to reach out over the miles and contact George or Emily. With all his might, he sent out the message in his head.

"Almost to the lake house. Where are you?"

As he sat and listened to the wheels roar against the pavement, a flash of insight flared in his mind. "Going to the bridge. They killed Joey."

"Oh God!" Travis wailed gripping his head. Andy sobbed loudly and gripped Travis around the waist. Mike swerved the car and shouted.

"Jesus! Oh my God," Teppy said holding her hand to her mouth in horror.

Janet gripped his arm. "What is it? Is it Trey? Is it Jack's little boy?"

Mike reached up and gripped her hand. "He's dead. Jack's boy is gone."

Janet began to cry along with Teppy. Mike wiped his eyes with his sleeve as he tried to keep the car steady on the road. He began to pray, something Travis rarely ever saw his dad do. He poured out his heart as he drove.

"Dear Jesus. We need your help. Our boy is out there and we are trying to save him, but we need you to protect him. Please, we ask for your grace and protection for Trey and Angie. Keep them safe. Cover them with your grace. Oh, God. Please help Jack and his family. We don't know exactly what happened, but if there is any way, help that little boy. Extend your hand of mercy and rescue him. He's just a little boy..." Mike's voice broke. Travis reached up and laid his hand on his dad's shoulder feeling his grief and brokenhearted pain.

"They're taking him out to the bridge. If there's any way for them to help him, it'll be out there," Travis said quietly. Mike patted his hand and nodded.

"I think you're right, buddy. Alright, we are almost there. When we get there, I am going to get out and put the money in the house where they told me. All of you are going to stay in the car and don't even think about trying to tell me otherwise," Mike said emphatically. No one said a word as they continued up the road that led back toward the lake. Empty vacation homes stood silently on either side of the narrow lane. Travis left his hand on his dad's shoulder. As they turned into the driveway and stopped, Mike looked back at him.

"I don't want you to come," Mike said.

"I know. But it's safer if we do. You know that," Travis said.

"We're coming, Dad," Teppy added emphatically.

"Our superpowers can help you, Dad," Andy offered.

Janet looked around. "It doesn't seem like anyone else is here. Good. Just go in there and leave the damn money and let's get back to town, or maybe just go out to that bridge."

Mike switched the car off. He leaned over and picked up the duffle bag he had placed the cash in and then reached up to turn off the dome light. He opened the door and got out with Travis. Teppy and Andy followed behind holding hands.

"I'm not staying out here alone," Janet whispered opening her door and coming around the front of the Vista Cruiser.

The family looked around and around but saw nothing moving except the bare branches of willows and cottonwoods against the starry sky. The temperature had dropped more and their breath made small clouds puff in front of their faces. Travis saw his dad reach behind his back and pull out the handgun, keeping it close to his leg as they walked toward the front porch. Travis and Andy climbed the stairs behind their dad as Janet moved in close behind them. The floor boards on the porch creaked as they walked across. Mike opened the screen door and turned the doorknob. The door opened with a groan and the group stepped inside. The moon was shining now and its silvery light glowed in the cold living room. Chairs and couches were pushed to the side or tipped over. There was a broken picture frame hanging cantilevered on the wall, the dead eyes of the pioneer woman in the portrait staring into the darkness. Mike took out a small flashlight and shined it around the room. Heavy drapes were pulled closed, resting on wrought iron rods with sharp arrowhead fittings on the end. The light sparkled on them as Mike panned the small beam around the room.

"This place gives me the creeps," Teppy whispered.

They walked toward the kitchen and the oven where the idiots had instructed them to leave the money. Janet gasped as she tripped. She looked down and picked up a pair of jeans and a t-shirt that belonged to Trey. Her eyes were wide with pain and terror as she hugged them close to her chest, breathing in her son's scent. Mike gripped the handle of the stove and opened it. It scraped and moaned like a lost soul, screeching loudly in the still of the cold house. He laid the bag on the wire rack and closed the door to equally loud grinding. Mike turned and gripped Teppy's hand, motioning her to go. Janet reached back to try and grasp Travis's hand. He wasn't there. She wheeled around and screamed. Two cloaked figures with bright gold masks stood in the shadows on the edge of the kitchen. One strong arm was around Travis's neck, a pistol pressed to his temple. Andy squirmed in the other man's arms. A hand was around his mouth and the other had a Bowie knife held to his neck.

"We did what you asked. The money is there. Let them go," Mike demanded.

A muffled voice laughed. "See, we figure these two brats of yours are worth another couple hundred grand. Damn, and then there's your super fine daughter. Bet she's tight. Who would be stupid enough to bring their kids with them?"

"I don't have any more money…you have it all. Just let them go. We'll leave and you can take it."

"We figure you can come up with more. If not, then we will just take these boys and add them to your nigger boy we already have and make it a family affair."

Mike took a step toward the men and heard the trigger of the pistol clicked back. The other man pulled Andy's hair and forced his neck up. A trickle of blood oozed from the knife edge."

"No! You're hurting him!" Janet screamed.

"Get back, asshole or we will cut off his head just like Tooter."

Travis reached over in the darkness and gripped Andy's hand and closed his eyes. Teppy reached over and grabbed her dad's. Travis could feel the cold steel pressing against his head. But in his mind, the steel was much warmer. It was burning hot. He felt the energy arc between Andy and himself. He pulled his head away from the barrel of the pistol as it glowed bright orange.

"Yaaah. Fuck, it's burning," the voice shouted loosening his grip on Travis as the metal of the gun seared into his flesh, cooking him. Travis spun like the wind and gripped the man's hand who was holding the knife close to Andy. He pushed Andy away from his grasp, gripped the man's hand and drove the glowing knife blade into the man's thigh. The other man ran over to the fireplace and grabbed the poker and ran up the stairs to the landing above, hiding in the shadows. Teppy grabbed the shovel from the hearth and ran up the stairs. Mike moved with blinding speed and grabbed the heavy curtain rod and yanked it free, drapes cascading to the floor.

"Teppy!" Janet whispered loudly.

She closed on the figure in the shadows, brandishing the shovel above her head. He charged forward, leaping off the landing with the poker aimed at Travis. Mike hurled the curtain rod like a javelin. It sailed through the air like a bullet, catching the man in his snarling mouth, ripping through his gut and protruding out his ass, nailing him to the wall like a boar on a spit. His wide eyes frozen in shock as blood and gore boiled from his open mouth.

"Oh my God!" Janet screamed, frozen in the middle of the room, turning her head to the side to wretch.

The other man stood in the middle of the room, still gripping hard to Andy's hair, disbelief paralyzing his face. Mike turned to find something to use as a weapon. A flash of metal in the moonlight caught his eye and he swiveled in midair and turned toward the other man in time to see the head of an axe cleave the man's skull in half. The gold mask broke apart as the axe head drove all the way down to his clavicle. Blood and brain splattered in a fountain, dropping the man to his knees, falling forward in a dead heap. Travis stood behind the man, his breath coming in gasps, chest heaving, his face covered in blood.

"Fuck me," Mike whispered.

"He shouldn't have tried to hurt my brother," Travis said in gasps.

Mike walked slowly toward Travis and wrapped his arms around him. "You did good, buddy. Jesus, remind me not to piss you off."

"What are we going to do?" Janet said. "They're dead. We killed them. It was self-defense but..."

With no words, Mike, Teppy, and Andy walked toward the body fallen in front of them and reached down and touched the heel of the boots. Then they walked to the man skewered by the curtain rod and touched his shoulder.

"Come on, we need to get out of here," Mike said. He took Janet's hand who stood immobile trying to comprehend what just happened. As she stood there, a small curl of smoke began to waft out of the dead man's open mouth and nose. Travis looked over at the other corpse and saw it shimmering in the silvery light, like the coals on a barbecue grill.

"What's happening?"

"We have to go now!" Mike ordered. The family scrambled to the door and down the front porch steps. When Travis reached the back door he stopped and turned and ran back into the house.

"Travis!" Mike hissed. Janet started to turn back as well but Mike stopped her.

Travis moved like the wind inside the house. The bodies were blazing, consuming themselves from the inside out. The drapes were burning along with the couch. He vaulted to the kitchen in one large leap and wrenched the oven door open and grabbed the duffle bag. He turned to leave and a wall of fire rose up between the kitchen and living room. Travis turned and ran for the large window in the kitchen. He tried to wrench it open but it was nailed shut. He backed up and ran at the widow and crashed through it like it was made of waxed paper. He landed on his feet and tore toward the car, his dad standing in front of it open-mouthed.

"We forgot the money," Travis said holding up the duffle bag. Mike shook his head and ran around the car to get in. He backed out of the driveway and burned off up the road as a huge explosion rocked the car, an orange cloud of fire billowing into the air.

"How did you know to touch them like that?" Janet asked in awe, still struggling to swallow her revulsion.

"Not sure. But I knew we needed to. Just popped into my head," Mike said.

"This shit just got real," Teppy said breathlessly.

Andy leaned over to Travis who was brushing glass and wood shards out of his hair. "That was so freakin' cool," he whispered.

61 JL

The needle still protruded from his arm as JL lay in the steamy water of the big bathtub. His head had been killing him all day, which was so unfair considering it was the most important day ever. He had orchestrated such a coup d'état, a way to purify this land and town for many, many years. All of his work, his study and understanding of his great-grandfather's journals, his sacrifice and planning…it all culminated tonight. When he offered up the half-breed whelp of Carl Washington along with his unborn grandchild, the Spirits would cleanse the water, the land, the people. The unfit would be cast out and Cowhill and the surrounding beautiful land would return to its pristine birth.

That debacle at the parade had almost ruined everything. How dare these idiots blame him for anything other than saving the town from its certain demise? What the hell had happened there anyway? From what Junior and Toy had said, it seemed half the town was on fire by the time the fire department arrived and began to take charge. It was those damn kids, he told himself. The mutant satanic worshipping spawn were unexpected, but Azarel had promised they would be removed as well.

The offerings were secured and ready for the ceremony. He had sent Cecil Evans and Daryl Wilkes off to the lake house to take care of Mike McGee. No sense in letting him turn up and be problematic tonight. Part of him regretted not being able to pay that son of a bitch back in person. He let the image of choking Mike with a thick cord while he rode his ass like a cheap whore flow over him, feeling the pleasure rise in his cock. The mixture of *Sernyl* and morphine tonight with the cocaine bumper had made him ravenously horny. He had already released twice tonight and still he felt the burn.

He had called Joe and LaFonda to come over earlier. He and Joe had penetrated the girl front and back as she writhed and moaned underneath them. She lay satiated on the bed as Joe repositioned himself and slid inside JL's ass. As Joe rode deep and hard within him, JL reached over to the nightstand and grabbed the gleaming razor. It flashed across LaFonda's neck with such speed, nothing but a red smile opened in her neck. Her eyes flew open, but no words, as her blood boiled out. Joe continued moving within him, oblivious to what had happened. As he climaxed and fell forward onto JL, his hands became sticky and warm. He looked at them and saw the blood. He stepped back as JL rolled off LaFonda, his mouth opening in a silent scream. JL's hand flashed again, opening Joe's throat from ear to ear. The college student grabbed at his neck and then fell on top of the slain coed. JL moved behind the big defensive end and slid his erection within, something Joe had never been willing to do before. JL gripped the man's shoulders and thrust again and again until he released within him. He smiled, thinking how clever he had been to tie up this dirty loose end. The vinyl sheet he had placed beneath the bedspread would catch the blood and make the clean up so much easier. They could be disposed of tonight along with the other sacrifices. He pulled Joe's bulk up onto the middle of the bed on top of the girl and gripped the edge of the bedspread, wrapping them within. He used duct tape to secure the vinyl around the spread making on very large bundle, drip-proof and easily moved. Well, as easy as shifting almost 400 pounds ever was. But that was for Junior and the others to figure out.

Now soaking in the soapy tub, JL felt the golden glitter behind his eyes sparkle to life. As he looked, Azarel sat in the tub on the far end, his large muscled legs gripping around his. The angel spoke.

"My brother. Tonight you will purge the stains of the past away in one glorious offering to the Earth Mother. The blood will flow and purify the stains of the past. The sinners plunged beneath the flood will lose all their guilty stains. You must offer the boy and the baby and destroy the satanic children as well. With sword and fire, you must sacrifice them all just as Josiah and Jephthah did."

"I will, holy brother," JL said. "May I ask, will this sacrifice heal me as well? I fear my mind is being destroyed by your holy angel dust."

"Fear not. You will be restored. Your devotion will be rewarded. The Earth Mother will make you whole and shower you with blessing upon blessing. Tonight, you will see her in all her radiance." The angel moved forward and kissed JL, his touch burning like a hot coal on JL's lips. JL leaned his head back as the angel's face lowered to his lap. JL's hands slid into the long golden wavy hair, pressing his face down lower and lower.

"Dad?"

The voice broke the sanctity of the moment. JL looked up annoyed to see Theo standing in the bathroom. His son looked in disgust at his erection poking up above the steamy water.

"What is it, son?"

"Um, Junior got some guys to clear off that, whatever it is, on your bed. We've got everything else ready so I thought you would want to, you know, get out and get dressed."

JL stood and motioned for Theo to hand him a towel. Theo handed his had the towel and stood back as he crawled from the tub. "Help me dry off, son," he said with more of a command than a request. Theo took another towel and began to dry off his father's back and backside. His dad turned around and Theo stepped back, unwilling to continue. JL smiled.

"Always so sensitive."

Theo moved back and rested against the bathroom counter, trying not to watch as his father bent over to dry his feet. His arms were folded tight against his chest. The constant ache in his belly burning and sending more and more acid splashing up into his throat. He burped and leaned over to the sink to spit.

"Dad, have you seen Mom? You said she was up in Dallas shopping, but I called and she's not there. I haven't seen her for a couple of days now. Did she go somewhere else?" Theo asked.

"You know, I'm not sure. Last time I saw her she was out in the garage," JL said mysteriously.

"What do you mean? Did she leave? Her car is still here."

JL smiled and walked naked into the bedroom and donned the long black cloak. He picked up the heavy headdress, its gleaming skulls and horns shinning white in the dim light. He fastened the golden mask to his face and stood in front of the full length mirror. His large hairy belly parted the robe, causing his dwindling erection to stand obscenely out from his legs like a small elephant trunk.

"The time has come, son." JL moved out of the bedroom and made his way down the stairs. The living room was filled with similarly robed men, golden masks glittering in the firelight of the hearth. Dozens of men filled the large room, more than he had ever seen dressed so before.

He smiled and lifted his hands to the company. JL made his way down the grand staircase like a Viking king or Egyptian pharaoh, but the illusion was ruined as his snakeskin Justin boots and knee-high tube socks peeked from the hem of his robe. The men below bowed their heads in reverence as he descended. Theo watched, fastening the black cloak around himself, holding the golden mask in his hand as he walked down the stairs behind his father. His dad moved into the middle of the gathering of men who reached out their hands and placed them on JL's back, shoulders, and chest, imbuing him with their blessing.

Theo walked into the empty kitchen, turned and stepped into the cavernous four-car garage. He scanned the room, all vehicles present and accounted for. It was cold out here and as he turned to go back inside, a flash of scarlet caught his eye. He moved to the large chest freezer against the wall and saw that a small triangle of red cloth hung out of the corner of the chest. Theo touched the fabric and frowned. He gripped the lid of the freezer and raised it high, crying out as it slid up. Caroline Martin lay within, blue and frozen, clad in her favorite red dress with the full skirt. Her dead brown eyes stared upward in a half-lidded gaze. A broken wine glass stem stuck out of her neck.

"Time to go," Junior Bidwell said standing in the doorway in his robe and mask.

Theo slammed the lid to the freezer and fastened on his mask, lifting the hood over his head.

62 George

George gripped Mary tightly as the truck tore down deserted roads toward Scatter Branch. He never liked riding in the back of pickups that much anyway. Riding in the dark on this November night didn't make it better. He was so cold, it felt like his fingers would break off. He looked over at Emily who looked utterly lost without Travis. He knew the feeling. Vince wrapped his arms around her, but the couple looked uncomfortable and off-balance. George imagined that Vince had longed for a moment like this for long time. Now that it was here and Emily Moon rested between his legs with his arms wrapped around her, he doubted it had played out the way it had in his fantasies.

Orion rode high in the sky as the truck turned off Hwy 24 and navigated the small back road toward the newly reformed bridge. George could feel his heartbeat accelerate. Coming back to this place was almost like coming home in some strange way. They belonged here and yet it was utterly strange and haunted. The truck bumped along the dirt road, tipping and tilting, sending the large cache of Tim's various outdoor gear cascading over their feet and legs. *The man had a lot of shit*, George thought.

Tim had cut the lights on the truck as they turned onto the road and the stars seemed brighter than ever. The rising moon lit up the back of the truck as it rolled to a stop in the clearing they had stopped at only a few days before. It seemed like a year. Tim opened the door and stood by the side of the truck lending a hand to the kids clambering out. They gathered on the edge of the road and waited for Jack. He was carrying the small boy tightly, wrapped in the quilt from his bed. His face was set in taut lines of utter despair. He looked at Tim who walked up beside him and placed a hand gently on his back and the two of them began walking toward the bridge.

The familiar thrum of the place began to echo in George's ears. He gripped Mary's hand tightly as they walked in procession with the men toward the bridge. In the rising moonlight, the boards gleamed silvery grey as they stretched across the expanse of the river, flowing fast tonight, its caramel water lashing at the footings holding up the bridge in the center of the stream. In the far distance, an amber glow permeated the darkness coming from the old barn that peeked over the hill on the far side of the river. As the group stepped onto the bridge, Tim spoke.

"Um, hello. Alien being or whatever. We really need your help. Please, can you heal this little fella like you did with me? I know it's a bigger deal than just regrowing my nut, but he's just a little boy. He never hurt no one. Can you help..?"

A dim green glow began to oscillate like a searchlight at the airport, its beam sliding across the landscape. When the light landed on the small group on the bridge, it stopped and illuminated them, bathing their faces in its soft emerald luminescence. The thrumming increased, almost to a pounding within their heads, causing the group to wince and step back.

A verdant dome engulfed Jack whose face went blank and then his head snapped back, his spine rigid. His arms slowly lowered and the quilt-covered bundle hovered in the air. Joey's body continued to float toward the far side of the river toward the source of the light as Jack's hands remained held in front of him still carrying their precious cargo. Then, a green rainbow arc of power burst forth from somewhere on the riverbank below and like a shockwave from a thermonuclear test, it blasted through the party like an x-ray, knocking them backward off their feet.

George looked up. He was lying flat on his back on the bridge alongside everyone else. As he leaned up on his elbow, he saw the group still and motionless, stacked like cord wood on the bridge. Tim began to move in front of him and sat up. As he looked over at Jack, he crawled to his side and began frantically searching. He shook Jack by the shoulders.

"Where's Joey?" Jack, where is he?" Tim whispered in a loud rasp.

Jack shot up and looked around wildly. He climbed to his feet and began to run toward the far side of the river as the sliding clack of a shotgun loading snapped in the air.

"Y'all are tresspassin," a low growl barked. "Git back in that truck and clear out now. Last chance."

"I'm not leaving without my boy," Jack said. The shotgun blast plastered the boards two feet in front of Jack's boots, causing him to hop backwards.

"Goddamn it. Where is my son?" Jack yelled. This time, a rifle fired, and struck the bridge less than a foot to the right of Jack's feet. Tim ran up and grabbed Jack and began to pull him back.

"No. Stop it. I have to…"

"We're not leaving but we are getting off this bridge right now," Tim hissed, pulling Jack backwards, following the teenagers that had run for their lives when the shooting began. They gathered near the tailgate of Tim's truck, sides heaving. The sound of a car lumbering up the dirt road drew their attention off the bridge. The group turned to see a station wagon stop, all four doors flying open. Travis ran to Emily and grabbed her in a tight hug. Mike ran over to Tim and Jack.

"Where is your boy?" he asked.

Jack looked back toward the bridge and pointed. Mike looked around toward the bridge, scanning to see.

"I can't see him."

"The light took him," George said as Mike stared trying to understand. "We went out there and the light just surrounded us and took him."

A small voice from the back of the group spoke. "I can feel him again. He's there," Andy said walking up to Jack and gripping his hand. "He's going to be okay." Jack fell to his knees and hugged the boy tightly.

Tim pulled Mike to the side. "We've got another problem. JL has some good ole' boys out here with guns guarding the far side of the bridge. They've already shot at us."

"What? Mike, we need to call the FBI or something," Janet demanded.

"Maybe. But not yet," he answered with finality. Another vehicle began to roll up the road and the assembled group defensively moved behind Jack's truck and ducked down. The old Ford stopped and person after person poured out of the car. A big thick teenage boy moved into the light.

"Damon?" George whispered. "What are you doing here?"

"I don't really know. All of these folks just sort of showed up near your house tonight and we all just sort of knew we had to come out here. Shit, I don't even know some of them." George looked around and saw Emily's mother holding the hand of a young girl. Andy ran forward and hugged the girl. There was Yvonne Davis and Naomi Cantor, the high school drama teacher. George looked around and Don and Doug climbed out of the car. Doug wore a thick scarf tied in an elaborate knot at his neck. A stocking cap sat jauntily on the back of his head. They ran over to Vince and grabbed his neck and hugged the boy, then turned to Travis, George and the girls and gave hugs all around. Last out of the car was Sarah who ran to Vince and fell into his arms.

"Oh my God, what are we doing back here?" Doug said. "And don't look at me. I look like Crackle from the Rice Krispies box."

"Not completely sure, but it has to do with Trey and Angie and now Joey. We felt like something bad had happened," Don said.

"It did," Travis said. George looked at him in the brighter light of the clearing.

"Hey, how did the other thing go?"

"Don't ask," Travis said.

"What's all over your hair and the side of your face? Is that blood?" Emily asked reaching up to his cheek. Travis grabbed her hand and held it. He reached over and gripped George's hand as well. A moment later, the two staggered back and stared at Travis.

"You should have seen him," Andy said. "And my dad. It was awesome."

"Holy shit," George said in awe. "Remind me never to fuck with your family."

Sarah moved around the group to Jack. "The EMT's took Lori and Candy to the hospital. They both were okay, just bad concussions. The babies are all fine too. But I had to come out here, I hope it's okay." Jack gave the girl and big hug and kissed the side of her head.

"Hey!" Vince said with mock indignation.

Tim gathered the group together and spoke in a low voice that caused them to stand very close in order to hear.

"Alright. For some reason all of you are out here. We all pretty much know this is where the light ended up. It's like some of that thing is in all of us and from the look of what happened downtown today, there must be quite a few others. Most of those just seemed to have figured stuff out today. Seems like most of you must have known about it for a while now." The group nodded.

"I don't know about you, but it seems like this thing wants us out here tonight. It can't be a coincidence that Trey and Angie are in danger out here tonight too. Not to mention what happened to Joey. That light took him when we brought him out here. We didn't know what else to do. We just knew that if there was a chance to bring him back, it would be out here."

"Like your ball," Andy said. A couple of the group chuckled.

"That's right," Tim said involuntarily gripping his crotch. "So whatever JL has planned for the kids is about to happen and we have to get across the river to help. Those guys with guns, we can take care of them if we stick together and use these powers. But we need to be careful. So, right before we go whup some redneck ass, everybody join up and concentrate with all your might. Think 'Save Trey and Angie.' Think 'Save Joey.' Think 'Stop JL Martin.' I think the rest of it will take care of itself. Remember to stick together and don't think just because you have powers that you can't get hurt because you can."

The group gathered in a circle and held hands. They began to concentrate and settle their minds into the mantra 'Save Trey and Angie,' 'Save Joey,' 'Stop JL Martin.' The thrum and vibration filled their minds and as they concentrated, the circle lifted two feet off the ground, their heads tilted upward. The energy built and grew within them, stronger and more aware than ever before. Their minds coalesced into a single multi-celled unit. A minute later, the light dimmed and the party felt their feet touch the ground. Tim headed to his truck and began to rummage around in the back.

Soon the group assembled. Tim and Jack stood at the front, both armed with compound bows and a quiver of arrows. Mike held a frog gig on the end of a long pole. Travis held a long handled double-headed axe. George, Damon, and Vince held machetes. The remaining group held a collection of ballpeen hammers, small sledges, claw hammers, hunting knives, and shovels. Andy and Jessie held small hatchets.

"I've been telling him he needed to clear all this crap out of his truck for a year," Jack said. "Glad you didn't listen."

"Why should I start now?" Tim added with a grin.

The tiny army lined up in a wedge shape behind the tall wall of dead Johnson grass near the edge of the river beside the bridge.

"Everybody ready?" Tim asked. The group nodded together.

"Remember," Travis said. "Guns don't work very well when they get really hot."

The group came out from behind the wall of grass and crouched low and stepped out onto the bridge. They moved quietly and as a unit making it all the way to the middle of the bridge before they were spotted.

"So y'all are just a bunch of dumb asses, or something," a voice yelled, more tense than before. "We warned you."

A collection of chambers were loaded, triggers pulled back. Jack and Tim crouched low and reached behind their backs to load their bows. The other members of the group hovered low behind the men. The night was filled with the boom and rapports of gunfire that sailed high over the heads of the group. In the distance, very faint glows of orange began to shine in the darkness. The glows brightened and flared to lava-like orange. Screams and curses filled the air. Deputy Dick Sparks ran toward the edge of the bridge with his shotgun aimed at the small crowd wearing thick black gloves, his face illuminated by the bright red glow of the metal gun barrel. When he pulled the trigger, the gun exploded into his face ripping off half his head in the process. He dropped like a rock and the others on the far side of the river scattered like mice.

The group rose and ran like the wind toward the scurrying men on the far said. Tim stopped and pulled back the eighty-pound bowstring like it was a toy Indian bow from Stuckey's and fired. The arrow struck one of the fleeing men in the temple and pierced his skull, slamming into the head of the man running beside him and nailing both of them to the trunk of a large walnut tree by their heads. Jack lowered his bow and sent the arrow flying over 400 feet in one second, knocking Sid Stewart off his feet and fastening his body to the side of the ancient barn.

From the side, two men emerged both brandishing baseball bats. As they swung the bats, Damon Reed moved with lightning speed to the left while Vince rolled to the right. They swung the machetes low and wide slicing off both legs at the knees, their bodies dropping to the ground. As they opened their mouths to scream, Mike and Jack grabbed their heads and twisted them around 180 degrees with loud pops.

"Look out!" Emily whispered loudly.

The men ducked low as James Hilton from the Charcoal Broiler flew toward them with a pitchfork, leaping down from a low branch. In a split second, Travis bent the axe behind his back and hurled it. The blade drove deep into the man's chest as George swung his machete high and wide, slicing the man's skull in half right below the eyes. Two additional men ran headlong toward the boys. Mike stood and threw his frog gig, the trident tip catching the first man in the stomach, pinning him to the ground. The other man pulled up, staring at the carnage and turned to leave. Mary caught him in the side of the head with her shovel knocking him backwards twenty feet. Jack wheeled and launched an arrow though his left eye. The group instinctively gathered into a circle back to back, slowly rotating defensively.

From a clump of bushes on the right, a black handgun stretched into the air and fired. The bullet struck Damon in the right shoulder knocking him to the ground.

"Y'all are trespassing and are under arrest for murder and . . ." Andy and Jessie spun like the wind and caught the shooter in the head with their hatchets, burying them deep into his neck, his head falling forward like a dropped melon.

"Are you alright?" George said to Damon reaching for the wound in his shoulder.

"Yeah," the boy winced. "Went all the way through. I'll be okay. Hurts like a bitch, though."

Jack gripped the boy with his hand on top of George's. The remainder of the group did the same. A warm green glow enveloped Damon's shoulder and the boy's grimace turned to a small grin.

"I'll be damned. It feels fine now," he whispered.

"Come on everybody. Gather up," Jack said. He was splattered with blood. George looked around the group. Most of the faces were splashed with blood and gore, but the eyes were focused and sharp. "Let's get close to that barn. No sounds."

Trey's arms ached. He tried to move and pain seared through his hands. He looked over and looked at his right hand. It was held by a metal cuff to the wooden cross. His palm had been nailed through, crucified. He looked to his left and saw the bloody mess in the palm of that hand as well. His ankles were similarly fastened to the cross. His feet rested on wooden blocks and were nailed in place as well. He looked to his side. Angie lay on a hastily constructed platform of plywood. She was naked except for her floral bikini panties. Her arms and legs were trussed down with chains and cords. Only her expansive belly remained free. He looked down at his body. Surprisingly, it seemed like all the rest of his parts were still in place. He wondered how much longer than would be true.

They appeared to be on some sort of platform in the back of the large barn under a roof that soared twenty feet in the air, disappearing in blackness. The room was dark except for two large burning wire buckets of wood on either side of the platform. Along the edge of the platform, shiny white skulls decorated the stage. They looked real and Trey didn't want to think about that. He concentrated on the nail in his right hand, wondering if he could move it. He concentrated until it felt like this head would explode, but it only caused his hand to throb more. He looked over at Angie again. This time her eyes were wide open in wild horror. He sent his thoughts to her. 'I'm here. We are still alive.' She nodded and continued to look at him. He looked over at his hand and then back to Angie. She nodded in understanding. Trey concentrated again on the large nail driven into his hand. As he watched, the nail began to slowly lift away from his palm and continue to lengthen. The pain was excruciating, but he kept staring and thinking. Just as the heavy nail dropped to the platform, strong hands gripped Trey's face and brought his attention back to the front.

"None of that, brother," Theo said, his lips close to Trey's. "You don't want them pounding more nails into you. Just be a good boy." Trey felt Theo lick the side of his face.

Trey saw a procession of black clad men with golden masks file into the barn. At the end of the queue, a large robed figure festooned with an elaborate headdress of a human skull and antlers fastened to a misshapen grotesque golden mask. The man's large belly poked out from the robe revealing his naked groin underneath. Curiously, the man was wearing cowboy boots with thick athletic socks pulled up almost to his knees, ruining the illusion of a mystical shaman. Someone must have pushed play on a cassette player, because soon, a wailing chant and drumming filled the barn in front of the platform was a five-pointed star dug into the soft earth of the barn. Trey watched as two of the robed figures produced a small bucket and walked to the star and began to traverse the outline while pouring the contents of the bucket onto the star. The dark liquid that poured out looked hideously like blood and Trey did not like thinking of how they had come by so much.

The robed figures began to walk in a circle around the star, chanting words Trey didn't understand. A part of him felt certain the participants had no idea either. The foreign sounding words seasoned with a thick Texas accent seemed almost other-worldly.

Terra mater, Dómine. Adjuva nos mundare aquas. Laetamini in terra. Disperdite tyrannorum. Ut, per naturale eius debent implere quod meretrix cum virga, et fortes eius: Cum inundatio ex semine. Pedicabo ego canis canis, donec ululat.

From somewhere, Trey felt voices speaking into his mind. He closed his eyes and focused on the voices. As he listened, a warm, comforting calm descended on him. It wrapped around his heart and filled him with hope. He looked over at Angie. Her eyes were filled with tears but he knew she felt it too. Her hand moved slightly and she crossed her fingers. Trey smiled and closed his eyes again.

"We are here. We will save you.
* We are coming…"*

The robed men continued to chant and circle the star. Trey noticed than many of them carried slender rods in their hands, much like short cane fishing poles. As the next chanting began and the circling continued, some of the figures broke away from the group and walked up on the stage. As they neared Angie, several of them raised their masks and spit on the girl. She screamed and tried to move away. The bonds held tight and the gag in her mouth kept most of the scream stifled. As they neared Trey, the men swung the rods in a big sweeping motion, whipping them into Trey's thighs, knees, belly and chest, raising angry red welts on his skin. Some of the men stood and opened their robe and urinated on the boy, splashing piss onto his stinging chest and stomach. One large figure wearing Converse high tops managed to spray his piss directly into Trey's face, low mocking laughter muffled behind the golden mask. Red cut marks soon crisscrossed his chest and thighs, the cuts weeping blood. The chanting changed and continued.

Na'ashjéii Asdzáá, Lava quod est. Sana quod est. Nostras aquam. Enischythei androprepís spóron mas; Confirma nostra virili semine. Lava a perfidia. In terram fructiferam, fac nobis. Adeptus peccatorum in infernum.

The robed man with the large headdress moved onto the platform. Trey's eyes opened wide as he spied the large curving knife the man held at his side. He raised his hands and the music and drumming was turned down. The robed figures stopped circling and stood in front of the platform.

"Brethren. The angel Azarel has assisted us today in bringing this holy sacrifice to fruition. Tonight we use this offering to cleanse our land and water, and set up the holy order of God's chosen people, his anointed white children, to rule and inhabit this land. Tonight, with this sacrifice, we will banish the interlopers and make this place once again the Promised Land for God's true children. We offer up this bastard nigra tonight and his evil spawn in tribute to the Earth Mother, Toci, Asherah, Artemis, *Na'ashjéii Asdzáá*. May our offering be as a sweet smelling incense unto you."

With that, the man in the headdress turned and looked at Trey. His cold bloodshot grey eyes shone through the holes in the mask. Trey knew those eyes. He tried to gather enough moisture in his mouth to spit at the man, but there was no saliva to be found. JL Martin brought the large knife forward. Trey pulled and writhed on the large X-shaped cross, pulling at the remaining nails in his hand and feet, but he kept coming forward. The tip of the knife pierced Trey's chest near his sternum and he screamed. JL continued to drag the blade down and then up to the left, across his chest to his right nipple, then at an angle down to the left and then connected the star, leaving a trail of blood oozing from the cuts. He gripped Trey's scrotum and pulled it hard away from his body, the edge of the knife resting against the sensitive flesh.

"Horse-hung…just like your daddy," JL hissed.

The barn doors exploded open, shattered on their hinges. The heavy beam across the doors splintered and fell to the ground as Mike McGee, Jack Tanner, and Tim Murphy burst through.

"Get away from my boy, you redneck motherfucker!" Mike shouted as he hurled the frog gig spear like a bullet. It sailed above the cloaked figures and drove deep into JL's meaty ass. The man howled and dropped the knife, whirling around to see the crowd of teenagers and adults swarming into the barn.

"Kill them!" JL shrieked in a high, womanly voice as he staggered around attempting to pull the spear from his buttocks.

Tim and Jack fired arrows into the middle of the robed men, scattering them like chickens. Jack caught Jim Measles in the throat, dropping him like a sack of concrete. The robed men took shelter behind corral fences and in horse stalls. Some turned and rushed headlong into the teenagers. Mary, Teppy, and Emily, now armed with crescent-shaped sickles spun in a circle, like mini-tornados, shredding three of the robed men to hamburger, blood and bone flying in all directions. The girls stood in the middle of the barn back to back, their sides heaving, blood spatter covering their faces, daring others to approach them. Travis swung his axe over his head, slamming it down at a fleeing Randy Hamm. The heavy axe head caught Randy near the neck, dividing him in half from collarbone to groin. George and Vince plowed into the throng hacking with their machetes, flying in every direction with the speed of a whirring sawmill blade, limbs and heads littering the straw covered floor. Don swung his large ballpeen hammer through the air catching Lloyd Massey in the forehead just as he pulled his revolver from his back waistband, aiming it at Doug. The resounding crack sounded like a bowling ball hitting a strike, sinking deep into his brain and dropping the man in his tracks.

"Duck!" Doug yelled. Don dropped to the ground as Deputy Alvin Sparks, gold mask thrown aside, leapt from the corral gate behind Don, his service revolver firing. Andy, Jessie, Emily, and Teppy put their hands up in the air and suspended the man in mid-air. The bullets hung in the air briefly then dropped to the straw. Mike hurled a nearby pitchfork at the man, skewering him in the belly before he dropped hard to the ground. Yvonne Davis and Naomi Cantor dropped to the floor to avoid another charging robed figure armed with a sawed-off shotgun. As the man blasted a hole in the stall door behind them, Yvonne swung her small sledge hammer at the man's knees disintegrating his patella. Naomi spun and caught the man's face on the edge of the hand grass whip she was carrying and sliced half his features away in one blurred swipe.

Sheriff LeRoy Hines pulled his mask off and brandished his side arm, limping from some injury he had already sustained. He held up his sheriff's badge and bellowed like a moose.

"I'm the law. I'm the law. Stop right now or I will shoot." Tim Hines spun in every direction like a madman, pointing his gun, shooting randomly at anything that came into sight. From the left, Vince gripped a long ago discarded circular saw blade and flung it like a Frisbee, faster than lightning. The blade caught the sheriff underneath his massive gut and opened his belly as if it were a zipper, spilling his intestines in a slithering plop on the straw floor.

Greg Benton took a long look at the carnage in the barn. He ripped his mask from his face and took off for the barn doors. But as he neared the right door at a full run, Janet stuck her foot out sending him careening through the air. On the other side of the door, Miranda Moon took one of her large wooden knitting needles she used for her afghan work out of her backpack and hurled it like a knife thrower at a side show. It caught Greg in the left eye and came out the back of his head, dropping him in his tracks. Miranda was horrified and looked up at Janet who gave her a defiant thumb's up.

JL Martin finally managed to pull the harpoon from his ass, hurling it to the ground. He looked around and found his discarded knife and grabbed it, turning toward Trey who still hung beaten and bloodied on the cross. As he drew the knife back, Travis, George, Mike, and Mary stretched out their hands, a bright green shield of light glowing around Trey. JL ran at the boy ready to plunge his knife into his chest. But as he hit the light barrier, the knife glanced off. At the same time, flying from the side of the platform, Theo Martin struck his dad sending him flying off the platform.

"I'm not gonna let you hurt him anymore," Theo said diving after his father. The two began scrambling and tackling one another, punching and scratching at each other's face. Theo landing a jaw-shattering blow on his father's face sending him flying backward.

Jack and Tim had their hands full now with Buck, Lonnie, and Cal Matlock. The men had discarded their bows since they were out of arrows. Trey stared as he watched Angie's father and brother press in on Jack and Tim. The Matlocks had them pinned down, firing quick rounds from their handguns over and over. The men dodged and hid fast enough to avoid the bullets, but the Matlocks seemed to have an endless amount of ammo and continued to shoot at the men as they took cover.

Buck reloaded and shouted to Cal and Lonnie. "Move over there, closer to that little faggot," he said motioning to Doug hiding on the other side of the corral wall.

Men and teenagers ran like rabbits around the barn, shots, shouts and screams filled the air. Cal and Buck worked closer and closer to Tim and Jack, strafing the area with constant gunfire. One of the bullets struck Tim in the thigh, sending him sprawling on the floor. The two Matlock men ran forward. Out of the shadows behind them, Doug Ailes ran forward in blinding speed with a large wheat scythe. Like a ninja, he spun faster than the wind and harvested three heads from the Matlock men, sending them spinning like Fourth of July pinwheels, spraying the walls of the barn crimson. He stood bloodied, chest heaving over the headless bodies like the Grim Reaper.

"Don't call me a fag," Doug shouted in his high voice. He looked up at Jack and Tim. "They ruined my scarf too!" he said ripping it from his neck and dumping on the corpses.

Over on the side of the barn, JL and Theo Martin continued to fight each other. The massive headdress hung awkwardly from the side of JL's head. Theo finally pinned his father to the floor, slamming his fist over and over into his father's face, his nose exploding in blood.

"You killed my mom. You ruined everything. I'm not letting you touch Trey. I love him," Theo yelled.

JL gritted his teeth and lunged for Theo and gripped his head between his forearms, pressing his hands on the side of his head. Theo grasped and clawed at his father's large hands but soon his grip loosened and his arms fell at his side. JL slid his hands around his son's throat and began to squeeze until Theo's eyes bulged out, his face turning bright red, blood vessels in his clear blue eyes bursting. JL stopped short of choking the life out of him, dumping Theo in a heap on the barn floor.

"You have always been a disappointment, son. I don't have time for your bullshit tonight."

JL climbed underneath the platform and hid. *His moment would come soon enough* he thought to himself. In the far corner, Tim and Jack fought Jerry Morgan and Cecil Evans with such ferociously fast punches, it looked like they had six arms each. In the end, the robed men hit the dirt looking like five pounds of ground chuck.

"I think y'all have caused us just about enough trouble for one night, a voice said from the platform area. Jack and Tim looked up. One by one, the others came out from their hiding places and moved to the middle of the barn floor.

Junior Bidwell and Toy Benton stood on the platform. Their faces were dripping in blood. Junior had already lost an ear. Toy had an ugly gash on his forehead that dripped a constant flow of blood into his eyes that he kept trying to wipe away with his sleeve. Toy stood over Angie. The frog gig harpoon in his hand aimed right at her large expectant belly. The girl writhed and squirmed, her screams still muffled by the rags gagging her. Junior stood beside Trey, a large buck knife in his hand resting on Trey's jugular.

"The first sign of any of your alien funny business and I end him," Junior said with a sneer.

"You oughta just cut off his dick, let him bleed like a stuck pig," Toy said. "Just try it," Toy said as Jack and Tim took another step toward the platform. I will pop her like a piñata."

"We don't care about this shit like JL. We were just going along for the ride. Figured no one would miss a few niggers from town. But now, we are just gonna jet out of here. He is the crazy one. We are gonna walk out of here and then you can have your half-coon son back."

Mary Washington walked into the light of the barn and faced the men on the platform. She remembered their voices, their touch, and their stink. She moved in closer and stared at them with utter contempt.

"Look, Toy. It's that Washington bitch. Hey honey, did you come back for some more of this?" he said gripping his crotch, waggling his tongue.

"Her cunt was like warm honey," Toy said. "I could have rode her all night."

George walked up beside Mary, Travis on the other side. Jack, Tim and Mike began to move toward the stage.

"I SAID NO!" Junior shrieked slicing down with the knife, cutting into Trey's neck. A fountain of blood sprayed against Junior's face. Janet and Mike screamed holding their hands out along with the others in the barn. Trey was wrapped in a green glowing blanket as Junior and Toy were lifted ten feet in the air. Mary stepped forward and smiled at the men.

"You want some more of me? How 'bout I go all 'Carrie' on your redneck ass!" With that, Mary raised her arms and then flung them down. As she did, every farm implement and tool in the barn flew at the two hovering men and slammed into their bodies, nailing them to the back wall of the barn like a hide stretched out for tanning. Blood leaked from dozens of punctures, cuts, divots, and impalings that fastened them to the barn. George grabbed his machete and took off for Junior, ready to chop him to a hundred pieces, but Mary grabbed his hand and looked at him.

"I took care of it, honey. Just let it go now. They gone." George looked at Mary, his head tilting to the side in complete devotion and he hugged her close.

"Let's get them out of here," Mike said walking to the stage to jump on it.

With a guttural scream, JL Martin burst from the shadow behind the cross and drove the knife deep into Trey's chest. Trey's eyes flew open in wide-eyed shock as he looked down and saw the huge knife protruding from his chest. Blood gushed from the deep wound, flowing across the tracks of the star already carved in his chest. Trey's head dropped to his shoulder, eyes still frozen open.

"NO!" a dozen voices screamed. Janet and Mike leaped to the cross. JL Martin took one giant step and leaped into the air brandishing a pistol. He began firing as he flew above the group, hitting George in the chest, knocking him backwards.

A sudden brilliant emerald light blasted through the barn, illuminating every corner and holding JL suspended in midair. The group slowly turned and looked back toward the bridge. A glowing form was walking toward the barn, tall and dark. Whoever or whatever it was, it was carrying a smaller being, glowing equally bright. The glow continued to intensify as it moved toward the barn. Another shockwave like the one earlier that night pulsed from the being and arced through the group in the barn. It held each one rigid, hovering several inches from the floor. Then, like a giant siphon was turned on, a glowing ember of light slid out of each person hovered and gathered together into one large mass. The glowing orb hovered above the being's head shining its light down on him and the child he held.

The thrum filled the room, pulsing like a giant heart through each one. As their feet touched the earth, their vision returned. Mary gasped and ran forward. Staring, Jack walked forward and took the child from the dark man, grinning intently. As Jack's arms wrapped around Joey, he fell to the ground sobbing, rocking the boy back and forth as Tim and others gathered around.

Mary gazed into her father's eyes and fell into his arms, crying like a baby. Travis and Emily looked at the scene, stunned. Then looked back at George who lay motionless, blood leaking from his mouth, his eyes dead and glassy. Travis gripped him tight and wailed along with Emily. The girl looked up at the platform, Mike and Janet collapsed at the foot of the cross, their bodies shaking in grief.

Tim looked up at Carl holding Mary. "So good to see you big fella. And you are so naked. But, can you help the others? Please?" Tim took off his coat and slipped his flannel shirt over his head and handed it to Carl who tied it around his waist like a country loincloth.

Mary turned and for the first time noticed George bloodied and silent, lying limp in Travis's arms. She screamed and ran to his side, trying to figure out where to place her hands in all the blood. She looked back at her father and screamed again. "Help us!"

Carl went quickly to George and laid his hand on the boy's chest. A large glow surrounded his chest as Carl pressed tightly to the boy's wound. Five seconds later, George gasped and his eyes flew open. Mary, Travis and Emily stared at the hole in his chest, blood receding. The wound grew smaller and then a spent .45 slug dumped out of the hole and then sealed. Carl walked quickly to the platform, leaping forward and moving close to Trey. Tears ran from his eyes as he took the boy's face in his hands and kissed his head. He gripped the large knife and slid it out, dropping it to the platform with a thud. His hand pressed tenderly against his son's chest. He laid his head onto Trey's forehead and his body began to glow green then white, enveloping Trey within the glow. When the light subsided, Carl stumbled backward and Mike caught him. The men looked at each other and then back to their son. Trey's blue-green eyes shown bright in the firelight burning in the barn. His hands were free and healed. He stood small and shrunken in that moment, more little boy than football star. He fell into his parents arms and bawled like a baby. Carl turned toward the girl on the table. The others had managed to get most of the cords off of her. Only the chains remained. He held his hand above them and they vibrated and fell to the floor of the barn with a loud rattle. He held his hand to the girl's head in a benediction of celestial healing and helped her sit up. Miranda Moon and Yvonne Davis moved behind her and held her up. Trey finally pushed past his parents and stumbled to Angie's side and held her close.

Trey looked up with most of the others and saw JL Martin still hovering high in the air above all of them. Far in the distance, sirens began to wail. JL looked down at the scene glaring at the people below.

"I think it's time we get on with that purification ceremony you are so big on," Carl said lifting his hand toward the man. A single coal of light flew from Carl's hand and zoomed toward JL's open mouth. It disappeared within and his body began to shake. "We need to go, folks," Carl said reaching out for Mary's hand. She held on to George's hand as she steadied him. Mike took off his coat and put it on Trey, Janet did the same with hers for Angie and they helped the teenagers off the platform, looking up at JL Martin in the air above them as they did. A thin stream of flame began to emanate from his mouth, his nose, and his eyes. The others gathered close around and they left as a group. The fallen acolytes of JL Martin were glowing bright orange and bursting into flame all over the barn and in the fields surrounding it where they fell. As Mike helped Trey down the steps of the platform and around the edge, they tripped over the fallen form of Theo Martin. Trey stopped and looked at the boy.

"Just leave him," Mike said. "He's as much part of this as any of them."

"No. Not the same," Travis said leaning down and gripping the collar of Theo's shirt, pulling him behind him as his dad helped him outside.

As they left the barn, Travis and Emily and Andy turned to see JL Martin grab the sides of his head, his mouth opened in a fiery blood-curdling shriek until his skull burst apart like a month-old Halloween pumpkin. Then, the flames wrapped around his form like a marshmallow held too close to the flame. The others within the barn burst into flame as well creating a hellish glow within the old evil structure. The meadow beyond glowed with bright orange fires as well.

As the group approached the bridge, the green glow brightened down on the riverbank. A metallic doorway stood open. Jack moved close to the edge of the bank and looked down at the chamber beneath. Joey pointed at the doorway.

"That's where I went. That's where I got fixed."

"That's where I got fixed too. I got out of that barn, was about dead from all the blood loss. I was trying to hold my guts together when I saw that doorway open. I crawled down there and fell inside. It's about the last thing I really remember until this little guy showed up. I was feeling all y'all for quite a while. I knew my girl must know I was still out there somewhere," Carl said hugging Mary tight. When he let her go, she moved back over to George and snuggled close to him. "I let you out of my sight for a couple of minutes and you go hook up with this white boy?"

Mary's eyes flashed. "Ooo, I know you ain't about to give me a lecture about hookin' up with white folks?"

"I heard that," Mike said. Sirens were very close to them now, though on the far side of the river near the Martin home. "I think we need to get out of here and fast."

As the group made it to the middle of the bridge, Carl stopped. His body went rigid and he floated off the boards on the deck of the bridge. A large glowing orb flew out from his chest and sailed back toward the open door of the chamber down on the riverbank. It joined with the other mass of lights and slowly sunk within. Then from the river, greenish glows flew out of the water and sailed toward the chamber hovering above. High pitched giggles and lower voiced laughs filled the air as the lights scampered up through the muddy water and hovered near the door. Then, one of the greenish lights shimmered and formed the outline of a young black girl who grinned up at Carl who was still floating in the air, but looking down at the apparition.

"Thank you, Carl," the image seemed to say to all who were present. "I'll tell daddy you done good." With that the green shape faded into a large glowing mass. The light flew up into the sky and then plunged down and struck the ground with a thunderous blow. The earth cracked open and zigzagged up the hill toward the barn, now consumed in fire. It opened up a crater underneath the barn and the structure began to crumble inside. The fault zipped up the hill and soon a large cracking, splintering sound filled the night along with the wail of sirens. Flames shot through the roof of Twelve Oaks. The roof began to crumble and fall in on itself as the fault opened into a huge cavern that consumed the building as it burned and fell within like the House of Usher.

Carl hit the ground and Mike reached out to steady him. Tim reached over and grabbed the still unconscious Theo Martin, throwing him over his shoulder like a sack of potatoes. The group ran for the other side of the bridge. As it did, the boards and rivets began to buckle and pop like gunshots. The far side of the bridge began to tumble into the river as the group raced overhead across. As Jack and Joey jumped off the bridge on the far side, the last of the beams and joists fell with a mighty crash into the murky water and was carried off into the night. Then a beam of white shot into the sky like a searchlight and the silver chamber rose from the muddy riverbed, large, sleek and intact. It flashed into the night sky like a silver comet, blowing back another shockwave that threw the company of people on the far side onto their backs on the cold, hard ground. A voice filled their minds.

I learned much. My gratitude for allowing my essence to coexist within you. Care for each other. Make your world better. Don't be afraid to stand. You are all made of stars, my brothers and sisters . . .

The voice trailed off, even though it seemed there was more to the message. When the group woke, flashing red and blue lights across the river sparkled in the night. Mike and Jack urged everyone to get up. They gathered the group around the back of Tim's truck. Mike looked around at the group, his body was cut and beaten, covered in blood and he had never felt better in his whole life.

"I don't know what to say to all of you. I'm pretty sure Jack feels the same. You saved a lot of lives tonight. I want to hug every one of you for about a week. I know there are going to be a lot of questions coming at us in the next few days. But after what we just saw, I just think the less we remember, the better, if you know what I mean. We all came out here looking for Trey and Angie. Don't bring up young Joey here or Carl. Just be as surprised as everyone else. Theo Martin, I don't know what to say about him other than he's a lucky son of a bitch, way luckier than he deserves. Hopefully he's smart enough to keep his mouth shut too. Kids, I hope you don't get in any big trouble at home. Maybe you all should come up with a story you can stick to together."

"Maybe, if you can get away, next Saturday night...let's try and have an impromptu get together at my place. Might be good to check in with each other. That way if you need to talk about any of this, would be a good place. Say 6:30? Try and come, or tell someone you can't so we know how you are doing," Jack said looking around. "We better scoot."

The group dispersed and got into the cars quietly, making sure not to use their lights. The cars started up one after the other and turned back toward Cowhill. Trey and Angie sat in the back of Mike's car with Andy in between his mom and dad in the front. Tim dumped Theo roughly into the back of the truck and climbed in with Jack holding tightly onto Joey. Most of the teenagers crowded into Damon's jalopy and took off following the others. Teppy took the rest in her car. Mary sat close to George while Emily hugged tightly onto Travis beside her in the front seat.

"Since when did my little brother start acting like Trey?" Teppy asked with a grin.

"Hey you just got home . . . no reason to be insulting," Travis said. Emily smiled.

Mary leaned over and whispered into George's ear. "I'm not complaining, but this was one sorry-ass date you took me on. I think you owe me another one."

"Hey could you give me a break? I just got through dying and everything."

Epilogue

Jack and Lori's living room was filled to bursting on Saturday, December 2nd. The Green Light Group showed up and helped decorate the Tanner's Christmas tree and spent the evening together catching up with one another and hearing each other's various stories of how the last week had gone.

Surprisingly, law enforcement officials, including the FBI that descended on the remains of JL Martin's property at Twelve Oaks did not question any of the group other than Mike McGee and Jack Tanner. Even then, they were mostly looking for insights to JL's activities in the community and the rumors they were following up regarding some secret society he was involved with. So far, the community had plenty of harsh things to say about JL Martin as a businessman and person, but no one opened up about the Black Knights of God. The church JL had started closed its doors and the congregation dispersed to other community houses of worship, mostly in other nearby communities.

The sudden disappearance of so many men from the community was chalked up to an act of God. The fault line or sinkhole that had opened up and swallowed Twelve Oaks was studied in depth by geologists and other scientists from East Texas State and other universities with little consensus. The painstaking removal of the earth and eventual removal of the spontaneously combusted human remains would take a month. Mass funerals were planned for many of the missing and presumed dead.

Carl's sudden reappearance he explained as recovery from a car accident where he had temporary memory loss. He claimed to have been staying with a distant relative in Segoville. He had not sought medical attention and appeared to be in perfect physical shape other than some unexplained scars to go along with those from Vietnam. Mary Washington had made a statement that she had never gotten a look at her abductors or rapists and that part of the case remained cold and unsolved. The authorities had so many mysteries to explain, they didn't invest any time at all in the Washingtons.

On the other hand, Theo Martin had been interrogated non-stop for over a week it seemed. He continued to hold fast to the story that he knew little to nothing of his dad's business or other activities. He claimed the parties and gatherings at Twelve Oaks seemed just like regular social affairs to him. He denied any knowledge of secret societies or plans to abduct or harm people. He did mention that his father had been acting strange and had taken to using a large amount of various drugs to combat the constant pain he had. JL's medical records confirmed he was suffering from terminal brain damage that cause large vacuoles to form in his brain. It was hypothesized by the medical authorities that he may have damaged his brain due to continual use of phencyclidine.

Most of the kids in the group had escaped serious groundings and retribution. Most of the parents seemed to buy the story of going over to one another's homes to escape the chaos of the disastrous State Football Championship parade. The fact was, so much was disrupted that day, many parents lost track of their children for a short time and were so happy to have them back unharmed. They didn't dig very deeply into where they had been. Phone lines in town had collapsed with so much traffic and with the power outages that also resulted from the fires and destruction downtown, it was virtually impossible to ignore the fact that the whole community had suffered an evening of missing time for the most part as they scrambled to try and get life back to normal.

Janet and Miranda helped Lori in the kitchen along with several of the teenagers. Lori had made a bit pot of chili and with the help of the others, they had a virtual feast. There were hot dogs, pizza, chips and dips, a big salad, Easy Cheese and crackers, and even some fondue. Mike, Carl, Jack, and Tim had grilled the hotdogs and some steaks Tim had brought over. It was a mild day and still plenty warm enough for barbecuing. Trey joined them at the grill, helping himself to a beer from the keg Tim had also brought along. But soon the other teens were calling him to quarterback the pick-up game of touch football in the backyard. For a bunch of band nerds and non-sports types, they played hard and tough. Don Edwards and Doug Ailes made a gang tackle on Trey that knocked the wind out of him for a moment, much to the delight of the others. Trey laughed and told them it was a good one, but he didn't get sacked again.

Mike and Janet had insisted that Trey and Angie be checked out in the ER after the ordeal they had been through. It was again explained as car accident. Tim had even done the kid's the courtesy of taking Trey's vehicle out on a road behind his property and intentionally rolling it over and banging it up to make the story more believable. As horrible and excruciating as their ordeal had been, by the time they were examined, there were almost no signs of trauma at all. The nail holes in Trey's hand, the cuts and marks from the rods, and obviously, the fatal stab wound had all vanished. What was confirmed, however, was that Angie was not only pregnant, she was very pregnant. The ER staff estimated her at 36 weeks. Even though they spent a great deal of time chiding the teens for not getting prenatal care started sooner, they had to admit Angie seemed the picture of health. The bit of unexpected news: Trey and Angie would be having twins, which caused Trey to almost faint and Mike to utter a string of expletives.

Angie was dealing with the tragedy of losing a number of her family members and the relief that much of her family was now dead. Angie's mother was beyond consolable and blamed Angie for everything, telling her she never wanted to see her again. Mike and Janet brought her home and put her in Teppy's old room. Trey made an attempt to move in with her, to which Janet told him she would be performing a second circumcision if he even tried it until the two teens were married. Trey argued that was the silliest thing he had ever heard until he saw his parents' faces, and he acquiesced. The two planned a simple wedding for Saturday, December 16, in the new stylish banquet room at the Cowhill Country Club, 100% paid for by an anonymous donor who had left over $5,000 in a plain envelope in Trey's locker. Interestingly, there were no objections brought up regarding a mixed-race wedding at the country club. The wedding was going to cost less than half of that with the remainder going toward setting the kids up in their own place when the time was right according to Janet.

The steaks simmered on the grill, smoke billowing in the soft winter wind. Mike thanked Tim for the keg and filled another Solo cup. Jack held his cup up and the men made soft clicks on each other's glass in a group toast.

"How's it going downtown at the store?" Mike asked. "I've been meaning to walk down there and check everything out, but it's been so damn busy."

"It's clicking along. They razed the barber shop and have already started rebuilding the shops there on the west end of the square. Lots of stuff got damaged of course and we will be dicking around with the insurance for a while, but honestly, not too bad considering. Most of the front window glass has been replaced in the stores. It's been very quiet, though. Tons of looky-loos, but almost no real business. Everyone is still shocked about Dale Maguire and Gordon Carpenter."

"Did they ever figure out how that shovel handle ended up his ass like that?" Mike asked.

"No, but several have suggested it might have happened before the big riot thing, pointing a finger at Rachel Swenson. Lots of bad stories going on right now about those two. But we all remember the images from that vision thing. It's most likely true. She ran off down to San Antonio to live with her grandmother," Jack said. "So Carl, any more insights into what all happened for you all those weeks?"

Carl took a long drink of his beer and shook his head. "Nah, not a lot. I mean, I do remember just being there in that ship or whatever it was. It felt like the ship itself was kind of alive, you know. It took care of me somehow and healed me. Kept me fed and alive somehow."

"What happened when you needed to take a shit?" Tim asked in his usual delicate style.

"Hell if I know but I guess it took care of that too." The men laughed. "How's your little man doing, Jack?"

"Rowdy as ever. Keeps telling Lori she's having a girl. I'm pretty sure he's right about it too."

"He, um, say anything more about his experience?" Carl asked.

"No. I'm starting to think the light took away the memories of him being attacked. When I asked about it, he acted like he didn't know what I was talking about. Guess I'm pretty grateful for that," Jack said.

"Things getting better for you and Dee," Mike asked Carl.

"Mmm, she coming around. That stuff almost broke her for sure. But I think she's almost back to normal."

"So let me ask you guys. Have you been sleeping very well the last week?" Jack wondered.

"Now that you mention it, no, not really. I keep waking up every night. It's been weirding me out a little," Tim said.

"Me too," Carl added.

"You guys having any dreams about bridges or green lights?" Jack joked.

"No, thank God," Mike said. "I just keep getting woken up, almost like someone is talking to me in my sleep."

"That's what it's like for me too," Tim agreed. "It's always the same thing too. Just a dumb word said over and over."

The men all looked at one another, nodding in agreement.

"What the hell is a Microsoft?" Tim asked.

Mike flipped the steaks and took them up from the grill. Janet came out to get them and the hotdogs and yelled for the kids to come in and get some food. The men let them run ahead and decided to go in after the masses were finished. He shook his head as he watched the group run inside.

"You know, I don't even like kids that much and now it seems like we have more than ever. These kids come by all the time and now, not to mention Trey and Angie's babies are coming," he joked.

"I know what you mean, we got more kids in the store during the lunch hour now than I've ever seen before."

"You still have those titty magazines out for everybody to see?" Carl asked.

"Jack made me move them behind the counter now. Said we were being a bad example or something." Tim said looking over at Jack. "But I made a sign that said you can ask us for them and everything."

"But the kids have stopped swiping them," Jack said.

"Hell, that was their only chance to learn about tits. Oh well, now that I am going to be a dad, guess I better be more respectable."

The men turned to go inside, laughing at Tim's continued promise to be a shining example of a good father. Mike grabbed Jack by the arm and motioned for him to stay back.

"Yeah?" Jack said.

"I just wanted to ask you…um, do you still have the feelings? You know, like we did that night. All powerful and able to do stuff and all that?"

Jack shook his head. "No. Seems like all that is gone. I have to say, I miss it."

"Me too. Especially in the bedroom," Mike chuckled.

"You know it. Damn, it was like being fifteen again." They went inside and joined the others in the kitchen.

The big group ate and talked, laughing and remembering stories of all that had happened in the past few months. All that they had been through wove them together as a family. The unspoken connections might have changed, but they still lingered in some ways. Mike looked at the teenagers and felt so glad they remained friends. The group that had been formed within them made them belong to something dynamic, something special that only they really understood. Being a teenager, especially one that isn't particularly popular or athletic or good looking can be lonely. These kids didn't seem that way at all anymore.

After the meal, some of the kids said their goodbyes and made their way home. Vince and Sarah walked back toward her house on Church Street. Don and Doug took off with Damon Reed and Yvonne Davis that had become something of a new couple. Andy and young Jessie Allen played with Joey in his room. George, Mary, and Emily joined Travis out in the front yard sitting at a picnic table on the side lawn under a bare elm tree.

"Your parents look pretty happy today," Emily said to Mary handing her some ChapStick from her purse.

Mary put the ChapStick on and nodded. "It's getting better. It's still kinda weird having Daddy back. We had almost got used to him being gone."

"It's super weird having Angie at home. I mean, I just wish Mom and Dad would let Trey move in with her into Teppy's old room. It's not like it can get much worse, you know."

"Parents are always funny about sex like that," Emily said.

"Look who knows so much," George teased. "Thank you, Ann Landers." Emily stuck her middle finger up and gave a tight-lipped smile.

"Well!" George gasped.

"So G. You've never said much about getting shot and all that. I've waited a week. You gonna tell us or what?" Travis asked.

George shrugged. "There's just not much to tell. I remember the bullet hitting me. Felt like I was hit in the chest with a sledgehammer. Hurt like hell. Then everything went all sparkly and then dark. Next thing I know, Mary's dad is standing in front of me practically naked and everyone was all freaked out and crying."

"Well excuse us for caring about your ass," Mary joked.

"Remember anything since then?" Emily asked.

"Yeah. One thing."

"And? Spill the beans, brother," Travis demanded.

"I kinda saw Fred."

The three teens stared at George who looked down at the table. "He looked good. Pretty much like he did before. He hugged me and said how good it was to see me. It felt like this warm, cozy blanket of love or something was all around us. But he said, 'you can't stay little bro. Not your time yet. Tell Mom and Dad I love them…' or something like that."

"Holy crap," Travis said. Mary wiped a tear from her eye. George sat forward again.

"So, hey. I know we kind of did this before, but can we just try again to use our powers? Maybe just something easy while we are all sitting here?"

"They're gone, man. Good Night, John-Boy. Smell you later," Travis said emphatically.

"I don't know," Mary began. "The other night, it did seem like I was able to make my Mom stop going on and on about doing the dishes."   "Probably just a coincidence," Travis said.

"Well, thanks a lot, Negative Norman," George said. He pulled a small flashlight from his pocket and placed it on the table. "So, the battery is dead. Let's just see if we can make it turn on. Okay? And Travis, don't be a dick and not try. Really try, okay?"

"Fine. I'll try. I want the powers to come back like the rest of you. I mean, I was really used to them. My grades are missing them too."

"If you would just study with me…" Emily began. Travis acted like he was gagging.

"When there's so much quality television to watch?"

Mary giggled. "Hey, are we ever going to go back out to the airport?"

"Now you're talking," Travis said.

"Hmm, without your powers, do you think you'd be up to it?" Emily said. Travis took her hand and placed it in his lap. She pulled it back quickly. "Really? Right now?" They all laughed.

George placed his hand on the little flashlight and waited for the others to do the same, like contacting a dead relative on the Ouija board. The four closed their eyes and concentrated. After a minute of deep hard concentration, a loud fart ripped along the picnic bench and Emily pushed Travis hard, causing him to fall off into the yard.

"Hey, I was concentrating VERY hard!" Travis said laughing while Emily fanned the air.

Unnoticed on the table, the tiny bulb in the flashlight glowed, then dimmed and went out.

An unfamiliar car pulled up on the curb. The teenager than climbed out of the bright red 1979 BMW Alpina B6 was very familiar. Theo Martin walked up to the group at the table, hands in the pockets of his tight 501's, and smiled.

"Hi kids."

The group stared at him not speaking, unbelieving that he was actually standing in front of them talking.

"You've got some balls," Travis said standing up, fists clenched.

"How dare you …" Emily started. Theo put his hands up in surrender.

"Not trying to start something. I just wondered if Trey was over here. I need to talk to him."

"Why would he want to see you?" Mary asked looking Theo up and down.

"It's important. So, is he inside?" Theo asked heading for the door. Before he could step on the porch, Jack and Mike came out the door, heading directly for Theo.

"Are you kidding me?" Jack said.

Mike walked up to Theo, grabbing the brown curls on the back of his head, tipping his face back. His nose was inches from Theo's. "I ought to nail you to the fence just like you did to my boy," Mike hissed in a low growl.

"I had nothing to do with that," Theo said, his eyes wide with fright. "I tried to stop him. I was never going to let him hurt Trey."

"What about Carl and Mary, you piece of shit?" Jack snarled. Theo looked up and saw Carl Washington coming down the stairs towards him. His mouth opened wide and he grasped at Mike's hands and tried to pull away. Carl came up to the boy with a bemused look on his face.

"You know, this one didn't touch my girl when the others did. I don't recall him doing anything to me either. He's either chicken shit or has some morality that father of his never did."

"I'm so sorry, Mr. Washington. I never ... I kept telling him to stop doing all that crazy ..."

Trey stood on the front steps of the Tanner house watching the scene in the front yard. He came up to his dad and laid a hand on his shoulder. "It's okay, Dad. I'll talk with him."

"You don't have to spend two seconds with this sorry sack of shit."

"I know. But I think I need to. Why don't y'all go inside? You can stare out the window if you want while we talk. We'll be fine."

Mike let Theo go with a rough shove. He couldn't put his finger on it, but Trey was different since everything happened. He seemed more mature, more patient. Maybe the thought he was about to be a dad of twins had scared the crap out of him. Who knew? The group make their way into the house, Mike standing on the porch longer than anyone else staring at Theo. The boys sat on the picnic table.

"Okay. What's on your mind, Theo?"

"Um, thanks for letting me talk to you, Trey. I heard about your big news with the baby and all that. Congratulations," he began.

"Cut the small talk. What's up?"

"I just wanted to tell you to your face how sorry I am. I should have told someone. I should have never just gone along with all that fuckin' bullshit. It's hard when it's your dad and all that. But I still should have done something about it."

"Can't argue with you there," Trey said.

"My sister, Carlene, came up from Houston to help me out. My dad left everything to me in the will. It made my other sisters, Aubrey and Sheridan, so mad they already left town. I told them I was going to make it right but they just called me a cocksucker and took off. I'm probably going to move down to Houston with my aunt after the school year is done."

"That's all great, Theo. Why do I care about any of that?"

"I know. That's not what I came to say. Um, did you hear back from any colleges yet? You know, about scholarships?"

"It's looking pretty good. Got a bunch of offers. Best ones are probably from USC, Ohio State, UT, and Georgia."

"Wow. That's great, I'm really glad. Any idea which one you are going to accept? Letters of Intent are due in February, right?

"Yeah. Believe it or not, I'm thinking about going with Georgia. Just feels right."

"That's sweet. I wish you all the best there, buddy." Trey stiffened at the word and Theo held up his hand to show he took it back.

"I came here to tell you…I have all this money now and I hate it. I mean, I don't hate it, but I hate how I got it and what my dad did to get it and all that. So, I am working with some lawyer guys and I am setting up some funds. One of them is going to try and clean up all shit dad's companies did down in Norton. I'm setting up some college scholarship funds for kids from Norton too. I'm also working on getting some money to your folks; Carl, Jack and Tim, all of you. I can't just give it to you or you will be all fucked up with taxes and stuff. But I can help you all out. Help your dad with his store, or Carl to start up new businesses, or pay for everyone's college. It will all be working with the law firm, y'all won't have to be dealing with me. I just want to make a difference for good, especially for all y'all that were hurt by us. I don't know what else I can do, but maybe this will help out in some small way. Bottom line, if y'all need some help, I am fixing it so you can contact the lawyers and they can help you without it costing you a dime. Please say it's okay. Please say you will let me help." Theo eyes were pleading. He extended his hand toward Trey who looked at it but didn't move.

"I don't know if anyone is going to want anything from you. But then, you trying to clean up Norton and help kids out from there, or pay for college is pretty nice. Some of them," Trey pointed toward the house, "Will just say you are trying to salve your conscience. Trying to make up for being a monster and a son of a bitch."

"They'd be right," Theo said.

Trey sighed. "Nobody gets to pick their parents. Look at me. But I think you do get to pick what you do with your life. You've had everything in the world handed to you and it made you sick and lonely most of the time. Maybe that's why you went along with all that shit. If you are for real, you really mean to make it better, then you better not fuck around with these people. If you mean business, you better come through for them. It would take you ten lifetimes and more money than Rockefeller to make up for all the hurt you been part of."

Theo looked down at his hands and then up at Trey. His clear blue eyes swam. "I know. I look at the family and friends you have …I would give up all the money just to have that. I hope you know how lucky you are."

"I'm beginning to figure that out," Trey said. "You aren't a bad guy like your dad, Theo. I always liked you. But you gotta understand, most of them in there, they can't get over this very fast, if ever. They may never trust you. I don't know why I should, but part of me does think this whole thing changed you too. So if you really mean it, if you really want a family that loves you and will stand by you … earn it. You can't be a dick anymore."

Theo smiled. "You always got a way with words, McGee. I really love you, you know?"

"Yeah. I hope you find what you're looking for Theo." Trey got up to leave. He took a few steps toward the house and turned back. Theo still sat on the bench, head down. Trey walked back and stretched his hand out and lightly held the side of Theo's head. Theo's head raised up and tears streamed down his face. Trey bent down and kissed the top of his head and went inside.

Travis, George, and Emily had been watching the two young men in the front yard from the window in Joey's room while Andy and Jessie played with him. When Trey touched Theo, Emily reached over and gripped Travis's hand. Travis reached up and put his arm around Emily and pulled her close.

"Wow, you've got a great airport built here, Joey," Andy said. The youngster had used all his blocks and Legos to construct an elaborate airport terminal. Several toy airplanes were staged at gates around the runway he had made from a set of Childcraft Encylopedias.

"Time to fly," Joey said. He sat back on his heels and stretched his hands out. The teenagers watched in wonder as the toy airplane lifted off from the runway and flew around the room.

$$x^2$$

Angie went into labor on January 1, 1979. She delivered a baby boy after a remarkably short three hours. Three minutes later she delivered a little girl. The boy was dark, with tiny brown curls and amazing blue-green eyes. The little girl was blonde with light brown eyes. They named the boy Nathan Carmichael, the middle name for Trey's dads. The girl they named Natalie Da'nay, because Angie liked it and thought it would have really pissed off her dad. Mike blubbered like a baby when he held the twins while watching the Rose Bowl. When they left the hospital two days later, they moved into Teppy's old bedroom with the babies. But a week later, Trey found another note in his locker at school. An envelope with a key to a house four doors down from his parents. The note just read: *Thought you could use some room now you are the man of the house – T.* There was no rent for the house. Mike and Carl helped Theo fix up a few things but it was a nice little first house.

Jack and Lori's baby came a month later. Another quick and easy delivery, the couple named the little strawberry blonde girl, Ella Grace. Joey was over the moon crazy about her. Tim and Candy welcomed their baby the next week. Jackson Dakota Murphy was a big strapping 9 lbs boy with a full head of curly brown hair and bright blue eyes that would eventually turn green. Dr. Will White, who delivered both babies, found it hard to explain the easy deliveries and how alert and mature they seemed. Along with the McGee twins from the month before, he had never seen such perfect little babies. When Angie brought in Nathan and Natalie for their one-month check, he'd been stunned to see them so bright-eyed, holding their heads up, and smiling.

Trey accepted the scholarship offer from the University of Georgia to play football for the Bulldogs. After much long discussion, Trey agreed to wait to move Angie and the twins to Athens until after his freshman year was over. Trey left in his new Black 1980 Trans Am, an anonymous graduation gift, on July 26th. He moved into Reed Hall and met his roommate, a big thick 6'1" tailback with the funny name, Herschel. It would become a household name soon enough. The Dawgs went 6-5 in 1979. When 1980 rolled around, Trey returned to school, this time with Angie and his twins who looked more like three-year olds than toddlers. He and Herschel remained close friends. The football gods smiled on the Bulldogs who went undefeated and closed out the season on the twins' second birthday in the Sugar Bowl with a win over Notre Dame to become National Champions. Herschel Walker would go on to win the Heisman Trophy and the Doak Walker Award in 1982.

Mike McGee held off contacting Theo Martin's lawyers until 1986. He had been driving to work and the radio news was going on and on about a new company that was getting ready to launch its IPO. Many were saying this company was going to be dynamic, others said it would be a boondoggle. When Mike heard the name of the company, he almost crashed into a fire hydrant on the corner of Pecan and College Streets. He pulled over and listened to the rest of the news report about the launch of a new computer software company called Microsoft. He called up Carl and the two of them went to lunch with Jack and Tim. Jack confirmed he'd heard about the company too. Mike contacted Theo Martin's lawyers and described the men's desire to purchase stock in the new company on March 13th. He asked for the outlandish sum of

$25,000 he wanted to invest. On March 25th, a messenger delivered the paperwork showing that the four men were the proud owners of 1190 shares of Microsoft stock. Janet along with the other wives raised their eyebrows at the investment, rattling off a number of better bets than a funny sounding company no one knew anything about. Twenty-five years later, the four's initial 1190 shares would multiply to over 342,000 with a net worth of $13 million.

True to his word, Theo Martin spent the next few years investing and working with engineers and scientists to clean up the toxic land in the Norton Community. Theo restored the roads and infrastructure, set up building projects for new homes, restored the old school into a community center, and set up trust for college scholarships for students from the community. Although still a decidedly black neighborhood, integration began to work its way into Norton and Cowhill until the stigma of living across the tracks mostly disappeared except for the old folks who couldn't let go of the past. Theo Martin moved to Austin, not Houston, and went to the University of Texas along with another Cowhill alum, Bo Williams. The two of them became business partners and started a company, Martin-Williams Investments, and continued to grow JL Martin's fortune into even more. The two never married and it was rumored they were more than business partners, vacationing together, even living together in a massive home on Lake Travis. Eventually, Theo had a family as well, two boys and a girl. No explanations were ever given on who the mother or mothers were. He and Bo parented the children, raising plenty of eyebrows, but their great wealth went a long way toward silencing any real controversy.

The Twelve Oaks site became the new haunted place of interest in the Cowhill area. Plenty of stories cropped up around the sudden disappearance and earthquake that had consumed the house and a large number of Cowhill residents. It took weeks for the excavation to be completed, but in the end, there were no real remains to be found. Charred boots and a few teeth were the only evidence at all of humans in the great home, other than the bodies of Hazel and Dub, the house staff, and curiously, Caroline Martin who was found in a freezer. Theo explained to the authorities he had discovered his mother's body only moments before the earthquake and he was certain his father had murdered her. Eventually, the FBI and others agreed and the case was closed.

Curiosity-seekers continued to make their way out to the property to see the site. The expanse where the bridge had been, the crumbling remains of the barn roof that stuck up at a strange angle from the green grassy meadow. The ghostly pool house windows creaked sadly in front of the cracked concrete hole. Rumors were that Theo Martin planned to return to the property and restore his family home. Those rumors were not true.

On clear summer nights, high school kids came to the place in pickups and cars to see if the green light would appear. Others would sing the old song . . . *"Red light, yellow light, green light bridge . . . "* It was almost a ritual, to visit this place of local legend, to see if any of the old stories were true.

In 1982, on a foggy night in early fall, Jimmy Earwood and his new girlfriend Nelda Potts, were making out in the back of his mother's Plymouth. The radio was playing Loverboy's "Working for the Weekend." Jimmy had successfully unhooked Nelda's bra and was working on sliding his jeans down over his own big backside when Nelda gasped and pointed. Coming out of the fog on the far side of the river, a black robed figure glided along the bank. Its head was large as if horns grew from the side of it. Jimmy and Nelda grasped hands as the figure moved out from the bank and through the emptiness where a bridge once stood moving ever closer to them with hands outstretched. As the fog parted, moonlight shown down, sparkling bright on a twisted golden face.

$$x^2$$

About the Author

Larry Black grew up in rural Texas before moving to Oregon in 1990. He has worked as a teacher, financial analyst, medical transcriptionist, small business developer, and business manager. He and his wife divide their time between Oregon and Hawaii, spending as much time as possible with their sons, their families, and grandchildren. This is Larry's first published novel.

$$x^2$$